THE
MIRROR
OF HER
DREAMS

MORDANT'S NEED

THE
MIRROR
OF HER
DREAMS

STEPHEN R.
DONALDSON

A DEL REY BOOK
BALLANTINE BOOKS · NEW YORK

A Del Rey Book
Published by Ballantine Books

Copyright © 1986 by Stephen R. Donaldson

Manufactured in the United States of America

Quality Printing and Binding by:
Berryville Graphics
P.O. Box 272
Berryville, VA 22611 U.S.A.

To Ross McGuire Donaldson:
for love,
laughter,
and just enough dignity.

CONTENTS

THE
MIRROR
OF HER
DREAMS

"Steeped in the vacuum of her dreams.
A mirror's empty till
A man rides through it."
—John Myers Myers. Silverlock

PROLOGUE: TERISA AND GERADEN

T he story of Terisa and Geraden began very much like a fable. She was a princess in a high tower. He was a hero come to rescue her. She was the only daughter of wealth and power. He was the seventh son of the lord of the seventh Care. She was beautiful from the auburn hair that crowned her head to the tips of her white toes. He was handsome and courageous. She was held prisoner by enchantment. He was a fearless breaker of enchantments.

As in all the fables, they were made for each other.

Unfortunately, their lives weren't that simple.

For example, her high tower was a luxury condominium building over on Madison, just a few blocks from the park. She had two bedrooms (one of them a "guest room," fully furnished and entirely unused), a spacious living room with an impressive view west, a separate dining room which contained a long, black, polished table on which candles would have gleamed beautifully if she had ever had any reason to light them, and the kind of immaculate modern kitchen displayed in remodeling catalogues.

Her home cost her father what the people she worked with would have called "a small fortune," but it was worth every penny to him. The security guards in the lobby and the closed-circuit TV cameras in the elevators kept her safe; and while she was living there she wasn't mooning passively around his house, gazing at him and his business associates and his women with those big brown calf-eyes that seemed too inert, or even too stupid, to intend what he read in them: the awareness of unlove that saw all his pampering and expense as a form of neglect. So he was glad to be rid of her.

And she thought she was glad to be living where she was because the bills were paid, and she could afford to work at the only job she felt herself competent for, the only job in which she thought her life might count for something: she was the secretary for a modern-day almshouse, a mission tucked away in a small ghetto only a fifteen-minute walk from the shining windows and reflected glory of her condo building; and she typed letters of mild explanation and appeal, vaguely desperate letters, for the lost old man who ran the mission.

Also, she thought she was glad to be living where she was because she had been able to decorate her rooms herself. This had been a slow process because she wasn't accustomed to so much freedom, so much control over her environment; but in the end what it came to was that her bedroom, living room, and dining room were decorated completely in mirrors. Mirrors had a seductive beauty which spoke to her—but that wasn't the point. The point was that there was virtu-ally no angle in her apartment from which she couldn't see herself. That was how she knew she existed.

When she slept, her mind was empty, as devoid of dreams as a plate of glass. And when she was awake, moving through her life, she made no difference of any kind to anybody. Even the men who might have considered her beautiful or desirable seemed not to see her when they passed her on the street, so blind she was to them. Nothing around her, or in her, reflected her back to herself. Without dreams—and without any effect—she had no evidence at all that she was a material being, actually present in her world. Only her mirrors told her that she was *there*: that she had a face capable of expression, with brown eyes round with thwarted softness, a precise nose, and a suggestion of a cleft like a dimple in her chin; that her body was of a type praised in magazines; that both her face and body did what was required of them.

She was completely unaware of the enchantment which held her. It was, after all, nothing more than a habit of mind.

As for Geraden, he was in little better condition.

He was only an Apt to the Congery of Imagers—in other words, an apprentice—and he had been given a task which would have threatened a Master. In fact, the opinion of the Congery was sharply divided about his selection. Some of the Masters insisted this task belonged to him because all their auguring seemed to imply that he was the only possible choice, the only one among them who might succeed. Others argued that he must be given the task because he was the only one of their number who was completely and irredeemably expendable.

Those who claimed that the act of bringing any champion into being was inherently immoral were secretly considered toadies of that old dodderer, King Joyse—and anyway they were only a small minority of the Congery. Apparently, all auguries indicated that the realm couldn't be rescued from its peril without access to a champion brought into being through Imagery. But how that translation should take place—and, indeed, who that champion should be—was less sure.

The Masters who considered Geraden expendable had good reason. After all, he wasn't just the oldest Apt currently serving the Congery: he was the oldest person ever to keep on serving the Congery without becoming skillful enough to be a Master. Though he was only in his mid-twenties, he was old enough to appear ridiculous because he had failed to earn the chasuble of a Master.

He was so ham-handed that he couldn't be trusted to mix sand and tinct without spilling some and destroying the proportions; so fumble-footed that he couldn't walk through the great laborium which had been made out of the converted dungeons of Orison without tripping over the carefully arranged rods, rollers, and apparatus of the Masters. Even rabbity Master Quillon, who had surprised everyone by casting aside his self-effacement and speaking out loudly (as King Joyse might have done, if he weren't asleep half the time) against the immorality of wrenching some champion out of his own existence in order to serve Mordant's need—even Quillon was heard to mutter that if Geraden made the attempt and failed, the Congery would at least gain the advantage of being rid of him.

In truth, this capacity for disaster rendered moot the central ethical point. Normally, the Master who had made that particular glass could simply have opened it and brought the champion into being. But Geraden had again and again shown himself incapable of the simplest translation. He would therefore have to do exactly what King Joyse would have demanded: he would have to go into the glass to meet the champion, to appeal for the champion's help.

His advantages were a willing heart, ready determination, and a quality of loyalty usually ascribed to puppies. His short chestnut hair

curled above his strong brow; his face would have well become a
king; and the training of being raised with six brothers had left him
tough, brave, and little inclined to hold grievances. But his expression was marred by an almost perpetual frown of embarrassment and
apology, occasioned by the petty mishaps and knowledge gone awry
that harried his heels. His instinctive yearning toward the questions
and potential of Imagery was so potent that his unremitting
dunderheadedness left a gloom on his spirit which threatened to
become permanent until the Congery elected by augury and common sense to send him on the mission to save Mordant's future.

When that happened, he recovered his ebullience. Where he had
formerly worked for the Masters with a will, he now labored in
fervor, doing the things their art demanded—mixing the sand and
tinct with his own hands so that the glass would welcome him, stoking the furnace with wood he cut himself, shaping the mold and
reshaping it a dozen times until it exactly matched the one that had
made the mirror in which the Masters watched their chosen champion, pouring the hot liquid while blood hammered like prayer in his
veins, sprinkling the specially ground and blended powders of the
oxidate. At every failure of attention, error, or mischance, he
groaned, cursed himself, apologized to everyone in sight—and then
threw himself back into the work, hope singing to him while sweat
soaked his clothes and all his muscles ached.

He had no more idea than Terisa did that she was under an enchantment. And if he had known, he might not have cared, so consumed was he by the opportunity the Masters had provided—an
opportunity which might be a sentence of maiming or even death.

She wasn't the champion the Congery had chosen.

She didn't so much as inhabit the same world as that champion.

In theory, at least, Geraden's mirror would have had to be entirely
different.

BOOK ONE

ONE: CALLING

T he night before Geraden came for her, Terisa Morgan had a dream—one of the few she could ever remember. In it, she heard horns: faint with distance, they reached her through the sharp air over the hills covered with crisp snow like the call for which her heart had always been waiting. They winded again—and while she strained to hear them, again. But they came no closer.

She wanted to go looking for them. Past the wood where she seemed to be sitting or lying as if the cold couldn't touch her, she saw the ridge of the hills: perhaps the horns—and those who sounded them—were on the far side. Yet she didn't move. The dream showed her a scene she had never seen before; but she remained who she had always been.

Then along the snow-clogged skirt of the ridge came charging men on horseback. As the horses fought for speed, their nostrils gusted steam, and their legs churned the snow until the dry, light flakes seemed to boil. She could hear the leather creaking of their tack, the angry panting and muttered curses of their riders: the ridge sent every sound, as edged as a shard of glass, into the wood. She yearned to block out those noises, to hear the horns again, while the three men abruptly swung away from the hills and lashed the snow toward the trees—directly toward her.

As their faces came into focus for her, she saw their fierce hate, the intent of bloodshed. Long swords appeared to flow out of their sheaths into the high hands of the riders. They were going to hack her into the snow where she stood.

She remained motionless, waiting. The air was whetted with cold, as hard as a slap and as penetrating as splinters. In the dream, she wasn't altogether sure that she would mind being killed. It would bring the emptiness of her life to an end. Her only regret was that she would never hear the horns again, never find out why they spoke such a thrill to her heart.

Then from among the black-trunked trees behind her came a man to impose himself between her and the riders. He was unarmed, unarmored—he seemed to be wearing only a voluminous brown jerkin, pants of the same fabric, leather boots—but he didn't hesitate to risk the horses. While the first rider swung his blade, the man made a sidelong leap at the reins of the mount; and the horse was wrenched off balance, spilling its rider in front of her second attacker. Both horse and rider went down, raising clouds of snow as thick as mist.

When a low breeze cleared her sight, she saw that her defender had snatched up the first rider's sword and spitted the second with it. He moved with a desperate awkwardness which showed that he was unfamiliar with fighting; but he didn't falter. In furious assault, he stretched the first rider out against the trunk of a tree before the horseman could strike back with his long poniard.

Watching, Terisa saw the third rider poised above the young man who fought for her—mount firmly positioned, sword hilt gripped high in both fists. Though she understood nothing of what was going on, she knew that she ought to move. In simple decency and gratitude toward her defender, if for no other reason, she should fling herself against the rider. He wasn't looking at her: surely she would be able to reach his belt and pull him out of his saddle before he struck.

But she didn't. In the dream, a small, vexed frown pinched her forehead as she regarded her passivity. It was the story of her life, that mute nothingness—the only quality she could ascribe to her uncertain existence. How could she act? Action was for those who didn't seriously doubt their own presence in the world. During the more than twenty years of her life, her opportunities for action had been so few that she typically hadn't recognized them until they were past. She didn't know how to make her limbs carry her toward the rider.

Yet the man who fought for her did so for no reason she could see except that she was being attacked. And he didn't know his danger: he was still trying to wrest his blade from the body of the rider he had just felled, and his back was turned.

Startling herself and the horseman and the sharp cold, she cried, "Watch out!"

The effort of the warning jerked her into a sitting position. She was still in bed. Her shout made her throat ache, and an unaccustomed panic pounded through her veins.

She recognized herself in the mirrors of her bedroom. Lit by the night-light plugged into the wall socket behind the bed, she was hardly more than a shadow in the glass all around her; but she was herself, the shadow she had always been.

And yet, while her pulse still labored and a slick of sweat oozed from her face, she thought she heard beyond the comfortless noises of the city a distant calling of horns, too faint to be certain—and too intimate to be ignored.

Of course, nothing was changed. She got up the next morning when her alarm clock went off; and her appearance in her mirrors was as rumpled and wan as usual. Though she studied her face for any sign that it was real enough for men on horseback to hate so fiercely, it seemed as void of meaning as always—so unmarked by experience, decision, or impact that she was dimly surprised to find it still able to cast a reflection. Surely she was fading? Surely she would wake up one morning, look at herself in the mirror, and see nothing? Perhaps, but not today. Today she looked just as she remembered herself—beautifully made, but to no purpose, and slightly tinged with sorrow.

So she showered as usual, dressed herself as usual in the sort of plain skirt and demure sweater her father preferred for her, breakfasted as usual—watching herself in the mirrors between bites of toast—and put on a raincoat before leaving her apartment to go to work. There was nothing out of the ordinary about the way she looked, or about her apartment as she left it, or about the elevator ride down to the lobby of her building. The only thing out of the ordinary was the way she felt.

To herself, so privately that none of it showed on her face, she kept remembering her dream.

Outside, rain fell heavily onto the street, flooding the gutters, hiss-

ing like hail off the roofs of the cars, muffling the noises of traffic.
Dispirited by the gray air and the wet, she tied a plastic bandana over
her head, then walked past the security guard (who ignored her, as
usual) and out through the revolving doors into the downpour.

With her head low and her concentration on the sidewalk, she
moved in the direction of the mission where she worked.

Without warning, she seemed to hear the horns again.

Involuntarily, she stopped, jerked up her head, looked around her
like a frightened woman. They weren't car horns: they were wind
instruments such as a hunter or musician might use. The chord of
their call was so far away and out of place that she couldn't possibly
have heard it, not in that city, in that rain, while rush-hour traffic
filled the streets and fought the downpour. And yet the sensation of
having heard the sound made everything she saw appear sharper and
less dreary, more important. The rain had the force of a determined
cleansing; the streaked gray of the buildings looked less like despair,
more like the elusive potential of the borderland between day and
night; the people jostling past her on the sidewalk were driven by
courage and conviction, rather than by disgust at the weather or fear
of their employers. Everything around her had a tang of vitality she
had never seen before.

Then the sensation faded; and she couldn't possibly have heard
rich horns calling to her heart; and the tang was gone.

Baffled and sad, she resumed her sodden walk to work.

At the mission, her day was more full of drudgery than usual. In
the administrative office, seated at her desk with the ancient typewriter crouching in front of her like a foul-tempered beast of burden,
she found a message from Reverend Thatcher, the old man who ran
the mission. It said that the mission's copying costs were too high, so
would she please type two hundred fifty copies of the attached letter
in addition to her other duties. The letter was aimed at most of the
philanthropic organizations in the city, and it contained yet another
appeal for money, couched in Reverend Thatcher's customary futility. She could hardly bear to read it as she typed; but of course she
had to read it over and over again to get it right.

While she typed, she seemed to feel herself becoming physically
less solid, as if she were slowly being dissolved by the pointlessness
of what she did. By noon, she had the letter memorized; and she was
watching in a state that resembled suspense the line of letters her
typewriter made, waiting for each new character because it proved

that she was still there and she couldn't honestly say she expected it to appear.

She and Reverend Thatcher usually ate lunch together—by his choice, not hers. Since she was quiet and watched his face attentively, he probably thought she was a sympathetic listener. But most of the time she hardly heard what he said. His talk was like his letters: there was nothing she could do to help. She was quiet because that was the only way she knew how to be; she watched his face because she hoped it would betray some indication of her own reality—some flicker of interest or concentration of notice which might indicate that she was actually present with another person. So she sat with him in one corner of the soup kitchen the mission ran in its basement, and she kept her face turned toward him while he talked.

From a distance, he appeared bald, but that was because his mottled pink skin showed clearly through his fine, pale hair, which he kept cut short. The veins in his temples were prominent and seemed fragile, with the result that whenever he became agitated they looked like they might burst. Today she expected him to rehash his latest letter, which she had already typed nearly two hundred times. That was his usual pattern: while they ate the bland, thin lunch provided by the kitchen, he would tell her things she already knew about his work, his voice quavering whenever he came back to the uselessness of what he was doing. This time, however, he surprised her.

"Miss Morgan," he said without quite looking at her, "have I ever told you about my wife?"

In fact, he hadn't, though he referred to her often. But Terisa knew some of his family history from the previous mission secretary, who had given up the job in defeat and disgust. Nevertheless she said, "No, Reverend Thatcher. You've mentioned her, naturally. But you've never told me about her."

"She died nearly fifteen years ago," he said, still wistfully. "But she was a fine, Christian woman, a strong woman, God rest her soul. Without her, I would have been weak, Miss Morgan—too weak to do what needed doing."

Though she hadn't considered the question closely, Terisa thought of him as weak. He sounded weak now, even when he wasn't talking about his failure to do better for the mission. But he also sounded fond and saddened.

"I remember the time—oh, it was years ago, long before you were born, Miss Morgan—I was out of seminary"—he smiled past her left shoulder—"with all kinds of honors, would you believe it? And I had just finished serving an assistant pastorship at one of the best churches in the city.

"At the time, they wanted me to stay on as an associate pastor. With God's help, I had done well there, and they gave me a call to become one of their permanent shepherds. I can tell you, Miss Morgan, that was quite gratifying. But for some reason my heart wasn't quiet about it. I had the feeling God was trying to tell me something. You see, just at that time I had learned that this mission needed a new director. I had no desire for the job. Being a weak man, I was pleased by my position in the church. I was well rewarded for my work, both financially and personally. And yet I couldn't forget the question of this mission. It was true that the church called me to serve them. But what did God call me to do?

"It was Mrs. Thatcher who resolved my dilemma. Putting her hand on her hip, as she always did when she meant to be taken seriously, she said, 'Now don't you be a fool, Albert Thatcher. When Our Lord came into the world, he didn't do it to serve the rich. This church is a fine place—but if you leave, they'll have the choice of a hundred fine men to replace you. Not one of those men will consider a call to the mission.'

"So I came here," he concluded. "Mrs. Thatcher didn't care that we were poor. She only cared that we were doing what we could to serve God. I've done that, Miss Morgan, for forty years."

Ordinarily, a comment like that would have been a prelude to another of his long discussions of his unending and often fruitless efforts to keep the mission viable. Ordinarily, she could hear those discussions coming and steel herself against them, so that her own unreality in the face of the mission's need and his penury wouldn't overwhelm her.

But this time what she heard was the faraway cry of horns.

They carried the command of the hunt and the appeal of music, two different sounds that formed a chord in her heart, blending together so that she wanted to leap up inside herself and shout an answer. And while she heard them, everything around her changed.

The soup kitchen no longer looked dingy and worn out: it looked well used, a place of single-minded dedication. The grizzled and tattered men and women seated at the tables were no longer reduced to mere hunched human wreckage: now they took in hope and possibility with their soup. Even the edges of the tables were more distinct, more tangible and important, than ordinary Formica and tubed steel. And Reverend Thatcher himself was changed. The pulse beating in his temples wasn't the agitation of uselessness: it was the strong rhythm of his determination to do good. There was valor in his pink skin, in the earned lines of his face, and the focus of his eyes was so distant because it was fixed, not on futility, but on God.

The change lasted for only a moment. Then she could no longer hear the horns, even though she yearned for them; and the air of defeat seeped slowly back into her surroundings.

Filled with loss, she thought she would start to weep if Reverend Thatcher began another of his discussions. Fortunately, he didn't. He had some phone calls to make, hoping to catch certain influential people while they were taking their lunch breaks; so he excused himself and left her, unaware that for a moment he had been covered by glamour in her eyes. She returned to her desk almost gratefully; at her typewriter, she would be able to strike the keys and see her existence proven in the black characters she made on paper.

The afternoon passed slowly. Through the one, bare window, she could see the rain still flooding down, drenching everything until even the buildings across the street looked like wet cardboard. The few people hurrying up and down the sidewalks might have been wearing rain gear, or they might not: the downpour seemed to erase the difference. Rain pounded on the outside of the window; gloom soaked in through the glass. Terisa found herself typing the same mistakes over and over again. She wanted to hear horns again— wanted to reexperience the tang and sharpness that came with them. But they had been nothing more than the residue of one of her infrequent dreams. She couldn't recapture them.

At quitting time, she put her work away, shrugged her shoulders into her raincoat, and tied her plastic bandana over her head. But when she was ready to go, she hesitated. On impulse, she knocked on the door of the tiny cubicle Reverend Thatcher used as a private office.

At first, she didn't hear anything. Then he answered faintly, "Come in."

She opened the door.

There was just room in the cubicle for her and one folding chair between his desk and the wall. His seat at the other side of the desk was so tightly blocked in with file cabinets that when he wanted to

leave he could barely squeeze out of his niche. As Terisa entered the
room, he was staring blankly at his telephone as if it sucked all his
attention and hope away.

"Miss Morgan. Quitting time?"

She nodded.

He didn't seem to notice that she hadn't said anything. "You
know," he told her distantly, "I talked to forty-two people today.
Thirty-nine of them turned me down."

If she let the impulse which had brought her here dissipate, she
would have that much less reason to believe in her own existence; so
she said rather abruptly, "I'm sorry about Mrs. Thatcher."

Softly, as if she hadn't changed the subject, he replied, "I miss her.
I need her to tell me I'm doing the right thing."

Because she wanted to make him look at her, she said, "You *are*
doing the right thing." As she spoke, she realized she believed it.
The memory of horns had changed that for her, if nothing else. "I
wasn't sure before, but I am now."

His vague gaze remained fixed on the phone, however. "Maybe if
I call her brother," he muttered to himself. "He hasn't made a contribution for a year now. Maybe he'll listen to me this time. I'll keep
trying."

While he dialed the number, she left the cubicle and closed the
door. She had the impression that she was never going to see him
again. But she tried not to let it bother her: she often felt that way.

The walk home was worse than the one to work had been. There
was more wind, and it lashed the rain against her legs, through every
gap it could find or make in her coat, past the edges of her bandana
into her face. In half a block, her shoes were full of water; before she
was halfway home, her sweater was sticking, cold and clammy, to her
skin. She could hardly see where she was going.

But she knew the way automatically: habit carried her back to her
condo building. Its glassy front in the rain looked like a spattered
pool of dark water, reflecting nothing except the idea of death in its
depths. The security guards saw her coming, but they didn't find her
interesting enough to open the doors for her. She pushed her way
into the lobby, bringing a gust of wind and a spray of rain with her,
and paused for a few moments to catch her breath and wipe the
water from her face. Then, without looking up, she headed toward
the elevators.

Now that she was no longer walking hard, she began to feel

chilled. There was a wall mirror in the elevator: she took off her bandana and studied her face while she rode up to her floor. Her eyes looked especially large and vulnerable against the cold pallor of her skin and the faint blue of her lips. So much of her was real, then: she could be made pale by wind and wet and cold. But the chill went too deep for that reassurance.

As she left the elevator and walked down the carpeted hall to her apartment, she realized she was going to have a bad night.

In her rooms, with the door locked, and the curtains drawn to close out the sensation that she was beneath the surface of the pool she had seen in the windows from the outside, she turned on all the lights and began to strip off her clothes. The mirrors showed her to herself: she was pale everywhere. The dampness on her flesh made it look as pallid as wax.

Candles were made of wax. Some dolls were carved of wax. Wax was used to make molds for castings. Not people.

It was going to be a *very* bad night.

She had never been able to find the proof she needed in her own physical sensations. She could easily believe that a shadow might feel cold, or warmth, or pain; yet it didn't exist. Nevertheless she took a hot shower, trying to drive away the chill. She dried her hair thoroughly and put on a flannel shirt, a pair of thick, soft corduroy pants, and sheepskin moccasins so that she would stay warm. Then, in an effort to hold her trouble back, she forced herself to fix and eat a meal.

But her attempts to take care of herself had as much effect as usual —that is to say, none. A shower, warm clothes, and a hot meal couldn't get the chill out of her heart—a detail she regarded as unimportant. In fact, that was part of the problem: nothing that happened to her mattered at all. If she were to die of pneumonia, it might be an inconvenience to other people—to her father, for example, or to Reverend Thatcher—but to her it would not make the slightest difference.

This was going to be one of those nights when she could feel herself fading out of existence like an inane dream.

If she sat where she was and closed her eyes, it would happen. First she would hear her father talking past her as if she weren't there. Then she would notice the behavior of the servants, who treated her as a figment of her father's imagination, as someone who only lived

and breathed because he said she did, rather than as an actual and
present individual. And then her mother—

Her mother, who was herself as passive, as nonexistent, as talent,
experience, and determination could make her.

In her mind, with her eyes closed, Terisa would be a child again,
six or seven years old, and she would hobble into the huge dining
room where her parents were entertaining several of her father's
business associates in their best clothes—she would go into the dining room because she had fallen on the stairs and scraped her knee
and horrified herself with how much she was bleeding, and her
mother would look at her without seeing her at all, would look right
through her with no more expression on her face than a waxwork
figure, and would make everything meaningless. "Go to your room,
child," she would say in a voice as empty as a hole in her heart.
"Your father and I have guests." Learn to be like me. Before it's too
late.

Terisa had been struggling to believe in herself for years. She
didn't close her eyes. Instead, she went into her living room and
pulled a chair close to the nearest wall of mirrors. There she seated
herself, her knees against the glass, her face so near it that she risked
raising a veil of mist between herself and her reflection. In that position, she watched every line and shade and flicker of her image.
Perhaps she would be able to keep her reality in one piece. And if
she failed, she would at least be able to see herself come to an end.

The last time she had suffered one of these attacks, she had sat and
stared at her reflection until well past midnight, when the sensation
that she was evaporating had finally left her. Now she was sure she
wouldn't last so long. Last night, she had dreamed—and in the
dream she had been as passive as she was now, as unable to do
anything except watch. The quiet ache of that recognition weakened
her. Already, she thought she could discern the edges of her face
blurring out of actuality.

Without warning, she saw a man in the mirror.

He wasn't reflected in the mirror: he was *in* the mirror. He was
behind her startled image—and moving forward as if he were floun-
dering through a torrent.

He was a young man, perhaps only a few years older than she was,
and he wore a large brown jerkin, brown pants, and leather boots.
His face was attractive, though his expression was foolish with surprise and hope.

He was looking straight at her.

For an instant, his mouth stretched soundlessly as if he were trying to shout through the glass. Then his arms flailed. He looked like he was losing his balance; but his movements expressed an authority which had nothing to do with falling.

Instinctively, she dropped her head into her lap, covered it with her arms.

The mirror in front of her made no noise as it shattered.

She felt the glass spray from the wall, felt splinters tug at her shirt as they blew past. Like a flurry of ice, they tinkled against the opposite wall and fell to the carpet. A brief gust of wind as cold as winter puffed at her with the broken glass, then stopped.

When she looked up, she saw the young man stretched headlong on the floor beside her chair. A dusting of glass chips made his hair glitter. From his position, he looked like he had taken a dive into the room through the wall. But his right leg from mid-calf down was missing. At first, she thought it was still in the wall: his calf and his boot seemed to be cut off flat at the plane of the wall. Then she saw that the end of his leg was actually a couple of inches from the wall.

There was no blood. He didn't appear to be in pain.

With a whooshing breath, he pushed himself up from the floor so that he could look at her. His right calf seemed to be stuck where it was; but the rest of him moved normally.

He was frowning intensely. But when she met his gaze, his face broke into a helpless smile.

"I'm Geraden," he said. "This isn't where I'm supposed to be."

TWO: THE SOUND
OF HORNS

ithout quite realizing what she was doing, she pushed her chair back and stood up. Involuntarily, she retreated. Her feet in her moccasins made faint crunching noises as they ground slivers of glass into the carpet. The wall where the mirror had been glued was splotched and discolored: it looked diseased. The remaining mirrors echoed her at herself. But she kept her eyes on the man sprawled in front of her.

He was gaping at her in amazement. His smile didn't fade, however, and he made no attempt to get up.

"I've done it again, haven't I," he murmured. "I *swear* I did everything right—but any Master can do this kind of translation, and I've gone wrong again somehow."

She ought to be afraid of him: she understood that distinctly. His appearance there in her living room was violent and impossible. But instead of fear she felt only bafflement and wonder. He seemed to have the strange ability to bypass logic, normalcy. In her dream, she had not been afraid of death—

"How did you get in here?" she asked so softly that she could barely hear herself. "What do you mean, this isn't where you're supposed to be?"

At once, his expression became contrite. "I'm sorry. I hope I didn't frighten you." There was tension in his voice, a fear or excitement of his own. But in spite of the tightness he sounded gentle, even kind. "I don't know what went wrong. I did everything right, I

swear it. I'm not supposed to be here at all. I'm looking for someone—"

Then for the first time he looked away from her.

"—completely different."

As his gaze scanned the room, his jaw dropped, and his face filled
up with alarm. Reflected back at himself from all sides, he recoiled,
flinching as though he had been struck. The knotted muscles of his
throat strangled a cry. A fundamental panic seemed to overwhelm
him; for a second, he cowered on the rug, groveled in front of her.
But then, apparently, he realized that he hadn't been harmed. He
lifted his head, and the fear on his features changed to astonishment,
awe. He peered at himself in the mirrors as if he were being transformed.

Spellbound by his intense and inexplicable reactions, she watched
him and didn't speak.

After a long moment, he fought his attention back to her. With an
effort, he cleared his throat. In a tone of constrained and artificial
calm, he said, "I see you use mirrors too."

A shiver ran through her. "I don't know what you're talking
about," she said. "I don't have any idea what you're doing here.
How do you know I'm not the right person?"

"Good question." His grin stretched wider. He looked like he
enjoyed the sight of her. "Of course you can't be. I mean, how is that
possible? Unless everyone has misunderstood the augury. Maybe this
room pulled me away from where I should be. Did you know I was
going to try this?"

Terisa didn't want to repeat herself. Instead of continuing to mention that she had no idea what he meant, she asked, "Why don't you
get up? You look a little silly, lying there on the floor."

One thing about him pleased her immediately: he seemed to hear
her when she spoke, not simply when it happened to suit his train of
thought. "I would like to," he said somewhat sheepishly, "but I
can't." He gestured toward his truncated right leg. "They won't let
go of my ankle. They *better* not let go. I would never get back." His
expression echoed the mercurial changes of direction in his mind.
"Although I don't know how I'm going to face them when I do get
back. They'll never believe I haven't done it all wrong again."

Still studying him for some sign that what was happening made
sense, she inquired, "You've had this problem before?"

He nodded glumly, then shook his head. "Not this exact problem.

Forcing down his confusion and abashment, he achieved a semblance of dignity.

"Please don't judge Mordant by me. The need is real. And it's urgent, my lady. Parts of the realm have already begun to die. People are dying—people who don't have anything to do with Imagery or kings and just want to live their lives in peace. And the threat increases every day. Alend and Cadwal are never exactly quiet. Now they're forming armies. And King Joyse doesn't do anything. The heart has gone out of him. Wise men smell treachery everywhere.

"But the gravest peril doesn't come from the High King of Cadwal or the Alend Monarch. It comes from Imagery." He gathered passion as he spoke. "Somewhere in the realm—somewhere where we can't find them—there are renegade Imagers, Masters of mirrors, and they're opening their glasses more and more to every kind of horror and foulness. They're experimenting on Mordant, trying to find in their mirrors those attacks and evils which will be most virulent to the peace, stability, and life that King Joyse forged in his prime. And these Masters seem to have no fear of the chaos that comes from unleashing powers that cannot be controlled.

"Before this winter ends, the realm will begin to crumble. Then there will be war on every hand—war of every kind—and all good things will be in danger.

"My lady," he said straight to her, "I don't have any power to compel you. If I did, it would be wrong to use it. And you aren't the champion the Congery expects. I've been such a fumble-foot all my life that my presence here might be just another one of my disasters.

"But I *might* be right. You understand mirrors." He gestured around the room. "You might be the help we need. And if you are, we're lost without you.

"Please. Will you come with me?"

She stared at him, her mouth open and her mind dumbfounded. *Dying. War. Every kind of horror and foulness. We're lost without you.* What, me? She had never heard of Mordant—or Cadwal, or Alend. The only countries she knew of that still had kings were thousands of miles away. And nobody anywhere talked about mirrors as though they were doorways into different kinds of reality. *You may be the help we need.* What was he talking about?

As carefully as she could, she said, "This doesn't make any sense. I know you're trying to explain something, but it isn't working. None of this has anything to do with me." You don't even know my name. "I can't help you."

But Geraden shook his head, dismissed her protest. "You don't know that for sure. You don't—"

Abruptly, his gaze narrowed as if a new thought had struck him, and he scrutinized her face. "Are you happy here?"

"Am I—?" The unexpected question made her look away from him, as though he had insulted her—or shamed her. Without warning, her fear was replaced by a desire to cry.

She peered hard into the nearest mirror, trying to reassure herself. Geraden occupied all the reflections, however, although she didn't want to see him. From where she stood, there was no glass or angle that didn't cast his image at her.

In spite of his strangeness, his reflection appeared more real than her own.

"Are you necessary?" he asked.

What a question. She stared deep into her own eyes in the mirror and pinched the bridge of her nose to hold back the tears. She was probably the most replaceable fact of Reverend Thatcher's life. If she evaporated, he would notice her absence immediately; but his concern would last only until he found a new secretary. And days or even weeks might pass before her father became aware that she was gone. Then he would raise an enormous hue and cry, offering rewards, accusing the police of negligence, having security guards fired —but only to disguise the fact that he really didn't care one way or the other what had become of her. And she belonged to no one else.

"Are you—?" He faltered for an instant, then persisted. "Forgive me. I've got the strongest feeling you aren't happy. You don't *look* happy. And I don't see anyone else here. Are you alone? Are you wedded?" At least he had the decency to sound embarrassed. "Are you in love?"

She was so surprised—and he was squirming so badly—that she began to laugh. She remained close to tears; but laughing in front of him was an improvement over crying. The fact that she wasn't crying enabled her to turn from her reflection to face him directly.

"I'm sorry." She had some difficulty suppressing her laughter. "I guess it's not easy being in your position. You should have had them tie a rope around your waist, instead of holding on to your foot. That way, you would at least be able to stand up."

"My lady"—again he spoke formally, and again his voice seemed to catch hold of her—"you are not happy here. You are not needed. You are not loved. Come with me." He extended a hand toward her. "You are an Imager. It may be that my glass was formed for you from the pure sand of dreams."

"I'm not an Imager," she replied. "I don't dream very often."

Her protest was automatic, however, not urgent. She was hardly listening to herself. Because her dreams were so rare, they made powerful impressions on her.

And in her dream she had remained passive and unimportant while three riders had charged forward to kill her and a man she didn't know had risked his life to save her. A man like Geraden. Everything she disliked about herself held her back—her unreality, her fear of her father and punishment, her inability to have any meaningful effect on her own life. But Geraden still held out his hand to her.

She couldn't help noticing that it was nicked and bruised in several places, and one of his fingernails was torn. Still she thought it was a good hand—sturdy and faithful.

It made her think of horns.

Their call carried her fear away.

"But," she went on, and each word was a surprise to her, conjured by unexpected music out of the ache in her heart, "I think I would like to find out what's been hiding on the other side of my mirrors all this time."

In response, his face lit up like a sunrise.

THREE: TRANSLATION

I don't believe it," Geraden murmured to himself. "I don't *believe* it." Then, an instant later, he said excitedly, "Quick, before you change your mind. Take my hand."

She didn't believe it either. What was she doing? But his excitement made her want to laugh again. And in her memory the horns called clearly, ringing out over the cold snow despite distance and the intervening hills—called to her.

Quickly, so that she wouldn't have time to change her mind, she moved closer to him and put her hand in his.

At once, she became self-conscious. "Is that all there is to it?" she asked. "Don't you have to wave your arms or say magic words or something?"

His grin grew wider and happier as he clasped her hand. "That's all. The invocations and gestures have already been made. And the ability is born, not made. All you have to do is move with me." Balancing himself on the knee of his truncated leg, he got his left foot under him. "And"—his expression sobered slightly—"watch your step."

He began to push himself backward, drawing her with him.

As he did so, his right calf disappeared by inches: the flat plane remained stationary, so that as he slid his knee backward more and more of his leg was cut off. He seemed to be using his foot and leg to probe a place behind him—a place that didn't exist.

When his right leg reached far enough, he was able to straighten his knee. Smiling and nodding to Terisa, slowly pulling her after him, he raised himself until he was almost upright. "You might find it easier," he said, "if you close your eyes." Then he shifted his weight to the other leg.

At that moment, his face went wide with dismay as he lost his balance and started to fall.

His plunge wrenched her forward, toward the wall—toward the plane where first his leg and now his entire body seemed to vanish. Instinctively, she tried to jerk free. But though he flailed for support, his hand held hers in a grip she couldn't break. She tried to cry out, flung up her arm to ward off the impact—

The last thing she saw of her apartment was the splotched plaster where her broken mirror had once been glued. While she was still trying to release the cry of panic trapped in her throat, her marginal grasp on actuality failed, and she faded out of existence.

At once, she passed into a zone of transition where time and distance contradicted themselves. She felt eternity in an instant—or maybe she felt an instant that took forever. Her fall became a vast and elongated plummet down from or up to the heights of the world, even though the plunge carried her no more than half a step forward. She studied the sudden darkness intimately, despite the fact that it was so brief she could hardly have noticed it.

And then, with the same sensation of instantaneous eternity, of huge brevity, she saw Geraden again: he seemed to snap back into existence as though he had been lit to life by the abrupt orange illumination of the lamps and torches.

She recognized it—and immediately forgot it.

He was still falling, his face stretched in consternation; he had misjudged the step behind him. And his hand still gripped hers. She couldn't recover. Even if she had been braced, she might not have been strong enough to stop his collapse toward the gray flagstones.

So she landed on top of him. Because she was trying to get her arms between herself and the impact, she accidentally planted an elbow in his stomach as she hit. His mouth gaped pain, and the breath burst from his lungs. But his body protected her: she flopped onto him and then off again. As a result, she came to rest on her back beside him, her face turned toward the massive old vaulted stone ceiling.

For a moment, the perceptual wrench had the effect of blindness: she stared upward as though she hadn't observed the difference between this place and her apartment. Past her feet, and up two steps from her sprawling position, stood a large mirror in a polished wooden frame. The glass was nearly as tall as she was; it was tinted with a color that only showed at the edges of its surface; instead of being made flat it had been given a faintly rippling curve. On some level, she was aware that what she saw reflected in the mirror wasn't the ceiling above her or the wall behind her. It also wasn't the living room of her apartment. Yet in other ways she was no more conscious of the mirror than she was of the stone on which she lay.

Then, distinctly, she heard someone say, "Where did you get her?"

"You were invisible in the mirror. How did you do that?"

"Where did you go?"

Slowly through her stunned surprise leaked the information that she was stretched on the floor in the center of a circle of men.

What? She thought dumbly, as if her throat were choked with astonishment. A circle of men. *Where?*

There must have been twenty or thirty of them, all staring down at her. At a glance, she saw that some of them were old and others weren't: all of them were older than she was. They wore a variety of cloaks and robes, cassocks and jerkins—warm clothing to compensate for the coolness of the air. Each of them, however, had a chasuble of yellow satin draped around his neck.

Some of them peered at her in amazement and horror. She felt that way herself. "Fool!" one of them rasped. Another muttered, "This is impossible."

Others were laughing.

At her side, Geraden gaped for air. A delicate shade of purple spread up from his corded neck over the tight lines of his cheeks.

"Well, Apt," one of the laughing men said through his mirth, "here is another fine disaster." He was tall, strongly built in spite of his leanness. His nose was too big; his cheekbones were too narrow, too flatly sloped toward his ears; his black hair formed an unruly thatch on the back of his skull, leaving his forehead bald. But the humor and intelligence in his pale eyes made him keenly attractive. He was wrapped in a jet cloak, which he wore with an air of insouciance. The ends of his chasuble hung as if he might start twirling them at any moment. "With all the realm in danger, we send you questing for a champion to save us. But for you this is nothing more than an opportunity for dalliance.

"My lady," he went on, addressing Terisa, "it may be that you found young Geraden appealing enough to lure you here. But now that you *are* here, I think you will discover that Mordant has better men to offer." With a laughing flourish, he bowed over her formally and extended his hand to help her to her feet.

Mordant, she echoed in the same dumb, choked surprise. He did it. He actually brought me to Mordant.

Geraden whooped a breath and began to pull air past the knot in his stomach.

Instinctively, Terisa turned toward him. At the same time, however, one of the men who hadn't been laughing crouched beside Geraden. This man had a face the color and texture of a pine board. His eyebrows were as thick and stiff as bracken, but there was no other hair on his head anywhere. His girth appeared to be nearly as great as his height. "Shame, Master Eremis," he muttered, reaching one heavy arm under Geraden's head and shoulders to support the young man as he hacked for breath. "Find some other cause for amusement. What has happened here is either disaster or miracle. Certainly it is unprecedented. It needs seriousness."

Master Eremis' smile reached halfway to his ears. "Master Barsonage, you have no sense of play. What can any man or Master do about Apt Geraden's pratfalls and confusions except laugh?" He turned his attention back to Terisa. His offer of help hadn't wavered. "My lady?"

"We can weep, Master Eremis," a guttural voice responded from the circle. "You have admitted yourself that we are doomed if we do not find the champion augured for us. I care nothing for King Joyse and his petty realm"—at this, the thick man supporting Geraden made a hissing noise through his teeth—"and I do not care who knows it. Let him sink into senility, and let Alend and Cadwal butcher each other for the right to replace him. But *we* have no other hope, the Congery of Imagers. This blighted Apt has just failed us."

Terisa wanted to turn to see who had spoken. But she was held by the smile and the eyes and the extended hand of Master Eremis. He was looking at her, *at her*, as if she were real—as if she were really present in this high chamber of cut stone, where the air held a tang of winter and the light came from oil lamps and a few torches; impossibly present here when she had no physical right to be anywhere at all except back in her apartment, staring at herself alone in her mirrors.

The magnetism of his look compelled her. She couldn't refuse him; he gave her the tangible existence she had always doubted. Gazing back at him in surprise and wonder, she let him take her hand and draw her easily to her feet.

"You're wrong," Geraden coughed. His color was improving. With Master Barsonage's help, he tried to sit up. "All of you. She's the right one."

The reaction was loud and immediate: most of the men started talking at once.

"What? A woman? Impossible."

"Are you blind? Look at her. She isn't even *armed*."

"This is not the champion you were sent to bring. Do you think we are as foolish as you?"

"But this proves it! Think of the implications. King Joyse and Adept Havelock are right. They *are* alive."

"Leave the boy alone. I'm sure this was just another accident."

The guttural voice added, "What nonsense. Do not be irresponsible. You have made a ruin out of our trust. Do not try to disguise your failure by pretending success." Terisa saw the speaker now: he was a heavyset man with a crooked back, hands that looked strong enough to break stones, a white beard spattered with flecks of black, and a fleshy scowl etched permanently onto his face. To the other Masters, he concluded, "I argued and argued that we should not pin our hope on this hapless puppy, but I was outvoted. This"—he pointed a finger as massive as the peen of a hammer at Terisa—"is the result."

Master Eremis laughed again and made a placating gesture. But before he could reply, Geraden protested, "No, Master Gilbur." Coughing, he struggled out of Master Barsonage's hold and pushed himself to his feet. "It isn't my fault this time. Think about it—"

Unfortunately, the attempt to stand, talk, and cough simultaneously confused his balance. He stepped on one of his own feet and fell to the side, pitching heavily against two Imagers. They were barely able to catch him. Several men guffawed; this time Terisa could hear their bitterness. They had seen him do things like this before.

When he regained his balance, he was flushed and glowering with embarrassment.

"Apt Geraden," Master Eremis said kindly, "you have not had an easy time of this. But what is done is done—and we are no nearer to the champion we need than we were when you began. It might be wiser if you did not vex the Congery further by arguing against the obvious."

Grimly, Geraden straightened the disarray of his jerkin. "What's obvious," he began sourly, "is that I haven't gone wrong the way you believe. You haven't considered—"

"Boy," Master Barsonage growled behind him, "watch your tone. We are Masters here. We are not required to hear the insolence of an Apt."

At once, chagrin rushed over the anger and embarrassment in Geraden's face. "I'm sorry. I didn't mean—" He flung a look of misery and contrition at Barsonage. "But this is so *important*."

"We are aware of what is important," rasped the heavyset man, Master Gilbur. "Credit us with that minimum of intelligence. The rest we will be able to reason for ourselves."

Terisa was only marginally attentive to what was being said. As soon as Eremis stopped looking *at her*, she was nearly overcome by a sense of unreality. None of this was possible. Where was she really? Was this what happened when her tendency to fade away was pushed to its conclusion? Deliberately, she concentrated on what she could see, trying to convince herself of her surroundings.

She had her back to the mirror on the stone dais: instinctively, she felt that was one glass into which she didn't wish to glance. Master Eremis had positioned her in an almost proprietary way at his side; the rest of the Imagers were clustered around Geraden, Barsonage, and Gilbur. And they all stood near the open center—the dais itself occupied the center—of a large, round chamber with a flagstone floor. Crude-hewn gray granite formed the walls and ceiling. Several huge torches burned in sconces set around the distant walls; but most of the light came from oil lamps hanging from the four thick pillars that supported the high vaults of the ceiling. Within the area marked by the pillars, the center of the chamber was ringed by a carved wooden railing with benches like pews outside it, facing inward. The benches could have seated forty or fifty people.

This, she guessed, was the official meeting hall of the Congery of Imagers. That seemed reasonable—which was good. If it were reasonable, it might also be real.

She would have liked to wander away from the group of men, do a little exploring on her own. But part of her did hear what the Masters were saying. She heard the appeal in Geraden's voice, the weight of sarcasm with which Master Gilbur responded. Though she had only known Geraden for—what was it? ten minutes now? twenty at the most—she felt loyal to him. He had talked and listened to her and smiled as if she actually existed. Meeting the flustered contrite-and-urgent supplication in his eyes, she said to the Masters, "I think you ought to give him a chance. There must be some reason why I agreed to come with him."

At once, she winced inwardly and wanted to apologize to Geraden, because Master Eremis let out a peal of laughter. "There must indeed, my lady," he chortled. "I was wrong to speak of dalliance, for that surely was no part of this Apt's appeal. He has many virtues, but grace and wit are not among them. Since we have no reason to believe that you were brought by force, there must indeed be some reason why you are with him." Several of the Imagers chuckled at Eremis' jest; but Geraden could do nothing except duck his head to hide his misery. "Well, speak, Geraden," the Master went on. "What is it that you believe we have not considered?"

For a moment, Terisa thought that Geraden would refuse to answer. She had watched her father embarrass her mother on any number of occasions, and the only outlet her mother had found for her resentment had been a refusal to speak. But Geraden set aside whatever humiliation he felt. Excitement surged into his gaze, and he took a step forward almost as if he were jumping.

"Master Eremis"—he turned his head—"Master Gilbur"—again, he faced Eremis, Terisa, and the mirror—"you know I'm only an Apt, and you laugh because I make a lot of mistakes. But you haven't thought about what she *means*." He made an open-handed gesture toward Terisa. "Why is she here? *How* did she get here?

"Master Gilbur, you taught me how to shape that mirror. It's exactly like the one you made. You know they're exactly alike because what you see in this mirror is the same as what your mirror shows. They're the same.

"Master Eremis, have you ever heard of a mirror that could translate things it didn't show?"

This question took several of the Masters aback. Gilbur scowled like the clenching of a fist; Eremis' mouth twisted thoughtfully; Barsonage raised his eyebrows so far that they appeared to grow back over his skull. A small man with a face like a rabbit's nodded vigorously.

Now Geraden was speaking to all the Imagers at once. "The greatest Masters we know of have never been able to make mirrors that show one thing and translate another. Adept Havelock in his prime couldn't do it. Even the stories about arch-Imager Vagel don't mention any power as strong as that.

"Think about it, Masters. Either I've stumbled by accident onto the greatest achievement in the history of Imagery. Or I'm already the greatest Master since the first mirror was shaped." Abruptly, he stopped, fixing his gaze squarely on Eremis.

"Or what, Apt?" Master Gilbur growled. "Surely you do not expect us to stomach either of those alternatives?"

"Or," Geraden said slowly, still holding Eremis' eyes, "another power intervened. Maybe it was the same power that shaped the augury. It took me to a place I could not have reached with that mirror. A place where I could find the champion the augury intended instead of the one you chose."

He was nearly whispering, and his brown eyes shone intently. "She's the one I should have been sent to bring back. She's the one who can save us."

For an instant, all the Congery stared in silence at Geraden and his assertion. Then the rabbity Master announced in a high, thin voice, "I said so. I have said so from the beginning. This proves it. They *are* real."

"Oh, forsooth," retorted Gilbur trenchantly. "The Apt speaks cleverly, but he defies reason. *She* our augured savior? *She* the power to rescue us from Imagery gone mad? Look at her, Masters. What are her powers? How will she fight in our defense? In what way is she superior to the champion we have chosen?"

As he spoke, he aimed a thick forefinger at the glass behind Terisa.

Several of the men shifted their attention there. Even Master Eremis turned and gave the mirror a glance.

Involuntarily, Terisa obeyed Gilbur's pointing.

Her first impression was confirmed: the mirror didn't reflect anything that she could see here—or that she had ever seen.

The tinted and faintly rippled glass showed a scene distant enough to be quite large, but not distant enough to weaken its primary figures. In the middle ground of a stark and alien landscape lit by the scarlet glow of an old, red sun stood a metallic shape which her mind instantly labeled a "spaceship." Forming a defensive perimeter around the ship were a number of manlike forms, also metallic: a moment passed before she realized that they actually were men, men in armor. They were under attack; but the destructive beams that chewed pieces off the landscape only glanced from the helmets and chestplates of the defenders. She couldn't see the effect of the fire they returned, but it must have been adequate: they weren't driven back toward their ship.

The central figure of the scene, however, wasn't the ship or one of the fighters. Rather, it was another metal-clad individual who occasionally waved his arms or shifted his attention as though he were directing the battle. He was heavily armed: strange weapons hung on his hips, and strapped to his back was a rifle the size of a small cannon. But more than his armament, it was his stance that conveyed a staggering sense of power through the glass. He stood the alien ground as if he meant to decimate whole populations in order to claim it.

Terisa understood at once that he was the champion, the strong and violent being Geraden had been sent to find.

That was the kind of help Mordant needed? The danger was *that* severe? And Geraden wanted these men to take *her* seriously as an answer to their problem, an augured savior? Suddenly, she realized that Master Gilbur was right. If Geraden considered her a sane answer to a problem of that scope, he was out of his mind.

What kind of lunacy had possessed her to take his hand? She should absolutely have gone to the phone, called security, and accepted the consequences. The strain of having to face her father would have been preferable to the impossibility of where she was now.

It affected her like dizziness. What was she *doing* here? She turned away from the mirror in a blur and seemed to lose her balance. Then she found herself gazing up into Master Eremis' face as if she were asking him for help. Though she didn't know him at all, she felt his intelligence, his strength, his effectiveness. His humor was built on confidence, and it promised results even when he was jesting.

He met her appeal for a moment, and the corners of his eyes crinkled as though he were about to start laughing again. But he didn't. Instead, he let a good-natured frown crease his high forehead. "Masters," he said in a musing tone, "it is a subtle question. We must not dismiss it lightly. Apt Geraden makes a point which deserves consideration."

Over Master Gilbur's growl of exasperation, Eremis went on, "That his taste in champions is suspect I grant you. But there is simple truth in his words. Either he has stumbled by chance into a miracle. Or he has secretly made himself greater than us all." Master Eremis put aside the protests of the Congery with a delicate wave of his fingers. "Or there is a power at work here which we do not comprehend—and which we must take into account.

"I propose," he continued promptly, "that we adjourn for the present. We must have time to think. Mordant's need is urgent, but it does not require foolish haste. What say you? Perhaps tomorrow we will understand these things better.

"Master Barsonage?"

Terisa was faintly surprised to hear him suggest rather than announce an adjournment: she had assumed automatically that he was the leader of the Congery. But that role seemed to belong to the thick, bald man with the eyebrows like scrub and the pine-yellow skin. When Eremis addressed him, he glanced around the Masters for a moment, taking a consensus. After most of them had indicated their assent, he said, "It is likely a wise idea. I doubt that we will gain much insight into whether Apt Geraden is the victim of accident, genius, or intervention. But we must determine what we will do about it. Those of us who are already weary of argument will need rest before facing that debate."

Brusquely, he concluded, "Let us meet again tomorrow."

Master Eremis grinned his approval. "Very good." Then he turned to Terisa and extended his hand. "My lady, will you accompany me? Someone must offer you the hospitality of Orison. I will see you honorably quartered, as befits a woman of your obvious importance." He gave the word *importance* a slight, jesting stress, teasing either her or Geraden. "And there are many things of which I wish to speak with you."

He was looking squarely at her again, and she doubted that she could have refused his offer even if she had wanted to: his direct attention was seductive and compelling. It seemed to make her throat dry and her knees unsteady. Involuntarily, she reacted to him as if he were the first man who had ever looked at her in that way. As far as she knew, he *was* the first.

But when she raised her hand to take Eremis', Geraden suddenly said, "My lady, I prefer that you accompany me." His manner had become formal.

At once, an astonished silence dropped over the Masters; they stared at Geraden as though he had just insulted Eremis. The flush

on Geraden's skin betrayed that he was conscious of his audacity.
Nevertheless the muscles of his jaw bunched stubbornly, and his eyes
didn't flinch.

Master Eremis raised an eyebrow; Terisa felt his concentration
shift from her to Geraden. But after a brief flick away his gaze returned to hers. "Come," he said in an appealing—and commanding
—tone. "The Apt has played his part in these matters, but now he
must leave them to those of greater rank, ability, and experience.
You will not complain of my company, I think, my lady."

She almost went with him. She wanted to—or thought she wanted
to—or perhaps she had no idea what she wanted, but if she went
with him he might be able to answer that question for her.

The Apt wasn't prepared to let her go, however. "My lady," he
said, his voice clenched around his anxiety and determination, "Master Eremis believes that you do not exist."

His assertion fell into the silence like a personal challenge, as if he
were daring the Master to battle.

And a small sting of panic touched Terisa's heart.

Vexation replaced the humor in Eremis' face. He swung scowling
away from her; his tall body seemed to poise itself for a scathing
retort. But an instant later he drew back a step, his self-control restored.

"That is not properly true, my lady," he said coldly, without a
glance at her. "I believe that you did not exist until you were translated from the mirror."

"And therefore," Geraden went on, "he believes that you are an
object, my lady, an artifact of Imagery—a thing to be used, not a
woman to be respected."

That was too much for Master Eremis. "Faugh!" he spat. "I will
not debate the meaning of Imagery with a puppy too hapless to earn
a chasuble and too witless to respect his betters." He dismissed Terisa. "Go with him. He will drive me to distraction if you do not."

Turning away, he strode through the crowd of Masters. A moment
after he disappeared behind one of the pillars, Terisa heard the thud
of a heavy wooden door.

Geraden didn't look at her. His gaze was fixed on the flagstones.
He was so hot with embarrassment that beads of sweat stood on his
forehead.

FOUR: THE OLD DODDERER

rrogance," one of the Imagers muttered. Another smiled his relish for Eremis' discomfiture; but most of the Congery felt otherwise. Master Gilbur gave a heavy shrug of disgust. The rabbity man twitched his nose.

They were glaring at Geraden.

Trembling inside, Terisa studied him too. Softly, hesitantly, she asked, "What do you mean, he believes I don't exist? Or I didn't exist until I was translated from the mirror?" That idea hit her too hard, too deeply. Was the uncertainty of her being so plain that even strangers could see it? "It doesn't make any sense. None of this makes any sense. You don't even know who I am."

At once, Geraden began to apologize. "I'm sorry, my lady. I keep treating you badly, when that's the last thing I want." He met her gaze with an expression of brave distress—unhappy about his talent for doing or saying the wrong thing, but determined to face the consequences. "I should have let you go with Master Eremis. I don't know what came over me."

Before she could protest, That isn't what I meant, Master Barsonage intervened. "Apt Geraden," he said, "we have little patience for your contrition just now."

"I'm sorry," said Geraden again, reflexively.

"It is a tale," the Master went on in a tone like a bar of lead, "we have heard many times. Silence it, therefore, and heed me instead. I will not command you not to speak to the King, since I know you would not obey me. I will say this, however. She is here through your agency. She is your responsibility. Give her the courtesy of Orison's hospitality as well as the Congery's respect. She is a mystery to us and must be well treated.

"But"—he clamped a hand onto Geraden's shoulder—"do not answer her questions, Apt."

At that, Geraden's eyes widened. Ignoring Terisa, Barsonage tightened his grip and his tone. "As a mystery to us, she is dangerous. Do not betray Mordant or the Congery to her until we are sure of her."

Geraden's gaze slid away from the Master's. He studied the stones under Terisa's feet and said nothing.

Very quietly, the thick man asked, "Do you understand me, Apt? I am the mediator of the Congery. If I dismiss you, you will never again be considered for the chasuble of a Master."

None of the other Imagers made a sound. Some of them looked vexed; some seemed to be holding their breath. The air in the room was still too cold for comfort.

Geraden's shoulder twisted under the mediator's grasp; then he straightened himself against the pressure. "I understand you, Master Barsonage." He sounded faraway and forlorn. "The lady is my responsibility."

"In all ways."

"In all ways."

Slowly, Master Barsonage released his hand. "Admirable," he muttered. "Good sense becomes you."

"Ha!" snorted Master Gilbur. "Admirable, indeed." He was glaring blackly at Geraden. "If you believe that he will keep his word, Barsonage, you have become old in your wits."

At that, Master Barsonage put his hands like barrel staves on his sides. "Let me caution you against such statements, Master Gilbur. We are little trusted now—and less when you speak with such contempt. Apt Geraden springs from the honest and honorable line of the Domne. The sons of the Domne have always been true."

Abruptly, then, he turned away from Geraden and Terisa. "These meetings consume too much time," he said in a friendly way to no one in particular. "Again I am late for my noontide meal." Slapping at his girth, he asked, "Masters, will you join me?"

Several of the Imagers assented; Gilbur and others declined with varying degrees of courtesy. The Congery began to break up as Masters left the open center of the chamber, moving toward the doors beyond the pillars. After a few backward looks and a murmured comment or two, they left Terisa and Geraden alone.

He continued staring at the stones under her feet as if he were ashamed.

She blinked at him, feeling vaguely stupid. No one was going to answer any of her questions? No one was going to tell her why Master Eremis thought she didn't exist? Surely she had a right to protest?

As a little girl, however, she had occasionally made the mistake of protesting, of trying to stand up for herself. *It isn't fair why do I always have to go to bed you never want me around!* The reactions she had received taught her at an early age the folly of what she was doing. Her parents had wanted her to impinge on their consciousness as little as possible. Her father, in particular, had seldom been gentle when she had called his notice down on herself. Following his example, most of his servants had treated her with bare tolerance. And the numerous private schools to which she had been shuttled at his whim all had specific instructions where she was concerned. A passive child was only dismissed from attention; an assertive one was punished. And it was punishment that had first convinced her that she might not be real. Over the years, she had learned to let herself feel less and less of the emotions that led to demands and rejection.

So instead of indulging herself in some kind of outcry, she did the next best thing: she watched the flush of Geraden's shame and said nothing.

When he finally raised his head, he looked miserable.

"I'm sorry, my lady. This isn't what I thought was going to happen at all. I knew they would have to be convinced—especially Master Gilbur. But I didn't think they—" He grimaced. "It isn't fair to drag you into this and then refuse to answer your questions. It just isn't fair. And it's *my* fault again, of course."

To keep him talking, she asked, "How is it your fault?"

Glumly, he muttered, "I didn't tell them about your mirrors."

There seemed to be no point in reminding him that she couldn't possibly understand what he meant, so she said, "Why didn't you?"

He shrugged. "I meant to. But at the last second I had the strongest feeling—" His voice trailed away, then came back more strongly. "I just don't trust Master Eremis. Or Master Gilbur either, for that matter. I don't want to tell them anything."

Terisa considered him for a moment. "But you're still not going to answer my questions." Thanks to her years of training, her tone betrayed almost no bitterness.

With a wince, he replied, "No. I can't. You heard him. I think he's wrong, but that doesn't make any difference. He can have me dismissed. I've been trying to become a Master since I was fifteen. I can't give it up." Again he said, "I'm sorry."

Glowering, but unable to meet her gaze, he stopped. His dire expression made him look younger than he was—in fact, younger than she was herself. Unexpectedly, she found that she wasn't angry at him, not even down in the secret places of her heart where she kept her dangerous emotions hidden. He seemed to be upset as much on her behalf as on his own. That was a degree of consideration to which she was unaccustomed.

In response, she surprised herself by inquiring, "Do you think I exist?"

He looked at her sharply, the glower suddenly gone from his face. "Well, of course. Isn't it obvious? In fact, you're the proof of what King Joyse and Adept Havelock have been saying all along. Masters like Eremis and Gilbur believe the mirrors create what we see in them. Those things only exist when they're translated out of the glass. But that never made any sense to me. And now it sounds like nonsense—now that I've gone into a mirror for myself and met you." Excitement improved his appearance considerably. "That was a shock—when I stepped into the glass expecting to find the champion and found you instead—but it convinced me you're real. Everything in the mirrors is real."

Then he caught himself; the excitement faded from his face. He became distant and wary, ashamed again. "But I'm not supposed to answer your questions."

Terisa almost laughed. Out of nowhere, he made her feel good—better than she had felt for a long time. Already, he had convinced her that if she kept him talking he wouldn't be able to refuse her. He took her too seriously to refuse her. "Apt Geraden," she said, "if I'm real, I must be important. Even if I'm an accident, I must be important. Don't you think it might be a good idea to ask me who I am?"

His eyes went wide: mouth agape, he stared at her. Apparently, he had been so wrapped up in her translation and his argument with the Imagers that he had forgotten the simple courtesy of asking for her

didn't find reassuring; but the other addressed Geraden like a familiar comrade, asking him if there were any Masters remaining in the
chamber.

When Geraden shook his head, the guard relaxed his stance.
"Then we're off duty for a while. Listen, Geraden. Argus and I have
a small keg of ale waiting. What do you think? Would you and"—he
flicked a suggestive glance at Terisa—"your companion like to join
us for a drink?"

"I think, Ribuld," Geraden replied good-humoredly, "that you
and Argus forgot how to think the day you decided to be soldiers.
For your information, my 'companion' is the lady Terisa of Morgan,
and she isn't likely to spend her time swilling ale with the likes of
you. The King is waiting to meet her right now."

"Too good for us, is she?" muttered Argus. But Ribuld gave him a
solid elbow-jab in the ribs, and he stepped back, a look of apoplexy
on his face.

Grinning, Geraden drew Terisa on down the passageway.

"Don't let them worry you," he said softly as they walked. "Those
two look terrible, but they're good men. They trained with my
brother Artagel. I'm going to try to get them assigned to keep an eye
on you."

"Why do I need guards?"

"Because—" he began. This time, however, he realized what he
was doing right away. "For the same reason I'm not supposed to
answer your questions. Mordant has too many enemies. The Congery has too many enemies. And King Joyse—" Again he stopped, a
look of unconscious pain on his face. "Whether you're here by accident or not, you already have enemies yourself. As long as I'm responsible for you, I want to be sure you also have guards—guards
who're going to take you seriously. Ribuld and Argus will do that for
me because I'm Artagel's brother."

After a moment, he muttered, "Master Barsonage made a big mistake telling me not to answer questions."

In silence, she walked with him down the corridor.

The corridor was built of the same gray blocks of granite that had
formed the walls and ceiling of the Congery's chamber; and it led to
several turns, a few doors, a stair, and then into an enormous square
hall large enough to be a ballroom.

This place had a smooth floor, the stones closely fitted so that there
were no gaps; balconies around the walls, where musicians might sit

to play, or from which high lords and ladies might watch the dancing; several huge hearths for warmth. In each corner, broad stairways curved gracefully upward out of sight. But the place was lifeless. It had an atmosphere of disuse, even of neglect: the people and musicians, the excitement and color that might have given it gaiety had gone away. The hearths were cold; and the only light came from narrow windows high above the balcony on one wall, with the result that the hall was full of gloom. The windows permitted a glimpse of sullen clouds.

Terisa shivered as Geraden headed her toward one of the stairways. "This isn't the direct route," he commented. "But we wouldn't be able to get across the courtyard without ruining your clothes." She was fortunate to be as warmly dressed as she was. What she could see of the sky through the windows looked like winter.

The stairway took them up one level. From there, he led her through a sequence of passages, short stairways, and halls that created a haphazard impression, as if the massive stone pile through which they moved had been constructed randomly, by lumps. But his instinct for mishap didn't include any uncertainty about where he was going: he knew this place intimately.

As they walked, they began to encounter more and more people. Many of them were guards, on duty or on errands; but many more seemed to be the inhabitants of the building. Old men leaned on their brooms in the corridors, stirring small piles of dust with diligent inattention. Girls scurried here and there, carrying linens or buckets or mops. Boys sprinted past, probably pretending that they were involved in something urgent so that no one would stop them and put them to work. As for the men and women—

Terisa found that she could easily estimate their rank by their clothes. Everyone was warmly dressed; but the sweeps and chambermaids wore woolen skirts, wool shawls over their blouses, and heavy clogs, where the ladies had on floor-length gowns of taffeta or satin and supple leather boots, with jewels in their hair or about their necks. The charmen and grooms dressed themselves as Geraden did, in jerkins, pants, and boots, perhaps with a long dagger sheathed at their belts, but the lords wore elaborately woven surcoats over flowing shirts and tight hose, with sabers in ornamented scabbards on their hips. And the intermediate degrees of station could be defined at once by the presence or absence of a sword or a décolletage, by the length of a gown or the embroidery on a surcoat.

In spite of their elegance, however, even the finest lords and ladies didn't look like they had ever been to a ball. Almost without exception, they comported themselves like people who lived under a shadow.

Several of the individuals Terisa and Geraden encountered greeted him, either by name or by title.

All of them stared at Terisa as openly as they dared.

After a while, self-consciousness made her realize that they had probably never seen anyone like her before. The idea was startling—and unsettling.

Shortly, Geraden led her up a series of stairs that doubled back and forth as if they occupied the inside of a tower. They led to a high, carved door with a guard stationed on either side. These men were better kempt than Argus and Ribuld, though they appeared no less experienced and dangerous; but they acknowledged Geraden with the same familiarity.

"This is the lady Terisa of Morgan," Geraden said. "Will you announce us? I think the King will want to meet her."

The guards made halfhearted efforts to conceal the way they ogled her. One of them shrugged: it was his duty to ward the King, but he clearly couldn't think of any reason to believe Geraden was dangerous. The other knocked on the door, let himself into the room beyond, and closed the door behind him.

A moment later, he returned. "You can go in. But be careful. The King and Adept Havelock are playing hop-board. If the Adept decides you've disturbed his concentration, he might do something unpleasant."

Geraden gave the man a sour smile. "I understand."

His hand lightly touching Terisa's arm, he moved her toward the half-open door.

The room they entered surprised her. It was the first richly appointed chamber she had seen in this place, and although it was about the size of her living room and dining room combined, it was warm. A thick rug, woven in an abstract pattern of lush blues and reds, covered most of the floor. Blond wood paneling had been set over the stone walls, and each panel was elegantly decorated, some with carving, others with fine black inlay-work. Candles burned in brass holders set into the walls; small five-branched candelabra stood on ornamental tables in the corners of the room and on both ends of the mantelpiece above the hearth. Hot coals glowed under the flames in the fireplace.

Two old men sat opposite each other at a small table in the center of the room. One of them wore a purple velvet robe that covered him like a tent. He appeared lost in it, as if it had been made for him when he was young and powerful, and no longer fit him now that his frame had withered. That impression was reinforced by his stark white hair and beard, by the faint blue tint his veins gave his skin, by the arthritic swelling of the knuckles of his hands, and by the watery azure hue of his eyes. A thin circlet of gold held his hair back from his face.

"King Joyse," Geraden whispered to Terisa.

The other man had lost most of his hair, and what was left of it stuck up from his pate in unruly tufts. His hawk nose gave his face a fierceness which was belied by the constant trembling of his fleshy lips. His eyes seemed to be looking in slightly different directions. He wore a plain, dingy surcoat, which had once been white, with— as far as Terisa could tell—nothing under it. But over his shoulders was draped a yellow chasuble.

"Adept Havelock," breathed Geraden. "Some of the Masters call him 'the King's Dastard.' "

Both men were concentrating intently on a playing board set between them. It was composed of alternating red and black squares, but only the black squares were in use. On them sat small round counters: the King's were white; Havelock's, red. As she noticed the board, Terisa saw Havelock make a move, hopping one of his men over two of the King's and removing them from the board.

They were playing checkers.

A jolt of recognition went through her, upsetting her disproportionately. After all, it was only a minor game—one of the few she had ever played. One of her father's valets had taught it to her in his spare time when she was ten years old; and they had played together at intervals for nearly a year, until he lost his job. He had been a square-cut young man with an odd kindness in his eyes and an infrequent grin. The truth was that she had never really enjoyed the game itself: she had played so eagerly because she had a tremendous crush on him. His attention and his little courtesies to her had charmed her completely. When the man was fired, she had somehow mustered enough courage to ask her father why, but he had refused to give any explanation. "It's none of your business, Terisa. Go and play. I'm busy."

Remembering that valet now, she felt an unexpected sense of loss, as if in her small world she had just suffered an important bereavement. The life she was used to had been taken away from her as easily as one of her father's whims, and nobody would tell her why.

The game disturbed her for other reasons as well, however. It was something familiar in a place where nothing was familiar. What was it doing here? What was *she* doing here? Precisely because it was familiar—because it didn't fit—it seemed to make what was happening to her less real.

Geraden took a step forward, but neither King Joyse nor the old Adept looked up from the game. After a moment, he cleared his throat. Still neither of the players took notice of him. He glanced back at Terisa and shrugged, then ventured to call attention to himself.

"My lord King, I've brought the lady Terisa of Morgan to you." He hesitated briefly before adding, "I've told her you must meet her."

Adept Havelock remained hunched over the board, unheeding of everything except his game. But the King raised his head, turned his moist blue gaze toward Geraden and Terisa.

He seemed to take a moment to focus his eyes. Then, slowly, he began to smile.

Terisa thought immediately that he had a wonderful smile. It contained none of the artificial good humor or calculation she might have expected from a ruler. Instead, it lighted his face with a clean, childlike innocence and pleasure: it made him look like a young boy who had unexpectedly found a secret friend. Irrationally, she felt that her entire life would have been different if she had seen anyone smile like that before. She couldn't stop herself from smiling back at him—and didn't want to.

With a slight quaver of age in his voice, he said, "If you have told her that I must meet her, Geraden, then surely I must. It would be unforgivably discourteous if you spoke anything less than the truth to such a lady—and so it would be equally rude if I failed to make what you have told her true."

Carefully, he pushed his chair back and rose to his feet. His movements were unsteady; standing, he appeared more than ever lost in his voluminous robe. But his smile remained as pure as sunlight. "My lady Terisa of Morgan, do you play hop-board?"

Terisa was fixed on King Joyse, but at the edge of her attention she thought she saw Geraden wince.

For the moment, his reactions were irrelevant to her. Buoyed by the King's smile, she replied, "I haven't played since I was a girl." That was true—if she didn't count all the games she had played against herself in the years after the valet was fired, games she had played in an effort to be content with her own company. "We called it checkers. It looks like the same game."

" 'Checkers'?" King Joyse looked thoughtful. "That seems an odd name." Then he smiled again. "But no matter. Perhaps when Have-lock has finished giving me his customary drubbing, you will consent to play a game or two with me? I would be delighted to be able to hope—however briefly—for an honest victory."

"My lord King." Geraden sounded tense and worried, as if his introduction of Terisa to King Joyse were going seriously wrong. "I told the lady Terisa you would want to meet her because she came here by translation."

Geraden's interruption appeared to sadden the King. His smile changed to lines of fatigue and melancholy as he looked toward the Apt. "I see that, Geraden," he said quietly. "I'm not blind, you know."

"I'm sorry," Geraden murmured. "I just meant that she's impor-tant. I had to bring her to you." He was hurrying. "The Congery sent me into the mirror this morning to try to get the champion they wanted. But I didn't find him. I found her instead. She might be the answer to the auguries."

Adept Havelock continued to ignore Geraden and Terisa. Scruti-nizing the board, he reached out finally and moved one of the King's men, hopping one of his own. Then, triumphantly, he responded by demolishing a whole line of opposing pieces and arriving at the last row, where he crowned himself with severe emphasis.

Grimly, forcing himself to speak in spite of his embarrassment, Geraden went on, "She proves you've been right all along. The mirrors don't create what we see. The Images really exist."

King Joyse studied Geraden for a moment. Then he sighed wea-rily and turned to Terisa. "My lady," he said, "please pardon me. It appears that this urgent young man will not allow us the freedom to play hop-board just now.

"Be reasonable, Geraden," he continued, shifting his attention
back to the Apt. "You know that I agree with you. But what does her
presence here truly prove?" The quaver in his voice persisted: he
sounded like he was rehearsing an argument so old that he would no
longer have gotten any satisfaction out of winning it. "Surely it's
possible that you found her instead of the champion you sought
because of one of your unfortunate mishaps? Or perhaps you've
touched on an unsuspected strength in yourself, and you found her
instead of the champion because she was what you wished to find? In
what way does her translation demonstrate the fundamental nature
of Imagery—or of mirrors?"

Geraden looked first startled by the King's argument, then
vaguely nauseated. "But I *saw*—" he protested incoherently. "It
wasn't the same."

King Joyse watched him mildly and waited for him to pull his
thoughts together.

With an effort, Geraden said slowly, "I made that mirror myself. I
saw the champion I was supposed to find in it. He was right there in
front of me when I stepped into the glass. But during the translation
everything changed. I arrived in a room that was totally different
from the Images. *She* is totally different. What you're saying is that I
made her up—by some kind of accident, either because I didn't
know what I was doing or because I didn't know my own strength.
How is that *possible*?"

In reply, the King shrugged—a bit sadly, Terisa thought. "Who
can say? Centuries ago, no one believed that Imagery itself was possible. Even a hundred years ago, no one believed that Imagery might
threaten the existence of the very realms which made use of it.

"Geraden," he said to the pain on the Apt's face, "I don't claim
that she does *not* exist. I only observe that her presence here doesn't
settle the question."

Geraden shook his head and tried again. "But if you think that
way—and you push it far enough—you can't prove *any*thing exists.
You can't prove I'm here talking to you. You can't prove you're
playing hop-board with anybody but yourself. You might not be
playing it anywhere except in your own mind."

At that, the King smiled, then grimaced humorously. "Unfortunately, I'm confident that my games of hop-board are real—and my
opponent as well. The drubbings I receive are too painful for any
other explanation."

"Very wise," remarked Adept Havelock unexpectedly, without raising his eyes from the board. In lugubrious concentration, he moved two or three of King Joyse's men to other squares; then with his crowned piece he jumped them all, hitting each square emphatically as if to compensate for his wall-eyed vision. "Only hop-board is real. Ask any philosopher. Nothing else"—he fluttered one hand in dismissal—"signifies."

Without meaning to, Terisa smiled at the fond grin King Joyse directed toward Havelock. The Adept's way of playing checkers made it clear that he wasn't in his right mind; nevertheless she found the King's affection for the old Imager catching. Watching them, she forgot for a moment that the present conversation had anything to do with her.

But Geraden was too vexed and unhappy to enjoy the King's playful attitude. "My lord King, this isn't a joke. The realm is tottering, and all of Mordant is waiting for you to do something about it." He gathered momentum as he spoke, until his urgency seemed to clear away his smaller uncertainties, contritions, and anxieties. "I don't know why you haven't, but the Masters finally couldn't wait any longer. They—" He caught himself. "*We* are doing our best to find an answer. And we have. *I* think we have, anyway. The lady Terisa isn't the champion we were expecting—but that probably doesn't matter. There's a reason she's here instead of what we were expecting, and I don't think it has anything to do with accidents. I'm *not* an arch-Imager in disguise. And mirrors don't have minds of their own."

As she studied his intent expression, Terisa caught a glimpse of what made him so accident-prone. He was too many things at once—a boy, a man, and everything in between—and the differing parts of himself seldom came into balance. She found him attractive in that way. Yet the perception saddened her: she herself wasn't too many things, but too few.

The King was watching Geraden as well; and the lines of his old visage seemed to hint at a sadness of his own. But they also suggested interest and perhaps a kind of pride. "So much confidence is remarkable," he commented. The quaver in his voice made his nonchalance sound unsteady, feigned. "You've spoken of what you've seen, Geraden. Tell me what you've seen that gives you this confidence."

Geraden hesitated, glancing at Terisa in appeal as though he believed she knew what he was about to say; as though he felt it would be more convincing if it came from her. But of course she had no idea what he had in mind. After a moment, he returned his gaze to King Joyse.

"My lord King," the Apt said, his own voice shaking with determination and alarm, "she is a Master of Imagery."

At that, the King fixed a watery and unreadable look on Terisa—a look which could have indicated surprise or boredom.

Without a glance at the other people in the room, Havelock swept all the men off the board and began to set up a new game.

"I believe," Geraden went on softly, "her power pulled my translation away from where I thought I was going."

The assertion was so absurd that several moments passed before Terisa realized she was expected to answer it. Then, helplessly, she began to blush under the scrutiny of the two men.

Close to panic, she replied, "No. No, of course not. That's crazy. I don't even know what you're talking about."

Carefully, Geraden said, "I found her in a room entirely walled with mirrors."

"So what?" A distant, self-conscious part of her mind was surprised by how this ludicrous conception frightened her. "Everybody has mirrors. A lot of people use them for decor. They're just pieces of glass—with something on the back to make them reflect. They don't mean anything."

In response to her alarm, King Joyse murmured as if he were trying to comfort her, "Perhaps in your world that is so. Here the truth is otherwise."

But Geraden was already saying as definitively as he could, "Each of her mirrors showed her own Image exactly. They showed *my* Image exactly. And she isn't hurt. *I'm* not hurt. I ought to be raving by now. Or my mind should be completely empty. But I'm all right. She's all right.

"They were *her* mirrors."

An amazed dismay stopped Terisa's mouth. She felt she couldn't understand what was literally being said to her. *Each of her mirrors showed her own Image exactly.* Here that wasn't true. Suddenly, her grasp on the ordinary details of life—the plain facts which showed that she was in contact with reality—was threatened, denied.

And King Joyse peered at her with an intent interest that made everything worse. "Is this correct, my lady?" he asked as if she had just claimed to be some kind of exotic insect. "The story is told that an Imager once chanced to form a flat mirror which showed the exact spot on which he stood. Therefore he saw himself in the glass—and was immediately canceled. His body remained where it was until its balance failed, but his spirit had entirely ceased to exist. It was lost in translation. How do the people of your world avoid this fate?"

Groping for sense, she countered, "That's impossible. Mirrors can't hurt anybody. They just show you what you look like. Except reversed. Like a pool of water. Haven't you ever looked at yourself in a pool of water?"

Both men studied her oddly. In a soft, musing tone, King Joyse said, "We're taught from childhood to be wary of Images. We don't seek them out."

Without any particular forewarning, Adept Havelock pounded his fist on the table, then picked up the checkerboard and threw it at the ceiling. The checkers made a sound like wooden rain against the granite of the ceiling and fell back to bounce noiselessly in the blue-and-red rug.

Tottering to his feet, the old Imager roared, "Horror and bal-locks!" His eyes squinted ferociously at both the King and Geraden; patches of scarlet burned on his face; his fat lips shook like wattles. "She's a *woman*!" He struck a wild gesture in her direction with the back of his hand. "Are you and every man jack feeble-wit Imager of the Congery *blind*? She is female, fe-fe-*fe*-male." Saliva sprayed from his mouth. "Oh, my groin!"

Because she didn't know what else to do, Terisa stood and stared at him.

"Look at you!" Still using the back of his hand, he hit King Joyse across the chest—a blow which was more dramatic in intention than in effect. "And you!" With his other hand, he struck Geraden. "Or here!" Awkwardly but quickly, he bobbed toward the floor like a poorly constructed rooster, then pulled himself erect. "And here!" Another bob. "And here!" Each time he stood upright again, he brandished a checker in his open palm. "All *men*, every one! Every one of them!"

But when his hand was full of checkers, he flung them down again. "By the hoary goat of the arch-Imager," he shouted as if the three people in front of him had insulted him beyond mortal endurance, "*she is a woman!*"

Moving with an attempt at vehemence which his frail lim couldn't support, he stamped/shuffled to the outer door of the ch ber, jerked it open, and slammed it shut again without leaving. Then, somewhat unsteadily, he retrieved the checkerboard from the floor and set it squarely on the table. Oblivious to everyone else, he took his seat and began to study the empty board as if an intense game were in progress.

King Joyse sighed delicately.

Geraden said, "I'm sorry."

Terisa wasn't quite sure why. Her heart pounded as if she had somehow escaped a crisis.

"No matter, my boy," replied the King, patting Geraden's shoulder absentmindedly, as though the Apt had in fact committed some minor offense. For a moment, his gaze seemed to swim out of focus while he thought about something—or perhaps he was simply taking a quick nap on his feet. Then he nodded to himself. Smiling irrelevantly in Terisa's direction, he said, "Geraden, it occurs to me to be surprised that the Congery released the lady Terisa in your company. She is here by Imagery—and some of the Masters, I know, are jealous. Also, I suspect that they would always prefer to keep what they do secret from me. Yet here you are. How do you account for that?"

Geraden made an effort to look at the King squarely; but his discomfiture was too strong for him.

"Did you tell the Masters that she may be a Master herself?"

The Apt swallowed thickly. "No."

"Ah," King Joyse said mildly. "That explains it, then. Of course they let her go, thinking her to be just another of your mishaps. But why didn't you tell them?"

A slow flush spread over Geraden's face. Muscles knotted in his forehead. His embarrassment was so acute that it nearly brought tears to Terisa's eyes. But he clamped his jaws shut and didn't answer.

"My boy, that may have been foolish." The King's hand still held Geraden's shoulder; his expression was kind. "You've been trying for—what is it now? ten years?—to become an Imager, a member of the Congery. How can you hope to succeed, if you risk angering the very men who control the knowledge, skill, and position you crave?"

"My lord King." Geraden forced himself to let the King see the sharp pain in his eyes; and a sudden dignity came to him. "If I had told them, they would have commanded me to keep all this secret from you. Then I would have been compelled to disobey them di-
·tly—and my hope of a chasuble would be lost forever." There

was an undercurrent of bitterness in his voice. "I can't bear disloyalty to the King of Mordant. I can't give up my dreams. So I act like a fool. They'll believe I didn't notice her mirrors—or didn't understand the significance of what I saw."

In response, another of the smiles that had first touched Terisa's heart lit the King's face. For a moment, his age, weakness, and uncertainty fell away, and he became simply happy.

"Thank you, Geraden. It pleases me to see such loyalty, especially in a son of my old friend the Domne. I'll try to arrange that you don't suffer for it.

"Now"—his expression grew thoughtful—"let us consider. How best to do it?

"Tell me." Slowly, he lowered himself back into his chair across the table from Havelock. His robe settled about him like a tent with the ridgepole cut. "How did the Masters react to the lady Terisa of Morgan's arrival?"

Relieved by the King's attitude, Geraden relaxed visibly. "That's easy. You could guess all of it if you wanted to. Everyone was astonished when she came out of the glass. Master Gilbur was furious. I'm sure he thinks I'm criminally perverse instead of"—he grimaced—"just unlucky. Master Eremis was . . . well, amused."

"Among other things, I don't doubt," the King commented. "Master Eremis," he explained to Terisa, "has an eye for loveliness which never fails him."

Geraden nodded and went on. "Master Quillon saw her appearance the same way I did, as proof you've been right about Imagery all along. But nobody listened to him.

"Master Barsonage made me responsible for her. He told me to give her all the hospitality and courtesy of Orison. But he told me not to answer any of her questions. Here she is, taken out of her own world for no reason except because I asked her to come, and put down in a place she has no way to understand, and he commanded me not to give her the simple decency of an explanation."

Terisa hardly heard him. She was wondering, Is that why he looked at me, *looked* at me as if I were real? The idea was so new that it seemed to be full of mysterious importance. Did he think I was lovely? Do you think I'm lovely? Is that possible?

"Unless, of course," the King returned quietly, "she is a Master Imager and had already chosen us before you met her."

Geraden scowled. "What difference does that make? Haven't I been saying all along I think she's an Imager? She still deserves—"

"No." King Joyse's tone was mild and certain. "You make an assumption which may be unjustified.

"Master Barsonage's command was not unreasonable. When the Alend Monarch sends his ambassador to negotiate our treaties, and to probe my intentions, he understands much of his world and much of my own. We have that in common. Yet I do not make him privy to everything I know or think or hope, neither for policy nor for courtesy. I do not invite him into the secret places of Orison, or into the secret places of my heart. To do so would be dangerous—too dangerous for any responsible justification. Not knowing his secrets, I could not predict or control the use he made of mine. Still less would I answer any questions which an ambassador from the High King of Cadwal might venture to ask.

"The same reasoning applies to the lady Terisa"—he looked toward her—"if you will pardon me for speaking of you as if you were absent." Returning his gaze to Geraden, he continued, "If, as she says, she comes from a world in which mirrors have no meaning, and is therefore ignorant of us, then it is at best unkind to refuse her answers. But in that case—mark this, Geraden—it is also folly to have brought her here at all. I speak not of morality now, but of the simple question of our practical need. If she is not an Imager, what use can she possibly be to us?"

Geraden held himself still and didn't reply.

Adept Havelock continued to study his blank board, deaf to whatever was being said.

"Conversely, if she *is* an Imager—a Master of mirrors strong enough to wrest your translation away from its apparent Image— then she is here for purposes of her own, which we do not know. She is like an ambassador: similarly to be respected, and similarly dangerous.

"Would you say, my lady," he asked Terisa unexpectedly, "that I've summarized the dilemma fairly?"

She stared at him, unable to follow his reasoning. In order to make sense of it, she had first to presuppose the existence of magical mirrors which didn't reflect whatever was in front of them but instead showed alternative worlds or realities. Then she had to take seriously the notion that her own mirrors, the mirrors in her apartment, were like that, giving *her*, Terisa Morgan, power over the reality and even the sanity of other people. The whole argument collapsed into non-sense before it reached the lofty conclusion King Joyse asked her to endorse.

Instinctively, she turned to Geraden. He was her only connection to her own life, with its ordinary facts and limitations. You saw me, she wanted to protest. You saw my apartment. There's nothing magic about it. You didn't lose your mind. None of this has anything to do with me.

His attention was on the King, however. "But if she's that strong," he said slowly, "an Imager more powerful than we can imagine, then it's folly for us to risk offending her. We don't know her purposes—they might be good or bad for us. But they're sure to turn bad if we don't treat her well. We need her friendship, not her anger. We need to be open and decent with her."

Smiling softly, King Joyse glanced back and forth between the Apt and Terisa as Geraden spoke. When he was done, the King replied, "Your reasoning has merit. It is fortunate that only rulers are re-quired to make those decisions."

"My lord King?"

"Apt," said King Joyse, his tone still mild but now faintly sad as well, "here is my command. You are no longer responsible for the lady Terisa of Morgan. Your King thanks you for what you have done—and relieves you of any further interest in the matter. Your duties lie with the Congery, to which you are pledged. You will have no more reason to see or speak with the lady Terisa, and certainly no reason to answer any of her questions.

"You may go. The lady Terisa will remain with me."

Geraden's face went white: if he had closed his eyes, he would have looked like he was about to faint. But his eyes contradicted his pallor. They flamed with a quick, unflinching anger that seemed to burn all the boyishness out of him.

Softly, he said, "You consider me unworthy."

At that, the King's features crumpled into a grimace. He made an abrupt, dismissing gesture. "Oh, get out." For the first time since Terisa had met him, he sounded like a querulous old man. "You're breaking my heart."

The muscles of Geraden's face twitched. "Yes, my lord King," he said between his teeth. Roughly, he turned to Terisa and bowed. "My lady."

She had no reply. He was too hurt—and his hurt was too real. She

was lost in it. He needed a response from her; but her responses
were hidden behind years of silence and passivity.

When he started toward the door, his foot came down on the edge
of one of the scattered checkers. His ankle twisted, and he stumbled,
nearly fell. Embarrassment darkened his cheeks. His ears were crimson as he made his exit.

Watching the Apt go, Havelock began to giggle in a high, mad
voice, as if his mirth were a place where reason or compassion
couldn't reach him.

When he subsided, no one spoke for a moment. Then the King
said, in an unsteady attempt at nonchalance, "Well, my lady Terisa of
Morgan. We must give some thought to you. You must be made
comfortable, with all the hospitality Orison can manage, as befits a
guest of your station and importance. And then perhaps you'll consent to a game or two of hop-board? I'm really very tired of Havelock's incessant beatings."

Geraden had been hurt for nothing. There was no reason for anybody to take precautions against her. To her own astonishment, she
heard herself say, "I'm not your lady. My name is Terisa Morgan,
and I'm not anybody's lady. You didn't have to do that to him."

King Joyse tried to smile, but failed to lift the sadness from his
face. "My lady, I am the King. I will call you by whatever name I
choose. And I hope that someday you'll understand."

With as much sarcasm as she had ever dared use, she returned,
"But you're not going to explain it to me. You don't want to answer
any of my questions."

Instead of replying, King Joyse slowly lowered his frail bones to
the floor and started crawling around the room, picking up checkers.

FIVE: WARDROBES
FULL OF CLOTHES

ike a baffled child, Terisa shook her head, blinked her eyes. Unfortunately, nothing changed. Adept Havelock went on peering at his board as if in his mind he were already playing future games. The King continued to collect the scattered checkers, moving on his hands and knees.

The panic which had been gnawing at the back of her mind suddenly got worse. She shouldn't have spoken so sarcastically, so assertively. She was dependent on these people. With one cross word, she could be dismissed from existence. The King could have her thrown into another of those mirrors, and she might end up somewhere even more impossible. The world of the Congery's chosen champion suggested itself to her imagination. Or she might arrive nowhere— might simply dissolve into the gray, unacknowledged, pointless nothing she had feared and fought for most of her life.

I'm sorry, she thought involuntarily, while her alarm increased. Let me stay. I'll be a good girl, I promise.

At that moment, King Joyse braced his arms, levered his legs under him, and tottered to his feet. Moving to the table, he dropped the checkers he had collected in front of Havelock. Then he turned his clean, good smile on Terisa.

"Pardon me, my lady. What have I been thinking about? I'm rude to neglect you in this way. You must be fatigued from your translation, eager for rest and refreshment. Do you have any special requirements in sustenance or comfort? No?" His apology sounded sincere, but his questions were perfunctory. "Then I'll summon someone to guide you to your rooms and care for you."

Still smiling, he hunted around him with an increasingly aimless air until he happened to slip one hand into a pocket of his robe, where he found a silver bell with a wooden handle. He rang it vigorously. Almost immediately the outer door opened, and one of the guards stepped into the room.

"My lord King?"

"Ah, thank you." For an instant, King Joyse appeared confused, as if he had forgotten what he was doing. His damp eyes blinked at the bell in his hand. Then, abruptly, he said, "A maid for the lady Terisa of Morgan."

"At once, my lord King." The guard saluted by tapping his mail shirt with his fist and left the room.

Havelock reset the checkerboard, although King Joyse hadn't retrieved all the pieces.

"Again I ask your pardon," the King muttered without glancing at Terisa. He scrubbed his hands over his face, sighed, and lowered himself back into his chair. "My wits aren't what they were." His smile was gone, replaced by sadness. "Be honest with me, my lady. Do you have family? Are there those who will be grieved by your absence? They shouldn't be made to suffer for our necessities. I'll command Geraden to find some way to translate a message for them, to reassure them. Poor boy, it will keep him out of trouble. What message would you have sent, my lady?"

"There's—" she began, but her voice caught. There's nobody. She didn't say that, however. She was lost in this situation, and her fear and her ignorance fed on each other. Nevertheless an unfamiliar part of her was almost trembling with anger at the way she was treated. With an effort, she cleared her throat. "There's only my father."

"How can he be reached?"

Forced to the truth, she said thinly, "He'll never notice I'm gone."

When she said that, the King's gaze flashed at her. For an instant, she couldn't see the white of his hair, the weakness of his stature, the blue tinge of his wrinkled old skin: she saw only the direct strength of his eyes. He was looking at her as though she had somehow moved him.

"Then perhaps"—phlegm made his voice husky—"you may wish to consider it fortunate that you are here."

Carefully, trying to keep her panic under control, she said, "I don't know how to consider it. I don't have enough information. When do you think you might be willing to tell me what's going on?" Then she held her breath in the quick rush of alarm which accompanied temerity.

"Ah, my lady." King Joyse sighed and spread his hands. His swollen knuckles made the gesture appear at once world-weary and decrepit. "That surely depends upon yourself. When will you make clear the truth of your origins, your skill in Imagery, your purposes?"

A weakness that felt like vertigo grew in her head. For some reason, it didn't cloud her mind—it simply made her want to lie down. "You mean," she said wanly, "you're not going to tell me anything until I can prove that I exist—that I wasn't created by any mirror— and until I show you everything I know about Imagery—and until I tell you why I pulled Geraden away from what he thought he was doing when he tried to translate that champion"—in fact, all the things she couldn't possibly do in this crazy situation—"and until I make you believe it."

Down in the pit of her stomach, she felt a giddy and unexpected desire to laugh.

The King didn't shirk her gaze. Nevertheless the lines of his face became sadder and sadder. She was causing him pain which he didn't choose to explain. After a moment, she had to turn away, unable to go on challenging his peculiar vulnerability. The sound of someone knocking at his door came as a relief to her.

The guard reentered the room, bringing a woman with him.

At the sight of her, King Joyse frowned involuntarily, as if he had made a mistake; but at once he rubbed his expression clear. "Saddith. Just the one I wanted."

The woman was shorter than Terisa, with bright eyes, a pert nose, long brunette hair tumbling over her shoulders in natural waves, and a spontaneous smile. She wore a russet skirt that went down to her ankles and a shawl of the same color and material over her shoulders —like the other women Terisa had seen, she was prepared for the cold. But her blouse was open several buttons below the hollow of her throat, and her ripe bosom stretched the fabric. Looking at her, Terisa thought that she must be the kind of woman whom men noticed—the kind who never had any reason to doubt her own reality. The arch of her eyebrows and the angle of her glances suggested that she knew what she was doing.

She scanned Terisa quickly, her eyes wide as she noted Terisa's unfamiliar clothes, a small frown between her brows as she took an inventory of Terisa's face and figure. Then, almost instantly, she shifted her attention. "My lord King," she replied, dropping a graceful curtsy. "You asked for a maid."

"None better," he said, making an effort to sound jovial, "none better. Saddith, this is the lady Terisa of Morgan. She is the guest of Orison. My lady, Saddith will attend upon you as your maid. I'm confident that you'll be pleased with her."

"My lady," Saddith murmured, her eyes now downcast. "I hope that I will serve you well."

Nonplussed, Terisa fell back on her customary silence. She hadn't expected to be assigned a servant. On the other hand, she luckily had some acquaintance with servants. At least she knew how to live with them—how to spend her time without disturbing the rhythms of their activities, how to keep her requests for actual service to a minimum.

"The lady will be using the peacock rooms," King Joyse went on. He sounded more and more distant—perhaps because of the distance in Terisa's head, perhaps because his own interest was wandering. "She'll need a wardrobe. The lady Elega will be able to assist you. Or better the lady Myste—they're more of a size, I think. Whatever food or refreshment she asks, serve her in her rooms.

"My lady"—he had returned his gaze to the board and was studying the checkers—"we will speak again soon. I look forward to testing your prowess at hop-board."

The guard held the door open. Saddith looked up at Terisa expectantly. It was obvious that she had been dismissed. But she felt too tired to understand precisely what that meant. The stress of strangeness was wearing her out. And now that she thought about it, she was probably long overdue for some sleep. She had spent a whole day at the mission, typing that letter over and over again, then returned to her apartment for what she had known was going to be a bad night. But she had had no real conception *how* bad. . .

Fortunately, Saddith came to her rescue. Terisa let the maid's touch on her arm guide her out of the King's chamber.

The guards closed the door behind her.

"This way, my lady." Saddith gestured down the hall, and Terisa automatically started walking in that direction. The maid moved with her head demurely bowed; but she cast repeated speculative glances at Terisa. As they descended the stairs, she asked, "Have you made a long journey to Orison, my lady?"

Terisa shook her head. "I don't know. I came through a mirror—I think." How far was that? It seemed like forever.

"Imagery!" Saddith responded with polite astonishment. "Are you a Master, my lady? I have never known a woman who was a Master."

In spite of her sleepiness, Terisa sensed an opportunity for information. "Don't women do things like that here?"

"Become Imagers?" The maid laughed delicately. "I think not, my lady. Men say that the talent for Imagery is inborn, and that only those so born may hope to shape glass or perform translations. They believe, I'll wager, that no woman is born with the talent. But what is the need for it? Why should a woman desire mirrors"—she gave Terisa a coy smile—"when any man will do what she wishes for her?"

From the stairs, they entered a wing of the immense stone building that Terisa hadn't seen before. Many of the rooms off the long, high halls seemed to be living quarters, and the people moving in and out of them apparently belonged to the middle ranks of the place—merchants, secretaries, ladies-in-waiting, supervisors. Terisa pursued her question with the maid.

"So you don't know anything about mirrors—or Imagery?"

"No, my lady," replied Saddith. "I only know that any Master will tell me whatever I wish—if I conceive a wish for something he knows."

"That must be nice." Terisa thought she understood what she was hearing; but the idea was too abstract to seem real. No man had ever found her that attractive.

"My lady"—Saddith appraised Terisa's figure again, nodding to herself at what she saw—"the same is true for you, if you choose to make it so."

You mean, Terisa thought, if I unbuttoned my shirt King Joyse would tell me whatever I wanted to know? Helpless to stop herself, she started laughing.

"Perhaps," Saddith said, "in your world women have no need of that power." She sounded faintly distressed by the idea: jealous of it? threatened by it?

"I don't know," Terisa admitted. "I don't have any experience."

Saddith looked away quickly; but before her face turned it betrayed a glimpse of mirth or contempt.

After a while, she led Terisa up another series of stairs into what appeared to be another tower. Past a landing at the end of a short hall, they reached a wide door made of polished wood. Saddith opened it and ushered Terisa into her assigned rooms.

It took no great effort of perception to see why they were called the peacock rooms. Their walls were decorated with an ornate profusion of peacock feathers, some hanging like plumes over the dark mahogany tables, others displayed in rich fans where other decorators might have put pictures or tapestries, still others forming a kind of canopy over the large, deep, satin-covered bed. The sizable room Terisa had entered was apparently a sitting room or parlor, its stone floor masked by rugs woven into peacock patterns, its cushioned couch and chairs painted with peacock blue and almost-black purple; but the bedroom could be seen through an arched entryway to her right. A door to the left suggested a bathroom.

The lamps set around the walls were unlit, as were the candles in their holders on the tables; but the rooms were bright with afternoon sunlight which streamed in through several glassed windows in the sitting room and bedroom. That, however, was the only glass to be seen; though she looked for them almost at once, Terisa couldn't discover any mirrors—not above the dressing table in the bedroom, not even in the bathroom.

She shivered. Both the sitting room and the bedroom had substantial fireplaces, but neither was lit. The sunshine on the rugs made their colors burn cheerily, yet outside the windows the sky looked pale, unwarmed. The air in the rooms was too cool for comfort. And the absence of mirrors seemed to have the force of a premonition. How would she be able to tell that she was still here, still real?

"Brrr," said Saddith. "Orison did not know of your coming, my lady, and so no one thought to warm these rooms." She went at once to the sitting room hearth and began setting a fire, using wood and kindling from a firebox close at hand.

Terisa looked around her quarters. In the bathroom, she noticed dully the basin, tub, and bucket (all apparently fashioned of galvanized tin), as well as the cunning arrangement of copper pipes which provided running water (none of it warm). In the sitting room, she tested the cushions of a chair. In the bedroom, she looked into two large wardrobes, which smelled pleasantly of dry cedar but contained nothing. She didn't approach the windows, however. In fact, she refused to glance at them. What she had experienced was already alien enough; she wasn't ready to find out what the world or the weather outside Orison was like.

She had been right the first time: there was nothing in her rooms that she could use for a mirror.

As she returned to the sitting room, the fire was beginning to crackle. Saddith rose to her feet. "With your permission, my lady, I will leave you now. The King speaks truly. You are near to a size with the lady Myste—although," she commented with a coy smirk, "she lacks some of your advantages. I must speak with her about clothing suited to your station. And I am sure that she will be able to make some contribution to the things needed for your toilet."

She looked at Terisa expectantly.

A moment passed before Terisa realized that Saddith was waiting to be dismissed.

This wasn't how her father's servants had treated her. Surprised, and rather gratified, she mustered her courage to ask, "Don't you use mirrors for anything except Imagery? They don't have to be made out of glass. How about polished metal?"

Unexpectedly, Saddith shuddered. "The Masters say the same— but how are we to believe them? Imagers have not always wished other folk well. Perhaps all Images are dangerous. Everyone knows that it is worse than death to see oneself in a glass. Perhaps the danger is not in the glass, but in the Image." She made a gesture of refusal. "We do not take the risk."

"Then how do you see yourself? How do you know what you look like?" How do you know you're real?

At that, the maid chuckled. "My lady, I see what I need in the eyes of men."

When Terisa nodded her permission, Saddith moved toward the door. In a moment, she was gone.

Terisa was alone for the first time since she had sat down in front of the mirrors of her apartment.

She was aware that she had some hard thinking to do, but that wasn't what she did. She was overloaded with strangeness, and she wanted to escape. Still avoiding the windows, she went into the bedroom. The air wasn't warm enough yet to encourage her to take off her clothes, so she simply slipped her moccasins from her feet and climbed into bed.

Clutching the coverlet tightly about her shoulders, she curled herself into a ball and went to sleep.

When she awoke, she passed straight from her usual blank slumber into a state of crisis.

There were no mirrors. No mirrors. The walls were decorated with peacock feathers, and she couldn't see herself anywhere. The bed was rumpled, but that had never been enough to tell her who she was—anybody could have rumpled the bed. If she were to see herself now she might bear no resemblance to what she was expecting, that was why she *had* to find some reflection of herself, had to prove somehow that—

The light had dwindled almost to twilight: it was barely enough to bring back her recollection of this place. With an effort of will, she took hold of her fear. Where she was didn't match the way she remembered it. She had an impression of changes—subtle, insidious, vast in implication—of ways in which reality had been rearranged. The dying of the light was the first one she was able to define, and she clung to it because it was reasonable, an indication of nothing more portentous than passing time.

Then she noticed there was a fire in the bedroom hearth.

It hadn't been set recently: the flames were small over a deep bed of coals; the bars of the grate shone with cherry heat; the air was warmer than it had been.

That, too, could be explained, she told herself, insisted to herself. Judging by the light, she had been asleep for several hours. Someone had come in and lit the fire for her while she slept. It was that simple.

But the idea that people had been changing things around her while she slept was too frightening to be simple.

She pushed her feet out of bed and sat up. The soft, woven texture of the rug under her soles reminded her of her moccasins. She put them on, straightened her sleep-creased flannel shirt, and stood up.

Nothing terrible happened. Her body felt normal. The stone and mahogany and feathers showed no signs of dissolution, of translation. Her panic took a few steps backward, and she began to breathe a bit more easily.

All right. Someone had been here while she slept. Probably Saddith. That was easy to check.

Although movement seemed to require an unreasonable amount of courage, she went to the nearest wardrobe and opened it.

It was full of clothes.

At a glance, most of them appeared to be gowns, but she saw robes, skirts, blouses, shawls, and a shelf or two of undergarments. They were the kind of clothes she had seen the ladies of rank wearing around Orison.

The other wardrobe was also full. And on the dressing table she found an impressive array of combs and brushes, fired clay jars containing creams and rouges, crystal vials of perfume.

Her fear actually turned and walked away, though it stopped in the middle distance to keep an eye on her. A little girl who had once enjoyed playing with her mother's dresses and cosmetics gave a small smile. She almost caught herself thinking, This might be fun after all.

But then from the sitting room she heard a woman's giggle, a man's rumbling whisper. As startled as if she had been caught doing something forbidden, she practically ran out of the bedroom.

The woman was Saddith, and Terisa's sudden appearance took her by surprise: an involuntary twitch nearly made her drop the tray she was carrying. "My lady!" she said, rolling her eyes comically. "I thought you were still asleep."

The man was one of the guards Geraden had introduced her to earlier—Ribuld, the one with the scar down the middle of his face. He, too, had been surprised by Terisa's entrance: his hand on Saddith's shoulder, and the disarray of her shawl and hair, suggested that he hadn't been expecting an interruption; had, in fact, been intending to enjoy himself as much as possible while Saddith's hands were trapped by the tray she carried. Nevertheless he promptly showed Terisa a grin which was probably intended to be reassuring.

In the doorway behind Saddith and Ribuld stood Argus, Ribuld's companion. "Better and better," he muttered with a gap-toothed leer. "One for each of us."

Terisa froze, caught by instinctive alarm.

As soon as Saddith regained her own equilibrium, however, she took pity on Terisa's fright. "Mend your manners, clods," she said mildly. "My lady is not diverted by your sort of humor." Without apparent effort—or malice—she swung one clogged foot sharply against Ribuld's shin.

Gasping and grimacing, he hopped backward. For an instant, he clutched at his shin with both hands. Then he forced himself to stand upright. A scowl of mingled chagrin, anger, and amusement puckered his scar.

Behind him, Argus sniggered like an adolescent.

"My lady," Saddith went on primly, "do not let these louts distress you. They are neither as fierce nor as manly as they would have you think." Argus faced this remark with open astonishment; Ribuld tried to ignore it. "And they will not dare to displease you. Though they are plainly dull, between them they possess wit enough to know that if they displease you *I* will be displeased, and then"—she gave the guards an arch smile over her shoulder—"neither of them will ever walk normally again."

This time, both men made studious efforts not to react.

"Now, my lady," continued the maid, "I have brought some small supper for you, if you care for food. Not knowing how you are accustomed to dine, I thought it best to begin simply. But if this fare is not to your liking, I will gladly bring you whatever I can."

Saddith's mastery of the situation enabled Terisa to unfreeze. Geraden had told her that he meant to try to have these two men assigned to her, for her protection. So far, he hadn't shown himself to be possessed of especially good judgment. On the other hand, he had been relieved of responsibility for her—which seemed to imply that Argus and Ribuld weren't here at his request. With an effort of concentration, she found her voice. "What're they doing here?"

"Those two?" Saddith sniffed disdainfully. "I cannot imagine. That is to say, I know precisely *what* they are doing. But why they have chosen to do it here, I have no idea. Doubtless King Joyse told the guard captain that you should be warded, either for protection or for honor, and the captain displayed his poor sense by assigning those two the duty."

In his loud whisper, Argus muttered, "I don't think we should let her talk about us like that, Ribuld. She would sing a different tune if we had her alone."

"If we had her alone, you overgrown slophog," Ribuld replied with equal subtlety, "she wouldn't need to act like this. You wouldn't be scaring the lady Terisa with your lewd attentions." Then he looked at Terisa and changed his manner to a loose approximation of respect. "The truth is, my lady, we're not on duty."

"No?" Saddith was moderately surprised.

"The captain doesn't know we're here—and I'm sure the King doesn't. We're doing this for Geraden. He stopped by the wardroom earlier this afternoon and asked us to look after you. As a personal favor. He didn't say what he was worried about, but he was obviously worried."

He shrugged his heavy shoulders. "If you don't want us around, you can tell us to go away. We might do that. But I think we might want you to explain it to Geraden first. He may be the clumsiest man in Mordant, and too young for his age on top of it, but we don't like to disappoint him."

"You might say," Argus added with an attempt at formal enunciation and pious sentiment which his missing teeth doomed to failure, "that he comes from a good family."

This explanation left Terisa groping. She didn't know what to do. Helplessly, she looked to Saddith.

The maid considered Terisa, glanced sardonically over at the two guards, then sighed. "Oh, let them stay, my lady. There is less harm in them than they might want you to believe. And I doubt that they would willingly insult Geraden by displeasing you. As this lout says"—she indicated Argus with a toss of her head—"the family of the Domne is well regarded—and especially Artagel, who is said to have the sharpest sword in all Mordant." She winked knowingly at Terisa. "Among other things." Then she resumed, "Even a brave man might blanch if he insulted Geraden and had to face Artagel in consequence."

It was Geraden who had wanted to answer her questions, Geraden who had seemed to care what happened to her. Now he had defied —or at least subverted—King Joyse's orders by arranging protection for her. As if she were giving him a vote of confidence, she murmured, "All right."

In response, Argus nudged Ribuld and grinned. "What did I tell you? She wants us. Under those funny clothes, she's got the itch. She's just too fancy my-lady-Terisa to show it yet."

Saddith turned on him and started to unleash a retort, but Ribuld forestalled her by grabbing Argus' arm and jerking him toward the door, growling, "Oh, shut up, limpwit. There isn't a woman in Mordant desperate enough to itch for the likes of you." Argus tried to protest; but Ribuld opened the door and thrust his companion out into the passage. In the doorway, he paused long enough to say over his shoulder, "We'll be out here all night, my lady"—struggling to sound respectful against his natural inclination—"if you need us for anything."

The door cut off Argus' burst of laughter.

Saddith rolled her eyes in affectionate ridicule, then moved to set her tray down on one of the tables. "As I was saying, my lady, if this fare is not to your liking, you need only tell me. The cooks of Orison are an unruly lot, but I am sure they will attempt to provide whatever you wish.

"First, however," she went on, "you must have light." Briskly, she went to the hearth, found a twig among the kindling, lit it, and used it to begin lighting the candles and lamps.

As the illumination in the room grew, the glow from the windows seemed to fade to darkness almost immediately, closing away any view Terisa might have had of the world outside. Unexpectedly, she felt a mild disappointment. She had missed an opportunity to look out and see what Orison was, where and how it was situated, what kind of environment surrounded it. Earlier, she had shied away from that knowledge; now she wanted it. Her nap must have done her more good than she realized.

That probably also explained why she did seem to be a little hungry. Dismissing the question of the windows, she went to look at the food.

It was familiar and surprising: as familiar as the language spoken by the people of this strange place; as surprising as the fact that these people spoke a language nearly identical to her own. To all appearances, the plate held a thick slice of ham garnished with borage and accompanied by brown bread, Swiss cheese, and string beans; the goblet contained a pale red wine. And, in fact, the ham was unmistakable, as was the bread. Under closer inspection, however, the borage smelled more like thyme, the beans were of a slightly different shape and color than any she had seen before, and in spite of its firm texture the cheese tasted like tofu. The wine carried a gentle tang of cinnamon.

Perhaps she should have feared that the food of this world would make her sick. In view of Geraden's belief that she had enemies, perhaps she should have feared that the food was poisoned. But such considerations seemed entirely unreal. The people she had met looked like normal human beings. They spoke her language. And, as far as she was concerned, she certainly wasn't substantial enough to be an object of malice. With no more hesitation than she had showed walking across the room to look at the food, she sampled the beans and found that they tasted like asparagus. Then she started on the bread and wine.

"Does it please you, my lady?" Saddith had finished lighting the candles and lamps in both the sitting room and the bedroom, and now stood watching Terisa.

"It's very good," Terisa replied like an obedient girl.

The maid smiled her approval. "Then I will leave you now, my lady. If you do not wish to rest, and the evening seems long, summon me." She indicated a bellpull which Terisa hadn't noticed because it was hidden behind one of the peacock feather displays. "We will find some entertainment for you. Perhaps you will want me to help you try some of your gowns. Several of them will become you nicely, I think. Or perhaps you will want other company. Both the lady Elega and the lady Myste wish to meet you, although they thought to wait until tomorrow so that you could spend tonight recovering from your translation. Both would be fascinated to make the acquaintance of a woman of Imagery."

Terisa ignored this reference to her purported mastery of mirrors. "Who are Elega and Myste?"

"They are my lord King's daughters. He has three, of whom Elega and Myste are the eldest and youngest. The second, the lady Torrent, lives with her mother, Queen Madin, in Romish of Fayle. The Queen is the daughter of the Fayle."

That answered Terisa's question. She didn't know what Romish or Fayle were, any more than she understood Domne or even Orison. But she knew now that she didn't want to meet Elega or Myste tonight. She didn't want to see anybody who would bring her more questions and no answers. She only wanted Geraden—or possibly (a piquant thought) Master Eremis, who may have considered her lovely. Since she couldn't ask Geraden to take any more risks for her, she declined Saddith's offer. "I think I'll rest tonight."

"Very good, my lady." Saddith gave a polite bow and started to leave the room.

But at the door she paused, one hand on the latch. With a roll of her eyes, she indicated Ribuld and Argus. Then she showed Terisa the bolt which locked the door and pantomimed pushing it home.

Terisa smiled her relief and gratitude. "Thanks. I'll remember that."

Saddith replied with her own arch smile and made her exit, closing the door quietly after her.

At once, Terisa went to it and bolted it. Through the heavy wood, she could faintly hear Saddith, Ribuld, and Argus bantering with each other. She was tempted to listen, simply because she didn't understand how any woman could have that kind of relationship with men. Nevertheless she withdrew toward the table where her food waited for her; and in a step or two the laughing voices became inaudible.

She was alone.

In an odd way, she was grateful for the presence of Argus and Ribuld outside her door. They weren't exactly reassuring in themselves, but they—she realized this slowly—were the first people in this impossible situation to reappear after an absence. Geraden had lured her out of her own life into a room full of Masters, but in a short time they had all gone away. He had then taken her to the King, and he had been sent away. Next she had been put in Saddith's charge, and King Joyse and Adept Havelock had fallen into the past. Each new person she met might have been created solely for that meeting; might have ceased to exist as soon as she moved on to someone else.

It was conceivable that none of this was real at all.

Ribuld and Argus, however, spoke of Geraden as though he had a continuous existence of his own, apart from her. They were substantial enough to have a relationship with Saddith which didn't include her, Terisa. Therefore they implied that what was happening to her had continuity, solidity, a dependable fidelity to its own premises and exigencies. They implied that if she were able to retrace her steps she would find the King's suite and the Masters' chamber where she had left them; that Geraden was alive and active somewhere not too far away, trying to do something about his concern for her; that however crazy her circumstances seemed they could be trusted as much as she had ever trusted her own world.

This was rather a large conclusion to draw from a small fact. Nevertheless she accepted it provisionally. It made her a little less afraid.

An entirely unmetaphysical concern impelled her to walk through her rooms again to verify that there were no other entrances. Then she sat down and ate her meal with at least an approximation of pleasure.

By the time she was done eating, the wine had made her slightly drowsy. But she was still too restless to consider going back to bed; so she decided to sample some of the clothes Saddith had brought for her.

Many of them frustrated her: they hooked or laced or buttoned so inconveniently that she couldn't put them on without assistance. Despite that, however, they struck her as finely made and elegant. And the robes and gowns she was able to don for herself made her long for a mirror so that she could see what she looked like. Was it possible that this exposure of breast or slimness of waist, these billowing sleeves or that intricate lace would make her beautiful? Immersed in what she was doing, she didn't notice the passage of time.

She was wearing a floor-length burgundy robe, made of deep velvet, with a wide, black sash and a hood she could have pulled over her head to hide her face, and had just decided to take it off and return to bed for some more sleep, when the wooden backing of the wardrobe in front of which she stood shifted and began to move aside.

Scraping against each other, the back panels opened on a well of darkness.

From the darkness a figure emerged.

If his advance was intended to be silent, it failed significantly: he made bumping and shuffling noises all along the way. Hanging gowns and robes that blocked his path he thrust unceremoniously aside.

She could hear him muttering to himself, "Softly, softly." His voice was old and thin, unsteady when he whispered. "Sneaking into the bedchambers of beautiful women. Hee hee. Oh, you're still a devil, you are. Mirrors are only glass, but lust and lechery last forever."

Only then did he notice that the front of the wardrobe was open—that Terisa stood staring at him with her hands over her mouth and a look in her eyes which might have been either terror or hilarity.

"What're you doing here?" she breathed. "What do you want?"

His thick lips shaking, Adept Havelock flinched as if she had threatened to strike him.

In spite of the alarm pounding in her throat, she felt forcibly the conflict between his ascetic nose and sybaritic mouth, the disfocus of his hot eyes. His self-contradictory visage made him look wild—an appearance aggravated by his few remaining tufts of hair. And yet he seemed to be doing his best to calm her. His hands made reassuring gestures; his whole stance was unthreatening, even deferential.

"Luscious," he said, as though he meant, Forgive me. "All women are flesh, but you are its perfection." I didn't mean to frighten you.

"Ha ha, sneaking into bedchambers." I'm not going to hurt you.
"Lust and lechery." You can trust me.

He was a madman—that much was unmistakable. Unfortunately,
the knowledge wasn't much help. So he was crazy. So what was she
going to do about it? She had no idea. Studying him warily, she
retreated a step or two to give herself more space. Then she said,
"There are two guards outside my door. They're both big, and
they've got longswords. If I shout"—she faltered and almost panicked when she remembered that the door was bolted—"they'll be
here before you can touch me."

Palms toward her, his hands continued to make placating movements. Parts of his face expressed a fear of which other parts were
ignorant: his eyes rolled, and his lower lip drooped, exposing
crooked, yellow teeth; but his nose and cheekbones looked too determined to admit fear.

"This winter chills my bones," he told her as if it were a high
secret. "No one understands hop-board."

Though they were speaking softly, he put a finger to his lips. Then
he turned back toward the wardrobe and beckoned for her to follow.

"You want me to go in there?" Tension made her voice jump like
his. The darkness behind the clothes was too deep to be measured.
"Why?"

As persuasively as possible, he replied, "The King tries to protect
his pieces. Individuals. What good are they? Worthless. Wor-r-r-r-
rthless. It's all strategy. Sacrifice the right men to trap your opponent."

While he spoke, he kept beckoning, urging her toward him.

"No, I'm sorry." The idea of entering the unknown place behind
the wardrobe was even more frightening than the Adept's unexpected appearance. "I can't go in there." She was familiar with dark,
closed spaces. Despite her best efforts to forget them, she remembered every detail of the times her parents had punished her by
locking her into a lightless closet. She had learned a great deal about
her own unreality during those times. In that closet she had first
started feeling herself fade, drifting out of existence into the effacing
black. "It's too dark."

"Ho ho ha," he responded in a tone of supplication. He could
only look at her with one eye at a time, and the lines of his face
twisted into a plea. "Dark and lust. We snuff the light so no one will
see how we revel. You don't need light to see flesh."

Reaching into a pocket of his surcoat, he pulled out an irregular piece of glass about the size of his palm. He held it so that she couldn't look into it; but she had the impression it was a small mirror.

He murmured something, passed his hand over the glass, and a beam of warm, yellow light as bright as sunshine shot straight out of the surface.

He shone it around the wardrobe. It showed her that the darkness was a stone passage angling downward inside the wall of the room.

Havelock flashed his light down the passage to demonstrate that it was safe. Then he beckoned to her again vehemently, at once asking and demanding that she go with him.

"No," she repeated. "I can't. I don't know what you want. I don't know what you're trying to do to me." Groping for some response which might penetrate his demented intentions, she asked, "Does King Joyse know you're here?"

That was evidently the wrong thing to say. At once, Havelock became the furious old man who had thrown his checkers at the ceiling and stormed around the King's chamber. "Bother Joyse and all his scruples!" the Adept raged, so angry that he was barely able to keep his voice down. His face turned an apoplectic red. And yet he did keep his voice down: he retained that much self-awareness. "He plays as badly as his daughters! Women and foolishness."

Flailing his arms, he made gestures that practically shouted, Come with me!

To defend herself, she replied, "Geraden warned me that the King has enemies. Are you trying to betray him?"

At once, Havelock stopped. He stared at her as though he had been stung. For a second, his whole face expressed nothing but astonishment and dismay.

Then a look of cunning came into his eyes.

She seemed to feel danger pouncing toward her. But it was imprecise: she didn't know how to react. So she stood where she was, helpless as a post, while he raised his glass and shone it directly into her face.

It was as bright as the sun; it made her throw up her hands and reel backward to protect her eyes.

She stumbled against the bed, nearly lost her balance. But before she could either fall or jump aside, Havelock clamped one bony hand around her wrist and jerked her toward the wardrobe.

He wasn't as strong as he seemed. If she could have planted her feet, found some leverage, she would have been able to break his grip. He was too quick for that, however. Keeping her off balance, he impelled her across the floor, into the wardrobe and the opening of the passage.

SIX: A FEW LESSONS

ith her free hand, she clutched for something to hold her back. But suns of blindness exploded back and forth across her vision: she couldn't see anything to grasp. Then she hit the stone of the passage, and cool air breathed up at her out of the unseen depths. Havelock slowed, giving her feet time to fumble for the downward stairs.

Argus and Ribuld would probably have been willing to rescue her from this madman. Unfortunately, her door was locked, and she didn't have time to shout for help.

Her sight cleared quickly, however. Havelock's glass hadn't done her any real damage. In a moment, she stopped bumping against the walls, stopped lurching on the stairs. The Adept pulled her after him as firmly as he could, but now she was able to exert some control over her rate of descent.

His glass revealed all there was to see of where they were and where they were going. The passage was narrow and low: if she had been any taller, she would have been forced to stoop. There were sharp turns and branchings whenever the stair had gone down another ten or fifteen feet. At a guess, the branchings led to other hidden entrances in other suites and chambers. But the main passage continued downward.

The absence of cobwebs and accumulated dust implied that these stone tunnels were used with some frequency.

The air became slowly cooler as Adept Havelock dragged her after him.

Unaccustomed to such exercise, her knees began to tremble. She felt she had been laboring down the stairs for a long time when the Adept arrived at a heavy, ironbound wooden door that blocked his way. It had been left unbolted, but he didn't open it immediately. Instead, he tugged her close to him. Then he released her wrist.

Shining on the door and the stone blocks of the wall, his light cast comic shadows across his face. "Remember hop-board," he whispered intensely. "Nothing else signifies."

A gesture and a murmur snuffed his glass. In the sudden dark, she heard his surcoat rustle as he returned the small mirror to his pocket. Then he pushed open the door and walked into the lamplight beyond it as if he didn't care whether she followed him or not.

From the doorway, she looked out at a large, square room.

It was furnished—and cluttered—like a study of some sort. A heavy pillar thrust down through the center of the floor, the flagstones of which weren't softened or warmed by any rugs or coverings. Around the pillar, however, stood a number of tables, some of them tilted like an artist's worktable, others flat and piled with papers and rolls of parchment. Stools waited at all the tables, although most of them were being used to hold stacks of old books or layer after layer of loose documents. Under the tables, the floor was furred with dust. Opposite Terisa, an entryway without a door led, apparently, to other rooms. Near the entryway was a rumpled bed, with several blankets tossed haphazardly over the stained gray sheets, and no pillow.

The light came from oil lamps around the walls and the pillar. Their glow showed clearly the two features of the room that most caught Terisa's attention.

Off to one side was a small table with two chairs and a checkerboard. All were at least as richly made as the ones King Joyse used. But there weren't any pieces on the board.

And the walls were lined with doors like the one through which Havelock had just entered the room. They were all bound with iron and heavily bolted. Orison, she realized, must be honeycombed with secrets.

Ignoring her completely now, the Adept moved to the checker table, seated himself with his back to her, and hunched over the board as if he were absorbed in a game.

Terisa cleared her throat to speak, then caught herself. She and
Adept Havelock weren't alone. A man whom she had somehow
failed to notice at first turned on his stool, leaning his elbow on the
desk beside him and propping his cheek against his fist. "Ah, there
you are." He wore a plain gray robe that looked warm enough to
combat the chill in the room (a chill that the Adept didn't appear to
feel, in spite of his inadequate garments), and that increased his ability to blend into the background. But over his shoulders was draped
the yellow chasuble of a Master.

Looking at him sharply, she realized that she had seen him before.
He had a rabbity face with bright eyes, a nose that twitched, and
protruding teeth. She wasn't likely to be mistaken about him. He was
the one who had agreed with Geraden that her appearance before
the Congery proved something.

"Geraden finally condescended to reveal who you are," he commented, his sarcasm distinct but not severe. "The lady Terisa of Morgan." He didn't seem particularly impressed. On the other hand, his
tone was polite: he clearly intended no offense. "I am Master Quillon.

"Adept Havelock—" Master Quillon paused to glance around
him. "Incidentally," he interpolated, "these are his rooms, not mine.
I believe I would find some way to have them cleaned. Even if I had
to do it myself." Then he returned to what he meant to say. "Be that
as it may, however, he has asked me to tell you a bit about Mordant's
history—the background, so to speak, of our present problems."

When he said that, Terisa's head filled up with air and started to
float. Sudden hope and relief danced together in her chest. At last,
somebody was going to tell her what was going on.

A moment later, however, her expectations fell out of the top of
her head into the pit of her stomach with a leaden thud. *Havelock* had
asked Master Quillon to talk to her? Abruptly, she demanded,
"How?"

The Master looked at her inquiringly. "How?"

"How did he ask you that? How do you know what he wants?"

Master Quillon twitched his nose and shrugged, his cheek still
resting on his fist. "He has his lucid moments. And you must remember that he has been like this for years. We have had time to become
accustomed to him. Occasionally he is capable of making himself
understood."

Well, she thought, that seemed true enough, as far as it went—if dragging people down stairs by main force counted as "making himself understood." But as an explanation it didn't suffice. "Then why?" she asked. "Assuming that you're right—that you haven't missed what he really wants—why do it? Both Master Barsonage"— she stumbled fractionally over the name—"and the King told Geraden—no, they *ordered* him not to answer any of my questions." What she was saying felt increasingly audacious to her, increasingly dangerous. When had she started talking to people like this? But her momentum kept her going. "Why disobey both of them? Whose side are you on?"

In response, he blinked at her as though the logic of his position were self-evident. Nevertheless he was slow in replying. "It is not as simple as you make it appear. In spite of his"—the Master glanced at Havelock—"um, his affliction, Adept Havelock is still the nominal head of the Congery. And there are those among the Imagers who consider his past services to us—and indeed to all Mordant—so great that they continue to deserve gratitude and respect, even compliance. Would you flaunt your father's wishes if he began acting somewhat strangely in his old age?"

Fortunately for Terisa, that was intended as a rhetorical question. Without waiting for an answer, Master Quillon went on, "In addition, there are times when you must define your loyalties. Master Barsonage is an honorable man who tries to be impartial, but in his heart he stubbornly fears the consequences of any decision or action. As for King Joyse—" He sighed. "Years have passed since he showed any significant grasp on what happens around him, and his judgment is suspect."

This didn't satisfy her, but she had pushed her temerity as far as it would go. The old habit of reticence and deference, her emotional protective coloration, reasserted itself and held her back. Master Quillon clearly meant to talk to her, and yet she was irrationally afraid that by speaking she had forfeited what he wanted to tell her, what she needed to know.

Nevertheless her doubts refused to go away. Cautiously, she took a different approach. Indicating the Adept, she asked, "Why do they call him 'the King's dastard'?"

Quillon sighed again and straightened himself on his stool. "My lady"—he gestured vaguely around him, as if he were suddenly tired of the whole thing—"will you sit down?"

Obediently, she located a free stool and moved it to the desk

nearest him. She wasn't accustomed to the robe she was wearing—it
made her feel awkward climbing onto the stool, as though it were a
high perch. But when she was seated with her back supported by the
edge of the desk, she was steady enough.

Master Quillon began.

"I will assume that you know nothing about us or our troubles."
He still looked like a rabbit, and his nose seemed to twitch whenever
he collected his thoughts; but the way he spoke contained a note of
dignity. "If that is untrue, please do not be insulted. There is no
other way that I can respect whatever secrets you may have.

"It is difficult to know how or where to begin. We have, in a sense,
two histories—that of the kingdoms and that of Imagery—which did
not become one until relatively recently—in fact, until King Joyse
and Adept Havelock forced them together. You can hardly believe
it, I am sure, looking at them now, but in their prime they bestrode
Mordant and the rest of our world like heroes, shaking it into a new
shape simply because they believed that the job needed to be done.

"Both histories, however, are histories of fragmentation.

"In fact, there was no Mordant—and no Congery, for that matter
—until King Joyse created them. Oh, there was a region which went
by the name 'Mordant,' but it was nothing more than a collection of
petty princedoms caught between the ancient power of Cadwal to
the east and the newer strength of Alend to the north and west.
These princedoms were what we now call the Cares—the Care of
Armigite, the Care of Perdon, and so on—but they were in reality
less substantial than what the Alend Lieges call baronial holdings.
They survived only because together they served as a kind of buffer
between Alend and Cadwal, which were always at war.

"Alend and Cadwal are actually contiguous along the last eighty
miles or so of the Swoll River, but that area is impassable, a swamp to
the sea and along the coast—" He started looking around the room
as he spoke, and after a moment his explanation trailed off. "Havelock," he asked distantly, as though he were talking to himself, or
didn't expect an answer, "do you have a map? There must be one in
this chaos somewhere. I ought to show her where these things are in
relation to each other."

Adept Havelock didn't glance up from his board. Concentrating
fiercely, he rearranged the pieces he imagined in front of him, and
began to study the new configuration.

"Well, never mind," murmured the Master. Returning his attention to Terisa, he resumed. "Even without a map, I am sure you will understand the point. Because of the swamp, Cadwal and Alend can only approach each other through Mordant, which is, essentially, a fertile lowland between the Pestil and Vertigon rivers. Alend is too mountainous—Cadwal, too dry. Therefore they have desired Mordant for centuries, both for itself and as a large step toward defeating each other.

"To put the matter simply, the princedoms of Mordant survived by being conquered back and forth, generation after generation—and by always siding with whichever of the two powers happened to be absent at the time. Because Mordant existed in pieces, each piece was easily taken, but hard to hold. Cadwal, for instance, might make itself master of the Care of Perdon, or of Tor. Alend might take Termigan or Domne. At once, the Perdon—the lord of the Care—or the Tor, the Termigan or the Domne, would swear eternal allegiance to his new prince. At the same time, he would begin looking for ways to betray that prince. So Cadwal would sneak into Termigan, or Alend into Tor, and the people of the Care would be liberated, amid great rejoicing. At once, however, a new prince would replace the old. And so the entire process would begin again, varying only in detail when Cadwal or Alend made a convulsive effort to conquer the whole region. And so the Cares endured.

"Of course, all that bloodshed was terrible. Naturally, a certain number of men voluntarily fought and risked their lives. But they were a small minority of the victims. The peasants of Mordant were constantly being hacked down or conscripted, raped or driven from their land—brutalized in any way the whims of the tyrants suggested. The only reason Mordant was not entirely depopulated was that both Cadwal and Alend needed what they could grow in the fields and on the hills of this lowland, so they were forced to import labor—usually slaves, especially from Cadwal—to replace the lost peasants. These laborers invariably found that life as a peasant was better than life as a slave or a coerced servant, and so they learned loyalty to the Care in which they found themselves. In that way, the population of Mordant was renewed.

"But such things are only bloodshed and tyranny. Mordant's plight was made much worse by Imagery.

"Am I boring you, my lady?"

Terisa was surprised by the realization that she had yawned. The wine, a long day, and reaction after the shock of Havelock's appear-

ance and behavior were making her drowsy. Nevertheless she shook
her head. "I just wonder what all this has to do with me."

A bit acerbically, the Master retorted, "It 'has to do' with you
because you are here. It will affect everything that happens to you
while you are among us."

"I'm sorry. Please go on."

"Very well," said Quillon stiffly. His nose twitched for a moment.

"In those days, it seemed that every man of any consequence had
in his service, or his employ, an Imager of some kind—or else he
served or was employed by an Imager. Cadwal itself was raised to
greatness by the first arch-Imager. And as recently as the past century
the Alend Monarch used an entire battery of Imagers to bring the
Alend Lieges into confederacy.

"Here again the situation was fragmented. The talent which can
make an Imager is not common, but neither is it rare. And in times
of war, it seems to breed under every hedgerow. As a result, Cadwal
has at times mustered armies in which *every* captain was seconded by
an Imager. Alend has been nearly as powerful. And of course every
lord in Mordant was defended by an Imager who depended on him
for support, patronage, or facilities.

"As I am sure you can imagine, the glass which makes mirrors is
not something that can simply be poured out in a patch of sand
behind some cottage. To study, develop, and use mirrors requires
equipment, tinct, furnaces, and much else as well, and so any Imager
not born wealthy has always been forced to ally himself with wealth
in some way.

"But I digress.

"I wonder, my lady," he said slowly, "if you possess the knowledge or experience to imagine the havoc dozens of Imagers can
wreak, fighting each other and armies as well as innocent men and
women who happen to get in the way. Consider it, if you can. Here
stands an Imager whose glass shows a sea of lava. At his word, mol-
ten stone floods outward, devouring its own carnage as it moves.
There stands an Imager whose glass shows a winged leviathan which
can consume cattle whole. At his word, the beast is translated here to
rage and ravage until he calls it back—or until some other Imager
conceives a means to kill it. And they are only two men. Consider
fifty of them, or a hundred, great Imagers and small, all dedicating
what mirrors they have to battle and bloodshed.

"Perhaps in your world Imagery is used for other purposes. Per-

haps it provides food for the hungry, water against drought, energy
and power to better the lot of all men. That has not been our history.

"One consequence"—he sighed—"is that the knowledge of Imagery—the understanding of what it is, and why it works, and how it
might be used—has advanced little from one generation to the next.
Imagers have tended to guard their secrets zealously, as protection
for their lives, and so the dissemination of new ideas, insights, or
techniques has taken decades. In fact, it would not have occurred at
all, if the making of mirrors were not sufficiently arduous to require
Apts. But each Imager must have help, and so he must teach some
youth with the talent how to give that help. In that way, slow progress has been made.

"It is a barbarous history, my lady." This time, his sarcasm was
directed elsewhere. "We are not traditionally a humane or scrupulous people.

"King Joyse has attempted to change us completely.

"Havelock"—he turned on his stool to face the Adept—"some
wine would be a kindness. All this talk is thirsty work."

At once, Havelock pushed himself out of his chair and hobbled
away to the opposite side of the room, behind the pillar. When he
returned, he was carrying a stoneware decanter and a clay goblet.
The goblet looked like it hadn't been cleaned any time during the
past decade.

Unceremoniously, he thunked the decanter down beside Master
Quillon and thrust the goblet into his hands. "We have a barbarous
history," the Adept said, waggling his eyebrows at Terisa, "because
we drink too much wine. Wine and fornication don't mix."

Returning to his table, he started playing his invisible game again.

Master Quillon peered morosely into the goblet. Finally, he wiped
it out with the sleeve of his robe. Muttering to himself, he poured
some of the wine and passed the goblet to Terisa. Then he raised the
decanter to his mouth and drank.

She wanted a drink herself. But the dark smear on Quillon's sleeve
dissuaded her.

"As I say," he began again, wiping his lips with the ends of his
fingers, "King Joyse set himself the job of changing everything.

"I can tell you quite simply what he did. First he conquered all the
princedoms of Mordant, some by force, some by persuasion. And
when he had made Mordant into a separate, sovereign realm, he
began waging an odd war against both Alend and Cadwal. In battle

after battle, raid after raid, for the better part of two decades, he took no territory, conscripted no soldiers, slaughtered no peasants. In fact, he did nothing to upset the ordinary structures of power in either country. All he did"—the Master rubbed his nose vigorously to make it stop twitching—"was to take prisoner every Imager he could find and bring his captives here, to Orison. At the same time, he offered universal patronage and safety to every Imager who would surrender voluntarily. In the end, he had collected them all—or we thought he had. From the western mountains of Alend to the eastern deserts of Cadwal, there were no Imagers anywhere but here.

"And when he had them all together, he did not do what Cadwal and Alend desperately feared. He did not try to weld all that talent for Imagery into his personal fighting force. Instead, he created the Congery. And he gave it work to do—peaceful work. Many of his assignments involved the study of specific problems. Could Imagery be used to relieve drought? Could mirrors put out fires? Could Imagers build roads? Quarry granite? Fertilize soil?

"Questions of wealth King Joyse left to Alend and Cadwal." Master Quillon was digressing again. "Alend had gold. Cadwal had gems. Mordant did not need them. Crops and cattle, food and fabric and wine, these were Mordant's strength and wealth.

"But overriding such work was another, larger assignment. King Joyse commanded the Congery to define an ethic of Imagery. He commanded the Imagers to answer the great moral question of Imagery: are the beings and forces and things that come out of mirrors created by translation, or do they have a prior existence of their own, from which they are removed by translation?

"All very simple, is it not? Nothing to it." Quillon took another swig from the decanter, wiped his lips again. "As you might guess, my lady, I am much harder pressed to explain *how* the King did these things.

"If the reports of him are true, he did it, essentially, by being the kind of man for whom other men—and women as well—were willing to die.

"He was born to the princedom which is now his Demesne, and he became the lord in Orison—though Orison was smaller then—at the age of fifteen, when his father was caught trying to betray the Cadwal tyrant who then held the princedom—was caught and slowly pulled limb from limb by oxen in front of young Joyse and all his family, as if that sort of lesson would teach them loyalty. He was little better than a boy, but already he possessed a quality which made a strong and, um, perhaps wise"—he glanced at Havelock—"Imager become his faithful friend. What the boy did after that, he and his Imager did together.

"What they did first was to sneak away in the middle of the night, leaving his family to bear the brunt of the Cadwal prince's displeasure.

"Naturally, this did not raise the esteem in which his people held him. So they were rather surprised when he returned at the head of a force from neighboring Tor, threw the Cadwals out, and personally separated the prince from his head.

"Tor had happened to be in a period of independence at the time. And it was somewhat more accustomed to independence than the other princedoms, being situated with the mountains at its back and Perdon, Armigite, Domne, and Termigan around it—therefore difficult to conquer. Young Joyse had insisted to the Tor—who was himself still young enough to be audacious—that the only hope for his people, and for all Mordant, was a union of the Cares against both Alend and Cadwal. And the Tor had liked this idea. He had also liked young Joyse. On the other hand, he had not liked to risk too much of his Care. So he had given Joyse scarcely two hundred men to use against more than two thousand Cadwals.

"Joyse and his Imager and those two hundred men, however, required only three days to free the Demesne. Before sunset of the third day, a new flag flew over Orison—the pennon of Mordant.

"You may wonder how that was done. I can tell you only that King Joyse and his forces made extensive use of the secret passages for which Orison has always been famed. It seems Orison has been a stewpot of plots and counterplots since its first tower was erected," Master Quillon commented by the way. "Also, their attacks were directed from the beginning at the Cadwal Imagers rather than at the soldiery. In fact, he spared as many of the soldiers as he could. When he was done, he offered them a choice between service with him or freedom. Those who chose his service became the kernel of the guard which eventually unified Mordant, and which has since successfully defied both Alend and Cadwal for decades.

"At this time, his people reversed their earlier ill opinion of him and became correspondingly enthusiastic.

"With considerably more support now from the Tor, young Joyse set about liberating Perdon. Then the three Cares turned their attention to Armigite, and to Termigan. Domne fell to them almost without effort—it has always been the least of the Cares, though the Demesne is smaller. Finally, in the most savage and costly battle he had yet faced, Joyse freed Fayle from Alend and became King.

"I will not protract this tale with details. You can imagine, I am sure, that all the Cares swore allegiance to King Joyse, but did not all keep their oaths, until he taught them to do so. You can imagine that most of his first success grew from the fact that neither Alend nor Cadwal were expecting what he did, and so the truly cruel wars for Mordant's independence were fought later, when his enemies understood what had happened and rose with all their strength against him. It is enough to say that twenty years passed before our King's hold on Mordant was secure enough to permit him to begin the work of collecting Imagers.

"That was thirty years ago," murmured the Master, peering into the mouth of the decanter to see how much wine was there. "For those of us who remember any part of it at all, it was grand. Even young boys, as I was, thought that everything the King touched took on a kind of sanctity, the stature of heroism and mighty deeds."

The contemplation of his tale—or the effect of the wine—was making him increasingly morose. His jaws chewed indecisively. Perhaps he didn't know how much more he should tell Terisa. Or perhaps he was simply debating another swig from the decanter.

"Go on," she said quietly. She wanted to learn how the King of Quillon's tale had become the frail old man she had met—a man so ineffective that even people who had worshiped him when they were boys now disobeyed him almost for no reason. "Tell me what happened."

Master Quillon made a face. "Well, of course, with his friend to advise and guide and assist him, the first thing he did was to start collecting Imagers. And the Imagers were so accustomed to hiding their secrets from each other, to looking at everyone else as an enemy, that most of them were reluctant to be collected. In addition, Cadwal and Alend naturally did everything in their power to preserve their access to the resources of Imagery. All three kingdoms existed in an ongoing state of war—undeclared war, but war nonetheless—and at times King Joyse had to hammer at his enemies until they broke. But he also used every possible kind of cunning and stealth. He broadcast bribes. He sent out small bands on lightning raids. He suborned messengers, counselors, captains, anyone who might know the whereabouts of a man he wanted. He even went so far as to kidnap the families of Imagers and hold them hostage until the Imagers surrendered. It was at once more complex and more difficult than the process of forging Mordant out of its separate Cares. It cost him another twenty years."

Again, he stopped. This time, however, he took an abrupt pull from the decanter and resumed his narration.

"But the bulk of the job had been completed five years earlier. Only one obstacle remained. The Alend Monarch and the High King of Cadwal, it will not surprise you to hear, did not trust King Joyse. They feared what he was doing, even though after each of his raids and battles he left their kingdoms essentially as he had found them. In their eyes, that was insane behavior, and insanity does not inspire confidence in the bosoms of mortal enemies. And, of course, if he had Imagers and they did not they would be defenseless against him.

"The High King of Cadwal, however, was both more prompt and less scrupulous than the Alend Monarch in his response to the threat. High King Festten, who still rules Cadwal from the great coastal city of Carmag, where the minarets rise high above the rocks and the sea, and where every exotic vice known to man is nurtured in the soil of riches and power"—Master Quillon didn't appear to think well of Carmag—"Festten began collecting Imagers of his own. He formed a force of perhaps thirty men, each of them powerful in Imagery, and set over them the arch-Imager Vagel. In addition, he gave his personal champion of battle, the High King's Monomach, responsibility for the protection of his Imagers. Guarded by the Monomach's incomparable prowess, this cabal dedicated itself solely to the arts of violence, and to the defense of Cadwal, and to the defiance of King Joyse."

Without warning, Adept Havelock raised his head as if he had suddenly decided to listen to what Master Quillon was saying.

"Five years passed before the King found means to break the cabal," the Master went on. "And then most of its members had to be slain. They had become too *acclimatized*," he muttered sourly, "to Cadwal's arid morals and lush pleasures. They could not accept transplantation. At the time, it was believed that the arch-Imager had perished also. But now he is thought to be alive—alive and in hiding somewhere, plotting malice.

"The High King's Monomach, of course, was executed for his failure, and another was chosen to take his place."

With a wide movement of his arm, Havelock wiped his board as though he were sweeping all his men off onto the floor. Then he rose to his feet. Walking over to Terisa and Quillon, he touched her sleeve, leered, and nodded in the direction of the still-open door which had admitted her to this room. When she stared back at him, he rolled his eyes and beckoned determinedly. "Time and tide wait for no man," he said as if he were in one of his lucid phases, "but everybody waits for women."

"No, Havelock." Quillon spoke with more firmness than Terisa had expected from him. "Doubtless you know better than I. But I am going to tell her the rest."

For an instant, ferocity came over the Adept's face. He clenched one eye closed so that he could scowl murderously at Master Quillon with the other. But Quillon didn't flinch, and Havelock's mood changed almost immediately. His expression relaxed into a fleshy smile.

"Wait for me, Vagel," he said in a high voice, like a child at play. "I'm coming. Hee hee. I'm *coming*."

Casting a wall-eyed wink at Terisa, he turned away and began rummaging through the clutter on one of his desks.

The Master shrugged. Tilting back his head, he drank what remained of the wine and set the decanter down beside him with a thump. His eyes were starting to look slightly blurred, and two red spots on his cheeks matched the end of his nose.

"That was ten years ago, my lady," he said in a glum tone. "For five of those years, we were relatively secure. The defenses King Joyse had created kept us relatively safe. Most of Mordant lived in relative peace. The Congery thrashed out the worst of its conflicts, both of personality and of trust, and became relatively unified, especially as the older generation—the men who remembered fondly what life had been like before King Joyse came along—passed away. By creating the Congery, of course, King Joyse could not control or limit the birth of the talent for Imagery anywhere in the world. But he had control of the *knowledge* of Imagery. Talent could find its outlet only by coming to Orison and accepting the servitude of an Apt.

"Alend and Cadwal were relatively quiet. Most of us"—his sarcasm returned—"were relatively immune to the disorder of the

King's domestic affairs. For five years, we did not notice, because we did not want to notice, that his spark was dying out. Perhaps because he had nothing enormous or heroic left to do, he was ceasing to be the man so many of us had loved.

"But eventually we had to notice. Oh, we *had* to." Master Quillon became more bitter by the moment. "We could not ignore that there was something evil running loose in Mordant.

"An Imager had begun to translate horrors and abominations out of his mirrors and unleash them to rampage across the land wherever they could find victims."

In the cool of the room, a sensation of tightening scurried from Terisa's scalp down the length of her spine.

"It is easy to assume that he is Vagel. That is as reasonable a guess as any. He was always expert at finding in his glasses men and monsters and forces of destruction. And he did not trouble his conscience much about the consequences of his translations. But no one knows where he finds the patronage, the resources, to make such mirrors.

"We would also assume that he found them in Alend or Cadwal—but all his Images strike deep into Mordant, and it is inconceivable that such mirrors could be made elsewhere and then brought here across those distances without some word of the matter finally reaching the ears of Orison.

"But if not in Cadwal or Alend, then where? Who in Mordant would level such a threat against the realm? And why does King Joyse do nothing about it?

"Perhaps in the early years of the peril, patience and caution were indicated. After all, the attacks did not come often. Either Cadwal or Alend appeared to be the likely source. It seemed understandable that the King was waiting for his spies or his friends to discover the secret and bring it to him, so that he would know what to do.

"But the attacks grow worse, and no explanation comes. Instead, his spies and friends bring word that Alend and Cadwal have learned what is happening from *their* spies and friends, and are mustering their forces to take advantage of Mordant's danger. Armies gather beyond the Vertigon and Pestil rivers. Raids probe the Cares, testing their defenses. Angry because they are compelled to defend their own without assistance from King Joyse, some of the Cares begin to mutter against him. And still the abominations being translated against us worsen, both in magnitude and in frequency. The arch-

Imager, if it *is* he, forms mirrors at an unheard-of rate as well as in perfect secrecy. And still the King does nothing.

"Well, not nothing, exactly," the Master muttered as if he had acid in his mouth. "He plays more and more hop-board.

"The Congery, of course, has not been blind to the problem. Even if we did not hear the same reports that reach every ear in Orison, we would have our auguries—and we have learned a great deal about auguring since our efforts were united.

"We can see Mordant dying, my lady, slaughtered by forces which we understand, but which our King, in founding the Congery, has forbidden us to act against. He will not allow us to be a weapon. Though he will do nothing to save Mordant, he is quick enough to march into our laborium and shatter any glass that offers a means of defense. He only permitted us to search for a champion because we agreed, after much squabbling debate, that whatever champion we chose would not be translated involuntarily, but would rather be approached with persuasion and given the opportunity to refuse.

"In short, our King has brought us to the verge of ruin. Unless more men become disloyal—and do it soon—Mordant will return to the days when it was nothing more than a battleground for Alend and Cadwal. And if Vagel is strong enough by then, he will join with one and devour the other, and so will make himself ruler over all the world."

Brusquely, Master Quillon picked up Terisa's goblet and tossed down the wine she hadn't tasted. Into the goblet, he muttered hollowly, "I, for one, do not relish the prospect."

She was listening to him so closely that she didn't notice Adept Havelock until he touched her sleeve.

He was grinning like a satyr.

"I remember," he whispered. His breath smelled like swamp gas. "I remember everything."

"He remembers everything," growled the Master sardonically. "Mirrors preserve us."

"Yes," Havelock hissed. "I remember." His grin was more than lascivious—it was positively bloodthirsty.

Quillon sighed disconsolately. "You remember, Adept Havelock," he murmured as though he were playing his part in an especially dull liturgy.

"Everything."

Abruptly, the Adept gave a capering jump that made his surcoat flap above his scrawny knees. He followed it with a pirouette, then confronted Terisa again, grinning like murder.

"I remember Vagel.

"He had a glass that poured fire. I had one full of water. He had a glass with a raving beast. But the beast could not breathe water. He had a weapon that fired beams of light which tore down walls and turned flesh to cinders. But the beams only changed water to steam. I *remember*.

"I remember the chamber where I cornered him. Shall I tell you how many candles were lit upon the table? Shall I count for you all the stones in the walls? Shall I measure the way the shadows fell into the corners? Shall I describe everything that I saw in his last mirror?

"It was perfectly flat, but because of its tinct and shape it showed a place among the sharp hills and fells of the Alend Lieges. A high summer sun shone on the meadow grass of the hillside—and on the waterfall, so that it sparkled in the distance. I saw butterflies of a kind which do not come to Mordant, and they danced among the daisies and dandelions. Above the waterfall stood tall fir trees. I saw it all.

"Mark me, my lady." He glared intensely into Terisa's face, but one eye or the other necessarily scrutinized the pillar behind her. "I remember Vagel well. I heard his scorn as he laughed at me, and I saw him step into the glass as though he had nothing to fear. I saw first one boot, then the other come down among the grass, crushing the blades. I saw his robe flare ebony under the summer sun. I saw the waterfall blocked from view by his shoulder as he took a stride or two on the hillside.

"Then he turned and beckoned for me to follow him.

"He beckoned to me, my lady." Havelock's hands made fierce scraping movements, tearing the air in front of Terisa like hungry claws. "He *beckoned*, and his scorn was still on his face. So I followed him, though every Imager knows that a translation which does not go anywhere is madness." His voice began to scale upward in pitch. "Wait for me, Vagel. I'm coming. I'm coming. Ah." His groan came out strangled, like a scream.

"I'm an Adept. I opened his glass. I stepped into it. But when I did"—his voice was now a high, falsetto croon—"he plucked the sun down from the sky and drove it into my eyes, and deep inside me everything was made light. Light, my lady, hee hee. Light." From his throat came sounds like a little girl locked in a closet trying to comfort herself.

Master Quillon coughed. His eyes were red with wine or grief. In a husky voice, he said, "My lady, you asked why some men call him 'the King's dastard.' That is because they think him a traitor to his own kind—to other Imagers.

"Well, it is true that he betrayed many Imagers to King Joyse. In his mind, the King's purpose outweighed their right to freedom. But his greatest act of treachery was to the Imagers gathered around Vagel in Carmag. It was he who broke that cabal. Concealing his identity and loyalty, he joined the arch-Imager as simply another crafter of mirrors hungry for power. For three years—his life always in the deadliest jeopardy—he served and studied Vagel, acting the part of an avid disciple, but in truth learning the cabal's defenses and plans. And when he had taught himself how to counter them, he sprang his trap, admitting King Joyse and a squadron of his guard into the keep where the Imagers lived and plotted.

"But the arch-Imager," Quillon continued sadly, "had one power which Havelock lacked. He was able—we know this now, though at the time we considered it impossible—to translate himself *within* our world by means of flat glass. When Havelock attempted to follow Vagel, the wrench of a translation which went nowhere cost him his mind, as it has cost the mind of every man but Vagel who has attempted it. For that reason, we believed the arch-Imager dead when Havelock returned raving to King Joyse and no trace of his foe could be found.

"As I say," the Master sighed, "Adept Havelock has his lucid moments. But for ten years now the King's chief friend and counselor has been a madman."

The Adept had been growing increasingly restive during this speech. When Quillon finished, Havelock suddenly flung his arms out violently, as if he were ripping a veil in front of him. Then he grabbed Terisa's arm and dragged her off her stool, pulling her in the direction of the open door. "Come on, woman!" he roared. "I can't stand the suspense!"

Suspense? Terisa's thoughts were too full of the things she had just heard. She forgot herself. Apparently, she didn't like being hauled around like a disobedient child. She took a couple of quick steps to catch up with the Adept, then planted her feet and twisted her arm in an effort to break his grasp.

It was easier than she expected. His old fingers slipped from her arm; he nearly fell as he stumbled away from her.

Her heart pounding—not so much at the exertion as at the shock of her own audacity—she turned back to Master Quillon.

He studied her with interest, his head cocked to one side and his nose twitching.

"I want to thank you," she said before her nerve failed. "This is a big help. I won't give you away."

He inclined his head gravely as if her promise were bigger than she realized. "That would be much appreciated, my lady."

"I don't know anything about your mirrors," she went on at once. "I'm not an Imager. But I think the worlds you see must be real. The place I come from isn't something Geraden and a piece of glass invented by accident."

Master Quillon shrugged, and his depression returned. "I hope you are right, my lady. I believe you are. But the arguments on the other side are difficult to refute. If your world is real—and if you are no Imager—then how was it possible for Geraden's translation to go so far awry?"

"I don't know," she repeated. "It's all new to me. But"—she was astonished to hear herself say this—"I'm going to try to find out."

Perhaps simply to keep herself from saying anything else so much unlike her image of who she was, she yielded to Havelock's dramatically mimed impatience and turned to follow him back into his secret passage.

"Nothing else," the Adept muttered at her darkly. "Only hopboard signifies." When she had entered the passage, he closed the door. In the darkness, he fumbled around for a moment before producing a light from his piece of glass. Then he hurried upward, taking the stairs as rapidly as his old legs could manage.

She found climbing the stairs easier than descending them because she had a better chance to find where she was about to put her feet; but Havelock complicated the ascent by jerking his light from side to side and shining it far ahead of him rather than holding it steady. He was becoming more tense by the moment. His exertions made his breath rattle raggedly in his lungs, but he refused to slow his pace.

"What's the hurry?" she panted after him. The elevators of her apartment building hadn't prepared her to run up stairs.

He paused at an intersection and flashed his light in all directions. Then he squinted down at her for a moment. "The trouble with women," he gasped, heaving for breath, "is that they never shut up."

As he started upward again, the stone corridor suddenly felt more constricted, narrower. The beat of feet on the stairs seemed like the labor of her heart, reverberating almost subliminally from the walls. The ceiling was leaning down at her. He was crazy; it was crazy how he managed to communicate things he didn't say. Where had this urgency come from, this panic? She didn't understand why she rushed to keep up with him—or why she tried to muffle her breathing at the same time.

Surely they had passed her rooms by now? It wasn't possible that she had been dragged so far down without a better sense of the distance.

She nearly collided with him when he stopped.

"What—?"

At once, his arms flailed furious shushing motions. He stood with his light aimed at his feet and his face in shadow, concentrating hard —listening. In the reflection from the gray stone, she saw that his lips were trembling.

Then she heard it: from somewhere far away, a faint, metallic clashing sound, a dim shout.

Havelock spat a perfectly comprehensible obscenity and threw himself up the stairs, dousing his light as he ran.

For a fraction of a second, she remained frozen as darkness slammed down through the passage. Then she sprang instinctively, as quick as fear, after the Adept, straining desperately to catch him before he left her alone in the dark.

His raw panting loomed ahead of her, almost within reach. She stretched, stretched—and her fingers hooked the fabric of his surcoat.

That was enough. He made a sharp, unexpected turn; she was able to follow, guided by her small grip on his clothes.

His turn took them toward a glow of lamplight, but the illumination came too late. Half a heartbeat after his feet thudded on wooden boards instead of stone, she tripped over the rim of the wardrobe door and sprawled headlong to the floor of her bedroom.

There were peacock feathers everywhere. They floated through the air, swirled in small eddies across the rugs, draped themselves delicately over the edges of the bed. One of them wafted into her face, blinding her while a harsh voice gasped, "My lady!" and iron rang like a carillon.

The voice sounded like Ribuld's.

She snatched down the feather in time to see him parrying frantically, sparks raining from the length of his longsword.

He and Argus fought with all their strength against a third man who held the entryway to the bedroom, blocking them from her.

The feathers were part of a decoration which this man had torn down to use as a shield.

He wore a cloak and leather armor so black that he was difficult to see: he confused Terisa's sight like a shadow cast on an uneven surface; all his movements looked like the flitting and darting of a shadow. Only his longsword caught and held the light, gleaming evilly as it struck fire from the opposing blades.

He seemed to be at least a hand shorter than Ribuld or Argus, slimmer than either of them. Yet his blows were as strong as theirs.

It was clear that they weren't winning.

Both of them were already badly battered. Argus had a vivid bruise under one eye, and his knuckles were bleeding. Ribuld had sustained a cut to the joining of his neck and shoulder. Notches and tears marked their mail: their opponent had been able to hit them at will.

Now Ribuld reeled away from the force of the attack. Losing his balance took him out of his assailant's reach, but it also fetched him heavily against the side of the fireplace. He stumbled to his knees.

Argus tried to surge forward, his sword hammering for the man's skull. The man was defter, however: his longsword leaped to catch Argus' blow and turn it. Then he smashed his now-tattered shield into Argus' face. Before Argus could counter, the man in black dealt him a kick to the groin which nearly pitched him on his head.

When he hit the floor, he hunched over and began retching.

As smooth as a shadow, the man turned toward Terisa.

Now she saw his face. His eyes shone yellow in the lamplight; he had a nose like the blade of a hatchet; his teeth were bared in a feral grin. She had the indistinct impression that there were scars on his cheeks.

His cloak seemed to billow about his shoulders as he clenched the hilt of his longsword in both hands and raised his blade against her.

"My lady!" shouted Ribuld again.

Charging like a ram, he launched himself at her attacker's back.

She had risen to her hands and knees, but she couldn't move. None of this made any sense. She could only watch as the man in black swung away from her and accepted Ribuld's assault.

Their blades met so hard that she thought she could hear them break. The sound of the iron was the sound of shattering. But this time Ribuld and his longsword held: it was the man in black who was forced to slip the blow past his shoulder and parry the return stroke.

He parried so well, however, that Ribuld had to skip backward to keep his hands intact.

The attacker followed at once, hacking at Ribuld from one side and then the other. Ribuld took the blows with his blade. Sparks spat over his forearms, but he didn't appear to feel the burns. He was retreating again, but under control this time, looking for an opening.

Abruptly, the man jumped away from Ribuld—jumped toward Argus. While Argus gaped horror at him, helpless with pain, the man whirled his sword to lop off Argus' head.

"No!" Desperately, Ribuld tried to catch his opponent in time. But desperation made him reckless. He had no defense when the man in black changed the direction of his stroke. The flat of his blade hit Ribuld in the face and leveled him.

"Now, my lady," the man said in a voice like silk, "let us end this."

With his longsword poised in front of him, he strode into the bedroom.

For some reason, Terisa thought that this time no one would rescue her, that no young man would appear out of her dreams and risk his life to save hers. If she wanted to live, she would have to do something to save herself—shout for help, jump to her feet and flee into the secret passages of Orison, something. Yet she remained lost, unable to understand why anyone would attack her with such hate, unable to move.

Fortunately, at the last moment Adept Havelock hopped out of his hiding place in the wardrobe and fired his glass into her assailant's eyes.

The man gave a roar of pain and recoiled. For an instant, he stood with his forearms crossed over his eyes, his longsword jutting at the ceiling. Then he snarled a curse. Though he plainly couldn't see a thing, he brought his blade down and started forward again, probing the air for someone to strike.

In the other room, Argus heaved himself into a crouch, reached for his sword. "Now," he grunted, in sharp pain and ready for murder. "Now I've got you."

Terisa's attacker froze. If he could have seen Argus, he would have known that he was safe: Argus was barely able to crawl. But the man couldn't see. He hesitated momentarily while he listened to the sounds Argus made; then he whirled away from Terisa, took an immense, acrobatic leap which carried him over both Argus and Ribuld, and found his way to the door. A second later, he was gone.

Groaning, Argus nudged Ribuld's inert form. "Go after him, you fool. Don't let him get away."

Terisa stared about her, too stunned to think in logical sequences. Ribuld and Argus had tried to defend her—and had almost been killed for their pains. The wood of the door was splintered around the bolt. If the man recovered his sight and came back— The Adept was out of his mind, of course, but he understood what took place around him to some extent, at any rate.

"Havelock," she murmured vaguely, "did you know this was going to happen?"

He wasn't there. He had already left. The door hidden in the back of the wardrobe was closed.

SEVEN: THE DUNGEONS OF ORISON

he events of the next half hour had blurred edges and imprecise tones. Her nerves jangled like badly tuned strings, and her pulse refused to slow down. With so much adrenaline in her veins, she should have been more alert, had a better grasp on what was happening. But everything seemed to leak away as soon as she focused her attention on it. Reality had become like sand, trickling through her fingers.

"Get help," Argus coughed in her direction. He hadn't moved from Ribuld's side; he was hunched there, barely able to hold himself up with his arms. "If he comes back—"

That was probably intended to mean something. Hadn't she just been thinking the same thing herself? But now she was unsure of it.

Her instinct was to simply run away. Use the Adept's secret passage and find her way back to Master Quillon. She wanted warm arms around her. She wanted someone who knew what he was doing to take care of her. Surely Master Quillon would be able to comfort her? So she felt that she was doing the hardest thing she had done in years when she made her way around Ribuld and Argus to the bell-pull behind one of the feather displays. From there, she was exposed to the open door. But she didn't know how else to call for help.

She tugged on the satin cord of the pull as hard as she dared. Then she returned to her bedroom.

An impulse she didn't immediately understand made her rearrange the clothes in the wardrobe and then close the door, concealing the secret passage.

Before long—or perhaps after a long time, according to how she happened to feel at the moment—her summons was answered. But not by Saddith. The woman who appeared in the doorway had the look of a chambermaid; she was older than Saddith, however, blowzy with sleep and hasty dressing, and in no good humor. Nevertheless after one glance at Ribuld and Argus, at the scattered feathers and the broken door, she forgot her irritation and fled.

For a moment, she could be heard squalling into the distance, "Ho, guards! Help!"

"Fool woman," Argus muttered through his teeth.

Ribuld was stirring. His hands rubbed at his face, then flinched away from his bruised forehead. "Daughter of a goat," he groaned. "Who *was* that bastard?" Weakly, he propped himself up on one elbow and peered around the room. When he saw Terisa, he gave a sigh of relief and sank back to the floor again.

"I'm dying," Argus whispered thickly. "Hogswill unmanned me."

"Forget it," replied Ribuld in a prostrate tone. "Won't change your life."

Shortly, Terisa heard nailed boots hammering the stone of the outer corridor—a lot of boots. Brandishing his longsword, a man dressed like Ribuld and Argus sprang through the doorway. He had five companions behind him, all ready for a fight: they looked clenched for violence, like the three riders in her dream. But there was no fight available. They scanned the rooms quickly, then gathered around Terisa's defenders. "What happened?" one of them asked, awkwardly jocose. "Did you two lechers finally meet a woman tougher than you are?"

Before Argus or Ribuld could answer, another man stamped into the room. From his close-cropped, gray-stained hair to his out-thrust jaw, from his swaggering shoulders to his hard strides, he bristled with authority, though he was shorter than Terisa—nearly a foot shorter than any of the men around him. He was dressed as they were, with the addition of a purple sash draped over one shoulder across his mail and a purple band knotted above his stiff, gray eyebrows. His eyes held a perpetual glare, and his mouth snarled as if it had long ago forgotten any other expression.

He scanned the room, assessing the situation, then stalked up to Terisa and gave her a rigid bow. "My lady," he said. In spite of its quietness, his voice made her want to flinch. "I'm Castellan Lebbick, commander of Orison and the guard of Mordant. I'll speak to you in a moment."

At once, he turned on Argus and Ribuld. Without raising his voice, he made it sound like a lash. "What's going on here?"

They struggled to their feet. Uncomfortably, they tried to explain the situation. As a personal favor, Apt Geraden had asked them to keep an eye on the lady Terisa of Morgan, in case she got in trouble. He said he didn't know what kind of trouble. But they were off duty, so they decided to do what he asked. Nothing happened for a long time. Then the man in black appeared in the corridor. He walked up to them and told them to let him in, he had business with the lady Terisa. When they asked him what his business was, he snatched out his sword, broke the door open, and tried to kill her. After that, he gave up and ran away.

Listening to them, Terisa realized that neither Argus nor Ribuld knew she had been out of her rooms. In fact, neither of them had seen Adept Havelock. Because of this, they weren't able to account for her attacker's flight. Glancing toward Terisa as if he believed she were responsible, Argus mumbled something about a light, then winced at the way Castellan Lebbick looked at him.

Ignoring her, the Castellan sent the six guards out of the room at a run to rouse the rest of the watch and begin a search for the man in black—"Although," he muttered as they left, "he's probably halfway to oblivion by now." Then he returned his attention to Ribuld and Argus.

"Let me get this straight. He fought the two of you away from the door long enough to break it open. He got as far as the doorway to the bedroom. He knocked one of you out and disabled the other. Then he panicked and ran away. Doubtless he was terrified by how easily you were overcome. Maybe everybody who serves the King is like you. I'm surprised he didn't die of fright."

Ribuld and Argus hung their heads.

"My lady?" Lebbick asked grimly.

Terisa didn't answer. Now she understood why she had closed the wardrobe. Havelock had taken the risk of angering both the King and the Congery by providing her with some of Mordant's history, and she didn't mean to betray what he had done for her.

"Very well," the Castellan growled. "Let that pass for the moment. Explain this, you ox-headed louts," he demanded of Argus and

Ribuld. "Why didn't you tell anyone what you were doing here? By the stars, I've spent my life training lumps of dead meat to understand the importance of communications and access to reinforcements. If you believed Geraden enough to think the lady might be in danger, why didn't you take the simple precaution of arranging to be able to call for help?"

The bruise on his forehead gave Ribuld an excuse to raise his hand in front of his face. "We didn't believe Geraden. You know *him*. We were just doing him a favor. For Artagel's sake."

"Pigswallow," retorted Castellan Lebbick. "*I'll* tell you why you didn't tell anyone. If you reported what you were doing to your captain in order to arrange reinforcements, he would report it to me —and *I* would report it to the King. Since the King didn't see fit to command guards for the lady himself, he might have been moved to wonder"—the Castellan's voice sounded capable of drawing blood— "what *business* it is of yours to meddle in his decisions."

"We didn't mean any offense," Argus protested. "We were just—"

"I know. Spare me your excuses. I'll take care of Geraden. *You* report to your captain. Tell him about this—and count yourselves lucky I don't have you clapped in irons. Go on."

Argus and Ribuld obeyed, hardly daring to groan. Neither of them looked at Terisa. Carefully—but promptly under the Castellan's glare—they retrieved their swords and hobbled out of the room.

"Now, my lady." Lebbick rounded on her. "Maybe we can discuss this matter a bit more openly. I'm sure King Joyse will be relieved to hear you were able to drive off your attacker—alone and unaided— after two of my guards failed. But he might like to know how you did it. And I'm sure he'll want to know what it is about you that brings on that kind of attack in the middle of the night."

He moved a step closer to her, his chin jutting. "Who are you, my lady? Oh, I know the story—Orison doesn't keep things like that secret. Apt Geraden brought you here by an accidental translation. But who *are* you?" His eyes held hers, as piercing as awls. "What game are you trying to play with my King?"

He sounded so angry that she started to tremble.

Another step brought him close to her. If he extended his right fist, pointed his heavy index finger at her, she knew exactly what would happen next. She would begin to babble:

I'm sorry I didn't mean it I won't do it again I promise please don't punish me *I don't know what I did wrong*.

Fortuitously, another guard sprinted into the room at that moment and jerked himself to a halt. He was a young man, and his fear of Castellan Lebbick's temper showed all over him.

"Excuse me, Castellan, sir," he said in a tumble. "I didn't mean to interrupt. I have a message from the King."

Lebbick took a deep breath and closed his eyes as if he were controlling himself with great difficulty. Then he turned his back on Terisa.

The guard swallowed heavily and stared back at the Castellan like a bird caught by a snake.

"A message from the King," Lebbick rasped venomously. "You said you had one. Try to remember."

"Yes, sir, Castellan, sir. A message from the King. He has stopped the search."

"*What?*" A flick of the whip.

"The King has stopped the search, sir."

"Well, that makes sense. In times like these, a potential assassin in the castle is a trivial problem. Did he give a *reason* for stopping the search?"

"Yes, sir." The guard's skin was chalky. "He said he doesn't like all this running around in the middle of the night."

For a moment, Castellan Lebbick's shoulders bunched with outrage. Yet he spoke softly. "Is that all?"

"No, sir. He also said"—the guard looked like he would have been happier if he could have fainted—"he wants you to leave his guests alone." And winced involuntarily, as if he expected to be struck.

The Castellan swung his arm, but not to strike the guard. He slapped himself, hard, on the thigh. He growled far back in his throat. He made a loud, spitting noise.

Abruptly, he faced Terisa again.

Like the guard, she winced.

"My lady, be warned," he said. "I'm the Castellan of Orison. I'm responsible for many things, but above everything else for the King's safety. He suffers from an unnatural faith in his own immortality. I'm not similarly afflicted." His jaws chewed the words like gristle. "I'll obey him as much as I can. Then I'll take matters into my own hands."

Turning on his heel, he stamped away.

As he passed the guard, he paused long enough to say, "I want the

lady guarded. This time, do it right." And at the door he stopped
again. "Keep this closed tonight. I'll have the bolt repaired in the
morning."

Then he was gone.

The guard gave Terisa a sheepish shrug—half chagrin at his own
timidity, half apology for the Castellan's brusqueness—and followed
his commander out of the room, pulling the door shut behind him.

As he left, he seemed to take all the courage out of the room with
him.

Without warning, everything changed to alarm. Gripping her robe
tightly closed, she hurried to the door to listen. She clearly heard the
voices of several men outside her room: they were issuing the orders
and making the arrangements to have her guarded. Still she felt
vulnerable, helpless. A total stranger had tried to kill her. Urgently,
she moved a chair to prop it against the door. Then she placed another chair inside her wardrobe to block Havelock's passage.

After that, she didn't know what to do.

For a long time, she couldn't relax or concentrate. High King
Festten had had his Monomach executed for failure when Adept
Havelock betrayed the arch-Imager's followers. Havelock had lost
his mind when he tried to chase Vagel into a flat glass. Master Quillon was willing to tell her stories like these, even though both King
Joyse and the Congery prohibited it. For some reason, Castellan Lebbick didn't trust her.

How could all this be happening to her?

But later, unexpectedly, she felt an odd upswelling of joy. Apparently, Geraden had brought her to a place where she *mattered*. The
fact that she was here made a difference. Castellan Lebbick took her
seriously enough to get angry at her. Master Eremis had *looked* at her.
It was even conceivable that he thought she was lovely.

That had never happened to her before.

Eventually, she was able to sleep.

Sunlight streaming in through her windows awakened her the next
morning. At first, she doubted everything. Wasn't this the bed in her
apartment, the place where she belonged? But the sun made the rugs
on the floors bright, shone on the peacock ornaments of the rooms,
lit the feathers scattered by the man in black. That much of what she
remembered was real, at any rate.

The sunshine had the pale color of cold. And the air outside her blankets was chill. She hadn't thought to build up her fires before she went to bed, and they had died down during the night. Holding her breath, she eased out of the warm bedclothes and hurried into the thick velvet robe she had worn the previous night. The stone felt like ice under her bare feet: with a small gasp, she hopped to the nearest rug.

When she looked toward the windows, she hesitated. She wasn't sure that she was ready to see what lay outside. The view might confirm or deny the entire situation.

On the other hand, she felt vaguely foolish for having postponed the question this long. Anybody with a grain of normal human curiosity would have looked outside almost immediately. What was she afraid of?

Unable to define what she was afraid of, she moved to the windows of the bedroom.

The diamond-shaped panes of thick glass—each about the size of her hand—were leaded into their frames. A touch of frost edged the glass wherever the lead seals were imperfect, outlining several of the diamonds. But the glass itself was clear, and it showed her a world full of winter.

From her elevation, she was able to see a considerable distance. Under the colorless sky and the thin sunlight, hills covered with snow rumpled the terrain to the horizon. The snow looked thick—so thick that it seemed to bow the trees, bending them toward the blanketed slumber of the hills. Where the trunks and limbs of the trees showed through the snow, they were black and stark, but so small against the wide white background that they served only as punctuation, making the winter and the cold more articulate.

When she realized how high up she was, however, her view contracted to her more immediate surroundings.

She was indeed in a tower—and near the top of it, judging by her position relative to the other towers she could see. There were four including hers, one arising from each corner of the huge, erratic structure of Orison; and they contrasted with the rest of the castle, as if they had been built at a different time, planned by a different mind. They were all square, all the same height, all rimmed with crenellated parapets—as assertive as fists raised against the sky.

Their blunt regularity made the great bulk of Orison appear haphazard: disorganized, self-absorbed, and unreliable, beset with snares.

In fact, the general shape of the castle was quite regular in its outlines. Orison was rectangular, constructed around an enormous open courtyard. Terisa could see it clearly because her windows faced out over one of the long arms of the rectangle. One end of the courtyard—the end away from her tower—was occupied by what she could only think of as a bazaar: a large conglomeration of shops and sheds, stalls and tents, wagons carrying fodder—all thoroughly chaotic, all shrouded by the smoke of dozens of cookfires.

The other end of the courtyard looked big enough to serve as a parade ground—as long as the parade didn't get out of hand. There men on horseback, children playing, and clusters of people on their way to or from the bazaar churned the mud and snow.

Large as the courtyard was, however, the structure of Orison was high enough to keep it all in shadow at this hour of the morning. The open air must have been bitterly cold: Terisa noticed that even the children didn't stay outside very long.

The other regular feature of the castle was its outward face. Since her window looked over the courtyard, she couldn't see the details of the walls, but she could see that Orison had no outer defenses: it was its own fortification. The whole edifice was built of blunt gray stone, presenting a hard and unadorned face to the external world on all sides.

Within its outlines, however, the castle looked as though it had been designed more for the convenience of its secrets than for the accommodation of its inhabitants. Mismatched slate roofs canted at all angles, pitching their runoff into the courtyard. Dozens of chimneys bearing no resemblance to each other gusted smoke along the breeze. Some sections of the structure were tall and square; others, squat and lumpish. Some parts had balconies instead of windows; others sported poles from which clotheslines hung. She couldn't resist the conclusion that King Joyse had attached the four towers to his ancestral seat, decreed the shape in which Orison was to grow, and then forgotten about it, letting a number of disagreeable builders express themselves willy-nilly.

Now, at least, she understood why she had found Geraden's and Saddith's routes through the castle so confusing. Truncated passages and sudden intersections, unpremeditated stairs and necessary detours were part of Orison's basic construction.

As far as she could make out, the only way into the courtyard from outside was along a road which led through a massive set of gates in

the long arm of the rectangle below her. These gates were apparently open, admitting wains pulled by oxen to the courtyard. But her
angle of vision didn't let her see whether the gates were guarded.

As she studied the scene, her breath misted the glass. She wiped it
clear again with the sleeve of her robe. Then she touched her fingers
to one of the panes. The cold spread a little halo of condensed vapor
over the glass around each fingertip; a sharp, delicate chill seeped
into her skin. That, more than the immense weight of Orison's piled
stone, made everything she saw seem tangible, convincing. She was
truly *in* this place, wherever it was—and whatever it might mean.
She was here.

Shortly, her musing was interrupted by a knock at her sitting room
door. Because she didn't want to stand where she was indefinitely,
thinking the same thoughts over and over again, she went to answer
the knock. On her way to the door, however, she hesitated again.
Did she really mean to open that door and admit everything that
might be waiting for her? Someone was trying to kill her. He might
be outside.

But what choice did she have? None, if she wanted to learn anything more about what was happening to her. Or if she wanted
breakfast.

Her heart began to beat more the way it should—more like the
heart of a woman whose life was at risk—as she pulled the chair away
from the door and opened it.

Two guards she hadn't seen before saluted her.

Saddith was with them, holding a tray with one edge propped on
her hip.

A gleam in her eye and a saucy tilt to her head indicated the spirit
in which she had been conversing with the guards; her blouse was
buttoned to a still lower level, giving out hints of pleasure whenever
she moved her shoulders. But as soon as she saw Terisa her expression became contrite and solicitous.

"My lady, are you all right? They said you were, but I did not
know whether to believe them. That woman and I traded duties for
the night. I did not know that you would be attacked—or that she
would be such a goose. She should have stayed with you. I brought
your breakfast. I know you are upset, but you ought to eat. Do you
think you could try?"

Terisa met the maid's rush of words and blinked. She was relieved
to see Saddith again. Saddith was safe; she was real. "Yes," Terisa

said when Saddith paused for an answer. "I am hungry. And I'm afraid I've let the fires go out. Please come in."

With a nod and a wink for the guards, Saddith shifted her tray in front of her and entered the sitting room.

As Terisa closed the door, she heard the guards chuckling together.

Saddith heard the sound as well. "Those two," she said in good-natured derision while she pushed aside the supper dishes to clear room for breakfast. "They doubted me when I told them that the sight of you would make their knees melt—whatever it did to the rest of them. Now they know I told the truth."

Then she indicated a chair beside the table where she had set her tray. "Please sit down and eat, my lady. The porridge will warm you while I build up the fires again. Then I think we must find you something better to wear."

Terisa accepted the chair. Neatly arranged for her delectation, she found grapes, brown bread, a wedge of deep yellow cheese, and a steaming bowl that appeared to contain a cracked-wheat cereal. Remembering the previous night's meal, she began to eat quickly, pausing now and then to relish the combination of the tart cheese and the sweet grapes.

But Saddith didn't stop talking as she worked at the nearest hearth. "What was he like," she asked, "this man in black who attacked you?" She seemed to be excited and pleased about something. "Orison is full of rumors already. He was taller than Ribuld, and so strong of chest that my arms might not reach around him. He had a hunter's face, and a hunter's glee, with enough power in his hands and thighs to batter Ribuld and Argus as if they were boys." For a moment, she hugged her breasts. Then she sighed wistfully. "So the rumor goes. What was he really like, my lady?"

Slowly, unsure of what she was going to say until she said it, Terisa replied, "He was terrifying."

"Perhaps if I had not traded duties I might have chanced to see him." Saddith thought about that for a moment with a quizzical expression on her face. Then she laughed. "No. I was better where I was."

Terisa had spent enough time listening to Reverend Thatcher to know a hint when she heard one, so she asked politely, "Where were you?"

Gaiety sparkled in Saddith's eyes. "Oh, I should not tell you that."

At once, she strode energetically into the bedroom to rebuild the fire there.

But almost at once she stuck her head past the doorway to ask, "Do you remember what I said last night, my lady? 'Any Master will tell me whatever I wish—if I conceive a wish for something he knows.' Perhaps you thought I was boasting." She disappeared again. For a minute, Terisa heard her working over the fire. Then she came back into the sitting room. "I will be truthful with you, my lady. I did not trade duties with anyone. I asked that woman you saw to care for you, so that I might have the night to myself—without interruption.

"I assure you that I did not waste the opportunity." Saddith grinned. "I spent the night with a Master."

Terisa had never heard anyone talk like this before; the novelty of the experience made her ask, "Did he tell you what you wanted to know?"

It was Saddith's turn to be surprised. "My lady, I did not share his bed because I lacked knowledge." She giggled at the idea. "I shared it because he is a Master."

With a toss of her head, she went back into the bedroom.

Unexpectedly, Terisa found that she couldn't concentrate on breakfast. The maid's frankness disturbed her. It reminded her that she knew next to nothing about men—about the things they did to women; about what pleased them. She had never been an object of desire or tenderness.

Pushing the tray away, she went into the bathroom and made as much use as she could stand of the soap and cold water. Then, her skin tingling under the robe, she joined Saddith in front of the wardrobes to search for appropriate clothing.

Apparently by chance, Saddith chose the wardrobe that didn't contain a chair blocking its back panels. Almost at once, she selected a simple but striking scarlet gown that looked long enough to sweep the floor.

Hesitantly, Terisa said, "I'm not sure I can wear that color. Wouldn't it be better if I just used my own clothes?"

"Certainly not, my lady," replied Saddith, firmly but not unkindly. "I do not know how these things are considered where you come from, but here it is plain that your clothes are not becoming. Also you do not wish to insult the lady Myste, who has been very generous. Here." She draped the gown in front of Terisa. "It is not the best of all colors for your eyes," she commented analytically. "But it does well with your skin. And it accents your hair to great advantage. Will you try it?"

Feeling at once a little excited and a little foolish, Terisa shrugged.

Saddith showed her the series of hooks and eyes that closed the gown at the back. Then Terisa put aside her robe and pulled the heavy scarlet fabric over her head. It was a snug fit: Saddith's earlier observation that the lady Myste "has not some of your advantages" seemed to mean she had smaller breasts, which weren't so much exposed by the gown's deep neckline. But it was warm. And it felt flattering in a way that Terisa couldn't define.

She wanted a mirror. She wanted to see herself. The look in Saddith's eyes—half approval, half gauging uncertainty, as if Terisa now appeared more attractive than the maid had intended or wished—that look meant something, but it didn't have the same effect as a mirror.

For Terisa's feet, Saddith produced a pair of fur-lined buskins with firm soles. They didn't exactly complement the gown; but they, too, were warm, and the gown was long enough to hide them.

She was just starting to thank the maid when she heard another knock at her door.

Saddith went to answer it, Terisa following more slowly.

When the door was opened, it revealed Geraden outside.

He had a pinched, white look around his mouth and eyes; a bright red spot marked each cheek, like embarrassment or temerity aggravated by fever. At first glance, he appeared miserable: he must have had a bad night. But when he saw Terisa, his face broke into the helpless, happy smile she remembered from their first meeting.

For a long moment, he gazed at her; and she gazed back; and he grinned like a puppy in love. Then he cleared his throat. "My lady, you look wonderful."

Her reaction was more complex. She was glad to see him: partly because, like Saddith, Adept Havelock, and the others, he had come back, demonstrating his capacity for continuous existence; partly because she thought she liked him (it was hard to be sure because she had so little experience); partly because he was one of the very few people here who seemed to care about what she thought or felt. In addition, she was immediately worried by his appearance of distress. And by his presence outside her door. King Joyse hadn't just ordered the Apt not to answer her questions: he had also said, *You will have no more reason to see or speak with the lady Terisa.* Geraden had already shown himself loyal to his King—and yet he was here in direct disobedience.

And nobody had ever told her that she looked wonderful before.

Flustered, she felt herself blushing. With a gesture at her gown, she said, "I feel like I'm going to a costume party."

Glancing back and forth between Terisa and Geraden, Saddith gave a quiet laugh. "What is a costume party, my lady?" she asked to disguise her amusement.

Terisa tried hard to get her confusion under control. "It's a party where people dress up in fancy clothes and pretend to be somebody they aren't."

For some reason, her response brought the strain back to Geraden's eyes.

"La, my lady," Saddith said at once as if that were the reaction she had been waiting for, "it must be greatly amusing. But if you will excuse me, I will return your trays to the kitchens. Please call for me at need. If you do not call before then, I will come whenever the lady Elega or the lady Myste asks to see you.

"As for you, Apt Geraden," she said in a tone of kind mirth as she gathered the dishes together and carried them toward the door, "a word of friendly advice. Women do not generally admire a man who gapes."

Laughing, she left the room, hooking the door shut with her foot.

But Geraden ignored Saddith's exit. Gazing at Terisa now with an intensity that matched the color in his cheeks, he asked softly, "Are you pretending to be somebody you aren't, my lady? What are you pretending?"

She turned her head away. "I thought I told you to call me Terisa." This was absurd. Why was she in such a dither? And why was he asking her such silly questions, when he must be risking some kind of serious punishment by defying the King? "I'm not pretending anything. I'm just wearing this dress because the lady Myste offered it and Saddith said she would be insulted if I turned it down."

Then she faced him. "Geraden, what are you doing here? King Joyse told you not to see me. You'll get in trouble."

At that, a pained smile made his mouth crooked. "I'm already in trouble. It probably won't get any worse.

"You've met King Joyse. These days, he doesn't punish anyone. I don't think he has the heart for it. Or maybe nothing matters to him

that much anymore. The worst thing he might do is turn me over to
Castellan Lebbick." Geraden sighed. "I guess Lebbick is a good man.
Artagel says he is. But he isn't exactly gentle. And he's already
started on me. Because I asked Ribuld and Argus to guard you."
That was the source of his distress: Castellan Lebbick must have
abused him severely. "He spent half the night at it. I kept wanting to
apologize, even though we both knew I was right."

Abruptly, he shrugged. "At least now I'm not afraid of him anymore. After last night, all he can do is lock me up. But he isn't likely
to do that to a son of the Domne—not without a better reason."
Slowly, he made the tight lines of his face relax, and his smile improved. "For a while, anyway, I don't have anything to worry
about."

Her heart twisted for him: she could guess what being scathed by
the Castellan might be like. "But why?" she asked. "Why did he do
that to you? What does he think you did wrong?"

"Well," mused Geraden, "I suppose he does have a point. He
wants to know why I thought you might be attacked when the idea
apparently never occurred to anybody else in Orison. It's his job to
know everything that happens here. What do I know that he
doesn't?"

"What did you tell him?"

He snorted quietly. "The truth. Mordant is under siege by Imagery. King Joyse won't let the Congery fight back—but even if he
did, the Imagers are so divided they might not be able to accomplish
anything. Cadwal and Alend are drooling for a chance to strike at us.
And in the meantime the King has taken to acting like a man who
left his head in the other room. Who in his right mind would *not*
want someone as important as you guarded?"

Again, the Apt mustered a crooked smile. "Castellan Lebbick
didn't like it when I said all that."

He was putting up a brave front; but the rest of his face still looked
as pale as wax around the hot spots of color in his cheeks. Wanting to
comfort him, Terisa said, "I can imagine what that must have been
like. He was here for a while last night. After everything was over."

"I know." Without transition, his expression became morose, almost grim. "That was something else he wanted me to explain. How
did you manage to save yourself, after both Argus and Ribuld were
beaten? And why didn't you answer the question when he asked it?

"He has a point there, too, my lady." He began to pace in front of her without looking at her. "Even Artagel couldn't beat both Argus and Ribuld at once. They may not look like much, but they're really pretty good. And you got rid of a man who beat them all by yourself. Do you have any idea what kind of conclusions Lebbick draws from that?"

"No," she breathed. "I don't have any idea about any of this."

"Well, I'll tell you. He thinks you're in league with that man. Or rather, that man is in league with you. He fought his way in here to meet you for some reason—maybe to give you a message, or to let you know what preparations are being made by your allies. But it doesn't have to go that far. Maybe you *aren't* allies. You still got rid of him without being hurt. That took *power*." The whole notion seemed to offend him to the point of nausea. "I tried to tell him it was impossible. I wanted to protect you. But when you get right down to it"—he stopped pacing and faced her squarely, his trouble in his eyes—"I don't have any reason to think it's impossible. Except you keep saying it is."

"What do you mean?" she protested. "Of course it's impossible." She had only wanted to commiserate with him; she hadn't intended to admit anything that might force her to betray Adept Havelock and Master Quillon. "I don't know anything about Imagery, or Mordant, or"—she saw again in her mind a wild grin, as sharp as hate, and a nose like the blade of a hatchet, and yellow eyes—"that man who tried to kill me."

"My lady," he countered, "I found you in a room full of mirrors! And it was a room where no known translation could have taken me —unless it was you who did the translating. You were sitting in a chair right in front of the glass, and you were staring at me, concentrating on me. I thought I could feel you calling me.

"My lady," he repeated in misery and appeal, "I want to believe you. I want to trust you. But I don't know how."

Terisa hadn't had much time to adjust to the new rules and emotions of her situation; the sheer seriousness of Geraden's reaction took her by surprise. She was unprepared for the way she was affected, not by his argument, but by his distress.

"I'm sorry. I didn't know you would feel that way about it. Come here."

Turning, she walked quickly into the bedroom, toward the wardrobe with the hidden door.

She still didn't intend to betray Adept Havelock and Master Quillon. She had no way to evaluate any of the conflicting factions or exigencies that she had already met in Orison, no way to know which side she might actually want to be on. But what Havelock and Quillon had done for her was better than the treatment she had received from either the Congery or the King, and she didn't mean to repay kindness with exposure.

When Geraden joined her, she pulled open the wardrobe and showed him the chair she had wedged there. Then she removed the chair to let him see the secret door.

"Oh," he said uncomfortably. "You've got one of those."

"I didn't know it was here when they gave me these rooms," she began. "But in the middle of the night"—she swallowed hard, hoping she would be able to say enough without saying too much— "Adept Havelock came through that door. I don't think he wanted to scare me, but he talked about hop-board and"—she faltered for an instant—"and lust until I wanted to scream. So he was here when that man attacked. And he had a piece of glass that let out an intense light. When that man was done with Argus and Ribuld, he came at me. But Adept Havelock shone the light in his eyes. He was blinded. He had to forget me and get away."

She met Geraden's astonishment as well as she could. "I probably should have said something to the Castellan. I certainly wasn't trying to get you in trouble. But Adept Havelock saved me. And he seemed to want to keep what he was doing secret. When I found out Argus and Ribuld hadn't seen him, I decided not to tell anybody he was here."

Then, changing the subject promptly, she went on, "And I'm not an Imager. Where you found me, mirrors don't do what they do here." She couldn't have borne the embarrassment of trying to explain why she had decorated her apartment in mirrors, but she had another argument ready. "When you arrived in my room, you must have noticed the broken glass. It was all over the rug. You even had some in your hair.

"You did that."

His mouth hung open. "I?"

"Two objects can't occupy the same space at the same time," she recited. "Your translation put you in the same space as my mirror. If I was trying to translate you, it was a failure. The glass was ruined, and I wasn't going to be able to send you back, or go with you. But glass isn't like that where I come from. There's nothing magic about it. When you arrived, it just broke.

"Do you see? I'm telling the truth. The translation was from your side. I've been telling you the truth all along."

For a long moment, he frowned intently while he absorbed what she had said. Then, slowly, starting at his mouth and rising to his eyes, a grin lit his face. "Of course," he breathed, beaming wonder at her. "I shouldn't have questioned you. Of course I saw the broken glass. Why didn't I think—?" With every sentence, his distress lifted and the weight of worry on him seemed to grow lighter. "I should have figured it out for myself."

Exuberant with relief, he put his hands on her shoulders and pulled himself close to her to kiss her cheek. But his enthusiasm tipped him off balance; he missed, knocking his cheekbone against hers instead.

"Oh, I'm sorry, I'm sorry," he babbled in immediate chagrin. Backing away, he waved both hands as if to assure her that he meant no harm. "I'm sorry, my lady. Please forgive me." Then he raised one hand to his mouth. "Oh, shatter it all to slivers. I bit my tongue."

Terisa rubbed her cheekbone; the blow had startled more than hurt her. Secretly, she wanted him to try to kiss her again. She was as lost as he was, however. The best she could do was to say with mock severity, "Apt Geraden, if you don't start calling me Terisa I'm going to tell Castellan Lebbick that you forced your way into my rooms and tried to knock me unconscious."

At that, he began to laugh. His laugh was strong and clean, and it blew most of the chagrin out of him. "My lady," he said finally, "I've never called a woman like you by her given name in my whole life. I've got at least three brothers who think I'm still young enough to spank—and I'm sure they would try it if they heard me call you anything except 'my lady,' no matter how badly you threaten me. Be patient. You can probably tell I've still got a lot to learn."

She, too, had a lot to learn. But she knew enough to say, "I'll try," and smile at him as if she knew a great deal more.

She was relieved to see him looking happier—and to have escaped the subject of Havelock so easily.

For a moment, he stood and gazed at her in silence, enjoying what he saw: her smile, the tumble of her hair against the scarlet fabric on her shoulders. Then he shook his head and recollected himself. He ran an unself-conscious hand through his hair, touched his own cheekbone, and said, "Actually, I do have one official reason for being here. I was just supposed to send you a message, but I can stretch a point by delivering it myself. If anybody asks, that's why I came.

"The Congery wants you to know you won't have to attend their meeting today. That's a polite way of saying you aren't invited. They want to talk about you, and they don't want to be"—he grimaced humorously—"inhibited by your presence while they do it. In fact, I'm not invited either. They don't want to have to spend the whole meeting arguing with a mere Apt."

As he spoke, his tone and manner became more serious. When he paused, he did so with an air of hesitation, as if he were unsure of how she would react to what he wanted to say. "My lady," he went on slowly, "I'm already disobeying the King, as you pointed out. And I really don't think I can get into any worse trouble. So I thought"—his gaze dropped to the floor as though he were forcing himself not to stare at her—"since all the Masters will be in their meeting, and nobody else is likely to stop us"—involuntarily, his eyes rose to hers again, and she saw trepidation and suspense in them —"I might try to answer some of your questions by showing you the laborium. Where the mirrors of the Congery are kept."

His audacity made her catch her breath. It was dangerous to flout authority: she knew that intimately. People who disobeyed were punished. In a rush as she forced the air out of her chest, she asked, "Are you sure that's a good idea?" Then, feeling her apparent ingratitude, she added, "I mean, it's too much. Too many people are angry at you already. If you do that for me—"

She stopped.

"I'm willing to take the chance." His open face projected a sober intensity which suggested that he didn't make his offer lightly—that he had thought through the implications of what was involved more clearly than she had. "I started thinking about it when King Joyse called off the search. If he can't even be bothered to let his guards try to find a man who attacked you—" His voice trailed into an uncomfortable shrug. In the set of his features, she saw how deeply his King had disappointed him. "Anyway, it's not as dangerous as it sounds. After all, I'm not offering to give you the kind of information you could use—if you were an enemy of Mordant. If you're an Imager, you'll already be familiar with everything I can show you. And if you aren't, you won't be able to do anything with what you learn."

"Then why—?"

"Because I owe it to you. I'm the one who brought you here. If you're the wrong person—or even if you *are* the right person but you don't want to help us—it's my responsibility to get you back where you came from. I want you to understand enough about Imagery to know what that means."

He paused, took a grip on his courage, and continued. "But that's not all. Even if you want to go back—and I want to take you back— the Masters won't permit it. Even if they decide you actually are the wrong person, they won't be able to ignore the importance of what you represent. They won't want to let you go.

"Right now," he said carefully, "while they're in their meeting, might be our only chance to get to the right mirror and try to take you home.

"I don't want you to go," he added at once. "I believe you're exactly the one we need. I don't know how or why, but you are. If you want to go, I'll beg you to stay. But"—he sighed—"you have the right to go, if you want to. It would be immoral to keep you here against your will."

He amazed her. The question of whether it would be possible for her to return to her apartment, her job at the mission, her infrequent dinners with her father hadn't seemed particularly substantial to her. Other matters dominated her attention. But behind the relatively tentative surface of his offer, he was asking her something fundamental.

She glanced down at her gown—at the rich scarlet fabric against her skin, at the snug neckline. Already? she protested. It's too soon. I'm not ready.

Nevertheless the risk he was willing to take in the name of her *right* demanded a different answer.

"I'll go with you," she said, although her pulse was heavy in her throat and she felt light-headed. "It might be a good idea if I knew what my choices were."

Geraden smiled bleakly. "In that case, we should probably go now. If we delay, we might miss our chance. There's really no telling how long that meeting will last."

Terisa wished she could take hold of his arm to steady herself. She had a mental image of women in gowns clinging closely to the arms of strong young men and looking happy there, supported and secure. But he gestured politely for her to precede him; she complied by walking toward the door.

He held the door for her, then closed it after her. Outside, he greeted her guards by name, and they replied in a tone of friendly commiseration, as if they knew all about his ordeal with the Castellan. But they didn't move to follow her.

Feeling a resurgence of fright, she hesitated, looking back at them.

"Don't worry," Geraden answered her concern. "Nobody is going to attack you in Orison in broad daylight." On this point, he sounded confident. "Nobody would dare."

She wanted to ask him how he could be sure. But this was his world, not hers. She ought to trust what he told her.

Carefully, she moved toward the stairs.

For a while, she and Geraden didn't speak. As he guided her through the halls, she seemed to recognize the route Saddith had used yesterday. Based on what she had seen from her windows, she guessed that Geraden's destination was on the opposite side of the huge open rectangle of Orison: in order to reach it without traversing the mud and snow of the courtyard, he had to take her around through the halls. Once again, they encountered any number of men and women of every rank. But now, instead of staring at Terisa, they deferred to her and bowed their respect, as if her gown marked her as a great lady whom they didn't happen to know.

Every salutation made her more self-conscious. She wasn't accustomed to being noticed so much. To distract herself, she asked Geraden if assassins commonly roamed Orison at night.

"Actually, no." Sensitive to the tone of her question, he treated it humorously. "It isn't common at all. If it were, Castellan Lebbick would have piglets. He takes his duties *very* seriously."

"Then why did King Joyse call off the search last night?" As she spoke, she remembered the oddness of the orders which had been reported to Lebbick. The King didn't *like all this running around in the middle of the night.* And yet he had known exactly what to expect of his Castellan—and had thought enough of Terisa to protect her from Lebbick's zeal. "I got the impression attacks were something that happened all the time—not worth the trouble of trying to pursue."

Geraden shook his head at once, scowling. "Orison has *always* been safe—ever since King Joyse conquered the Demesne. I would have expected him to call out the entire guard, instead of letting that man get away." A moment later, however, he admitted, "But this is an impossible place to search. It has too many rooms. I don't think anybody knows how they all interconnect. And then there are the secret passages. As long as he had a head start, it would take a miracle to find him."

Even after Havelock blinded him? she wondered. But she didn't raise the question aloud.

"What *I* want to know," Geraden went on after he had worried for a while, "is, how did he know where to find you?"

That wasn't something which would have occurred to Terisa. "How did Argus and Ribuld find me?"

"That's not the same thing. They knew you would have someone to look after you, so they asked around the maids until they heard Saddith had volunteered. Then all they had to do was locate her. Nobody was trying to keep where you were secret. But how did *he* learn where that was? He's an assassin hiding in Orison. Who did he talk to? He must have talked to someone. He must," Geraden said more slowly, "have an ally living here. Someone who could ask questions without making anyone suspicious. Or else—"

"Or else?"

They took a stairway down to a lower level, turned through the base of one of the towers, and continued on around the courtyard. "Or else," he rasped, "he's one of the people of Orison himself. He lives here like anybody else—and presumably serves the King—or acts like he serves the King—and then at night he sneaks around trying to do murder. He might be someone I know."

"Is that possible?"

He shrugged stiffly. "Orison is a big place. And it's open all the time, especially to anybody who lives in the Demesne. Nobody keeps track of all the people here. Although Castellan Lebbick tries, of course." His thoughts were elsewhere. "My lady, you had better keep your eyes open. If you see anybody who resembles him at all, tell someone right away."

Frightened by the prospect, she spent a few tense minutes staring hard at every face she saw, searching it for signs of yellow eyes and scarred cheeks and violence. But slowly she talked herself into calming down. The man would be a fool to show himself where she might encounter him. And if he did, she wouldn't have to make a special effort to recognize him. She could see him again anytime she wished, simply by closing her eyes.

Then another stair took them down to the huge, empty hall, the ballroom fallen out of favor, which they had crossed the day before. There were several entrances to the hall; but she recognized the corridor that led down to the meeting room of the Congery.

The air grew colder.

"In the old days," Geraden commented as he guided her into the corridor, "before King Joyse unified Mordant—and before Orison was built as big as it is now—these used to be the dungeons. Back then, half of every castle must have been dungeons. But King Joyse gave all the torture chambers, most of the cells, and a hall that used to be a kind of guardroom to the Congery. All that space became the laborium." There was a note of pride in his voice. "You've seen the old examination room. That's where the Masters hold their meetings. We'll stay away from there."

Terisa remembered the downward stair; but she quickly became lost among the doors and turnings that followed. She had no idea where she was when he opened another of the stout, ironbound doors which characterized the dungeon, and a glare of light and heat burst out at her.

This must have been the former guardroom: it looked large enough to sleep a hundred people. Now, however, it contained no beds. Instead, it was crowded with two large furnaces built and roaring like kilns; firewood stacked in cords; piles of finely graded sand; sacks of lime and potash; stone conduits and molds in many shapes polished to a metallic smoothness; worktables supplied with scales, pots, small fires, retorts; iron plates and rollers of arcane function; and shelf after shelf affixed to the walls and laden with any number of stoneware jars in a plethora of sizes and colors.

Working about the room were several young men dressed like Geraden: they tended the furnaces, polished pieces of stone, measured and remeasured tiny quantities of powders from the jars, cleaned up the messes they created, and generally sweated in the heat. One of them saw him and waved. He waved back, then closed the door, sealing the noise and fire of the hall out of the corridor.

"You don't want to go in there," he said. "You'll ruin your gown. But that's where we make the glass for our mirrors. The Apts do most of their work there. If a boy wants to be an Imager, but he just doesn't have the power for it in his blood, his inability usually shows up here, before the Masters teach him any of their real secrets. Beginners do the menial chores, like keeping the furnaces at a steady temperature. The more advanced ones learn to mix tinct and prepare molds."

"Is that what you do when you aren't disobeying the King?"

He grimaced, then fell into a wry grin. "It was. The one advantage of being older than all the other Apts is that I already know everything they're being taught. I just can't seem to do it right. So now I'm sort of a formal servant for the Masters. I normally attend all the meetings, not because they care what I think, but so I can run errands, take messages, things like that. They don't trust me to carry glass"—Terisa heard a tone of sadness behind his smile—"so they do that themselves."

He didn't let himself brood, however, on the consequences of his awkward instinct for mishap. "Come on," he said in a brighter voice. "I want to show you some mirrors."

He touched her arm; and again she wanted to take hold of his, for encouragement and support. The excitement he seemed to feel at the prospect of mirrors affected her strangely: it made her want to hang back—made her reluctant to face a risk that might be more dangerous than either of them knew.

"What do the Masters do?" she asked wanly.

"Research, mostly." His eyes watched the way ahead and sparkled. "They're supposed to be finding proof that Images really do or really don't have an independent reality. But some of them would rather figure out how to predict what Image a particular configuration and color of glass will show. Most research is just done by trial and error. Unfortunately, the Congery hasn't been any better at predicting than at proof. As a more attainable goal, Imagers like Master Barsonage are trying to determine how much one mirror has to vary from another before it shows an entirely unconnected Image.

"But the Congery does practical research, too. That's also King Joyse's idea. He wants Imagery to be useful for something besides war and ruin. Not so long ago, some important progress was made—" Geraden swallowed, frowned to himself, and admitted, "Actually, Master Eremis did it. He shaped a glass that shows an Image where nothing seems to happen except rain. Nothing at all. The Congery checked the water, and it's fresh. So now we have a good local solution for drought. That mirror can be taken anywhere crops are dying and provide water." Being fair to a man he didn't like, the Apt pronounced, "It's quite a discovery.

"More recently, of course," he added with even less enthusiasm, "we've spent most of our time worrying about King Joyse's collapse."

Perhaps to shake off uncomfortable thoughts, he guided Terisa forward with a quickening stride.

Down the corridor, along an intersecting passage, they soon came to a heavy door like the door of a cell. Her step faltered: the door was guarded. But he gave her a reassuring smile, saluted the guards casually; and one of them bowed appreciatively to the lady in the scarlet gown while the other opened the door, ushering her and Geraden into a small, well-lit room like an antechamber, with entryways in the massive walls leading to other rooms.

"These used to be cells," he explained, "but the Masters had them rebuilt to make a place where mirrors could be displayed—as well as protected."

When the guards had closed the door behind him, she whispered, "Why didn't they stop us?"

He grinned. "As a matter of protocol, the laborium is under the command of the Congery. Master Barsonage didn't give orders to keep us out because it never occurred to him I might bring you here.

"Come on."

His excitement was growing. Turning to lead her through the nearest entryway, he caught his toe in the long hem of her gown and fell toward the wall as though he meant to dash his brains out against the stone.

At the last instant, however, he contrived to tuck his dive into a roll. He hit the wall with an audible thud; but the impact wasn't enough to keep him from bouncing back to his feet at once—or from apologizing profusely.

"Don't worry about me," she said quickly, expressing concern to keep herself from laughing. "Are you all right?"

He stopped himself with an effort. "My lady, if I got hurt every time I did something stupid, I would have died by the time I was five. That's the worst part about being such a disaster," he went on ruefully. "I do any amount of damage to everybody and everything around me, but I never really hurt myself. It doesn't seem fair."

For a moment, she did laugh. Then she swallowed it. "Well, you didn't hurt me. I'm glad you didn't hurt yourself."

He gazed at her as if the sight made him forget why they were here. "Thank you, my lady," he said softly, earnestly.

But he recollected himself almost at once. "Let's try this again."

With elaborate care, he turned away and walked through the nearest entry into the chamber beyond.

Following him, she found herself in a room which had been enlarged by joining it with three or four other cells. The light came from plentiful oil lamps, which didn't smoke. Aside from the lamps, however, and the slim pedestals that held them, the room contained nothing—no decorations on the walls, no rugs on the floors—except three tall objects hidden under rich satin coverings.

Happily, Geraden pulled off the nearest cover, revealing a glass.

Like the only other mirror she had seen in Orison—the one that had brought her here—this one was nearly as tall as she was; the glass wasn't quite flat or quite clear, and it wasn't perfectly rectangular; it was held in a beautifully polished wooden frame which gave it a secure base on the floor and still allowed it to be tilted from side to side as well as from top to bottom.

In addition, the glass reflected nothing of the stone or the lamps in front of it. It didn't even show Geraden.

What it did show was a fathomless seascape under a bright sun. For an instant, she could have believed that the Image was simply a painting brilliantly contrived to create the illusion of three dimensions. But the waves of the sea were moving. They rolled toward her out of the distance until they came too close to be seen. Small caps of froth broke from their crests and dissolved away before her eyes.

The Image was so real that it made her stomach watery.

"Master Barsonage shaped that one several years ago," Geraden explained. "It's the kind of mirror King Joyse wants the Congery to concentrate on. Something useful, practical. Master Barsonage was searching for a world of water—an Image Mordant could use in case of drought. Or fire. The story is that he extrapolated this glass from a small mirror Adept Havelock once had. If that's true, it's an amazing achievement—to reproduce exactly every inflection of curve and color and shape on such a different scale." With his fingers, he ran a stroke of admiration down the side of the frame. As he re-covered the glass, he added, "Unfortunately, the water has too much salt for our soil and crops."

Shaking her head in gingerly astonishment, as if her brain were a bit loose in her skull, she followed him into the next room.

This chamber was roughly the same size as the one they had just left. It was similarly lit with lamps on pedestals. But it contained four satin-covered mirrors.

"I don't mean to lecture you," he was saying. "If you really are an Imager, I'll bore you. And if you aren't, I'll just confuse you. Stop me if I get carried away."

He considered for a moment, then selected a mirror.

When he uncovered it, she gasped involuntarily and stepped back. From the glass stared a pair of eyes as big as her hands.

They glared at her hungrily, and the teeth under them seemed to drip poison as the mouth gaped in her direction. She had an impression of a body like a gargantuan slug's hulking behind the eyes and the mouth—an impression of a dark, cavernlike space enclosing the body—but she couldn't look away from those eyes to confirm the rest of the Image. They were eyes that wanted, insatiable eyes, consuming—

Geraden stooped to the lower corner of the mirror and nudged the frame. At once, the eyes receded a few dozen feet, and Terisa found herself blinking her horror at them from a safer distance. Now it was plain that she was looking at some kind of huge, sluglike beast in a cave.

"This is how we adjust the focus." He nudged the frame again: the Image retreated farther. Then he pushed lightly on the side of the frame, and the Image panned in that direction, revealing the mountainside where the cave opened. "The range is limited, of course. But once a true mirror is made—one that works, instead of just throwing distortion in all directions—we can look at its whole Image —in this case, the whole mountain—by adjusting the focus. If we have that much patience."

He stood up and tugged the cover back over the glass. She hardly noticed the darkness gathering in his mood. "The story is that King Joyse captured this mirror during his wars for Mordant's independence. The Imager who made it had already translated that"—he shuddered—"that abomination, and it was busy eating an entire village, hut by hut.

"But that was in the days before Adept Havelock lost his mind. When King Joyse captured the glass intact, Adept Havelock was able to reverse the translation.

"The Congery was founded to keep Imagery under some kind of control. So that no more mirrors like this one would be made."

Terisa's arms and legs felt weak, and her head was full of air. "How—" she asked faintly. "How could something like that get through?"

"Oh, size is no problem. Imagers discovered long ago that once a mirror reaches a certain size—about the size of the ones you've seen —it can translate anything. Nobody knows quite how that works. But if you had a glass focused at the right place at the right time, you could bring an avalanche through it.

"Come on."

Without looking at her, he strode into another room.

Viscerally expecting the slug-beast to lift its own cover and come after her, Terisa followed him. Mordant was being threatened by things like *that*? There were people at work here mad or malicious enough to translate things like *that*? Then he was badly mistaken. Mordant didn't need her. It needed the champion in Master Gilbur's mirror. And all the armored men who fought under him. And all the weapons from his ship.

She trailed right on Geraden's heels because this whole situation was crazy and she had to get out of here.

He led her into a chamber larger than the previous ones: apparently, an extra cell or two had been used to make it. Six covered mirrors stood on the smooth stone floor, but four of them had been set back against the walls, leaving room in the center for the remaining two. Those two were the same size. Under their coverings, they seemed to have the same shape.

As he considered the mirrors, his face clenched into an unself-conscious scowl. "We usually keep the flat mirrors here," he said toward one of the side walls. "This is the largest display room, and we have more of them than of any other kind. But the Masters had some moved out to make room for these two. The Congery does a lot of experimenting with flat glass, trying to find some way to use it —or at least understand it."

Abruptly, he moved toward one of the mirrors against the wall. "Here." He sounded angry; she couldn't tell why. "I'll show you what happened to Adept Havelock."

With a rough jerk, he pulled the cover off the glass in front of him.

Involuntarily, she winced.

Nothing terrible happened.

The mirror did in fact appear to be flat. Its color, the sand from which it was made, the slight irregularity of its edges—she guessed that these things determined what Image the mirror showed. But because it was flat its Image existed in this world rather than some-where else.

Something about the scene looked vaguely familiar.

"It's dangerous," muttered Geraden. "I don't know who shaped it, but if it was an accident it was dangerous to make. And even if it wasn't an accident, it's dangerous to keep."

She was looking at what appeared to be a place where roads came together. The roads were deeply packed in snow, of course, and were only marked by the wheel tracks cut into them by passing wagons. But lines of stark, winter-stripped trees made the roads more obvious than they would otherwise have been against the piled white background. The Image was so vivid that she could see cold aching among the outstretched limbs of the trees.

On the other hand, she had no idea why it was dangerous.

Had she seen those trees or that intersection from her windows this morning?

Apparently so. "You can see that place from your rooms," Geraden explained. "That's where the one road out of Orison branches south toward the Care of Tor, northeast toward Perdon, and northwest toward Armigite. But why would anybody bother to shape a glass that shows a place we can already see from here? If someone is coming it doesn't exactly give us a lot of warning. As I say, it could have been an accident. Or else whoever did it was trying to produce a mirror that would show Orison itself—and only missed by that much."

"Who would do that?" she asked.

He shrugged. "Someone who wanted to spy on King Joyse.

"But what makes this dangerous—more dangerous than most flat mirrors—is that we're so close to being able to see ourselves in it. If we took this mirror out to that spot and stood in front of it, we would see ourselves in the Image. And we would be lost forever, erased—caught in a translation that took us away without shifting us an inch from where we stood."

He dropped the cover to the floor and stepped back to consider the glass. "I guess we're lucky that didn't happen to Adept Havelock. *He* was lucky, anyway. He's just crazy—he hasn't been erased. But if we tried to use this glass now—if we tried to translate ourselves out to the branching of the roads—we would end up like him. The stress would destroy our minds.

"Nobody knows exactly why." He began to sound more and more irritated, vexed with himself. "The people who believe that Images don't exist—that mirrors create what we see—argue that the stress comes from being in a created place that exactly resembles a real place. You expect reality and don't get it, so your mind snaps."

"And what if Images are real?"

"Then it's the translation itself that does the damage. I guess you could say translation is too powerful to be used so simply. If you want to get from here to there"—he gestured at the scene in the mirror—"you need a horse, not Imagery. Because you aren't using the true power of translation, it rebounds against you instead of taking you safely where you want to go.

"Anyway, something like that happened to Adept Havelock." Geraden turned his back on the glass, and now she caught the flash of anger in his eyes. "That's why the Masters want to understand flat mirrors. They're so dangerous—and fundamental.

"Come on," he growled. "I've dragged my feet long enough."

Brusquely, he moved to the two mirrors in the center of the room. Now she understood him. He was angry because he was conflicted: he was acting against his own wishes as well as the King's, forcing himself to do what he thought was right despite his belief that Mordant needed her.

And he was risking the accusation that he was a traitor in order to give her a chance to go home.

Despite the warmth of her gown, a chill went through her as he pulled one of the covers off, and she recognized the glass that had stood in the Congery's meeting room the day before—the glass that had brought her here.

Its Image was both different and unchanged. The fighting had stopped. The metallic figures had enlarged their defensive perimeter and were holding it unchallenged. But the alien landscape, red-lit by its old sun, was unaltered, as was the tall ship in the center of the scene.

Like his men, the armored figure who dominated the Image had moved: he now walked the perimeter, pausing briefly at each defensive station as if to check how his forces were placed. Again, his power was almost palpable across the distance between the worlds. He looked like a man who conquered whole continents almost daily, as a matter of course.

Geraden gave her a glance, measuring her reaction. Then he lifted the satin from the second glass.

She saw at once that it was identical to the first. The shape was the same; the tint was the same; the curvature was the same. Even the curved and polished wooden frames were indistinguishable. And yet the Images weren't the same. Under a red-tinged light, against a stark background, a colorless metal helmet with an impenetrable faceplate looked in her direction as if the eyes hidden in it were studying her coldly.

A moment passed before she realized that both mirrors showed the same scene: the first reflected the ship from some distance, while the second depicted the commander of the defense in extreme close-up. Looking at both mirrors, she could see that each portrayed exactly the movements of the commander's helmeted head: only the perspective was different.

Softly, Geraden muttered, "It's too bad we can't hear thoughts through the glass. It would even help if we could hear language. But of course most of the Masters believe there aren't any thoughts or language in there to be heard."

He adjusted the focus of the second mirror carefully until it duplicated the first. Then he stepped back to stand beside Terisa. Still he avoided her gaze.

"I made one of those," he said. "The one we used yesterday. It's a duplicate. Master Gilbur created the original. I couldn't use his. Imagers learned a long time ago that there's some kind of essential interaction between a mirror and the talent of the man who shapes it. So I made a copy." He snorted sourly. "It took me half a year because I kept doing things wrong.

"Can you tell which is which?"

She shook her head. The question didn't matter to her. She cared only about his distress and her opportunity. It might really be possible for her to go back to her world, to her apartment and her job and her father—

—and the man with her wanted her to stay. He wanted it so intensely that the bare thought of letting her go hurt him.

"Actually," he murmured, "nobody else can. But Master Gilbur and I don't have any trouble. Any Imager can always feel his own work. The one I shaped makes my nerves tingle." He pointed to the glass on the left. "That one.

"My lady." At last he forced himself to face her. He held his arms clenched over his chest, as if to keep them from reaching out. His scowl had become a knot of worry and pain. "Are you sure you want to do this?"

"Geraden—" Now that he was finally willing to meet her gaze, she wanted to look away. She had never learned how to refuse other people. If she did what was expected, or asked, or even suggested of her, she could at least fit herself to her circumstances. But she didn't belong here. It made no sense.

As well as she could, she said, "Please understand. I'm no Imager. None of this could possibly have anything to do with me. You didn't force me to come with you. You just asked me to come, and I came. I don't know why," she admitted. "I guess I just wanted to believe my life didn't have to be the way it was. I didn't want to just *sit* there. But now I know I made a mistake. You don't need me. You need that champion. I think the best thing for me to do is just go back where I came from."

"It's your right." Behind its dismay, his voice held a note of dignity and even command which she remembered vividly. The importance of what he was saying lit his eyes. "But you *are* needed here. Mordant's peace will be the first good thing to be lost—and the smallest. In time, the Congery will be perverted, and Orison will be torn down stone from stone, and what remains of the realm will be reduced to nothing but bloodshed and treachery."

Somewhere in his voice, or his words, she heard a reminder of horns, calling out to her heart in dreams and changing everything.

"You give us hope," he continued. "You say you aren't an Imager. Maybe you aren't. And maybe you just don't know yourself yet. Maybe you just don't know yet that you're more powerful than any champion.

"I can't explain it—but I believe you're here because you *must* be here.

"And"—all at once, he relapsed into normalcy, and his gaze clouded—"you make sense out of my life. As long as I can believe in you, it's all been worthwhile."

His insistence should have repelled her, frightened her. It was so unreasonable. *She* was necessary? *She* had power? *She* made sense out of his life? No. It was easier to believe that she had already lost herself, faded away into dreams. Or that she had never existed—that the translation had created her.

Nevertheless what he wanted and offered moved her. His appeal and the reminder of horns moved her.

"Aren't we getting a little ahead of ourselves?" she said unsteadily. "We don't know yet whether this is going to work. We should find that out first, before we worry about anything else."

He studied her hard, trying to gauge her emotions. Then he nodded. "You're right, I suppose." Suddenly decisive, he said, "Here—
hold my hand. I'll go first, just in case something goes wrong." At
the same time, he stepped closer to his mirror. "You can anchor
me."

She became increasingly conscious that the air in the room was
cold. She looked at his hand, the glass, the hard lines of determination on his face. Now that she had gained her point, she found
herself hesitating. "Don't we have to go through some kind of ritual
first?" Her ambivalence felt absurd, but she couldn't control it. As
soon as she made anything that resembled a choice, she lost confidence. "There must be magic powders—or spells—or something?
Aren't there?"

"Is that how Imagery is done in your world?" he demanded with a
glare.

"No, of course not. I mean, we don't have Imagery. I keep telling
you. We don't have magic." Self-consciousness flushed her cheeks. "I
just thought you must need preparation."

He made a visible effort to unclench himself a bit. "I'm sorry. I
didn't mean to snap at you. Imagery is in the way the glass is made
and shaped and colored. That's the preparation. Then it either works
or it doesn't, depending on whether the person who tries it has the
power. If we wanted to translate something out to us, that would be
different. There are words and gestures that trigger the process. But
we aren't going that way. Right now, all we have to do"—he attempted a smile which didn't succeed—"is do it."

Again, he extended his hand to her.

This time, she took it.

What she was doing made her feel sick.

He drew her to the mirror and braced his free hand on the frame
to keep it—or himself—steady. "First I'll just stick my head in," he
murmured, thinking aloud, "and take a look around. Then I'll come
back, and you can decide what to do next. Hold on tight," he added
to her. "As long as we've got a grip on each other, you can pass in
and out of the glass as well as I can."

Abruptly, he dashed his forehead at the surface of the mirror.

And his head vanished, cut off as cleanly as a knife-stroke at the
neck. Beyond the glass plane, the Image of the back of his head
blocked part of the landscape and the ship.

Instinctively, she braced herself against his weight.

He had pushed himself forward too hard: he was losing his balance, starting to fall. His hand pulled on the frame of the mirror, shifting the focus of the reflection. As he toppled forward, she saw one of the armored defenders aim a hot shaft of light at him.

Somehow, she jerked him back. He pitched out of the glass and stumbled away from it, then caught himself with his feet splayed and his knees locked.

All the color was gone from his cheeks: he was as white as flour paste. Panic and astonishment stared out of his eyes.

"Are you all right?" she asked.

"He shot at me," whispered the Apt hoarsely. "He almost hit me."

"I saw him. I saw the back of your head."

"Glass and ruination." He swallowed repeatedly. "If I had gone there the first time. Instead of finding you. They would have killed me before I could open my mouth."

Her heart began to hurt as the implications struck her. The mirror that had impossibly taken Geraden to her when it should have put him in front of the champion now did what it was supposed to do. "I don't believe it." That mirror was her only doorway home. She was stuck here. "I want to try."

"My lady!" His surprise and fear turned instantly to dismay. "You'll be shot! They might not miss twice."

"Come on." Without thinking, she grabbed one of his hands and tugged him toward the mirror. She was stuck here forever. There was no other way she could get back to her own life. "I've got to try."

He twisted out of her grip, then clapped his hands to her shoulders and shook her. "No!" He was shouting at her. "I'm not going to let you kill yourself!"

"I've got to try!" she yelled back at him. It was quite possible that she had never yelled like that at anybody in her entire life. "Let me go!"

Wrenching away from him, she swung around toward the mirror —and tripped on the hem of her gown. Helpless to stop herself, she fell as if she were diving straight at the glass.

Apparently, he got one hand on her just in time to make the translation possible. Instead of shattering the glass, she passed into it.

The transition felt shorter this time: it didn't have as much impact on her as the one that had taken her out of her apartment. It was quick and timeless, vast and small, as if eternity had winked at her while she went by; but this time its familiarity made more of an impression on her than its strangeness.

Then she landed hard enough to jar her breath away on a hillside of thick, rich grass dotted with wildflowers.

More precisely, her body from the waist up landed on the grass. She must have been lying with her stomach across the bottom edge of the mirror's frame, because she was cut off at the navel: everything beyond that straight, flat severance was gone. She could feel her legs. They gave her a sensation of movement. Someone was holding them. But she had left them in another world.

This world was warm and tangy with springtime. A low breeze made the bright heads of the wildflowers dance and cooled the touch of the open sunlight on her hair; the sky was so blue it looked whetted. The hillside sloped down to her right toward a fast stream almost big enough to be called a river. The water ran like crystal over the gold background of its rocks and sand and gurgled happily to itself as it rushed past.

She saw now that she was in a valley that closed sharply as the ground rose ahead of her. A few hundred feet away, the valley became a narrow defile, almost a chasm, mounting toward the mountains in the distance; and this cut was given both a marked entryway and a guard by the tall, rugged, ponderous stone pillars like sentinels which the hills had set on either side of the stream. Shaded by the steepness of its walls, the defile looked dark and secretive—and also inviting, like a place where it would be possible to hide and be safe.

Her heart went out to it at once. Because she had grown up in a city, she had seldom seen a place so beautiful before. For a moment, she simply stayed where she was and inhaled the scent of spring grass, the tang of wildflowers.

Soon, however, she thought of Geraden. This wasn't an alien landscape where men in armor shot beams of fire at people. And it certainly wasn't her apartment. She wanted to show it to him.

Too full of wonder to call out, she began to crawl backward.

As she did so, more and more of her body disappeared past the plane of translation. And Geraden was unceremoniously trying to help her. Her chest vanished; then her shoulders.

Shortly, she found herself on her hands and knees in front of the mirror.

The stone under her palms felt cold. The air in the room was cold. Even the lamplight seemed cold.

The scene in the glass had scarcely changed at all. The commander was conferring with the defender who had fired at Geraden. Perhaps they were trying to understand the man's head which had unexpectedly appeared and then vanished before their eyes. Perhaps they thought they were faced with some new trick by the people they were fighting, the natives of the planet.

"My lady," Geraden panted as if he had been wrestling for her life, "are you all right? What happened? I couldn't see you. I didn't see them shoot at you. They didn't seem to know you were there. What happened?"

"Geraden—"

She was so shaken and cold that she could hardly lift her weight off her arms, hardly get her legs under her. The change was too abrupt, too complete. It left her gasping, disoriented. Springtime—? A stream dancing in sunlight—? No, not here. Not in this converted stone dungeon. And not in the mirror, where men of violence discussed their work.

Somewhere inside her, the translation was still going on, still happening. Now, however, she knew what it meant. Doubt accumulated in her nerves: she was on the verge of failure. It was the sensation of fading, of losing existence, concentrated to crisis proportions: it was the pure moment in which she lost her hold on herself, on actuality, on life. This was what she had been falling toward ever since she had begun to be unsure of her own being.

It was happening to her now.

Although Geraden hovered beside her, urgent to know what she had seen, she couldn't shift her attention to him. She was staring at the glass he had left uncovered—the flat glass that showed a snow-clogged meeting of roads—

The Image in that mirror had changed.

The way she stared made him turn.

When he saw the mirror, he gasped. "That's impossible. How did you—?"

He fought to control his amazement. "I *know* that place. I've been there—I practically grew up there. We used to play there when I was a boy. We called it the Closed Fist. It's in the Care of Domne. It can't be more than five miles from Houseldon." Through his confusion and surprise, his voice shone with pleasure. "That valley is a jumble of rocks inside. A great place to climb. And there must be a hundred little caves and secret places to hide. We had the best games—"

She believed him: she had just been there herself. She recognized the contours of the ground, the shape of the valley. The hillside was blanketed in snow, ice choked the stream, the pillars wore frost like thatches of white in their gray hair. But the scene was the same. Only the season had changed; spring had become winter.

Now Geraden was gazing at her as if she had done something wonderful. "My lady," he said in awe, "I don't know how you did that. It isn't possible. Mirrors can't change their Images. But you did it. Somehow.

"You're an Imager. You're certainly an Imager. Nothing like this has ever been done before. It's a good thing for us you're here."

The color was back in his cheeks.

She had no idea why he had jumped to the conclusion that she was the cause of this impossible change. At the moment, however, that was secondary. She couldn't think about it yet. Other things staggered her.

She had just seen the same scene in two different mirrors. A scene he said was real. But she had seen it in two different seasons. One of the mirrors was wrong. This was winter, not springtime. The mirror that showed the Closed Fist in springtime was wrong.

A sensation of fading drained her heart. It was Geraden's mirror. The mirror that had brought her here. That glass reflected Images that didn't exist.

When she realized that she also was an Image that didn't exist, she nearly collapsed to her knees again.

EIGHT: VARIOUS ENCOUNTERS

W hy isn't it possible?" She sounded small and weak, and her head was spinning.

Exaltation had taken hold of Geraden; he didn't seem to be aware of her distress. "Nobody knows how to change Images. It isn't possible. The Image is part of the glass. But you've just done it. You're the augured champion."

He didn't know what she had seen in the other mirror. His mirror. He didn't know she had proof that she didn't exist. Her hands made unself-conscious warding gestures, pushing ideas away. The implications were horrifying.

On the other hand, she didn't *feel* horrified. She felt distant, as if she were floating off. The sensation that she was fading grew stronger. Or perhaps she was now more acutely sensitive to it. She had no idea why she was still present in the room with him.

The mirror that had brought her here showed Images that weren't real.

"You said it's a real place. Didn't you? But I've never seen that place before." Her voice had a brittle edge to it; a tinny pitch of hysteria. She was struggling to recover the sense that she existed. "I've never been there. I can't change Images if I don't know how." She hugged her elbows and tried to sound calmer. "Otherwise it would be easy to get back to my apartment."

That argument reached him in spite of his elevated state. He thought about it, frowning intently. "But you *must* have done it. If you didn't—That only leaves me. *I* can't even do simple translations. I've never been able to do anything like that."

"Have you ever tried?" Whatever she said no longer mattered. Her life was growing farther and farther away.

He stared at her: for a few seconds, he seemed to take her question seriously. Then he shook his head. "No, of course not. It's nonsense. An Image is a fundamental part of the glass itself. That's why mirrors have such limited range. They can't be focused away from what they are." Abruptly, he peered more closely at the glass. "But this one was," he muttered in bewilderment. "It changed while we were right here in the room. So it isn't nonsense. One of us must have done it." He stepped back, his manner abstract and intense with thought. "Unless there's somebody in Orison who has that much power. And he's here."

"That is absurd, Apt Geraden," a crisp voice commented. "The impossible is the impossible. There must be another explanation."

Geraden whirled.

Terisa turned also, floating around from far away.

In one of the doorways stood Master Eremis.

He wore the same jet cloak under his chasuble which she had seen the previous day. Again, she was struck by how little conventionally handsome he was: his large nose and narrow, sloping cheeks made his face look like a wedge; the thick, black hair perched on the back of his skull emphasized the baldness of his high forehead. But in his case the conventions lost their usual meaning. He was tall, lean, and strong, his pale eyes shone with intelligence and humor, the smile on his lips promised secrets. And the way he *looked* at her made her hold her breath.

She had been told that he might consider her lovely.

Without warning, her pulse began to beat with excitement in her skin. Inexplicably, the sensation that she was fading lost its urgency.

As grateful as if she had been rescued, she waited to find out what he would do.

For a moment, he looked at the changed mirror, frowning in concentration. "Yes," he murmured, "that is impossible." Then he turned his attention back to Terisa and Geraden.

"Freshen my memory, Apt. Perhaps I recollect incorrectly. Did or did not Master Barsonage command you to give no knowledge away to the lady?"

Geraden glared at the floor and didn't respond.

Insouciantly, Master Eremis came forward. Before she had moved into her own apartment, Terisa had seen a variety of men who were reputed to be powerful, her father's guests; but none of them had projected the commanding confidence Master Eremis did. Only her father's presence had been comparably effective—and his manner had been considerably less attractive. He had lacked the sparkle of play or passion that would have made her mother's marriage to him comprehensible. As Eremis approached, he spoke to Geraden, but the interest gleaming in his eyes and smiling on his lips was directed at her.

"Well, no matter. I think it a stupid command. The first rule of good courtesy is to deny beautiful women nothing. Nevertheless you are fortunate that the rest of the Masters are too interested in their debate to be vigilant. Master Barsonage might well strip you of your place if he learned what you have done. But he will not learn it from me."

"Thanks," Geraden muttered ungraciously. The Master's sudden appearance seemed to reduce him to the stature of a sullen boy.

Eremis glanced at Geraden. "My forbearance does not please you? I wish I could persuade you that you have no truer friend on the Congery than I am. You know that I opposed the decision to let you attempt an approach to our chosen champion. Do you believe that I did so because I despise either you or your abilities? You are wrong. The champion is dangerous. I was arguing for your safety, Geraden."

"I might have an easier time being grateful if I understood," Geraden said through his teeth, still glaring at the floor. "What good is my safety to you?"

"Shame on you," laughed the Master. "Bitterness is not becoming." He moved behind Geraden and put his hands like a fond parent on the Apt's shoulders. From that position, he gave Terisa a conspiratorial grin. "Your safety is no 'good' to me personally. But I value your intelligence—and your stubbornness. It would not please me to see those qualities wasted.

"Also"—he squeezed and patted Geraden's shoulders—"the fact that you are safe means that you can now give me formal introduction to this"—his gaze left hers and went down to her neckline, resting there deliberately for a moment before returning to her face —"delectable lady."

Stiffly, Geraden said, "I'm sure you know her name by now."

"Ah, but I have not heard it from you. You are her translator. As Master Barsonage observed, you are responsible for her." The particular way he looked at Terisa made the weakness she felt seem more pleasant. "I want you to introduce me to her properly."

Geraden flicked a glance at her. His mouth was twisted into a snarl. Nevertheless he complied. "My lady, may I present Master Eremis. His home is Esmerel, one of the most renowned castles of Tor." He was as rigid as an iron bar. "Master Eremis, this is the lady Terisa of Morgan." Then, in a tone of muffled ferocity, he added, "She is a guest of King Joyse and under his protection. Castellan Lebbick has her well guarded."

Once more, Master Eremis laughed. "Geraden, you are as graceless as a child." He gave the Apt's shoulders another pat and moved away from his back. "But I mean to show my friendship in a way that will surprise you.

"Now," he went on, returning his attention to the mirrors, "there is the question of how Images can be changed. I doubt that a substitution has been made." He stroked the flat glass lightly with his fingertips. "At the same time, a more fundamental change is inconceivable. This requires thought."

He didn't appear to be interested in thinking about the question at the moment, however. "In the meantime," he said unexpectedly, facing Geraden again, "I naturally wonder what inspired you to bring the lady Terisa here. Your glass and Gilbur's are uncovered. This leads me to suspect that you had some aim of enabling her to leave us—or of proving to her that departure is impossible. I dismiss the first. It is absurd. Even you, Apt, would not risk your life, your future with the Congery, and the survival of Mordant, only to undo everything the next day."

Geraden met the Master's gaze without flinching, but the muscles of his jaw knotted.

"I conclude, therefore, that her departure is now impossible. Some change has taken place within the glass, closing the door which you opened—somehow!—to bring the lady Terisa here.

"Yet that, too, is impossible." He smiled as if the idea pleased him. "We have impossibilities everywhere. Here is a challenge for you, Apt. As I hope I have made plain, I appreciate your intelligence. Your capacity for disaster exerts itself in practice rather than theory. Consider this question: is it theoretically possible to project or transpose the Image of one mirror onto another?" He sounded like a teacher raising issues to which he already knew the answers. "Would that explain the impossibilities which seem to surround the lady Terisa?

"Study the matter and let me know your conclusions. For my part, I will take up the question with the Congery. You will advance yourself much if you reach an answer more promptly than the Masters do."

Before Geraden could reply, Master Eremis shifted his concentration to Terisa. "And now, my lady," he said, resuming his previous manner, "perhaps you will do me the kindness to accompany me to my chambers. The space which Orison allows me is not lavish, but I can offer you hospitality and comfort." At once casual and intent, he moved closer to her. "There are many matters that I think we can profitably discuss."

His smile and his nearness seemed to have strong male implications which made the blood rise in her face. She studied his expression until her breathing quickened and she couldn't look away.

"We will not bore you, Apt, by requiring your attendance," the Master murmured over his shoulder. "You have more pressing responsibilities to pursue."

With one hand, he reached out to her. His fingers were long and slim, artist's fingers, their knuckles delicate, their tips made to stroke and probe and know. His index finger touched the skin of her shoulder at the edge of her gown and gently traced the fabric down into the hollow between her breasts.

"My lady, shall we go?"

Involuntarily, her lips parted as if they were waiting for him. She felt too hypnotized and malleable to move, transfixed by his magnetism and the light in his eyes. But if he had put his arm around her, she would have gone with him anywhere.

"Master Eremis"—Geraden's voice was so tight that it cracked—"what is the Congery debating? If the Masters are trying to make a decision about the lady Terisa, all three of us should be there. I know a lot more about her than I did yesterday." He sounded at once desperate and angry, yet he kept himself under control. "And she might want to speak for herself."

The Master raised an eyebrow; one corner of his smile knotted. "Apt Geraden," he said softly, without looking away from Terisa or removing his finger from the V of her gown, "this is insufferable. I have dismissed you. If you find yourself unable to grow up, return to

Houseldon and ask the Domne to put you back among your toys and
nursemaids. Orison is no place for children."

"Master Eremis." Geraden's tone made Terisa look at him. In his
face, she saw an inchoate hardness, a capacity for strength that hadn't
come into focus. "I've been wrong about a lot of things. I make any
number of mistakes. But I've never served the Congery wrongly." A
secret ferocity mounted behind his words. "Something impossible
has happened in this room. The Masters need to know what I've
learned—what the lady Terisa can tell them. What are they debating?"

"Tinct and silver, boy!" Eremis wheeled away from Terisa sharply.
"Are you blind as well as deaf?" An instant later, however, he restrained himself. "Oh, very well," he growled. "Perhaps if I answer
you, you will be content to leave us alone.

"Because they are muddled and ineffectual, those pompous
Imagers will today arrive—with much protestation, consideration,
expostulation, and inspiration—at the astonishing conclusion that it is
not possible to arrive at a conclusion concerning the lady Terisa of
Morgan. You cannot explain whether you came upon her by accident
or power. Therefore you cannot possibly know whether the power
was yours or hers. And nothing she may say for herself can be
trusted. *If* she is real in her own existence, and not a creation of
Imagery, then she will have her own reasons for any answer she
gives. Her motives will most assuredly not be the same as ours. And
if she is in fact made by the glass—as seems apparent to me—then all
her reasons and answers will be shaped by the Imager who caused
you to find her. By someone who chooses to remain secret because
he is the obvious enemy of the Congery and Mordant.

"Therefore intelligent decisions concerning her cannot be made as
matters stand.

"I anticipate that the Masters will achieve this remarkable insight
in another hour or two—well before Master Barsonage is in danger
of missing more than one meal.

"Tomorrow they will debate what action should be taken in this
dilemma. And by that time I will have spoken to them concerning
the lady Terisa's latest impossibilities.

"Apt, are you satisfied?"

Once again, Geraden didn't meet the Master's gaze. His strength
appeared to have deserted him. With his head down and his shoulders sagging, he looked like he might begin to kick his boots against

the stone in chagrin. But he didn't retreat. Terisa noticed particularly that he didn't accept his dismissal and leave the room.

"You can forget about accidents," he said, his voice muffled by the way he held his head. "The mirror that brought her here has been closed. There's power at work. And it has something to do with the lady Terisa.

"She says she's not an Imager. She says there *are* no Imagers in her world. She uses the word *magic*—there is no magic in her world. And when I was there I saw evidence that she didn't draw me to her.

"But that doesn't mean she has no power *here*."

Terisa winced at this argument. When Master Eremis turned his attention away from her, she began to recover some of her ability to think. As a result, she wished that she could have told Geraden what she saw in his mirror before he tried to argue with anyone. Her proof might have saved him from making a fool of himself.

Unfortunately, it was too late to save him now. "I believe," he went on, speaking more slowly and tensely, "that there's something crucial about her. We need her. *I* know I don't have any kind of undiscovered talent. I would not have found her if she weren't vitally important."

Then he did look up at the taller man. He appeared to be chewing the inside of his cheek to steady himself. His expression was anxious and abashed, but his gaze didn't falter. "Master Eremis, I believe she's too important to become just another one of your women."

"You insolent puppy!" spat the Master. For an instant, he seemed to grow taller, as if he were cocking himself to deliver a blow.

Suddenly, however, he burst out laughing. "Oh, Geraden, Geraden!" he chortled. "Is it any wonder that I wish you well? You are beyond price. Tell me, boy." His voice took on an edge of glee, as if he were playing at outrage. "Is it actually possible for you to look at this lady"—he indicated Terisa with a broad sweep of his hand— "and *believe* that she could ever be 'just another' woman to any man?" Throwing back his head, he laughed again, loudly and thoroughly.

That was what was wrong with her father, of course. He never laughed. In an odd way, Master Eremis' mirth filled her with sadness. It represented a loss. If she had grown up in a family where people laughed, things might have been entirely different. She might have been entirely—

Almost inevitably, this sorrow brought back the sensation that she was fading.

It had remained with her despite the Master's gaze, his touch. Now it was growing stronger and changing: safety was being transformed into danger. It made her turn her head as if she knew what was happening.

In quick horror, she saw that the flat glass which Geraden had uncovered was shifting.

While she gaped at it, the impossible Image of the Closed Fist modulated as though the mirror were a kaleidoscope of winter. Bleeding out of itself, the stream became roads; the pillars stretched limbs and spread out as trees; the sloping virgin snow slumped into ruts and mud. After only a moment, the scene became unmistakable: it was the intersection outside Orison, where the roads from the Cares came together; it was the mirror's original, real Image.

This time, however, there were riders on the northeast road. At least ten men on horseback flailed their mounts and the snow as if they were frantic to reach Orison.

As if they were being pursued.

"My lady," breathed Geraden in astonishment.

Then he gasped, "Glass and splinters!"

Master Eremis also gazed at the mirror, his eyes bright; but he said nothing.

From out of nowhere, a black spot sprang like a predator at one of the riders. It was small, hardly larger than a puppy by comparison, too small to hurt him. Nevertheless it communicated force and fury like a shout across the distance. The rider flung up his arms and plunged from his horse as if he were screaming.

None of his companions turned back to help him. They only goaded their mounts harder, straining toward the castle. His horse veered off the road and fled with a frenzied gait, disappearing past the edge of the glass.

A cold fist clutched at Terisa's stomach and twisted it hard.

She was so frightened she failed to notice that she was no longer fading.

Another black spot appeared out of nowhere.

The whole scene seemed to jump toward her as the spot sprang. Geraden had moved to the edge of the mirror: he was adjusting its focus, bringing the Image closer. Now she could see that the spot was a gnarled, round shape with four limbs outstretched like grappling hooks and terrible jaws that occupied more than half its body. Bounding from whatever invisible perch it had launched itself, it struck a rider in the chest. At once, its limbs took hold; its jaws opened and began ravening.

The mirror showed the man's agony distinctly as he toppled backward in a useless effort to avoid having his heart torn out. It showed the exact shape of the stain his blood made gushing into the snow.

Pointing at one of the riders, Geraden cried, "The Perdon! He'll be killed!"

"Perhaps not!" countered Master Eremis. "They have fled this attack for some distance. If they can outrun the range of the mirror which translates those abominations, they will be safe."

Terisa couldn't tell which one of the riders was the Perdon. All of them looked the same to her, clenched by cold fear and riding for their lives; the eyes of all their horses flashed white panic. She was holding her breath in unconscious alarm, trying to brace herself for the next black spot that would spring out of the empty air, trying to bear the sight of those jaws.

But Master Eremis was right. From that moment until the riders passed out of the Image, out of this flat glass's reach, no more of them were attacked.

Geraden stood with his fists knotted at his sides, panting between his teeth. "Thank the stars. Thank the stars."

Pressure in her chest made her draw a shuddering breath. Abruptly, she wanted to throw up. She couldn't find enough words to ease her nausea. "What *were* those things?"

Master Eremis shrugged. "Translated things such as that have no names for us. I have a more interesting question." The fire in his eyes was eager, avid. "At last report, the Perdon refused to leave Scarping because he believed that matters along the Vertigon required his constant attention—rumors from Cadwal, sneaking spies, hints of armies, forays by bandits. Yet now he is here. What has happened to drive him from his Care?"

Without waiting for an answer, he took hold of Terisa's arm. Brusque with concentration, he drew her away from Geraden and the mirrors. "Come. I want an explanation."

Geraden followed with a bleak expression on his face.

Hurrying, Master Eremis' long legs set a rapid pace; she had difficulty keeping up with him. After a moment, however, he seemed to notice that she was struggling. He shortened his strides a bit, smiled at her, and tucked her arm through his so that she could support herself on him.

Even then, she was glad he didn't try to talk to her. Most of her attention was consumed by the necessity to fight down nausea.

He guided her up out of the dungeons, across the unused ballroom, and into the main halls of Orison, along Geraden's route of the previous day toward the tower in which King Joyse had his quarters. In a large chamber like a waiting room in front of the stairs upward, he stopped. Only a few people occupied the chamber, and most of them had the needy and inward look of petitioners—a look which she recognized almost automatically because she had seen so much of it in the mission. But there were more guards here than she remembered. They told Master Eremis readily enough that the Perdon was already with King Joyse.

They also made it clear that no one else had been invited to attend that meeting.

Almost at once, Castellan Lebbick strode into the room, heading for the stairs.

Master Eremis detached himself from Terisa and accosted the Castellan. "Can it be true, Lebbick?" He towered over the shorter man; his intent curiosity couldn't conceal an air of superiority. "Is the Perdon here? This is strange news. What crisis could possibly inspire that bulwark of Mordant to abandon his domain to the Cadwals?"

"Master Eremis," Castellan Lebbick replied trenchantly, "that is the King's business."

Attacking the stairs, he climbed out of sight.

The Master glared after him. "Unconscionable lout," he muttered to no one in particular. "I require an explanation."

Terisa glanced at Geraden. He stood a little distance away, his good face marred by a mixture of alarm and bitterness. If he had an answer for Master Eremis, he didn't offer it.

No one else in the waiting room had anything to say. The guards stood motionless, apparently meditating on their duty—or perhaps on their lunch. The petitioners were absorbed in themselves. Terisa steadied her respiration and tried to push gnarled, round shapes with terrible jaws out of her mind.

The Imager's impatience mounted visibly. He seemed to have trouble holding himself still. Abruptly, he announced as if everyone around him were eager for his opinion, "There is a crisis in the Care of Perdon. That much is obvious. But I doubt that it is the crisis itself

which brings the Perdon here. He is not a man who would readily
flee trouble—or admit weakness. No, I think it is our illustrious
King's response to the crisis which forces the Perdon to Orison. I
will wager a dozen gold doubles that he hazarded this journey because he was furious. And he will be more so when he departs."

As if on cue, a shout echoed downward, a roar of anger:
"No!"

Clattering metal, a man appeared on the stairs. He was big and
brawny, and made bigger by the iron pallettes on his shoulders
above his breastplate, the gorget around his neck, the brassards
about his arms. On one hip, he had a longsword that appeared heavy
enough to behead cattle; on the other, a fighting dagger. His head
above his eyebrows was perfectly bald; but his eyebrows themselves
were red and thick, red tufts of hair sprouted from his ears, and his
wide mustache was so shaggy that food and drink had stained the
fringe over his mouth black. The haste of his arrival showed in the
spattered mud on his legs.

His blunt face knotted like a club, he pounded downward as if he
were looking for someone to attack.

Behind him hurried a woman. Her sky-blue gown and resplendent
jewelry marked her as a high lady; but she moved as though she had
no interest in the dignity of a long dress or the good manners of
necklaces and earrings. Framed by her pale skin and the short crop of
her pale blond hair, her violet eyes flashed vividly.

"My lord Perdon!" she protested, demanded, as she descended.
"You must try again! You must not give up. Surely it is just a failure
of understanding. You must explain it to him again. *We* must explain
it to him until he grasps its importance. My *lord*!"

"No!" he repeated, his voice like the shout of a breaking tree.
From the stairs, he stamped into the center of the chamber, then
whirled to face her. Shaking his fists at the ceiling, he roared, "He
has given his answer! *He will not command it!*"

The force of his anger made her halt. Her skin was so pale that it
might have been drained of blood. Yet she didn't flinch. "But he
must!" she replied. "I say he *must. Some* attempt must be made in
Mordant's defense. I am certain that Castellan Lebbick tries to reason
with him even now. Return with me, my lord. It is vital that you do
not fail."

The Perdon clamped his hands together in front of him, holding
down his fury; his brassards gave out a muffled clang against his

breastplate. "No, my lady," he said thickly. "I will not endure it. Let him play hop-board until the realm *crumbles*!" His fists made a fierce hammering motion, pounding hope to the floor. "I fought at his side for ten *years* to make Mordant what it is. I will not grovel asking him for what he should volunteer.

"You tell him *this*, my lady. Every man of mine who falls or dies defending him in his blind inaction, I will send *here*. Let him look to their wounds, or their bereaved families, and explain why he will not"—he couldn't contain himself—"*command it*!"

"My lord Perdon." Master Eremis sounded suave and easy—and authoritative enough to catch the attention of everyone in the chamber. "I gather that our admirable lord, King Joyse, has done something foolish. Again. Will you tell me what it was?"

His tone made the blond woman flush, but she bit her lip and didn't retort.

The Perdon turned. "Master Eremis." For a moment, his eyes narrowed, gauging the Imager. Then he spat, "Paugh! It surpasses belief. I would not have believed him capable of it.

"I will not speak of the horrors that befell my men within the hour —horrors hardly a stone's throw from the gates of 'our admirable lord.' They are Imagery, and I am sick of such things. I fought with King Joyse in part so that the abominations of mirrors would be ended.

"I will not speak of them because there is nothing to be said"—his hard gaze glittered—"except by the Imager who causes them.

"But you must know that our borders have been raided for some time now. *I* have not kept the matter secret. All along the Vertigon, from end to end of Perdon, North and South, bands of marauders have ridden out of Cadwal despite the season to strike and burn whatever they happen to find. Then they flee. My protests to that fop Festten's regional governor have been met with shrugs. The marauders damage him also—he says. Since its wars with Mordant, Cadwal no longer has the strength to control banditry—he says. And I, Master Eremis"—he hit his breastplate with one fist—"*I* am left to guard every mile of the Vertigon with enough men for no more than a small fraction of the job.

"Lacking support or counsel from Orison," he went on with massive sarcasm, "I set out to solve this problem as best I could.

"Among my patrols, I included riders who were trained as scouts and spies, so that when marauders were found—or sign of them was found—they could be followed in secret. I wanted to know where those pieces of rabble went to ground. If I could discover their camps, I would not mind raiding a bit into Cadwal myself, to root some of those bandits from their holes."

Master Eremis nodded. "Sound thinking, my lord Perdon. But I gather you were surprised by what you learned."

"Surprised?" the Perdon growled. "Death's hatchetmen, Master Eremis! We are speaking of Cadwal. I should not have been surprised.

"Nevertheless," he went on darkly, "I was not altogether prepared in my mind for the reports which eventually came to me. Some of my scouts were lost—doubtless because they let what they were doing be discovered. Others were gone so long that I gave them up before they won home. But those that lived all told the same tale.

"It was natural, I trust, that I had believed these marauders to be petty bandits and butchers. Their bands were not overlarge. They wore the rags and equipage of men who have grown poor enough to be careless of bloodshed. They struck in motley fashion, as though they meant to overwhelm opposition or be slaughtered without discipline or forethought. They were only a serious trouble to me because they came from Cadwal. And because they were so *many*.

"But I was wrong, Master Eremis." His fists bunched, and his anger rose again. "I was wrong. Will you believe it? After forays of two or four or even ten days, all the bands my men followed rode at last to *the same camp*."

Terisa glanced at Geraden and saw that his face was losing color rapidly.

"And in this camp," the Perdon continued, "they mingled freely with Festten's soldiers, men plainly wearing the uniforms of Cadwal. The supply wains bore the High King's sigil. The tents where the officers and supplies and support were housed were of Cadwal design."

"Indeed," murmured Master Eremis. "Perhaps your surprise is understandable, my lord Perdon. *I* am astonished." He didn't sound astonished. "How large was this force?"

"Estimates vary. My scouts did not observe it under favorable conditions. And some of them were inclined to panic, where others remained too phlegmatic. But I am convinced that it could not have numbered less than fifteen thousand fighting men."

One of the guards in the chamber let out a low whistle; Terisa didn't notice who it was.

"All this *in winter*," snarled the Perdon. "They mean to throw themselves at our throats as soon as the weather shifts."

"You see how the matter stands, Master Eremis," said the blond woman. "The King *must* be made to admit reason. This threat cannot be ignored."

"Between North Perdon and South," the Perdon rasped, "I have little better than three thousand men. To my certain knowledge, Orison has at least five thousand, all sitting idle in their camps under the command of Castellan Lebbick."

"More nearly eight thousand, I think," Master Eremis commented.

"Eight? Yet when I asked for support"—the Perdon ground his teeth to keep himself from shouting—"the King refused. He has refused repeatedly, but at first I could not believe it. Finally I came in person to demand help. I lost seven men along the road, within sight of his walls. And still he refused." The brawny lord shook his mustache. "With an invasion force poised on his eastern border, waiting to take advantage of the chaos of Imagery which assails us from within, and doubtless more peril being plotted in Alend, he refused."

"It is inconceivable," the pale woman breathed to herself. Her violet eyes looked distracted and urgent. "He must command it. How can he not?"

Geraden was frowning hard, deep in thought. What he was thinking made him look sick.

"For ten years, I fought beside him," finished the Perdon. "I trusted him. Now I learn that to him it means nothing."

Master Eremis studied the armored man. "Then perhaps," he said quietly, "it will not amaze you to learn that I have the same problem."

Both Geraden and the blond lady showed their surprise. The Perdon arched his red eyebrows. "You, Master Eremis?"

"Indeed." Glancing around him casually, Eremis moved to the Perdon's side and placed a hand on the pallette protecting the Perdon's shoulder. "Our plights are remarkably similar, my lord. Will you accompany me to my quarters? The battles of Perdon will not be fought in the next hour or two, and I have some excellent Termigan ale. Commiseration will benefit us both."

For a moment, the Perdon stared at Master Eremis as frankly as Geraden and the lady did. His blunt mouth formed the word, *commiseration*, as though he had never heard it before. Then his expression closed. Carefully, he said, "I thank you. Your offer is kind. I could drown my anger in a hogshead of good ale, if you have it."

The Master laughed. "I have that—and a great deal more, which I think will please you."

His face blank, the Perdon replied, "Then I am yours, Master Eremis."

"Good!" At once, Eremis bowed to the blond woman and Terisa. "With your permission, my ladies." His salutation was abrupt: he was clearly eager to leave. As soon as the Perdon also had bowed, Master Eremis steered him out of the chamber.

Slowly, as if involuntarily, Geraden and the lady in blue looked at each other. They both appeared stiff, awkward. She had more self-possession, however. After a few moments, she asked, "Now why would he do such a thing, Apt?"

Geraden shifted his weight uncomfortably, though he refused to drop her gaze. "I don't know, my lady. The Perdon has the heart and soul of a soldier. And he has fought Cadwal too long. Master Eremis knows he doesn't trust any Imager."

She looked away. Cupping her hands about her elbows, she gripped them tightly. "I *hate* it when he looks at me like that. He smiles and jests, but all I see is scorn."

"I don't exactly love it myself," muttered Geraden. "But that doesn't explain what he thinks he has in common with the Perdon."

They fell into a discomfited silence. Now that he didn't have to meet her gaze, he scanned the stone floor. She watched the corridor down which Master Eremis and the Perdon had departed as if she wanted to run after them and demand an answer. Considering Geraden and the lady, Terisa thought suddenly that they had known each other for a long time. The lady was about his age and seemed to Terisa to be a fitting companion for him. The intensity of her violet eyes, especially, seemed appropriate to his awkward intensity of spirit.

Abruptly, the lady gave a start of embarrassment. Turning to Terisa, she said, "Oh, I *am* sorry. How very rude of me. You have been standing here all this time, and I have not been courteous enough to speak to you. You must be the lady Terisa." She produced a smile that appeared genuine, if somewhat tentative. "I know the gown,"

she explained. "If the Apt's manners were any better than mine"—
the glance she cast in his direction suggested a scorn of her own—
"he would have introduced us. I am Elega. King Joyse is my father."

"Oh, yes." Terisa recognized the name. Because she had never
met a king's daughter before and had no idea what kind of salutation
was expected, she said what she had so often heard her mother say:
"How nice to meet you." Then she winced internally because her
voice sounded just like her mother's.

Fortunately, the lady Elega hadn't known Terisa's mother. "Myste
and I," she continued, "have wished to meet you since we first heard
of your—shall I call it your 'arrival'? The present circumstances are
not of the best. Matters which you have overheard leave me somewhat distracted, I fear." Despite her words, the way she regarded
Terisa implied that she had found something to compensate her for
her father's distressing treatment of the Perdon. "But I would be
pleased"—she smiled—"and Myste would be delighted, I think, if
you would visit us in our rooms. You may be unaware of the interest
you have aroused in Orison. My sister and I are always eager for new
friendships. And I tell you frankly, my lady"—she lowered her voice
as if she were imparting a public secret—"Mordant is a man's world.
We women are not often given enough to occupy our talents. So
your acquaintance would have a special value to us.

"My lady, will you come?"

Terisa was momentarily frozen. Then she shook herself in disgust.
Why did she feel threatened when she was asked for the simplest
statements and decisions? It was her mother in her. Her mother
would have said, *What a nice idea. When would you like us to come? I'm
sure that would be lovely. My husband is so busy these days. Shall I call you
next week?* For that reason, Terisa gazed at Elega as straight as she
could and said, "I'm not doing anything right now."

A second later, she realized how that would sound to Geraden,
and a sting of chagrin turned her face crimson. He wasn't looking at
her: his expression had gone flat, like nonreflective glass. Only the
slight, stretched widening of his eyes betrayed that he had heard her.

Now she remembered why it was natural to fear even simple statements and decisions. They caused trouble.

Apparently, however, the lady Elega considered the assertion a
natural one to make in Geraden's company, even though Terisa
might be presumed to have come here with him for some reason or
another. Her smile seemed as unconstrained as her earlier dismay

allowed. "Thank you, my lady. Have you eaten? We can have a quiet lunch together. I am certain that we have an enormous amount to talk about."

Yet she stiffened when she turned to Geraden. In a tone of dutiful politeness, she asked, "Will you join us, Apt?"

The corners of his jaw bunched. He shot a glance at Terisa and murmured, "No, thanks." His voice was studiously neutral. "I think the lady Terisa has had enough of my company for one day. Give the lady Myste my greetings."

Abruptly, he sketched a bow toward her and headed out of the waiting room.

As he passed through the entryway, he bumped into a doorpost with his shoulder and stumbled until he caught his balance. Several of the guards chuckled at his departing back.

The lady Elega put a hand to her mouth to hide a smile. "Poor Geraden." Then she shook her head, dismissing him. "We must go upward, my lady." She gestured toward the stairs and started Terisa in that direction. "My sister and I share rooms a level above the King's. We are told that we must live there so that we will be at least as safe as our father. But I believe," she said cynically, "the true reason is so that anything of importance will reach him before it reaches us—and stop." Trying to blunt the edge of her words, she added more humorously, "As I said, Mordant is a man's world."

In a small voice, Terisa said, "You should call me Terisa." But the suggestion was abstract; her heart wasn't in it. Part of her remained with Geraden. It pained her that she had hurt him. He was the only one she knew here who made sense to her. And part of her was still nauseated. Had the Perdon told King Joyse about those fatal black spots? Of course he had. He must have. And *still* the King refused to act? If he had only *seen*—

"Terisa. I will," the lady Elega said with satisfaction. "And you must call me Elega. I hope we will be great friends."

"Have you known him long?" asked Terisa. That was better than the memory of jaws and blood.

"Apt Geraden?" Elega laughed, but her mirth sounded brittle. "You will hardly believe it, but he and I were once betrothed."

"Betrothed?"

"Yes. Astonishing, is it not? But his father, the Domne, although no fighter—unlike the Perdon—is one of my father's oldest and most trusted friends. Because of"—a hitch in Elega's voice unexpectedly made Terisa think that the King's daughters might also have been warned against revealing too much—"of his wars, my father wed late. Though I am his eldest, I was born only a year before Geraden, who is the Domne's seventh son. Later, during a difficult period of those wars, my father sent all his family to the Care of Domne for safety. I spent several seasons in the Domne's home in Houseldon, and Geraden and I were natural playmates." The memory didn't amuse her. "For that reason, thinking us well suited, our parents arranged a match."

One flight of stairs took them to the level of the King's suite. Elega passed his high, carved door and took another stairway upward. "I would have been better pleased with one of his brothers," she continued. "All women seem to favor Artagel, and to see Wester is to love him. But both lack ambition. Nyle is more to my taste. Sadly, women are often given little say in these matters."

"What happened to your betrothal?"

"Oh, I flatly declined to marry him. He is quite impossible, Terisa." Elega made no effort now to conceal her scorn. "It is bad enough that he cannot be trusted to walk out of a room safely. But in addition he is *such* a failure. He has already been serving the Imagers for three years longer than any other Apt since the Congery was founded, and he is no nearer a Master's chasuble than he was when he began.

"His determination must be respected—and his desire to better himself. But I am the daughter of Mordant's King, and I do not mean to spend my life cleaning sheds in the Care of Domne, or sweeping broken glass after Geraden's disasters.

"Do you know?" She giggled suddenly. "The first time he was to be formally presented to my father—we had all ridden out to visit the Domne, some twelve or fourteen years ago now—he was so eager that he had no better sense than to attempt a shortcut across a log which spanned a pig wallow. When he reached us, he was carrying more filth on his person than he left in the wallow."

Terisa nearly laughed. She could imagine him as clearly as if she had been a witness: mud caked to his hair, his face, his clothes; water and fruit rinds dripping off him. He was exactly the sort of person to whom something like that would happen.

A second later, however, her emotions turned until she was close to tears. Poor guy, she murmured to herself. He deserves better.

"No, Terisa," Elega concluded. "Apt Geraden will make an honest husband for some dull woman with her mind in her belly, a strong passion for motherhood, and much tolerance for accidents. But I will not have him."

In silence, Terisa replied, That's your loss. She never said such things aloud.

From the top of this flight of stairs, they approached another door as high as the King's, which may have been directly below it. But this one wasn't guarded: there was apparently no other way up to this level of the tower, and so whatever protected the King would also ward his family.

Then Terisa remembered the secret passages. Maybe no place in Orison was safe from anyone who knew them well enough.

Smiling, Elega went to the door and swung it open to admit her guest. "You are welcome here, my lady Terisa of Morgan," she announced formally. Then she turned and ushered Terisa into the suite of rooms where she and her sister lived.

In a small way, Terisa was surprised to see that these rooms weren't as richly furnished as the ones King Joyse used. The thick, woolen rugs looked more like the work of villagers than the creations of artists—rugs for use rather than display. The divans, chairs, and settees had sturdy frames that emphasized their expanse of cushion rather than their maker's craftsmanship. Some of the end tables in the first room had the look of having been built for children to stand on; the dining room table which she glimpsed through another doorway had seen better days.

Her own background being what it was, she couldn't help wondering why King Joyse kept his daughters in this less luxurious style. But Elega was already explaining that detail. "Formerly, these rooms were those used by our family, while the ones below were reserved for the private business of the kingdom—receptions, small audiences, discreet parties, and the like. The Queen, my mother, had no taste for personal ostentation, but she recognized the importance of visible wealth in the craft of governance. For that reason, the public rooms were designed for show rather than comfort." This arrangement clearly suited her, as far as it went. The way she wore her jewelry revealed that her interest in her father's affairs had nothing to do with wealth or luxury.

Terisa started to ask why the King had moved downstairs—or why, for that matter, the Queen (had Saddith said her name was Madin?) no longer lived in Orison. But asking personal questions wasn't one of her strengths; and before she was ready to take the risk, a woman wearing a flowing gown of yellow silk came out of the back rooms.

"Ah, Myste." The look Elega gave her sister was at once fond and a bit condescending, as if she loved Myste but didn't hold her in very high esteem. "I have brought a treat for us. This is Terisa—the lady Terisa of Morgan. She looks well in your gown, does she not? We will have lunch together. Terisa, may I introduce my sister, the lady Myste? She is perhaps the only person in Orison more *avid*"—she stressed the word humorously—"to make your acquaintance than I am."

This made Myste blush. She was, as both King Joyse and Saddith had observed, very nearly the same size as Terisa, although slimmer in certain dimensions. In much the same way, she very nearly resembled her sister, although she lacked the contrast between Elega's vivid eyes and her pale skin and hair. Standing together, they were outdoor and indoor versions of each other. The deeper blond of Myste's hair might not have looked like fine gold by candlelight, but it would have a burnished richness in sunshine. The tone of her skin promised that it would tan well. At the same time, the less dramatic color of her eyes seemed suited to peering across distances under bright light rather than to penetrating the secrets hidden in corners and conversations.

The faraway quality of Myste's gaze was apparent when she entered the room: her thoughts might have been in another world. But it was strangely emphasized when Elega introduced her to Terisa. All at once, she did look avid, so poised for wonder that she was almost trembling—and yet her eagerness seemed to pass through Terisa in order to fix itself on something behind her, some set of possibilities that she cast like a shadow. This impression was so strong that she instinctively looked around, half expecting to find someone at her back.

"My lady." Myste bowed to the floor in a pile of yellow silk as if both to honor Terisa and to hide her blush.

Terisa almost panicked. Helpless and alarmed, she cast a mute appeal toward Elega.

In response, Elega put a hand on her sister's shoulder. "That is well done, Myste," she said somewhat dryly. "Nevertheless it appears that so much homage makes Terisa a little uncomfortable. I call her Terisa by her own request. Surely she will want you to do the same."

"Please," Terisa begged immediately. This time, she was acutely sincere.

The lady Myste rose. Apparently her blush was a sign of excitement rather than embarrassment: she didn't show any shame or self-consciousness. Her gaze, however, now seemed to be better focused on Terisa. "You are very welcome here, my lady," she said in a kind voice. "I am sure I will be able to call you Terisa in a moment—when I have calmed the beating of my heart." She laughed in a way that immediately reminded Terisa of King Joyse's smile. "Forgive me if I have discomfitted you. Perhaps you do not realize the honor you do us. I have so much that I wish to ask you."

"It *is* an honor," Elega put in before Terisa could protest. "By the standards of Mordant, we are merely two women living with our father because he has found us unmarriageable. The lords and personages who pass through Orison do not feel obliged to call upon us or keep us informed. It was only by chance that I happened to be with the King when—"

More urgently, she went on, "Myste, you will not believe it. Father has outdone himself." In a few scathing sentences, she told her sister about the Perdon's audience with King Joyse. Then she concluded, "Fifteen thousand men, Myste. The Perdon has but three thousand. And yet Father will not reinforce him.

"He has gone too far. This must stop."

"Elega, he is our father," Myste demurred. "Of course we do not understand his intent. How can we, when we know so little of what he knows and fears?" Unlike Elega, she didn't complain of her ignorance: she was simply stating a fact. "But we must not be quick to judge him. High matters are abroad in Mordant. It appears that war is near. A chaos of Imagery threatens us. And the lady—" She glanced at Terisa, blushed again momentarily, and forced herself to say, "Terisa." Then she gave Terisa a sweet grin. "Terisa has come to us out of a mirror. It is rumored that she comes in answer to augury. We must not be quick to judge."

"Myste, you are incurable." A small frown pinched Elega's forehead. "If the High King's Monomach broke in upon us, butchered me before your eyes, and raised your skirts with his sword, you would say that we must not be quick to judge him."

"I trust," the lady Myste said gravely, but without irritation, "that the High King's Monomach has more honor."

"Oh, you are a fool!" cried Elega softly. Her violet eyes flashed in her pale face. But at once she put her arms around her sister and hugged her until her own vexation faded. When she stepped back, her social graces were restored. "Yet even a fool and a great lady from another world"—she smiled to show that she was playing— "must have lunch. I will summon it."

She went to a nearby bellpull and gave it a tug. Then she retreated to another room.

A short time later, Terisa heard her speaking softly to someone, probably a domestic. And not long after that a maid laden down with trays appeared in the dining room and began to set the table.

In the meantime, however, Terisa was alone with Myste.

The particular quality of Myste's gaze—and attention—made her nervous. She found that she liked Myste readily, but she didn't want the lady to look at her. The way Myste seemed to see things that existed through or behind or beyond Terisa gave her the impression that she was starting to fade again. Involuntarily, she remembered that the mirror which had brought her here was false.

"There's so much about all this I don't understand. Why is the King—your father—why is he being so passive? What reason could there be for not supporting the Perdon?"

"Ah, my la—Terisa. There you touch on a question which has sundered this family to its heart, and still we have no answer." The lady gestured toward a divan. "Will you sit?"

They sank deep into the comfortable cushions, and Myste went on, "You have not been among us long. And it appears to be our policy that we must not reveal too much of ourselves to you." Her frown expressed her disapproval as effectively as her admission itself did. "You may be unaware that our father has *three* daughters. Our middle sister, Torrent—accompanying our mother, Queen Madin—no longer lives with us. They make their home in Romish—or in a manor just outside Romish, I believe, for I have not been there— with Mother's family among the Fayle.

"Two years ago, that was not true. We were together then. And I was glad of it, though I cannot say that we were happy."

Terisa remained still, said nothing. She sensed what kind of story was coming. The mission had taught her how to listen to stories like that.

"I think you would like our mother, my—Terisa. She is a woman who knows her own mind—a fact which upon occasion gave our father no little exasperation." Myste smiled at the memory. "If you listen to Elega, she will lead you to believe that there are not five such women in all Mordant. But it is my opinion that she misjudges. It is my opinion that women simply lack the courage to follow their dreams." As she said this, her gaze seemed to be aimed through the opposite wall, as if the stone were translucent. "Nevertheless none would deny that Queen Madin is one of the few who know themselves enough—or are brave enough—to insist upon their own wishes.

"This accounts, I think," she commented as a digression, "for the fact that she permitted Elega to break her match with Geraden of Domne, though the King himself had made it. Our mother was glad to have a daughter who knew her own mind.

"Now Madin," the lady resumed, "loved Joyse from girlhood—long before he became King of Mordant—and he loved her. In fact, it is said only a little in jest that he began the campaigns which led to his kingship in order to rid himself of the obstacles that thwarted his passion for her. Therefore when he had established the Demesne under his rule, and had brought the Care of Fayle to freedom in his service, he threw himself at her feet and begged that she would enter his possession, as her father the Fayle had done.

"To his astonishment"—Myste smiled again—"she refused him. She did not deny that she loved him utterly, but she would not have him for husband or for lover. He had set his hand to war as a farmer to a plow, and he must not release it until his fields were furrowed and planted. But while his grasp was upon that handle, his time and his life belonged to bloodshed. She was prepared to share him with many things, she said, but not with a mistress as avaricious as warfare, where every spear and arrow and blade of his enemies hungered for the riches of his heart. If his will did not change—and if he were still alive—let him only send word to her when his wars were done, and she would come to him anywhere in all the world.

"Well, he is a man. Of course he was furious. But he is also a good man. When he had been furious for some little while—a time which he describes in days, but which she reports as a *little* while—he laughed loudly and long. He avowed that there was no other woman alive to suit him as well as she did, and he swore on his oath that, whatever happened, her own steadfastness would provide her a minimum estimate of his. Then he rode away, bragging—as young men will—that he meant to conquer both Cadwal and Alend before the next winter.

"Sadly, he did not fulfill that boast. Many years passed before he could call himself King without fear that the title would be ripped from him in the next day's battle. And when that was accomplished, he turned himself to a different kind of warfare, the struggle to unify all Imagery in the Congery. Upon occasion, he visited her so that she could see he had not changed toward her. But his wars were not done.

"At last, she had had enough. Departing Romish on horseback with no other companionship or protection than her maid, she rode the hills and forests of Mordant until at last she found where he fought. He and his men, Adept Havelock among them, had just ended a battle with a malign Imager, and he was covered in ash from head to foot. Yet she rode up to him—as he tells it—as though they were being presented to each other in the audience hall of Orison, and she said, 'My lord King, how much longer will this go on?'

"He looked at his men, and he looked at her. For a moment, he says, he was tempted to make some foolish retort. She was a woman riding abroad with no one but a maid beside her, and five of his men had just been slain. But he thought better of it. Instead, he handed her down from her mount and took her into his tent and explained to her all that he was doing and all that he had left to do.

"When he was done, she said, 'My lord King, this may occupy another ten years or more.'

"He nodded. Her estimate was accurate.

"'That is too much,' she said. 'I have had enough of waiting. Is there any man in your camp qualified to perform a wedding service?'

"My father says that he gaped at her for fully an hour before he understood, but she insists that he did not appear to have lost his mind for more than a moment or two. Then he let out a yell and embraced her so boisterously that the tentpole broke and the tent collapsed upon them.

"Nevertheless it was he who insisted that they return at once to Orison for a full and elaborate marriage rite. He says that she deserved no less. In her view, however, he wished primarily to take her away from the danger of battles to the safety of his Demesne.

"Their union"—Myste glanced at Terisa as she continued, and Terisa saw both happiness and sorrow in the lady's face—"was what some have called 'gleefully contentious.' Certainly both of them knew their own minds with a vengeance. To those who observed them, each compromise they achieved seemed to be twenty years in the making. But we also saw how his eyes shone behind his bluster when she contradicted him. And we heard the warmth and loyalty with which she always spoke of him when he was absent. I call it a good marriage, Terisa.

"Its ending," she sighed, "was both slow and sudden."

"What happened?" Terisa was thinking about her parents, trying to find some point at which their relationship had had anything in common with what she had just heard.

Sadly, Myste said, "He became passive. The spark faded in him. More and more of the time which should have been occupied with governance, he spent closeted with mad Havelock, playing—so he said—hop-board. Fewer and fewer decisions were made. Perils and signs of peril were ignored. His people were not given justice. Not all at once, but over a period of years, he became what some men call him—an old dodderer. He retains only enough of his rule—and of the loyalty of his followers—to guard that he will not be usurped. The rest he has let go.

"This has been a grief to us all, but for our mother it has been a blow to the heart. As she valued her own mind, so she prized his. Yet now he only argued with her over trifling matters, such as whether his daughters should be taught hop-board in place of needlepoint. This she bore until she had had enough. Then she confronted him.

" 'Old man,' she said—by her wish all her daughters were present —'this must stop. There is evil Imagery at work. Your enemies gather as thick as jackals at your heels. Unrest grows close to rebellion among the Cares. And while all this transpires, you play hop-board with that fool Havelock. I say it must stop.'

" 'My dear,' he replied, as though she had wounded him unjustly, 'you refused to marry me for years because I was at war. Do you wish me to go to war again?'

" 'I was young then, and unwed,' she retorted. 'Now by my own choice I am your wife. As King of Mordant, you are my husband. I have accepted your kingship, and I expect you to do all that your kingship demands. The duty is yours and must be met.'

" 'As it happens,' he answered with a touch of his old hardness, 'I *am* King of Mordant. And no one but the King is fit to tell me where my duty lies. I have already consulted myself on the subject, and I follow my own advice exactly.'

"At this, our mother rose from her seat. 'Then you will follow it without me. I love you as utterly as death, and I cannot bear to watch the ruin which you are making of yourself and everything that you once held precious.'

"My father watched her go. When she was gone, he wept fiercely, as though he had been torn out of himself. But he did not say one word to explain himself, or to reassure her, or to call her back.

"Torrent went with her because she believed her to be in the right. Elega remains here—"

By this time, the lady Elega had returned. "I remain here," she interrupted, her eyes flashing, "because something must be done for Mordant—and it will not be done in Romish. Whatever action may be possible to save the realm, it will be taken in Orison. I mean to be a part of it, if I can.

"For her part," she continued, barely muffling her scorn, "my sister remains here because she dreams that the King will one day rise up to defend his kingdom—if only we are willing to trust him long enough."

Myste sighed again. "Perhaps."

At once, Elega became apologetic. "Forgive me, Myste. I should not speak so harshly. His treatment of the Perdon has upset me. Perhaps the true reason you remain here is so that whatever happens he will have the comfort and company of at least one woman who loves him."

Or perhaps, Terisa thought, she does it because at least one member of his family ought to be willing to witness what happens to him. Her own mother had stayed with her father until her death, but there hadn't been any steadfastness in that. Steadfastness required decision, and her mother had been incapable of it. She had simply been chosen by her husband, and she had accepted his right to do so. That may have been the only way she knew how to believe in herself.

Then Elega turned to Terisa. "But we did not invite you here to tell you such stories." She forced herself to sound more good-humored. "As my sister has said, there is so much that we wish to know of you. And lunch has been set for us. Shall we eat as we talk?"

Almost without thinking, Terisa replied, "I really don't have much to tell you." The contrast between her own background and the story she had just heard shamed her somehow, like a demonstration of how insubstantial she had always been. Against the threat of violent death she had no reality at all. "You're being very kind. But I'm only here by accident. I'm not an Imager. We don't have Imagers—where I come from. Something went wrong when Geraden made his mirror. Or during his translation." Again, she found herself sounding like her mother. But what else could she say? "I don't know why I ever let him talk me into coming with him."

Then, so that it would all be said and done with, she concluded, "I would have gone back already. But the mirror changed somehow. He can't make it work anymore."

She stopped. Her heart beat in her throat as if she had just uttered something dangerous, and the strange desire to weep which had touched her when she thought of Geraden in the pig wallow returned.

Gaping through her as though someone a few rooms away were performing a prodigious feat, Myste breathed, "Is it possible? Oh, is it possible?" She seemed to think that what she had just heard was more marvelous than any other revelation could have been.

In contrast, Elega flung her head back as if a menial had slapped her face, and her eyes flared. Slowly, her voice under rigid control, she asked, "Do you mean to say, my lady, that you have no reason here? No purpose? That you have not come to play a part in Mordant's need? Do you wish us to believe that you are nothing more than an ordinary woman? That this 'accident,' as you call it, should not have happened to you?"

Terisa didn't want to answer. The thrust of Elega's demand was hurtful. She had created this situation for herself, however, and she mustered her courage to face it. In that way, at least, she could try not to be like her mother.

"I'm not a lady. I'm a secretary in a mission." She held her back straight and her head up. "They need me. Not many people can afford to work for what they pay me. But I'll lose my job if I don't get back soon. Reverend Thatcher can't take care of everything alone.

"That's all. I live in an apartment. I eat and sleep. I go to work. That's all."

For a moment, she thought that Elega would scorn her. Myste was whispering, "That's wonderful. It's wonderful." Her gaze was coming into better focus on Terisa. "I have always wished that such things were possible." But Elega's face was made feverish by the intensity of what she felt, and she had drawn herself up as if she meant to spit acid.

"You should have gone after the Perdon," Terisa said dully. "He and Master Eremis are the ones you want."

In response, the lady tried to smile.

It was a sickly expression at first, but Elega mastered her features and forced them to serve her. With an effort of will, she softened her posture. "My lady, this is unnecessary. We belong to none of the factions of the Congery. We have no secret allies among Mordant's enemies. We will not manipulate or betray you. We are women like yourself, not self-serving men hungry for power. We can be trusted. We are perhaps the only people in Orison whom you may safely trust. This pretense is unnecessary."

Myste looked at her sister at once. "Elega, Terisa has no reason to lie to us. I am sure that she has not. It is not a pretense."

With a savagery that would have done Castellan Lebbick credit, the lady Elega flashed out, "*It must be.*"

An instant later, she recollected herself. Once again, she tried to smile. Now, however, she looked like a woman bravely suppressing an impulse to throw up.

"I'm sorry," Terisa said. "I'm sorry."

NINE: MASTER EREMIS AT PLAY

T he ladies Elega and Myste struggled to engage Terisa in a desultory conversation while they ate lunch together, but they weren't very successful. Myste smiled as if she had a secret behind her faraway gaze; she asked Terisa polite questions about what she had seen and done in Orison. Elega masked a towering impatience by picking at her food and filling the silences with trenchant descriptions of the life Terisa could have expected to lead, had she been born and reared in Mordant—a safe life, insufferably protracted by her essential irrelevance to her own fate. Both of them were obviously not saying what they had in mind.

It was also apparent, however, that both of them were constrained, not by Terisa, but by each other. The quick, stark moment of their disagreement had been intense enough to shock them, make them retreat from her as well as from each other. She felt an active relief when Myste at last suggested that Saddith be summoned to conduct Terisa back to the peacock rooms.

In a state of pronounced awkwardness, the three women awaited an answer to their summons. Fortunately, Saddith's arrival was prompt. A few moments later, Terisa had said a stiff farewell to the ladies Myste and Elega and was on her way back to her rooms.

Saddith had kept her eyes lowered in the presence of the King's daughters. Now, however, she studied Terisa frankly. At first there was uncertainty in her eyes, but it slowly gave way to a look of spice and humor.

When she and Terisa had passed the King's rooms, and were out
of earshot of the guards, she said in a cheerful, probing tone, "Well,
my lady. You have met the lady Elega and the lady Myste. They are
the two highest ladies in Orison. What do you think of them?"

I think, Terisa mused, they're both miserable. But she didn't want
to say anything like that to Saddith.

Terisa's silence seemed to confirm the maid in her opinion. To
hide a smirk, she glanced down at her unbuttoned blouse, the cloth
stretched open by the pressure of her breasts. "I think," she said with
satisfaction, "that they have forgotten who they are."

"What do you mean?" As she walked, Terisa found herself watching the faces of everyone who passed by, looking for some sign of
the man who had attacked her. That was preferable to thinking about
what she had seen in the mirrors of the laborium.

"They are the highest ladies in the land," explained the maid.
"They have position and wealth, rich gowns and rare jewels. All the
finest men of Mordant are theirs by right. But what use do they make
of their opportunities? The lady Elega scorns suitors. She does not
wish a man—she wishes to be one. And the lady Myste will not leave
behind her a nursery girl's dreams of romance and adventure."

Saddith laughed softly. "They are properly clad and placed to be
who they are. But they are too bloodless for it. Neither of them is
woman enough to rule the King's court as it should be ruled.

"Some day, my lady," she added confidently, "I will stand among
them. I will be as high as any of the ladies of Mordant.

"The contrast will not be to their advantage."

The maid's bluntness was strange to Terisa. She wasn't accustomed
to servants who spoke so freely. Curiosity impelled her to ask,
"Don't you like what you're doing now?"

At that, Saddith glanced sharply at Terisa as if to gauge the intent
of the question. Whatever she saw, however, reaffirmed her faith in
Terisa's innocence; she relaxed at once and replied candidly, "It is
well enough for what it is, my lady. Before I became a maid, I was a
scullion in the kitchens of Orison. And before that, I served ale in a
tavern near where the army of Mordant is encamped. And before
that"—she grimaced—"I fed chickens and swept floors in the village
where I was born—one of the lesser villages of the Demesne. The
place of a lady's maid in Orison is well enough, indeed. For what it
is.

"But it is not enough for me."

Terisa considered this. "What do you mean?"

Saddith replied with a lubricious grin, and her eyes sparkled. "My lady, it is in their beds that men put aside their pretenses and become the enslaved children that they are in their hearts. When I learned this, the village of my birth could no longer hold me. A soldier of Mordant could not bear to be parted from me, and so he found me a place in the tavern near his camp. A cook of Orison could not bear that my body should suffer the grimy hands of soldiers, and so he found me a place in his kitchens. The dear son of an overseer could not bear to displease me, and so I was given the work of a maid. The beds of men have lifted me this high, and they will lift me higher.

"Do you remember, my lady, that I spent last night with a Master? Already, my position in Orison rises."

Her complacency made this information sound to Terisa like an announcement in a foreign language. Under no circumstances would she have revealed to anyone that Master Eremis had touched the curve of her bosom.

"He believes," Saddith continued, "that he took me to his bed to reward me because he had asked for a service and I had met it well. But that is only his pretense to himself, by which he preserves the illusion of will and power. He bedded me because he could not do otherwise. He has begun to share his confidence with me. Soon he will find that his pretense disappears in public as it does when we are alone. Then he will find some place for me, to raise me closer to himself. But it will be a place of my choosing, not his—and I assure you, my lady," she concluded with relish, "that I will choose a place that will open my way to the strong sons of the lords of Mordant."

They were nearing the tower where the peacock rooms were. For a moment, Terisa said nothing, though she was conscious of Saddith's gaze on her, half expectant and half amused. She wanted to ask, Does it really *work?* Can you live like that? Can you be happy? But the words stuck in her throat. Without quite intending to speak aloud, she said, "I've never met anyone like you before."

"That is plain, my lady." The maid tried to reply gravely, but she was almost chortling. "Yet you may rely on me to assist you," she went on, speaking now more like a kindly sister. "If you wish it, we will make of you a formidable woman"—she smiled behind her hand—"eventually."

Terisa ascended the stairs to her rooms with her head full of haze. She had apologized to the King's daughters. For what? For not being a powerful Imager, come to save the world? Or for simply not being substantial enough to deserve their interest in her, their friendship or alliance?

Did she want Saddith to help her become *formidable*?

"I'll think about it," she murmured belatedly as she and Saddith approached the guards standing outside her door. "This is all so new to me. I need time to think."

"Certainly, my lady." Saddith spoke as a proper servant, but the looks with which the guards regarded Terisa conveyed the impression that Saddith had winked at them. "Let me help you undress, and then you will be alone as long as you wish."

One of the guards made a sound in his throat as though he were choking. Helpless to do otherwise, Terisa blushed again as Saddith ushered her into her rooms. As soon as the door was closed, she turned to see if Castellan Lebbick had kept his word.

He had: the bolt was fixed.

The rooms had also been cleaned and tidied. The strewn peacock feathers of the previous night were gone. A decanter of wine and a few goblets had been set on a table near one wall.

She was relieved when Saddith unfastened the hooks at the back of the gown and the pressure around her chest was released. Her lungs felt tight, as though she hadn't taken a decent breath for hours. Gladly, she dressed herself in her flannel shirt, corduroy pants, and moccasins. Then she waited as patiently as she could until Saddith had built up the fires, replenished the lamps, and made her departure.

At once, Terisa bolted the door. Then she went to the wardrobe with the concealed door and made sure her chair was still propped securely against that entrance. It was impossible that she would ever be *formidable*. She didn't want any man to look at her as Master Eremis did.

Unless Eremis himself did it again. Just once. So that she might have a chance to learn what it meant.

But when she went to one of her windows to gaze out over the winterscape of Orison and try to make some sense of her emotions, the face she remembered most vividly was Geraden's—his expression flat and neutral, held rigidly blank because she had hurt him and he didn't intend to show it.

During the afternoon, as the sun westered toward the cold, white hills, she was watching a squad of guards exercise their mounts in the courtyard when she chanced to see a figure that looked like the Perdon stride out into the wet snow and mud. Men on horseback were waiting for him, their shoulders wrapped in heavy cloaks against the weather. He sprang onto a beast they held ready for him. With as much speed as the horses could manage on that footing, they rode out of Orison.

To her, he looked like a man who had made up his mind.

After breakfast the next morning, she gave herself a bath, put on her own clothes, and tried to decide what she was going to do. For some reason, she hadn't been troubled by the sensation that she was fading —even though she had spent the evening alone with her fears and the strangeness of her situation; even though her existence seemed to be more doubtful than ever; even though there were no mirrors anywhere, no kinds of glass in which she could see herself reflected. Nevertheless her problem remained. The mirror that had brought her here was false. She wasn't an Imager—and Mordant needed help at least as powerful as an Imager's. A man in black had tried to kill her. She had seen men torn apart like raw meat by creatures out of nowhere. People who counted on her were going to get hurt.

She had to do something about it.

Well, *what*, exactly?

She still had no idea.

For that reason, she jumped up and ran to answer it when she heard a knock at her door. It sounded like an offer of rescue.

Unbolting the door, she pulled it open.

Master Eremis stood outside.

He had Geraden with him.

"Good morning, my lady," the Master said cheerfully. "I see that you have slept well. Your eyes are altogether brighter this morning —which I had not thought possible. I must confess, however"—he leered at her—"that I prefer yesterday's apparel. But no matter. I have come to escort you to the meeting of the Congery."

This was too sudden. Her heart was still pounding in reply to his unexpected presence. "The Congery?" she asked as if she were deaf or stupid. "Am I invited?"

Instinctively, she turned to Geraden for an answer.

The Apt's face was deliberately blank. He looked like a man who had taken an oath to stifle his emotions. Apparently, he still felt hurt, but didn't want to show it. Or was he just trying to keep his reactions to Master Eremis under control? She couldn't tell.

Nevertheless he was the one she trusted to tell her what was happening.

He didn't quite meet her gaze. "Actually, neither of us is invited," he said neutrally. "But Master Eremis wants us to go with him anyway."

"I do, indeed," said the Master. "I have told you that I mean to show my friendship toward you. And today the Congery will attempt to decide what action the lady Terisa's presence and Mordant's need require. Surely that discussion will be of some interest to you, my lady?"

Because she had hurt him—and because she had no idea where she stood with Master Eremis or the Congery—she tried to find some way to ask Geraden what she should do. But the words wouldn't come. Eremis' smile seemed to stop them in her throat.

Geraden scanned the room. Still neutrally, he said, "It may not be pleasant. At least half the Imagers are going to be offended when we show up without being invited. But Master Eremis doesn't seem to care about that. And the opportunity is too important. I don't think we should miss it."

Listening to him gave Terisa the odd impression that he had aged since the previous day.

In an effort to show him how much she appreciated his reply, she said, "All right," without a glance at Eremis. "I'll go." Then she stood still under the Master's quick frown of vexation, although it made her heart quake.

Unfortunately, Geraden's gaze didn't rise above her knees; he didn't see that she was trying to apologize.

Master Eremis got even with her by giving her an exaggerated bow in the direction of the door and saying, "If you will so graciously condescend, my lady?" His mockery was plain, but his quick smile took the sting out of it. The way he looked at her reminded her of his finger's touch on the curve of her breast. Before she was altogether sure of what she was doing, she returned a shy smile of her own. Somehow, she accepted his arm, and he escorted her out of the room.

Geraden followed without expression.

At once, one of the guards stepped forward to call attention to himself. "Master Eremis."

Eremis paused, cocked an eyebrow. "Yes?"

"Castellan Lebbick's orders. We're supposed to know where the lady is at all times. Where are you taking her?"

Terisa was a bit surprised. No mention of those orders had been made the previous day, when she had left her rooms with Geraden. She glanced at him and saw that he, too, was surprised. His blankness lifted, and he concentrated as if he were thinking hard. The exertion improved his appearance considerably.

But this discrepancy in the guards' behavior was something that Master Eremis obviously knew nothing about. "I have invited her to a meeting of the Congery," he answered smoothly—acid under a satin surface. "Doubtless Castellan Lebbick—by which I mean King Joyse—will also wish to know what the Congery means to discuss in her presence." He wrinkled his nose in distaste. "And doubtless his spies will tell him shortly after the event. Come, my lady."

As though she were dressed for a formal ball, he took her grandly down the stairs.

His route toward Orison's former dungeons was the same one Geraden had used yesterday. As they walked, he bent his tall form slightly over her, at once deferential, proprietary, and courtly. They must have looked like they were sharing secrets. She didn't have anything to say, however; all the talk was his. She was looking among the people they passed in the halls for any face that might remind her of the man who had attacked her. So he caught her completely off guard by commenting casually, "The Perdon and I discussed you at some length yesterday, my lady."

She was too startled to respond. Surely she wasn't the kind of woman men *discussed at length*?

He chuckled as if she had said something clever. "He has a—what shall I call it?"—he savored the word in anticipation—"a *vast* experience of women, but he and I disagreed as to which of your many attractions would prove to be the most delectable. I have promised to give him an answer when he returns to Orison."

The idea made her shiver. What did he mean? Something intimate and presumptuous—but what? Her mind remained stubbornly blank on the question. How would he touch her? What emotions would he draw out of her? She was too ignorant: ignorant of men, of course, but also of herself.

Unconsciously, she held his arm as though she were cold and needed warmth.

Crossing the disused ballroom with Geraden behind them, they took the corridor which went down to the laborium of the Congery. Again, she lost her bearings immediately among the doors and turns; but at last she recognized the straight passageway leading to the former torture chamber which the Imagers now used for their debates. The guards outside saluted, then opened the massive wooden door for Master Eremis, Terisa, and Geraden to enter the meeting hall.

From its perimeter, beyond the four heavy pillars that supported the ceiling, the large, round chamber seemed to clench around the Masters who had already gathered there. But when Eremis took Terisa toward the curved circle of benches and the better light of the lamps, her perspective changed; the space began to feel a bit less oppressive, a bit less like a crypt buried under a pile of old stone.

There were at least ten Imagers staring at her and Geraden as Master Eremis led them forward. A few of them sat on the benches, leaning toward or away from the carved railing that circled the center of the chamber; the rest stood around the dais. Two days ago, that dais had held the mirror of her translation. No mirrors were present now, however. As a result, the dais looked more like what it had once been: a raised platform to display the interrogation of prisoners.

Terisa had no trouble identifying Master Barsonage: she remembered his bald head, his eyebrows like tufts of gorse, his face the color and texture of cut pine, his wide girth. And two or three of the other Imagers she recollected vaguely: they must have been standing nearby when Geraden had pulled her out of the glass. But most of the Masters had a strange and hostile appearance, as though they were prepared to judge her sight unseen. To put her to the question without mercy.

"What is this, Master Eremis?" Master Barsonage asked darkly. "Did we not explicitly determine that neither Apt Geraden nor the lady should take part in our discussions?"

Geraden studied the groins of the ceiling.

"You did, Master Barsonage," replied Master Eremis in good humor. "But I am prepared to persuade the Congery otherwise."

The mediator frowned sternly. "This does not please me. It is frivolous. Our survival—and indeed the fate of all Mordant—hinges on the choices we must make. We have not the time"—he faced Eremis squarely—"and I have not the patience to reopen finished decisions."

Several of the Imagers nodded, muttering assent. Eremis didn't appear popular among them.

"Let us not be hasty," a familiar voice put in, as if the speaker were meek and disliked calling attention to himself. "For my part, Master Barsonage, I am willing to hear Master Eremis. Perhaps he has too little concern for the dignity of the Congery, but surely he is not frivolous."

Until she heard his voice, Terisa didn't realize that Master Quillon was sitting on one of the benches halfway around the circle from her. His gray robe and nondescript demeanor blended into the stone background. Involuntarily, her gaze leapt to him, at once glad to see someone she thought of as a friend and fearful that in his presence she wouldn't adequately keep his secret. But he didn't meet her look. His bright eyes watched the other Masters, and his nose twitched alertly.

"In any case," drawled Master Eremis, "it is my right to bring whatever I see fit before the Congery. That is one of our rules, Master Barsonage, as you well know."

An Imager said, "That's true." Another agreed.

Master Barsonage made a snorting noise, but he didn't trouble to argue the point. Turning away, he resumed his conversation with the Masters standing near him.

For a moment, Master Eremis grinned at the mediator's back. Then he drew Terisa toward an empty bench and seated her there, with the railing between her and the center of the chamber. With a gesture, half brusque, half cheerful, he commanded Geraden to the bench as well. Eremis himself remained on his feet, however. From her seat, Terisa received an exaggerated impression of how much taller he was than any of the men near him.

The room didn't seem as cold as it had been two days ago.

Alone or in small groups, more Imagers arrived. She noticed now that two or three of them were young enough to be recently elevated Apts—as young as Geraden. Among the others was someone else she recognized: heavyset Master Gilbur, a scowl cut deeply into the thick flesh of his face under his black-flecked white beard, his crooked back counterbalanced by the power of his hands. She remembered his voice, as guttural as the bite of a saw. But young or old, familiar or otherwise, they all stared at her and frowned at Geraden. Apparently, none of the Masters had improved his opinion of the Apt and her. As he passed, Gilbur rasped rhetorically, "What foolishness is this?"

Shortly, she heard Master Barsonage murmur, "Well, we are here. Let us begin." Imagers shuffled themselves to the benches, their yellow chasubles dangling. There was no escape: all the doors were closed. And they were strutted and bolted so that they could only be opened from inside. The Congery valued its privacy. If Master Eremis hadn't brought her here so confidently, she would never have come. She had nothing in her that might enable her to outface twenty-five or thirty antagonistic men.

As soon as all the Masters were seated and the mediator was alone beside the dais, he said abruptly, "Be brief, Master Eremis. We have more important questions to confront."

In response, Master Eremis resumed his feet. His smile appeared easy, impervious to insult; but his skin had an underhue of blood, and his pale eyes glittered dangerously. "Master Barsonage," he said in a conversational tone, "with deference to your age, place, and experience, I doubt whether your questions are more important than mine.

"No one here has failed to note that I have brought with me two persons expressly prohibited from this meeting—Apt Geraden and the lady Terisa of Morgan." He didn't glance at either of them: he was playing to the Masters. "They *are* the questions we must confront. He is the issue of power, for we still have no understanding of how he contrived to find her in a mirror focused upon our chosen champion."

Geraden lowered his head and covered his face with his hands.

"She represents action—the action we wish to take for our own preservation and the saving of all Mordant. Who belongs in our discussion, if they do not?

"First let us consider Apt Geraden—"

"Paugh, Eremis!" Master Gilbur interrupted rudely. "All this has already been said. A child could make the same arguments. Come to the point."

"The point, Master Gilbur?" Eremis waggled his eyebrows. "Do you wish me to forgo the fine speech I have prepared for this solemn occasion? Very well. I will trust to your penetrating good sense and make no further defense of my proposal.

"I propose"—suddenly, he raised his voice until it rang around the stone walls—"that Apt Geraden be granted the chasuble of a Master!"

While his shout died away, the Imagers gaped at him. Geraden's head jerked up, his eyes were wide with emotion. Terisa thought, *I mean to show my friendship toward you*. So this is what he meant. Master Eremis had been planning to gain recognition for the Apt, to see that he was finally rewarded for his years of devotion. She couldn't understand why the expression in Geraden's face was neither pleasure nor gratitude, but rather a kind of fear.

Then through the silence she heard a faint sound like muffled laughter. Scanning the circle, she saw Master Quillon biting the side of his hand to keep himself quiet.

Several other Masters were less successful. One of them let out a guffaw like the burst of a ruptured wineskin, and half the chamber broke into chuckles and hoots of laughter.

Slowly, Geraden's skin turned red until it looked hot enough to catch fire.

Master Eremis' grin was like his gaze—at once sharp, ominous, and vastly amused.

The mediator didn't laugh. He faced Master Eremis, his chin outthrust. Without effort, he made himself heard through the glee of the Imagers. "Master Eremis, it is not kind to humiliate the Apt in this way."

"*Humiliate*, Master Barsonage?" returned Master Eremis instantly in a tone of protest and outrage, though he didn't lose his grin. "I am entirely serious." More laughter greeted this assertion. In response, he began to shout at all the Masters together. "Apt Geraden has accomplished something that no Imager before him has ever achieved! Even the arch-Imager Vagel could not use glass as *he* has! Will you laugh at him? By the pure sand of dreams, you will *not*!" His voice quenched the mirth around. "Geraden is as worthy of the chasuble as any of you, and I will have my proposal answered!"

Still he didn't lose his grin.

"Oh, forsooth," said Master Gilbur before anyone else could speak. " 'I will have my proposal answered.' " His sarcasm was as heavy as a truncheon. "You dream, Eremis. You have put your head into a flat mirror and brought it out as mad as Havelock. Make Geraden a Master? Must I explain even this to you?"

"You must indeed," Master Eremis replied like sweet poison,

while the rest of the Congery watched him in various states of uncertainty and annoyance. "I ignore the offense, but I must have the explanation."

"Have it, then," Gilbur growled. "We could not accept him to the Congery, were he the greatest Imager in recorded time. We do not have his loyalty. While his body serves us, his heart and mind belong to King Joyse. It is no secret that when he left with her two days ago he took her straight to that old dodderer. But what did he say to her along the way? Ask him that, Eremis. What did he say of us to the King? Ask him *that*. And how has he served our interests with her since then? Master Barsonage commanded him not to reveal anything to her until the Congery had made its decisions. I will wager that command was broken before Apt Geraden and the lady left this chamber."

The muscles at the corners of Geraden's eyes flinched at every word. Yet he didn't lower his head or look away. Instead, he grew pale, as though his emotions were being honed out of him, leaving him focused and sharp. Holding her breath for him, Terisa thought that at any moment now someone was going to mention the flat glass which had changed. Then he would be asked to explain what he and she had been doing there.

"Apt Geraden." Master Barsonage was gazing at Geraden, his eyes level and solemn. "You must reply to this."

Geraden's jaws knotted, and he jerked to his feet. His deliberate blankness had failed him like an inadequate mask. "Master Barsonage," he said, biting down on his voice so that it wouldn't shake, "I am loyal to King Joyse—as all of us should be. He created Mordant. He gave us peace. He made the Congery to be what it is. But he"—his voice snapped for a second—"he has no allegiance to me. I kept your command, Master Barsonage, while I took the lady Terisa of Morgan to the King. But when I reached him, he paid as little attention to me as you have. He gave me your same command. And he dismissed my responsibility for the lady.

"Master Gilbur implies that I'm a spy for my King." Acid leaked past his control. "I'm not. What purpose would it serve? If I tried to tell him the secrets of the Congery, he wouldn't listen."

Stiffly, he sat down.

Terisa heard his hurt and his need. At the same time, she remembered her dream of winter, in which three horsemen rode to kill her, and a young man dressed like Geraden fought to save her. She had remained motionless in that dream, as passive as she had been all her life.

Remembering, she stood up.

"He's telling the truth." She was trembling, but she didn't let that stop her. "He obeyed you. And King Joyse dismissed him. He told him not to answer any of my questions." Then, impelled by a secret flash of anger or adrenaline, she added, "The King didn't give me any answers either. He feels the same way you do. He doesn't trust me."

Master Quillon stared vacantly at nothing.

For a second, Geraden's face shone with relief and gladness. The vitality that made him so likable was restored. But the smile Master Eremis turned on her looked as gentle and friendly as the strike of a hawk.

Abruptly, her courage failed. She sat down and bowed her head, trying to hide behind her hair.

"Thank you, my lady," Master Barsonage said quietly. "Apt Geraden, it is my opinion that you are owed an apology—by Master Gilbur, if no one else."

Master Gilbur made a hoarse spitting noise and muttered, "Do you consider that dogswater the truth?"

"Since it is unlikely"—Master Barsonage whetted his tone—"that Master Gilbur, or any other Master, will do so, I must apologize for them. Any son of the Domne deserves better treatment than you have received."

"It's not important," murmured Geraden. Then he raised his voice. "I would be satisfied if the Congery simply decided to treat the lady Terisa with more consideration."

"Very good," Master Gilbur whispered harshly. "He is not content with an apology from the mediator of the Congery. Now he must try to teach us our priorities and duties."

"Have done, Master Gilbur!" snapped Barsonage at once. "This does not become you. Apt Geraden's manners are not what we must decide here. It is his elevation to the chasuble of a Master."

Master Gilbur replied with a glare that would have split a wooden plank.

The mediator faced him for a long moment. But what Master Barsonage saw seemed to unsettle or alarm him: he was the one who looked away. The silence in the chamber became strained as he frowned into the distance, looking for self-possession.

"You have made your proposal, Master Eremis. Do you wish to speak further?"

"I will let Apt Geraden's evident merit speak for itself," replied Master Eremis. Bowing to the Congery, he sat down.

"Very well. Masters!" Barsonage called out formally, "you have heard the proposal. Shall it be accepted? What is the will of the Congery?"

Terisa was beginning to understand, partly from Master Gilbur's irritation, but mostly from Master Eremis' strange fierceness, that there were more things going on here than she could identify. Ulterior motives were at work. She watched in unexpected suspense as the Imagers voted by show of hands.

For a moment, she thought that Geraden had won. A number of hands were favorably raised, though most of them—with the exception of Eremis'—appeared to be reluctant. Master Quillon's was not among them, however. He was watching Geraden, and his eyes held a look of understanding and empathy, but he only raised his hand to vote against the proposal.

He was in the majority. When Master Barsonage had finished counting, he announced that the proposal was defeated.

Oh, Geraden, Terisa said to him silently. I'm sorry. But she didn't have enough nerve to speak aloud.

"Masters," Eremis enunciated softly but distinctly, "you will regret this."

Master Gilbur replied with a snarl of derision.

"Apt Geraden," said the mediator in a way that suggested his self-possession was still in doubt, "the vote has been taken. I must ask you to leave us now."

To Terisa, Geraden had never looked more like a man with whom the Congery would have to reckon. "Master Barsonage," he said as he rose to his feet, "you must make the lady Terisa a party to your decisions. It is her right to know and understand what is done here." Perhaps she had hurt his feelings the day before; that didn't appear to affect his sense of justice. "And it's folly to deny her. If she's simply a woman accidentally translated, then she can't do any harm. And if she's an Imager secretly—if she's the augured champion of Mordant's need—then you're wrong to risk angering her against us."

His assertion still in the air of the chamber, he turned sharply away from the Imagers and left the meeting hall.

Master Eremis shook his head and sighed. He was smiling at no one in particular.

Geraden's departure twisted Terisa's stomach. She was already in knots when she realized that no mention had been made of the flat glass with the impossibly shifting Image.

"Master Barsonage," rasped Gilbur, "may we dismiss this woman also and go about our work? There are reasons for haste. And I do not enjoy spending entire days in debate."

"You are in haste, Master Gilbur," put in Master Quillon unexpectedly, "but you are also hasty. We must not be too quick to set aside the questions Apt Geraden has raised."

"Masters," Eremis said, "I will give you good reason why we must accept the lady Terisa of Morgan among us. It has come to us from her own mouth. King Joyse desires her ignorant. If that is *his* policy, then surely it must be *ours* to inform and enlighten her. Why else do we have these debates, if not to break the mute inaction which our King imposes upon us?"

"Master Eremis"—Quillon's voice had an edge which he usually kept hidden—"do you propose that we commit treason?"

"If it is treason," the tall Master responded, "to fight for our survival—and for the defense of all Mordant—then I will propose it. But for the moment I advocate only that we permit the lady Terisa to remain during our debate."

"You make all matters complex," said Master Barsonage stiffly. "I do not like the direction in which you take us. But with Master Gilbur I wish to reach the meat of the question, so that I will no longer have to guess what is in your mind.

"Masters, you have heard the proposal. Shall it be accepted? What is the will of the Congery?"

This time, Quillon and Gilbur were on opposite sides of the vote. Once again, however, the former was with the majority. By a significant margin, the Congery elected to let Terisa stay.

Suddenly, there were too many eyes on her, too many men looking to see how she would react. She lowered her head to hide her disconcertedness. It was Geraden who should have been allowed to remain.

"Very well." The mediator sounded tired. "Now we turn to the matter which must be decided today."

"At last," breathed Master Gilbur.

"I will not remind you of the debate which brought us to this point," Master Barsonage went on. "It is enough to say that we must choose a policy—or a course of action—to meet the unexpected outcome of Apt Geraden's attempt to translate our chosen champion. We decided on that attempt because it was demanded by our circumstances—and because it appeared to be supported by augury. And we decided to send Geraden into the glass out of respect"—here Master Gilbur snorted again—"out of *respect*, I say," the mediator snapped, "for our King's belief that what is seen in mirrors is not created by Imagery, but rather has its own existence outside our knowledge.

"But that has gone entirely awry. And we have realized that it is impossible for us to know what role the lady Terisa of Morgan will play in the fate of Mordant. Therefore we must now choose where we will stand. Will we accept the consequences of what we have done and await its outcome? Or will we choose some other policy or action to meet our dilemma?

"Masters, you must decide."

Without rising, Master Eremis said immediately, "I say that we must accept the consequences of what we have done and await its outcome." Now he spoke as if he wanted to avoid provoking an adverse reaction. "As I have observed repeatedly"—he permitted himself no sarcasm—"the lady Terisa represents an enormous and unprecedented display of power, which we do not understand. We must not take further risks until we have learned more of her."

"Is this *you*, Master Eremis?" a younger voice interposed. The speaker was an Imager of about Geraden's age; he didn't hesitate to be sarcastic. "You sound craven. We have already determined that we cannot know *what* the lady represents. So we cannot make our choices on that basis. In our peril, it does not matter that Apt Geraden did something unprecedented. It matters only that he *failed*. The augury itself is sound. It must be, or we have no understanding of Imagery. Only the Apt failed. We must try again."

A flash of passion showed in Eremis' eyes, but he didn't retort.

Quietly, Master Barsonage asked, "And did you never fail when you were an Apt?"

"I did not make a lifetime of it," retorted the young Imager. "As well you know."

"In any case," Master Gilbur cut into the discussion, gathering force as he spoke, "whether Apts are prone to error is not at issue here. I agree that we must try again. *I* will try again. Using the original glass, of which Apt Geraden's is a copy, I will translate our chosen champion to us"—abruptly, he shook his huge fist at Master Quillon—"and *blast* the King's scruples, whatever they are! He will sit and play hop-board with that madman Havelock until the ground cracks under him and all Orison is swallowed in ruins. If Mordant is to endure, *we must have power!*"

"Well said, Master Gilbur!" two or three of the Imagers applauded. But Master Barsonage faced Gilbur with undisguised dismay.

Terisa felt a jolt like a moment of vision as she saw the armored figure again in her mind: though the landscape he faced was alien to him as much as to her, he confronted it as though he were in the habit of victory; and his strange weapons gave him all the strength he needed.

"Then you also," another Master said, "advocate what Quillon calls treason? Or do you mean to enter the glass and ask the champion to come to us?" A pause. "He will shoot you."

"I do not fear 'what Quillon calls treason,' " Master Gilbur returned. "Do none of you understand the *reason* we are in such peril? It is not Mordant which is truly threatened. It is the Congery. We are in peril because all men who have ever hated King Joyse or loved power covet what we represent—all the resources of Imagery in the world we know. And they dare act on what they covet because King Joyse has abandoned us. He created the Congery, and he shackled it with rules which serve no purpose but his own, and now he has cut it adrift. We must fend for ourselves or die."

"I agree." Master Eremis continued to speak carefully. "But how must we fend for ourselves? That is where we differ."

"Master Eremis," Gilbur grated, "you differ from everyone. You have no sense."

Tentatively, as though he wished to avert hostility, Master Quillon asked, "Would it help, perhaps, if we looked again at the augury?"

"Would that help you?" Master Gilbur answered in a nasty tone. "Have you forgotten what it shows? Or do you believe it may have changed?"

Quillon seemed unwilling to take offense. "I would like to be sure that it has not."

"As would I," said another Imager.

"In addition," Master Quillon went on, "there is the question of interpretation. Perhaps the experience of the past few days will teach us to read the augury more clearly."

A handful of men around the circle promptly indicated their assent.

Master Barsonage sighed. "It will take a moment to have the glass brought here. Masters, we do not vote on this. Any of you has the right to make such a demand—if the demand is seconded."

"I wish to see the glass," one of Master Quillon's supporters said at once.

"And I," said another.

"Very well." The mediator nodded toward someone Terisa couldn't see; the sounds of the door as it opened and closed carried distinctly through the chamber.

No one spoke while the Congery waited. Perhaps this was part of the Masters' protocol. Or perhaps none of them wanted to commit himself until Quillon's request had been satisfied. Master Barsonage stared beyond the circle. Master Gilbur ground his big hands together as if he were practicing breaking things. Master Eremis leaned back on the bench and gazed nonchalantly at the ceiling like a man whose good manners kept him from whistling. Master Quillon appeared to be making a conscious effort not to twitch his nose, but he didn't succeed. The other Imagers exhibited varying degrees of impatience, curiosity, assurance, and alarm.

Terisa had the impression that she ought to be more worried. There were undercurrents in this debate which she was able to sense but not define. They might be dangerous. People were plotting—and plots meant harm. What she felt, however, was a small, hesitant eagerness. She wanted to see the augury that had led Geraden to her.

It was brought into the chamber by two Apts, carrying it between them on a beautifully polished wooden tray nearly five feet on a side. As the Apts passed near her on their way toward the dais, she saw that the tray was covered with pieces of broken glass. These pieces had all been laid flat on the wood, and none of them touched each other; but they didn't appear to have been arranged in any other way.

So softly that no one else could hear him, Master Eremis murmured to her, "Perhaps Apt Geraden neglected to explain how auguring is done, my lady. There are two arts: to create a flat glass of the proper kind, accurately focused; and to interpret the outcome. In simple terms, a flat mirror is made that shows some person, place, or event from which the augury is to be extrapolated. For example, if we wished to determine whether our future contained a war with

Cadwal, we might attempt to create a glass focused on Carmag—a glass in which High King Festten could be seen. Mirrors show places, but it is people who cause wars. Then the mirror is dropped. If it has been correctly made, it breaks into fragments that show pieces of what will come from the Image on which it was focused.

"This glass was created by Master Barsonage." He smiled sardonically. "For that reason, none of us ask whether it was correctly made." Then he added, "The other difficulty, as you will see, is to interpret the results. I have always suspected, my lady, that augury exists primarily in the mind of the interpreter."

Once the Apts had set their burden down on the dais, most of the Masters left the benches and crowded around it. Only Gilbur and his most outspoken supporters apparently felt no need to look at the broken glass again. Everyone else cast at least a glance at the augury. Taking her arm confidently, Master Eremis guided Terisa among them until she stood at the edge of the dais. The Apts had stepped back: the tray of glass was clearly displayed in front of her.

The mirror had broken into dozens of fragments.

Each of them showed a different Image.

And all the Images were moving. When she first looked at them, they seemed to be groping blindly toward each other, as if they aspired to some kind of wholeness.

Pieces of what will come.

The sight made her momentarily dizzy: it seethed like migraine. She felt that she was going to fall. But she closed her eyes and pushed down her queasiness. When she looked again, she held herself steady by concentrating on one or two Images at a time.

—of what will come.

At first, she was startled by how many of them she recognized—and by how precise they were, despite their small size. In one, King Joyse hunched over a game of hop-board, a game that had collapsed into chaos; the men scattered everywhere. He stared at it as if he were determined to make sense of the confusion, and his hands moved aimlessly over the board. In another, Geraden had begun to step into a mirror; but his body blocked the Image within the Image. In another, he appeared again, this time standing surrounded entirely by mirrors, all of them reflecting scenes of violence and destruction against him. And in yet another, the armored warrior in the alien landscape fired his weapons past the edge of the glass.

But in fact those were only a small handful of the Images. The

others reached beyond her experience. One shard showed a castle—
she guessed it to be Orison—with a smoking hole torn in one side
and a look of death about it. Several pieces of glass held Images of
battle: men on horseback hacking at each other so vividly that she
could see the blood in the wounds; figures that looked like kings
rampaging; soldiers on foot spitted by spears; corpses trampled; carnage. Smoke blotted out the sun. And other Images were of things
that could only have come into existence through Imagery: rocks
falling from the sky as if off the side of a mountain; creatures so hot
that whatever they touched caught fire; devouring worms. Villages
were razed. Castles fell. Crops burned. Men, women, children died.

And yet here and there in the squirming mosaic were scenes of
peace, perhaps even of victory: a plain purple pennon set on a hillside; a celebration that might have been a wedding, taking place in a
high ballroom; farmers planting a field still scarred by battle.

Then another Image caught her eye.

Three riders. Driving their mounts forward, straight out of the
glass, driving hard, so that the strain in the shoulders of their horses
was as plain as the hate in the keen edges of their upraised swords.
Fixed on her across the gulf of augury and translation, and riding
hard to hasten the moment when she and her future would come
together.

The riders of her dream.

Of course.

At once, a wonderful and ludicrous calm came over her. It lasted
for only a moment; but while it endured she lifted her head, half
expecting to hear the heart-tug of horns. Of course. Why hadn't she
thought of that before?

Not the riders. She didn't know what they meant. She hardly
cared. But the *future*. Mirrors didn't simply span distance or dimension: they had the capacity to span *time* as well. *Pieces of what will come.*
That was why she had been able to see the same Image in two different seasons, the same scene in spring and winter: time. What she had
witnessed wasn't proof that the mirror that had brought her here was
false; she had seen only another demonstration of the potential that
made augury possible.

And that meant—

From across the dais, Master Quillon asked blandly, "Does this
shed any light for you, my lady?" as though he were inquiring only
out of politeness. "I confess that it baffles me."

"The secret of interpretation, my lady," Master Eremis murmured, "is to read the flow of the Images. Their movement is not random. There is a—perhaps it might be called 'current'—which runs from crisis to action to outcome. Unfortunately, this current is not easily discerned. We see Mordant's danger. We see the importance of Geraden. He is in august company—King Joyse, High King Festten, the Alend Monarch. And he is the only individual who appears twice. The champion we thought he would bring to us is here. Also, we see scenes we do not understand." He pointed at Geraden surrounded by mirrors. "And we see outcomes—ruin and hope. But how the Images flow is harder to determine. Does Apt Geraden lead to hope, or to ruin? What does King Joyse meditate upon while his enemies ride against him?"

"In brief," Master Gilbur rasped from his seat, "nothing has changed. The augury tells us only what we have already seen."

"When we decided that Apt Geraden should attempt to translate our champion," explained Master Barsonage, overriding Gilbur, "the logic of it seemed plain enough. He clearly could not be the cause of ruin. Ruin confronted us already. Therefore he must be a source of hope.

"Now," he sighed, "the interpretation is less obvious."

"Oh, forsooth." Master Gilbur was growing steadily angrier. " 'Less obvious,' indeed. Nothing has been more obvious. The Apt's involvement in our plight *is* the path which leads to ruin. Only the champion you see before you offers any hope."

Through his teeth, the mediator replied, "That is what we must decide."

For another moment or two, the Imagers stood around the dais. Some of them whispered among themselves. Others pointed out details of the augury which their companions might have missed. Then, slowly, they returned to their benches. Still holding Terisa's arm, Eremis steered her back to her seat.

But when the Masters were in their places again, a silence fell over the Congery. Everyone except Gilbur seemed lost in thought—perhaps frustrated that the augury didn't provide a clearer answer, perhaps hesitant to consider the drastic solution Master Gilbur had proposed. And he continued glowering about him as if he were determined not to speak first.

At last, an Imager Terisa didn't know asked, "Is there no middle ground? Must we either do nothing or risk doing too much?"

"No," another muttered. "The King has not left us that choice. Our *plight* is extreme. By governing Mordant like a madman, he has made the situation too grave to be met on any middle ground."

"I have heard a rumor," said a third Master portentously. "It is said that the Perdon came yesterday to speak with King Joyse. He reported an army of thirty thousand Cadwals mustering against him beyond the Vertigon, and he demanded reinforcement.

"He was refused."

The shocked expressions of several of the Imagers showed that this story hadn't reached them. Master Eremis smiled vacantly.

"Nevertheless," Master Barsonage put in more loudly than necessary, trying to shore up a weak position, "he is the King. That decision was his to make. We do not know what reasons he may have had for his refusal."

"True," retorted Master Gilbur. "And I, for one, do not care. When an assassin tries to strike a knife into my heart, and the man who is sworn to protect me steps aside, I do not ask for his reasons. First I fight the assassin. And when I have defeated him, and have bound them both in irons, and perhaps broken a few of their limbs for good measure, *then* I ask my sworn protector what his reasons may have been."

"Master Gilbur." The mediator swung his bulk to face Gilbur squarely. A combination of anger and fear stained his skin. "How have you become so savage? Your arguments I understand, but not the tone of hatred in which you utter them. Whatever else we may say of him, we must say that King Joyse created the Congery. He made us who we are."

"Who we are," sneered Gilbur. "Divided and useless."

Grimly, Master Barsonage continued, "We cannot make our decisions now on a basis of blind passion. What causes your loathing of him, Master Gilbur?"

Master Gilbur clenched his hands together until the knuckles whitened.

"Personally," drawled Master Eremis, "I believe that good Master Gilbur once had the insolence to ask for the hand of one of the King's daughters in marriage. Quite understandably, King Joyse laughed at him."

A few of the Imagers might have been tempted to laugh, but Master Gilbur silenced them by surging to his feet.

"Am I savage, Master Barsonage? Do you hear hatred in my voice? Do I display loathing? I have cause.

"As you know, I was one of the last Imagers brought into the Congery in the days before the defeat of the arch-Imager Vagel. But the story of how I was brought to the Congery has never been told.

"I have given my life to my researches, and in those days no other question interested me, although of course I knew of the King's invitation to all Imagers to leave their private laboriums and join him in Orison. I did not know, however, that another Imager had moved secretly near to my lone cave in the Armigite hills. This corrupt wretch coveted my research—and he attacked me, seeking to wrest what I knew from me. I defended myself, but he had taken me by surprise, and I could not win. In our struggle, a portion of the ceiling of my cave collapsed, pinning me under a block of stone I was unable to shift. My attacker snatched what he desired most of my possessions and fled.

"As it happened, he fled straight into the arms of King Joyse. The King had learned of my attacker before I had, and he was riding toward us to deal with the man when I fell. Instantly, my attacker turned his power against the King. But he was no match for Adept Havelock in those days, and he was killed.

"Weakened by the damage it had suffered, the ceiling of my cave continued to fall. But King Joyse risked his life to enter and lift the stone and carry me to safety. He could not heal the harm done to my back—the harm which marks me still. But he restored my health, recovered my researches, and gave my life purpose in the Congery."

"And for this you hate him?" asked Master Barsonage incredulously.

Master Gilbur slashed the air with hooked fingers. "Yes! Oh, he was wise in the creation of the Congery. He was strong and valiant in the making of Mordant. And he was good to me. But he did not teach me to look upon his subsequent weakness, his folly, his refusal to act, as though such things were anything except *betrayal*.

"I despise what he has *become*, Master Barsonage. If you or I slipped into our dotage, the servants of Orison would tend us in our beds, and our responsibilities would pass elsewhere. Our incontinence or loss of mind would do no hurt. But *he* remains King. And he takes no action except to prevent any action that might offer us hope.

"You should be savage, as I am. The man in all Mordant whom we have most cause to love has *betrayed us*!"

His shout echoed through the chamber. At once, however, he sat down. Into the silence, he growled softly, "I have been attacked and broken once. We must have power to defend ourselves."

Then he bowed his head into his hands and sat still.

No one spoke. Master Eremis shifted in his seat as if he wanted to say something, then thought better of it. Master Quillon appeared to be shrinking: he might have been making a conscious effort to disappear into the background. The mediator clenched his arms over his heavy chest like a man who felt like raging and did not intend to let himself go. Some of the Imagers watched the rest of the circle as if they were looking for hints. Others studiously avoided anyone else's gaze.

Terisa listened to the tension and wondered what the implications of being real were. What did it demand of her? What should she do?

Abruptly, Master Gilbur hit the rail in front of him so hard she thought she heard the wood crack. "Balls of a dog!" he roared. "Will you sit there forever? If you consider me wrong, say so. Does not one of you possess bowels enough to tell me to my face that I am wrong?"

At once, the young Imager who had jeered at Master Eremis said loudly, "I second Master Gilbur's proposal. We must call our champion to us."

His words broke a dam: suddenly, the air was full of voices urging that the matter be put to a vote.

Still gripping himself hard, Master Barsonage waited until quiet was restored. Then he said stiffly, like a breaking board, "Very well. This is madness, but it must be answered. I know my duty. You have heard the proposal. Shall it be accepted? What is the will of the Congery?"

Terisa counted the show of hands as rapidly as she could. Master Barsonage, Master Eremis, Master Quillon, and several others voted against the proposal.

They were in the minority. Master Gilbur had won.

The mediator snarled his disgust.

As if shocked by what it had just done, the Congery relapsed into silence. Imagers blinked at each other uncertainly. A grin of anticipation bared Master Gilbur's teeth; but he savored his victory and said nothing. Nobody seemed to know what to do next.

Then Master Eremis rose to his feet. If anything, his manner was more nonchalant than ever; but Terisa saw in his face—especially in his eyes—a new excitement, a taste for the game he was playing.

"I am surprised," he drawled. "This *is* madness, as Master Barsonage has said. I will not challenge the vote, however. It is conceivable, I suppose, that my judgment may be in error." He flashed a smile to which no one responded.

"Be that as it may," he continued, "you must next decide *when* to attempt this translation. Let me beg for a delay. Six days should suffice."

Master Gilbur jerked up his head as though he had been poked in the ribs. Master Quillon watched Eremis like a small animal staring at a snake.

"A delay, Master Eremis?" asked Barsonage. "Six days?" A quickness had come into his attention; his distress receded. "If Master Gilbur has his way, we will begin the translation at once. Why should we delay?"

"Why should we not?" Master Gilbur retorted trenchantly. "The peril thickens around us like quicksand. Thirty thousand Cadwals are poised against Perdon. The Alend Monarch alone knows what treachery he contemplates. We are attacked by Imagery of all kinds—and in all places, as if our enemy has no limitations of time and distance. In six days we may all be dead. But doubtless we will bow to the wisdom of our esteemed Eremis."

"Master Gilbur"—once again, the insouciant Imager looked hugely and secretly amused—"I advise you to watch your tongue. If you do not, I will watch it for you. In order to watch it well, I will remove it from your head."

Gilbur replied with a bark of laughter.

"Master Barsonage," Eremis went on smoothly, "I do not make this request lightly. Here is my reason. Yesterday, after his audience with King Joyse, I spoke with the Perdon. We spoke at some length, and we agreed that Mordant's plight is dire, that the King's passivity is insufferable, and that some action must be taken in spite of him.

"Our own dilemma is severe, Masters," he said to the circle, "but consider the situation of the Cares. It is Perdon that will die first when Cadwal comes to war, Fayle that has always been the first victim of Alend's aspirations, Termigan and Armigite and Tor that will have their people decimated. Therefore the Perdon promised that he will summon all the lords of the Cares to Orison—with the exception

of the Domne, of course, who is too great a friend of the King's—so
that they can try to determine an answer to their common need. And
so that they can try to forge an alliance with us."

Terisa saw dismay on Master Quillon's face. On the other hand,
the mediator listened with visibly increasing enthusiasm.

"They will meet during the night of the sixth day," Master Eremis
continued. "I have been asked to confer with them, to speak for the
Congery."

"What? In *six days*? For messengers to ride out and the lords to
reply?" an angry Master demanded. "At this time of year?" A mutter
of agreement rose around him. "If the Armigite is sent for, he may
possibly ride the distance in time. Batten is little more than forty
miles distant. But the Fayle? The Tor? That is madness. Under the
best conditions, the Termigan has seldom made the journey to Orison in less than *ten* days."

"Nevertheless," Master Eremis replied, as suave as poison, "the
Perdon has promised it. Will you call him a liar?" Then he smiled. "I
do believe, however, that he had decided on this gathering—and had
sent out his call—well before he spoke to me. I merely persuaded
him to include us in his proposed alliance."

At once, he resumed what he had been saying. "Masters, I believe
that we must not ignore this opportunity to find support for what we
do. If we ally ourselves with the lords of the Cares, explaining to
them what we propose for Mordant, we will not risk their opposition
to our champion. And we will gain friendships across Mordant which
may prove of great value in the coming strife."

Terisa found herself gazing up at him as though her face shone.
The boldness and possibilities of what he proposed took her breath
away. He was trying to fight for Mordant in a way that made sense to
her.

"Also," Master Barsonage put in promptly, "it may be that the
lords will propose a defense which will make the calling of our champion unnecessary. And we will have six more days in which to be
sure of what we do. Master Eremis, I congratulate your foresight and
initiative. This is well done."

"Is it?" demanded one of the younger Imagers. "By what right
does Master Eremis speak for us in front of the lords of the Cares?"

"As Master Barsonage has said," Master Eremis said with a gleam
in his eyes. "By right of foresight and initiative."

"But you oppose the calling of our champion," another man protested. "How can we be sure that this is not some ploy to undercut our decision? How can we know that you will advocate our knowledge and position fairly to the lords?"

"Masters," Eremis answered in a tone of good-natured sarcasm, "the lords will not agree to bare their hearts before the entire Congery. However we may look at the matter, we are the creation of King Joyse, and all men who fear his present *policy* fear us as well."

"My question remains," retorted the man who had just spoken. "How can you be trusted to form an alliance for us, when you oppose what we mean to do?"

For a moment, Master Eremis looked around him—at Master Barsonage, at Master Quillon, whose eyes seemed to bulge with stifled distress, at the Imagers who challenged him. Then he shrugged. "Very well. I will take one of you with me, to ensure that I deal rightly with your decisions. I will risk the ire of the lords.

"Master Gilbur, will you accompany me in this?"

Surprise echoed around the circle. Gilbur gaped. But he quickly nodded, murmuring, "I will."

Master Barsonage permitted himself a sigh of relief. "Master Gilbur, I take that as a second. Masters, it has been proposed that we delay the translation of our champion for six days, until Master Eremis and Master Gilbur have spoken to the lords of the Cares. Shall it be accepted? What is your will?"

The vote was almost unanimous.

Terisa began breathing more easily, as if a threat had been averted. Six days. Anything could happen in six days.

But Master Eremis wasn't done. Still standing, he said, "One matter more. The lords of the Cares will come to Orison openly, as befits their station. But they will meet in secret."

The mediator nodded briskly. "I understand you." The postponement appeared to have restored his confidence, his command of the situation. "Masters," he said in an incisive voice, his jaw jutting, "my lady Terisa of Morgan, no one must speak of this. No one. Whatever your private opinion of us, and of what we mean to do, you must not speak." He addressed the circle generally, but his gaze was fixed on Terisa. "The lords will not trust us if any word of this meeting precedes them. If King Joyse interferes, all hope of any alliance will be lost. We do what we do, not to aggrandize ourselves, but to save Mordant. We must not be betrayed." Slowly, he moved until he was standing at the rail in front of her: his eyes held hers. "My lady," he said quietly, "you must not speak of *anything* you have heard today."

He gave her a wry smile. "Geraden will question you, I do not doubt. If you become acquainted with her, you will find that the lady Elega is insatiably curious. Castellan Lebbick desires to know everything that takes place in Orison. Even King Joyse may bestir himself to take an interest in you.

"My lady, you must say nothing."

She tried to meet his eyes, but they were too demanding. He was asking her to make a choice and stand by it—asking her to accept at least a small share of the responsibility for Master Eremis' success. A passive share, perhaps, but a choice nonetheless. Wasn't that what people who believed in themselves did?—made choices and stood by them?

She hesitated because she wasn't ready to promise that she wouldn't talk to Geraden.

Fortunately, Master Eremis came to her rescue. "Master Barsonage," he said kindly, "I am certain that we can trust her."

The mediator glanced at Eremis, frowning as if he disliked his thoughts—as if something in Eremis' words or tone suddenly raised a host of questions. A moment later, however, he shook his head and turned away.

"Masters," he said distantly, "are there other matters we must discuss here?"

No one said anything.

"Then let us have done. I think that we have cast enough votes that will shape Mordant's future for one day."

Leaving the center of the circle, he passed between the pillars, unbolted a door, and walked out of the chamber.

Terisa looked for Master Quillon. He wasn't present. Apparently, he had already left.

Master Eremis took her arm and raised her to her feet. "Come, my lady," he said privately. "This is only your third day among us, yet already I feel I have been waiting a long time to offer you my hospitality."

She couldn't resist the way he pulled her arm through his and hugged her to his side. She sensed triumph from him, and anticipation, a secret, whetted enthusiasm. He was moving events too quickly. His confident vitality as he paraded her out of the chamber ahead of most of the Masters made her thoughts swirl.

When she was that close to him, his physical impact on her dominated everything else. He gave off a slight scent of perspiration and cloves, and she could feel muscle working over bone under his jet cloak. Where did his confidence come from, his power? And what did he see in her? Why did he go to such lengths to lay claim to her? She didn't understand him at all.

That made his hold on her stronger. His confidence was like a display of magic, enchanting because it was at once so attractive and so far beyond her experience.

As a result, she walked at his side as if his strength and her uncertainty were a kind of charm, entrancing her in ways she couldn't define.

He made her want something she didn't know how to name.

Still escorting her formally, he took her up out of the laborium and into the public passages of Orison. Once past the ballroom, however, he moved her in the opposite direction from the route to which she was growing accustomed—the route back to her rooms. As they walked, he explained that they were entering a section of the castle devoted to the personal quarters of the Masters—a section that King Joyse had had rebuilt when he first began to form the Congery, so that his Imagers would have fitting, perhaps even sumptuous, places to live, places that would show the respect in which their occupants were held. But she only paid attention to the sound of his voice, not to what he said. At once fascinated and alarmed, she concentrated on him physically as though his voice and his scent and the hard grasp of his arm were a spell that might solve the problem of her existence at last.

Leaving the ballroom behind, they began to pass more and more people. She saw a knowing leer in some of the greetings Master Eremis received from men of rank, a smile of congratulation or envy. Guards rolled their eyes at the ceiling; a few of them were bold enough to wink. Ladies and chambermaids studied her as if they were trying to grasp what made her desirable.

The sensation that she was enchanted and real caused her to feel unexpectedly bold. Undaunted by the way people looked at her, she said, "That was a nice thing you tried to do for Geraden."

"Do you think so, my lady?" She heard the grin in his tone. "You are delightfully naive. A child's spirit in a woman's body." With his free hand, he stroked her forearm; his touch seemed to leave trails of intensity on her skin. "I doubt, however, that Quillon takes a similar view. Unless I am quite mistaken, he considers me cruel."

His mention of Quillon sparked a quick protective reaction in her. There was little in herself or her circumstances of which she was sure; but she was sure that she didn't want to betray either Master Quillon or Adept Havelock. She felt Eremis probing on that point, and she replied immediately—perhaps too immediately—"Quillon? Which one was he? I haven't been introduced to very many of the Masters."

He responded with an easy laugh. "No matter, my lady. I assure you that he is of no significance whatsoever."

With a wave of his hand, he indicated that they had arrived at his quarters.

They had just entered a short hall like a cul-de-sac, with a door or two on either side and one at the end. The stone of the walls was the same almost-smooth gray granite that appeared everywhere in Orison, but the door bore no resemblance to the dungeon doors of the laborium. It was of rosewood, polished to a high sheen so that the bas-relief carved into it was unmistakable: a full-length rendering of Master Eremis himself, complete with a sardonic smile and a look of extraordinary knowledge in his eyes—a look, Terisa realized a moment later, that was achieved by embedding subtle pieces of ivory in the wood.

"I hope you will always be able to find me, my lady," he remarked. "The doors of the Masters are marked with their characteristic signs and sigils. But Orison is large, and signs are easily confused. Anyone who knows me will always know which door is mine."

Deftly, he unlatched the door and steered her into his chambers.

His use of the word *sumptuous* hadn't prepared her for the room she entered. After the relative starkness of the halls and stone outside, the opulence of the furnishings seemed exotic and exquisite. Both light and warmth were provided by perfumed oil fires cunningly hidden in brass shells as large as urns, their sides cut into delicate open filigree. The main piece of furniture was a huge divan swathed in satin and piled with pillows; and before it stood a long, low table, its engraved brass top suspended by chains from rosewood legs at each corner. But there were two or three armchairs in the room as well, each cloaked in satin to match the divan. An ornate washstand and basin, also of brass, filled one niche. Nearby was a wooden cabinet that held what appeared to be wine decanters. The floor was softened by several layers of rugs, the uppermost of which cast a solid sweep of crimson against the predominant blue of the furniture and the canary drapes that covered the windows. The fabric masking the ceiling was also canary; but the tapestries on the walls picked up all three colors, using crimson primarily to focus attention on what they depicted—scenes of women in various stages of seduction.

Grinning his welcome, Master Eremis released Terisa's arm and bolted the door. "Joyse treats his Imagers well, as you see, my lady," he commented. "Mordant, however, is not natively wealthy. For centuries, the Cares produced nothing grander than wheat, grapes, and cattle—and farmers to tend them. Our King's wealth—like his power—is the result of war." He glanced around him smugly. "Doubtless some Cadwal noble previously had the use of these riches. That pleases me."

He moved to the washstand to rinse his hands and sprinkle a few drops of water on his face. When he returned to her side, Terisa smelled a renewed scent of cloves. "Be comfortable," he said, gesturing toward the divan. "Do you like wine?" His smile was fading, and there was an avid smolder in his eyes.

The tang of incense, and the smell of cloves, and the expression on his face shifted the balance of her excitement and alarm, made a sensation like panic rise in her throat. Groping for something to say, some way to gain time so that she could try to think, she blurted out, "There was something I didn't understand about the mirrors. When Geraden was showing them to me."

He frowned, perhaps at her mention of Geraden, perhaps at her uncertainty. To cover whatever vexation he felt, he went to the cabinet, took out two goblets, and filled them with a wine as crimson as the rug. Then he came back to her, placed one of the goblets in her hands, and drank from his. He was smiling again, and the urgency in his eyes had receded a bit, become more wary.

"Frankly, my lady," he said, "no one understands what you saw. No mirror, flat or otherwise, can change its Image. Since it is impossible, I would not have believed it if I had not seen it myself.

"Doubtless you noticed that we did not discuss that change in our debate today. There is nothing to be said about the impossible, now that it is gone. Most of the Masters did not believe me when I described what had happened. Especially"—he spoke in a musing tone

—"since I did not recognize the new Image and could not identify it."

"Oh, Geraden recognizes it. It's called the Closed Fist. He says it's somewhere in the Care of Domne." As soon as she said the words, she felt that she shouldn't have. She had a strange feeling that she had betrayed a secret—that she had betrayed Geraden. But Master Eremis' virile presence compelled her to speak. He bowed slightly over her, listening as though he were waiting for her to finish so that he could take hold of her. She needed time. At once, she explained, "But that isn't what I meant."

As if involuntarily, she told Master Eremis what she hadn't told Geraden. She told him what she had found in the glass that showed the champion: not violence, not her apartment, but the Closed Fist in springtime.

Her hasty admission interested him, although it didn't appear to interest him quite as much as she had hoped. His frown now was one of thoughtful consideration. "That *is* strange," he admitted. Slowly, he took her to the divan and seated her so that her side was warm against his, with his arm on the cushions behind her and his torso leaning toward her. "Did Geraden have this experience also?"

She shook her head. "He tried." Her senses were full of incense, cloves, and baffled desire. "He wanted to see if he could take me back where he found me. So that I would at least have the choice of leaving. But when he went into the glass, he was with your champion."

"Indeed?" He cocked an eyebrow. "Then it was for you that the translation went astray?"

She didn't want to think like that. "Or Geraden does it for me. He probably doesn't even know he's doing it. He doesn't know he has the power." She remembered the way he had left the meeting hall—the way he had spoken out for her; the authority of his first appeal to her. To herself, she murmured, "They should have accepted him as a Master."

"Then," Master Eremis said firmly, "it is well that this changing of Images was not publicly debated. Unable to believe such power of Geraden, the Masters would have concluded that you are the powerful Imager they both fear and want.

"But you are no Imager, as we both know. I will speak quietly to Masters who may be trusted, and we will attempt to explain the things you do not understand."

While he spoke, his arm tightened around her; now his lips brushed her hair. "Are you satisfied? I am ready to begin exploring the territory of your womanhood."

She felt that she had no choice, that all choices were being swept away. Her body yearned against her clothes. She inhaled his warm breath as his mouth came down and covered hers firmly.

Then somebody knocked at the door.

The knocking was quiet at first, a few gentle taps. Master Eremis ignored it. His tongue stroked her lips, giving her a taste of kisses she had never experienced. But the knock became more insistent. Soon the person outside the door was hammering at the wood.

"Whelp of a dog!" Eremis jerked himself off the divan. Chewing curses under his breath, he strode to the door, unbolted it, and yanked it open.

Terisa saw Geraden standing in the doorway.

She was breathing harder than she should have been, and she could feel her face burning.

He didn't look at her—or at Eremis: he kept his gaze studiously fixed on a vacant spot between them. "Master Eremis," he said in a controlled tone, "how may I serve you?"

"*Serve* me?" snapped the Master. "Why do you imagine that I have any need of you at all? Go away."

"I'm in your debt. For no apparent reason, you proposed me for the chasuble of a Master. I'm done with my other duties. I want to repay you somehow."

"Very good. I accept your indebtedness. Repay me"—with a visible effort, Master Eremis refrained from shouting—"by leaving me alone."

At that, Geraden raised his eyes. Steadily, he said, "The lady Terisa deserves better."

Then he turned and walked away.

Master Eremis cursed again and started to slam the door. He caught it before it closed, however, shut it gently and restored the bolt. When he turned back to Terisa, there was a distant, peculiar smile on his face—a smile that might almost have been one of admiration. "That boy is a challenge," he murmured. He sounded like he was speaking to himself; but the glance he gave Terisa showed that he was aware of her. "I must think of something truly special for him."

A moment later, he shrugged the question away and looked at her more directly. The intensity came back into his eyes. He returned to the divan, drained his goblet, then seated himself close beside her again.

Without quite meaning to, she shifted a little away from him. By turning more to face him, she was able to raise her goblet like a barrier between them. Her cheeks still burned: for no clear reason, the sight of Geraden made her feel that she was doing something she should have been ashamed of. *The lady Terisa deserves better.* What did that mean? He knew too little about her to say something like that.

And yet the way he said it—*the lady Terisa deserves better*—touched her. It made her withdraw a bit from the Master leaning expectantly over her.

"That reminds me." Her voice was soft, even tentative; but inwardly she seemed to be growing bolder all the time—so bold that she could hardly recognize herself. She actually met his avid gaze as she said, "He told me you don't believe I exist. Remember? And you said you believed I didn't exist until I came out of the mirror. That's something else I don't understand."

"In what way?" Eremis' tone expressed deliberate patience.

She tried to explain. "I don't know anything about Imagery. I don't really understand anything about it. But I'm trying. It's easier for me to believe that a mirror is like a window. It lets you see from one place to another. Or from one world to another." She hoped he couldn't see the way her heart was beating, the way her breath came unsteadily from her chest. She didn't want him to know how important this question was to her. "It's much harder to believe that a piece of glass *creates* what you see in it."

Please. Do you really *think I didn't exist until you saw me for the first time?*

"Ah." He nodded in recognition. "As you must know by now, my lady, that is the fundamental confusion which divides and weakens the Congery. And Joyse further muddies the issue by insisting upon 'ethical' questions, such as, by what right do we translate Images out of their natural existence? But that is extraneous. The matter cannot be resolved until the essential point is known. Is a mirror a 'window,' as you call it, or are the Images seen in the glass brought into being by Imagery itself, by the act of making and shaping the mirror?"

As he spoke, he moved incrementally closer to her, leaned closer to her. His arm was around her again so that she couldn't retreat, and his spell renewed its power. She had never realized before that the delicate aroma of cloves was sensuous. She could no longer hold his gaze. Instead, she watched his mouth as if in spite of her uncertainty—not to mention her recent embarrassment—she wanted him to kiss her again.

"The true difficulty, however, is not a failure of understanding, but of imagination." He took the goblet from her and put it aside. His voice became lower, huskier. "The evidence of the truth is plain, but we do not accept it because, as you have observed, it is harder to credit."

His mouth dipped to hers, kissed her lightly: once; again. The second time, she responded as if she knew what she was doing.

"My lady," he breathed, "it is plain that you did not exist before you were incarnated by translation. Glass is dumb. Mirrors depict Images. They do not transmit sounds. If you come to us from another world"—again, he kissed her—"complete in its own existence"—and with each kiss her response improved—"how is it possible that we speak the same language?

"Since Geraden created the glass that conceived you, I must admire his taste in women."

This time, his mouth took hold of hers and didn't let go. His tongue parted her lips. She was leaning back among the cushions: his arm hugged her there, half reclining. For a moment, all her senses were concentrated on his kiss—and on learning how to kiss him herself. It was true: the mirror had created her. She was free. What she did no longer mattered. At first she didn't realize that he was unbuttoning her shirt. But his kiss was so potent—and his hand, so adept—that she felt no wish to stop him.

"Master Eremis," a voice said, "my lady Terisa, would you like something to eat?"

Eremis sprang to his feet, rage flaming in his eyes. Terisa pushed herself out of the cushions and looked up at Geraden.

This time, he had entered through a doorway which led to some of the inner rooms: he must have used a servants' entrance. Once again, his gaze was fixed away from both her and the Master. In his hands, he carried an ornate brass tray on which he had arranged a large wedge of cheese, some bread, and several bunches of grapes.

"While you discuss the fate of Mordant," he commented in a voice so determinedly nonchalant that it sounded fierce, "I thought you might like something to eat." As he spoke, he moved forward into the room. "It's been a long time since breakfast."

"Excrement of a pig!" the Master snarled softly. His hands hooked into claws. "This is insufferable! Must I bolt the doors on my own servants in order to keep you *out?*"

"I've already told you." Geraden's deference was comparable to his nonchalance. "I'm in your debt. I'm just trying to find some way to repay you."

Though she fought to hide it, Terisa could hardly refrain from laughing. The Apt's second interruption wasn't embarrassing: it was absurd. And the butt of the absurdity was Master Eremis, who looked angry enough to tear Geraden's heart out for too small a cause. Standing ridiculously polite and out of place in the middle of Eremis' seduction room, Geraden reminded her why she liked him so much. She was barely able to keep her face straight.

As if sensing that he appeared foolish, Master Eremis pulled himself erect. "Apt, I believe you," he rasped, jabbing one finger like the point of a spear at Geraden's face. "You seek to repay me. But *revenge* would be a better word, would it not? You blame me because the Congery laughed when I proposed you for the chasuble, and now you wish to 'repay' me by driving me mad.

"Listen to me, boy." He managed to look calmer as he spoke, despite the struggle between control and ferocity in his voice. "I wish you to go away and leave me alone. I have been your friend, whatever you believe. But you will sacrifice my friendship if you continue to torment me. And you will not enjoy my enmity."

If Geraden felt the force of this threat, he kept his reaction to himself. Without looking at Terisa, he asked—deferentially, nonchalantly—"My lady, do you want to be left alone?"

As soon as he confronted her with his question, she found that she couldn't answer. She liked him. She wanted to give him a reply that pleased him: it would have made her feel good to please him. But her body had come so close to learning what its womanhood meant —to Master Eremis, at least, and perhaps thereby to herself. She was trembling inside, and her legs felt too weak to lift her off the divan. Her yearning hadn't gone away.

"Are you blind, Apt?" The Master was almost whispering. "The *only* thing she wants is to be left alone."

"Then"—for an instant, Geraden's control nearly cracked, and a spasm of pain leaped across his face—"I must go." His tone became formal in compensation. "Please forgive this mad intrusion. I have misjudged."

Master Eremis made a stiff gesture of dismissal. Geraden turned and left the room the same way he had come.

"Fool." Eremis glared after the Apt. "He believes that he is safe to play games with me. I do not play games." Abruptly, he swung toward Terisa. "My lady, be warned. I do not play games."

She met his gaze until it seemed to make her tingle. If what she did no longer mattered, then why did she ache this way? Perhaps her yearning was stronger than she realized, and it was changing her. Or perhaps she felt an inchoate desire to defend Geraden. Whatever the reason, she amazed herself by saying, as if she were accustomed to comment on the behavior of the people around her, "I can understand why he thinks you do."

To her surprise, her remark caught his interest. His anger receded, and an inquiring look came into his face. It made him even more attractive than his intent desire. "Do you, indeed? I am taken aback." His tone was sardonic, but kindly. "What have I done to convey such an impression?"

She made an effort to answer him accurately, in part because she enjoyed being free to say what she thought, in part because his question flattered her by conferring substance on her ideas. "You don't show much respect for people when you talk about them in private, so when you act respectful in public you don't sound sincere. And you aren't consistent. You seem to do things"—her boldness was positively dizzying—"like propose to make Geraden a Master, not because you believe in them, but because you like surprising people."

His eyes widened humorously. "Not consistent, my lady? I? You were not present when the Apt's role in the translation that brought you among us was debated. You have not heard how consistently I have always defended and supported him." He took evident pleasure in questioning her. "How am I not consistent?"

She considered the matter. This couldn't last: surely he was about to become angry at her. That was what happened whenever she called attention to herself. She didn't want to lose this moment. Trying to minimize the risk, she replied carefully, "I was surprised when you chose Master Gilbur to go with you to that meeting with the Perdon. He doesn't seem to like you very much."

That surprise came back in a rush when Eremis burst out laughing.

For a moment, he was too amused to speak. She had apparently touched a point on which he was exceptionally pleased with himself.

Chortling loudly, he returned to the divan and sat down beside her again, sprawling back into the cushions and stretching his arms above his head.

When he was able to stop laughing, he drew himself erect, put his hands on her shoulders, and held her for a kiss. "Ah, that was a fine jest, my lady," he replied, enjoying her mystification, "and the richest humor of it lies in its secrecy. I will wager that all the Congery was equally surprised." Only the hint of calculation in his eyes, the way he seemed to gauge the consequences of what he did, prevented him from looking as unabashedly happy as Geraden sometimes did. "None of those fools knows that Joyse was not the one who saved Gilbur's life when his cave collapsed. *I* was."

While she gaped at him—while her thoughts reeled and her conception of everything that had taken place during the meeting of the Congery changed—he pulled her to him and captured her mouth again with his.

He stopped her breath in her chest. But as soon as his kiss eased she panted, "Wait a minute. Wait. I don't understand."

Placing kisses on her eyes, her forehead, the corners of her mouth, he eased her back into the cushions. "What do you not understand?"

"You and Master Gilbur are working together." Her chest heaved. "You planned that whole meeting." You were playacting all the time. "Why did you pretend to be enemies?"

"Because, my precious"—his tongue licked at her lips between phrases—"some of those dunderheaded Imagers truly do not like me. Ideas and hopes are frequently rejected simply because I am the one who presents them." His warm breath seemed to fill her lungs. "The truth would have turned them against Gilbur as well." She felt his hand once more on the buttons of her shirt. "The lie that he was saved by King Joyse gave him credibility, so that he was able to swing the vote."

Reclining against the pillows and his arm as though she were helpless, she still asked, "But why? Why do you want that champion? He's dangerous."

Master Eremis withdrew enough to let her meet his gaze. His expression was serious, and he spoke candidly. "Arms and war are dangerous. Power is dangerous. But nothing else can save us.

"You do not know the Perdon. You have seen his rage, however. He loves his people. He is proud of Mordant—and of his place in the realm. And yet his King has refused him aid. Impelled by desperation, he will go to any extreme to defend what he loves."

She thought she heard a knock at the door. For an instant, Master Eremis stiffened. But the sound was tentative, and it wasn't repeated.

"I will also," he went on. "I sneer at my fellow Masters, but that is only because a talent for Imagery is not a guarantee of intelligence or courage. I love the potential the Congery represents. I would gladly do battle in its defense. And I, too, have been refused. My King denies me his aid.

"I will not hesitate at a lie or two in order to gain the strength I need."

She wasn't sure of what she saw in his eyes or heard in his voice. His manipulation of the Congery was too easy; his explanation for his lies was too tidy. But his nearness and his strong touch took hold of her. His scent of cloves and his kisses were more persuasive than logic.

Her lips answered his as well as they knew how. Slipping under her shirt, his hand cupped her breast. His caress made her nipples ache. Instinctively, she arched her back, pressing her breasts closer to him. He pushed her shirt aside, and they were bared. Then his mouth left hers, and he breathed thickly, "My lady, I was not wrong. You are made for a man's delight," and his tongue reached out to her breast until his lips closed over the nipple.

Willing to risk almost anything now, she put her arms around his head and held it where it was so that he wouldn't stop what he was doing.

She was so amazed that she did nothing but stare when Saddith walked into the room.

Like Geraden, the maid studiously didn't look at Master Eremis or Terisa. She held her face slightly averted, and her expression was perfectly bland.

"Master Eremis—" she began.

He bounded off the divan violently, his arm cocked as if he were expecting Geraden and intended to hit first and ask questions later.

"Master Eremis," she repeated, flinching, speaking quickly to ward off his outrage, "this intrusion is inexcusable, I know, but you must forgive me. I had no choice. You did not answer the door. My lady, you must forgive me. I have no choice."

"No *choice*?" As soon as he recognized Saddith, he lowered his arm. Nevertheless he needed a moment to control his anger. "You are a servant. Why is it a matter of *choice* for you to enter my rooms unbidden?"

"Forgive me. I know that what I have done is inexcusable." Because Saddith's face was so bland, and her tone was so neutral, she didn't sound particularly contrite. "But I have been commanded to fetch the lady Terisa. The lady Myste wishes to speak with her. She is the King's daughter, Master Eremis. I could not refuse to obey her. You have the power to insult me—perhaps even to hurt me." She also didn't sound particularly fearful. "But if the lady Myste complains of me to Castellan Lebbick—"

Eremis interrupted her. "You could have told Myste that you were unable to find the lady." He had already regained his self-possession, however. He sighed. "But that may have been too much to expect of you." He turned to Terisa. "My lady, you must go. Kings' daughters are capricious—and our King lets his do what they will. It is not safe to ignore them."

Only his eyes betrayed him. They had gone dark and murderous.

Terisa wanted to wail in frustration—and also in unexpected fright. His ferocity was suddenly as vivid as her father's. She felt giddy, almost wild, close to tears—or laughter. Her relief was as acute as her sense of loss, her alarm.

Because she had no idea what else to do, she mutely began buttoning her shirt.

TEN: THE
LAST ALEND
AMBASSADOR

S till trembling weakly, full of confusion and trying not to show it, Terisa left with Saddith.

Master Eremis unbolted the door and bowed her out of his rooms. As he did so, his smile displayed a familiar blend of amusement and concupiscence: he might have been proof against his recent vexations. If she hadn't seen his eyes, she wouldn't have been scared.

She breathed an instinctive sigh of relief when the door closed because it had been Saddith, not Geraden, who had interrupted the Master the third time. She didn't like to think of so much anger aimed at the Apt.

For her part, Saddith appeared untroubled by Eremis' ire. Instead of betraying any kind of embarrassment or concern, her expression suggested a barely concealed satisfaction.

Terisa wanted to ask, Why does the lady Myste want to see me? More than that, she wanted to ask, How did you manage to come for me at just that moment? But as soon as she and Saddith left the cul-de-sac of Master Eremis' quarters, Geraden accosted them.

He made no effort to restrain himself. He was gamboling like a puppy.

"Saddith, you're a wonder!" Grabbing her by the arms, he danced her in a circle until he stumbled against the wall and almost knocked her to the floor; then he planted a loud kiss on her cheek and released her. "I'm in your debt. Forever! How did you *do* it?"

Without waiting for an answer, he turned, practically prancing, toward Terisa.

She kept on walking.

She couldn't tell what he saw in her face, but whatever it was, it sobered him rapidly. For once, however, he didn't apologize. "I know it was none of my business." He controlled his glee for her sake. "I just had the strongest feeling—" He gave her a wry grimace. "We've talked about my 'feelings.' I told you they're always wrong. But I have to do what they tell me anyway. I can't ignore them. I just can't. And this time I had the strongest feeling you were in some kind of danger."

"Danger, indeed," Saddith replied derisively. "You mistake those 'feelings,' Apt. You had the strongest 'feeling' that you wish to bed the lady yourself, and you could not bear to think that any man would do so before you. Perhaps also," she added with a leer, "you feared that once she had tasted Master Eremis' lovemaking she would have no interest in yours."

At Saddith's words, Geraden's eyes filled up with chagrin, and he began to blush like a little boy.

Suddenly, Terisa's trembling got worse. She had come so close— so close to something she couldn't name, some vital awareness of who or what she was. Master Eremis had told her that she didn't exist. And yet his touch—She was shaking all over. Her voice shook. "Do you mean to tell me Myste doesn't want to see me? You made that up?"

The Apt winced, but it was Saddith who said, "Certainly *not*," in a tone of humorous indignation. "I am not a liar, my lady." With evident difficulty, she suppressed a desire to laugh. "The lady Myste has most assuredly asked to speak with you. I spent some considerable time searching for you before I encountered Apt Geraden and he told me where you were."

Reassured by this support, Geraden admitted, "But it *is* true that Myste isn't the kind of lady who would insist on seeing you right away."

Saddith nodded. "I believe she truly does not know what it means to be the daughter of a king."

"If she had known where you were," Geraden continued, with some of his personal happiness bubbling up past his self-command, "I'm sure she would have insisted on waiting until Master Eremis was done with you."

"Nevertheless," concluded the maid, "I made him believe it. In future, he will be wise to be more careful about his designs."

Geraden couldn't help himself: he threw back his head and laughed.

Saddith joined him.

In their distinct ways, they both sounded so pleased that the tension which made Terisa tremble loosened itself involuntarily. She wanted to laugh as well. "He got so angry." At the moment, she felt it would have done her a world of good to laugh. "Maybe he isn't used to frustration. He looked pretty silly."

The thought of Master Eremis looking *silly* started Geraden and Saddith again.

Paying no attention to where they were going, they nearly ran into Master Quillon.

Because of his self-effacing gray robe and unassertive demeanor, he seemed to appear in front of them out of nowhere. His smile didn't close over his protruding teeth. "Ah, there you are, Apt," he said at once. "Come with me. I have need of you."

Terisa felt that his tone boded ill for Geraden.

"Master Quillon—" Geraden was nonplussed. "I've finished my duties. I wanted to spend the afternoon—"

"Precisely," the Imager cut in. "You wanted to spend the afternoon helping me. I am determined to finish my researches before Master Gilbur summons his champion and we are all required to put aside our personal concerns for the sake of the war which will ensue. Come."

Abruptly, he turned and started down the hall.

"Master Quillon!" Geraden protested. "It's customary to let Apts do what they want with their time when they've finished their duties."

The Master paused. The way he bared his teeth gave him an air of lugubrious savagery. His eyes glittered coldly. "For shame, Geraden," he said, speaking more mildly. "Sloth does not make a Master. Work does. How will you ever learn, if you are unwilling to make an effort?" Then his face tightened. "This is not a request, Apt. Come with me."

Walking briskly, he moved away.

Geraden cast a look of appeal and apology at Terisa.

"*Go*, Geraden," whispered Saddith. "Do not be a fool. What will become of your wish to be a Master? You hurt no one but yourself by disobeying."

The Apt grimaced, nodded, threw up his hands, and trotted after Master Quillon.

Saddith laughed again, this time at Geraden, but her mirth was not unkind. "He is a good boy, my lady, with many attractive qualities." She grinned. "Even his awkwardness might prove piquant. But in your place I would not trouble with him. You can aim higher.

"If you are already able to interest Master Eremis"—now she was serious, perhaps even a trifle vexed—"making no more effort than you do, you can most certainly aim higher. As an example, consider Castellan Lebbick. You will hardly believe it, having tasted a little of his tongue—and his temper—but he is uxorious to a fault. And now his wife of many years has died, after a protracted illness. *There* is a man in grave need of a woman. If I could attract his notice, I can assure you I would not remain a servant in Orison much longer."

"Saddith, what should I do?" Terisa asked on impulse. Now that Geraden was gone, she felt an urgent need to talk to him. Despite Master Barsonage's instructions, she wanted to tell Geraden everything. And she wanted to know how he would answer Master Eremis' reasoning. But she couldn't discuss any of those things with the maid. "I'm not an Imager. I don't know anything about men." Then, remembering Eremis' hands—and his mouth—she added, "Master Eremis and Geraden hate each other."

"My lady," replied Saddith, trying to speak lightly, "I would make certain that Master Eremis does not come to hate *me*."

An open window somewhere let a draft of cold into the corridor. Terisa shivered. Saddith was silent along the way to their destination.

Terisa expected the maid to take her to the suite the lady Myste shared with her sister, in the tower above King Joyse's rooms, but Saddith led Terisa back to her own quarters. Myste was waiting there.

Saddith exchanged her customary badinage with the guards, then opened the door and ushered Terisa inside. They found the lady Myste standing in front of one of the windows. Despite the chill outside, sunshine emphasized the summer tone of her hair and skin, making her more obviously beautiful than she had been in her own rooms, in Elega's company. Nevertheless she gazed out over the castle and the desolate winter as though she longed to be anywhere except where she was.

Her face retained its faraway expression, but she left the window and smiled when Terisa entered the room. "My lady," she began, then corrected herself, "Terisa, it is good of you to come so promptly." She hadn't lost the strange excitement with which she had greeted the idea that Terisa was far from being an Imager or a woman of power, was in fact nothing more than a mission secretary. "I hope I have not called you away from anything you would rather do. I fear I have nothing urgent in mind. For Elega everything is urgent, but I want nothing more than a little quiet talk."

This greeting took Terisa aback. She felt instinctively that Myste was one of the few people here who didn't have some kind of outlandish or even lethal expectations of her—one of the few with whom it might be possible to have a simple friendship. But for that precise reason she wasn't sure how to respond. She knew so little about friendship.

Fortunately, Saddith came to her rescue. Dropping a curtsy, she lied, "The lady Terisa was already returning here when I found her, my lady. She had attended a meeting of the Congery, but it was ended.

"And it is well past time for a meal," she went on. "Shall I bring you something to eat? You will be able to talk at your leisure."

For a moment, Terisa expected Myste to answer Saddith. Myste was the King's daughter. But then she realized that these were *her* rooms: hospitality was her responsibility.

"Please," she said quickly. "I'm hungry." Hurrying to recover her manners, she asked Myste, "Are you? I don't know what Saddith can bring us, but I'm sure it won't take long."

The lady continued to smile. Her gaze was direct—and distant, as if it passed straight through Terisa's eyes and mind to something beyond. "Thank you. You are kind."

"Very well, my lady," said the maid. "I will return shortly." On her way to the door, she turned so that her back was to Myste and gave Terisa a sharp look—a look that seemed to say, *Wake up. Pay attention. This woman is the King's daughter.* Then she left, closing the door quietly behind her.

From Terisa's point of view, however, the fact that Myste was the King's daughter really made no difference. What mattered was that she, Terisa, suddenly wanted Myste's friendship so strongly that the desire made her ache. She had never had a *friend*—

Oh, of course, she had had friends: playmates in her early years; girls who spoke to her in the halls and whispered gossip during school. But from the first her parents had never encouraged friendships. In particular, they had never allowed her to visit the homes of her young playmates, had never invited any of those girls to their home. And this separation had carried on into the numerous private institutions to which she had been sent, exclusive schools dedicated more to forming moral character than to nurturing comradeship. Or perhaps the distance that kept everyone away was something she had carried in herself—a gulf of passivity and doubt that no one knew how to cross; an unhealed wound.

She didn't want to lose this opportunity.

Awkwardly, she gestured toward two of the chairs. "Would you like to sit down?" Then she remembered the decanter on one of the side tables. "Would you like some wine?" But she sounded so disconcerted to herself that she couldn't endure it. "I'm sorry," she said, abandoning the pretense that she knew what she was doing. "I'm making a mess of everything. I'm so new at all this. I don't think I've ever had a guest in my apartment."

Myste had no way of knowing that this was the literal truth, but she accepted it anyway. "Please do not apologize. I think you do amazingly well. Consider what has happened to you in the past three days. You have been taken to a strange and alien world. You have been put down in the middle of a castle full of conflict, machination, and treachery. Half the people around you seem to believe that you can save them from war and chaos. An attempt has been made on your life. If I were in your place"—her tone became wistful—"I would be proud to manage half as well."

Without warning, Terisa's eyes filled with tears. Myste's understanding took her completely by surprise. "Thanks." Gratefully, she tried to explain. "Most of the time, I think I must be losing my mind. Everybody wants me to do something, and I barely understand what's going on."

"Here." Myste took Terisa's arm and guided her to one of the chairs. Then the lady produced a delicate handkerchief from the sleeve of her gown and handed it to Terisa. "It is a lonely thing which has happened to you. You must think that everyone you meet plots against you in some way. And now you have been taken to a meeting of the Congery. I doubt they reacted well when you told them you are not an Imager."

Terisa nodded, wiping her eyes with the handkerchief. "They're all doing it. The Congery doesn't want me to talk to the King. He doesn't want me to talk to the Congery. None of them want me to talk to anybody else." She almost said, Except Master Quillon and Adept Havelock. "And the Masters are all scheming against each other. Master Eremis—" He kissed me. He kissed my breasts. "Castellan Lebbick yells at me." She hesitated for a second, then blew her nose on the fine fabric. "Even Geraden wants to turn me into an Imager."

"Ah, Geraden." Myste's voice suggested a smile. "I cannot speak for the others, but him, at least, you can trust. You may doubt his judgment. His luck is disastrous. Nevertheless you can trust his heart. It is agreed everywhere that the Domne has no bad sons."

After a pause, she added, "I would like to be your friend, Terisa."

Terisa met the lady's eyes. They were focused on her now, not distant at all, and the expression in them was direct and kind.

So that she wouldn't start crying again, Terisa looked away. Myste's offer touched her too deeply to be acknowledged. How was it possible for someone like her to have friends? Evading the important point—and hating herself for doing so—she said, "You have a better opinion of him than Elega does."

Myste smiled again; but as she did so her gaze slipped back into the distance, and her face resumed its faraway cast. Quietly, she replied, "I have a better opinion of many things than she does. She is a king's daughter, and she desires the importance of a high place in the affairs of Mordant. She does not forgive her father—or the society around her—or anything else which she imagines stands between her and her natural right to plot and manipulate and betray as much as any prince. She does not forgive Geraden for the mistaken judgment which once betrothed him to her." Then she shrugged. "I think better of being a woman. I think better of those who hold power in Orison." Her tone was gentle and reassuring, but soft, as if she were speaking in another place, perhaps to someone else; and there was a note of yearning in what she said that didn't entirely agree with her words. "I think better of myself."

Terisa nodded as though she understood. "Was that what you wanted to talk to me about?"

"Oh, no," Myste replied easily. "Or perhaps it was. I have nothing special to say. But I would like to know everything about you. You are a pleasure and a wonderment to me. You consider yourself an ordinary woman—and I believe you," she hastened to add, "I believe what you say of yourself, though it is difficult for me to call any woman from another world ordinary—and yet you find yourself here, in the great crisis of Mordant's history. If your world has no Imagery, such a translation must seem extraordinary.

"For my part, great things have never happened to me. I have never been to a world other than my own. Indeed, I have hardly been out of Orison in the past few years. What is your world like? How did you live your life there?" She became more animated as she spoke, bright with curiosity. "How does it feel, to step through a glass and find everything changed? What do mirrors do in your world, since they have no magic?"

"Please. One thing at a time." In spite of herself, Terisa smiled at Myste's fascination. "We don't have anything magic. Mirrors just"— she groped for an adequate description—"just reflect. They show you exactly what you put in front of them. If they're flat. If they aren't flat, they still reflect what you put in front of them, but they distort it.

"In my apartment—" There she faltered. She had never admitted to anyone, I had my walls covered with mirrors so that I would know I existed. Lamely, she finished, "I had a lot of mirrors."

"Then you must be very wise," murmured Myste as if she were clinging to every word.

"Wise? Why?"

"You are able to see yourself exactly as you are. You are able to see everything exactly as it is. I have no such vision. And those who look at me do so with their preconceptions of a king's daughter— perhaps even of a woman—and so their vision is confused. None of us see anything exactly as it is."

"We do the same thing," objected Terisa. "We have the same preconceptions. But we only look at the surface. All we care about is the surface." She made a deliberate effort to be candid. "Maybe I've been able to see what I look like. But I don't know what that means. It doesn't help me know who I am."

Myste seemed to find this notion both humorous and appealing. "Then you are not wise?"

Slowly, Terisa replied, "I don't think I've ever known anybody who was wise." Unless Reverend Thatcher's ineffectual dedication counted as wisdom.

At that, the lady laughed. "Then you are surely mistaken, Terisa. You yourself are already the wisest woman in Orison, for you have not been misled by those who believe in their own wisdom. You know the difference between what is seen and what is unseen, and you do not attempt to judge the one by the other."

"Do you call that wisdom?" Terisa wanted to laugh simply because Myste was amused. The lady's mirth betrayed her kinship to her father: her smile was almost as infectious and likable as his. "Doesn't the fact that I don't understand *anything* count against me?"

Myste went on laughing. "Of course not. Mere understanding is the business of kings, not of sages—or of ordinary women. And it is always mistaken. It depends upon a knowledge of things which cannot be known—a knowledge of what is unseen.

"I must tell you, Terisa, I wish that Elega had less understanding and more wisdom. You are wiser than she."

They were silent for a moment while they relapsed to seriousness; then Myste asked, "Where does such wisdom come from? Tell me about your world. What are its needs and compulsions? How do you spend your days?"

A few minutes earlier, that question would have frozen Terisa. But Myste's friendly manner defused the frank pressure of her curiosity. Almost before she knew what she was going to say, Terisa began talking about her work in the mission.

She had never discussed it before. Words seemed to tumble headlong after each other as she described the mission's work, the human wrecks and relicts it served, the facilities, the surroundings; and her own job, her typing and filing and drudgery, her relationship with Reverend Thatcher; and her reasons for doing the work, because she had believed that in a place like that even she would be able to make a difference, because she could afford to accept the meager pay, because she hadn't considered herself capable of anything more demanding or ambitious. She babbled about it all until the discrepancy between what she was saying and the sparkle of Myste's attention stopped her. The lady absorbed every sentence as if she were hearing a tale of heroism and romance. Abruptly, Terisa said, "I'm sorry. I didn't mean to go on like that."

"It is a wonderment," sighed the lady. A gleam still shone in her faraway gaze. "Forgive me if I repeat myself. But that such a strange world exists! And you have a part in it."

"A little part," Terisa commented, "and getting less by the minute. Reverend Thatcher must have replaced me by now." And her father had no reason to want her back.

In her excitement, Myste rose to her feet. "But that is just the point." She began to pace the rug, her eyes searching everything except her companion. "You are an ordinary woman, and you say that your life in your world was utterly ordinary, however brave and self-sacrificing it may appear to me. I, too, am an ordinary woman.

"I am a king's daughter—but what of that? It is an accident of birth. Its effect upon what is seen is merely that I am able to dress well and command servants. Its effect upon what is unseen is—I hardly know whether it has any effect. It seems plain to me that I am an ordinary woman—and that this is good.

"Yet I am surrounded by people who are not content. Her lack of involvement makes Elega savage. Geraden causes himself misery striving for a Mastery he will never attain. Half the Congery wishes to retreat into pure research. The other Masters yearn for power over Mordant. Castellan Lebbick's life has revolved around a woman, and yet in his grief he despises all women. Alend and Cadwal struggle against the peace which has done them more benefit than all their generations of warfare.

"Terisa, I do not consider my father's passivity a good thing. I do not *understand* it. I am his daughter enough to know the importance of striving and risk. Passivity is not content. But surely we must acknowledge that it is not a terrible thing to be who we are.

"You are the proof of this." Her voice had risen to a pitch of affirmation. "By your own insistence, you are an ordinary woman, with no experience of power, and no talent for it. Yet your life is not meaningless. Great forces are at work in Mordant, and you are involved in them. There is no life which does not possess its own importance, no life which may not be touched by greatness at any time—yes, be touched by greatness and have a hand in it."

For a moment, Terisa stared at Myste. With an urgency which surprised her, she wanted to say, *Greatness?* That's ridiculous. How could I have anything to do with *greatness?*

At the same time, she wanted to weep harder than she had ever cried in her life.

Fortunately, Myste realized almost at once what she was doing.

Puncturing her own seriousness, she smiled; her manner relapsed to its more usual diffidence. "In her heart," she said with a verbal shrug, "Elega considers me mad. She thinks that such romantic notions render me unfit for my own life." A note of sadness entered her voice. "But my father did not despise what I believe. He loved me for it, and it was a bond between us." Her face hardened. "Until he changed, and it became impossible for any of us to speak with him."

Terisa was holding her breath, clamping herself rigid to restrain what she felt. But that wasn't necessary anymore, was it? She was free, wasn't she? The past didn't exist. What she said or did didn't matter. She could tell Myste the truth. By degrees, she released the air from her lungs.

"My father didn't change. He's always been like that."

"Do you mean passive?" asked Myste. "Lost and uncaring?"

"No. I mean impossible to talk to."

Tentatively, like a small animal coming out of a burrow after a storm, she began to smile. She had just spoken critically of her father, as if she had the right to do so—and nothing terrible had happened. Maybe friendship was possible after all.

Myste sat down beside her again. The lady's expression was soft and reassuring. "Tell me about him."

By chance, Saddith found that moment to knock on the door and come into the room, carrying trays of food.

Unable to sustain the way she felt in front of the maid, Terisa stood up at once—more abruptly than she intended—to thank Saddith and help her set out the meal.

If Myste was taken aback by the shift in Terisa's manner, she didn't show it. Apparently, she recognized that something important had happened—something that required privacy. She didn't pursue the conversation. When Saddith had served the food and left again, Myste made a polite show of enjoying her meal, and while she ate she kept her curiosity still.

Grateful for Myste's consideration, Terisa spent a few minutes concentrating on her food—a stew baked in a thick pastry shell. Then, to keep the conversation safe for a while, she asked a practical question in which her mission work had taught her to be interested: How did Orison manage to feed so many people so well in the dead of winter?

Myste replied by describing the system that provided Orison with all its food and supplies. After generations, even centuries, of an economic system based on warfare, in which powerful lords fought for the privilege of taking what they needed by violence, Mordant had been reduced almost to destitution, despite its abundance of natural resources. One of King Joyse's most important acts had been to replace war with trade. Essentially, he had established Orison as the principle buyer—and seller—of everything Mordant needed or produced. All the villages of the Demesne, and all the Cares of Mordant, traded with Orison; and Orison used its profits from these transactions to buy what its own people needed, so that its wealth acted as fertilizer to grow more wealth for the kingdom. A similar system applied to trade with Cadwal and Alend—which needed the resources of Mordant too badly to refuse to barter with King Joyse— and those profits were likewise plowed back into the soil and society of Mordant. As a result, all the Cares had come a long way from the fierce poverty that had marked the beginning of King Joyse's reign.

Terisa didn't entirely absorb the details, but she appreciated Myste's explanation nonetheless. She had criticized her father without being punished. When the lady was done, Terisa commented, "This sounds silly—but I've just realized that I haven't been outside since I got here." She glanced toward the window, with its thick glass and its tracery of frost. "I don't have any idea what's out there."

Myste put down her fork and dabbed at her mouth with her napkin. "It must be quite a shock for you. As strange as your world seems to me, ours must appear equally strange to you. And we have been so strictly instructed"—she betrayed a moment of embarrassment—"not to reveal our 'secrets' to you. Your ability to accept such things—Well, I have already said that you amaze me.

"How does it feel, Terisa? I have no experience with translation." There was a rapt undertone in her voice. "I have never stepped through glass into a different creation. It is another of my romantic notions," she admitted, "that such an event in anyone's life must be fundamental in some way, changing them as much as it changes where they are."

"No," Terisa said at once, remembering a sensation of impersonal vastness, of temporary eternity, of fading, "I don't think it changed me at all." She almost added, I wish it had. "It didn't last long enough.

"It was like," she went on, suddenly sure of what she meant, "dying without any pain. All at once, your whole life is gone, everything you ever knew or understood or cared about; you don't exist anymore, and there's nothing you can do about it except maybe grieve. But it doesn't hurt.

"I'm not talking about physical pain," she explained, "or even emotional pain. It just doesn't hurt. Maybe because there's a whole world around you to take the place of the one you've lost. Do you understand? I think that's the only reason I can bear it."

In response, Myste smiled vaguely—not as if she weren't listening, but rather as if what she heard triggered a wide range of ideas and yearnings. "I do not really understand. Elega would say that you are talking nonsense. Translation is a physical passage, nothing more. But there is something in what you say"—her hand closed unconsciously into a fist—"something that is not nonsense to me."

"Perhaps it is only death which gives life meaning."

But I didn't die, Terisa protested instinctively. That isn't what I meant. I was never there.

The impossibility of explaining herself any better, however, kept her silent.

"Terisa," Myste went on, quietly, distantly, without looking at her, "you have given me a great deal to consider. You say that you are not wise"—slowly, she became less abstracted, more present in the room and in Terisa's company—"but I have met very few fools who challenge me to examine my life so closely."

"Don't blame *me*." Terisa didn't know what Myste meant—and at the moment didn't care. She couldn't suppress a grin. "I didn't do it on purpose."

At that, Myste started laughing. Happily, Terisa joined her.

They were still chuckling together like old friends when Saddith knocked on the door and reentered the room. She was red-cheeked and panting, as if she had run up several flights of stairs. "My lady Terisa," she said breathlessly, "my lady Myste, the King summons you.

"There is news. Important matters are afoot. Your presence is commanded in the hall of audiences. All the high lords and ladies of Orison must attend."

"That is news indeed, Saddith," replied Myste. Her immediate excitement made itself clear in the way her eyes focused on the maid. "My father has not summoned Orison to the audience hall in more than a year. What occasions this gathering?"

"An ambassador has come, my lady," Saddith answered through her panting. "An Alend ambassador—in the dead of winter! He must have paid an awful price in time and men and supplies. And they say it is Prince Kragen himself! What could possibly compel the first son of the Alend Monarch here, through such hardship at this time of year, and across so much distance, when all Mordant knows that Alend desires war, not peace?"

Myste dismissed that question. "And he asks an audience with King Joyse?"

"Asks, my lady? He *demands*. Or so it is said."

"And the King consents to grant what the Prince demands," Myste continued. "That is well. Perhaps it is very well. Perhaps the affairs of the realm begin to interest him again.

"Terisa, we must go." She was already moving toward the door. "This must not be missed."

Because of the background Master Quillon had given her, Terisa caught some of the importance of Saddith's news. She followed without hesitation.

Perhaps this was what being free meant. She could criticize her father and follow her friend and even share in her friend's excitement without having to worry about the consequences.

When they had descended into the body of Orison, Myste turned in a direction new to Terisa. This part of the castle was more open than many of the other halls: the ceiling was higher; the walls, farther apart; the floor, worn smooth by generations of feet. Windows between the arched supports of the ceiling shed winter sunlight on large, colorful pennons fixed so that they jutted out from the stone; under the banners guards stood at attention, their pikes braced by their feet. As a result, the place seemed more formal, less inhabited, than the rest of Orison.

A number of men and women, however, were headed in the same direction as Myste and Terisa. Some were clearly officers of the guard; others wore the rich attire of high rank. Almost everyone saluted or greeted the lady Myste in some respectful or friendly way. She replied with faraway politeness: like her eyes, her attention was aimed ahead. Quite a few people, on the other hand, stared openly at Terisa. What she was wearing made her stand out in the crowd as badly as if she were naked.

Self-conscious now, she looked around and noticed that Saddith was no longer with her. Apparently, the servants of the castle hadn't been commanded to attend the Alend ambassador's audience. She regretted that: she could have used Saddith's worldly advice and support.

The stream of people approached a set of peaked doors, perhaps a dozen feet tall, opening out of the formal corridor. When she and Myste passed between them, Terisa found herself in what was unmistakably the hall of audiences.

It had the look and size of a cathedral. The stone walls were hidden by carved wooden screens, panel after panel around the room, each of them depicting characters and scenes Terisa couldn't identify; and the screens rose into elaborate spikes and finials reaching twenty or thirty feet toward the vaulted ceiling. The deep brown of the wood had the effect of making the hall dark, but it also seemed to distance the ceiling and fill the very air of the chamber with an impression of authority. The light came from two narrow windows up near the ceiling at the end of the hall, from rows of candles set around the walls and in tall holders here and there, and from batteries of cresseted oil lamps in the corners. The spiced oil of the lamps gave the air a sandalwood tang.

Down at the far end, opposite the doors, stood a structure that could only be King Joyse's seat: an ornate mahogany throne on a wooden pediment four or five steps high, dominating the space before it. A large part of the floor before the throne was clear, except for a wide, thick strip of rich carpet which led from the doors to the first step of the throne; but this open space was closed on three sides by benches like pews, in which the people entering the hall seated themselves.

They all stopped talking as soon as they passed through the high doors. The atmosphere of the hall seemed to silence them.

When she looked about her, however, Terisa saw that the hall of audiences hadn't been designed entirely to inspire respect. Above the screens on all four sides of the hall ran a balcony; the guards stationed there were archers rather than pikemen.

Those were the only guards in the hall, except for two at the doors and two more on either side of King Joyse's seat. But they were enough to make Terisa crane her neck as Myste guided her forward and wonder how many assassinations had taken place in Orison before King Joyse or his ancestors had conceived this protective arrangement. It was a convincing defense. As long as the guards remained loyal to their King, he probably had nothing to fear from anyone he met in the audience hall.

Following the lady Myste, Terisa bypassed the benches ranked on three sides of the open space and moved toward the King's seat. On each side of the pediment, a row of chairs reached toward the benches—special places for those who wielded the King's power or had the King's favor.

To the right of the throne, the nearest chair was already occupied by Castellan Lebbick. His perpetual glare and the purple band knotted around his short gray-stained hair made him look like a fanatic.

Fortunately, Terisa wasn't expected to sit near him. The first seats were taken by officers under his command; most of the rest had been filled by Masters, among them Gilbur, Barsonage, and Quillon. (Quillon? Why wasn't he working with Geraden?) Myste led Terisa to the left of the throne, where they joined the lady Elega and several men, most of them old, who resembled counselors more than courtiers. Myste introduced them by such titles as "Lord of Commerce" and "Lord of the Privy Purse." They gaped at Terisa as if she had just arrived from the moon.

Elega showed more enthusiasm. "I am glad you are here," she whispered, drawing Terisa into a seat beside her. "I feared that you would be found too late—or that Myste might not consider a call to audience worth obeying." She spoke as though she meant no insult, and Myste appeared to take none. "Kragen himself, Terisa! The first son of Margonal, the Alend Monarch, and Prince of the Alend Lieges. Imagine! He has come this entire distance from Scarab in deep winter. His purpose must be both mighty and terrible. Now my father will rise to the stature of his Kingship"—her vivid eyes flashed —"or he will forfeit what little respect he still holds in Mordant."

"Elega, he is our father," murmured Myste under her breath. "Even if he loses his mind completely, he still deserves our respect."

Elega gave a soft snort of derision. "Let him abdicate his rule when he loses his mind. Then we will respect him as our father without despising him as a failed King."

Terisa noticed Lebbick glowering at them as if he heard and hated every word.

His glare struck such a chill into her that several moments passed before she realized that the doors to the hall had been closed.

Around the balcony, each of the guards unlimbered his bow and put an arrow to the string. Instinctively, Terisa clutched at Myste's arm. But the lady shook her head and smiled in reassurance.

Now the Castellan was on his feet. Facing the seated people, he said formally, "My lords and ladies, attend." He didn't raise his voice, but his tone cut to the farthest corners of the hall. "You are commanded to this audience by Joyse, Lord of the Demesne and King of Mordant."

On cue, King Joyse appeared from behind the tall construct of his seat. He had on what appeared to be the same robe of purple velvet he had been wearing when Terisa last saw him. His white hair was held in place by a circlet of gold; but his beard looked like he had slept on it and forgotten to comb it. Now, however, a brocade strap across his chest over his right shoulder supported a tooled leather sheath which held a longsword with a double-handed hilt and a jeweled pommel. The weight of the sword made him seem even more frail than before, more withered inside his voluminous robe. He was walking very slowly.

He was followed immediately by Adept Havelock.

The people in the hall rose to their feet and bowed while King Joyse ascended the pediment and sat down on his throne; then, responding to some signal Terisa missed, they raised their heads and stood in silence before their King.

At the same time, Adept Havelock walked into the open space before the seat and began to dance.

From one foot to the other he hopped, shaking his head, gesturing with his arms, kicking up his heels behind him.

His dingy surcoat, tattered at the hem, and his stained chasuble, his bare feet and the ratty tufts of hair protruding from his pate made him look like a derelict, a piece of human flotsam that had recently been retrieved from some gutter. His beaklike nose confronted the gathering with a fierceness that his unsteady, sybaritic mouth and confused eyes rendered foolish.

His expression was so lunatic that Terisa nearly laughed aloud. Luckily, she didn't. Everyone else stared at Havelock—or avoided staring at him—in misery, disgust, or horror. Someone she didn't see muttered audibly, bitterly, "Hail the King's Dastard." Castellan Lebbick fixed the Adept with a glare that threatened to make his surcoat catch fire. Even Myste's tolerance wasn't equal to the way Havelock capered: she frowned and bit her lower lip, and her eyes were bright with anger or tears.

Nevertheless he reveled in the reaction he caused—or he was proof against it. In one hand, he carried a smoking silver censer shaped like a large baby rattle, and he shook fumes of incense around him while he pranced. Soon his dancing took him close to the people standing in front of their pews. At that point, he began to single out individuals for special attention. He jumped up and down in front of them, flourished his censer until smoke made them cough and their eyes water. And he shouted in a liturgical tone, as if he were intoning specific prayers for each of the people he faced:

"Rut in the halls!"

"Hop-board is the game the stars play with doom!"

"Twelve candles were lit upon the table, twelve for the twelve kinds of madness and mystery."

"All women are better clothed naked."

"Dandelions and butterflies. We are nothing more than dandelions and butterflies in the end."

King Joyse slumped in his seat, propping his elbows on the arms of the throne and supporting his head with both hands.

"Hail King Joyse!" Adept Havelock went on piously, still dancing in front of people, still forcing them to breathe his incense. "Without him, half of you would be dead. The rest would be slaves in Cadwal." He had chosen a pretty young woman to receive this utterance. "If you are dead from the waist up, and the lower half remains alive"—he grinned savagely—"you will still be of service."

The woman looked pale enough to faint. Instead of collapsing, however, she tittered nervously behind her hand.

At once, the Adept stopped. He peered at her in astonishment and indignation; with his free hand, he scratched one of the bald patches on his skull. Then he snorted, "Ballocks!" and tossed the censer away over his shoulder. It cracked open when it hit the floor, and a block of incense fell onto the thick carpet. In a scalding tone, he snapped, "Do not trouble to say anything more, my lady. I can see that I am wasting my time."

Abruptly, he turned from her and stalked toward the place where he had made his entrance. "Do you hear me, Joyse?" he shouted up at the King. His arms flailed fury at his sides. "*I am wasting my time!*"

A moment later, he disappeared behind the pediment.

The hall of audiences was shocked. Apparently, the people of Orison still weren't accustomed to Havelock's quirks. In one or two places among the pews, a different kind of titter began; it was stilled immediately. The mediator of the Congery had a lost expression on his face. Master Quillon covered his eyes with one hand. A scowl of

vindication twisted Master Gilbur's face. Elega's eyes flashed anger.
Myste looked like she wanted to weep.

Behind the incense of the censer and the perfumed oil of the
lamps, Terisa smelled the stink of burning fabric. Spilled incense was
making the carpet smolder.

King Joyse seemed to be shrinking inside his robe. The watery
blue of his eyes was bleak.

Castellan Lebbick was the first to act. Bristling with anger, he
stamped away from his chair, went to the burning patch in the carpet,
and ground out the fire with his heel. Then he faced the King, his
fists cocked on his hips.

"Perhaps you know the meaning of the Adept's display, my lord
King." He sounded savage. "I don't. He would be more understandable to me if you had him *chained*."

At once, however, he regained his self-control. Without any pretense of transition, he said, "My lord King, Prince Kragen of Alend
has requested this audience. He says that he comes as ambassador
from his father, Margonal, the Alend Monarch. Shall he be admitted?"

For a while, King Joyse didn't reply. Then he sighed. "My old
friend is wiser than I. All this is a waste of time. But since it must be
faced, let us do it and be done." He made a tired gesture. "Admit
Prince Kragen." A moment later, he added, "And sit down, all of
you. You exhaust me."

Lebbick glanced up toward the balcony and nodded. Then he returned to his chair.

Obeying her father promptly, Myste sat down. Terisa followed her
example. The Castellan himself took his seat. Shortly the rest of the
gathering did the same.

Elega was the last. She remained on her feet for a few seconds,
staring up at the King as if she were trying by force of will to make
him behave as she wished. He didn't meet her gaze, however, and
after a moment she, too, resumed her seat, muttering darkly to herself.

At the same time, the high doors swung open. From somewhere, a
cornet sounded a fanfare. Everyone looked toward the doors as three
men came striding into the audience hall.

One of them led the way, with the others a step behind him on
either side, and Terisa at once took him for the Prince. His bearing
was confident, and his stride expressed regal self-assertion. His black

hair curled out from under his spiked helmet; his black mustache shone as if it had been waxed; his black eyes gleamed with vigor. In contrast to his swarthy skin, his ceremonial helmet and breastplate were of polished and gleaming brass, and a sword in a fine brass sheath was belted to his hip. The silk flowing around his limbs picked up the same contrast, giving off glimpses of light and dark as he moved.

He looked like a man who wouldn't hesitate to demand an audience of anyone.

Judging by the fact that the two men behind him seemed more wary as well as less assured, Terisa guessed that they were bodyguards. The Prince ignored the archers poised around the balcony above him: his companions didn't.

He strode forward until he was close enough to the throne to show that he considered himself King Joyse's peer, but not so close that the guards would take him for a threat. There he stopped. He gave King Joyse an elaborate bow—which his well-trained companions matched—then announced, "Hail, Joyse, Lord of the Demesne and King of Mordant. I bring you greetings from Margonal, the Alend Monarch and Lord of the Alend Lieges, whose ambassador I am." Like his smile, his tone was perfectly courteous. "Great matters are afoot in the world. The times are perilous, and it well befits rulers to consult with each other as brothers, to meet the danger. My father has sent me to Orison to ask many things—and to propose a few which may be of interest."

King Joyse didn't stand or in any other way acknowledge the Prince's salutation. Gruffly, he muttered, "Kragen, is it? I know you." The tremor of age in his voice made him sound petulant.

The Prince's smile shifted a few degrees. "Have we met, my lord King?"

"Yes, we have, my lord Prince." King Joyse articulated the title sourly. "You should remember. It was seventeen years ago. You led several squadrons of Alend horse to protect one of your Imagers from me. When I beat you, I had to have you bound to make you accept defeat—yes, and gagged to make you keep your insults to yourself. You were an overeager puppy, Kragen. I hope that seventeen years have made you wiser."

Now Prince Kragen wasn't smiling. His men weren't smiling. One of them whispered something Terisa couldn't hear. Nevertheless Kragen's manner remained suave and sure. "My thanks for the reminder, my lord King. I doubt that I am much wiser, since I have always been too ready to forget my defeats. For that reason, I am not bitter. Howsoever, it is well that I have come as an ambassador instead of as an opponent, is it not? Since I am an ambassador, you will not need to have me bound and gagged in order to save yourself from an overeager puppy."

At that, Castellan Lebbick made a noise between his teeth that could be heard across the hall. Though he sat back in his chair with his arms folded, he gave the impression that he was ready to spring at Prince Kragen's throat.

King Joyse scowled. "I have often said," he answered the Prince slowly, "that a puppy is more deadly than a dog. A dog learns from experience. A puppy has none, and so his behavior cannot be predicted."

The Alend ambassador's eyes had a yellowish cast, like a tinge of anger. Yet his manner remained unruffled. His stance suggested that he was incapable of quailing. "My lord King, do you keep hunting dogs? I do not know if you enjoy the sport. It is one of my passions. Among my people I am not considered a poor master of the hunt. I can assure you that it is never the puppy that brings down the stag."

The King's hands gripped the arms of his throne. "That," he snapped, "is because dogs hunt in *packs*."

"Oh, Father," Elega groaned softly.

The indignation of Prince Kragen's companions was becoming stronger than their training—or their good sense. One of them put a hand on his sword; the other turned his back halfway to the King and whispered hotly in Kragen's ear. But the Prince stilled them both with a sharp cut of his hand. He appeared determined not to take public offense.

"My lord King, it seems that you harbor some enmity toward me —or perhaps toward the Alend Monarch himself. If that is true, it may have a bearing on my mission. I am prepared to discuss it openly, if you desire. But would not a more private audience be better? That was my request, as you will recall."

"That was your *demand*, as I recall," rasped the Castellan.

"Nevertheless," King Joyse said as though he were following a different conversation, "I apologize for calling you a puppy. You have become wiser than you admit. In that, you resemble your father."

In response, Prince Kragen brought back his smile. "Oh, I think

you misjudge the Alend Monarch, my lord King," he drawled. "He
has become openly fascinated with wisdom over the years. My mission to you is evidence of that."

The Castellan continued to glare at Kragen. "The Alend Monarch," he said in an acid tone, "has caused more death in Mordant
than any man except the High King of Cadwal. Come to the point,
my lord Prince, and we'll judge your father's wisdom for ourselves."

For the first time, Prince Kragen shifted his attention away from
the King. Still smiling, he said, "You are Castellan Lebbick, are you
not? If you do not keep a civil tongue in your head, I will have you
garroted."

Terisa stiffened. Despite his casual manner, the Prince was convincing. She heard stifled gasps around the hall. The guards tightened their grips on their weapons; Lebbick's officers poised themselves. Myste was alarmed; but Elega watched the Castellan or the
Prince—Terisa couldn't tell which—with admiration and envy on
her face.

Lebbick's expression didn't flicker, yet he looked more like a
threat of violence with every passing moment. Slowly, he rose to his
feet. Slowly, he turned toward the King. Then he waited in silence
for the King to speak.

King Joyse had slumped back in his seat. He seemed to be shrinking. Wearily, he said, "I wish you *would* come to the point, Kragen.
I'm too old to batter my wits against yours for the rest of the day."
To the Castellan, he added, "Sit down, Lebbick. If he is puppy
enough to attempt harm to anyone or anything in Orison, he'll deserve what happens to him. I'm confident you'll feed his liver to the
crows."

Castellan Lebbick glanced at Kragen, then bowed his acquiescence. "With pleasure," he murmured as he sat down.

Terisa heard Elega and several other people sigh. Some of them
were relieved; the rest sounded disappointed.

More sternly, King Joyse went on, "We have little reason to love
Alend. I ask you simply, Kragen: Why are you here?"

As if nothing had happened, the Prince replied, "I will answer you
simply, my lord King. The Alend Monarch wishes to know what
takes place in Mordant. He wishes to end the chaos of rumor and
implication. And"—Kragen paused for an instant of drama—"he
wishes to propose an alliance."

The reaction in the hall was as strong as he could have desired.

Unable to restrain herself, Elega sprang to her feet—as did the Castellan, two of his officers, and Master Barsonage. Master Quillon gaped. Whispers of surprise spattered toward the ceiling. Clapping her hand to her mouth, Myste stared up at her father with excitement and hope.

Terisa had no reason to share Castellan Lebbick's hostility. As far as she was concerned, the Prince had just spoken the first sensible words she had heard in the hall of audiences.

"An alliance?" snapped Lebbick. "With Margonal? Sheepdung!"

One of his officers demanded, "Does the Alend Monarch think we have lost our minds?"

But another cried, "But if we are allied against Cadwal? The High King musters his armies beyond the Vertigon. The Perdon should hear this!"

At the same time, Master Barsonage protested, "An alliance? An alliance against our doom?" He looked almost frantic. "My lord King, you must accept!" For an instant, Terisa thought he was going to shout, You must accept, so that the Congery will not need to call its champion!

More quietly, but with equal fervor, the lady Elega was saying, "Bravely said, Prince Kragen! Bravely done."

But King Joyse said nothing until the hubbub stilled itself. He didn't appear surprised. In fact, he hardly seemed to be interested. His face was tight, as if he were stifling a yawn.

At last the hall became quiet again. Castellan Lebbick and the others seated themselves reluctantly, as though pushed down against their will. Soon, every eye was fixed on King Joyse.

Muttering under his breath, he pulled himself straighter in his seat. His circlet had been nudged askew, and a few strands of hair hung down over his eyes. "An alliance, Kragen? After several dozen generations of war? Why should I agree to such a thing?"

"My lord King, I have not the least idea," the Prince replied equably. "I have no facts. But the rumors coming out of Mordant suggest that you are in need. They suggest that the need is growing dire. Therefore it occurred to the Alend Monarch to offer his assistance."

"What does the Alend Monarch think our need is?"

The Prince shrugged delicately. "I must repeat that he hears only rumors. But the import of these tales seems clear." He nodded past

Lebbick toward the Masters. "It appears that some—perhaps many—
of your Imagers have turned against you."

"Impossible!" Master Barsonage objected at once. "You are offensive, my lord Prince."

King Joyse ignored the mediator. "And what does the Alend
Monarch think to gain from this alliance?"

"Your trust, my lord King."

That made sense to Terisa.

King Joyse had a different reaction, however. He sat forward, his
incredulity plain on his face. "What? *Trust?* He does not wish to rule
half of Cadwal? He does not desire Imagers of his own?"

"As I have said," Prince Kragen explained patiently, "the Alend
Monarch has given himself to wisdom. He understands that things
may happen between rulers who trust each other which are impossible otherwise. Of course he desires the resources of Imagery for his
people. Of course he desires the wealth of Cadwal, so that he can
purchase more of what Mordant has and Alend lacks. But he sees
that these wishes will not be fulfilled without trust. And trust must
begin somewhere.

"He offers you his assistance and asks nothing in return. If what he
wants can be achieved, it will come of its own accord when his cooperation has taught you to know him better."

"I see." King Joyse leaned back again. "Doubtless that explains
why Margonal has an army of tremendous size gathering beyond the
borders of Fayle and Armigite. I mean, of course, that I have heard
rumors of such an army."

"Then you have also heard," the Prince answered smoothly, "that
High King Festten musters a massive assault against you. Doubtless"
—he allowed himself a hint of sarcasm—"he means to take advantage of your weakness—I mean your need—to crush your kingship,
enslave the Cares, and capture all Imagery for himself. I think you
will understand, my lord King, that the Alend Monarch cannot permit Cadwal such a victory. Whether or not you accept his alliance, he
must oppose the High King. In forging the Congery, you have created something which must not be surrendered."

"That is true," acknowledged the King. "That is true."

For a long moment, he stared at the ceiling with his mouth open,
stroking his beard as though he were deep in thought. His eyes
closed, and Terisa thought suddenly, Oh, no, he's going to sleep!

Abruptly, however, he looked back down at Prince Kragen and smiled.

His smile seemed to light his face like a touch of sunshine.

"My lord Prince," he said as if he were happy for the first time since the audience began, "do you play hop-board?"

Terisa's throat closed against a mounting sense of panic as Kragen replied, "Hop-board, my lord King? I am unacquainted with it."

"A game." The wobble in the King's voice began to sound like ardor. "I find it most instructive."

With a noise like a slap, he clapped his hands together. Instinctively, Terisa flinched. Myste and Elega stared worry and consternation up at their father.

Almost at once, two of the wooden screens across the hall parted, revealing a door in the wall. The door was already open, and through it came two servants carrying a small table between them. Two more followed, each bearing a chair. Heads bowed, they brought their burdens forward to the long run of carpet and set the table and chairs down roughly midway between the Prince and the base of King Joyse's throne. While the lords and ladies of Orison gaped, the chairs were placed at the table as if to accommodate Kragen and the King. Then the servants withdrew, closing the screens and the door after them.

Terisa's alarm tightened another turn. She recognized that table, those chairs: she had last seen them in King Joyse's private apartment.

His checkerboard was set up on the table, ready for play.

"Oh, Father," Myste whispered, "have you fallen to this?"

Elega's cheeks were hot with color. "He is *mad*," she answered. "Mad."

But King Joyse ignored the reactions of his people. Sitting forward eagerly, he said to the Prince, "On the surface, it is a simple game. A child can master it. Yet it is also subtle. In essence, you force your opponent to win battles against you so that he will lose the war. Will you play?"

"I?" Prince Kragen betrayed some surprise of his own. "As I have said, I am unacquainted with this game. I will gladly watch it played, if that is your wish. If," he commented casually, "you can find no better use for this audience. But I cannot play."

"Nonsense." The King's voice held a note that Terisa hadn't

heard before—a note of hardness. "I insist. Hop-board is an excellent gauge of persons."

"And I must decline." Kragen spoke firmly, yet he had begun to sweat. "My lord King, I have spent nearly thirty days in the snow between Scarab and Orison because the mission entrusted to me by the Alend Monarch could not wait another season. I do not like to let it wait another day. If I must, however, I will. Shall we meet again tomorrow, privately?"

King Joyse dismissed this speech with a toss of one hand. Coughing to clear his throat, he said, "I mean to be as fair as I can. I will not play you myself. Though I am hardly the equal of Adept Havelock, I have had much experience. No, my lord Prince." His tone became sharper. "I have not seen you measured for seventeen years. Your strengths and abilities are unknown to me. I will match you against another who is similarly unknown."

With no forewarning except her own imprecise alarm, Terisa heard the King say formally, "My lady Terisa of Morgan, will you be so kind as to test Prince Kragen for me?"

Now everyone in the hall was staring at her. Her face grew hot. She looked up at King Joyse. In front of all these people—? Fear made her vision acute, immediate, as if there were no distance between them; every line of him was distinct. She could see the veins pulsing in the thin old skin of his temples. His watery eyes seemed weak, almost lost. The hair straggling across his features caused him to appear faintly ludicrous.

But he was smiling.

And his smile hadn't lost its power. It reassured her, like a promise that he meant her no harm; an assertion that she was too valuable to be mistreated; a belief that she would acquit herself well, whatever he asked of her. It was innocent and clean, and she couldn't resist it.

Without consciously making the decision to move, she rose to her feet and went toward Prince Kragen.

At once, she wished she had remained seated. She understood too much of what was happening to be calm, but not enough to be sure she was doing the right thing. And virtually all of the important people in Orison were going to watch her do it. The daughter of her father wouldn't have done this. She could hardly bring herself to meet the Prince's gaze.

His black brows were knotted over his eyes, and he seemed to be chewing the inside of his cheek. His easy and confident manner had deserted him: he didn't smile at her, bow to her, greet her. The hint of yellow in his eyes darkened as his anger increased. He was strung so tight that she expected him to pull out his sword at any moment.

She went as near to him as she dared—no closer than ten feet. Then she stopped.

"My lady"—King Joyse seemed to be speaking from the far end of a tunnel—"may I present Kragen, Prince of the Alend Lieges and son of Margonal, the Alend Monarch? My lord Prince, this is the lady Terisa of Morgan.

"My lady, I am sure that Prince Kragen will grant you the first move." With one hand, the King motioned her toward the chair which faced Kragen and the audience.

The Prince turned back to King Joyse. "Do not waste your time, my lady," he said. "I will not play."

"I think you will." King Joyse no longer sounded old—or innocent. He sounded like a sovereign who was nearing the end of his patience. "Please be seated, my lady."

As if she were helpless, Terisa went to the chair King Joyse had indicated. She pulled it back, sat down, and focused her eyes on the checkerboard, all without risking a glance at Prince Kragen. If she met his eyes, she felt sure he would scathe her to the ground. The whole hall was focused on her. The air around her was heavy with alarm and doubt.

But surely she wasn't helpless? If the mirror had created her, everything she believed about herself and her past might be an illusion. In that case, she belonged here. She had been created to be where she was, and the things she had to do wouldn't be too much for her.

"You are mistaken, my lord King." Though he spoke quietly, Kragen's voice was as passionate as a shout. "I understand you now. When I came to you as my father's ambassador and desired an audience, you determined at once to humiliate me. You chose this public occasion when I wished a private meeting. And you meant from the first to confront me with this"—he swallowed a curse—"this *game*. You had it ready and waiting for your signal. Doubtless you have chosen the lady Terisa of Morgan because in some way she increases the mockery. Really, my lord King, I am surprised that you troubled to wait until I had explained my mission before beginning this charade.

"It is enough. I will return to the Alend Monarch and inform him that you do not wish an alliance."

"You will not." The King's tone made the back of Terisa's neck burn. "You will sit down and play."

"No!"

"By my sword, *yes*! I am King in Mordant yet, and my will rules!"

Before the Prince or his bodyguards could react, Castellan Lebbick gave a small signal. Around the balcony, archers raised their bows, pulled back the strings.

All the arrows were aimed at Kragen.

"Treachery!" one of the bodyguards spat. Fortunately, he retained enough sense to leave his sword in its sheath.

"Treachery, is it?" rasped Castellan Lebbick with evident relish. "Keep a civil tongue in your head, or I'll have you fed to the hogs."

Slowly, Prince Kragen turned in a complete circle, studying the balcony, the screens, the arrangement of the pews and seats; there was no escape. He faced King Joyse again. His expression was flat, closed. The people in the hall watched him without a sound.

Then the lady Elega cried, "Go!" as if she were in torment. "Leave this madness! You are an ambassador. Your mission is one of peace. If he has you killed, the execration of all Mordant will hound him to his grave!"

The Prince didn't glance at her. He didn't speak.

In one swift motion, he seated himself across the table from Terisa and folded his arms over his chest, glaring at her as if his gaze were a spike which he meant to drive through her.

King Joyse said nothing. Castellan Lebbick sneered and said nothing. Master Barsonage fretted in his seat. Master Quillon seemed to have disappeared from her range of vision. Neither of the King's daughters moved. No one came to Terisa's aid.

It was up to her to save the Prince.

She didn't look into his face: she concentrated on the board. It seemed impossible that she had ever played this game before. The servant who had taught her had been fired. Perhaps he had been a friend of hers without quite intending to be. Perhaps that was why he had been fired. Close to panic, she thought, Why? Not, Why is King Joyse doing this? But, Why am I?

She knew the answer. Because the King was behaving like a lunatic, and a humiliation like this would make war with Alend inevitable. Because Mordant couldn't afford a war with Alend. Because Cadwal was already mustering. Master Quillon had given her the answer. He was watching her keenly. And Geraden had showed it to her in a mirror. Because gnarled shapes with terrible jaws had been sent out of nowhere to tear men apart.

If her past didn't exist, what did she have to lose?

After a long moment while sweat gathered on her scalp and fright clogged her chest, she reached out and made her first move.

At once, Prince Kragen unfolded one arm, picked up his matching piece, and slapped it down in a move which mirrored hers. His gesture betrayed the dark stains spreading through the silk under his arm.

She nodded to herself, and a bit of her tension relaxed. What else could he do? He knew nothing about the game. He was in her hands.

Like a distant calling of horns, the realization came to her that there was a way out of this dilemma.

She made another move.

Kragen copied it.

Quickly, so that she wouldn't falter, she moved again. He copied her again.

After a few more moves, she was able to turn in her seat and look up at King Joyse. Her heart pounded as though she had just taken an important risk, done something that would make a difference.

"It's a stalemate."

The passion on his face resembled apoplexy. He was almost bursting with rage. Or else he was tremendously amused—she couldn't tell which.

The Prince took his cue promptly. Rising to his feet without so much as a glance at Terisa, he gave King Joyse an ironic bow. "I thank you, my lord King. It is indeed a most instructive game. An excellent gauge of persons. The Alend Monarch will be fascinated to hear of it.

"Now with your permission I will withdraw. I fear that the journey from Scarab has exhausted me. I cannot continue without rest."

He nodded to his bodyguards; they bowed also. Then he turned and started for the doors.

King Joyse swallowed his emotion with difficulty. "Go rest, if you have to." He sounded petulant again, like a disenchanted child. "You're more of a puppy than I thought."

Prince Kragen's stride checked for an instant; his shoulders bunched. Shocked by the suddenness with which the ambassador's mission had been refused, the people in the hall stared at him—or at King Joyse.

But the Prince didn't stop. The doors were opened for him, and he stalked out of the hall of audiences.

Before anyone else could react, Elega was on her feet. Lightning flared in her eyes. Her cry rang against the high ceiling of the hall: "Father, I am *ashamed*!"

As quickly as her long, heavy skirts and petticoats permitted, she ran after the Prince.

No one else said anything. No one else dared.

Softly, King Joyse sighed. With both hands, he pushed the hair out of his face and resettled his circlet. Then he scratched his fingernails through his beard. "That saddens me," he murmured as though he didn't know that everyone in the hall could hear him. "I have always been proud of you."

Weakly, he climbed to his feet and stepped down the stairs from the throne.

When he started toward the back of the pediment, Myste said in a quiet, aching voice, "Oh, Father!" and went after him.

Terisa should have been proud of herself. She had achieved a victory of a sort. In spite of that, however, Myste was in pain, and Elega was furious; and King Joyse had become so much less than he was, so much less than he needed to be. Terisa was left with a hollow feeling like a stalemate in her heart.

The memory of horns was gone.

ELEVEN: A FEW DAYS WITH NOTHING TO DO

erisa would have had trouble finding her way back to her rooms by herself: she wasn't familiar with this section of Orison. But Castellan Lebbick didn't leave her alone. As soon as the lords and ladies began to depart, muttering and arguing their astonishment among themselves, he assigned one of the guards to escort her.

The walk seemed longer than she remembered; but eventually she was in her suite, with the door bolted behind her, and she had her first chance to think about everything that had happened to her today.

From her windows, she was surprised to see that the sky was clear and the snow-packed roofs and towers of the castle were gilded pink, while dusk shrouded the ground and the distant hills. She hadn't realized that so much of the afternoon was gone. For a moment, she forgot everything else and simply watched the sunset, entranced by the way it made Orison look like a place in a fairy tale—old stone immured in winter and darkness, and yet reaching like hope or dreams toward the light and the sky and the delicate touch of the sun's glory. Now she was able to remember the sound of horns. For a long moment, she ached to leave the castle, not to escape back to the illusion of her old life, but to go out into Mordant's world and find the spot among trees and hills where it was possible to hear hunters or musicians calling joy and passion into the cold.

How had the augury known about the riders in her dream?

She could think of an answer, of course. If she had been created by a mirror, then a mirror had also created her dreams.

For some reason, that didn't help.

She had so much to tell Geraden. Regardless of the way she felt about Master Eremis, Geraden was the only one she trusted to help her decide what to do.

Some decision had to be made—that was obvious. Some action had to be taken. King Joyse was on the path to self-destruction—a path more dangerous than the passivity people ascribed to him. She knew now that he wasn't passive. By refusing to shore up Perdon's defenses, as much as by humiliating Prince Kragen, he was working actively toward Mordant's ruin.

Clearly, Mordant needed a leader strong enough to take command of circumstances—and intelligent enough to be constructive. Not Castellan Lebbick: he was too fiercely loyal to the King. And not the Congery as a body. Despite the power it represented, it was too divided to be effective. Adept Havelock? He was mad. Master Quillon? She didn't know what his motives were, but she couldn't imagine him leading the struggle for Mordant's survival.

That left Master Eremis.

Geraden wouldn't like the idea, of course. But maybe she could convince him. If they agreed to help the Master, she might get the chance to spend more time with him.

The thought brought back the sensation of his mouth on her breasts. She hugged herself with her arms and shivered. Saddith had asserted, *Any Master will tell me whatever I wish—if I conceive a wish for something he knows.* And she had said, *The same is true for you, if you choose to make it so.* Well, why not? She lacked Saddith's experience— and expertise. But Eremis found her desirable.

No one had ever found her desirable before.

While the sun set and darkness swallowed the castle, she turned away from the window, poured a goblet of wine, and made herself comfortable to enjoy what she was thinking.

Later, Saddith brought her supper. The maid wanted to talk: Orison was full of rumors about Prince Kragen's audience, and she had heard them all, but she wanted to know the truth. Terisa found, however, that she was too tired—as well as too self-conscious—to do the subject justice. The day's events had exhausted her emotional resources. And her reveries of Master Eremis had put her in the mood for sleep. After a few halfhearted apologies, she dismissed

Saddith. Then she ate her supper, drank one more goblet of wine, hung up her clothes in the wardrobe which didn't have a chair propped in it, and went to bed.

She fell asleep almost at once—

—and was awakened by a dull, wooden pounding. Dreams she couldn't remember fogged her brain: she felt sure, with a certainty like cold, congealed oatmeal, that what she heard was the sound of her clothes knocking on the door of the wardrobe, begging to be let out—frantic to dissociate themselves from the false petticoats and misleading gowns which had been loaned to her to seduce her from herself. Something about that didn't make sense, but she couldn't figure it out: the oatmeal was too thick to stir.

The pounding was repeated. After a long, stupefied moment, she realized that it came from the wrong wardrobe.

It came from the door to the secret passage.

At first, she was so mush-headed with sleep and fatigue that she didn't consider answering the knock. At this rate, she thought as clearly as she could, I'm never going to get any rest. Does everybody here spend all night sneaking around behind everybody else's back?

The problem didn't go away when she ignored it, however. The knock was repeated; a muffled voice croaked, "My lady!"

As far as she knew, only Master Quillon and Adept Havelock knew about that passage.

If the pounding became any louder, the guards outside would hear it.

"All right," she muttered as she pushed back the covers and stumbled out of bed, "I'm coming."

Fortunately, the fire in the hearth had burned down. As a result, the air was cool—and that reminded her that she was naked. Her head began to clear. She detoured to the safe wardrobe, pulled out her clothes and put them on. The pounding began again. "I'm *coming*," she replied as loudly as she dared.

As soon as she had unwedged the chair, the door opened, and lamplight spilled out of the wardrobe.

Though her eyes weren't accustomed to the light, she had no trouble identifying her visitor. Master Quillon shrugged past the hanging clothes and stepped out of the wardrobe. "My lady," he whispered with some asperity, "you are a sound sleeper."

"I'm sorry." She made no effort to sound sorry. "I'm still not used to having people break into my room in the middle of the night."

"I would rather be asleep myself," he retorted. "Some things are more important." Anger made his nose twitch. In the lamplight, he looked more than ever like a rabbit. But the intensity of his manner didn't suit his face. It gave his eyes a manic gleam, like the gaze of a cute pet gone rabid. "Have you seen Geraden since Prince Kragen's audience?"

He took her aback. His demeanor was frightening. Intimations of danger suddenly filled the air.

"Is he missing?"

"Missing? Nonsense. Why would he be missing? I only want to know if you have spoken to him at any time today—at any time since I separated you."

Terisa took a deep breath, tried to steady herself. "What's going on?"

Half snarling, Quillon demanded, "My lady, *have you spoken to him?*"

"No," she retorted defensively. "I haven't seen him. I haven't spoken to him. What's going on?"

Master Quillon glared at her for a moment. Then he sighed, "Good," and his face relaxed a little. "That is good." But his gaze didn't release her.

"My lady, you heard a great deal in the meeting of the Congery. And I will venture to guess that you heard a great deal more from Master Eremis. You must not speak of these matters to Geraden. You must tell him *nothing.*"

"What?" A pang went through her; alarm closed around her stomach. She had been looking forward to seeing him again, to spending the day with him, to telling him everything. "Why?" He's the only one I can talk to!

"Because," the Master articulated distinctly, "that is the only way we can keep him alive."

"*What?*"

"As long as he is ignorant, his enemies may not risk exposure by killing him. If you tell him what you know, he will surely act on it. Then he will become too dangerous, and he will be killed."

"Killed?" She was reeling inwardly. The floor and the lamplight seemed to tilt. "Why would anybody want to kill him?"

"My lady," he returned heavily, "it must be obvious to you that your presence here cannot be an accident. You were translated through a glass which could not have been used for that purpose.

How was that done? No mistake or blunder can explain it. You insist that you are not responsible. Then who is?

"My lady, you are important." Abruptly, Master Quillon turned and began to push his way back through the wardrobe. His voice was obscured by clothes. "Geraden is crucial."

For a moment, she stared after him while he entered the passage and closed the door, cutting off the light. Then she wrenched herself into motion. The thought that Geraden's life depended on her silence was so sharp that it nearly made her cry out. Thrusting garments aside, she reached the door and jerked it open.

Master Quillon was on the stairs below her. He turned at the noise she made, looked up at her. The angle of the lamplight left shadows like pools of darkness in his eyes. "My lady?"

"Who are his enemies?"

She couldn't see his expression. His voice was flat. "If we knew that, we would be able to stop them."

Before she could speak, he turned away again and continued his descent. His silhouette twitched like a marionette.

"Who are his friends?"

The echoes of Master Quillon's feet didn't answer.

When she could no longer hear his sandals on the stair, or be sure of the glow of his lamp, she left the passage. Closing the door, she wedged the chair against it again.

After a while, she went back to bed.

By the next morning, she had made at least one decision.

She wasn't going to talk to Geraden.

Unfortunately, that wouldn't be as easy as it sounded. Her desire to confide in him was strong. And she knew he would be hurt by her silence.

In order to protect him, she would have to avoid him for a while.

So she got up early. Despite her inexperience, she managed to build up the fires in her hearths. Gritting her teeth against the cold, she bathed thoroughly. Then, defying the awkwardness of clothes that hadn't been designed to be put on without help, she struggled into a demure, dove-gray gown which, she hoped, would enable her to blend into the background.

She intended to ask Saddith for a tour of Orison—as complete a tour as possible. If she were occupied doing something Geraden didn't expect and couldn't predict, and if she were camouflaged against accidental discovery, she might win herself a day's respite from choices and crises.

Getting dressed alone took some time, however. When she was done, she didn't have to wait long for breakfast. Saddith soon knocked on her door and entered when it was unbolted, bringing a tray of food with her. Today she appeared a bit more cheerful—or perhaps a bit more highly spiced—than usual: there was more sauce in her smile, more zest in her step. On impulse, Terisa said, "You look happy. Did you have another night with that Master of yours? Or have you found someone better?"

"Why, my lady," Saddith protested, fluttering her eyelashes, "whatever do you mean? I am as chaste as a virgin." Then she grinned. "That is to say, I am as chased as most virgins dream of being."

Giggling at her own humor, she began to set out Terisa's breakfast.

As she ate, Terisa proposed the idea of a tour. The maid agreed at once. "However," she said, studying Terisa critically, "we must first repair your dress. If it was your intention to appear as if you had spent the night in your gown, wrestling for virtue, you have succeeded. Really, my lady, you must let me assist you with such things."

"I didn't think it was that bad." Terisa was in a hurry to get going: she didn't want to take the chance that Geraden was on his way to see her. But a closer look at the gown convinced her that Saddith was right. Wryly, she assented to the maid's ministrations.

That was a mistake. Saddith took only a few minutes to adjust and refasten the gown; but as she finished there was another knock at the door.

Terisa's heart sank. She wasn't ready for this. Was she going to have to lie to him? She didn't think she could bear to lie to him.

Saddith, of course, had no idea what was in Terisa's mind. With a sprightly step, she left the bedroom to answer the door. Terisa heard her say in a teasing tone, "Apt Geraden, what a surprise. Have you come to repay me for my help yesterday? For that we must have privacy. Or do you mean to spurn me, preferring my lady Terisa?"

Geraden's laugh sounded a little uncomfortable. "Come now, Saddith. You can do better than me. In fact, you *do* do better than me. The best *I* can do is ask the lady Terisa to talk to me. Is she free?"

"Geraden," Saddith answered with mock severity, "no woman is *free*."

Chuckling to herself, she returned to the bedroom, where Terisa waited as though she were cowering. "My lady, Apt Geraden is here. He will be better company than I for an exploration of Orison. He is male, even if he is awkward, easily embarrassed, and only an Apt. I will leave you to him."

No, Terisa tried to say. Please. But Saddith was already on her way out of the room. She aimed another riposte at Geraden and closed the door behind her.

For a moment, Terisa remained where she was, wishing stupidly that she knew how to swear. But she couldn't stand there, paralyzed, forever. Eventually, Geraden would come a few steps farther into the sitting room, and then he would see her. Feeling at least as abashed as she ever had in front of the barracuda-like young men whom her father had tried to interest in her—trying to marry her off so that he would no longer be bothered with her—she left the bedroom.

Geraden's grin nearly ruined her good intentions: he looked so happy to see her that she wanted to break down immediately and tell him everything. It was all she could do to glance at him and force her mouth into a smile.

"I'm sorry I didn't get to see you again yesterday," he began at once; he couldn't swallow the pleasure bubbling up in him. "I don't know what came over Master Quillon. He isn't usually that unreasonable. He took me down to his private workshop and put me to work grinding sand, of all things. That job is so menial and mindless even new Apts don't usually have to do it. Then the message came that Prince Kragen was here and King Joyse was going to give him an audience. I thought that would save me. Despite whatever came over him, Master Quillon wouldn't expect me to go on grinding sand at a time like that."

He grimaced. "I was right, as usual. I didn't have to grind any more sand. Instead, he handed me instructions for the most complex tinct I've ever heard of and told me to prepare it three different ways. 'For experimental purposes.' Some Masters never let Apts do work that sophisticated. And it's been years since *any* Master gave me a job like that. I didn't know whether to be grateful or cut my throat.

"Anyway, I didn't finish until after midnight. I'm still not sure I got any of them right.

"I guess I missed all the excitement."

Terisa's throat felt like cotton wadding. She swallowed roughly. "You must have heard about it."

He nodded slowly, studying her: the strangeness of her manner cooled his ebullience. "Did you really play hop-board against Prince Kragen?"

Unable to face him, she went to the window. The clear sky of the previous evening was gone: now low clouds as heavy as stone covered the castle and the surrounding hills, making everything gray. In that light, the gown she had chosen seemed as drab as her spirit.

"Yes."

Geraden whistled his appreciation. "Amazing! And he didn't know the game. How did you manage to maneuver him into a stalemate? *That* was impressive. The Alend Monarch ought to give you a title for treating his honor with so much courtesy." Then his tone darkened. "Judging by the rumors, that was the most intelligent thing anybody did in that disaster. If King Joyse had half your sense, there would still be hope for us."

Oh, Geraden. Hating herself for what she had to do, she took advantage of the opening he had unintentionally given her, the chance to deflect—or at least postpone—his inevitable questions. Without turning her head, she said bitterly, "But that's the point, isn't it? He doesn't have any sense. As far as I can tell, he arranged that whole audience for just one reason—to make fun of the Prince. He *wants* a war with Alend."

Then she did turn, forcing herself toward him because she was ashamed. "Geraden, why are you loyal to him? Maybe he was a great king once—I don't know. But there's none of that left." She spoke as if during the audience she had been capable of refusing the King's smile—as if she could have refused it now. "Why don't you give him up?"

The quick hurt in his eyes made her want to run into the bedroom and hide her head under the pillows. Lamely, she concluded, "That's why the Masters don't trust you. Because you're loyal to him, and nobody can understand why."

"Is that what they told you?" he retorted at once. "They don't trust me because I still like to serve my King? I thought it was because I haven't done anything right since I was nine years old."

Stung, she returned to the window, leaning her forehead against the cold glass to cool the pain. Not talk to him? Not tell him the truth? How could she do that, even to save his life?

"I'm sorry," she heard him say, chagrined by her reaction. "I didn't mean it that way. This is just a sore point for me. As you can probably tell.

"But I have the strongest feeling—" He stopped.

She waited, but he didn't go on. Finally, she asked, "What is it this time?"

As if the words were being forced out of him by a deep but involuntary conviction, he replied, "I have the strongest feeling he knows what he's doing."

"Oh, Geraden!" She couldn't restrain herself: she faced him again, showing her irritation plainly. "Do you really think that starting a war with Alend is *wise*? Do you think that's a *good* answer to Mordant's problems?"

"No," he admitted glumly. "I've already told you my feelings are always wrong. I just can't ignore them." After another hesitation, he said, "I haven't told you about the first time I met him."

Thinking she knew what was coming, Terisa winced inwardly. "Would you like to sit down?"

"No, thanks." His manner was abstracted: his mind was on the story he meant to tell. "I spent too many hours yesterday hunched over a mortar. My back still hurts." He began to pace slowly back and forth in front of her.

"I must have been eleven or twelve years old at the time, and I had never been away from home. Oh, there was hardly a mile of Domne where I hadn't ridden or worked, trailing after my brothers, doing the jobs I was given, or"—he smiled—"trying to avoid my chores. I don't care what anybody else says. Domne is the most beautiful of the Cares—especially in the spring, when the apple trees and dogwood and redbud come out, and some of the hills as far as you can see are wooded in blooms—and I loved exploring it, playing in places like the Closed Fist, riding like wild around the skirts of the mountains."

He sighed happily. "But Houseldon was the center of my life. My father, the Domne, is a man who loves his home more than any place in the world. He prefers the company of his family to anyone else— even though people call him one of the King's dearest friends. Every year or two, he had to go somewhere to do something for King Joyse or Mordant, and he always took at least two of my brothers with him. That was how Artagel discovered his talent for fighting, which he would never have done at home. But I was always too young to go. I was my mother's baby, of course. And when she died, Tholden—he's my oldest brother—he and his wife took over as if they thought I was never going to grow up.

"In some ways, it's difficult to describe why I didn't take after my father. Tholden certainly did—when he becomes the Domne, even our father's beloved cherry trees will hardly notice the difference. So did Minick and Wester—he's the handsome one of the family. And the only reason I don't count Stead is that he would rather court every village girl in Domne than do his share of the shearing. Did I tell you that our family raises sheep? We do all kinds of farming, of course. All the Cares do. But wool and cloth are what we're known for." He sounded proud. "As soon as my brothers found out how clumsy I was," he continued wryly, "they refused to let me near the shears. But one summer I did so much herding that I knew every sheep within five miles by name.

"Looking back on it, I think my father's love should have been irresistible. He can still take off a sheep's wool in one piece so even it can be used as it is. His eyes light up when he sees a new seed sprout or a new crop come up. And he enjoys the company of his sons as if they were the best people in the world. He even manages to appreciate *my* good points—whatever they are. Whenever I go home, I spend the first five days amazed at my good luck and wondering why I ever left."

Then he shrugged and grinned. "I spend the *next* five days trying to figure out how to tell the Domne I have to leave again. Maybe it's because I never got to go with him when he traveled. I had to wait until he and my brothers came back and spent the next entire season telling stories about all the exciting things they saw and did. I was like Nyle in that. Except for me, he's the youngest. He had to stay home a lot, too. When Artagel went into training with the armies of Mordant, Nyle and I treated him like visiting royalty. We wanted him to tell us *every*thing.

"Or maybe it's because King Joyse sent Queen Madin and their daughters to stay with us for more than a year when I was five or six. What was happening, I think, was that the Alend Monarch and High King Festten were becoming desperate to defend their Imagers, and King Joyse was afraid they might try to stop him by attacking his family. Anyway, the lady Elega and I were about the same age, and we played together most of the time. Even then"—his fondness was evident—"she was so full of being a king's daughter that I hardly knew what to do with her. But I admired her for it. I loved her stories of wars and power, even though she credited herself with saving the realm more often than most five-year-old girls can manage. Young as I was, she made me ache to explore the whole world the way I did Domne.

"Or maybe it was simply that the most exciting thing I knew about my father was his friendship with the King.

"Whatever the reason, I haven't been content with the idea of being a farmer or sheepherder for as long as I can remember."

Abruptly, he stopped and looked at Terisa. "I'm sorry. I didn't mean to go into all that. I just wanted you to understand what kind of boy I was when I first met King Joyse."

"Don't apologize," she replied gently. She was grateful for anything that kept him from questioning her. And she liked hearing about his family. His background was as alien to her experience as Mordant and Imagery were; but it was also attractive—as strange and wondrous as a fairy tale. "If you didn't point it out, I would never know you were digressing."

He bowed playfully. "You are too gracious, my lady." Then he resumed his story.

"As I say, it was probably thirteen years ago. Mordant was approximately at peace because Adept Havelock wasn't ready to expose the arch-Imager and his cabal, and King Joyse was doing a royal circuit, getting ready for the days when his wars would actually be over. After Termigan, he came to Domne.

"The day he arrived, I was weeding corn in one of the fields near Houseldon. It was as far away as I could bear to be, and I only went that far because the field was on a hill that let me watch the road. I was so excited that I kept forgetting to look where I swung the hoe. By the time the King and his party finally rode into view"—he chuckled to himself—"I had left a swath of ruined corn right through the middle of the field.

"But that didn't bother me. As soon as I saw him coming, I dropped my hoe and ran.

"There's a stockade around Houseldon, mostly to keep the animals out, and unfortunately there was a large pig wallow between me and the nearest gate. However, one of my brothers in an enterprising mood had tossed a long log into the wallow as a shortcut, and I headed for it to save time.

"You can imagine what happened." He grimaced in mock disgust. "But I didn't stop. I absolutely *had* to meet King Joyse as fast as possible. It was the most urgent thing in my life. So I managed to arrive in front of our house just as the King and his people—Queen Madin with Elega, Torrent, and Myste, Adept Havelock in his scruffy chasuble, Castellan Lebbick and a handful of guards, two or three of the King's counselors, and a small number of servants—you see, I remember it all—I got there just as they were dismounting." He snorted. "I had cherry pits in my hair, orange peels on my clothes, melon rinds sticking to my feet, and I was still dripping mud.

"A lot of people laughed—except Elega, who got angry—but my father and the King didn't. The Domne said, 'My lord King, this is my youngest son, Geraden,' as if he had never loved me as much as he did right then. Then the King beckoned me to him. In spite of the muck, he put his hands on my shoulders and gripped me hard. 'I like you, boy,' he said. 'Come to Orison in a few years.' Just like that. 'You already have one fighter in the family, and Artagel does it well. You will be an Imager.' "

Again, he stopped pacing to face Terisa firmly. "He made me happier than I had ever been in my life. And I can't forget that. I'm not as loyal to him as I should be—he doesn't want me to talk to you, remember?—but he is my King, and I won't stop trying to serve him as well as I can."

Then he laughed self-consciously. "Anyway, that's the best explanation I can give you. At the rate I'm going, if you ask me any more questions, I'll never give you a chance to tell me what happened to you yesterday."

A pang went through her. Not quite able to meet his gaze, she said, "I like hearing about your family. Did you hear Saddith mention a tour? She was going to give me a tour of Orison. I would like to know this place a little better." Deliberately duplicitous, she added, "This room is starting to give me cabin fever."

Forgetting self-consciousness, Geraden became immediately sober and intent. "I'll gladly give you a tour. After yesterday, I can use the escape myself. But that meeting of the Congery is too important to talk about in public. With my luck, somebody would overhear us. Why don't you tell me what happened after I had to leave? Then we'll go."

If he secretly wanted to know what she had done with Master Eremis, he concealed the desire well. Nevertheless she needed some way to deflect him again and didn't have any better ideas, so she said, "Are you sure it isn't Master Eremis you want to hear about? You were eager enough to interrupt us."

She tried to make the words teasing—and failed completely. In fact, she sounded just like her mother, feigning playfulness to disguise the intended hurt in what she said.

Involuntarily, Geraden scowled to keep himself from flinching; his face darkened. "Was I wrong, my lady?" he asked stiffly. "Does Master Eremis mean you well?"

She couldn't answer that. She was too ashamed of herself. Softly, as if she were apologizing, she said, "Do you know what he did? He proved I don't exist. Or I didn't exist until you found me in the mirror. You must have created me somehow."

Suddenly, the Apt was angry. His eyes burned. "He convinced *you* of that? *You*. That must have been quite a display of logic. What did he actually say? What argument did he use this time?"

Surprised and a bit frightened by Geraden's reaction, she answered, "Language. Mirrors don't translate sound." Confusedly, she repeated the gist of what Master Eremis had said to her.

In response, Geraden threw up his hands. Stalking away to the window, he glared out at the winter. "That son of a mongrel," he rasped. "Why does he *do* things like this?" Then, roughly, he swung toward her again.

"That's all pigslop, and he knows it. It's an interesting argument, but it doesn't *prove* anything."

She stared at him dumbly.

"There is at least one alternative explanation. Translation changes things. That's part of the magic. Language isn't the only issue. When I put my head into that mirror—the one with the champion—I didn't have any trouble breathing the air. But surely a world like that would have different air than we do. Why would a mirror create alien landscapes, alien people, alien power, alien creatures—and not alien air? That doesn't make sense. I must have been changed by the translation so I could breathe. If those people hadn't been so determined to kill me right away, we might have been able to talk to each other.

"I can't prove that either, of course. But proof isn't the point. The

point is, the answer Master Eremis gave you isn't inevitable. There is
another explanation.

"It isn't love that makes him talk to you like that." His tone was
hard, like a clenched fist. He didn't seem to be aware that she was
panicking in front of him.

The past *was* real? She couldn't simply turn her back on it and go
ahead, as if she had a role to play and a right to play it? Then she
didn't belong here—and everything she did was too important. Her
mistakes might do serious damage: the risk she had taken for Prince
Kragen against King Joyse might have terrible consequences.

She hardly heard Geraden saying, "There's some reason why he
wants you to believe I created you. He wants something from you."
He grimaced bitterly. "He wants to bed you—but that isn't what I
mean. If it were that simple, he wouldn't take the chance of upsetting
you.

"My lady, what happened during the meeting of the Congery after
I left? What did they decide?"

She hardly heard him—but all at once the words came into focus,
and she grasped what he had said. The color drained from her face.
"Decide?" she breathed, trying not to pant. Even this might be
wrong, the decision to protect him. Maybe she shouldn't trust Master
Quillon. Or maybe Geraden needed to die—maybe he was a danger
to Mordant in some way she could never understand because she
didn't belong here. She didn't know enough: the right answer wasn't
available to her. A feeling of weakness washed through her, and
darkness swirled around the edges of her vision. Her knees started to
fold.

Somehow, Geraden crossed the distance between them. He was
holding her up, his hands clamped to her arms. "Terisa!" he hissed
like a blaze. "What did they decide?"

She couldn't stand. If he let her go, she would be lost. A moment
later, however, she found that the urgent need in his face brought
her strength back. He was more at risk than she would ever be.
Master Quillon was right about that: Geraden was too passionate and
determined to be safe. She couldn't let him be killed, couldn't give
his enemies an excuse to kill him.

But as she straightened her knees, took her own weight, she realized that there was no way out. She couldn't let him be killed. What
good was that? She also couldn't lie to him. It would be impossible
for her to lie to any man who looked at her like that. Even if she had

never existed before in her life, she would have become real at that
moment because of the way he stared at her, simultaneously outraged on her behalf and desperate for her help.

One after the other, she shrugged her arms free. Still feeling weak,
she said, "They told me not to tell you. They told me that if you
knew what the Congery was going to do your enemies would have
you killed."

As quick as a slap, astonishment stretched his face, and he recoiled
a step. "Killed—?" His eyes flashed from side to side, hunting for
comprehension. "Me? *What* enemies? Why would anyone—?"
Questions burst from him in fragments: he couldn't frame them
quickly enough to keep up with them. "And you—? They did *that* to
you? Who are—?"

Abruptly, he took hold of himself with an almost visible grip of
will, forced down his confusion. In a clenched voice, he murmured,
"You poor woman. You know something I don't, and you know I
need to know it, but you think it might cost me my life if you tell me.
And if I tell you I don't have any enemies—I can't *imagine* having any
enemies—you won't know who to believe."

She nodded. If he kept going, she was going to weep.

Without warning, he did something that amazed her down to the
ground. Nothing in her father's dour unlove or Reverend Thatcher's
weakness or Master Eremis' desire had prepared her for the way
Geraden unknotted his throat and swallowed his distress and gave
her a smile like a gift.

"You know, Terisa, a tour sounds like a grand idea to me." He
met his danger with a sparkle in his eyes. Dimly, she realized that he
was using her name at last. "I would love to show you around Orison. I don't know any of the secret passages everyone keeps talking
about, but I think I've explored almost everything else."

She was so relieved and glad that she went to him without thinking, put her hands on his shoulders, and kissed his cheek.

At once, his pleasure became so bright that she started laughing.

They were still chuckling together when they left her rooms a
moment later to begin the tour.

It took considerably longer than she had expected. In fact, it spread
out over several days. Geraden was familiar with a bewildering combination of routes which stretched through Orison from end to end
and top to bottom. He had never been able to win admittance to the

Congery and its secrets; but he could tell the story behind each of the pennons hanging outside the hall of audiences (each one was the standard of some commander who had been beaten by King Joyse in battle). Most of the high-ranking men and women he and Terisa met in passing either didn't know him or recognized him with amusement bordering on disdain; but every guard, maid, scullion, cook, sweeper, wine steward, armorer, apprentice, plumber, stonemason, and merchant from the deepest storerooms to the highest rafters of the castle seemed to be a friend or acquaintance, either of his own or of his family's. And his relationship with all those people was like his knowledge of Orison: he was as clumsy as a puppy, tripping on stairs or his own feet, bumping into walls, dropping things, and falling all over himself with enjoyment whenever someone made a particularly acute jest; yet he held his own among the scullions and armorers and sweepers, in spite of his instinct for mishap, by displaying an unfailing insight and humor that made many of them look at him with affection indistinguishable from respect.

Nearly exhausted after a few hours—and determined not to show it—Terisa asked him how long he could afford to stay away from his duties. "If they can't catch me," he replied with a shrug and a laugh, "they can't tell me what to do. And they can't punish me." Then he closed the subject by leading her away into one of the huge, hot kitchens where Orison's food was prepared; or perhaps (she couldn't remember after a while) it was into one of the long dining halls crowded with trestle tables where many of the people who worked for the castle ate their meals; or perhaps into one of the warrens of stone rooms and apartments, as crowded and complex as tenements, but scrupulously clean (kept that way by Castellan Lebbick's orders and under his supervision because he was determined that Orison would never fall siege to disease), where the people who served and maintained the castle lived.

Along the way, Geraden chatted amiably with her for a long time. Eventually, however, he became curious enough to wonder aloud why she wasn't asking more questions. "I've probably made it clear," he commented, "that I'm not going to let anybody tell me what to do where you're concerned." He was trying to sound casual. "I'll tell you anything you want to know."

She understood him. He was trying to find out how much she knew already. And where she had learned it.

His offer flustered her. She didn't want to betray what Master

Quillon had already done for her. Because she was in a hurry to say something—and because Master Quillon made her think of Adept Havelock, who reminded her of the arch-Imager Vagel and his cabal —she replied, "Tell me about the High King's Monomach."

That was such an odd response that Geraden stopped and peered at her. "Gart? Where did you hear about him?"

She winced at the blundering way she forced herself to prevaricate. In an effort to keep the falsehood to a minimum, she said vaguely, "One of the Masters mentioned him. They were talking about Vagel and Cadwal."

For a difficult moment, the Apt continued studying her. Then, fortunately, he shrugged and started walking again, deliberately accepting her explanation at face value.

"Cadwal is a strange country." His answer was typically rambling. "With its ships, it has more contact with the rest of the world than Alend does—and we've never had any. That trade brings in wealth like you'll never see here. But wealth isn't good for anything except to buy food, pleasure, or power. Well, food they get from us at reasonable prices—or they did until they started harassing Perdon's borders. Now they rely on brigand commerce. And in other ways power hasn't done them much good since King Joyse established Mordant and the Congery. So the Cadwals buy a *lot* of pleasure.

"On the other hand, the country is bitterly harsh. Most of it is ragged rocks and desert, and the regions with water also have the kind of winds that tear your skin off your bones. Conditions like that teach harshness—they teach anybody who can survive them to be strong and cruel.

"The strange thing is the way the Cadwals combine pleasure and harshness." Geraden thought for a moment before he explained. "The High King's Monomach is Festten's traditional champion—a personal defender and assassin. He's supposed to be the greatest fighter in the country—the strongest and cruelest product of the harshest circumstances and training. In fact, the Cadwals like to say the men who fail as the High King's Monomach's Apts are so strong that Carmag is built on their bones. But the reward they give the greatest fighter in the whole country isn't wealth or power—or even freedom. It's just pleasure. That, and the chance to get killed serving —or displeasing—the High King.

"For some reason, power and wealth in Cadwal—and control over pleasure—have always belonged to the sybaritic side of their culture.

High King Festten doesn't have an ancestor in the past ten generations who ever lived in a tent in the desert, or survived the wind that cuts the rocks, or measured his life with the edge of his sword. And yet his hold over Cadwal makes the Alend Monarch look like the mediator of the Congery." He flashed Terisa a grin. "As far as I can tell, the High King has always wanted to rule Mordant simply to save himself the cost of food, so he'll have more wealth free to spend on pleasure."

Carried along by what he was saying, Geraden seemed to forget the incongruous fact that she wasn't asking questions. Breathing a sigh of relief, she reflected that both the Congery and King Joyse had good reason to try to protect what they knew from strangers. For instance, if by some wild stretch of the imagination she were in league with Gart, this tour might prove priceless to her. During the second day, Geraden showed her the prodigious reservoir where rainfall, melting snow, and the waters of the small spring that fed Orison were accumulated and stored. That was information any enemy would have known how to use.

This realization increased her appreciation for what the Apt was doing for her. She knew she was perfectly harmless—but he couldn't be equally sure. His trust itself was a risk.

She began to feel that keeping secrets from him wasn't a very satisfying way to thank him. She didn't want him hurt.

The next day, however, he didn't arrive to continue the tour. Instead, he sent a message to let her know that Master Quillon had commandeered him once more. Somewhat to her surprise, she went back to bed and slept through most of the day.

But her dreams were of Master Eremis, and she was restless all night. When morning came she found herself hoping that Geraden would return. If he didn't, she might be tempted to take her questions and decisions in search of the man who had kissed her so intimately.

Where was he? Why had he left her alone? Didn't he want her anymore? Was she so unappealing that he had already lost interest in her?

Fortunately, Geraden knocked on her door soon after breakfast.

He had procured a thick sheepskin coat and boots for her, similar to the ones he was wearing himself. "Today," he said sententiously, a grin shining in his eyes, "the battlements." When she had wrapped

the coat around her gray gown, he bowed her out of the room with a
mock-courtly flourish.

As she was able to see from her windows, Orison didn't have a
defensive outer perimeter: the same stone served for the rooms and
halls inside and their protection outside. But that wall, as Terisa saw
when Geraden took her through it, was tremendously thick. Its outward faces were lined with battlements wide enough to carry supply
wains, high enough to make archers effective without exposing them
to counterattack, and massive enough to resist catapults and battering
rams; and it contained (so she was told) storerooms, guardrooms,
and passages. Now she was more baffled than ever by the fragment
of augury that had shown Orison with a smoking hole torn in its side
and a look of death about it. What kind of force was powerful
enough to do such damage to a wall like this?

From the battlements, Geraden took her up to the top of the tower
that held her rooms.

The air was as sharp as splintered glass, and her nose and ears were
chilled. At this elevation, the breeze seemed harsher than it was. The
heavy clouds of recent days had lifted slightly, but the increased
clarity made the cold worse. The snow packed into the crenellations
and corners of the parapet looked old and rotten, gnawed upon but
not consumed by the occasional touch of the sun. Her breath
steamed in front of her face; she hugged her arms inside the sleeves
of her coat and shivered. But she didn't try to persuade Geraden to
forgo this exposure. It offered her the best view she had ever had of
the countryside surrounding Orison.

The position of the sun enabled her to verify that the long rectangle of the castle ran roughly from northwest to southeast. She and
Geraden stood atop the eastmost tower. Churned mud showing
through the snow marked the road that left the gates in the north-
east-facing wall and branched almost within arrow shot of the castle,
one limb turning toward the south, the Broadwine River, and the
Care of Tor (as Geraden had explained several days ago), another
paralleling the Broadwine northeast into the Care of Perdon, and a
third swinging northwest toward the Care of Armigite. The river, he
assured her, could be seen in the distance at other times of year, but
in winter white snow and ice made it blend among the hills. Nevertheless it was the same river she had seen in one flat mirror, the river
that ran out of the narrow defile that he had called the Closed Fist. It
came down through the center of Domne, divided Tor from both

Termigan and Armigite, separated a portion of the Demesne from
Perdon, and finally split Perdon into its North and South regions
before joining the Vertigon on the border of Mordant.

It was odd, she thought as she shivered, how much safer this scene
looked here than it did in the glass that had let her, Geraden, and
Master Eremis witness the attack on the Perdon. Under the open sky,
it became almost impossible to believe in savage monsters and fierce
death. Surely things like that only existed in mirrors?

She didn't absorb much of what he was telling her. She would
need a map to get it all straight. Still her eyes devoured Orison's
surroundings. The castle dominated the snow-cloaked hills immediately around it, but those farther away were higher, more rugged,
and more interesting. Trees lined the roads after they branched and
went their separate ways; yet the hillsides around Orison were so
bare that she thought they must have been cleared. Geraden confirmed this: Castellan Lebbick wanted space in which to exercise his
men, and Orison's rulers had never wanted cover to hide an approaching enemy. There were woods in the distance, however—
trees as thick, black, and secretive as the ones in her dream. And the
roads seemed to lead to places so far away that they must be wonderful.

She wanted to say, Take me to Domne. Take me to Termigan and
Armigite and Fayle. Take me away from here. But the weather was
too cold; the snow, too deep. And she wasn't Prince Kragen or one
of his men: she couldn't travel under these conditions. When she saw
a group of riders coming up toward Orison from the south, she
remembered that she had never been on a horse before.

Squinting into the breeze to keep his vision clear, Geraden stared
out at the riders. After a long moment, he breathed softly, "Sand and
tinct! That looks like the Tor. The Tor himself. He hasn't been to
Orison since I came here." To Terisa, he added, "Some people say
he's too fat to travel. But I think he's probably just too old. He's at
least ten years older than King Joyse." Then he murmured distantly,
"If that's him, what's he doing here? At this time of year?"

As he spoke, Terisa felt the cold reach around her heart, and she
turned toward the stairs leading back into the tower. The Perdon
was keeping the promise he had made to Master Eremis.

But one of the Masters had said—or implied?—that the Tor was
incapable of making such a journey. There wasn't enough time? The
distance was too great?

Without warning, Geraden burst past her, half running for the stairs. "Come on!" he called over his shoulder. "That's definitely the Tor! He's got a litter with him!"

For a second, she was frozen. A *litter*? Then Geraden's urgency grabbed hold of her.

He took the descent two steps at a time. The long skirt of her gown made it impossible for her to keep up with him. But he glanced back at her from the first landing, saw her difficulty, and slowed his pace.

Nearly together, they hurried down out of the tower.

A few moments ago, she had been cold. Now she was hot. In spite of his haste, she stopped on the stairway to pull off her coat. He tried to calm himself, but his face betrayed his vexation at the delay. "I'm sorry," she murmured as they started moving again.

Before he could reply, he missed a step, let out a yelp, and dove headlong down the length of the stone stairs.

"Geraden!" She rushed after him in panic.

As she reached him, he got to his hands and knees and pushed himself off the floor. His head wobbled from side to side as if he couldn't remember which way was up. She took him by the arm, tried to lift him erect. "Are you all right?"

Although he looked stunned, he put his weight on her until he propped his feet under him. Then he was able to stand.

"Don't worry. If this didn't happen at least once a day, I wouldn't know who I was." Awkwardly, he lurched into motion. "Come on. I've missed everything else recently. I don't want to miss this."

His strides grew slowly steadier as he led her down more stairways toward the level of the gates.

Abruptly, the air turned cold again. They were approaching a high, wide doorway which gave access to Orison's enormous inner courtyard. Guarded doors made of heavy timbers and bolts stood ready to close the entrance if necessary; but they were open.

Shouts began to echo off the walls of the castle. Guards came running down the hall. More guards splashed out into the mire of the courtyard, running toward the gates. A moment later, Castellan Lebbick appeared. His commands carried more sharpness than the cold as he, too, headed for the gates.

"Put on your coat," Geraden whispered tensely.

As soon as Terisa had complied, he took her arm and drew her out into the open court.

Her feet sank into the mud up to her ankles. She groaned to think of damaging such nice boots, then had to forget about them in order to concentrate on pulling herself from step to step against the suction of the muck.

She and Geraden were in the southeast end, which was relatively clear. The shops of the bazaar and the wagons of the farmers were crowded to the northwest, and among them were pitched the tents of their attendants, as well as of the guards who were responsible for maintaining order and honesty. But even this half of the courtyard looked large enough to exercise several squadrons of horse.

The castle stood open. The gate itself, a tremendous construct of timbers the size of tree trunks and lashed with iron, had been raised, as it was every day. During the tour, Geraden had showed her the gigantic winches that cranked the gate up into the wall above its architrave. Ahead of her, the Castellan was forming his men into an honor guard to greet the lord of the Care of Tor. A trumpeter blew an announcement. Geraden took her as close as the guards permitted to the place where the Tor's riders would enter Orison and dismount. There they stopped.

The riders were on the road outside the castle. They had almost reached the gate, despite their mourning pace. She saw now that the men were all in black. The breath of the horses steamed silver in the iron cold, but their trappings were black. Black draped the litter that four of the mounts supported from their saddles. The man who led the group hid his face under a black hood, and a black cloak was wrapped around him.

This figure was so fat that Terisa wondered how his horse could bear his weight.

He led his riders toward Castellan Lebbick, then halted within the precise formation of the honor guard. Their horses seemed to sag under the burdens they carried.

"Greetings, my lord Tor," the Castellan said gruffly. His shoulders were braced as if they had the weight of the whole winter on them; the purple band across his forehead emphasized the anger of his eyebrows. "You are welcome in Orison. No matter what reason has brought you here at such a time, you are welcome."

Slowly, the Tor raised his black-gloved hands and lifted his hood, revealing thin white hair that straggled from his pale scalp, features the shape and color of cold potatoes, bleak eyes. His fat cheeks were hurt with cold.

In a husky voice, he rasped, "I will see the King."

The sharpness of the air made everything distinct. Terisa saw the shadow of a wince pass across Lebbick's hard face. "My lord Tor," he replied, "King Joyse has been informed of your coming. At present, he is busy with other matters." He couldn't keep his disdain for those "other matters" out of his tone. The King was probably playing hop-board. "I'm sure he'll grant you an audience shortly."

The clouds sealing the sky were the color of tombstones. Cold seemed to close around the courtyard. For a long moment, the Tor didn't move or speak. His eyes blinked as if he were going blind. Then, with a grunt of effort, he heaved his leg over the back of his horse and dismounted. The guards were silent. The champing of the horses and the squelching sound of his boots in the mud could be heard clearly as he moved like an old man among his people toward the litter.

From the litter, he lifted in his arms the black-draped shape of a man or woman who must have been taller than he was. He didn't look strong enough to bear so much weight; nevertheless he cradled the body against his belly, carrying it forward until he stood directly in front of Castellan Lebbick.

In the same dried-out, hollow voice, he said, "This is my first son. I will see the King."

Now the Castellan's distress was unmistakable. "Your son, my lord Tor? That's a terrible loss." Terisa remembered that Lebbick was acquainted with loss. "All Mordant will sorrow with you. How did he die?"

For a moment, a flicker of passion lit the Tor's speech. "His face was torn away by a wolf such as Mordant and Cadwal and Alend together have never known. Do you care to see the wound?" He extended the shrouded body toward Lebbick.

But almost at once his energy faded. Dully, implacably, he repeated, "I will see the King."

"That won't be possible." Castellan Lebbick sounded thick and hoarse, like a man in pain. "King Joyse doesn't yet grant you an audience."

Through the silence, the riders at the Tor's back muttered curses. How far had they ridden in order to present the Tor's slaughtered son to his King?

Abruptly, Geraden left Terisa's side. Striding through the mud as if he couldn't be held back by any slip or accident—as if he had forgotten his talent for mishap—he went toward the Tor. The boyish prance-and-fumble of exuberance and mistake was gone from his manner entirely. The way his chestnut hair crowned the strong lines of his face made him look incontestable, as sure of himself as if he had power and knew how to use it.

Ignoring Castellan Lebbick's fierce glare, he said, "My lord Tor, I am Geraden, youngest son of the Domne. In the name of my father and all his family, please accept my grief. King Joyse will see you. When he hears why you have come, he will see you."

"Geraden," the Castellan snarled in an undertone, "be warned. You forget yourself, whelp."

At once, Geraden turned toward Lebbick. "No, Castellan." He had become taller almost without transition, certain of his authority. "Be warned yourself. You may despise me as much as you wish. But the day has not yet come when you may despise the Domne. I speak in his name.

"In his name, I claim the responsibility. Let it crush me if it will. The King will see my lord Tor."

The Tor said nothing. He stood there with his son in his arms as though he had been stricken mute, unable to articulate his grief except by demanding the King's acknowledgment of it.

A snarl twisted Castellan Lebbick's mouth. His hands knotted at his sides. After a moment, he said softly, "You can try, whelp. Gestures like that come cheaply to those with no duty—to those who can ignore the consequences of what they do. It's my place to ensure that King Joyse is obeyed, and I will do it"—his fist beat the words against his thigh—"if I must."

Then he stepped aside. With a barked command, he ordered the honor guard to do the same.

Geraden put his hand on the Tor's arm to help support the great weight of what the man carried. Together, they moved toward the nearest open door. Perhaps a dozen guards took formal positions behind them and followed.

Terisa started after them.

The Castellan stopped her with a hard gesture. "No, my lady. There's harm enough here without your contribution." He spat the words like gusts of steam. "I won't expose my King's plight to a woman of your dubious allegiance."

Raising his voice, he instructed two of his guards to return the lady Terisa of Morgan to her rooms.

For a moment, she stood right on the edge of resisting him, though she had never done anything like that before and wouldn't have been able to do it if she had thought about it in advance. She wanted to go with Geraden. If anything could be done for the Tor, she ached to do it. But the quality of Lebbick's glare pushed her back. It was outraged and extreme, and it seemed to say that if she forced him to do her violence she would drive him mad.

She turned to the men he had assigned and let them take charge of her.

As she slogged through the mud, she heard Castellan Lebbick stiffly welcome the Tor's retinue and offer the riders and their mounts Orison's best hospitality. Then he went after the Tor and Geraden himself.

Back in her rooms, with her boots cleaned as well as possible and drying in the bathroom, she reflected that the Tor had obviously *not* come to Orison in response to any summons from the Perdon. On the other hand, what difference did the Tor's reasons for being here make now? His presence was what mattered. It worked in Master Eremis' favor.

Master Eremis wasn't a comfortable subject of contemplation. His absence gave her a secret ache of frustration and fear. Nevertheless thoughts of him were an improvement over the image of the Tor which remained with her—the fat old man standing ankle-deep in mud, his dead son in his arms and his eyes bleak with grief. When her mother had died, and Terisa had dared to cry, her father had hit her, once, to make her stop. Then he had gotten drunk for the first and only time she could remember. Then he had begun bringing other women into the house as though his wife had never existed. Terisa definitely preferred thinking of Master Eremis.

An hour or so passed before she realized how restless she was. She wasn't ordinarily a woman who paced, but now she caught herself tensely measuring the rugs and stone of the floor—waiting for Geraden. He had stood up to the Castellan. She felt that it was a long time since she had seen so much strength in him. Surely he would come tell her what had happened?

He did. Before lunchtime, she heard a knock on her door. When she answered it, she found Geraden outside.

He looked like a little boy. His eyes were still puffy from crying, and the expression in them was so forlorn that she wanted to put her arms around him.

She couldn't go that far. A lifetime of inhibition held her: she had never learned how to reach out to other people. But instinctively, without gauging what she did, she put her hand on his arm and breathed, "Oh, Geraden. What happened?"

He tried to compose himself, but the effort only made him harsh. "He got to see the King. Being the Domne's son is good for that, at least. I just didn't let anybody say no to me. But King Joyse didn't—"

Then his throat closed on the words, as if they hurt too much to come out. For a moment, his features knotted. He glanced rapidly at the guards on either side of the door. "Please, Terisa. I can't talk about it out here in the hall."

Her heart was beating double time. "Come in," she gulped. "I'm being stupid. I didn't mean to keep you standing there."

With her hand still on his arm, she drew him into the sitting room.

If he hadn't been struggling so hard to contain himself—and if she hadn't been so awkward—they might have hugged each other. But he looked untouchable in his distress, and she had to step away to close the door. When she turned back to him, he was standing with his elbows pressed against his sides and his hands in fists over his heart.

"Oh, Geraden," she murmured again. "Geraden."

"I don't know what's going on." His voice was still harsh, clenched. He was trying to shore up something inside himself. "I swear I don't understand it.

"It wasn't hard to get in to see him. All I had to do was ignore the guards at the door when they told me the King was busy. Under the circumstances, they weren't likely to stand in the Tor's way.

"King Joyse and Adept Havelock were playing hop-board. You probably guessed that. What else," he asked acidly, "would make him too busy to see the man who got him started on the road to becoming King of Mordant? But he didn't seem to resent the interruption. When I barged in, he left his game to welcome us. And he smiled the way he does—the way that makes you want to lie down in front of him so he can walk on you.

"Then he saw what the Tor was carrying. I told him who it was. And for a few moments there I thought I had finally done the right thing. For once in my life, I had *finally* done the right thing.

"He seemed to remember his strength and call it back from somewhere. Suddenly, he was taller, bigger, and his eyes flashed. 'How was this done?' he demanded. The Tor couldn't speak, so I said, 'Imagery. Some kind of strange wolf.' Gambling that I knew what I was doing, I said, 'Look at his face.'

"King Joyse lifted the cloth." Geraden shuddered. "It was terrible. But it would have been worse if the body hadn't been frozen for ten days while the Tor was on the road.

"When King Joyse saw it, he seemed to stand up inside himself. He took the body out of the Tor's arms. He raised his head as if he was going to howl. There was so much outrage and hurt in him that it practically shouted from his face. I thought that finally—*finally*—he was going to get angry enough to do something.

"I was wrong."

Geraden made no effort to muffle his pain. "Adept Havelock chose that moment to say, 'Joyse, it's your move.' As if he didn't know anyone else was in the room.

"And King Joyse just collapsed.

"His face crumpled, and he started crying—softly, almost not making a sound. 'Oh, my old friend,' he said. 'Forgive me. Forgive me.' Then he fell to his knees—he couldn't hold up the weight any longer." Geraden was weeping himself, with his elbows hugged to his ribs and his hands across his chest. "As carefully as he could, he rested the Tor's son on the floor. For a while, he bowed over the body. Then he got his feet under him again"—Geraden had to grip his determination in both fists in order to say the words—"and went back to his game."

For a while, Geraden stood still, fighting to regain control of his emotions while Terisa ached for him and the Tor and King Joyse and said nothing.

"After that," Geraden resumed with a shuddering sigh, "he didn't respond to anything. He didn't give any orders for the funeral. He didn't answer any questions. Maybe he forgot we were there. Eventually, he moved one of his pieces. As far as I could see, it improved Havelock's position.

"All this time, the Tor hadn't said a word. He looked too stunned, too hurt, to say anything. I thought he was going to fall on his face. But now he pulled himself together a bit. 'My son is dead,' he said as if maybe King Joyse had failed to notice that detail. 'Is this the best you can do?'

"The King still didn't respond. Adept Havelock said, 'Close the door on your way out.' "

Geraden shrugged. "Then Castellan Lebbick made us leave. Two of his men had to move the Tor by main force. But I was actually grateful. He did us a favor by getting us out of there."

Abruptly, the Apt ground the heels of his palms into his eyes to force down his tears and his pain and his weakness. When he looked at Terisa again, his glare was red-rimmed and lost. Certainty had deserted him. More than anything now, he resembled a young man who was being broken by his involuntary instinct for disaster.

"Castellan Lebbick was right," he said. "It would have been better if the Tor had been kept away. All I did was make his misery worse."

"I'm sorry," Terisa whispered, hating herself for her inability to help him, heal him. But there was nothing she could do for him except say, "I'm sorry."

Later that day, alone in her rooms in the middle of the afternoon, with nothing to do except brood, she was standing at one of her windows and musing out toward the road when more riders appeared.

This group was larger than the Tor's, more military in character. A trumpet announced the approach of the riders to the gate of Orison. Castellan Lebbick greeted them with an honor guard equal to the one which had met the Tor. Then they dispersed into the castle. But she still couldn't make up her mind.

Saddith brought news with her supper. "Have you heard, my lady? Both the Fayle and the Armigite have come to Orison. Both have demanded audiences with King Joyse. And both have been refused." The maid was proud of her information, as if it came from some high, secret source. "It is said that the Fayle carries messages from Queen Madin and the lady Torrent. And yet he has been refused.

"If the reports are true, he bears his disappointment stoically. Not so the Armigite. I have heard him. He wanders the halls, accosting whoever will listen and explaining his indignation." She tittered. "I am inclined to question his virility, my lady."

When Saddith left, Terisa found that she had reached her decision. King Joyse was unwilling to meet with the lords of the Cares: he was unwilling even to receive a message from his wife. He was too far gone. Master Eremis was right. Mordant could only be saved now if someone else took charge of events.

She would have to go to him, talk to him, tell him what she knew.

It was possible that she would have to tell him about her secret conversations with Master Quillon and Adept Havelock. Not to betray them, but to help him; the information might make him more effective.

She made this decision because she wanted to do what was right. She didn't mean to remain passive for the rest of her life. Her presence here made no sense—but as long as she *was* here, she had to make some effort to help. For Geraden's sake, as well as for Mordant's. He was too paralyzed—and too hurt—by his devotion to the King; he wasn't able to see past his dislike of the Master. He was blind to the one fact she saw clearly: Master Eremis was the only man who had any chance of uniting the Congery and the lords against Mordant's enemies.

But she wasn't thinking about Geraden—or about Mordant—when she finally reached her decision. She was thinking about the way Master Eremis had kissed her and touched her.

So the next morning, after a restless night, she got up early. She bathed. She washed and dried her hair. When Saddith brought her breakfast, she found that she couldn't eat it. Instead of risking nausea, she asked the maid to help her put on the gown she had chosen the previous evening—a confection of mauve silk which clung to her thighs and made the hollow between her breasts look deep and desirable. Then she dismissed Saddith for the rest of the day, saying that she meant to spend it with the lady Myste.

Saddith winked at this obvious fabrication, grinned her approval, and left as if she had plans of her own.

When the maid was gone, however, Terisa remained in her rooms for quite a while. She told herself that she wasn't hesitating—precisely. She was waiting for a decent hour. But the truth was that she had lost her confidence. Master Eremis was too much for her—too experienced, too adept, too powerful. Geraden had accused him of trying to manipulate her. He had certainly manipulated the Congery. The explanations he gave for what he did weren't entirely satisfying. And apparently he was no longer interested in her.

Nevertheless in the end her resolve held. Around mid-morning, she went to her door, unbolted it with an unsteady hand, and left her rooms.

One of the guards whistled at her softly through his teeth; she ignored him.

Descending from the tower, she panicked for several moments because she wasn't sure of the route back to Master Eremis' quarters. She hadn't paid close enough attention on the one occasion when she had visited those rooms. And she thought she saw a man following her—

She glimpsed him three or four times, on different levels of the castle. He seemed to disappear as soon as she spotted him. But he was tall; he looked strong. A gray cloak hid his clothes and covered his head, but didn't conceal the end of the longsword jutting down near his boots.

On the other hand, he didn't seem to be the man who had attacked her in her rooms. He wasn't wearing black. And he didn't keep after her. Instead, he seemed to forget her after a while. She didn't see any more sign of him.

After worrying about him probably more than he deserved, she put him out of her mind, concentrating her attention again on the problem of finding Master Eremis' quarters.

What she remembered of Geraden's tour helped. Eventually, she found her way into the section of Orison that had been set aside for the personal use of the Masters. After that, all she had to do was locate the polished rosewood door with the full-length bas-relief carving of Master Eremis.

As soon as she reached it, she raised her hand to knock—and stopped. She was breathing too hard. She needed a moment to become calm. But the carving on the door was really quite extraordinary. The eyes seemed to see everything, and the mouth promised pleasures which she might not like. He was much too much for her. If she had any sense left, she would admit that. She had no business taking a risk like this.

So she didn't knock. Gripped by the demented logic of the obsessed, she put her hand on the latch and eased the door open more quietly than the thudding of her heart.

Exactly as she remembered it, she saw the sumptuous room in which the Master had held her and kissed her. She saw the crimson of the uppermost rug made even more dramatic by the blue of the furniture and the yellow of the drapes. She saw the filigree-cut brass urns from which perfumed lamps provided light and warmth. She

saw the tapestries which covered the walls with scenes of seduction.
She saw the divan—

Master Eremis was on the divan. Fortunately, he wasn't facing in
her direction. He was lying forward, his attention focused on the
woman under him. The long, clean muscles of his bare back and
buttocks bunched and released to the rhythm of his movements.

The woman's legs were locked around his hips. Her arms clenched
his back. She made moaning noises deep in her throat.

Her clothes were scattered across the floor. Terisa recognized
them. But she didn't need the confirmation.

The woman was unmistakably Saddith.

She had seen something like this once before. Her parents had had
separate rooms. After her mother's death, she had begun using her
mother's room as a hiding place, a retreat, as if her mother were a
more comforting presence dead than alive. Of course she hadn't told
her father; he probably had no way of knowing what he was doing
when he took one of his women to her mother's bed. She had
watched for a while before she had realized what she was seeing.

Now she closed the door softly. Hugging the cold ache in her
heart, she returned to her rooms. Careful not to tear it, she finally
worked her way out of the silk gown and put it away. Then she got
dressed in her old clothes and went to the window to stare out at the
wilderland of winter.

She was still there near sunset when yet another group of riders
approached the castle. Like the one she had seen the previous afternoon, it was larger than the Tor's retinue—and less funerary. Again,
a trumpet saluted the riders as they approached the gate. Again,
Castellan Lebbick met them with a guard of honor. While they were
dismounting, she thought she recognized the brawny shape and bald
head of the Perdon. But she couldn't be sure.

TWELVE: WHAT MEN DO WITH WOMEN

S he didn't know how she was going to face Saddith again. Fortunately, when the maid brought her supper, old habits came to Terisa's rescue. She responded to Saddith's glow in the same pale, passive, covert way that she had so often dealt with her parents; she put on nonexistence like a cloak, so that nothing about her called attention to itself or disturbed the flow of Saddith's emotions and concerns. As a result, she was able to hear Saddith's hints and elation in safety, as if she felt nothing. And she had no trouble fending off the maid's cheerful, leering attempts to find out how she had spent her day.

It seemed quite possible to her that she did feel nothing. How would she have known if an emotion of any importance had taken hold of her?

Unfortunately, the habits that saved her exacted a price. The sensation that she was fading began to steal over her. A bad night loomed ahead—and she had no mirrors with which to defend herself.

After the maid had cleared away the tray and left for the night, Terisa took another bath, using the cold of the water and the warmth of the fire to create the illusion of physical actuality. Then she spent some time meticulously rearranging the lamps in the room, trying to bring out a reflection from the glass of the window. But the black night outside stubbornly refused to give her image back.

She was tempted to give up, let go of herself and take the consequences. But she had been fighting this battle for years. What did

Master Eremis have to do with her, anyway? He hadn't created her problem. Surely she wasn't foolish enough to believe that he could cure it?—that his touch on her body could restore what she lacked? Then why was she wasting her time feeling so miserable about him? Why was she—

—trembling in the middle of the room with her heart in an uproar simply because someone had knocked on her door?

She knew the answer to that one. Tonight was the night when Master Eremis and Master Gilbur were supposed to meet with the lords of the Cares.

For a moment, she wanted to ignore whoever was outside her door. But the knock was repeated, reminding her that she really had no place to hide. Mustering her scant resources of courage, she went to answer the door.

Master Eremis stood there grinning.

The way he looked at her still had too much power: effortlessly, it banished all question of fading, made her real in front of him—real for him. After all, what harm had he done her by making love to Saddith? His eyes promised that his attentions were worth having. Who else did she know who could kiss her with just that combination of ardor, experience, and glee?

And if he lost interest in her, she could bring him back by telling him about Adept Havelock and Master Quillon.

In self-defense, trying to take a stand against him, she said, "I don't want to go."

He came easily into the room, as if he knew her better than she did herself. "My lady," he said in a teasing tone, "you must."

"Why?" The effort not to lose herself in his bright gaze and his smile made her light-headed. "It doesn't have anything to do with me."

"Ah," the Master replied, "now there you are wrong." His manner became slightly more sober. "You must come with me as a demonstration of my good faith. You may be unaware of the ill repute which King Joyse has placed upon all Imagers. Either we are the creatures of his will, honest only as far as he is honest, or we retain allegiances to Cadwal and Alend which make us treacherous, or we are the source of the present peril. We are regarded in this way because the Congery was created by force rather than volition. I must persuade these unruly lords to trust me, and that can only be accomplished if I am honest with them. I must show you to them so that they will grasp what the Congery has attempted in the past—and what we mean to do now.

"My lady, this has a great deal to do with you. If you do not come with me, I will gain nothing from this meeting"—he made an attempt not to look too cheerful—"and all my efforts to save Mordant will be undone."

His hands twitched the ends of his chasuble playfully.

She remembered his hands. She had just begun to learn what they could do. Her heart was beating in her throat. She almost said, All right. I'll go with you. If you'll take me back to your rooms afterward. The words came so close to utterance that she felt giddy. She had to swallow more than once before she became able to nod her head.

He reached toward her. "My lady," he drawled as he took hold of her arm, "I was confident that you would understand."

The guards stopped him as he closed the door after her. They wanted to know where he was taking her. Castellan Lebbick's orders. Even though—she was only vaguely aware of this—Geraden was never questioned when she left with him. Master Eremis replied acerbically that the lady Terisa of Morgan had agreed to join him and several other Masters for a quiet supper in the quarters of the mediator of the Congery. Then he steered her away.

The set of his jaw showed that the guards had made him angry.

Holding her arm, he took her down out of the tower and through several of the main halls. She nearly missed her balance and stopped when she spotted the man in the gray cloak again. But he disappeared almost immediately; she lost sight of him before she could point him out to Master Eremis. Smiling apologetically to excuse her awkwardness, she walked on. The man in the gray cloak didn't reappear.

Master Eremis made no obvious attempt at stealth, but he moved along a route calculated to confuse the few guards they passed. Nevertheless it soon became clear that he wasn't taking Terisa anywhere near the Congery's private section of Orison. Nor was he moving toward the complex rooms and passages of the laborium. Rather, he was descending, circuitously but steadily, into a dank, disused part of the castle which resembled the place where Adept Havelock had his rooms—a place among the foundations of Orison. For a moment, she was struck by the wild thought that Master Eremis had something to do with Master Quillon and the Adept. But though the passages

Eremis chose were cold, empty, and untended, they were still public enough to be lighted: lanterns hung from the walls at distant intervals. The side corridors and chambers seemed to indicate that this part of the castle had once been inhabited. Perhaps Orison had settled as it was built higher. Or perhaps the foundations had begun to leak. Whatever the reason, these halls and rooms had clearly been abandoned for drier quarters on some other level. Master Eremis' boots splashed through ice-scummed puddles on the floor, and the sound echoed wetly. Terisa could hear water dripping in the distance.

She hugged her arms against the cold and tried to remember the way back, so that she wouldn't get lost.

Without warning, a dark shape seemed to materialize out of the wall. She flinched involuntarily. The nearest lantern was twenty or thirty feet away, and its dim light made the figure look as bulky and dangerous as a bear.

But Master Eremis chuckled through his teeth; and a moment later she made out a profile with a bald head, thick eyebrows, and a shaggy mustache. The man was wrapped in a fur cloak the same dark, wet color as the shadows. He probably presented such a bestial shape because he was still wearing his pallettes and gorget under the cloak.

Now that she looked harder, she saw the faint outline of a doorway behind him. He must have been waiting concealed there for Master Eremis to come along.

"Master Eremis," the man breathed. His greeting steamed in the cold. "They are all foregathered—even that hunchbacked dog you say we must endure to reassure the Congery. You are not what I call prompt." Terisa could see only half his face in the lantern light, but the one eye on that side glared at her. "Why do you bring a woman?"

"My lord Perdon," the Imager replied, "it is not as easy as you imagine to arrange for a meeting like this to take place in secret." The softness of his voice muffled his sarcasm. "Lebbick watches everything—or thinks he does. A number of plausible lies must be placed in a variety of ears. I will explain the woman."

The Perdon glowered at Terisa a moment longer. "Explain her well, Master Eremis." Then he shifted his gaze to the Imager. "When you persuaded me to this meeting, I promised that I would gather the other lords as quickly as possible. But the task of sending summons and receiving answer across such distances at this season seemed likely to take at least fifteen days. You assured me, however, that less time would be required. I must confess that I did not entirely believe you. Now I am astonished that you were right to such an impossible degree."

In surprise, Terisa nearly said aloud, *Fifteen* days? He told us *six*. He told the Congery you promised *six*.

The Master's grip on her arm kept her quiet. "Imagery has its uses," he commented enigmatically.

"Doubtless it has," said the Perdon. "And doubtless you will explain them, also—when you see fit. But one answer you must give me. I am troubled by the Tor's presence among us."

"Troubled, my lord Perdon?"

"Yes, Master Eremis." A clenched fist showed between the edges of the Perdon's cloak. "I do not trust him here. He has been too steadfastly the King's friend. I agreed to summon him only because I believed him too old—and too fat—to make the journey. His presence now alarms me."

At that, Master Eremis cocked an eyebrow. "Now you begin to alarm *me*. I begin to suspect, my lord Perdon, that it is not the Tor you distrust. It is me."

The Perdon's scowl didn't waver.

"This distresses me." Eremis let a glint of anger into his voice. "When you spoke of fifteen days, I knew that the time would be less because the Termigan was already on the road to Orison. I have a flat glass which chances to show his seat in Sternwall, and I saw him depart.

"When the Tor arrived, I did not hesitate to include him. Has no one spoken to you, my lord? Has the Tor himself not told you why he is here? He came to demand a response from our brave King because his eldest son was killed by some instance of vile Imagery. And the King has refused. He refuses even to hear the demand—as he has also refused audiences to the Fayle and the Armigite.

"The Tor loves his sons," Master Eremis concluded. "I believe he will be our ally now."

"Well," the Perdon murmured. "Well." He had turned his head. All his face was in shadow. "He has been the King's friend for forty years. But perhaps grief will make him bitter. Perhaps it is worth the risk to have him with us."

"My lord Perdon," said the Master dryly, "you have already im-

plied that I am late. If we do not go to them soon, the other lords
will become restive, and then we will have no one with us."

The Perdon's eye came flashing back into the light. He stretched
out his fist and touched the Imager's chest lightly. "Be warned, Master Eremis," he whispered. "I am the lord of the Care of Perdon. I
do not like manipulation—or abused trust. And I suspect that my
fellow lords have similar prejudices."

Then he turned and strode away down the corridor, his heels loud
against the stone.

For a moment, Master Eremis held Terisa where she was. "Someday," he said in a musing tone, "that rash lord really must be taught
to be more careful with his threats."

Almost involuntarily, as if the question were forced out of her, she
asked, "Why did you lie to the Congery? You told them it was the
Perdon's idea to meet tonight."

At once, he raised a finger to his lips. "My lady," he whispered, "I
have already explained that some of my fellow Masters do not like or
trust me. They only accepted the risk of this meeting because they
believed it to be based on the Perdon's honor rather than on my
foresight. Now I advise you not to utter a word until you are once
again safely in your rooms."

Still holding her arm tightly, he drew her after the Perdon.

They followed the hard echo of his bootheels until they had passed
another turn; then she saw light streaming from an open doorway
ahead. The door wasn't guarded: apparently, the lords of the Cares
still believed they were safe in Orison. The Perdon strode through
the doorway, and Terisa heard low voices greet him. A moment
later, Master Eremis took her into the light.

There he released her arm and gave her a small nudge forward.
She had the impression that he had stepped back—that he was using
her entrance to provide some kind of distraction.

The door opened on a room as plain as a cell and not much larger.
The light came from several lanterns set on a long, crude wooden
table which filled at least half the space. The heavy chairs around the
table made the chamber crowded.

As soon as she entered the room, Terisa noticed Master Gilbur: he
sat at the far end of the table, and his features were clenched in an
acid scowl, as if he had been trading insults with someone.

The Perdon was still on his feet, but the other lords were seated.
She recognized the Tor, of course. He sat near Master Gilbur. Out of

direct contact with the winter, his skin had more color; but his face still looked like a handful of mealy potatoes, and his eyes were glazed. There was an enormous flagon on the table in front of him.

Opposite him was a man whom Terisa took at once to be the Armigite, simply because of Saddith's description. The softness of his face made it appear fleshier than it really was, and his expression was petulant; his hair was darkened and pomaded into elaborate curls; his clothes were rich in a way that somehow suggested a lady's bedroom. He was the only man in the room who looked younger than Master Eremis: clearly, he had inherited his place rather than earning it in Mordant's wars.

Like the other lords, he was armed, but the slim blade at his side seemed essentially decorative.

The man next to him was a strong contrast: he appeared to have been chipped from a block of flint. Every line of his face, every glance of his eyes, every gesture of his hands looked like it had been made sharp by blows, hammered to a cutting edge. His skin had a dusty tinge that suited his flat eyes. His eyebrows seemed to have no color.

He must have been the Termigan. Terisa reasoned this because he wasn't old enough to be Queen Madin's father. The lord across from him—beside the Tor—was much more likely to be the Fayle. This man was at least the Tor's age; the sparse white hair on the back of his skull was cut short; he was as lean as a whippet. His face was so long, and had so much jaw, that he might have looked lugubrious if his eyes hadn't been so bright, blue, and precise. The way he sat— upright in his chair, with his arms crisply folded over his thin chest— implied the stoicism Saddith had attributed to him.

With the exception of the Tor—whose attention was fixed on his flagon—everyone was looking at her. The Fayle's keen gaze betrayed nothing; but the Termigan regarded her indignantly, the Armigite's face wore a sneer, and Master Gilbur's customary scowl was black and stormy.

The men and the lanterns made the room considerably warmer than the corridor.

No one offered any introductions. As soon as Master Eremis came into the room, just a moment or two after Terisa, the Perdon announced sourly, "Master Eremis says that he will explain her." The red hair of his eyebrows and ears bristled as he took a chair beside the Termigan.

"I would like an explanation," Master Gilbur growled at once. "What sort of legerdemain will you use to make us swallow her presence, Eremis?"

Under so much hostile scrutiny, Terisa felt her face growing hot. Anybody who looked at her closely would notice the sweat trickling down her temples. How had she become the linchpin of Master Eremis' plans? Why did everything he wanted in this meeting suddenly hinge on her?

"My lady"—his tone wasn't especially courteous—"be seated." He gestured her toward the chair beside the Fayle. Then he sat down himself, at the head of the table opposite Master Gilbur. His leanness, the thatch of black hair behind his high forehead, and the way his cheeks sloped like the sides of a wedge from his ears toward his large nose gave him the appearance of an exotic bird. In some ways, she had never seen him look less serious. The sparkle in his eyes counterbalanced the grim set of his mouth. His hands he folded together on the table in a conspicuously unsuccessful effort to appear grave.

"My lords," he said briskly, glancing at each of them in turn, "the problem is time. If we were not in haste, I would not have presumed to make decisions without your knowledge and consent. It is true that this winter may not break for another thirty days, or even fifty. But it may break in ten. In ten days, an army of considerable size may begin to march against us from Cadwal. And only a few days have passed since wise King Joyse saw fit to reject a proposed alliance with Alend, humiliating the ambassador to seal his refusal. The forces of Margonal will not be far behind those of the High King."

"That is true," the Armigite said with boyish bitterness. "If King Joyse had granted me an audience, I would have told him that Margonal's army musters not half a day's march from the Pestil. My commanders say that they cannot stand against it. When Alend decides to attack, I will be swept away. And King Joyse refuses to hear me!"

He would have gone on, but Master Eremis cut in smoothly, "Worse than armies, however, is Imagery. And Imagery does not wait for spring. All Mordant is already assailed. Strange wolves have slaughtered the Tor's son. Ghouls harry the villages of Fayle. Devouring lizards swarm the storehouses of the Demesne. Pits of fire appear in the ground of Termigan—almost within the fortifications of Sternwall."

The Termigan nodded bleakly. "That's why I'm here. I'm a soldier. I'm weaponless against pits of fire in the ground."

"We have no time, my lords," Master Eremis concluded. "For that reason, I have presumed to do what I have done."

He paused, and Master Gilbur growled, "Get on with it, Eremis. What have you done?"

Master Eremis' dour expression nearly broke. Suppressing himself stiffly, he said, "I have invited someone else to our meeting." Before anyone could react, he called over his shoulder, "My lord, you may come in now!"

Terisa gaped as Prince Kragen strode into the room, accompanied by his two bodyguards.

His bearing showed that his self-assurance hadn't been dampened. He no longer wore his ceremonial brass helmet, breastplate, and sword sheath. Black silk garments emphasized the darkness of his skin; his mustache gleamed. But once again he had a strong sword belted to his hip. His bodyguards were armed for use rather than show.

Seeing him, the Armigite blanched. The Termigan thrust back his chair and sprang to his feet, hauling at his sword. Master Gilbur's face darkened apoplectically. The Tor took a swig from his flagon and belched.

"This is surprising," commented the Fayle in a voice like the rustle of dry leaves. "You are not presumptuous by half measures, Master Eremis."

"Have you lost your mind?" the Perdon snapped at Eremis. "I warned you that we will not be manipulated. Will you admit the son of the Alend Monarch to our secret counsels?"

One of the bodyguards braced himself between Prince Kragen and the Termigan. Before the man could draw his sword, however, the Prince stopped him. "My lords," he said with a placating gesture, "hear me. You are surprised—but you are not threatened. Indeed, I am grateful that Master Eremis has provided me this opportunity to meet with you. After my treatment at the hands of your King, I was minded to depart Orison at once. But that would have ensured war between Mordant and Alend. And the Alend Monarch strongly desires peace. It is his greatest wish to form an alliance against the perils of Cadwal and Imagery. Therefore when Master Eremis asked me to remain in Orison, promising me a chance to speak to you, I allowed myself to be persuaded.

"My lords, I have been denied an alliance with Mordant's King. But surely the same end may be achieved by an alliance with Mordant's lords?"

"Alend is my enemy," the Termigan spat at once, still holding his sword. "I've had too many brothers and friends killed by Alends who thought it was their right to own our freedom. I didn't realize, Master Eremis, that you called us together to discuss treason."

"Oh, *treason*, forsooth." The Armigite fluttered his delicate hands, quickly recovering from his initial fright. "For myself, I am delighted to see Prince Kragen on grounds of friendship. What is your loyalty, my lord Termigan—to King Joyse, or to Mordant? You know what our King has done—and not done—to meet our need. I call it *treason* to obey him further. Mordant," he added piously, "is a higher service."

"My lord Termigan," Prince Kragen continued, "you must understand the Alend Monarch's position. As I have said, his desire for peace is strong. We have known peace since you fought so powerfully for our defeat—and we have learned that peace is better than war. But your King has not been content with peace. He has created the Congery.

"My lords," he said generally, "the Congery represents great danger. While your King held it strongly, so that it served the causes of peace, we were able to bear the threat. But now your King has become weak. Mordant is under attack by Imagery—and Imagery is not used in your defense. How are we to explain this? Either your King has gone mad and no longer cares to defend what he fought so long to win. Or he has gone mad and now wields the Congery against his own land, preparing his strength"—Master Gilbur started to protest, but the Prince overrode him—"so that in time he will be able to destroy us all!"

"*That* is a lie!" Master Gilbur barked, pounding the table. "Of course King Joyse is mad. But he does *not* use the Congery! By the balls of the arch-Imager's goat, we are *not* the cause of this peril!"

Prince Kragen didn't take offense. "You speak for yourself, Master Gilbur," he said mildly, "and for yourself I believe you. That the Congery desires our meeting augurs well for its honesty. To my mind, Master Eremis has proven himself true by bringing us together —and by gaining the Congery's permission to tell us what the Masters mean to do in Mordant's defense. Sadly, however, that changes nothing. Your King has become weak. Therefore Cadwal aspires to possession of the Congery. And therefore Alend must fight. We cannot permit so many Imagers to become a weapon in the hands of the High King.

"My lord Termigan, you have lost much in war against us. We also have lost much. But Mordant and Alend together will lose a great deal more if Festten becomes the ruler of the Congery."

"Well said!" cheered the Armigite. "Well said!"

The Perdon was looking hard at Master Eremis. After a moment, he said softly, "You are wiser than I realized, Master Eremis. If I had known that you are so farsighted, I would have come to you for counsel sooner."

Eremis' eyes glittered, but he didn't permit himself to smile.

The Prince's argument was enough to make the Termigan reconsider. He lowered his sword; frowning in thought, he stared at the table.

Unexpectedly, the Tor banged his flagon to the table. "Oh, sit down, my lord Termigan. So much upright anger makes me tired. Let us learn what more surprises are in store for us."

"Before we go further," the Fayle said dryly, "perhaps Master Eremis will explain why he has brought this young woman to hear what we say and decide."

Taken by surprise, Terisa's heart started to pound again.

Abruptly, the Termigan slapped his sword back into its sheath and sat down. His flat eyes looked at no one. "Yes, Master Eremis. Account for the woman. You ask us to accept too much too quickly."

Master Eremis opened his mouth to answer, but Prince Kragen was faster. "My lords, she is the lady Terisa of Morgan. I know nothing of her. Yet I am in her debt. During my audience with your King, she did all she could to spare me humiliation. For that, the gratitude of Alend is hers." He gave Terisa a formal bow. Then, his voice at once velvet and iron, he added, "My lords, I must ask you to treat her with respect."

Master Gilbur snorted softly.

The Tor peered past the Fayle at her through a blur of wine. "You were with that boy of the Domne's," he said thickly. "Geraden. When I arrived." Without warning, his eyes filled with tears. Blinking furiously, he leaned back in his chair, then slapped his hand down on the table. "Take my gratitude as well. Prince Kragen and I will see that you are treated with respect."

Gulping from his flagon, he slumped to the side as if he had lost consciousness.

"Very touching," the Armigite murmured without quite looking at Terisa. "What will we have next? Offers of marriage?"

The other lords, however, seemed to think better of the Tor than of the Armigite: they didn't acknowledge his sarcasm. Instead, they fixed their attention pointedly on Master Eremis, and the Termigan said, "I'll respect her well enough when I understand why she's here."

"My lords"—Eremis spread his hands in an expansive gesture—"I will tell you. Will you be seated, my lord Prince?"

"Thank you." Smoothly, Prince Kragen moved to a chair beside Terisa, between her and the Fayle. His eyes gleamed at her. "May I sit at your side, my lady?" he murmured. He didn't wait for her permission, however. As he sat down, she noticed that his hands were well manicured, but there were ridges of callus on his palms and fingers.

His bodyguards stationed themselves behind him.

"As you have heard," Master Eremis resumed at once, "she is the lady Terisa of Morgan. She was brought among us by Imagery."

No one reacted to this announcement: perhaps it was self-evident.

"Beyond that, you already know as much of her as I do—certain secondary details aside." He couldn't resist a leering grin that made the Armigite snigger. But he suppressed it quickly. "She reveals nothing. She has no discernible talent for Imagery. I brought her here so that you will understand what the Congery has done in an effort to answer Mordant's need—and what we now propose to do.

"My lords, our dilemma is yours, and we are not blind to it. Mordant is in great danger. And Kind Joyse has lost his senses. Therefore we have done what Imagers have always done. We have cast an augury.

"A great amount of time was required to do this. It is not a simple thing to create the glass needed for such specific augury. But when the glass was done, the augury was cast. As best we can, we have acted on what we learned.

"I will not trouble you with lengthy explanations of augury. It is enough to say that the matter of interpretation is difficult. Put simply, our augury shows Mordant's peril. It shows an alien figure of great power. It shows scenes of victory. And it appears to imply a connection between the figure of power and the Domne's youngest boy, Geraden.

"As it happens, this same figure of power is visible in one of Master Gilbur's most celebrated mirrors."

Master Gilbur gave the room an indiscriminate glare.

"We came to the conclusion," Eremis continued, "that this figure was the champion who would save Mordant—if he were translated in the right way. And we agreed—not without some debate—that it must be Geraden's task to perform the translation."

He leaned back and indicated Terisa with a nod. "She is the result. In some way that we cannot explain, Geraden's translation went awry." Then he paused to enjoy the perplexed frowns and muttering of the lords.

The Tor twitched in his seat. "I know that Geraden," he rumbled. "He is a good boy. A true son of his father." Absentmindedly, he yawned and took another pull from his flagon.

After a moment, the Armigite said in a tone of rising indignation, "Do you mean us to believe, Master Eremis, that Mordant is to be saved by this"—he waved the back of his hand in Terisa's direction—"this *woman?*"

"No, my lord Armigite." The Fayle's voice was as dry and brittle as ever, but it held an unexpected authority. "Master Eremis would never ask that of a man who has no wife and no daughters. He means us to understand the decisions which the Congery has made because of the lady Terisa's translation."

"Exactly, my lord Fayle." Despite his stern expression, the laughter in Master Eremis' eyes implied a comment on the Armigite's embarrassment. "It is my hope that seeing the lady Terisa will enable you to grasp why we have determined now to turn our backs on the obvious interpretation of our augury.

"Though he figures prominently in the augury, we have decided to forgo Geraden's assistance. Master Gilbur will perform the translation as soon as you wish him to do so."

Terisa thought the room was getting colder. But—she protested. But— That wasn't what the Congery had decided. Master Eremis was going too far.

The Tor made a soft snoring noise. The other men were more attentive, however. The Termigan stared at Master Eremis. The Armigite's mouth hung open. Prince Kragen's gaze darted watchfully around the room, gauging what he saw. The Fayle moved his lips as if he were talking to himself. In the surprised silence, Terisa could hear the creak of the bodyguards' leather as they shifted on their feet.

All at once, her sense of the situation changed. Despite his strange manner, Master Eremis had the ability to amaze her. Now she understood what he was doing. He was trying to forge an alliance, trying to place all three of the forces here—the lords, the Congery, and Alend's representative—into positions from which they would find it impossible to refuse him. Lacking the strength of the King, or even the authority of the mediator of the Congery, he was forced to resort to these subtle ploys. But the point of his maneuvering was to save Mordant.

Abruptly, Prince Kragen slapped his hand down on the table and crowed, "Bravely done, Master Eremis! You are audacious and resourceful, and you have my admiration. This is the union you offer us—Alend and the lords of Mordant and the Congery. I would not have believed there to be a man anywhere bold enough to make such a proposal—and clever enough to make it possible by bringing us together."

"Master Eremis is indeed audacious and resourceful," said the Fayle. "Our reward for forming the union he wishes is the chance to employ the Congery's champion as if he were our own."

"You say a 'figure of power,' " the Termigan put in brusquely. His tone suggested distaste, but his flat eyes revealed nothing. "What do you mean?"

"A moment, my lord Termigan," the Fayle insisted mildly. "I must claim precedence."

The Termigan closed his mouth.

"Emend me if I am mistaken, Master Eremis." The Fayle's blue eyes glittered like a bird's. "Has not King Joyse forbidden any translation that deprives its object of volition?"

"He has," snapped Master Gilbur. "The greater our need for Imagery, the more he strives to paralyze us."

"And is he aware that your champion will be brought among us involuntarily?"

Master Eremis spread his hands like a shrug. "My lord, that is one of many reasons why we must meet in secret. Our wise King will not lift his hand in Mordant's defense. But he will take Orison stone from stone to prevent a forbidden translation." Then Eremis indicated Terisa. "The last time we obeyed his commands, she was the result."

"I see," the Fayle replied. "Forgive my interruption, my lord Termigan."

"For my part," said the Perdon fiercely, "I favor anything that will keep Festten's butchers on their side of the Vertigon. I have sworn to send King Joyse my dead and wounded if I am attacked—and I will do it."

The Armigite looked like he was going to be sick.

The Termigan hadn't shifted his gaze from Eremis. Softly, he said, "Tell us about this 'figure of power,' Master Eremis."

"What is the need?" Gilbur demanded sourly. "He is *augured*. We must have him."

But Master Eremis answered, "He has weapons that hurl a destructive fire. His armor protects him from all attack. Seeing him in battle, we cannot imagine how even an army would be able to stand against him. Surely he will be proof against wolves and ghouls and devouring lizards. Pits of fire will not harm him. He will be able to fight this vile Imagery to its source."

"Better and better." Prince Kragen's smile shone like his mustache. "What *is* that source, Master Eremis?"

"I believe," Eremis replied as grimly as his private excitement allowed, "that he is the arch-Imager Vagel."

The Tor made a snorting noise. He raised his head, glanced around blearily for a moment, then heaved himself to his feet. "My lords, I must go to my bed. I have become too old for so much carousal."

"Do not go, my old friend," the Fayle remonstrated gently. "You must help us to a decision."

The Tor blinked hard. "What decision? I have none to make. I will not return to Marshalt. I am *old*, I say. These questions are too much for me. If King Joyse means to destroy Mordant, I will be here to assist him. I will stand at his side to the end." He made a small chuckling noise. "He deserves me." Then he began to shuffle his bulk toward the door. "My son always said I was a fool and a coward for not giving him more than two hundred men when he first set himself to become King. Now my son is dead. I should not have been so cautious."

Slowly, he lumbered out of the room.

To Terisa's surprise, the Armigite said, "The Tor is right. We should all go to bed. A decision like this should not be made quickly." His eyes showed white, and there was sweat on his upper lip. "What if we are discovered? What if Castellan Lebbick comes upon us? We need time. We must choose with care." His voice cracked. Struggling for dignity, he concluded, "I do not like decisions."

With considerable asperity, the Perdon snapped, "My lord Armigite, your father is groaning in his grave. Did he fight so many bloody-handed battles against"—he flicked a glance at Prince Kragen—"against foes of every description, simply to surrender his Care to a half-man who does not like decisions?"

The Armigite flushed, but was too nauseated to retort.

"My lords," the Perdon went on, "Armigite is bordered on the east by Perdon, on the west by Fayle and Termigan, on the north by Alend. We are enough. The Armigite cannot oppose us all. He will permit us to make his decisions for him."

There was a moment of silence while the Armigite squirmed and the Perdon looked hotly around him. Then the Fayle said, "Be explicit, my lord Perdon." He sounded like a dry husk. "What is the decision you propose?"

"I propose the union Master Eremis has offered us," replied the Perdon at once. "I propose that we join together to draw up a plan of battle—against Cadwal as well as against these attacks of Imagery. King Joyse we will ignore. When Prince Kragen has had time to ready his forces"—he spoke as though he could hear trumpets, and his bald head seemed to gleam with enthusiasm—"the lords of the Cares will march with him and the champion of the Congery for the preservation of the realm."

Master Eremis sat very still, trying not to smile. Down the table from him, Gilbur had covered his face with his heavy hands.

"That's eloquent, my lord Perdon." The Termigan's tone betrayed neither approval nor sarcasm. "I'm considered a loveless man. Certainly, I've got little use for any of you, my lords—and none for King Joyse. But Termigan is my *Care*. From the depths of its copper mines to the expanse of its wheat fields and the heights of Sternwall's towers, it is mine.

"Tell me this. When Cadwal is beaten, and the Imagery has been defeated, and Joyse is deprived of kingship, who is going to rule Mordant and Termigan? Who is going to have authority over my Care?"

Prince Kragen replied with surprising promptness, "The lady Elega."

Elega? Terisa thought as if she had been kicked.

"She is your King's eldest daughter, his rightful heir. And I have had the pleasure of her acquaintance in recent days. She understands power and rule better than you know." He paused. "And she is not Alend."

"A woman," groaned the Armigite, apparently seeking to regain lost stature. "Then you will marry her, and Margonal will become king over us."

Kragen's eyes glittered dangerously, but he didn't deign to retort. Instead, he asked the Termigan, "Is she acceptable to you, my lord?"

"My lords," interposed the Fayle. For the first time, he unfolded his arms and put his long, thin fingers flat on the table. The veins in the backs of his hands bulged crookedly. "This must stop."

At once, every eye in the room was on him.

"I have heard enough." He sounded old and tired; yet there was an undercurrent of firmness in his voice. "If you mean to accept this alliance, you must be content to do so against my opposition. Fayle will fight for the King."

In an apologetic tone, he added, "You must understand that I am the father of his wife. Queen Madin is a formidable woman. Whatever choice I make here, I must justify to her."

"Women and women!" The Perdon was on his feet, his features clenched in anger. "Must Mordant be destroyed because you cannot stand before your own daughter? Or because Prince Kragen is enamored of Elega? Or because"—he brandished his mustache at Terisa— "Master Eremis desires to bed this product of Imagery? My lords, such questions are not important! Our ruin musters against us while we debate petty considerations. We must—"

"No, my lord Perdon." Though the Termigan didn't raise his voice, he made himself heard through the Perdon's ire. "You'll do what you want. But you'll do it without me. My lord Fayle is too polite to say what he thinks. I'm not so courteous. There is some plot here. My lord Prince agrees with all this too easily. I *know* the Alend Monarch. When he closes his hand around Mordant, he won't release it—not unless the lady Elega has already agreed to become his proxy."

He got to his feet. "Make all the alliances you can. I trust no Alend or Imager." Roughly, he strode from the room.

For a moment, no one moved or spoke. The Termigan's unexpected declaration appeared to have shocked everyone. Terisa was reeling at the sudden collapse of Master Eremis' plans. He looked like he wanted to laugh; she interpreted that as fury.

"One thing more," said the Fayle. He, too, was standing. "Master Eremis, Master Gilbur—you must not translate this figure of power."

Master Eremis only cocked an eyebrow. The Armigite looked like he was trying to shrink down in his seat, so that he would be ready to duck under the table. But the Perdon stared accumulated outrage at the Fayle. And Master Gilbur demanded in quick anger, "*Not?*"

"You will violate the King's express commands. And more—you will violate the purpose for which the Congery was conceived. You must not do it."

"That purpose is Joyse's, not ours!" retorted Gilbur. "We will not allow some doddering old fool to tell us our duty." Abruptly, he hit the table so hard that the Tor's abandoned flagon toppled to the floor. "*We mean to survive!*"

"Then," murmured the Fayle sadly, "I must tell the King what you intend."

Terisa felt a sting of panic as she saw everything Master Eremis had tried to achieve backfire.

Prince Kragen was on his feet with his bodyguards.

The Perdon faced the Fayle across the table. "Do you mean to betray us, my lord Fayle?"

"No, my lord Perdon," the Fayle answered as though he were grieving. "I will say nothing of this meeting. I mean only to prevent the Imagers from betraying their King."

He should have looked foolish as he left the room: he was old and thin, and his erect carriage emphasized his peaked shoulders, his ill-proportioned head. The men he opposed were younger, stronger, handsomer. But he didn't look foolish. To her astonishment, Terisa considered him admirable. His loyalty touched her. She could imagine Geraden greeting the Fayle's exit with applause.

When the old lord was gone, Master Eremis threw back his head and let out a sound like the cry of a loon.

"Oh, control yourself, Eremis!" growled Master Gilbur. The hunchbacked Imager was plainly furious. "I warned you that this would happen. These *lords* forget every lesson of the past, but they remember that they do not trust Imagery. I have said from the beginning that we must take our own action and let the Cares fend for themselves."

"Yes, Master Gilbur," said Eremis. "You did indeed warn me. You warned me often." With a sudden push, he left his chair. Speaking rapidly, urgently, he said. "My lord Prince, my lord Perdon, you must excuse me." He ignored the Armigite. "Despite Master Gilbur's warning, I did not anticipate this outcome." His face was so knotted that Terisa couldn't read it. "Our fellow Masters are already at work, preparing the champion's translation. We must go to them at once, before the Fayle is able to bring down the King's wrath. If they are caught in the act of a forbidden translation, I fear that our kind King will reinstitute the practice of execution.

"My lord Prince, will you see that the lady Terisa is returned to her rooms?"

Without waiting for an answer, Master Eremis said, "Come, Master Gilbur," and hurried away.

Master Gilbur followed as quickly as his bent back allowed.

Terisa sat where she was, too confused to move. Why did she admire the Fayle, when he and the Termigan had ruined Master Eremis' efforts to save Mordant? And why was the translation already started? The Congery had agreed to wait for the outcome of this meeting.

"It is too bad, my lord Prince," the Armigite was saying, "that the courage to accept your offer of alliance is so scarce. I would be willing to discuss a private union. I would require protection against reprisals. In exchange, I would—"

His voice trailed away; no one was listening to him.

"My lord Prince," said the Perdon stiffly, "please forgive the failure of this meeting—and the insult. I can only assure you that Master Eremis and I meant well. It will not be wise to linger here. Shall I relieve you of the lady Terisa?"

"No apology is needed, my lord Perdon." Prince Kragen didn't appear as upset as Terisa expected. "It is true that my mission has met little success. Frankly, I do not see how Mordant and Alend can now be saved from war." He gave Terisa a sparkling black glance and grinned. "But perhaps my fortunes will improve. I am in the lady's debt. I will happily escort her."

"As you wish." The Perdon bowed brusquely, pulled his cloak around him, and left.

Almost at once, the Armigite scrambled after him, as though the younger lord were afraid to be left behind. When he reached the corridor, Terisa heard him call out to the Perdon, asking for company. She didn't hear the Perdon's answer.

"My lady." Prince Kragen had his hands on the back of her chair. "Will you come?" He was bowing slightly over her and smiling. "As the Perdon has said, it is not wise to linger."

She didn't know how to interpret his smile. It reminded her to some degree of Master Eremis'. At the same time, it suggested that the Prince was a better diplomat, better able to conceal his feelings. His self-assurance was as good as a mask.

She rose in compliance. She had learned her manners from her father.

He pulled the chair out of her way, then took her arm, holding her closely but without undue intimacy. With one bodyguard ahead of him and one behind, he guided her from the room.

Almost without transition, the temperature of the air dropped. The sound of dripping water seemed to creep around her.

"Are you warm enough, my lady?" the Prince asked softly. "You are not warmly dressed."

She should have murmured some noncommittal reply. But she had lost the ability to be as compliant as she appeared. In instinctive self-defense, she answered with a question of her own. "Do you really know Elega?"

She felt him stiffen. He was silent for a moment. Then he said politely, "My lady, it is customary to address me by my title."

"My lord Prince."

He let an easy laugh into the dank passage. "Thank you. Yes, it has been my great pleasure to make the acquaintance of the lady Elega. I have had considerable leisure since the debacle of my audience with King Joyse."

The boots of the bodyguards made crisp crack-and-spatter noises as they strode through puddles of water thinly crusted with ice. When the light of the lanterns was right, she could see her breath steaming. Without conscious boldness, she asked, "Then why are you interested in me?"

Again, he fell momentarily silent, as though he needed time to digest her question and marshall a reply. "My lady," he answered finally, "if another woman asked that question, I would know better how to respond. Can you be unaware that you have a face and form that would interest any man? Perhaps you can. Yet I suspect that your question had another meaning.

"If you are not a coquette—if your question is not meant to entice me—I will answer frankly. I am much impressed by the lady Elega. King Joyse has done more than he knows in producing such a daughter."

Terisa breathed an almost audible sigh of relief.

There was a hitch in the leading bodyguard's stride, a flicker of hesitation. Then he resumed his steady pace.

A chill reached both hands through Terisa's shirt.

"Few Mordants clearly understand, I think," Prince Kragen went on with apparent irrelevance, "that the rule of Alend is not hereditary. When my father, the present Alend Monarch, dies, I will not automatically assume his Seat in Scarab. Rather, the new Monarch will be chosen by contest from among all those who wish to vie for rule.

"Incidentally," he commented, "it is this method of choosing rulers that has preserved the confederacy of the Alend Lieges. Those unruly barons remain faithful to Scarab because they know that they or their families will always have another opportunity to win the Seat.

"This contest is not formal, of course. It has simply evolved. In former times, it was primarily a test of ruthlessness. Whoever butchered, poisoned, or terrified enough of his opponents into submission became Monarch.

"Peace has its benefits, however," he continued. His voice formed a murmuring undertone to the damp echo of bootheels. "And the Alend Monarch is devoted to wisdom, as I have said repeatedly. Now people who desire to rule Alend are not allowed to fester in private, scheming murder. They are publicly acknowledged, and they are tested in the service of the kingdom. Put simply, they are given opportunity to demonstrate that they are fit for the Seat." He chuckled briefly. "One mad old baron put his son forward in recent years—and then went privately about the business of trying to slaughter all opposition. His son was given the test of bringing the baron to justice.

"As it happens, he succeeded admirably.

"My lady," he said ruefully, "this mission is a test for me. And it does not provide much hope. You could safely wager, I fear, that I will not be the next Alend Monarch."

At once, however, he assumed a more cheerful tone. "But we were discussing the lady Elega. I mention all this so that you will understand me when I say that if she were an Alend the Seat of the Monarch would not be closed to her. I believe that she would stand high among the powers of the Kingdom."

The leading bodyguard hesitated again. This time, he nearly froze in mid-stride. Cold suddenly licked across Terisa's heart. She thought she heard the same thing he did—a quiet leather sound which reminded her of swords and sheaths.

Prince Kragen snatched at his blade. He had time to snap, "Beware! Guard the lady!" Then the darkness attacked.

Men charged out of a side passage. How many? She couldn't tell—five or six. Cloaks fluttered from their shoulders like wings. Their leather armor was so black it was difficult to see. Lantern light glinted on bare iron.

They struck straight for her through the opposition of the Prince and his bodyguards.

Swords rang, echoing in the passage. Baleful red sparks sprayed from the conflict of blades. Violence streaked her vision. She saw the head of the nearest bodyguard lift from his shoulders and away like a ball negligently tossed aside. Then a handful of hot blood slapped her face, and his corpse fell into her, driving her against the wall.

Slipping on blood and ice, she sprawled beside the body.

Two attackers drove Prince Kragen back. He was quick with his sword, stronger than he appeared; but his opponents were expert. He couldn't dispatch two of them at once. The force of their double-handed blows hammered him down the passage.

One of the attackers stretched out on the stone, coughing his lungs into a puddle of water. The other bodyguard still kept his feet—barely. He held one arm clamped to a gushing wound in his side; with the other, he flailed his sword at his assailant.

With a deft toss, the assailant flipped his cloak over the bodyguard's head.

Then Terisa lost sight of him. A black figure reared over her, sword poised.

The light caught his face. His nose was like the edge of a hatchet. A fierce grin bared his teeth. His eyes gleamed, as yellow as a cat's.

He was trying to kill her again.

This time, he was going to succeed. There was nothing she could do to stop him, and she still didn't know why he wanted her dead, she had no idea, it didn't make any *sense*—

"Stop!"

The shout caught him. It echoed in the corridor, wrenching him away from her to protect his back.

A drawling voice said clearly, "Five against three are coward's odds. But even a coward wouldn't attack a woman."

Fighting her eyes into focus, Terisa saw the man with the gray cloak advancing along the passage.

The obscure light left his features unclear: she couldn't tell if she had ever seen his face before. But his sword was in his hands. The smile on his lips didn't soften the glint of battle in his eyes.

An attacker drew his blade out of the cloak-blinded bodyguard and moved to join the man threatening Terisa. Her assailant gestured help away, however, sending his companion toward the struggle to kill Prince Kragen.

Black against gray, Terisa's enemy and the newcomer faced each other.

For a moment, they paused. The man in gray commented pleasantly, "It might be interesting to know who you are."

The man in black barked a laugh and exploded at his opponent.

Iron flashed and scraped. Blows resounded. The man in black was knocked to the wall. He recovered and countered as if he were immune to pain. With his cloak, he made an attempt to snare the man in gray. The ploy failed. Their swords clashed, caught and held, clashed again. Attacking, retreating, flinging their bodies from side to side, they wove quick sparks about them like fireworks.

The man in gray kept smiling, but his concentration was savage.

Terisa should have helped. She knew that. She should have gotten to her feet, picked up one of the fallen swords, tried to intervene. For Prince Kragen. Or the man in gray. But she didn't move. Instead, she lay on the cold, wet stone with her hands at her temples, terrified by the enormity of what was happening because of her.

She had no idea *why*. What had she done to deserve such hate? Or to be defended from it?

The man in gray moved with such speed that it was difficult to realize how graceful he was, difficult to follow the way his sword swept and cut as if it were avid in his hands. He and his opponent wove gloom and echoes and hot sparks around each other. In the space between one heartbeat and the next, he blocked his opponent's blade, then dropped one fist from his swordhilt and struck a back-hand blow that staggered the man in black.

Smoothly, almost contemptuously, Terisa's attacker brushed aside the onslaught that followed. He gripped her defender's blade with one gloved hand long enough to chop his elbow down on the man in gray's neck.

The man in gray staggered to the floor. He caught himself on one knee, countered a brutal assault, regained his feet. He was still smiling, *still smiling*. But his opponent had single-handedly beaten Argus and Ribuld. Sweat ran from his face. The lanterns showed a glare of desperation in his eyes.

Shouts rang along the corridor. He made the mistake of glancing to see what they meant.

His opponent responded with a belly-thrust so swift it couldn't be parried.

He parried it.

The convulsive effort cost him his balance, however. Although he stopped the next blow with his blade, it was so powerful that it knocked him on his back.

For a fraction of a second, he was as helpless as Terisa.

Then Prince Kragen sprang into the struggle, whirling his bloody blade.

The Perdon was only half a step behind him.

The man in black flung a look of yellow hate at Terisa.

An instant later, he leaped back. His hands and sword made a strange gesture.

Without warning, he disappeared. Before the echoes of combat died, he was gone from the passage as completely as if he had never been there.

The Perdon gaped. Prince Kragen dropped his sword in stunned surprise. The man in gray regained his feet, hunting the air as though he thought he might hear or smell some sign of his opponent.

Shivering, Terisa got her arms under her and pushed her chest off the floor.

The Prince was breathing in harsh gasps, near exhaustion, but he went to look at his men. When he saw that one of them had been beheaded, he clenched his fists over his heart, and his face twisted into a snarl. "They were my friends," he rasped. "I was in your debt, my lady. But now I think I have made repayment."

The Perdon spat, "Pigswill!" He wasn't talking to Prince Kragen. "Who were they? How could they know we would be here?"

Braced on her hands and knees, Terisa watched her rescuer wipe his sword and sheath it, then kneel in front of her to help her to her feet. He had a nice smile—he was trying to reassure her—and his face was strong. It reminded her of someone. Nevertheless his eyes were clouded with trouble.

"My lady, I am Artagel. One of Geraden's numerous brothers. He asked me to watch over you. I haven't done very well.

"Apparently"—he grimaced—"someone really wants you killed."

The smell of blood on her clothes was so strong that she simply couldn't help fainting.

THIRTEEN: FOLLY
IN GOOD FAITH

hen she came to, she suffered a moment of disorienta-
tion. Half of her seemed to be standing up: the other
half was upside down. She thought she was going to fall,
but something hard held her by the waist.

"We were betrayed," the Perdon rasped. "Does this not make you
suspicious? Perhaps in Alend the word 'alliance' has another meaning. What better way to fill Mordant with dissension than by bringing violence to an unprecedented meeting between the lords of the
Cares and the Masters of the Congery? This ensures that we will not
be strong enough to defend ourselves."

"My lord Perdon—" Prince Kragen began in a dangerous tone.

"And if we are not strong enough to defend ourselves," the
Perdon snarled, "where else shall we turn for help, but to Margonal
and you?"

"Two of my friends are *dead*!" the Prince retorted. His diplomatic
self-control was badly frayed. "If I desired dissension in Mordant, I
would have one of the *lords* killed, not any of *my men*!"

As her eyes squeezed into focus, she saw that she was indeed
upright; but her arms and torso dangled toward the floor. The backs
of her hands scraped lightly on the cold stone. A forearm clasped
about her waist kept her from falling on her head.

"If you must have traitors," Prince Kragen went on fiercely, "I
advise you to look for them among your fellow lords. Who gains if
the Cares are not united against their King?"

"Precisely, my lord Prince," demanded the Perdon. "Who?"

"Any lord who can hope to become King directly, without disloyalty to Joyse. The Tor does not mean to return to Marshalt. Queen Madin has had considerable time to forge a bond between her husband and the Fayle. Is it inconceivable that the road to power may be shorter if it does not pass through a union of the lords with Alend and the Congery?"

"Are you all right, my lady?" Artagel asked. He was the one holding her.

Now she understood: he had put her in that position because she had fainted. He helped her pull herself upright, and she found that she was able to keep her balance. Watching her closely, he withdrew his hands from her waist. A glance down the passage showed her that he had moved her a short distance from the scene of combat. Her clothes still stank, but now she was able to stomach that. She took a deep breath, pushed her hair back from her face, and murmured, "I think so. Thanks."

He gave her a fleet smile and at once turned away. "The alternative, my lords," he said, striding toward Prince Kragen and the Perdon, "is that you were betrayed by an Imager."

"I would like to believe that," said the Perdon gruffly. He seemed to regard Artagel as an equal. "But only Master Eremis and Master Gilbur knew the place of our meeting. And it was Master Eremis who brought that meeting about. If he desired disunion among us, he did not need to go to such lengths. All that was required was to leave us alone." He paused, then said, "I cannot speak so positively for Master Gilbur."

"And I," said Prince Kragen, "did not know that Imagery could do such things. Is it not true that such a translation would require a flat glass? And is it not true that translation through flat glass produces madness? Who could have performed the feat we have witnessed?"

No one had spoken to Terisa. She wasn't sure they knew she could hear them. But she replied, "The arch-Imager. Vagel."

For a moment, the three men stood still. Then the Perdon growled, "As Master Eremis said. But who in Orison—or in all Mordant—would be foolish or vile enough to ally himself with that fiend?"

"Let us look, my lords." Artagel moved past the Perdon and Prince Kragen toward the nearest of the fallen attackers.

Terisa followed, walking warily back into the memory of bloodshed. Artagel was kneeling over the body when she drew near him. He turned it onto its back; she flinched at the sight of the gory wound in its chest. Nevertheless she watched as he pushed aside the cloak in order to inspect the dead man's face and armor.

The hardened leather chestplate was so black that she couldn't make out any of the details Artagel appeared to be analyzing. She didn't know what he was talking about when he suddenly tapped the covering over the dead man's heart and said, "Here."

"I lack your eyes," growled the Perdon. "What is it?"

"A sigil." Abruptly, Artagel rose to his feet. "I've seen it before." His eyes held no expression; his face looked as hard as the stone around him. "This man is a Cadwal. The sigil indicates that he trains with and serves the High King's Monomach."

"Gart?" Prince Kragen asked incredulously. "*Here?* Was that Gart you fought?"

"I don't know who I fought." Artagel's voice was like his face, blank and rigid. "Whoever he was, he beat me. But this man is one of Gart's Apts. The others must be the same."

"Entrails and carrion!" spat the Perdon. "An Apt of the High King's Monomach!"

"But *here?*" the Prince persisted. "How could such men come here? How could they gain admittance to Orison? They could not simply enter the gates. Castellan Lebbick is not so lax."

Artagel nodded curtly. "They must have come the same way their leader vanished."

"Vagel?" Prince Kragen scowled in frank dismay. "Why did we ever believe the story that he was dead?"

The Perdon had no answer. At the mention of Lebbick, he had jerked up his head as if he were reminded of something important. Now he glanced rapidly back and forth down the corridor, trying to watch both directions at once. "I have a better question. Do we wish to be found here when the Castellan comes?"

The Prince became instantly alert. "Will he come? Are we not beyond earshot of his nearest guard?"

"That spineless fop, the Armigite," explained the Perdon. His voice dripped venom. "When we heard the sounds of attack that brought me to your side, he fled in the opposite direction, yowling murder. He must have missed his way, or the Castellan would already be here. In any case, we have little time."

"He will question me, whatever I do," mused Kragen. "My men are dead. But if I am not here, he will not be able to connect me to this bloodshed." Promptly, he made his decision. "My lord Perdon, Artagel of Domne—I thank you for my life. But I will not remain with you, to give us all the look of treachery. My lady, farewell."

Retrieving his sword, he slapped it into its sheath and ran. Swiftly, the sound of his strides receded into the distance.

"I will leave you also," the Perdon said to Artagel. "I do not know what role this woman means to play in our doom, but I will not risk an accusation of treason to protect her."

Muttering angrily, "Cadwals? Horsepiss," he rushed away after the Prince.

Terisa looked at Artagel and saw that the gleam was back in his eyes; he was smiling again. In reply to her gaze, he bowed humorously. "For my part, my lady, I haven't got anything worth hiding. Whatever happens, all Orison will assume I had something to do with this many dead bodies. I'm afraid I have that kind of reputation —I don't know why. In any case, I have a better opinion of Lebbick than most people do. But there's no reason why you should have to spend the rest of the night listening to him sneer at you." He gestured down the passage. "Shall we go?"

Again, she said, "Thanks." She wished he would take her arm: she needed the support. "I don't think I can face him. He doesn't like me."

"Nonsense." As if guided by inspiration, he slipped his arm through hers and braced her companionably. His tone jollied her along. "You don't know him as well as I do. Our good Castellan only insults the people he likes. And if he likes you a lot, he becomes positively scathing. His wife—rest her soul—was the only person in Orison who was ever able to get civility as well as affection out of him."

Together, they moved through the gloom toward the next lantern.

Almost at once, they heard running feet.

He was undismayed. Still grinning, he drew her into a side passage and along a different route back toward the inhabited levels of the castle. With apparent ease, he avoided encountering the guards. In a shorter time than she was expecting, he brought her to the tower where her rooms were.

By then, she had recovered at least some grasp on the situation. Artagel had saved her life. Because Geraden had asked him to keep an eye on her. Now he was taking her away from a session with the grim Castellan, in which she would have had to lie and lie and lie to protect Master Eremis, Prince Kragen, and the lords of the Cares. She should have started thinking about gratitude some time ago.

Off the top of her head, she couldn't imagine many ways to thank Artagel effectively. At least one small one was clear to her, however. So far, they had been fortunate: they hadn't been seen closely enough to expose the mess that blood and dirty water had made of her clothes. But to reach her rooms she would have to pass within arm's reach of the guards outside her door—

At the foot of the stairway, she stopped and disengaged her arm. A bit awkwardly—she wasn't accustomed to making decisions in this way, with a tall, strong man smiling at her quizzically—she explained, "I can go alone from here. We've been lucky so far. I don't think you want to be seen with me."

He cocked an amused eyebrow. "I don't, my lady?" The events of the evening hadn't seriously ruffled his self-confidence. "Well, I admit you aren't as clean as you should be. But I don't choose my friends on the basis of accidents like that." He chuckled. "If I did, poor Geraden would be at the bottom of my list."

His smile was disarming, but she persisted. "That's not what I meant. The guards are going to notice"—she twisted her mouth in disgust—"the way I look. And someone is going to realize that a woman covered with blood must have something to do with all those dead men. If you're seen with me, you'll be implicated."

"I know you aren't worried about that. But you should be. How are you going to explain it to the Castellan?"

He was unpersuaded. Lebbick didn't worry him. And she couldn't ask him to lie, either for herself or for Master Eremis. So she shifted to a different argument. "Do you know what he did to Geraden the last time he caught him trying to give me independent protection?"

At that, Artagel frowned thoughtfully. "You have a point, my lady. He tried to explain why he doesn't trust the guards, but I didn't understand all of it. It had something to do with the orders King Joyse gave the Castellan? Or the way he interprets those orders?" He shrugged. "Geraden has always had a subtler mind than I do. Is it true that the guards don't even ask where you're going when you leave your rooms?"

Terisa felt a new touch of panic. So she wasn't imagining it: the guards *did* treat Geraden differently than the other people who came for her. She nodded mutely.

"That doesn't make sense," Artagel commented. Then he shook his frown away. "But I'm sure it will eventually. That's Geraden's only fault. I mean, aside from clumsiness. He's too impatient. Things always make sense eventually, if you don't think about them too hard."

Smiling again, he added, "But you're right. I don't want to get him in any more trouble. I'll leave you here." For a moment, his expression grew sober. "I'm still going to keep an eye on you. I take him seriously when he's that worried. And this time he has good reason. The High King's Monomach is training his Apts better than he used to. If you need me, I'll usually be somewhere nearby."

He put on a jaunty grin. With a graceful and humorous bow, he saluted her. "Rest well, my lady." Then he strode away.

She smiled at his departing back. As soon as he was gone, however, she began to shiver again, as if she had brought the chill of the lower levels up with her. Shock and reaction were setting in.

She was alone. She would have no defense if more men in black appeared suddenly out of nowhere to attack her.

She was going to have to face Castellan Lebbick by herself.

She wanted to sit down. Her knees felt too weak to hold her. But she put her feet on the stairs and forced her legs to take her upward.

When the guards at her door caught sight of her, they became immediately tense with concern. One of them said, "My lady, are you all right? Do you need any help?"

She couldn't meet their eyes. As firmly as possible, she said, "No, thanks. I'm fine."

Trying not to hurry, she went into her rooms. At once, she bolted the door. Then she checked to be sure that the entrance to the secret passage was still blocked.

After that, she kicked her moccasins away and flung off her clothes in a rush of revulsion, alarm, and determination, unable to bear the touch of drying blood against her skin any longer. First she took a bath, splashing icy water over herself as though she thought she could sting or shock herself into being brave enough for what she had to do. Next she scrubbed her clothes thoroughly, almost brutally, and set them out to dry in front of the fire.

She intended to be ready for Castellan Lebbick when he came.

But she couldn't stop trembling.

He came early the next morning, a barely polite interval after she had finished breakfast. She was wearing her dove-gray gown because a cowardly instinct told her it would make her look more vulnerable, less deserving of abuse. But she met him in her sitting room as bravely as she could.

As always, he wore the symbols of his office—the purple band around his cropped gray hair, the purple sash over one shoulder across his mail. But his real authority was expressed in the glare of his eyes, the stiff swagger of his movements, the thrust of his jaw. If he had held no position in Orison at all, he would still have commanded the room when he entered it.

"My lady." His tone was as subtle as an iron bar. "I trust you slept well after your adventures last night."

She was determined to lie to him. It would have been better to face him squarely, but that great a display of courage was beyond her. After all, she had never lied to an angry man in her life. "What adventures?" She cursed herself for sounding so small and weak, but perhaps that would work to her advantage in the end.

Castellan Lebbick, however, appeared to be unsympathetic toward small, weak women. "Don't be coy with me, my lady. I do my duty under a number of disadvantages, but stupidity isn't among them."

"I'm not being coy." That was true, at any rate. She was doing everything in her power to refrain from running into the next room and hiding under the bed. Or from blurting out the truth. "I went out with Master Eremis. I came back alone. We didn't have any adventures. You can ask him. He'll tell you the same thing."

"My lady"—he feigned a tiredness which didn't show in his eyes —"I have no taste for manure this morning. Whatever you were doing, my night was longer than yours, and when I went to my bed it was cold. Do me the courtesy of being honest."

Her resolve was crumbling: she could feel it. The promises she had made to herself were all very well—but what did any of this have to do with her? Her father hadn't raised her to be strong. "I *am* being honest," she said without conviction, already flinching in anticipation of his retort.

It came quickly. "Dogshit! You haven't spoken a true word since you arrived. By the stars, woman, you will answer me! The Armigite came squalling out of the abandoned foundations of Orison—where he never should have been in the first place—and insisted there was a battle going on. Naturally, he had no idea who was involved. He has rotten fruit for brains. But an investigation was required, so it was done. We found two men dead—Prince Kragen's bodyguards, by some towering coincidence—and enough blood for a small war. But we found no explanation."

For two or three heartbeats, her mind went completely blank. *Two* men dead? There should have been six. Four Cadwals. She was on the verge of crying out, I'm sorry I didn't mean it it wasn't my fault *what happened to the four Cadwals?*

Fortunately, Lebbick didn't pause. "I questioned Prince Kragen. He put on righteous indignation and accused *someone* of having his men murdered. *Someone*, he said, wants to provoke a war. *Someone*"— the Castellan's reference to King Joyse was unmistakable—"wants to be sure he returns to Alend with every conceivable provocation. On top of that, those bodyguards were *friends* of his."

He clenched his fists. "My lady, I know how to get the truth from men like him. Some of the old engines of torture have been preserved. Unfortunately, he's an ambassador. I can't touch him.

"You are another matter."

Abruptly, her head cleared. She didn't become less afraid, but a sense of urgency made what she was thinking sharp and precise. Four bodies were missing. Someone had taken them. Probably in the same way her attacker had vanished. So Castellan Lebbick didn't know there were Cadwals in Orison. He had no inkling of the truth. Master Eremis was safe. Artagel was safe. If she didn't lose her nerve.

Her voice was almost steady as she asked, "You mean you're going to torture me?"

Instead of answering directly, he snarled, "After my discussion with Prince Kragen, imagine my surprise when I learned that you had returned *alone*"—his tone was pure vitriol—"from your supper with Master Eremis and the mediator of the Congery—and that you were covered with blood."

He cocked his fists on his hips. "Do you want me to believe that Prince Kragen's bodyguards killed each other in a contest for your affections? Will you ask me to credit that you *happened* to wander down to that part of Orison, and you *happened* to find those two bodies in all the miles of corridors down there, and you *happened* to slip and fall while their blood was still warm—all by the most monumental coincidence? No, my lady. I won't have it. You returned here alone and covered with blood. But you told no one what had happened, when the common sense of a small dog would have led you to report it to the guards. Therefore you want to keep what happened secret. You have something to hide. I'll have *that*, my lady."

The lash of his outrage brought up an unexpected anger from among the secrets of her heart. How much sarcasm was she expected to swallow in one lifetime? "Your guards must have been mistaken," she retorted. "Maybe the shadows fooled them. Or maybe they were half asleep. I wasn't covered with blood. I've never been down there. I don't know what you're talking about."

When she was done, she wanted to give out a crow of joy which would announce to the world what she had achieved.

But the Castellan behaved as if she hadn't spoken—or as if he hadn't heard her. Lowering his voice until it sounded like the thongs of a flail being stroked between eager fingers, he said, "I am the Castellan of Orison and commander of the King's forces in Mordant. Do you wonder how I came to this high position? It's simple. Midway through his wars for Mordant's freedom, King Joyse found me prisoner in the stockade of an Alend garrison near the borders of the Care of Termigan. I was hardly more than a boy, but I had been wed"—his throat knotted—"for nearly ten days. Our families were farmers and peasants of Termigan, and those folk wed early. So I had been a married man for ten days—and of those ten I had spent six in the stockade. As it happened, the garrison commander had ridden across my little farm, noticed my wife, and taken a fancy to her. Because I was foolish enough to resist, I was imprisoned.

"But I wasn't mistreated. No harm was done to me." He bared his teeth. "I was merely held spectator, so that I had to watch the great variety of things that were done to my wife, by the commander as well as most of the garrison.

"Then King Joyse surprised the garrison. We were released."

The Castellan's voice sank as he spoke. "When he observed the zeal with which I took revenge upon the commander, he gave me work which put that zeal to good use. And when I displayed a talent for that work, I rose in his service.

"Now he has lost his mind"—Lebbick was barely whispering—"and it's my duty to preserve his life and power for the day when he may recover himself and need everything he entrusted to me. Don't tell me any lies, my lady. If you don't give me the truth, I'll tear it out of you."

Terisa's throat had gone dry. She had trouble finding her voice. "The King told you to leave me alone."

"My lady"—a touch of the whip—"I'm rapidly losing patience for the instructions of a madman. My King was in full possession of his wits when he made me his Castellan and commander. That's the responsibility I intend to fulfill."

In a strange way, he frightened and moved her at the same time. But she couldn't afford to feel either fear or sympathy. She had to find some way to defend herself.

"I'm sure you will," she said as if her small fund of anger were equal to his. "But I think you learned your moral sense from that garrison commander. I've told you what I did. Before you call me a liar, you ought to find out if I'm telling the truth. Look at my clothes. They're clean. Ask Master Eremis. *Ask* him. Or have you already decided he's a liar too, without bothering to check what he says? You want to do your job the easy way, by bullying the weakest person you can find. If you did a little work, you might learn something different."

Then she stopped and held her breath while her heart shook.

A look of pain clouded his glare. "That's enough, woman," he said thickly. "When you've suffered the way my wife did, I'll permit that imputation. Until then, you don't have the right. You are an enemy of Mordant and King Joyse, and you don't have the *right.*"

She wanted to babble, I know I don't I didn't mean it that way. The pressure to give up everything and tell him what he wanted to know was maddening. Somehow, however, she kept it under control. Instead, she replied, "No, I'm not. I'm nobody's enemy. Not even yours. We have one thing in common. I'm just a spectator. I don't have anything to *do* with any of this."

For a moment, his jaws clenched, and his eyes darkened, and she thought he was going to let out a blast which would rip her to the bone. Yet he didn't. He was more dangerous than that: he knew what to do with his anger.

"Have it your way, my lady. I'll talk to Master Eremis—I'll check your story. I'll *persuade*"—the word was a snarl—"that pig-brained Armigite to go over every step of his tale with me. I'll talk to every guard in Orison who may have encountered Prince Kragen's bodyguards—or seen where you were going with Master Eremis. I've already studied the place where those men died. They could not have shed so much blood. And at least four people walked through the blood while it was wet. One of them had feet the size of a lady's." Though the threat was unmistakable, he emphasized it by raising one hand and cupping it lightly over her cheek. "I'll have the truth. I don't care how."

Turning sharply, he strode out of the room. The door slammed behind him hard. He was capable of hitting her like that. If Master Eremis didn't somehow convince him that she was telling the truth, she would be at his mercy.

But she had kept her promises to herself. She had done it, *done* it: she had fended Lebbick away from the truth. There was still hope for Mordant. Because of what she had done. She, Terisa Morgan—a woman who had never learned how to believe in herself. She had made a *difference*. The idea made her want to start singing. She imagined herself going to the window, flinging open the casement, and shouting out to the world below her—the muddy courtyard, the roofs clogged with snow, the smoking chimneys, the guards patrolling the battlements—"I did it! I lied to the Castellan!" The vision struck her as so ludicrous that she laughed.

She was having such fun that the quick knock at her door didn't interrupt her. "Come in!" she called without so much as pausing to wonder who might be there.

It was Master Eremis.

He had Geraden with him again.

The Apt wore a baffled expression: he didn't know why he was there. Nevertheless Terisa was instantly glad to see him. Although she couldn't tell him what she had just accomplished, she was free to smile at him, and she did that with unfamiliar pleasure.

He grinned back through his confusion, then shrugged in the direction of Master Eremis.

The Imager was scowling as though he wanted no one to realize that he had never been happier in his life.

Closing the door quickly, he strode toward her in a hurry. He seemed to give off an electricity of excitement and urgency, so that simply being in the same room with him made her nerves tingle and jump, ready to go off in any direction. "The Castellan," he demanded in a rapid half whisper as he crossed the peacock rugs. "He was just here. Why?"

The question closed her throat like a hand clamped around her windpipe.

She knew immediately what he was after: he wanted to know how much of his night's activities had been betrayed to Lebbick. But she didn't know how to answer. Geraden was staring at her, perplexed and alarmed by her consternation. She had been warned to keep everything secret from him. How could she reply without putting his life in danger—and without exposing what the Master was trying to do?

Eremis reached her and caught hold of her shoulders, gripped them so hard that he nearly lifted her from the floor. "Tell me!" he hissed furiously, his eyes sparkling. "Why was Lebbick here?"

She felt his power so strongly that for just a moment, perhaps no more than one or two heartbeats, she was nearly overwhelmed by an irrational desire to say, Why did you leave me last night? I wanted to go back to your rooms. But he needed more than that from her. And Geraden was watching. He needed better—and didn't deserve to be hurt.

Meeting the Master's strange gaze, she said as clearly as she could, "He doesn't know anything."

"Nothing?" He cocked an eyebrow, eased his grip on her shoulders. "Then why was he here?"

At that, her tension increased to the level of fright. Suddenly, a new dimension of uncertainty was added to the situation. Perhaps Master Eremis didn't know what had happened after he left the meeting. If he didn't, she should tell him, make him aware that Apts of the High King's Monomach had the power to appear and disappear in Orison. But again she couldn't talk about such things in front of Geraden.

Geraden was watching her with frank worry. If he felt any personal pain over the fact that she and Master Eremis were sharing secrets, it was secondary to his direct concern for her.

She had to say less than she meant. Striving for nonchalance, she replied, "The guards told him I went out with you"—she darted a glance at Geraden—"and came back alone. That made him curious."

For a second longer, the Master studied her, searching for the truth behind her words. Then he let her go, turned away, and started laughing as if he were having the best time of his life. "Curious?" he chortled. "That old lecher. I will wager gold doubles to coppers that he was more than curious. He must have been *avid*."

Geraden looked away. A dull flush spread over his face.

All at once, Terisa was ashamed of herself.

Fortunately, Master Eremis' mirth was quick to subside. "Well, the stars have smiled on us," he said, resuming his haste. "I am certain that the Fayle spoke to King Joyse. So it follows that the King said nothing to Lebbick. Either our illustrious sovereign has lost the capacity to understand what he hears, or he does not believe it, or he is unable to achieve a decision. We must act while he leaves us time."

Immediately, he started for the door. Over his shoulder, he said, "The Masters are gathering. Come."

Terisa remained where she was. This was too fast. She still felt obscurely ashamed. And she hadn't told Master Eremis all the things he needed to know.

For that matter, why was the Congery in such a rush to meet? Hadn't Master Eremis stopped it from summoning the champion last night? What had changed since then?

But Eremis wasn't prepared to wait. From the doorway, he snapped, "Geraden, bring her!" and stalked out of the room.

That brought the Apt's gaze back to hers. In a hurry himself, he whispered, "Terisa," as if the words were being wrung from him, "*what* is going on?"

"I can't tell you," she replied. She was trying to make sense. "I want to. It's too much for me." But what she really wanted was to reassure him. "I don't know what he was laughing about. I didn't spend the night with him."

He looked away. At first, she thought he was still in pain. Then she realized that he was just trying to hide his relief. When he turned to her again, his expression was clear.

"We ought to go." He tried not to smile. "He told me to bring you. I won't be an Apt much longer if I start disobeying commands this simple."

He made her feel better. "All right," she said. "I really don't know what the Congery is going to do. But we might as well not get ourselves in trouble."

Enjoying his helpless, idiotic grin, she took his arm. Together, they went after Master Eremis.

On her way down the stone stairs, she missed her moccasins. They were warmer and protected her feet better than the delicate buskins Saddith had recommended. But her discomfort wasn't enough to make her go back.

When she and Geraden left the tower and entered the main halls, they caught up with Master Eremis: he had stopped to talk to someone. His stance briefly obscured who that someone was; as her angle of vision changed, however, she recognized Artagel.

"That's Artagel," Geraden whispered quickly. "I've mentioned him. He's one of my brothers. I asked him to keep an eye on you—give you some extra protection. I would introduce you if we weren't supposed to be in a hurry."

His words left a trail of electricity across her mind. So Artagel hadn't told Geraden about last night. And if he hadn't told Geraden, he probably hadn't told anybody. There was a real chance that Master Eremis didn't know she had been attacked.

Artagel was leaning casually against the wall, a smile on his lips, his sword prominent on his hip. He seemed to be sneering politely at something the Imager had said.

Master Eremis shook his head. "Artagel, Artagel," he murmured sadly, "I thought we were friends."

"So did I." Artagel's smile might have been an insult. "But Geraden assures me you're no friend of his—so I'm no friend of yours."

The Master turned a gaze Terisa couldn't interpret on Geraden. Then he looked back to Artagel. "Do you always let him choose your friends for you?"

Artagel laughed easily. "Always. He's my brother."

For a moment, Master Eremis stood motionless. His back was to Terisa; the only face she could see was Artagel's. Somehow, the confident mischief in his eyes increased his resemblance to his brother. Abruptly, Eremis strode away. As he left, he said, "Geraden is mistaken. I am a better friend than he knows."

Artagel glanced past Geraden and Terisa and shrugged eloquently. As if he were speaking to the air, he commented, "He wants to hire me. He thinks he needs protection. In Orison, of all places. I wonder what he's afraid of."

Geraden snorted. "Probably his friends."

Artagel went on smiling. "Speaking of friends, did you know Nyle is here?"

"No." Geraden sounded surprised.

"I met him by accident. He didn't seem especially pleased to see me. But I got him to admit he's been here for eight or ten days now. I have no idea why he made a journey like that in the dead of winter. He said he just wanted to get away from Houseldon for a while."

"Sounds like one of your expeditions," Geraden muttered. Then he added, "He must be hiding. Otherwise I would have run into him. Do you suppose he's in some kind of trouble?"

"That's what I thought." Artagel pushed himself away from the wall. "You should go. I don't think Master Eremis is feeling patient today.

"My lady." He gave Terisa a bow and sauntered off down the hall, heading away from the laborium.

At once, Geraden tugged her into motion. "He's right. We'd better hurry."

She went with him as quickly as her skirts permitted, but her brain was spinning. After a moment, she asked, "Isn't Nyle one of your brothers? Why would he come here in the middle of winter and then not try to see you?"

He shrugged without looking at her, as if the question were painful.

She let it go. Instead, she asked, "What kind of 'expeditions' does Artagel go on?"

This proved to be a safe topic. "Didn't I tell you about him? He says he's too lazy to be a regular soldier, but the truth is that he hates to take orders. So he does what you might call piecework for Castellan Lebbick. Whenever he's in the mood, he volunteers for something. The Castellan sends him all over Mordant—and probably into Cadwal and Alend, too, but nobody says that out loud. He just came back a few days ago from stopping a smuggler who was selling our crops to High King Festten's army suppliers.

"When I heard he was here, I couldn't resist asking for some help. Did I tell you he's the best swordsman in Mordant?"

She shot a glance of concern and sympathy at him which—fortunately—he didn't notice. His brother may have been the best swordsman in Mordant, but the man in black was better.

The idea that Artagel could be beaten by a man who appeared and disappeared in Orison at will gave her a shiver of trepidation.

Shortly, she and Geraden crossed the vacant ballroom to the corridor that gave entrance to the laborium and descended the stairs into the former dungeon. Soon they were walking along the passageway that led to the Congery's meeting hall. Ahead of them, Eremis and another Master entered the chamber. The guards saluted correctly—they certainly betrayed no sign that King Joyse or Castellan Lebbick knew what the Imagers had in mind. Nevertheless Terisa felt a tightening in her chest as she and Geraden followed Master Eremis.

Two or three more Masters arrived after she and Geraden did; then all the doors were closed and bolted, and the Imagers gathered around the curved circle of benches within the pillars. She was starting to recognize more of them by sight. All the familiar faces were there. Except Master Quillon. That surprised her. She expected—no, there he was, already seated partway around the circle from her. He nodded at the floor as though he were half asleep.

He was the only man in the hall who wasn't staring at Geraden, Terisa, and Master Eremis with some degree of confusion, curiosity, or indignation.

The light of the oil lamps and torches flickered, making the Masters appear hot-eyed and hollow-cheeked, spectral.

Then Terisa's attention was drawn to the open center of the chamber. Some of the Masters in her way sat down; others stepped aside to make room for Eremis. She saw the tall mirror which had been set ready on the low stone dais.

The mirror of the champion.

The scene in the glass had changed: the spaceship was gone. But hadn't Geraden told her that mirrors focused on *places*, not on *people*? Had the ship taken off? Or was it simply out of sight? The alien landscape certainly seemed unaltered, despite the shift of details: it was stark, red, and dim, composed of jagged old rocks and sand under the light of a dying sun.

The metallic figures were clustered in the center of the Image— and they were fighting for their lives.

Black flame as liquid as water and as flexible as whips licked at them from all directions. Three or four bodies sprawled around the scene, their machinery and flesh still smoking from great, ragged gashes. The remaining men used the rocks for protection as much as possible and struck back at the black flame with the incessant fire of their guns.

The champion was distinct among them. His gestures directed the fire of his companions, and his huge rifle gave out blasts that chopped the edges of the landscape into new configurations.

He conveyed an impression of desperation that Terisa hadn't seen in him before. For the first time, she realized that he, too, was someone who could be beaten.

But Master Eremis took a different view of the matter. Rubbing his hands together vigorously, he said, "Excellent! Whether he exists in his own right or is a creation of the glass, he will have no cause to complain of our translation."

"Master Eremis, you presume too much!" The mediator of the Congery stood beside the mirror, his fists braced on his large girth and his pine-colored face mottled with anger. Apparently, his fear of what Master Gilbur and the others proposed had concentrated into ire. "Your arrogance is offensive. You call us together in urgent haste, you have this glass brought before us, and once again you bring Geraden with you without permission—as if our course were already decided. Our course is *not* decided. You were deputized to speak for us before the lords of the Cares. You have not told us the outcome of that meeting. You have not told us what was said—what position the lords take. Our course cannot be decided until we have heard a full report, both from you and from Master Gilbur.

"Also the lady has no place in this," he added grimly. "Correct your presumption by sending her and the Apt away."

"Oh, presumption!" the guttural voice of Master Gilbur growled before Eremis could reply. "It is not presumption. It is survival. We must act or die. Stop trying to shirk the situation, Barsonage. The woman does not matter. But look at Geraden!" He made a hacking gesture with one powerful hand. Every eye in the chamber turned to the Apt. "He is fumble-footed and disastrous. But he has never been stupid. *Look* at him."

Geraden appeared unaware of the way he was regarded. He was chewing his lower lip and thinking so hard that the effort made his eyes look wild.

"Where else would you have him? You have already blurted out all the information he needs. In a moment, he will guess the import of what we propose—and then he will be on his way to inform the King. Here, at least, he will have no one to tell."

As if to prove Gilbur right, Geraden abruptly faced Terisa. At that moment, no one else in the room seemed to exist for him. What he was thinking filled him with dismay.

"Is that what you couldn't tell me?" he whispered. "They've decided to call the champion? And Master Eremis had some kind of meeting with the lords of the Cares?" An instant later, he went further. "But they waited until after the meeting. Master Eremis went to suggest some kind of alliance. The Congery and the lords against King Joyse?"

She couldn't help him. Her heart pounded in her throat as she felt the danger suddenly thicken around him, but there was nothing she could do.

"I've got to warn him."

So quickly that she had no chance to try to stop him, Geraden headed for the nearest door.

With unexpected speed, Master Gilbur pounced after the Apt. In an effort to reach him, Gilbur struck him from behind. The blow made Geraden trip, so that he slammed against one of the pillars and sprawled to the floor.

At once, Master Gilbur knotted one great fist in the back of Geraden's leather jerkin, and wrenched him to his feet. "No, whelp," he grated. "You have heard too much. Now you will hear it all."

Blood trickled from Geraden's temple. The impact of his head left a small red stain on the pillar. For a moment, he struggled as though his heart were breaking. But he couldn't twist away from Gilbur's powerful grip—and his jerkin refused to tear. The fight went out of him, and he sagged into submission.

Terisa wanted to rage at Master Gilbur. The fact that she thought Geraden was wrong made no difference. In misery, she met his dumb pain. "I'm sorry."

"It's not your fault," he replied dully. "Somebody told you I would be killed if I knew what was going on. Whoever that was, it's his fault."

Terisa looked around quickly. Master Quillon hadn't raised his head. But Master Eremis' face showed an instant of honest surprise.

He recovered rapidly, however. Frowning, he said, "She was told the truth, Geraden. You will not believe it—but I brought you here to save your life. Now that you cannot leave, you will live."

Immediately, he turned to face the rest of the Imagers.

"Masters, if you will sit down and compose yourselves long enough to hear me, I will tell you what happened at my meeting with the lords of the Cares—and why we must act without delay on our decision to translate our champion."

His manner was commanding; he emanated urgency. After a moment, Master Barsonage said between his teeth, "Very well, Master Eremis. So far I will go with you. But there is much that I expect you to explain."

Scowling dourly, he left the center of the circle to Eremis.

The other Masters followed his example. Before she could be separated from him, Terisa caught Geraden's arm. Master Gilbur's controlling grip forced the two of them to a seat on the bench. At the same time, Master Eremis strode toward the dais.

Almost at once, he began.

"Masters, I can make this quite simple." His tone was soft, but it seemed to carry an echo to the farthest reaches of the room. "Our meeting with the lords of the Cares was broken up without useful issue because they do not trust us. They believe that we serve King Joyse and wish only to entrap them. Or they believe that we serve ourselves and wish only to make them serve us also."

"And Master Eremis is accused of arrogance," one of the younger Imagers put in. "Are the lords not arrogant?"

As softly as possible, Terisa whispered in Geraden's ear, "Don't worry. King Joyse already knows."

He gaped at her in surprise.

"Of course," Master Eremis went on with deceptive sarcasm, "the discussion itself was not so simple. First I must inform you that I have been more 'presumptuous' than you know. When I learned of the outcome of his embassy among us, I invited Prince Kragen of Alend to the meeting."

At that announcement, several of the Masters stiffened. Eremis had their complete attention now. The mediator glared at him furiously but didn't interrupt.

"I cannot honestly say that I trust any representative of the Alend Monarch. But he protests that he desires peace. And I am certain that he desires to preserve us from Cadwal. For that reason, I considered that his presence would cost nothing at worst, and at best would open the possibility of a much stronger alliance than one uniting only the Congery with the lords."

"The Fayle told him," Terisa explained to Geraden. "About the champion, anyway. Not about the meeting."

"Then why—?" For a second, he forgot to whisper. But the sharp glares of the Masters—and Master Gilbur's grasp on his jerkin— reminded him. "Why doesn't he do something?"

Visibly mollified, Master Barsonage murmured, "You surpass yourself, Master Eremis. You are entirely presumptuous—but you are not thick-witted. I feared that this gamble would make the lords unwilling to heed you. Was I wrong?"

Eremis sighed. "That is the second matter I must explain. The lords were indeed unwilling to heed me, but not because of Prince Kragen's presence. In truth, I think they would have listened to him well if I had not been there. Their hatred of Alends is less than their distrust of Imagers."

Several Masters expressed surprise. Others muttered angry curses. But Master Eremis raised his hands to ward off their reactions. "I do not mean to be unjust. Prince Kragen himself was much interested in our proposal. The Perdon was interested, even eager. But as for the others—" He shrugged. "The Armigite has too little sense to know his own mind. And the Tor was too steeped in wine to have a mind."

"Don't you understand?" Terisa returned, trying to make herself clear to Geraden. "That's why Master Eremis doesn't have any choice."

His gaze was dark with pain. Apparently, he didn't want to understand her as well as he did.

"I believe the Termigan could have been persuaded, under other circumstances," Master Eremis continued. "With the Perdon, he might have been enough. We would have had a base on which to build. But it is all made hopeless by the intensity of the Fayle's prejudice against Imagery."

"The Fayle?" asked Master Barsonage. "He has the reputation of a reasonable man."

Master Quillon was paying close attention now. His eyes glittered at everything he saw.

"Oh, he is *reasonable*," Gilbur put in, "if you call it reasonable that he rejected everything we proposed simply because we mean to call our champion without King Joyse's approval."

Another Master protested, "Are you serious? Why did he think you were meeting in secret? Why did he accept your invitation, if the King's approval is so important to him?"

"To spy on us," Master Gilbur growled. "Why else?"

The mediator was staggered. "Is this true?"

"It is," Master Eremis said crisply. "He admitted his intention to inform King Joyse, so that we would be prevented from any exercise of our own judgment or will."

Startled out of concentrating on Geraden, Terisa thought, That's not really the way it happened. Is it? But it was. The more she tried to remember, the more she had to agree with Master Eremis and Master Gilbur. It was only her personal reaction to the Fayle's dignity that misled her.

"Then why," Master Quillon inquired unexpectedly, "has the King done nothing to prevent us?"

Suddenly angry, Master Eremis whirled to face Quillon. "You ask me to explain *his* decisions? If I had *that* power, I could save Mordant single-handedly."

"We can't explain them," an Imager who hadn't spoken before said urgently. "We've got to act—before Lebbick and his men get here to stop us."

Geraden's face wore an intent frown, as if he were listening hard.

"Very well." Master Barsonage rose heavily to his feet. "I have conceded everything else." He had an air of defeat; even his eyebrows looked wilted. "I concede the need for haste also. Be plain, Master Eremis. What do you propose?"

Eremis turned to the mediator. The way he pivoted, balanced himself, and faced Master Barsonage conveyed so much sharp energy that he seemed to give off sparks. His expression was too intense for Terisa to interpret.

"Translate our champion," he said. "Now."

Master Barsonage nodded. For a moment, he said nothing. Then he asked, "Why?"

Master Eremis was ready. "To prove our good faith. We are not heeded because it is believed that we have no commitment to anything except ourselves. Or because as the King's tools we have, in effect, lost our minds as badly as he has."

Now he raised his voice so that it throbbed and thrilled in the chamber, as clarion and moving as a trumpet. "We have no way to convince anyone otherwise except by taking single and unselfish action in Mordant's defense. Only by opposing the evil ourselves can we show that we are worthy of trust and alliance."

That might have been enough to gain what he wanted. It was enough for Terisa: his electricity and passion swept her with him. But Master Gilbur didn't leave it alone.

"In addition," he rasped, "we must consider the possibility that Prince Kragen and the lords came to our meeting for an entirely different reason. We were created by Joyse. He set an example for Cadwal and Alend to follow. They think we are to be used as they see fit, and they maneuver against each other in order to *possess* us." His hands made fierce fists on the railing in front of him. "They want to own us as if we were things instead of men.

"We have no swords or soldiers." His voice lacked resonance, but it had the force to be terrifying. "We can never protect ourselves *unless we show our power!*"

Through the silence which followed his shout, everyone heard the hammering at the door. It sounded like the haft of a sword or the butt of a pike belaboring the wood.

Everyone heard the command:

"In the King's name, open this door!"

For a fraction of a second, Terisa had time to wonder why King Joyse had changed his mind.

Then Geraden jerked up his head. "*The Castellan.*" At once, he tried to gain his feet, yelling, "Castellan Lebbick! Break down the door! Stop them!"

Gilbur jerked him back. With one stone fist, the Master struck him so hard across the side of his head that his whole body flopped soddenly. His eyes glazed.

Terisa froze. Everything was happening at once. King Joyse had finally made a decision. Master Eremis' plans were in danger. *Geraden was hurt.*

Most of the Imagers were on their feet, shouting at each other frantically; but Master Barsonage sank to the bench. His face had no strength left: he looked lost. "Then it must be done," he murmured to no one in particular. "Or else we will cease to exist."

"Gilbur!" Master Eremis barked. A grin bared his teeth. "Do it now!"

Master Gilbur dropped Geraden and hurried into the center of the chamber, toward the dais and his mirror.

Several of the Imagers cheered. Others dithered in alarm. They all got out of Gilbur's way, however. They crowded past the pillars toward the walls, as far as possible from Castellan Lebbick's hammering and the mirror.

Eremis took Master Gilbur's place, lifting Geraden from the stone and holding both him and Terisa with a grip they couldn't break.

The mirror faced them directly. Geraden plainly had no idea what was going on—he couldn't even hold up his head—but Terisa had a perfect view.

Master Gilbur put his hand on the frame and deftly began to adjust the focus of the glass. After one heartbeat, the champion was centered in the Image. After another, he seemed to sweep forward until he filled the mirror.

The pounding on the door had become a heavy, rhythmic thud. Terisa could hear wood cracking. But the ironbound timbers were too stout to yield easily. Between blows, Castellan Lebbick shouted,

"Master Barsonage! Imagers! By the stars, I will have this door open!"

Master Gilbur shot a glance toward Master Eremis.

"Translate him!" Eremis hissed.

Geraden stirred, shook his head. Blinking rapidly, he tried to clear his vision.

Master Gilbur braced his hands against the edge of the mirror as though he were preparing to pull the champion through by main force. His guttural voice rasped words Terisa couldn't understand.

"Got to stop him." Geraden sounded like he was choking. Somehow, he fell forward over the rail. Climbing unsteadily to his feet, he stumbled toward Master Gilbur.

Master Eremis was no longer holding Terisa. Had he tried to grab Geraden and missed? Lost his grip on her at the same time? She had no idea: she didn't see him. Her attention was concentrated on Geraden.

Swinging her legs over the rail, she went after him.

He was too late. If he hadn't been stupefied by Master Gilbur's blow, he would have seen that he couldn't reach the glass in time.

In front of him, the surface of the mirror went dark as the champion surged through it.

His armor made him at least seven feet tall. His head showed no face, but only a thick plate that must have been a visor. The metallic skin that protected him was scored black in several places: it had been breached at least twice. Acrid smoke curled from the wounds. He moved as if he were hurt.

But his huge rifle was ready. As he caught his balance on the dais, he aimed the muzzle straight at Geraden's chest.

Terisa got her arms onto Geraden's shoulders. He was so weak and woozy that her weight pulled him to the floor.

The first shot went over them. The Masters shouted. At least one of them screamed.

Trying to pull her legs under her, fighting to stand, she suddenly found herself staring down the barrel of the rifle.

For a period of time as quick and intense as a crisis of the heart, she watched the champion's metal-clad hand tighten on the firing mechanism.

Then he jerked up the barrel, and the blast hit the ceiling.

Broken stone began falling into the chamber.

The champion unclosed one hand from his rifle, gripped her neck,

and forced her down on top of Geraden. "Stay there." His voice
blared like a megaphone, but it was barely audible through the thun-
der of collapsing rock. "I don't shoot women."

The next instant, he started firing again.

In a rush, the entire ceiling came down.

BOOK TWO

BOOK TWO

FOURTEEN: OUT OF THE RUBBLE

 astellan Lebbick suspected that he was foundering inside. Of course, life in Orison had been going from bad to worse for some time now; but suddenly the purpose of his life had sprung leaks in all directions.

Because of the Congery's gamble, he had several crises to deal with at once. But they were only symptoms; they weren't fundamental. As he strode to face them, he was smiling like a hawk; and only his wife—and perhaps King Joyse—had ever known him well enough to realize that this smile was a bad sign. To other people, he probably looked like he was in his element, eager for the conflicts or disasters that would provide an outlet and a justification for his rage. Only his wife and his oldest friend could have understood the particular ferocity of his grin.

Unfortunately, his wife was dead—miserably dead, killed by a long, hacking illness that cut her life out as slowly and effectively as a knife in her lungs. Nearly a year had passed, and he still missed her so acutely that it seemed to make his guts tremble.

And King Joyse had cast him adrift.

He had refused to hear the Fayle. One way or another, he blocked every vital act, interfered with every hope.

The Castellan clenched his teeth tighter, stretched his smile thinner, and refused to think about it. King Joyse was his reason for living. The passions that had led to the founding of Mordant, the ideals that had inspired the creation of the Congery—these things were the blood in his veins, the air in his chest. He was the King's hands. The King had rescued him—

Now the King *had refused to hear the Fayle*. He had abandoned it all to die, Mordant and passion and purpose, abandoned it to die miserably, hacking its life out while Castellan Lebbick cradled it in his arms and couldn't let go.

No, he was definitely not going to think about that. He had too many other problems in front of him.

That woman.

To himself, he chewed out a long, scathing curse. She was in everything somehow. The connections were there, if he could find them: she was doing this to Orison and Mordant somehow.

And she made the back of his throat ache with a desire he hadn't felt since the days of his wife's best beauty.

He wasn't going to think about that, either. He was going to do his job, *cling* to it until he recovered what it meant.

For a start, he was going to sort out the consequences of the latest catastrophe perpetrated by those pig-brained Imagers.

His task had the advantage of being both dramatic and subtle. All the crises were linked together in some way.

First in point of time, if not in degree of urgency, there was the matter of Prince Kragen's dead bodyguards.

Clearly, they had been killed for *some* reason. And they couldn't have shed all that blood by themselves. Furthermore, it seemed unlikely that they were responsible for tracking their own blood away from the places where they lay dead.

And that woman had returned to her rooms liberally besmirched with blood.

There was a band of renegade soldiers—or worse—loose in Orison. They were skilled and numerous enough—or worse—to kill trained bodyguards and carry away their own dead or wounded. They had friends to conceal them. They had something to do with that woman. And their purpose was to instigate a war between Mordant and Alend. Or worse.

That brought up other matters. What had happened to the man in black who had tried to kill her during the night after her arrival? He had escaped easily enough. Why hadn't he made another attempt?

What came next? An attack on the King himself?

And King Joyse *had refused to hear the Fayle*. The old lord had tried to warn the King of the Congery's intentions, and the King had refused to hear him. The Fayle had spoken directly to the Castellan because he had no other recourse.

Which raised the question of how the Fayle had come to know what those Imagers meant to do. He had flatly declined to answer when Lebbick had demanded an answer.

As for the Congery's crazy defiance of King Joyse's prohibition against forced translations, Castellan Lebbick knew who was responsible—or, more accurately, he knew whom he could blame. He had compelled the Fayle to mention a name or two. But they would have to wait. The results of that translation posed more immediate problems.

Apparently to defend them against Alend or Cadwal, the Imagers had chosen some alien man of war whom they had discovered in their mirrors—a soldier of commanding power, weaponry, and fierceness. So what did they expect after snatching a fighter like that out of his own life? A docile bow? A humble offer of service? They were lucky he had simply brought down the ceiling of their meeting hall, instead of murdering them individually as they deserved.

Judging by the way he had blasted an escape up out of the laborium and through the thick northwest wall of Orison to open air, he was certainly powerful enough to have murdered any number of people. In fact, Lebbick had at first feared he would turn and attempt to raze the castle itself. If that had happened, the Castellan would have had no choice but to hale whatever Imagers he could find to the defense. Completely unforewarned, his own forces and siege engines weren't in position for war.

Fortunately, the champion kept on going—away from Orison, lumbering madly through the snow like a rogue animal. Something about the way he moved suggested to Castellan Lebbick's experienced observation that he was hurt.

That left two exigent dilemmas, neither of which was the gaping breach in the wall. Of course, the breach was an enormous problem, and it was going to become urgent—but not yet. First the champion had to be pursued. That was obvious. His location had to be known, so that some effort could be made to control him, stop him. His present rampage would take him through the most densely populated region of the Demesne straight toward Batten and the heart of the Care of Armigite.

On the other hand, Master Quillon kept harrying the Castellan's heels like a ferret, thrusting his dust-caked face forward whenever

Lebbick paused and shouting that the woman and Geraden had been buried under the collapse of the ceiling.

Castellan Lebbick bared his teeth. "Do you mean you think they're still alive?"

"I don't know!" returned Quillon. "But they won't be if you don't get them out!"

Lebbick debated the question with himself. He didn't have enough men available to both pursue the champion and dig effectively in the rubble. Some time would be needed to call up reinforcements from the encampments among the hills around Orison.

One of those encampments, however, lay reasonably close to the path the champion appeared to be taking.

Without hesitation, the Castellan did his job. He sent one aide to summon all the guards of the castle to the ruined meeting hall. Another ran for the courtyard to get a horse, bearing explicit instructions for several detachments of the King's forces. Then Lebbick turned back to Master Quillon.

"This will be slow. We can't shift all that stone in just a few hours." Gauging the relative positions of the chamber and the breach, he commented, "It'll have to be shifted uphill. If that woman and Geraden aren't dead yet, they'll suffocate soon." Almost without malice, he added, "Unless you and the rest of the Congery can think of some way to be helpful for a change."

Unaware that he was smiling, he strode away.

Quillon went to find Master Barsonage.

He located the mediator on the floor outside one of the doors of the chamber. Those doors had saved the Congery. Not knowing what to expect from the champion, the Masters had retreated to the walls, and so they had been able to reach the doors almost instantly. As a result, only two of them were dead: one hit by the champion's first blast; another fallen under a block of stone. The rest were safe—including Master Gilbur and Master Eremis, although no one knew how they had contrived to get away in time.

But Master Barsonage didn't look particularly safe. He was covered with dust, chips of stone, and flakes of ancient mortar—as Quillon was himself—which gave him the appearance of a derelict. The rims of his eyes showed red through the caking dust; his mouth hung open; he sat with his hands dangling between his knees. He might have been in shock from a wound that didn't show because it was hidden by dirt.

"Barsonage!" snapped Master Quillon. "Get up! We must hurry."

For a moment, Master Barsonage didn't respond. He stared sight-lessly past Quillon as though the ruin of the chamber had made him deaf. But when Master Quillon began to fume, the mediator raised his head and blinked.

"Quillon," he croaked in recognition, his voice husky with dust and dismay. "I knew it was a mistake. From the first. We should never have tampered with someone that powerful. But there was no alternative. Was there? The augury—And everyone was against us. The lords, Cadwal and Alend, King Joyse—"

He lowered his head again. "It was a mistake."

"Never mind," Master Quillon cut in impatiently. "We all make mistakes. Come *on*."

Master Barsonage gave Master Quillon a look of blank incompre-hension.

"Geraden and the lady Terisa!" Quillon was practically hopping from foot to foot. "They are buried under all that stone!"

The mediator's expression didn't change. "So is Gilbur's glass. It is powder. We have no way to undo what we have done. Geraden's mirror has shown that it does not translate properly. And any other glass will be a sentence of death, either for our 'champion' or for the Image that receives him."

"Mirrors preserve us! Wake *up*, Master Barsonage! Forget the champion. We must rescue Geraden and the lady! Castellan Leb-bick's men will make the attempt, but it will be too slow. All that stone must be moved up and out. *It will be too slow*."

Slowly, Master Barsonage began to understand. "They cannot be alive," he muttered. "Under all that? It is impossible."

"They must be!" shouted Master Quillon so hard that his voice squeaked. "We have no other hope! *Come on!*"

Urgently, he reached down and tried to pull the much larger Imager upright.

For a moment longer, the mediator seemed unable to achieve enough resolution to get his legs under him. But then he muttered, "I suppose we must. Even if it is hopeless. After this disaster, how else can we show our good will?"

Puffing dust, he heaved himself to his feet.

As quickly as possible, Quillon took Master Barsonage toward the warren of converted cells where the mirrors of the Congery were displayed and protected. After a certain amount of dithering, the

mediator chose the glass Master Quillon had had in mind all along—
the tall mirror reflecting a fathomless seascape, nothing but water in
all directions. Strong under his girth, Master Barsonage picked up
the glass without assistance and carried it back to the meeting hall.

He was starting to move faster. His carriage became steadier.
When he and Master Quillon encountered other Imagers—retreating from the debacle, milling around in the halls—he issued commands with increasing authority, summoning the rest of the Congery
to his support.

The two Masters soon reached the chamber.

The nearest door stood open, letting winter blow dust and cold
and snow into the corridor.

Inside, the pile of rubble was substantial: it reached halfway to
where the ceiling had once been. To the stone of that ceiling had
been added a wide portion of the level above it, as well as all the
damage the champion had left behind him on his way up to and
through the outer wall. Much of the mound was composed of cut
granite—ponderous foundation slabs, huge monoliths from the inte-
rior of the walls and pillars, smaller pieces which the builders of
Orison had used like bricks—but the champion's rifle had reduced
enormous quantities of rock to powder and pebbles.

Now Master Quillon understood the Castellan's point better. The
only way the guards could clear the space was by somehow transport-
ing the rubble up and out of the hole. Even with the help of every
appropriate mirror in Orison, the job might take all day.

The whole place was in gloom, blocked from light by Orison's
bulk and the thickening snowfall. Nevertheless he could see the
cloud-clogged morning sky, the pall of dust in the air, the guards and
other servants of the castle who had already arrived and begun fighting the pile with shovels, picks, and crowbars.

He could see Artagel on top of the mound, wrestling like a madman to shift blocks and shards nearly as large as himself. His curses
sounded like cries.

At once, Master Quillon clambered up the side of the pile toward
Geraden's brother. Encumbered by the mirror, the mediator followed more slowly.

When he reached Artagel, Quillon caught at his arm. Artagel
brushed the Master aside without a glance. The fixed wildness in his
eyes made him look dangerous.

"Make room, Artagel!" barked Master Quillon. "We can do this better. It will be of no help to Geraden if you rupture yourself. We can reach him, but we need cooperation, not stupid single-mindedness."

"He is my brother," Artagel panted between exertions.

The Master spat an obscenity that sounded silly, coming from him. "I do not care if he is your mother, your father, and the bastard offspring of every act of fornication in all the history of Mordant. Help us or get away."

Artagel's fists clenched murderously; he forced them to relax. "Show me, Imager," he breathed through his teeth. "Show me you can do better."

By this time, Master Barsonage had gained the top of the mound. Master Quillon rasped at Artagel, "Then make room," as the mediator positioned his mirror beside the block Artagel had been trying to move.

Quillon helped hold the glass. While the mediator murmured the invocations that had gone into the shaping of this mirror, the two Imagers lowered the glass toward the block—

—and the block was translated away into the rolling sea.

Artagel gaped for a second. Then he started to grin.

More Imagers and many more guards were arriving. Several of the Masters had mirrors with them, Eremis among them. Master Quillon noticed Gilbur's absence; but he had no time to worry about that. While he and Master Barsonage shifted their glass, he shouted instructions to the guards. Rapidly, they organized themselves into teams around each mirror. Someone threw a shovel up to Artagel. At a nod from Master Barsonage, he began heaving rubble at the mirror, working to clear an approach to the next large piece of granite.

Powder and pebbles and hunks of rock large enough to shatter any glass passed into the Image and were swallowed by the sea. If Master Quillon had cared to do so, he could have watched the splash as each shovelful of rubble hit the water.

Glancing around the pile, he recognized the other mirrors as they were put to work. Only two of them were as large as the one he and Master Barsonage held, but they had all been intelligently chosen: none were flat; none showed scenes where the sudden appearance of huge heaps of rock would do any damage. The only possible exception was the glass Master Eremis employed with the flustered assistance of a young Apt. It reflected a gigantic and ravenous sluglike beast, with fangs that looked poisonous and malign eyes. The guards around Eremis shoveled rubble straight into the creature's face.

The creature appeared to be roaring in fury.

"Quillon!" Master Barsonage demanded. "Pay attention!"

Hurriedly, Master Quillon helped the mediator adjust his mirror to translate another large chunk of stone.

"Is there a chance?" Artagel asked. "Can they really be alive down there?"

"They must be," Quillon averred again. That conviction was becoming harder and harder to sustain, however.

Terisa knew she was alive.

The scant air she was able to draw into her lungs was thick with dust: they were full of it, and whenever that dry suffocation forced her to cough, the pressure against the edges and corners of rock gouging her chest threatened to crack her ribs. Every breath raised grit into her face, scouring her eyeballs, blinding her to the darkness. And she could feel the weight of the rubble pressing down on her, slowly compressing her until her weak flesh and bones would burst and break. In addition, the rocks were hot, charred by the champion's rifle. The air was so warm it ached.

She knew she was alive. But she had no idea why.

The champion had pressed her face-down on top of Geraden: she had been in no position to observe the way his metal-clad form and his destructive fire shielded her from the worst of the stone-fall. Blocks of stone came down on him and bounced aside, forming a pocket around her; slabs of rock were cut into pieces and powder which made a cushion over her body and Geraden's. In consequence, when he turned away to burn a path for himself out of Orison, the rubble that fell immediately onto her and Geraden came, not from the ceiling and the upper level, but from the sides of the protective pocket. And smaller pieces wedged the fall securely enough to hold it in place as more and more debris from the champion's rampage was added to the pile.

She was still breathing. Against all likelihood, there was still air trapped in the stone heap.

It wasn't going to last.

With a palpable shift, a hard ridge clamping the middle of her back pressed down another fraction of an inch. She struggled frantically, but couldn't move anything more than her fingers. The heat and the dust made her want to gag on each shallow breath she sucked through the rocks. Pain like the caress of flame increased in her lungs, her eyes, her outstretched limbs. To die like this, slowly, feeling it happen moment by moment, feeling the hurt grow worse with each feather-width change in the poise of the rubble—

Something like this had happened to her before. Sometimes, when her mother and father had been angry at her, they had locked her in the closet. No one had answered her cries, her timid or hysterical appeals, until she had been quiet long enough to appease her parents. And once—for an offense which might have been heinous or trivial—she had been thrust into the back of the closet and armfuls of clothes had been tossed in on top of her before the door was locked, so that the house would be insulated from any protest she might make.

There in the dark, she had had her first experience with fading.

The clothes had choked her, and the dark was locked and absolute on all sides; and suddenly she had understood that her distress and panic meant nothing, that sensations like fear and asphyxiation meant nothing—that the locked door and the piled clothes and the dark made her unreal. For the first time, she had felt herself losing reality, felt her existence leeching out into the enshrouding blackness.

She hadn't realized it at the time—perhaps she had never realized it—but this response to the crisis had protected her. It had prevented the dark and her parents' unlove from creeping *in*.

This time, unfortunately, there was no protection. Her mind was going to snap. She could feel a crazy desire to scream rising from the bottom of her stomach. Then she would inhale so much dust that the effort to breathe would tear her heart.

"Geraden." Her voice was a whisper, as desperate as the powder burning in her lungs. "Geraden. Can you hear me?"

But of course he couldn't hear her. She had been lying on top of him, but not in a position that afforded him any protection. And he had been on his back, facing the stone-fall. His head must have been crushed immediately. He must still be under her somewhere, but nothing there felt soft enough to be a body.

"Geraden." Her mind was definitely going to snap. "Geraden."

There was a way out, however. It came to her without drama, almost without surprise. She could fade now. She could let go of herself, of her long struggle against unreality, and allow the darkness to bear her away. Then she would be safe. Whether she lived or died, she would be safe because she would be gone.

As soon as the idea occurred to her, she knew it would be easy. That kind of failure would be easy. It had been calling out to her all her life, offering to protect her—offering her peace.

"Terisa?"

The word was a rustle of dry pain, so far away that she couldn't believe it.

"Terisa!" Impossibly weak, hurt, crushed—and stubborn, determined to reach her. "Are you all right?"

Sudden weeping closed her throat. Now she couldn't escape. Safety was impossible. He was here with her. She was too relieved to hear his voice. She had to stay.

"Terisa?" He fought to control his alarm. "Are you all right?" he coughed. "Can you hear me?"

"Geraden." Raw strain knotted her chest. "I can't breathe. I can't stand it."

"Don't try so hard." His whisper came to her from some place entirely out of reach. "Take shallow breaths. Make yourself relax. I'm getting air from somewhere."

Despite the awful distance between them, she could hear his distress. He, too, was being crushed.

"We're going to be rescued. They'll dig us out. All we have to do is wait."

"I can't. Can't." The pressure of rejecting her one chance for escape drove her toward hysteria. "Can't move. It's breaking my back. Geraden!"

"Don't think about it." His voice sifted like dust between the stones. "Put it out of your mind."

"I can't." She locked her teeth to keep from screaming.

"You can." Somehow, he managed to speak more strongly. "Nothing to it. Think about something else. Tell me what happened. I don't remember anything—after Master Gilbur hit me. Did he translate the champion? Did the Castellan stop him?"

Just for a moment, he startled her out of her panic. He didn't remember—? He had come back to consciousness without any notion of where he was or why—

"Terisa."

Until she heard the edge of need in his appeal, she didn't realize how much he was depending on her. If he lost her now, he, too, might start screaming.

Deep inside, she wailed, I can't I'm being crushed *I can't stand it!* Let me *go!* But she struggled to do what he was doing, struggled to think about him instead of herself. He didn't even know how he had come to be buried alive. "I'll try."

In quick, broken phrases, pieces of explanation like her breathing, she described the outcome of Master Gilbur's translation.

When she finished, he groaned, then fell silent. Before she could panic again, however, he said, "That proves one thing. You're definitely the one. The one who's going to save Mordant. The champion."

"What?" she panted. "What're you talking about?"

"It was always possible"—the words came out as if he were retching them—"you were just an accident. I went wrong somehow. But that means Master Gilbur was right. Now we know he wasn't. His champion isn't going to rescue us.

"You must be the real champion."

"That's crazy." She could feel the bones of her spine being squeezed to chips and splinters. The air was getting worse. *You can. Think about something else.* "Nothing's changed. I'm not an Imager. I don't understand anything. Master Eremis is the only one who can save Mordant."

The words trailed away. If he were still alive—He was right behind her when the champion emerged. Wasn't he? What if the collapse of the ceiling caught him? What if he were dead? A pang made her twitch against the press of stone. The ridge across her back settled closer to her.

"Master Eremis." Somehow, Geraden managed a snort. "You think he can save Mordant? If you can make me believe that, you don't need Imagery. You're powerful enough already."

She bit her lips to keep from crying out, I can't stand it!

When she didn't respond, he changed his approach. "Maybe you should tell me the stuff that was supposed to get me killed. I want to understand"—he seemed to be gritting his teeth—"why you trust Master Eremis."

"All right." I can't! *You can.* His voice was the only thing that kept the rock from breaking her apart.

With a clench of will, she fought to push the pain and the dust out of her mind, the close heat, the immuring weight of the stone. To take their place, she fixed her attention on images of Geraden—the line of his cheek, the way his hair curled above his forehead (*the blood trickling from his temple, the way Master Gilbur hit him, that good face smashed under the rubble*— No! not that, don't think about things like that), the quick potential for happiness and misery in his eyes. He was the reason she couldn't fail, couldn't fade. Picturing him helped her remember the things he wanted to know.

Her account was erratic, filtered and altered by the press of rock. Nevertheless she told him everything as well as she could. She related what he had already surmised about the decision of the Congery to translate its champion, as well as to send Master Eremis and Master Gilbur to a meeting with the lords of the Cares. Master Eremis had arranged that meeting, but had opposed the translation of the champion. Master Quillon was the one who had warned her not to talk to Geraden. *You can.* The meeting and its outcome. What she could remember about Prince Kragen. The attack of the man in black.

When she was done, she held her breath for a moment, hoping that would ease the pressure in her chest. But it didn't.

Geraden's reaction surprised her. Sounding even more distant and forlorn, he murmured, "So Quillon's a traitor."

"What do you mean?"

"He warned you not to talk to me because he knew I would tell King Joyse about that meeting. And about the champion."

"No." The dust was turning to stone in her lungs. She couldn't maintain her equilibrium, could not— "If you put it that way, all the Masters are traitors. They voted for the champion *and* the meeting. Master Quillon is just more loyal to them than to King Joyse. And he's been trying to keep you alive."

Geraden, help me.

He considered for a while. "There has to be a traitor on the Congery." The pain in his voice was growing stronger. "The man who attacked you had to know where you were going to be. That leaves out the lords and Prince Kragen.

"Ah!" he groaned sharply.

A moment later, however, he continued at a higher pitch, "Even if Eremis told them he was going to bring you, none of them knew you existed when you were attacked the first time. Only the Congery. And for that man to just disappear—It takes Imagery. Some Master wants you dead. He knows you're the only one who can save Mordant.

"If it isn't Quillon, it must be Eremis."

"No," she said again. *That isn't what I meant. You don't understand. I need him.* The rubble shifted again. She thought she could feel her ribs starting to give. *I need him to teach me who I am.*

On the other hand, the air seemed to be cooling. That was one small blessing, at any rate.

"He's trying to *save* Mordant. Can't you see that? He's trying to make alliances. Find ways to fight. Because King Joyse won't."

"No, I don't see that," Geraden replied distantly. "Don't you think it was odd for him to take you to that meeting? You didn't know he was going to do that. How could the man who attacked you know? And why did he rush off and leave you? Maybe he went to use the mirrors so that man could appear and disappear."

"No. No." *You don't understand. Pressure. Dust. I put on the sexiest gown I could find and went to his rooms by myself. Come on* —*think* *about it.* "You aren't being fair. You were with him this morning. When he came to get me. You saw the way he behaved. *He didn't know I was attacked.*

"It had to be set up in advance. How could he know how the meeting was going to turn out? He wanted it to succeed. He certainly didn't sabotage it."

"The Fayle was there," Geraden muttered. "He wouldn't have anything to do with illicit Imagery. Everybody knows that."

She wasn't listening. Her concentration was focused on what she was trying to say. It was important—she knew it was important. *You can.* If she survived this—and Master Eremis survived it—she had to talk to him right away. He needed to know there was a traitor on the Congery. "And how could he know where King Joyse would put me? The first attack had to be set up in advance too. But none of the Masters knew you were going to find me instead of the champion."

Geraden coughed thinly. Then she heard him gagging.

Instantly, everything else rushed out of her head. He was being crushed. "Geraden! Are you all right? What's wrong?"

For a time, he didn't answer. She saw him in her mind, dangling from Master Gilbur's grasp, falling, always falling, his head a smear of blood and splinters of bone. Again she struggled crazily, helplessly, to move.

"*Geraden.*"

"I'm sorry." To her amazed relief, he sounded better. "I didn't mean to scare you. The rock keeps shifting. It came down harder on my throat for a while. Are you having an easier time breathing?"

At first, she had no idea what he meant. If anything, the dust was thicker than ever. But then she realized that the air had become cooler—noticeably cooler than the rubble piled around her. It was almost cold.

"They're coming," he said. "They're going to rescue us. We're going to be rescued."

Unable to control herself, Terisa burst into tears.

It seemed to take forever. Then it happened all at once. The air grew colder and colder, cooling the rocks, cooling the desperate pressure in her lungs; but there was no other change except an increase in the shifting. That nearly pushed her into panic: every subtle movement threatened to break the bones of her back. She couldn't keep from sobbing. Nevertheless Geraden's nearness helped her. And she knew how to hang on when every part of her seemed to be fading.

And suddenly the weight on her simply vanished as though it were no longer real. She heard voices; more stone vanished. Hands came scrabbling through the debris to grab her arms with alarmed roughness and haul her upright.

She was still crying, but the tears washed the grit out of her eyes. She got her vision back in time to see Artagel pull Geraden out from under the place where she had been lying.

Master Quillon held her. "Are you all right, my lady?" He seemed to be weeping himself. "Are you all right?" His concern sounded as wonderful as the grip of his arms, and the cold, open air full of snow, and the freedom to move.

Geraden clung to his brother and coughed as if his lungs were torn. Yet he was breathing. Nothing about him looked crushed. Dust hid the traces of blood on his temple.

Falling snow made the air as dim as twilight, but she could discern what was left of the Congery's meeting hall. Beyond the shattered stumps of the pillars, the doors were open. Enormous quantities of broken stone still covered the floor. At least a dozen Masters—and many guards with shovels, picks, and crowbars—stood holding mirrors among the debris.

She caught a glimpse of Master Eremis; then he strode away as if he were in a hurry.

Abruptly, Artagel shouted, "We did it!" and the guards dropped their tools and started cheering.

"It was a terrible mistake," muttered Master Barsonage. Behind the dust caking his face, his eyes were red with weariness. He gripped a tall mirror that she recognized—the glass with the reflected seascape. The mediator's shoulders shook in exhaustion. "We should never have risked that champion. We were all mad. Castellan Lebbick has fifty men chasing him, but I doubt they will be enough. Still, we have been luckier than we deserve. We have lost only two Masters." He named men she didn't know. "And you are alive.

"Please forgive us, my lady," he finished unsteadily. "We were stupid—but we did not mean you harm."

Geraden rubbed a cloud of dust from his hair. "Tell that to Master Gilbur." He was smiling. "If he had hit me any harder, he would have broken my neck." But he seemed unable to keep his eyes in focus. "With your permission, my lady," he said to Terisa, "I think I'll lie down for a while."

Smoothly, as though it were the most graceful thing he had ever done, he fainted in Artagel's grasp.

There was a gaping breach in the ceiling of the chamber, and that section of the level above it had been gutted; but the worst damage was off to the side, where the champion had burned his way up and out through the wall. Snow swirled inward on an eddying wind. It was falling heavily enough to gather in Master Quillon's hair and form clumps on the mediator's wide shoulders.

Geraden believed that she was going to save Mordant.

When she looked up into the snow, she thought she heard the distant thrill of horns.

FIFTEEN:
ROMANTIC NOTIONS

S he was shivering. The temperature of the air seemed to drop rapidly—although that was just reaction, she knew, just her body and mind suffering the consequences of what she had been through. Her gray gown, so warm and self-effacing earlier, now gave her no protection at all. Granite dust coated every fiber of the material, covered every inch of her skin, made her hair feel like ruined wool.

On the other hand, she was able to understand why Geraden had fainted.

But someone thrust a rude, soldier's goblet in front of her face. She took it and swallowed deeply because she thought it contained wine.

The liquid turned out to be harsh brandy. A spasm knotted her chest. When she was done coughing and gasping, however, she felt better. More dirt had been washed from her eyes, and her lungs were clearing. She felt warmer.

Geraden remained unconscious. Artagel had stretched him out on the rubble, and a man in a gray doublet and baggy cotton breeches was examining him. After listening to his chest and feeling his pulse, the man sponged the dirt from his face, noticed and cleaned the wound on his temple, then took a vial from a leather satchel and poured some liquid between his lips.

Rising to his feet, the man announced quietly, "He sleeps." Apparently, he was a physician. "He does not appear seriously hurt.

Take him to his bed. Let him rest for an hour or two. Then awaken him for a bath and food. If he has any complaint—or if he is difficult to awaken—I will come at once."

Artagel nodded, and the man turned to Terisa. "Are you hurt, my lady?"

She tested her arms and legs. They felt unnaturally stiff, and she couldn't stop shivering, but nothing was damaged.

The physician watched her analytically. "Bruises and headaches must be expected. But if you discover any deep pains or swelling—or if you suffer dizziness or prolonged faintness—you must send for me."

Taking his satchel, he left the chamber.

Artagel scooped Geraden into his arms. "Take care of him," Terisa murmured. He gave her a smile and moved away, carrying his brother easily.

"Come, my lady." Master Quillon was still supporting her. "We will return to your rooms. You, too, will profit from rest, a bath, and food."

"Yes," sighed Master Barsonage. "We must all rest. And think. We must find some way to combat this champion. Now that his proper glass is broken, we have no good weapon against him."

Leaning on Master Quillon because her legs seemed to have developed ideas of their own, Terisa let him help her out of the meeting hall.

As soon as they gained the relative privacy—and the warmer air— of the corridors leading out of the laborium, she asked the question that was uppermost in her mind. "Is Geraden safe now? Do his enemies have any reason to kill him now?"

He hesitated momentarily. "My lady, let me first explain that I do not know what the enemies of Mordant hope to gain by the presence of this champion. For that matter," he added, "I do not know what *we* hoped to gain. I abide by the decisions of the Congery because I am an Imager—but that decision I do not understand. He appears to be a danger without aim, allegiance, or purpose. As such, his actions will be random in effect. Perhaps they will aid our enemies, perhaps us.

"Nevertheless," he continued, "it is clear that Geraden's immediate peril is now less. If you were to tell him everything you have heard, what action could he take that would threaten those who do not wish him well?

"And yet, my lady," he said pointedly, "the *reason* for his peril—I have never been able to say what that is. I do not know what it is that makes him a threat to his enemies, and so I cannot claim that their malice against him has been made less. The reason for his peril remains."

Master Quillon's words drew a shudder from her; but she accepted them. She needed to keep her mind moving. Since he seemed willing to talk, she asked, "Why didn't King Joyse stop them? Why did he wait so long before sending Castellan Lebbick?"

The Master cleared his throat uncomfortably. "My lady, the Fayle tried to warn King Joyse, but he was not heard. The King refused. Castellan Lebbick had no orders to intervene. He acted upon his own initiative, after the Fayle spoke to him."

"But why?" she pursued. "I thought King Joyse opposed that kind of translation. I thought that was one reason he created the Congery in the first place—so he could have all the Imagers in one place and make sure they didn't do any more involuntary translations."

Master Quillon gave a snort of exasperation. "If I were in a position to explain our King's actions and inactions, Mordant's need would be very different than it is now."

That was the best answer she was able to get out of him.

He took her through frightened, tense, and curious crowds in the direction of her tower. When they reached her suite, they found the doors unguarded.

"Wonderful!" he muttered angrily. "By the stars, this is perfect."

Confusion had begun to creep like fog through the cracks and crevices of her brain. Her reaction to what had happened was growing stronger. Like a woman with a head full of cotton, she asked, "What's perfect?"

"The guards." He stopped and cocked his fists on his hips; his head made twitching movements as his gaze darted in all directions. "They were all called to dig in the rubble. You are unprotected. If that butcher who desires your life should choose this moment to attack again, you are lost."

Obviously, what he was saying was important to him. Yet somehow she had missed the point. Carefully, she inquired, "How do you know about that?"

He looked at her sharply, his nose wrinkling. "My lady, you need rest. And I suggest a quantity of wine. But you are unprotected."

"I mean it." It was difficult to speak aloud. I didn't tell anybody. Artagel didn't. I'm sure Prince Kragen and the Perdon didn't. "How do you know I was attacked last night?"

"Last night?" Surprise made his voice squeak. "You were attacked last night? By the same man?"

She nodded dumbly.

"Ruination! By the pure sand of dreams, why does Lebbick bother to train the dead meat he uses for guards?" With an effort, Quillon controlled himself. Facing her squarely, he asked, "My lady, how did you survive?"

"Artagel saved me. Geraden asked him to keep an eye on me."

"Thank the stars," Master Quillon breathed fervently, "for that impetuous puppy's interminable interference!" Almost at once, he demanded, "Why did you tell no one?"

She blinked at him, unable to fathom his distress. This was going on too long. She wanted to lie down. To make him stop, she asked, "Who do you expect me to trust?"

For just a moment, he looked as miserable and desperate as a soaked rabbit. Then he shook his head and scowled. "I take your point, my lady. You are not in an easy position. Someday it will improve—if you live that long.

"Go to your rooms," he continued brusquely. "Bolt the door. I will guard you until Lebbick's men return to duty.

"As soon as I can, I will have your maid bring food and wine."

The fog was growing thicker. She stared at him blankly.

His expression softened. "Go, my lady." He took her arm to urge her toward the door. "You need rest. And if you remain standing here your mistrust will become unbearable to me."

Somehow, his strange mixture of concern and sorrow was enough to move her. She entered her rooms, and he closed the door behind her.

After that, however, the capacity to act abandoned her. She forgot to bolt the door. Standing in the center of the room, she looked at her windows. They were blinded by the storm. Snow mounted on the ledge outside the glass; snow caught the light from the room and reflected it back. Flakes swirled and swirled forward like bits of light, but behind them everything was dark, as impenetrable as stone.

After a while, she realized that she was lying on the rug.

She felt weak and light-headed, but clearer, less fog-bound.

Cautiously, she got to her feet and located the decanter of wine. It had been refilled, a fact that gave her a sensation of detached surprise until she realized that her bed had also been made, her fires rebuilt, her stores of firewood replenished—until she remembered that a long time had passed since she had left her rooms this morning. Plenty of time for Saddith to do that part of her job.

Because Master Quillon had told her to do so, she poured a goblet of wine, drank it, and poured another.

The wine seemed to increase her detachment as well as make her feel steadier. Now she wasn't surprised when she heard voices outside her door.

"How is she?" a woman asked.

"Quiet, my lady," replied Master Quillon.

"I do not like it that she is alone." The woman seemed to be hesitating. "But if she is resting a knock may disturb her."

"Try the door," the Master suggested. Terisa couldn't gauge his tone through the wood. "I think she did not bolt it."

"Thank you, Master Quillon."

The latch lifted, and the lady Myste let herself into the room.

She bolted the door before she turned and saw Terisa.

She had on a bulky cloak the color of old snow, too heavy and warm to be worn around Orison. Held closed by her arms, it covered everything from her neck to the floor and made her look like she was trying to conceal the embarrassment of having suddenly gained forty or fifty pounds. The flush of her cheeks and the perspiration on her forehead showed that she was in fact too warmly dressed. But she smiled, and her eyes seemed to sparkle with accuracy, as if she were seeing things in good focus for the first time in years.

"Terisa," she said, studying her quickly, "you are well. You need a bath"—she grimaced humorously—"but you are well. I am pleased." Her pleasure was unmistakable. "All Orison knows what you have suffered today. Taking that into consideration, you are impossibly well. Have I not tried to tell you that you are more special than you realize?"

This reaction left Terisa nonplussed. She was sure that she wasn't special. On the other hand, she was glad to see Myste. Although several days had passed since their last conversation, she remembered that the King's daughter wanted to be her friend.

Awkwardly, she asked, "Would you like some wine?"

The lady's smile became laughter, then faded to seriousness. "I would love some wine. But first"—she faltered as if a touch of fear made her stumble—"you must agree to hide me."

Terisa's detachment wasn't equal to the challenge. "*Hide* you?"

"Just until tonight," said Myste quickly. "Until after dark. Then I will be gone, and no one will know that you have aided me.

"If you will not," she went on, "I have no time for wine. I must go at once, hoping that I will be able to hide myself."

"Wait a minute." Terisa began to feel faint again. "Wait a minute." She made a warding gesture with both hands. "What do you mean, no one will know? Master Quillon already knows. He knows you're here."

"Yes, but who will he tell? The guards? Your maid? The Masters of the Congery are not inclined to tell such people anything. And if we manage matters properly, he will not realize the significance of what he knows until I am safely gone.

"Then"—the lady's expression was pained, but she held Terisa's gaze—"I will ask you to lie for me. When Master Quillon tells what he knows—and you are asked what became of me—say that I left again shortly after I arrived, and the guards failed to notice me. Or say only that you do not know where I have gone.

"Terisa, I would not ask this if I had any choice."

"No, wait a minute," Terisa said again. "I don't understand. Where are you going?"

Myste started to reply, then suddenly gestured for silence.

Terisa heard Saddith's voice. "Is my lady all right? I came as soon as I heard that she has been rescued."

"She will be all right," replied Master Quillon. "Before you see her, go call the guards who are supposed to be here. I have better things to do than stand outside her door for the rest of the afternoon. And bring food and wine."

"Yes, Master."

As Saddith moved away, Myste lifted her shoulders in an I-told-you-so shrug.

"She'll be back," Terisa hissed urgently. "*Where are you going?*"

The King's daughter looked uncomfortable, a little sad—and yet excited, burning inside with a personal fever. "If I tell you, you will be able to stop me. You must promise that you will keep my secret and not interfere."

Terisa stopped. Her mind had cleared enough to grasp that she was being asked to do something she couldn't evaluate, something that would have consequences she couldn't predict. She hesitated because she didn't know what to say.

Her silence deepened the pain in Myste's face. "Forgive me," the lady said softly. "I should not demand so much of you. Your own burdens are already severe. I will go at once."

"No!" Startled out of her uncertainty, Terisa answered, "Don't do that. I won't tell anybody where you're going. I'll hide you. I just want an explanation.

"The Masters translated their champion, and he went berserk. Geraden and I were buried alive. People are being killed. They appear and disappear. Everybody is betraying everybody else." Geraden thinks I'm going to save Mordant. "I feel like I'm falling apart. I would like to understand *some*thing."

To her relief, Myste at once gave her a smile and a nod. "I will gladly explain as well as I can. It would ease my heart. If you were Elega"—her smile became a wry grimace—"you would believe that I have lost my mind. Doubtless this is another of what she calls my 'romantic notions'—the worst of a bad lot. But I hope you will understand it.

"May I have some wine?"

"Of course."

Half flustered and half pleased, Terisa filled a second goblet and handed it to the lady. At the same time, Myste opened her cloak, shrugged it off her shoulders, and set it aside.

Under the cloak, she wore a heavy leather jacket with a masculine cut, pants stitched of the same material, and boots clearly made for traveling. The bulk that the cloak covered was caused by a number of sacks—apparently full of supplies—slung over her shoulders on a strap like a bandolier. Knives hung at her belt—a long fencing dagger and a short poniard.

She asked permission to sit. Terisa nodded at once and gladly took a chair herself: her knees seemed to be growing weaker rather than stronger.

"Terisa," Myste began after a long draught of wine, "I believed from the first that you would be willing to help me. I believe you will understand. But I do not willingly impose what I mean to do on anyone. I truly have no choice.

"Are you aware," she asked slowly, "that Orison is riddled with secret passages?"

Taken aback, Terisa said before she had a chance to think, "Yes. There's one in the bedroom."

Myste smiled inwardly, and the focus of her eyes drifted into the distance. "You have been among us for hardly ten days, and already you have learned so much. I would not have done as well. I have always been a woman who could live for years without learning such things. But Elega has a different spirit. By the time she was twelve, exploring secret passages had become her favorite pastime.

"She could not interest Torrent in this, so she often urged me to go with her.

"If you were to characterize us when we were girls," she commented, "you would say that Elega was bold; Torrent, timid; Myste, dreamy. In a sense, I found secret passages more exciting than Elega did. She would say that I found them 'romantic.' But in another sense I did not need them. I explored them with her enough to please my imagination. Then I was satisfied. Eventually, I began to ignore her urging.

"But I had learned enough for what I mean to do now.

"Terisa, you may not know that all the passages do not connect. They were built at different times, for different purposes. Most provide admittance to only a few locations in Orison.

"My knowledge of the passages is not extensive. The only entrance I am aware of to the one I need—the passage that goes where I need to go—is from the wardrobe in your bedroom. That is why I had no choice but to come to you."

Terisa was about to ask, You mean you want to go where Adept Havelock lives? But she remembered that the passage had several branchings and kept her mouth shut.

"If I have not forgotten what Elega and I learned together," Myste said carefully, "if I am not confusing imagination and memory, a branch of this passage leads down into the laborium, near the meeting hall of the Masters."

Terisa couldn't help herself. "Why do you want to go *there*?"

Firmly, the lady answered, "From there I may be able to leave Orison unseen through the breach in the wall. I know of no private exits, and Castellan Lebbick watches the public ones better than most people realize. If I do not get out unseen, I will be brought back involuntarily, and what I must do will come to nothing.

"Of course, the breach will be watched. But that duty will be new to the guards. They will be watching for enemies who desire to enter, not friends who wish to leave. And if this snowfall continues, it will cover me. Perhaps it can be done."

The sensation of fog began to fill Terisa's head again. She needed sleep—a bath, a meal, and sleep, in that order. Slowly, as if she were becoming stupid, she asked, "What do you want to do? What's so important that you have to sneak out in this kind of weather?"

Articulating each word precisely, like a woman controlling an impulse to rush, Myste said, "I mean to find that poor, lost man the Masters call their champion. He needs help desperately."

"*Help?*" Terisa nearly choked. "He needs *help?*"

Myste made a warning gesture, urging Terisa to lower her voice.

"He could have burned this whole place to the ground," she whispered intensely. He almost killed me, "and you think he needs *help?*"

He almost killed me. Even though he said, *I don't shoot women.*

"He could have," the lady returned promptly. "He could have killed us all. But he did not. Does that not say something important about him—something crucial to an understanding of him and his plight?"

"Yes!" Terisa hissed back. "It says he doesn't want to waste his power until he knows what kind of mess he's in—how many people he's going to have to slaughter to stay alive."

Suddenly, Myste was angry. She rose to her feet. "Perhaps you are right," she retorted. "Perhaps he seeks only to ration his capacity for slaughter. Do you think that Castellan Lebbick's soldiers will teach him restraint? No. They will harry him from murder to murder, searching for their opportunity to kill him in turn. If he is to be stopped, it will only be by someone who cannot harm him."

The lady would have gone on: she plainly had more to say. But she paused at the sound of voices.

"The Castellan sends his apologies, Master." Saddith's tone was pert and insincere: apparently, she didn't aspire to Master Quillon's bed. "He regrets that you have been held so long on guard duty. You will be relieved shortly."

She gave the door a saucy rap.

"Will you hide me?" Myste breathed.

"I said I would," Terisa retorted softly. Then she admitted, "I don't know how."

The lady picked up her cloak. "Let her in. I will conceal myself in one of the wardrobes." She didn't forget her goblet. "Try to keep her here for a while—long enough so that the guards will relieve Master Quillon. They will not know that I am here, so they will not expect to see me leave." Her excitement had returned. "But do not let her bring you clean clothes from the wardrobe. If she finds me there, she will surely talk about it."

Without a sound, Myste left the room.

Saddith knocked again.

For a moment that felt like an icicle in her stomach, Terisa was unable to move. This was worse than merely telling lies: this was active subterfuge. She had to trick Saddith. And she felt too weak and befuddled to so much as stand up, never mind trick anyone. The cold paralyzed her.

But the next instant a leap of imagination told her what was about to happen. Saddith would knock again. If there was no answer, she would turn to Master Quillon and ask him what to do. And Master Quillon would be concerned. He would say something like, "The lady Terisa may be asleep. But the lady Myste is with her. She should answer." Then Myste would be lost.

Stung by panic, Terisa got her legs under her and hurried to the door.

When it opened, Saddith sailed grandly into the room like a yacht on show, the lower buttons of her blouse straining to contain her breasts. Her demeanor made it clear that she didn't think very highly of Master Quillon.

She carried a well-laden tray to a table while Terisa closed the door. "That man," she said as if she intended to be overheard, "ought to be more civil. I can perform my duties very nicely without the benefit of his instructions."

Putting down her tray, she surveyed Terisa.

Her immediate reaction was a gleam of mirth and a quick giggle. "My lady, you look awful!" At once, however, she made an effort to swallow her amusement. "My poor lady, how terrible! To be buried like that. And to be recovered in such a state, with all those men around—!" She frowned. "What a shame that this dull gown was not damaged more. A few strategic tears would have done much to make your appearance more appealing."

The maid continued to babble, apparently controlling her desire to laugh by saying whatever came into her head. Until that moment, Terisa had had no idea what to do. But the sense of weakness which made her want to simply fold at the knees and forget everything came to her rescue like a flash of inspiration.

"I need help," she murmured. "I'm so weak." Her voice sounded wan and distant in her ears. "I want a bath, but I keep passing out when I try to get undressed." She had left enough dust on the rug to make that statement credible. "I can't seem to get warm."

Through the fog in her head, she felt remarkably clever. No one could say she was really lying. And she would gain precious time while Saddith arranged to have hot water brought to her rooms.

But her imitation of frailty was perhaps a little too convincing. With increased sympathy, Saddith came to her and took her arm. "My poor lady, lean on me. You should sit down." Gently, she moved Terisa toward a chair. "It will take me only a moment to begin heating water. Then we will remove that foul gown, and I will bathe you."

Unable to raise a reasonable objection, Terisa allowed herself to be seated.

Saddith went into the bathroom. Terisa heard running water; then the maid emerged carrying the tin bucket, which she set in the fireplace as close to the grate as possible. As she added wood to the fire, she announced, "It is too cold in the bathroom. I will bathe you here."

Pushing back the rug, she made room in front of the fire. Then she brought the tub from the bathroom and positioned it next to the hearth. After that, she began unfastening Terisa's gown.

For the first time since chidhood, Terisa had the experience of being undressed and washed like an invalid. It made her acutely self-conscious.

The result was undeniably pleasant, however—sitting in the tub before a hot fire while Saddith poured warm water through her freshly scrubbed hair. The relief of being clean and warm compensated for the embarrassment of Saddith's comments on her body. When she heard the unmistakable sounds indicating that guards were now on duty outside—unmistakable because Master Quillon complained peevishly about the delay as he left—she felt almost equal to her next trick, which was to get rid of Saddith without allowing the maid to bring her any clothes.

"This feels wonderful," she murmured. "I think I'll just soak here for a while," it'll be all right for you to leave, "and then go to bed."

Saddith nodded approval. "I will bring you a robe."

"No, thanks." Terisa barely escaped betraying her fright. "I don't need one. The fire's warm, and I have plenty of towels." Hoping it would help, she added shamefacedly, "I don't wear anything in bed."

"Nonsense, my lady," replied the maid. "What if you change your mind and decide to eat something before going to bed? You must not risk a chill."

Before Terisa could stop her, Saddith walked into the bedroom.

Terisa nearly fell out of the tub. Water splashed and steamed on the hearth as she scrambled to her feet.

But Saddith returned almost immediately with the burgundy velvet robe in her arms and a puzzled expression on her face.

"What's the matter?" asked Terisa, her heart hammering.

"Nothing, my lady." Saddith shook her perplexity away. "I cannot remember leaving your robe on the chair when I cleaned the room this morning."

Terisa felt so light-headed with relief that she almost collapsed. Myste was more quick-witted than she would have believed possible. "I got it out"—she seemed to hear herself from far away—"when I thought I was going to be able to undress myself."

"My lady," Saddith said reprovingly, "you must not stand there wet."

As calmly as if she were levitating, Terisa reached for a towel.

Saddith wound a second towel around her hair while Terisa dried herself. When she was done, she stepped out of the tub and let Saddith lift the robe onto her shoulders. "Thanks," she said again. "You can go now." She had lost the capacity to be subtle. "I'll be all right."

The maid studied her for a moment. Then she winked. "I believe," she said mock-seriously, "that I recognized the voice of one of your guards. He has a good reputation in these matters. You may find it restful—and rewarding—if you ask him to warm your bed. If I had come so close to death, I would be eager to remind myself"— she moved her hands suggestively down her thighs—"that life is worth living.

"He is the tall one with the green eyes," Saddith added, laughing happily as she let herself out of the room.

Immediately, Terisa rushed to the door and bolted it.

When she turned around, she found Myste standing in the door-

way of the bedroom. The lady's face wore a distracted and thoughtful expression.

"That was close," breathed Terisa. "I don't know how you can
think so fast."

"Hmm?" Myste murmured. Her mind was obviously elsewhere.
"Oh, the robe." With a shrug, she dismissed the subject. "Terisa, I
think it is not a good idea to leave that chair in your wardrobe."

"Why not?" Surprise and reaction gave Terisa's tone a note of
asperity. "*I* don't know where those passages go. I've got to do
something to keep people out of here."

A smile quirked Myste's lips. "I see your point. The precaution is
tempting. The difficulty is that the position of the chair announces to
anyone who sees it that you are aware of the passage. I want to ask
how you chanced to notice it—"

Terisa held her breath.

"—but you owe me no explanations. We must simply hope that
your maid will not volunteer what she knows to the wrong ears. I
assure you, however, that your life will become much more burden-
some if Castellan Lebbick sees a chair in your wardrobe."

"Oh." Terisa let the air out of her lungs in a sigh of self-disgust.
"You're right." Why wasn't she able to think of things like that for
herself?

At once, Myste became reassuring. "I doubt that you have any
cause for worry. Your maid has already told everyone she is likely to
tell. And Castellan Lebbick has had no reason to search your rooms."

"I hope so." Terisa made an effort to relax. Of course the Castellan had no reason to search her rooms. She was probably safe. And
Myste's kind refusal to pursue the question of how she had become
aware of the passage was another relief.

By degrees, she began to feel that her bath had done her a lot of
good. And a tray of food was waiting for her. When she sniffed it,
she discovered that she was hungry. Inviting Myste to join her, she
sat down to a meal.

Myste had left her cloak in the bedroom. Taking off her bandolier,
she accepted Terisa's invitation.

While they ate, Terisa returned to the subject of Myste's intentions. "You were telling me why you think the champion needs your
help. That's the point, isn't it? At least that's what I don't understand.
You don't even know him. What difference does he make to you?"

The lady cleared her throat with a swallow of wine. "You ask several questions at once. The truth is probably nothing more profound than that when I heard of his plight it wrung my heart—and when I thought that I might help him the pain turned to gladness. But I will try to give you reasons.

"That he needs help is obvious. Consider." Her gaze was fixed on something beyond the wall of the room. "He is a man of war, accustomed to hostility on all sides. Subjugation and destruction are his life. And now—suddenly, without explanation—he is alone in a world surely as unfamiliar to him as any he has ever conquered.

"You are aware of the great debate of Imagery. Do the people, places, and creatures seen in mirrors have independent existence, or are they merely like reflections in a pool of water, unreal apart from the glass in which they have been cast? Is the champion a man, deserving the rights and respect of a man? Or is he, in effect, nothing more than an animal—a being like a horse that can be decently, even honorably, deprived of its own will?

"Terisa, by either standard he must have help."

Myste's excitement impelled her to her feet. She began to pace the rug. "If he is a man—as my father would surely insist he is—then what the Masters have done is abominable. We cannot judge whether he is a good man. Perhaps he is a foul enslaver—that lies outside our knowledge. But any man deserves better than to be wrenched out of life, away from world, home, family, purpose, and explanation, to serve what are, essentially, the whims of Imagers. Think of him! He knows no one here, understands nothing. He was not invited to cast his lot among us. To him we must appear simply as enemies. He will fight us until weapons, food, and hope fail him. Then he will die.

"If he is a man, his death will be murder—

"If he is less than a man," she continued after a long pause, "a being comparable to a horse or a hunting dog, then it is his right to have help. There is a responsibility which accompanies the service we impose on animals. In exchange for what we take away, we give food, shelter, healing, perhaps even kindness. If we do not, few will call us admirable. Does not a champion with the mind and needs and desires of a man deserve at least as much consideration as a beast? Even if he did not truly exist until the moment of his translation, he is real now and should not be harried to death simply because, like an animal, he does not understand what we require of him."

Perhaps reaction to the day's events left Terisa punchy; perhaps her emotions were bouncing out of control. Whatever the cause, her heart lifted as she listened to the lady. She was glad that she had decided to help Myste, very glad. This was worth doing. Simply because she wanted confirmation, she said, "Maybe all that is true. But what does it have to do with you? Why do you think you have to sneak out of Orison and chase after him on foot in this weather?"

Myste frowned for a moment. Then she smiled self-deprecatingly. "There you touch me on my weakest point. I am a bundle of romantic ideas which defy common sense." As she spoke, however, she became stronger. "Yet I have always believed that problems should be solved by those who see them—that when a difficulty presents itself the person who becomes aware of it should answer it instead of trying to pass it to someone else." Her voice cast hints of passion like glints of gold in the firelight. "This is more true rather than less for a king's daughter. What is a king if not a man who accepts responsibility for problems when he sees them? And should his daughter not do the same?"

Her eyes flashing like Elega's, she faced Terisa. "But the truth," she said as intensely as a cry, "is that I *want* to go. I am tired of waiting for my life to have some kind of purpose."

At once, however, she made an effort to tone down her manner. " 'Romantic,' as I say." She laughed awkwardly. "But I cannot claim that I have been happy since the hall of audiences, since my father" —she was uncomfortable mentioning him—"forced you to play hopboard against Prince Kragen. When my mother and Torrent left, I remained in Orison because I thought I had a purpose. I wanted there to be at least one person at the King's side who would believe him if he chose to explain himself. Perhaps I could not help him solve Mordant's problems, but I could offer him the company and support of my willingness.

"But when for a whim he insulted an ambassador of Alend to the point of war—for a *whim*, Terisa!—and I went after him, he refused to hear me." She couldn't keep her emotion down. " 'My daughter and that Kragen mean to betray me,' he snapped. 'They have already begun. Do not hover. I am tired of daughters.' Then he slammed his door."

Again, Myste was silent for a while. But then she shrugged, and that small gesture seemed to restore her balance, her excitement. "I am still enough his daughter to want to take action when I see a need. And I do *not* want to watch him continue as he is going."

Terisa did the best she could to help. Slowly, she said, "When the champion first appeared, he nearly killed me. But he stopped himself. He said, 'I don't shoot women.' "

Myste smiled like a beam of sunshine through the storm piling snow over Orison.

The snowfall began to lessen shortly after sunset. Because she didn't want to risk departing Orison under an open sky and a clear moon, across an expanse of new snow in which she would leave obvious tracks, Myste left Terisa's room promptly. Her supplies over her shoulder under her cloak, a small oil lamp in one hand, she opened the hidden door and clambered through the wardrobe into the passage.

"Be careful," Terisa whispered after her. "If you get lost, and Castellan Lebbick has to send a search party down there to find you, we're both going to look pretty silly."

"Do not let him bully you," replied the lady almost gaily. "He only does it because he loves my father. I thank you with all my heart. I think I have not been this happy for years."

As an afterthought, Terisa asked, "What shall I tell Elega?"

With the lamp in front of her, Myste seemed to be standing on the lip of a well of darkness. "Tell her nothing." Her voice carried a hollow sound like an echo. "Watch her. If she truly means to betray the King, stop her."

How do you expect me to do that? Terisa demanded. But she didn't speak aloud. Myste was already gone.

Oh, well. Terisa closed the passage and got out of the wardrobe. Tomorrow she would have to go looking for Master Eremis. He needed to know how he had been betrayed. For some reason, the prospect of talking to him didn't appeal to her. She preferred to think about Myste.

She wanted to believe that someday she would have as much courage as the King's daughter.

As soon as she went to bed, she slept like a dead woman all night.

She was awakened early the next morning by the sound of horns.

It snatched her out of bed as if it were the call from her dreams, the distant appeal and ache of music or hunting. In too much of a hurry to notice that her fires had almost died out and the air was chilly, she strode naked out of the bedroom, looking for the source of what she had heard.

It came again.

It wasn't the call she remembered. It was the blare of a trumpet, the same solitary fanfare that had greeted the arrival of the lords of the Cares to Orison.

Now she recollected herself enough to feel the cold. Nevertheless she went to the window and looked out over the muddy courtyard.

The trumpet winded again. Apparently, each of the departing lords was being given a personal salutation. She saw the Fayle and his entourage emerge from the gate with the Perdon behind him, while the Termigan turned his horse away from the guards ranked formally behind Castellan Lebbick. Then came the Armigite, accompanied by his guards and courtiers—and by two or three women. Perhaps they were his mistresses or courtesans.

Last was Prince Kragen.

So he was leaving also. Apparently he—like the lords—had decided to remain only long enough to assess the consequences of what the Congery had done. Were they all abandoning Orison now because it was no longer safe, no longer proof against siege—or even against weather? Did Prince Kragen intend to bring down the war that the lords of the Cares fled?

How much was the translation of the champion going to cost Mordant in the end?

The cold of the stone against her arms and breasts made her shiver. The tempo of events was accelerating. She thought she heard a wild note of warning in the way the trumpeter blew his salute as Prince Kragen received his abrupt farewell from Lebbick and turned toward the gate, surrounded by his coterie of bodyguards.

Shivering violently, she left the window.

First she retrieved her robe and sashed it tightly; then she worked on her fires, stoking them with fresh kindling, blowing on the coals until the kindling caught flame, feeding the flames with generous quantities of wood. After a while, she began to feel warmer.

She had become surprisingly hungry during the night. But Saddith didn't usually bring her breakfast quite this early. When she had completely stopped shivering, she decided that she would get dressed, then ask one of her guards to call for the maid and a tray.

She wanted to wear her own clothes: she had had enough of gowns for the time being. To her bafflement, however, she couldn't find her moccasins. That was strange. When had she last worn them? The night before last, to the meeting of the lords. Where were they?

Had Saddith taken them for some reason?

Frowning, she finished dressing, put on the delicate buskins again, then went to the door and unbolted it.

The guards outside looked vaguely familiar: they must have had this duty sometime recently. They saluted her, and one of them asked if she needed anything.

"Can you call my maid?" she asked. "I want breakfast."

"Of course, my lady." A moment later, the man added, "Apt Geraden was here earlier, asking if you're all right. I won't be surprised if I see him again soon." He grinned. "Should I tell him you're ready for visitors?"

"Yes, thank you."

Smiling because Geraden must be well if his brother and the physician were willing to let him worry about others, she closed the door and returned to her windows to watch people—guards on duty, servants carrying supplies, men and women who had business with the few shops already open in the northwest end—watch them slogging through the cold and mud of the courtyard while she waited for Saddith or the Apt.

Soon there was a knock at her door. Before she could answer it, Castellan Lebbick stalked into the room and slammed the door behind him.

In the center of the rug, he stopped to face her. He had one arm clamped at his back, the other cocked on his hip. His jaws chewed anger; his shoulders were stiff with it.

Nevertheless he was smiling.

"My lady"—his tone was practically cheerful—"you are done lying to me."

To her surprise and relief, she didn't cringe. She had already outfaced him once. She could do it again.

"I would have come sooner," he commented in a conversational way, "but I've been busy. I'm sure you don't want to hear about it, but I'll tell you anyway.

"I was on my way to confront you again yesterday when the Fayle found me and told me what those pigshit Imagers were doing. After that, of course, I had to organize my men to help dig you and Geraden out of the rubble. I had to provide protection for the lords of the Cares and"—his mouth sneered—"Prince Kragen as well as King Joyse, in case that *champion* turned to attack us. I had to arrange to follow and trap him, so that he wouldn't do any more damage.

Since I knew where Eremis was, I didn't have to worry about him. But I had to spend hours and good men searching for Gilbur.

"I suspect you already know the outcome. I'm going to tell you anyway.

"Gilbur is gone. Vanished as completely as if he's mad and can use any flat glass he wants. The lords are gone. Since they think the Masters are insane, they aren't willing to stay and stand by their King. I had to let Prince Kragen go. He's an *ambassador.*" He grinned as though considering the prospect of tearing into her with his teeth. "In addition, the champion is free."

"Free?" The Castellan had made no mention of Myste. He wasn't saying the things Terisa expected. It was happening too fast. Why did he want to "confront" her? How could Master Gilbur have vanished? "What do you mean?"

"I mean, my lady," he replied like the edge of an axe, "that my men failed. Of course, I only sent fifty—but two hundred might have done no better.

"Oh, they found him easily enough. That strange armor of his doesn't include wings. In any case, I think he's wounded. So they should have been able to keep him. I didn't tell them to fight. I didn't want him provoked. I just wanted him to stay in one place until we had a chance to decide what to do with him.

"But his translation was planned well. Gilbur and Eremis must have been working on this for a long time." Now the fury in his grin couldn't be mistaken. "My men succeeded. They made him stop. But before they could do anything more than send a rider back to me, they were attacked. The air in front of them opened, and a cat the size of a small *house* jumped out."

In some strange way, the Castellan's ire sustained him, as if it were the food on which he lived.

"A beast that large would have been formidable under any circumstances. But this one, my lady—*this* one set fire to everything it touched. Flesh and iron were tinder for it, and it butchered my men like cattle. Only two escaped. They left it feeding on charred carcasses. I'm lucky I didn't send two hundred men. I can't afford to lose two hundred men.

"Since then," he went on more quietly, "I've been out there. The snow makes it easy to see that the champion and that firecat left in different directions. Clearly, they didn't do us the courtesy of destroying each other. Now we have two abominations on our hands, instead of just one."

Terisa shuddered involuntarily. Fifty men! And that was where Myste had gone— She nearly groaned aloud, *That's where Myste went!*

But all this had happened yesterday, and Myste hadn't left Orison until last night. The odds were great that both the champion and the firecat were so long gone that she would never catch up with them.

Taking a deep breath to steady herself, Terisa said, "That's terrible. I just don't understand what it has to do with me."

"My lady," he replied like a blade, "in some way you are responsible."

She started to protest, but he cut her off. "Yesterday morning, right after you left here with Eremis and Geraden, I took your advice. I did 'a little work.' I searched your room."

For some reason, she found that she had to brace herself against the wall to keep her knees from folding.

"I discovered a chair in your wardrobe." His satisfaction was as keen as his anger. "And I found these."

From behind his back, he produced her moccasins.

While she stared at them, he said, "You were able to wash the blood out of your clothes. But these are leather. You couldn't do anything about the bloodstains on the soles."

At that moment, a knock on the door interrupted him.

"Come in!" he snapped harshly.

The door opened, and Geraden entered the room.

Her attention jumped to him like a leap of the heart. For an instant, she saw his ready smile and the light of pleasure in his eyes, and she felt that she was already rescued, that his mere presence would be enough to save her. He was loyal to King Joyse—therefore logically on the Castellan's side against her. But she was confident that he would stand by her, whatever happened.

The next instant, however, his pleasure vanished in alarm as he grasped what was going on. Warily, he inquired, "Castellan Lebbick? My lady?"

Lebbick nodded in recognition. "Geraden. Is this an accident, or are you intruding on purpose? Are you in this with her?"

"In what?" asked Geraden.

For a moment, the Castellan studied him. Then Lebbick said sourly, almost bitterly, as though he were disappointed, "No, I don't believe it. You're capable of almost anything misguided or blind. But you know better than to betray your King. The Domne would birchwhip you to ribbons if you tried it."

"Are you accusing the lady Terisa of treason?" Geraden sounded a little frightened by his own temerity, but determined nonetheless. "Isn't that awkward? I mean, she isn't one of his subjects. He has no claim on her. How can she commit treason?"

Castellan Lebbick returned his gaze to Terisa. She met it so that she wouldn't look at Geraden, wouldn't let her need for him show in her face.

Softly, her accuser growled, "Why are you here, boy?"

"This morning," replied Geraden promptly, "the Congery will hold a funerary commemoration for the two Masters who died yesterday. The lady Terisa is asked to attend."

"In other words"—Lebbick's tone sharpened into a lash—"the Masters need to decide what to do about Eremis and Gilbur, and they don't want anybody else to know it." He didn't allow Geraden a chance to respond, however. "You can tell them the lady Terisa won't be coming. She's under arrest. You can visit her in the dungeon when I'm done questioning her."

Unable to restrain herself, she flung a mute appeal toward Geraden. She saw him mouth the words "under arrest" as if he were appalled. During the space between one heartbeat and the next, she believed that he would protest on her behalf, do something—that he might even jump at Lebbick and try to defend her physically.

But he didn't. He said, "I'll tell them." Turning away, he walked out of the room and closed the door behind him.

Geraden! He had abandoned her to Castellan Lebbick's anger. *Geraden!* When she needed him, he turned and walked away.

Her knees threatened to fail her. She could feel the courage running out of her like water from a broken jug. She had been so *sure* that he was her friend—

"I see I finally have your attention," the Castellan commented maliciously. "Yes, you're under arrest. For lack of anything better, you're accused of participating in the murder of Prince Kragen's bodyguards."

Really, it would have been better if she had never come here, if she hadn't let Geraden's smile and his earnestness (and his brief, unaccountable authority) persuade her to ignore her common sense. She had no business pretending that she had anything to do in this place, that she could make a difference.

"I'm going to lock you in the deepest, darkest cell I've got—the one with the biggest rats—and let you rot there until you tell me the truth."

Everybody was betraying everybody else; she was just a minor item on everybody's list. She couldn't defend herself because she couldn't figure it all out. And she didn't have anybody to betray because there was nobody on her side.

"If you get lonely, you'll be able to talk to your lover. Eremis will be in the cell beside you. If I have my way, you'll get to hear him scream."

That halted the downward spiral of her dismay. Eremis? Eremis was arrested? That was bad—worse than what was happening to her. He needed his freedom. Mordant needed him to be free. Especially now, with the hope of the champion turned to disaster and the lords gone back to their Cares.

"I wish you knew how silly that sounds," she said as if a total stranger were speaking for her. "I haven't done anything. I never do anything."

"Is that a fact?" Lebbick's sarcasm was as thick as blood.

"You're really doing a good job," she continued so that she wouldn't stop, wouldn't realize how dangerously she was behaving. "I'm probably the only person in Orison who is innocent of everything. And Master Eremis is probably the only one who doesn't deserve to be locked up."

"Sheepguts!" snarled the Castellan. "You're trying my patience, my lady."

"Which was never your best feature anyway," she retorted.

For a moment, he gazed at her in silence, perhaps in surprise; and for that moment she failed to realize she was giving him exactly what he wanted. Then his smile warned her. But of course the warning came too late. Her unpremeditated goading had already provided his anger the object it desired.

"No," he said almost mildly, "it was never my best feature." He was grinning like a barracuda.

Her audacity turned to fright. Instinctively, she tried to retreat; but the wall held her where she was.

"Of course, as you pointed out earlier, I don't have much proof. Yesterday I was too busy to question either the Fayle or that whelp the Armigite. And today they insisted on leaving. I couldn't refuse them.

"But I'm not stupid.

"The night before last—the same night my guards found Prince Kragen's men, after the Armigite warned them—the Fayle somehow came by the knowledge that Eremis and Gilbur intended to translate their champion. The same night, you left here with Eremis—and came back alone, covered with *blood*." He flung the word at her. "Of course, you're innocent. You innocently washed the blood out of your clothes, trying to get rid of anything that might connect you to those dead bodyguards. You innocently lied to me. But you innocently *forgot*"—he brandished her moccasins—"that your footwear would give you away.

"By some staggering coincidence, all of the lords except the Domne were here at the same time. Prince Kragen was here, the Alend ambassador. The next day the Congery rushed to its translation, hurrying to get done before I could interfere. When my men tried to stop that champion, he was rescued by another exercise of Imagery.

"What do you expect me to make of all this, my lady? Do you expect me to be impressed by the purity of your innocence, my lady, or by the sincerity of your lover's motives, my lady?"

He swore at her with intense relish. "I'll tell you what I make of it." His oaths were unfamiliar to her, but their passion made her quail. "First, it's obvious that this translation has been planned for a long time. Mirrors don't come into existence overnight. Although I don't know how they did it," he muttered half to himself. "Where's the glass that worked the translation?" Then he resumed his attack. "Since Eremis and Gilbur were the ones who spoke to the Fayle—and since Gilbur has disappeared now—it's obvious they're responsible.

"But what happened to produce two men dead and enough blood for five or six more?

"One of two things, my lady, both of them treason. Either Eremis and Gilbur met with the lords to plan the betrayal of Mordant by means of their champion, and Prince Kragen was caught spying on them, and his men died saving his life. Or Eremis and Gilbur met with Prince Kragen, and the lords caught them planning the betrayal of Mordant, and his men died saving his life. Either way, the Fayle spoke to me because what Eremis and Gilbur intended to do appalled him.

"How do I account for the quantity of blood—or the insufficiency

of bodies? The chair in your closet answers that. The men who
fought for you and *died* were removed into one of the secret passages.

"In fact, that chair explains a lot. It tells me how you contrived to
survive being attacked the first night you were here. Your allies—I
mean Eremis' allies—came out of the passage long enough to save
you. Then they went back into hiding."

A sensation of horror rose in her throat, choking her. He was so
close!

"In addition," he went on, "ordinarily, I would have said you
haven't been here long enough to become so deeply involved in
treachery. Eremis may be the greatest fornicator in all Mordant, but
even women usually need time to be so degraded. But you've had
more time than I realized—you've had all the time I thought you
were safely locked in your room.

"What do you think, my lady? Which evil did you share? Or is
there a third explanation, a worse crime?"

He stepped closer to her, aimed his rage straight into her face. She
flinched, but couldn't look away. His passion held her.

"What do you gain here? Is the way Eremis abuses his lovers
reward enough for you? Or do you have some other purpose? Did
the arch-Imager send you here to destroy us?"

Tossing aside her moccasins, he gripped her arms and ground his
fingers into her triceps.

"Who fought for the King, my lady? Is *everyone* a traitor?"

No leave me alone it's not my fault I don't know what you're
talking about!

He shook her as if he meant to fasten his teeth in her throat. "*Why
didn't you use your secret passage to come back to your rooms?* That way, you
would have been safe. No one would have known you had anything
to do with those dead bodyguards."

"Because that isn't where it goes!" she cried.

Then she stopped and stared at him while the blood froze around
her heart and a look of triumph filled his face.

"That's a start, my lady," he whispered between clenched jaws.
"Where *does* it go?"

She couldn't tell him that. If she did, she would expose Master
Quillon and Adept Havelock, as well as Myste. She had already said
too much.

This time she defied the Castellan deliberately. It was Terisa herself, not some audacious stranger, who said, "I don't deserve to be treated like this. If your wife were here, she would be ashamed of you."

After that, panic made her giddy. She saw the widening like a flare of madness in his eyes, but she didn't understand it. She heard him say, as if he were speaking in a foreign language, "Thank you, my lady. I haven't had this much fun since King Joyse let me punish that garrison commander." Through a veil of dread, she watched him let go of her arms, cock himself back, and swing the back of his hand at her head.

Instinctively, she jerked her head down, jerked her arms up.

Deflected, his blow was still hard enough to knock her to the floor. Pain began to roar in her ears. She had the impression that she was going blind: the only thing she could see was the Castellan staring at his hand as though it belonged to someone else.

The pain had a voice. It said distinctly, "What am I doing?"

Then she heard someone pounding at the door.

"Go away!" Lebbick roared.

"Your pardon, Castellan." A guard's voice. "The King's orders."

"The King?" Castellan Lebbick verged on apoplexy.

"He wants to speak with the lady Terisa. I'm instructed to take her to him." The man's tone conveyed a squirm in the face of Lebbick's rage. "He wants to speak with her now."

"She's under arrest. She should be in the dungeon."

"Castellan, I was specifically told to assure the lady she isn't under arrest."

The Castellan made a hoarse, strangled noise.

Abruptly, hands took hold of her and stood her on her feet. After a moment, she saw that they were his. "Someday, my lady," he said softly, "my chance will come. When that happens, you aren't going to escape me."

He left her to the support of the guard.

SIXTEEN: WHO YOUR FRIENDS ARE

n the whole, she reflected with a loopy clarity while pain clanged back and forth in her head and the guard held her upright, she liked being rescued. It was better than not being rescued. Definitely.

But what had inspired King Joyse to send for her now? How did he know she needed rescuing?

How did he know she was under arrest?

Considering how little information she herself possessed, it was truly astonishing how much everybody else seemed to know.

"Are you all right, my lady?" asked the guard.

She heard relief and concern in his tone. On the other hand, no one had mentioned Myste. Hadn't they missed her yet? She speculated on that until she forgot the guard's question.

He shook her gently and repeated, "Are you all right?"

Her vision appeared normal. Nevertheless she had the odd impression that everything was distorted. The angles where the walls met the floor looked false. The doorway was insidiously straight, not to be trusted. She was out of her mind, of course. She didn't object, however. This kind of craziness helped her bear the way her head hurt.

"My lady?" The guard's concern was becoming stronger than his relief.

Do you know—? she began, but no sound came out. She made an

effort to clear her throat, hold her head more upright. "Do you know why he hit me?"

"No, my lady." The guard was standing beside her with one arm around her back and the other hand on her shoulder. She still had no idea what he looked like. "I wasn't here."

"He hit me," she said precisely, "because I insulted him." Suddenly, she wanted to laugh. Or cry: it was hard to tell the difference. She had insulted him, *she*, Terisa Morgan. It was worth getting hit for. Maybe. "Oh, my head hurts."

"Here, my lady."

Carefully, the guard maneuvered her into a chair, then pressed a goblet of wine into her hands. She drank deeply; for a moment she felt spikes hammering through her skull. After that, however, she began to feel better.

With an effort, she said, "Thanks." Now what she wanted was a nap. But there was some reason why she couldn't take one. What was it? Oh, yes. "Did you say the King wants to see me?"

"Yes, my lady. When you're well enough to walk."

She turned her head to look at him and smile. She didn't remember ever having seen him before. He was a relatively young man with a thin face and earnest eyes—perhaps not the most promising candidate to convey a message that would infuriate Castellan Lebbick. But he had carried out his orders. And she was grateful for his courtesy.

"We might as well try," she said. "Maybe the walk will do me good."

Nodding encouragement, he assisted her to her feet. Then he gave her his arm to lean on. She took a few experimental steps and found that the condition of her head continued to improve. Incredible. Judging by appearances, it was actually possible to survive having a man like the Castellan furious at her. A man like her father. She could hardly believe it.

Moving cautiously, she let her escort guide her to the tower where King Joyse and his daughters had their suites. By the time she arrived at the high, carved door of the King's apartment, she felt reasonably stable—balanced between light-headedness and the aftereffects of Lebbick's vehemence.

The King's guards opened his door without question: clearly they were expecting her. One of them announced her while the other bowed her inward. In a moment, she found herself standing for the second time in the richly furnished chamber where King Joyse played his games of hop-board.

The room was lit by candles in candelabra and brass wall-holders, and the thick blue-and-red rug contrasted warmly with the decorated blond wood paneling of the walls, bringing out the carving and the delicate black inlay-work. An ornamental mantel framed the fireplace. On the hop-board table, a game was in progress. No one was playing, however.

"My lord King," the guard pronounced firmly, "here is the lady Terisa of Morgan." Then he withdrew, taking his companion and Terisa's escort with him and closing the door. But King Joyse didn't react. He sprawled in a gilt-edged armchair with his legs extended on a fat hassock and his head propped against the chair back. His purple velvet robe covered him like a shroud: it was starting to look as old and ratty as Adept Havelock's surcoat. A long sheet of parchment—an open scroll—was draped over his face; his arms dangled beside him, his swollen knuckles nearly scraping the rug. The floor around his chair was littered with more scrolls, some of them open, others haphazardly tied with string.

He was snoring decorously. The stiff parchment rustled whenever he breathed.

The King's Dastard wasn't present. Instead, King Joyse was being kept company by Geraden and the Tor.

Involuntarily, she gaped at them.

"My lady," rumbled the Tor. "It is a pleasure to renew your acquaintance." His fat overflowed his chair, and his plump hands gripped a flagon of wine as if he couldn't function without it. His thin white hair straggled disconsolately from his pale scalp. But his voluminous black robe was clean; his jowls were decently shaved. Although his small eyes were bleary, they seemed marginally less blurred than she remembered them.

Geraden met her surprise with a grin. Almost at once, however, his expression changed to distress. He jumped out of his chair and approached her. Lightly, he stroked the hot skin of her cheek. "That unscrupulous bastard," he whispered. "He hit you." Then chagrin overcame him. "I'm so sorry. It's my fault. I didn't think he would go that far. I thought I would be fast enough. I ran all the way—all the way—"

"Enough, young Geraden," the Tor interposed, peering morosely into his flagon. "You are a son of the Domne. Have more dignity."

"I don't understand." Terisa felt that she had abruptly become stupid. "What are you doing here?"

"As little as I can," the Tor replied as though she had spoken to him. "King Joyse keeps good wine and an excellent fire. I have no other needs.

"It was awkward, I admit," he mused, frowning to himself. "He refused to see me. After that cell, I felt as cold as my son. I wanted to be warm again. And I thought I would share a last flagon with my old friend the King of Mordant. Did I say that I would not leave him? I meant to say so. But he refused to see me. Very awkward."

Unexpectedly, he smiled. Under other circumstances, it would have been a happy smile; but it didn't touch the sadness in his eyes. "He underestimated me. I sat down outside his door and commenced howling. Not polite, deferential howling, I assure you, but howling to alarm the dead."

"You did that?" Geraden grinned in spite of himself, surprised out of his contrition.

The Tor nodded. "It is well that my family did not see me. They would not have thought better of me for it. But I succeeded." He glanced toward King Joyse and commented, "Since admitting me, he has found it impossible to make me depart."

This didn't make much sense to Terisa. She shook her head to clear it, but the movement had the opposite effect. She needed to sit down. Or lie down.

"But why?" She couldn't forget how the Tor had looked standing in the mud of the courtyard with his dead son in his arms, or what Geraden had told her about King Joyse's reaction to the Tor's son's death. "All the other lords left. Why do you want to stay?"

The Tor grimaced.

"Revenge."

Geraden was startled. "Revenge?"

"For most of my life," explained the lord in a husky voice, "I have been haunted by the knowledge that I did not give King Joyse my full support when he needed it. This would have been wise policy— if he had failed. But he succeeded, thereby making me a conniving ingrate in the eyes of all Mordant. I mean to be revenged for that."

"I don't understand," Terisa repeated weakly. Maybe the Tor was joking. But what kind of joke was it?

"The King needs a chancellor." The lord didn't raise his head. "Someone who can put two coherent commands together better than that mad Imager. As long as I sit here"—he flopped one hand on the arm of his chair—"and speak as though I had authority, I will be obeyed. Whether he wishes it or not, Joyse will no longer be a passive ruler. Either I will take action in his name, or he must take action to stop me."

Geraden's eyes gleamed appreciatively; but Terisa said, "Wait a minute." She was too slow: she had to catch up. She had believed that the Apt was abandoning her when he left her to Lebbick. "You're giving orders in the King's name." She turned to Geraden. "You came here—you ran here—to get King Joyse to stop Castellan Lebbick." Geraden nodded. She glanced over at the King. "Does he really want to see me?"

With the exaggerated care of too much wine, the Tor scanned the room as if searching for eavesdroppers. Then he said, "No." At once, one plump finger jumped to his lips to hush himself. In a thick whisper, he added, "But he would if he had any sense. He was asleep, so I took the liberty of speaking for him.

"Young Geraden is right," he continued sententiously. "The good Castellan should not be allowed to make decisions where women are concerned."

She felt that she hadn't stopped gaping at him. She wanted to say several things at once. What do you hope to accomplish? Oh, Geraden, I'm sorry! Do you really think he'll let you get away with this? But that wasn't the point, of course. The point was to make King Joyse declare himself—to make Mordant's sovereign take a stand that would reveal his true intentions. So she didn't ask any of her questions. Instead, she said sincerely, "I'm glad you did it. I needed rescuing."

The Tor gave her a lugubrious wink. To Geraden, he commented, "You see? Already my revenge begins to bear fruit."

"My father tells a lot of stories about you, my lord," said Geraden. "I don't think they do you justice."

But Terisa wasn't done. She turned to Geraden. Because she had become brave enough to tell lies—and even to speak insults—she was brave enough to say, "I'm sorry. When you left, I thought you were running out on me. I should have known better."

He met her gaze sharply, and his shoulders straightened. "That's right." His tone was earnest. "You should have known better. I would rather cut off my hands than run out on you."

Almost at once, however, he relapsed to self-consciousness. "I'm glad I did something right." His smile was embarrassed and happy. "Please don't count on it. It doesn't happen that often."

"Tush, young Geraden," the Tor interposed. "You malign yourself." He drained his flagon and waved it until the Apt found a decanter and poured more wine for him. "Your difficulty is quite simple. You have not found your true abilities. As the King's chancellor, I dispense advice freely to all. Born swordsmen make very clumsy farmers, as I am sure your brother Artagel would agree. Give up Imagery. A son of the Domne should not spend his life providing jokes for Imagers."

Geraden's face darkened, not with anger, but with pain. "I would if I could." The quick distress in his voice went straight to Terisa's heart. "I'm a disappointment to my whole family. I know that. But I can't—I can not give it up."

The Tor studied his wine with the air of a man who didn't want to meet Geraden's eyes. "At least you are your father's son. Take comfort in that. He, too, is stubborn. I have heard King Joyse say that he would rather break his head on a stone wall than argue with the Domne."

Privately, Terisa thought that if Artagel had been present he would have denied being disappointed in his brother at all.

Abruptly, the King made a snorting noise. A twitch of his head dislodged the scroll, and the parchment slipped aside, curling around itself among the others on the rug. Blinking, he raised his hands to his chest and flexed them as if they had gone numb. "The Domne," he muttered at the ceiling. "Stubborn man. Rather break my head on a stone wall."

In an effort to push himself upright, he fumbled at the arms of his chair, but he seemed too stunned with dreams—or too weak—to succeed.

"My lord King." Geraden went to him and helped him.

With awkward hands, King Joyse tried to rub the sleep off his face. Seen in this way, his old skin and watery eyes had a vulnerability which pained Terisa. He didn't look like a perverse or half-mad ruler who refused to defend his kingdom: he looked like a frail semi-invalid, nearly crippled by arthritis and age, who had lost most of the people he loved and now could barely keep his grip on reason.

But when he saw her—when he got his eyes into focus and saw who she was—he answered her unspoken concern with a smile of clean, uncluttered joy.

That was where the lady Myste had come by her look of sunshine: she had inherited it from her father. Terisa tried to distance herself from his transparent pleasure, but she couldn't. If he had simply smiled at her like that and done nothing to change the way she felt about him, she would have done anything for him.

Unfortunately, he spoke.

"My lady, have you come to offer me a game? How kind of you. I have a problem here"—he gestured toward his hop-board table—"that defies my poor brain."

Her disappointment was so acute that she had to turn her head away.

He levered himself upright in a way that suggested his legs weren't as weak as his arms. "Havelock set it up for me. If I understand him—which isn't always easy—he once found a solution. These are his notes." King Joyse nudged a nearby scroll with one foot. "Since I haven't been able to design a solution for myself, I've been reading his notes, hunting—" His voice trailed away as he lost the thread of what he was saying. His gaze shifted toward the Tor and Geraden as if he couldn't quite remember who they were. Then he looked back to Terisa and resumed, "—hunting for his answer." He shrugged. "Without success. Maybe you can give me some fresh ideas."

Memories of her game with Prince Kragen made her stomach twist. King Joyse had lured her into that situation with his smile. She didn't want to find herself in a similar mess again. Carefully, she said, "I'm sorry. I didn't come for that. The Tor"—she hoped the lord would forgive her for putting him on the spot—"had your guards bring me here."

"Ah, my old friend the Tor." King Joyse grimaced as though his mouth were full of bile. "He is one of the few mummers in this masque who defies prediction." He seemed to drift between colloquial and more formal diction according to his mood. "Who could have foreseen that he would feel compelled to force his service upon me, after all the indignities I have required him to suffer?" He didn't glance in the direction of the old lord. "This is not in the rules. It is enough to drive me mad, my lady."

"My lord King"—the Tor's voice was quiet and harsh—"I am sure you understand that I am not motivated by benevolence."

The King ignored him. "Nevertheless," he said to Terisa, working visibly to recover his equanimity, "we must all bear our burdens as

we can. Mine is hop-board." Again, he gestured toward the table.
"This problem beats me. Are you sure you won't take a look at it for
me? It's really quite demonic." Slowly, the skin around his eyes
crinkled with humor and enjoyment. "And I think you know something about it.

"Please?"

Without quite intending to do so, she faced the table. After all, it
wasn't entirely fair to say that his smile alone had seduced her into
her game with Prince Kragen. She had had her own odd reasons for
what she did. It wasn't fair to place all the blame on King Joyse.

When she saw the arrangement of the men on the board, she
understood his idea that she knew something about it. The position
was virtually a stalemate: it was the same position she had played for
against Prince Kragen. Whose move was it? If white's, the game
could go on; if red's, the only available play would complete the
stalemate.

"It's red's turn," answered the King, although she hadn't spoken.

"I see what you mean," she murmured. "There's no way out of
that. Adept Havelock must be joking."

"Oh, I don't think so. He doesn't have that kind of humor." King
Joyse frowned at the board. "There is a way out. I'm sure of it. I
simply can't imagine what it is."

Terisa shook her head. The subject of hop-board held no interest
for her. To dismiss it, she said, "I haven't played for years. The only
thing I can see is to back up and start over again. Try to avoid
arriving in this position."

He gave her another of his radiant smiles. "My lady, I wish life
were that simple."

Under the influence of his joy, she thought suddenly that she
caught Havelock's joke. "In that case," she said, "try this." Without
pausing to reflect, she took hold of the edge of the table and tilted it
back and forth just enough to slide most of the men off their squares.
In an instant, the impending stalemate became chaos.

Grinning, she turned back to the King.

He obviously didn't think what she had done was funny. A look of
nausea on his face, he stared at the board. His frailty came back over
him; his eyes filled as if he were on the verge of tears.

Hastily, she tried to explain. "I still think Adept Havelock was
joking." She indicated the board. "Does he have *that* kind of humor?"

King Joyse gave no sign that he heard her.

"I'm sorry. I didn't mean to upset you. It's just a game."

Without warning, his eyes flashed like steel glimpsed through water. "To you, it's just a game. To me, it's the difference between life and ruin."

Moving so feebly that he nearly tottered, he went back to his chair. The difficulty with which he lowered himself into his seat made her ache as if in some way it were her fault.

"My lord King," Geraden asked, "are you all right? Can I get anything for you?"

Slowly, King Joyse shifted his damp blue gaze toward the Apt. "I notice you haven't been paying much attention to my orders," he rasped acidulously. "I distinctly told you not to see or speak with the lady Terisa. I told you not to answer her questions. Do you call what you've been doing obedience? I expected better loyalty from a son of the Domne."

His accusation surprised Geraden. The Apt's head jerked up; his concern changed to a scowl. "My lord King," he replied slowly, holding his emotions like a bit clamped between his teeth, "I would obey your orders if I understood them. But they don't make any sense.

"You've lost interest in Mordant. You insulted Prince Kragen badly enough to start a war with Alend. You let the Congery summon that champion, when the Fayle did everything he could to warn you. We need all the friends we can get. I'm not willing to treat the lady Terisa like an enemy."

King Joyse looked too tired and old to keep his head up, but his gaze didn't waver. "Are you through?"

Geraden took a sharp breath. "No." Stiffly, he said like a formal confession, "My lord King, the day after you commanded me not to see or speak with the lady Terisa, I took her to the mirror which brought her here and attempted to return her to her own world." Then he stopped, held himself still.

Like Geraden, Terisa expected anger from King Joyse. She wouldn't have been surprised if he had sent for the Castellan. Apparently anticipating the same reaction, the Tor shifted forward in his chair, braced himself to speak.

But the King only sighed. He leaned back and rested his chin on his chest. Staring vaguely into the rug, he murmured, "One grows

old so quickly. This should have happened when I was younger. I
was strong enough when I was younger."

Terisa wanted to ask—gently, gently—What should have happened? But Geraden had been too shaken by the King's accusation
to let it drop.

"I tried to translate her back to her own world because I believe
all the things you used to say about the reality and integrity of what
we see in mirrors. I think she deserves the freedom to leave whenever she wants. If I had known you were going to let the Masters
translate their champion—if I had known you were going to turn
your back on the ideals you talked about when you created the Congery in the first place—I would have tried a lot harder to get her out
of here." What he was saying wasn't recrimination: it was an appeal.
Terisa could hear his heart in it. "Why did you do it? Their champion nearly killed us. He left a hole the size of a small mansion in the
northwest wall. We might as well invite Cadwal and Alend to besiege
us. And he's still out there, ready to tear down anybody who gets in
his way."

And Myste is out there, Terisa thought. Your daughter. She's trying to catch up with him.

"My lord King, the Fayle tried to warn you. Why didn't you let
him warn you?"

King Joyse didn't bother to glance at the Apt. When Geraden
finally fell silent, the King remained still for a moment. Then he said,
"Because I didn't see fit to do so." A tremor of bitterness and pain
ran through his voice. "Do you think you're qualified to make my
decisions for me? I was fighting to make Mordant and the Congery
whole long before you were old enough to fall on your face in pig
wallows."

Geraden flushed at this gibe, but couldn't retort to it.

"I let the Masters have their champion because I didn't choose to
stop them.

"Besides," King Joyse added sourly, "Eremis is under arrest. That
should make you happy. Lebbick will arrest Gilbur when he finds
him. The perpetrators are going to be punished. What more do you
want?"

"I want to *understand*," cried Geraden.

"Tush, young Geraden," the Tor rumbled unexpectedly. "I doubt
that the Domne has any thick-skulled sons. Surely you are not stupid.

It must be obvious by now that my lord King does not *wish* you to understand."

Geraden whirled to face the Tor. "But *why*? I'm just an Apt. I'll never become a Master. What harm would it do if I understood? Who would it hurt?"

The Tor lifted his shoulders fatly. Speaking half into his flagon, he asked, "How did I gain an audience with the King?"

Hauled up short, Geraden blinked at the old lord. Slowly, he said, "You howled outside the door until he let you in."

King Joyse snorted quietly.

In disgust, the Tor grimaced. "You cannot convince me that you are stupid. I insist that you are not. How did I gain an audience with the King when I first arrived in Orison?"

Geraden opened his mouth. "I—" Then he closed it again.

"Young Geraden"—the Tor emphasized each word—"the King does not wish you to understand. I suggest that you return to your quarters and beat your head against the wall until your skull cracks enough to let a little light shine in."

"Yes, go," King Joyse muttered at once. "I'm tired of being reminded how little my own people respect their King."

Sharply, Geraden turned back to the King. Now Terisa saw something wild in his eyes, something extreme enough to be dangerous. Nevertheless his balance had become steady, as if urgency improved his poise. "Actually," he said, "I should be used to this." His tone was almost calm. "I was always the youngest. My brothers didn't have the patience to explain things to me very often." Almost calm— and almost threatening. "I probably do better when I figure it out for myself."

Without glancing away from King Joyse, he asked Terisa, "My lady, will you come with me?"

"She will stay here," King Joyse answered for her. "I want to talk to her."

So he did want to talk to her. Terisa didn't know whether to be relieved or concerned. To Geraden, she said, "I'll see you later," trying to reassure him. "We'll think of something." Then she waited while he made up his mind to leave.

Before he left, he gave her a look like an iron promise—a look that hinted at passion and authority. Then he was gone.

As the door closed, the Tor sighed thickly. He emptied his flagon and settled his bulk more comfortably in the chair as though he intended to take a nap.

Terisa faced King Joyse.

Instinctively, she felt sure she knew why King Joyse wanted to talk to her. And she meant to take advantage of the opportunity. She was angry. Castellan Lebbick had hit her. King Joyse insisted on causing Geraden pain. Master Eremis had been arrested. She was angrier than she had realized.

Her voice shook slightly as she said, "You knew Master Eremis was arrested. Castellan Lebbick has been reporting everything to you." That seemed a safe deduction. "You knew he was going to arrest me. You *let* him attack me like that. If the Tor hadn't stopped him, I would be in a cell by now.

"I seem to recall hearing you argue I might be a powerful Imager —I was like an ambassador—I had to be treated with respect. Do you call this respect?"

As if he intended to answer her, he raised his head. He shifted in his chair to face her squarely. Now there was no petulance or bitterness in his expression. He looked grave with all the seriousness of his years, as intent on her as his watery gaze permitted—and so sorrowful that she was taken aback.

"My lady," he asked softly, "where is my daughter?"

So she was right. Her pulse beat faster. At last she had something somebody else wanted, something she could use. As long as she didn't betray Myste, this was her chance.

The prospect frightened her, but she clung to it with both hands. "Which daughter?" she returned despite the tremor in her voice. "You have several."

She expected indignation and anger—that was what she always expected—but King Joyse remained quiet. His expression didn't change. For a long moment, he studied her through the moisture in his eyes. Then he indicated the chair across the table from him. "My lady, will you be seated?"

At first she hesitated. Perhaps she would be stronger if she stayed on her feet. But his sadness was as persuasive as his smile. She went to the chair, pulled it away from the table to dissociate herself from hop-board, and sat down.

When she was seated, he said in the same soft, grieving tone, "My lady, my daughter Myste is gone. Where is she?"

Suddenly, her tongue was so dry that she could hardly swallow.

Like a frightened but stubborn child, she asked, "My lord King, why did you let Castellan Lebbick arrest me?"

The room seemed uncomfortably warm. Again, the King's eyes gave a hint of steel. He held her gaze until she faltered and looked down. Then he breathed almost inaudibly, "My lady, do not play this game with me. It is more dangerous than you imagine."

For a few seconds while her heart hammered and her stomach knotted, she nearly backed down. She didn't have the strength to face him. Anybody was stronger than she was. As she had with Saddith, she felt that vulnerability and weakness were her only defense, her only weapon.

But backing down now wouldn't accomplish anything. The King would still want to know about his daughter. He would still demand answers. If she gave up what she wanted, she wouldn't make herself safer. And it would be more difficult for her to avoid betraying Myste.

And she was too angry to give up. Deliberately, she raised her eyes to the King's again. "I don't have any choice. Geraden tried to take me back where I belong, but that mirror doesn't seem to work anymore. I have to play.

"Why did you let Castellan Lebbick arrest me?"

Something shifted in the background of King Joyse's expression, like clouds moving their shadows across a distant landscape. Without any definable change, his attention became sharper and more cautious.

"My lady"—his tone was caustic in an oddly impersonal way, as if he didn't mean it—"do you know who your friends are?"

She stared at him in surprise and bit her lip and didn't try to answer.

"Well, I don't either. Having you arrested would have been a good way to find out. It would have been very interesting to see who tried to help you, or communicate with you, or persuade me to let you go. But of course Geraden interfered. With his usual instinct for disaster. I already knew *he* was a friend of yours."

This reply startled her. It drew a different sketch of him—of the way his mind worked—than she was expecting: it seemed to imply that he was paying attention to what happened in Orison. "Wait a minute," she protested weakly. "Wait a minute. You mean you *planned* to have me arrested? It was just a ploy?"

"No, my lady." He waved one sore-knuckled finger at her. "You aren't playing the game. It's my turn now. Where is my daughter?"

Terisa drew a sharp breath. For a moment, she considered trying to extort information from him without revealing anything herself. In spite of his age, however, he looked too strong for that tactic. And it wouldn't be fair. He was Myste's father.

Carefully, she responded, "She came to see me yesterday afternoon. In my rooms. We talked for a long time."

He nodded. "I guessed that. But I don't understand it. What do you have that she wanted? What did she tell you?"

"No, my lord King. It's my turn now."

She had so *many* questions. Too many to remember them all at once. And she didn't want to waste an opportunity like this on the one she had blurted out a moment earlier. So she concentrated on the issue that had brought her to the King's suite—on Castellan Lebbick and his behavior.

"When I leave my rooms with someone—with Master Eremis, for example—my guards always want to know where I'm going. But when I leave with Geraden, nobody seems to care. Why is that?"

King Joyse snorted as if she had just made a particularly bad move. In the same caustic, impersonal way, he said, "You should have figured that out for yourself. I already know Geraden is your friend."

Right. Of course. She really *should* have figured that out for herself. A sense of panic rose in her. She wasn't thinking quickly enough.

Impatiently, the King continued, "You were speaking of my daughter, my lady."

"Yes." She needed to be smarter. Sharper. She was tempted to turn to the Tor for help. But she could hear him breathing deeply, heavily, as though he were about to snore. Groping for inspiration, she asked, "Can you be more specific?"

"Certainly," he snapped. "Where is she?"

Fortunately, his tone brought back her anger. All right. If that was the way he wanted to play. "I don't actually know where she is." She made an effort to sound sweet. "But you asked what I have that she wanted. There's an entrance to a secret passage in my wardrobe. She wanted to use it."

Again, he nodded. Apparently, Terisa was only confirming his own suspicions. "Why?"

Anger was a great help. She was being cruel to him—but only

because she had been so badly treated herself. "My lord King," she said stiffly, "the first night I was here a man tried to kill me. When he was chased away, Castellan Lebbick started a search for him. But you called it off." Despite her inexperience, she worked to match his tone. "Why?"

For an instant, King Joyse hesitated. The shadows shifted behind his eyes. Then he said trenchantly, "Because I didn't want him caught."

"What? Why not?"

"I didn't think he was stupid, so I didn't think he would lead Lebbick to his allies. And I didn't think he was a coward, so I didn't think he would tell me anything if Lebbick caught him. The only way to learn anything about him was to leave him alone and wait for what he did next." His voice grew harsher, but it still sounded impersonal, as if his ire were calculated rather than real. "Are you satisfied, my lady?"

"Why did my daughter want to use a secret passage?"

"Because"—Terisa's anger made her stronger than she would have believed possible—"she wanted to leave Orison."

That struck him, hurt him. "Leave Orison?"

"She knew you would stop her if you could, so she used that passage to get down into the laborium. Then she sneaked out through the hole in the wall."

"Leave Orison?" he repeated. "Why?"

"No." She clenched her fists to make herself ignore his distress. "Why did you make me play hop-board against Prince Kragen? You did everything you could to force a war. I didn't enjoy being used like that."

So suddenly that she had no chance to defend herself, King Joyse surged out of his chair. As if he had never been weak or old in his life, he knotted his hands in the front of her shirt and jerked her to her feet. "This is intolerable! She is my *daughter!*" His eyes ran as if he were weeping. "Her mother and one of her sisters left me. Her other sister holds me in contempt. *Where did she go?*"

Terisa should have broken then: she knew that about herself. She should have given up everything and betrayed Myste in simple fear. Her own anger should have evaporated.

But it didn't.

"Back to her mother," she retorted. Myste was her friend. "She wanted to be loyal. She wanted to help you. But when you insulted

Prince Kragen like that, you broke her heart. She was raised to be the daughter of a *king*, not some petty tyrant who likes war and can't be bothered to defend his own people. She—"

Terisa stopped. His anguish stopped her. His sudden strength collapsed. He let go of her shirt. His hands dropped. His eyes squeezed shut, but tears went on spilling past his old eyelids. "If you lie to me—" he rasped far back in his throat. "If you dare lie to me—" It wasn't a threat: it was a plea. Fumbling behind him, he found the arm of his chair and braced himself on it while he sat down. His robe covered him as if he were lost inside it. "My daughter, what have I done to you?"

"Why did you do it?" Terisa asked so that his pain wouldn't tear the truth out of her. "Why did you make me play hop-board against Prince Kragen?"

"To test him," he replied like a man who had no idea what he was saying. "No other reason. How could I trust him? Alend has been Mordant's enemy for generations. He has a personal grudge against me. If his mission were honorable, he would refuse to play. He would have no reason to brook that insult to the Alend Monarch. But if he intended treachery he would acquiesce because he could not risk my displeasure—risk expulsion from Orison before his work was done." He covered his face with his hands. "Oh, my daughter."

So it was true. He knew what he was doing, what was happening around him. The thought seemed to chill her blood. Where had she gotten the idea that it was too warm in this room? She wanted to shiver violently. Ignorance or senility had nothing to do with it.

He was intentionally destroying Mordant.

And yet his distress swept her anger away. She could fear him, but she couldn't be angry at him. "I'm sorry," she said, trying to be kind. "I guess this game is a stalemate too."

Roughly, he pulled down his hands. They shook as he clasped them together in his lap. He didn't look at her. Quietly and distinctly, he said, "My lady, I suggest that you give the matter more consideration before you once again attempt to end a stalemate by tilting the board." Then he indicated the door with a twitch of his head, dismissing her.

She turned to leave as if she were fleeing.

The Tor was awake. He watched the King with a look that resembled hunger. As she passed his chair, he gave her a firm nod of approval.

She had already closed the door behind her before it occurred to her to wonder how King Joyse had been able to guess that Myste had come to her for help.

SEVENTEEN:
TERISA TAKES
ACTION

he had the impression that she was hurrying inside, racing to keep ahead of her emotions, ahead of the consequences and implications of what she was doing. She needed to outrun the lie she had told King Joyse. She had caused him too much pain. Liars surrounded her. Even Master Eremis didn't trust her with the truth to any remarkable extent. It was possible that the King himself had been lying to her. Falsehood was her only weapon, the only way she could defend herself. She wanted to flee from it.

She had descended two flights of stairs and was about to enter one of the main halls before she realized that she had no idea how to get where she wanted to go.

She tried to swear at herself, but the unaccustomed words lacked conviction. Geraden's tour hadn't included the information she needed. She was off to a great start.

She scanned the hall in both directions. It was full of people; she might conceivably ask one of them for directions. But she had no idea how to approach them. What were they all doing here? Floor- and chimney-sweeps, stonemasons, supply porters, chambermaids, scullery maids, seamstresses, even blacksmiths: she understood the servants of the castle. But who were the rest of these men and women, these lords and ladies? Myste had made a point of explaining how much Mordant and Orison depended upon trade. Were these people all involved in commerce and finance?—warehouse managers? goods inspectors? tax collectors? shipment foremen? bookkeepers? supply allocaters? black marketeers? If so, her father would have felt right at home.

Her father, she firmly believed, wouldn't have hesitated to tell King Joyse any number of lies. She believed this despite the fact that she had never heard him utter an untruth.

Still running inside, she spotted Artagel.

Some distance away, he sauntered across the hall. Judging by his manner, he might have been unaware of her. But a moment after she noticed him—before she had time to raise her hand and wave—he changed course and came toward her.

"My lady." He gave her an amiable bow. "Have you recovered from your adventures already? If I had a similar experience, I would get into bed and not get out again for several days."

"Call me Terisa," she said to dismiss the subject of her recovery. She was in a hurry. What she had in mind was even more uncharacteristic of her than her conversation with King Joyse. If she paused or faltered, it would fall apart; she might never be able to pick up the pieces again. "Where are the dungeons?"

He cocked an eyebrow. "I can't call you Terisa, my lady. If I do, I'll be in danger of forgetting that Geraden is my brother. I'm not like Stead— Has Geraden mentioned that we have one brother who is absolutely insatiable for women? But I'm also not immune to beauty. Why in the world do you want to know where the dungeons are?"

Remembering the conversation she had overheard between him and Master Eremis, she hesitated. But she couldn't afford the luxury of hesitation. "Castellan Lebbick has arrested Master Eremis," she said, trying to sound like she knew what she was doing. "I need to talk to him."

That announcement widened his eyes. She saw him consider and reject a variety of responses in rapid succession—surprise, disapproval, curiosity. When he spoke, he had decided on unruffled amusement. "If Eremis is safely locked up, I don't think Lebbick will want him to receive social visits."

He had a good point. Grasping at possibilities that hadn't crossed her mind until that moment, she said, "But you can get me in. If we don't ask the Castellan's permission. If we just go to his cell. The guards will let you in," she concluded awkwardly, "because of who you are."

His expression became wary. "Maybe. But you'll be taking a chance. Even if Lebbick doesn't catch you, he'll still be told you were there. I assume there must be some *reason* why Eremis was arrested. You'll make yourself look like his accomplice. You'll make *me* look like an accomplice. What good is that going to do?"

For a moment, she froze. The matter was too urgent to be explained. King Joyse knew what he was doing. He was doing it on purpose. *My daughter, what have I done to you?* Master Eremis needed to know that. He couldn't act or plan accurately unless he knew what he was up against. And he was Mordant's only hope.

Unfortunately, that also couldn't be explained—to Artagel even less than to Geraden. The sons of the Domne were too loyal.

Impelled by her sense of haste, she tried another prevarication. "Maybe I'm being naive, but I think what's really wrong here is that none of the people who want to defend Mordant are willing to talk to each other. The Congery doesn't trust Geraden. The King doesn't trust the Congery. Nobody trusts Master Eremis. Castellan Lebbick doesn't trust anybody. And meanwhile the whole kingdom is going to hell." She was pleased to hear that she sounded like she knew what she was talking about. "I want to see if I can make people start talking to each other.

"I've just had a talk with King Joyse. Now I want to talk to Master Eremis. I think he's the key to the whole thing."

Artagel watched her while she spoke, a bemused smile on his lips. When she finished, he shook his head, not in refusal, but in wonder. "You amaze me, my lady. You make it so simple. There must be some reason why it's never been attempted." Then his smile broadened into a grin. "It might be fun. It might even work." Bowing extravagantly, he offered her his arm. "Shall we give it a try?"

At once grateful for his acquiescence and alarmed by her own behavior, she accepted his arm and let him guide her down to the dungeons of Orison.

The cells were physically close to the laborium. After the conversion of the original dungeons, the place where the Castellan kept his prisoners was separated from the workrooms of the Masters only by a masonry wall. Artagel took Terisa to the disused ballroom which was becoming so familiar to her—its emptiness a symbol of Orison's loss of heart. Beyond it, a passage paralleling the entrance to the laborium led to a corresponding stairwell. There, however, the similarities ended. The atmosphere of the dungeon was a world away from the laborium.

Ill-lit by torches guttering at intervals along the old walls, the place was dank and oppressive; she could feel the huge pile of Orison's stone impending over her. Straw that smelled of rot—and perhaps, faintly, of blood—covered the floor. It had originally been scattered to sop up whatever the prisoners of the castle spilled, but now it served primarily to control moisture. The corridor was narrow but direct: after a second downward stair, it brought Terisa and Artagel to the guardroom.

Here the men who were about to go on duty, or had just been released, or were taking a break could warm or refresh or relieve themselves; but the guardroom also served as part of the dungeon's defenses. Although the chamber was appointed like a crude tavern, with trestle tables and rough benches for the guards, a few beds against the walls, a large hearth in which a fire struggled against the wet chill of the stone, and a short bar from which a servingman provided ale and meat, it also gave the only admittance to the cells: no one could get in or out of the dungeon without passing through the guardroom. Racks of swords and pikes along the walls above the beds suggested that the men in the guardroom were expected to be ready to fight at a moment's notice.

Discipline was slack, however—perhaps because most of Orison's guards were exhausted by the previous day's exertions; perhaps because the dungeon wasn't the most vital or interesting part of the castle. One man sat honing his sword with the studious attention of diminished intelligence; the rest were less involved in their duties. Three guards at one table had obviously consumed more ale than was good for them; two more occupied beds, snoring in a perfect third; the rest threw dice in a corner of the room with more vehemence than pleasure.

Artagel frowned at what he saw, then changed his expression to an insouciant smile. His eyes glittering, he said to no one in particular, "What a collection of slovens and aleheads. I could walk every prisoner you have through this room singing, and you wouldn't notice until the Castellan locked you in irons."

Glaring with surprise, irritation, and stupidity, everyone who was awake turned toward him.

When the guards recognized him, however, their hostility vanished. Expressions of gruff humor stretched their faces. Several of

them guffawed hoarsely, and one riposted, "That's true. Who cares
about prisoners? But just try getting that woman past us."

"Anyway," another said, "the Castellan never comes here. Except
when he wants to question Master Eremis. We always have plenty of
warning."

"The fact is," explained a third, "Master Eremis is the only prisoner we've got. That's bad enough—but you don't know what misery is until you've spent an entire night turning away women who
want to see him." Staring straight at Terisa, he clutched his groin. "I
would give my left hand to know how he does it."

Terisa noticed that all the guards were now staring at her.

Suddenly, she wanted to forget the whole thing and go back to her
rooms.

Then one of the dicers rose to his feet. A purple band knotted
around his right bicep marked him as a captain of some kind. "Take
it easy, you louts," he drawled. "Unless I'm confused in my old age,
Artagel's companion is the lady Terisa of Morgan. She isn't one of
Master Eremis's toys—or yours either.

"My lady"—he gave Terisa a decent bow—"don't look so worried. You aren't in as much danger as you think. Artagel can unman
half the rubbish here before they get their hands on their swords.
And Castellan Lebbick would feed the other half to the pigs just for
touching an unwilling woman."

Artagel's answering smile made the captain straighten his shoulders. In a more rigid manner, he asked, "What can I do for you?"

She had no idea how to respond, but her companion replied easily,
"The lady Terisa is taking a tour of Orison. She wants to see the
dungeon."

The guard with the armband hesitated; his eyes narrowed. "The
Castellan isn't going to like that."

Artagel's smile stretched wider. "The Castellan isn't going to hear
about it."

Terisa was holding her breath. She felt rather than saw the men
around her stiffen.

"If he does," the captain observed slowly, "you won't be the one
who gets eaten alive. I will."

"That's probably true." Artagel seemed to enjoy himself more and
more by the minute. "But there's one consolation. You'll be safe
from me. Whoever tells Lebbick we were here won't be that lucky."

For a moment, Artagel and the guard captain measured each

other. By degrees, the guard's expression changed until it resembled Artagel's threatening grin. He unhooked a ring of keys from his belt and tossed it to Terisa's companion. "I don't have any idea why you want to talk to Master Eremis. I don't want to know. Just don't let him out."

" 'Talk to Master Eremis'?" Artagel was gleaming. "You aren't serious. I would rather lie down in a nest of snakes."

"That's a mistake," someone chortled. "There aren't any women in a nest of snakes."

All the men laughed—with the exception of the guard honing his blade, who frowned as though the people around him spoke a foreign language.

Artagel jingled the keys. "We'll be back soon." Then he said to Terisa, "Come, my lady," as though she weren't clinging tightly to his arm. Together, they crossed to the doorway which led to the corridors and cells of the dungeon.

Beyond the guardroom, she asked softly, "Would you really kill somebody who betrayed us?"

"Of course not," he replied negligently. "That's why we're safe. If they were really afraid of me, someone would talk."

For some reason, his tone didn't carry conviction.

Breathing deeply to ease the pressure in her chest, she inhaled the rotten air and tried to remember why she was here.

To talk to Master Eremis. To tell him what she had learned from the King. So that he would know better where he stood, what Mordant's true danger was. So that he could decide what to do, now that his attempts to unite the Congery with the lords of the Cares and Prince Kragen had failed.

To see him again, so that she could try to understand what he meant to her, why the mere thought of him was enough to make her nerves tingle.

Her heart laboring, she went with Artagel past a first turn in the passage, past a second, and into the area of the cells.

Perhaps because the dungeon itself was so obviously closed, the cells were relatively open. They didn't have solid doors to shut their occupants in. Instead, each of them was essentially a deep niche cut into the foundation stone of the castle, eight or ten feet deep and just wide enough to accommodate a low cot and a washstand against the back wall. A heavy iron grid bolted to the stone served as the near wall for each cell; a barred door in the grid provided entrance and egress.

All the nearby cells were empty: apparently, King Joyse's recent rule hadn't supplied the Castellan with a significant number of prisoners. Nevertheless the glow of a lamp some distance ahead implied that one cell, at least, was occupied. Terisa and Artagel walked toward it, their feet rustling through the straw on the floor. As they passed, the one lantern that provided dim illumination for this corridor made ghoulish shadows leap in and out of the cells on either side.

Before they reached his cell, Master Eremis said in a voice pitched to carry, "Astonishing. I thought that I would be left alone longer. The time is not right for a meal. Have more innocents been arrested? Has the Castellan already obtained King Joyse's permission to torture me?" He sounded almost jovial. "Can it be that I have been granted a visitor?"

"You're in good spirits, Master Eremis," commented Artagel dryly as he and Terisa reached the cell. "I hope you have reason. As I remember, the last time Lebbick locked somebody up down here, she was executed two days later. A Cadwal spy, I think she was. Before that, it was a brigand who lost both hands for his trouble."

At first glance, this cell seemed as empty as the others. A small oil lamp balanced on the washstand revealed that a rumpled blanket covered the dirty mattress on the cot; but the light didn't show Master Eremis. Instead, it reflected delicately in the fine trails of moisture dripping down the granite.

Then, however, a darker place—a place without reflections—took shape against the wall.

He was sitting on the end of the cot as far from the lamp as possible, and his jet cloak blended him into the shadows. Until Terisa's eyes adjusted, she saw the pale skin of his face and hands as nothing more than stains on the old stone of the wall.

He wasn't wearing his chasuble. He had given it up—or it had been taken from him.

"My lady," he murmured. Now his voice didn't carry: it was soft, almost intimate. "I wanted you to come."

That statement went straight into her heart. It was pitched to a key which made her whole being resonate. Nobody else except Geraden had ever said anything like that to her. And nobody else in the world had ever spoken to her with that specific magnetic vibration, that knowing and personal passion. In an instant, all her reasons for being here changed to suit the tone in which he said, *I wanted you to come*.

Without thinking, she said to Artagel, "Let me in. I need to talk to him."

Artagel glanced at her strangely. But the expression on her face must have convinced him not to argue with her. With a shrug, he stepped to the door, tried a few keys until he found the right one, then unlocked the Imager's cell.

Before either common sense or timidity could inspire her to question what she was doing, she entered the cell.

At once, Artagel closed the door. In a distant, noncommittal manner, he said, "I'll be nearby. Just raise your voice. If he tries to do anything, I'll kill him so fast he won't know he's dead until afterward."

Quietly, he moved a few paces away down the corridor.

Terisa paid no attention to him. She was focused on Master Eremis.

He hadn't left his seat on the end of the cot. He didn't speak. He was still hard to see in the dim light. Involuntarily, she slowed down as she moved toward him.

The cot was low: despite his height, his head only reached her shoulders. When she was near enough, however, he sat forward, drew her between his spread knees, and pulled her head down to take her mouth in an urgent kiss. She tasted wine and desire on his breath.

The strength of his embrace and the insistence of his tongue seemed to complete the change in her. She responded with everything he had taught her, trying to make her kiss as intimate as his. A long moment passed before she remembered that she had other reasons for being here: that without having planned to do so she had joined the ranks of King Joyse's opponents; that Mordant's fate might hinge on what she could tell Master Eremis. And they weren't really alone.

Deliberately, she pushed herself back a little way. Trying to recover her breath, she murmured, "That's not why I came."

"Is it not?" Still holding her with both knees and one arm, he raised his free hand to the buttons of her shirt. "It would be enough for me."

Again, he kissed her.

When he let her pull back once more, his deft fingers began to open her shirt.

"Artagel will see us." In spite of her anxiety, she kept her protest low. She wanted the Master to touch her.

"He will not if you do not raise your voice. Artagel is scrupulous."

His hand slipped inside her shirt. His fingers were cold, bringing her nipples erect at once, making her breasts ache for him.

His behavior and her own unexpected emotions confused her; she could hardly think. Nevertheless she made one more attempt to draw away. "I've just talked to the King. I came straight to you from him."

Somewhat to her chagrin—as well as to her relief—Master Eremis loosened his grip. "A talk with the King," he murmured, tilting his head back to peer into her face. "That is an honor which all Orison and half of Mordant would envy you. What did the old dodderer desire?" He caressed one of her breasts. "Does he have enough life left in him to covet my place?"

"Castellan Lebbick came to arrest me." She wanted to explain everything clearly, make the importance of what she had learned plain; but she felt that she was babbling. "The Tor and Geraden stopped him. But King Joyse wanted to talk to me anyway." Quickly furious at her incoherence, she halted, took a deep breath, then said distinctly, "He's not an old dodderer. He knows what he's doing. He's doing it on purpose."

The Master's sharp face betrayed no reaction; yet his sudden stillness suggested that she had touched on something important. Slowly, he lowered his hand. "My lady, you must tell me everything. Begin at the beginning. Why did Lebbick decide to arrest you?"

His attitude was like magic: it made her firmer, stronger. At once, her confusion receded. "I think it's the same reason he arrested you. You broke one of the King's rules, I know that—but I don't think it's the real reason. I think the real reason is that he figured out we went to a meeting with the lords and Prince Kragen. He believes we're all traitors."

It was his embrace that confirmed her, his expressionless face, the steady pressure of his knees. She might have been willing to tell him anything. Yet she made no mention of Myste or secret passages; she said nothing about Master Quillon. Instinctively, she focused on the attack after Eremis' clandestine meeting two nights ago; on the bloodshed that had led Castellan Lebbick to her; on the Castellan's

conclusions. Then she explained how the Tor and Geraden had rescued her from arrest.

After that, she had to be more careful. Acutely conscious that she
wasn't a good liar, she said, "He wanted to talk to me about his
daughter Myste. She's vanished. He thought I might know where
she's gone. I pretended I did to make him talk to me." Hurrying
once more to get past her falsehood, she described the answers King
Joyse had given to her questions.

Now Master Eremis did react. By the weak lamplight, she thought
she saw surprise, anger, excitement emerge in glimpses from the
darkness surrounding him. At one point, he breathed as if involuntarily, "That old butcher." At another, he whispered, "Cunning.
Cunning. I was warned, but I did not believe—" Calculations as
quick as his emotions ran behind his eyes.

When she was done, he thought soberly for several moments.
Without releasing her, he gave the impression that they had become
distant from each other. As though she weren't still clasped in his
arms, he said, "This will be a better contest than I anticipated."

Almost immediately, however, his notice returned to her. Tightening his embrace, he studied her face and said in a detached tone,
"You have done me a considerable kindness, my lady. I wonder why.
I have claimed you"—he squeezed her with his knees—"and you are
mine. No woman refuses me. But I can hardly fail to observe that
you are enamored of that puppy Geraden. And you risk more than
Lebbick's rage by coming here. Why have you done it?"

So she had done the right thing. She had helped him. The knowledge made her feel so weak, so ready for him, that she could hardly
answer his question. If she had been braver, she would have bent to
kiss him again. A kiss might be a better explanation than any ratio-
nale. But he needed this answer as much as anything else she had
told him.

Awkward with conflicting priorities, she said, "King Joyse is doing
everything on purpose. I don't know why—it's insane. But he's refusing to defend Mordant on purpose. Somebody has to resist him.
You're the only one who seems to have enough initiative—or intelligence—or determination—to *do* something. Everyone else is just
waiting around for King Joyse to finally wake up and explain himself."

The Master remained silent, untouched by her account of herself.

For an instant, she faltered. Then she blurted out, "You have enemies. There's a traitor on the Congery. You were betrayed."

In response, the lines of his face became stone. His eyes searched
her face; his whole body was still. "My lady"—softly, sardonically—
"you did not come to that conclusion alone. Who told you?"

Please. You can make me sure of myself. You can do anything with
me. She hardly heard herself say, "Geraden."

That was the wrong answer. She could feel the Master's quick
anger through her skin. "Now I understand you," he snapped. "You
are worse enamored than I realized. Of course *Geraden* believes there
is a traitor on the Congery. There *is* a traitor on the Congery." He
glared up at her. "But why did he reveal that fact to you?"

Before she could reply—before she could imagine what she had
done to infuriate him—his anger changed to surprise. "That cunning
son of a mongrel," he murmured. "Naturally he spoke to you. For
that reason alone, if for no other, you will never credit that he himself serves the traitor."

Now she was too shocked to speak. *He himself serves*—? It was cold
in the cell, too cold. She ought to button her shirt. No warmth
seemed to come to her from the Master. Could Artagel overhear
what was being said? Probably not: otherwise he would already have
a blade at Eremis' throat.

Geraden?

"My lady, you must learn to think more clearly." The Imager
sounded almost sympathetic. "I know that the young son of the
Domne is attractive to you. That is understandable, considering that
he created you. If you had not come to me of your own volition, I
would not say such things. I would simply give your fine body the
love it craves—the love for which it was made—and keep my
thoughts to myself. But if you wish to help me, you must use your
mind to better effect.

"Take into account whatever reasons Geraden may have given for
his belief that the Congery conceals a traitor, and add to them what
we have learned since. Along with his initial questions, Lebbick did
not fail to mention that Master Gilbur has disappeared. Does it not
seem likely, my lady, that he himself is the traitor?"

Yes, she thought, held by his arms and knees and his intent gaze.
No. How could he foresee that I would go to your meeting? How
could he know where I would be after the meeting, so he could
translate those men to attack me? (Don't translations with flat mir-

rors drive people crazy?) But those arguments no longer seemed to make sense. Gilbur was the one who had vanished.

"I confess," Master Eremis went on softly, "I did not foresee his treachery. Foolishly, I trusted him simply because he has cause to feel gratitude toward me. But when Geraden went into his glass, purportedly seeking our champion, and brought you to us instead, my eyes were opened.

"My lady, do you never try to understand why I do what I do? Did you never ask yourself why I involved Master Gilbur in my meeting with the lords of the Cares, when it was plain to all the Congery that he and I stood on opposite sides of every issue? I was trying to expose him, to give him means and opportunity to betray himself. And I succeeded—

"At a greater cost than I had anticipated," he commented. "Orison's wall breached. The champion gone. Myself arrested. And stripped of my chasuble by that officious lout Barsonage to prove the Congery's good faith to the Castellan."

He snarled in disgust, then resumed his reasoning. "Did you never wonder why I have placed so much value on Geraden's life? I wanted him alive so that I might try to gain his friendship, insinuate myself into his counsels, study his strange abilities.

"Did you never ask yourself why I attempted to have him admitted to the Congery as a Master? Surely that must have seemed gratuitous, even to someone who knew so little of Orison and its conflicts. In that I did not succeed. Oh, I gained a part of what I wanted—I learned how our good King had reacted to his first encounter with you. That information might have aided me, if I had possessed the key to understand it." His voice grew sharper as he spoke, more urgent and demanding. "But I did not accomplish my chief end, which was to tighten a snare around Geraden—to place him where he would be watched, even by fools who did not fear him, where his secrets might be forced into the open, and where the achievement of his lifelong dream might help blind him to his true talents."

"No." Terisa's protest was too strong to be kept still. "That doesn't make sense." The Master's assertion hurt everything in her chest. "What talents?" As though she were rising up inside herself, she demanded, "What makes you think that he and Master Gilbur have anything to do with each other?"

"Use your mind!" Eremis replied between his teeth. "It was Gilbur who shaped the mirror that first showed the champion. It was he who taught Geraden to copy that glass, he who watched and verified every step of the process, from the refining of the finest tinct to the sifting of the precise sand to the polishing of the exact mold. He must have seen what went wrong, what was changed, to produce the mirror which translated you here.

"Think. While he shaped his glass, Geraden showed abilities which have never been seen before, abilities which allowed him to twist all the laws of Imagery to his own purposes—abilities as great in their way as the arch-Imager's ability to pass through flat glass and remain sane.

"Gilbur must have known this. He must have witnessed it. Yet *he said nothing*. Something fundamental occurred under his nose, and he made no mention of it.

"What conclusion do *you* draw, my lady? What conclusion *can* you draw? Are you able to insist that I am wrong?"

No. She shook her head leadenly, and her heart reeled. This time she couldn't contradict him. In his logic, as in his physical magnetism, he was too much for her. If she accepted the proposition of Master Gilbur's treachery, then all the rest followed impeccably. *It was he who taught Geraden*— Why hadn't she thought of that for herself?

It was still possible, she argued dimly, like a woman who was about to faint, it was still possible that Geraden was her friend. That he meant her well. If he was as ignorant and accident-prone as everyone believed—

Clutching at straws, she breathed, "Maybe. Maybe you are. You saw what happened when he tried to stop Master Gilbur from translating the champion. Maybe he's being used and doesn't know it." Her temples were beginning to ache. "Maybe he was misled while he was making his mirror—maybe he thought it *was* an exact copy. How would he know if Master Gilbur lied to him? Maybe these 'abilities' are Master Gilbur's, not Geraden's."

Master Eremis shook his head. "That is conceivable." His face seemed to be growing darker. "Why do you imagine that I have relied on subterfuge rather than direct action? I have not wanted to risk harm to anyone who might be innocent. But remember two things, my lady.

"The first is a fact. It is Geraden who figures so prominently in the augury, not Gilbur. That cannot be meaningless.

"The second is a possibility. As it is conceivable that Geraden is being manipulated, so it is also conceivable that he and Gilbur feigned their conflict in order to disguise their relationship, thereby freeing Geraden to continue his work when Gilbur was forced to flee."

At once, Terisa retorted, "That's crazy!" so strongly that she surprised herself. She and Geraden had been buried alive together. "Master Gilbur almost got him killed!"

"Paugh!" Abruptly, the Master was angry again. "Gilbur could not have foreseen that—or caused it. He was busy with his translation." The pressure of his knees increased. "Do not insult my intelligence."

As quickly as it had come, her resistance evaporated. "I'm sorry," she said like a wince. Don't hurt me. His face had gone completely dark: she could see nothing but the outlines of his form against the wall. "I'm not used to thinking like this."

Unfortunately, that wasn't what he wished to hear. His grip felt like rock, bruising her flesh. In rising panic, she asked, "What do you want me to do?"

He didn't ease the clench of his knees or release his embrace, yet the vehemence of his posture softened. "Under other circumstances," he murmured harshly, "I would not ask such flesh to serve any purpose but its own. But I must have your help.

"This is what I want you to do." He undid the last buttons and jerked her shirt open. "I want you to pretend friendship for young Geraden." Her breasts were exposed to the cold air and his moist breath. "I want you to watch him for me, study him for any sign of betrayal or talent, scrutinize him for any word or deed or implication which may reveal his secrets to me.

"And tell him nothing. Do not tell him that you have spoken to me. Swear Artagel to silence if you must. Give no hint to anyone that we are allies."

Moving his head from side to side, he stroked his wet tongue across her nipples, bringing them to hardness, making them demand him. Then he put his mouth to work, sucking and kissing her breasts.

She couldn't resist him. She felt herself giving up balance, leaning into him, so that his hand and his lips would caress her more strongly. He made it imaginable that she could clinch her arms around his neck and hug herself to him.

And yet he asked her to pretend—to watch— The bare conception knotted her stomach. He was asking her to betray Geraden, *Geraden!*

She had already doubted him once today, and he had proved his faithfulness almost immediately. He had kept her sane and actual under the rubble of the meeting hall. Simply to admit the intellectual possibility that he might be dishonest felt like an essential injustice. He was more loyal than this. Didn't he deserve more loyalty?

How could she betray him?

How could she ignore Master Eremis' reasons for what he did, his commitment to Mordant's survival, his ardor?

Both he and Geraden were trying to tell her who she was.

Without raising his head—without ceasing his kisses and caresses, which seemed to draw her heart to the surface of her skin and inspire it with every touch—he whispered surely, "You are mine. I have claimed you. Whenever you think of another man—whenever you are tempted to doubt me—you will remember my lips upon your breasts, and you will cleave to me. You will do what I ask with Geraden."

"Yes." She was helpless to say anything else. What stubbornness she had left was already committed, holding her arms back from his neck, holding herself passive in his embrace. It would have been easier to give him her inexperienced passion and let him do what he desired with it. But she was too deeply sickened for that submission.

"You will do what I ask," he repeated as if in litany.

"I will do what you ask."

"When I am freed from this cell—for I will be freed. Do not ever doubt that I will be freed. If Lebbick does not recognize my innocence, I will free myself in spite of him. And when I am free, I will come to you. Then we will consummate these kisses, and I will take possession of your fine beauty utterly. There will be no part of your womanhood which I have not claimed—and no portion of my manhood which you have not accepted."

"Yes," she said again. For a moment, she wanted what he wanted, despite her nausea. "Yes." As if she knew what her acquiescence meant.

"In that case"—he leaned back without warning, dropped his arms, released his knees—"you must leave me. You will be of no help at all if Lebbick finds you here. If he does not stretch his authority so far as to imprison you, he will certainly do his best to make sure that we cannot meet and talk again. Button your shirt and call Artagel."

His change of mood and manner was so abrupt that she flushed with shame. "Yes." Why did she keep repeating herself, offering him her assent over and over again like an idiot child? "Yes." Her father's moods had been sharply and inexplicably changeable, flashing from tolerance to anger for reasons she could never understand. Because of the ache in her stomach and the heat in her face, she didn't look at Master Eremis again. She turned away; her hands shook as she hurried to do up her shirt and tuck it back into her pants.

For a moment, her throat refused to work. Then she whispered, "Artagel."

"Speak louder, my lady," Master Eremis suggested with cold mirth. "I doubt that he can hear you."

Louder.

"Artagel. I'm done." A croak in the back of her throat.

He wants me to betray Geraden.

Like a flowing shadow, Artagel appeared past the edge of the cell and reached the door. Then the door was open. "My lady," he murmured, offering her his hand, his arm.

With the Master's silence behind her like a wall, she moved to accept Artagel's support.

He drew her out of the cell, paused almost negligibly to relock the door, then took her down the passage, out of sight of Master Eremis' imprisonment.

"My lady," he growled as soon as they were beyond hearing, "are you all right? What did he say to you?"

The concern in his voice was so quick and true—so much like his brother—that her knees gave out, and she crumpled.

Sickness and shame. Desire and dismay. Master Eremis was right: she could never forget the touch of his lips and tongue; she was his; he could do anything he wanted with her. But what he wanted—! To spy on the person she most needed to trust, the man whose smile lifted her heart. To betray—

Artagel held her. *"Terisa."* His eyes were bright and extreme. *"What did that bastard say to you?"*

It hurt. She should have cried out in simple protest. But that would ruin everything. He was Geraden's brother. Despite his concern, the light in his eyes and the murderous half-smile on his lips, she couldn't tell him what was wrong. If she did, he would tell Geraden. She understood that clearly. He might be willing to keep one or two things secret from Castellan Lebbick for her sake, but he wouldn't keep secrets from Geraden.

To speak to him now would be the coward's way to betray Master Eremis, to withdraw her allegiance and aid, her new passion, without having the courage to face Geraden and admit that she had chosen his side by default, that she preferred his friendship to Eremis' love for no better reason than because she wasn't brave enough to do otherwise.

With an effort, she found her balance and took her weight on her legs, easing the urgency of Artagel's grasp. "I'm sorry." When he let go of her arms, she pushed her hands through her hair. "I guess I really haven't recovered from yesterday."

"Are you sure that's it?" Artagel's concern made his voice rough. "You were better before you went in there. You look like Eremis just tried to rape you."

He was so far from the truth that she let out a giggle.

That didn't reassure him, however. Her giggle sounded ominously hysterical. And she had trouble making it stop.

She would have to give him a more cogent explanation if she wanted to deflect his alarm. "I'm sorry," she repeated. Still giggling —and fighting it. "I don't know what's come over me. I've just had a lesson in humility.

"I told you I wanted to see if I could make people start talking to each other." Abruptly, the artificial mirth ran out of her, and she found herself close to tears. "That's going to be a lot harder than I thought."

For a moment, he studied her sharply. Then he took her hand, drew it through his arm to comfort her, and moved her again in the direction of the guardroom. "Don't worry about it, my lady. It was worth trying. It's still worth trying. Master Eremis just"—his smile was perhaps a shade too fierce to offer much consolation—"isn't very promising material to work with."

In an effort to distract him, she asked, "Is it true that you and he used to be friends? Before Geraden turned you against him?"

He shrugged. "Sort of. Not really. I was never actually able to like him, but I didn't have any reason for the way I felt, so I kept it to myself." He glanced at her. "Geraden understands these things better than I do. And he knows Eremis a lot better. You ought to talk to him about it."

She didn't meet his gaze. "You trust Geraden completely, don't you."

Without hesitation, he replied, "He's my brother."

"Is that the only reason?"

Her question made him chuckle. "No, my lady, that's not the only reason. It's at least two reasons—experience and blood. We have five other brothers, you know. I've watched him with all of them." Then his face darkened, and he turned her so that she had to look at him. "My lady, does Eremis think you shouldn't trust Geraden?"

Kicking herself, she countered, "That isn't what I meant. I don't know if you realize what a strange position you're in. As far as I can tell, you're the only person in Orison everybody trusts. Even Master Eremis wants you on his side." Her unexpected facility for lies—for using parts of the truth to disguise other parts—amazed and frightened her. "I want to know why you trust Geraden because I'm trying to understand *you*."

Apparently, he believed her explanation; but he still didn't know how to respond. After an awkward moment, he said in a tone of deliberate foolishness, as if her question embarrassed him, "It's clean living, my lady. Nobody trusts anybody who overindulges in clean living. I'm more dissolute than practically everybody else, so I'm easier to trust."

His reply was clearly intended as a joke, but she accepted it simply because she was relieved to get away from his seriousness. "I never thought about it that way," she murmured as she let him guide her down the corridor to the guardroom.

From the guardroom, they returned to the ballroom and the main halls of Orison. Now she wanted him to leave her; she couldn't go on talking to him and still keep her emotions hidden. With frustrating gallantry, however, he insisted on escorting her most of the way toward her rooms. She was unable to detach herself from his attendance until they reached the tower that held her rooms. After thanking him abruptly, she hurried up the stairs as if she were fleeing from him.

But of course what she really fled from was the danger he represented—the danger that she would betray the choice she had to make before she was sure of it. She had said *yes* to Master Eremis, and *yes* again; but the illness in her stomach was getting worse. Artagel bore just enough resemblance to Geraden—and she had been just dishon-

est enough with him—to make what the Imager wanted of her vivid
and appalling.

Pretend friendship.

Watch him.

Tell him nothing.

She feared she would throw up before she reached safety.

When she approached her door, however, one of the guards
stepped forward, gave her a stiff bow, and said with gruff courtesy,
"My lady, you have a visitor."

For a second, she thought her knees were going to fail again. A
visitor. Now? Oh, please. But she was tired of being so weak. Her
emotional nausea itself acted like a kind of strength, enabling her to
keep her legs under her, her head up, her voice quiet. "Who is it?"

The guard seemed discomfited. "We couldn't refuse to let her in,
my lady. You've never asked us to keep visitors out of your rooms."

His self-defense made no sense, but Terisa didn't try to understand
it. "Who is it?" she repeated.

"The lady Elega." At once, the guard added, "We couldn't refuse
her, could we? She's the King's daughter."

From a distance, Terisa heard herself say, "Of course not. You did
the right thing." But she wasn't paying much attention. The lady
Elega—Myste's impatient and discontented sister. Terisa hadn't spoken to her since their awkward, disappointing lunch. On that occasion, Elega had protested, *We are women like yourself, not self-serving
men hungry for power. We can be trusted. This pretense is not needed with
us.* When Terisa had refused to give up her pretense of ordinariness,
the lady Elega had looked the way Terisa herself felt now.

What does she want this time? Terisa wondered dimly.

Then it came to her, and a sting of adrenaline ran down her veins.
Myste.

With a pang of embarrassment, she realized that she was standing
slack-faced in the hall while one of the guards held her door open
and both men made obvious efforts to appear unaware of her distraction. Pushing herself into motion, she entered her sitting room as if
she were still in a hurry.

Elega stood before one of the windows, much as Myste had once
stood. And, like Myste, she was beautiful. But her beauty seemed to
be a reflection of the lamp- and firelight in the room, a contrast to the
lowering gray winter outside the glass. In its own way, her skin was
as pale as her short blond hair; and both emphasized the striking

violet flash of her eyes. Although she was clad and jeweled like a queen, her manner was too forthright, too assertive for ornaments. Nevertheless she had a queen's spirit, a queen's instincts.

She left the window at once. As the door closed, she moved a few steps toward Terisa; there she stopped. Her gaze reminded Terisa of another contrast between the King's daughters. Unlike Myste's, Elega's glances were so immediate and fiery that they threw what she saw into stark relief. Both, however, were able to convey an impression of excitement, a sense of possibilities. "My lady," she said in a low voice. "Terisa. I hope you will forgive this intrusion. I did not know when you would return—and I did not want to wait in the hall."

Terisa didn't feel equal to the situation. All she wanted to do was huddle near the fire to drive the cold out of her bones and drink wine until her stomach either calmed down or got rid of its distress. But she had to face Elega for Myste's sake. Responding almost automatically, she waved a hand toward the wine goblets and decanter, which Saddith had mercifully replenished. "Would you like to join me? I'm going to have some wine."

"Thank you." Elega obviously had no interest in wine. Nevertheless she accepted the goblet Terisa handed her as if she appreciated the gesture.

Terisa took a longer draught than good manners or wisdom suggested and refilled her goblet. Without thinking to offer Elega a seat, she sat down in the chair nearest the fire. The flames were oddly entrancing. She hadn't realized how cold she was. How long had she stood in Master Eremis' cell with her shirt open—?

"Terisa?" She heard Elega as clearly as a voice in a fever. "Are you well?"

With an effort, she pulled her attention away from the fire. "Too much is happening." Unlike Elega's, her own voice sounded muffled. "I don't understand it all." In an effort to be polite, she added, "Why don't you sit down and tell me what's on your mind?"

For a moment, Elega hesitated. Her doubts were plain in her face. I must look awful, Terisa thought vaguely. Abruptly, however, the lady became resolute. First she accepted a chair. Then she asked softly, firmly, "Terisa, where is Myste?"

It was symptomatic of Terisa's condition that she leaped from this question to the conclusion that King Joyse had somehow seen through her lie. With an inward wince, she replied suspiciously, "Did your father send you to talk to me?"

Elega raised her eyebrows in surprise. "No. Why would he?" Gradually her tone took on a tinge of contempt. "I doubt he knows that she is gone. And if he does know—and if he thought to have me ask for him the questions a father should ask—I would refuse. I am his daughter, but he has broken that duty for me by breaking all other duties for himself.

"No," she repeated, pushing the subject of her father aside, "I ask because I am afraid. My sister is not the wisest or the most practical woman in Orison. Her dreams often do not contain enough plain sense for ballast. I fear she has done something very foolish.

"Terisa, where is she?"

Terisa turned back to the fire to avoid Elega's vivid gaze. So her lie to the King hadn't been caught. That was a relief. Unfortunately, Elega's question still had to be answered.

Staring into the flames as though they might hypnotize her and thereby make her strong, Terisa murmured, "What are you afraid she's done?"

"I hardly know." The lady's uncertainty sounded sincere. "I freely admit I do not understand her, Terisa. She prefers dreams to realities. I know that she is hurt—as I am—by what our father has done, and especially by his humiliation of Prince Kragen. That the King of Mordant"—she forgot her concern for a moment in anger—"should actively seek war with Alend is abominable." Then she steadied herself. "But what Myste might do because of her pain, I cannot guess. Perhaps she has left Orison for some mad reason." Her tone tightened. "Perhaps she has gone after Prince Kragen, thinking to persuade him to ignore the extent of his insults."

Elega had come just close enough to the truth to frighten Terisa. Dimly, she asked, "What makes you think I know where she is?"

Again, Elega hesitated. When she spoke, her tone was carefully neutral, distinct but unaccusing. "First, because I doubt that anyone else in Orison would assist her in anything greatly foolish. She is the King's daughter. Orison's people value her too highly to help her into trouble.

"But primarily," she went on, "because I have seen how she responds to your insistence that you are only an ordinary woman."

Terisa gazed vacantly into the fire and waited.

"It was an astonishment to me," admitted Elega frankly. "I con-

sider that people are as ordinary or as exceptional as they choose to
be. Oh, I am assured that no one can conceive a talent for Imagery or
statecraft by effort of will"—she didn't sound entirely convinced—
"and it is true past argument that anyone who has the misfortune to
be born a woman must oppose the prejudices of all the world in
order to prove herself. Yet I believe that in the end I am limited only
by the limits of my determination, not by accidents of talent or
preconceptions of sex.

"Myste," she sighed, "thinks otherwise. She does not want to
open doors. She dreams that doors will be opened for her. And she
sees you, Terisa, as proof that into *any* life—be it drab and dreary
enough to numb the mind forever—a door of magic and mystery
may open, offering the least drudge an opportunity for grandeur."
Her tone suggested frustration rather than disdain. "In the meantime, it behooves us to be contented while we wait.

"I have no reason to believe that you know where she is. Yet I
think you do, if anyone does. You are a flame which she is too
mothlike to resist."

This view of Myste struck Terisa as so poignant—and so mistaken
—that she didn't know how to reply to it. If anything, Elega's ideas
seemed less realistic than Myste's, rather than more. And Terisa had
questions of her own about the King's eldest daughter. But that
wasn't the point, of course. What she thought didn't matter. In this
situation, only her promise to Myste mattered.

As if she were reading her answer in the flames and coals, she
murmured, "She came here yesterday because she wanted to get into
the passage behind my wardrobe." She felt rather than saw Elega
stiffen. "She used it to sneak out of Orison without being stopped."
Behind the soft snap of the fire and the distant soughing of wind past
the edges of the tower, the silence in the room was intense. "She
went back to her mother."

For a moment, Elega remained still—so still that Terisa couldn't
imagine what she was doing. Then, in a tone soft with surprise, as if
she had just received a revelation, the lady breathed, "That cannot
be true."

Anxiety twisted through Terisa. Half involuntarily, she turned to
look at Elega.

The lady had risen to her feet. Her eyes flashed as though their
violet depths were lit by lightning. Yet her demeanor remained
quiet, almost perfectly self-possessed.

"I believe that Myste has left Orison. Thank you for telling me how it was done. But she has no intention of going to the Care of Fayle, to Romish—to Queen Madin, our mother."

Because she was lying, Terisa wanted to protest that she wasn't: she wanted to use all her distress and fear to feign as much anger as possible. But she was restrained by Elega's eagerness. It bore so little resemblance to the reaction she had expected.

With slow caution, she said, "She was disgusted by what the King did to Prince Kragen. She couldn't stand to watch him destroy himself and Mordant anymore, so she decided to go back to the rest of her family."

"Terisa—" The lady's arms made a gesture of appeal, which she controlled abruptly. "Do not continue. That is unimportant now. A lie is an exercise of power, and I rejoice to see it. You are not passive —you are no longer content to hide behind a mask of ordinariness. You have decided to take your part in Mordant's need. That is a great step—a step which I can only hope Myste has taken also—and I honor you for it."

Nonplussed to the point of chagrin, Terisa stared at her visitor. Simply because she had to say something, she muttered, "I'm not lying."

Elega shook her head decisively. "I will attempt to persuade you this charade is not necessary with me." But then she paused. Her eyes scanned the room as if searching for the best line of argument. In an abstract way, like a woman digressing momentarily while she prepared her thoughts, she asked, "Terisa, what do you consider Orison's greatest internal weakness?"

Taken completely by surprise, Terisa said without thinking, "The water supply."

The lady didn't appear to be paying attention. "In what way?"

"If you poisoned the reservoir, the whole castle would be helpless." Not permanently, of course. The small spring under the walls supplied some water. The open roof and the collecting pipes could bring in large quantities during any heavy snow- or rainfall. But for a few days, at least—

Why were she and Elega having this conversation?

Smiling, the lady Elega returned to her chair, seated herself, smoothed out her skirt. The electricity of her gaze made Terisa shiver. Without transition, she said in a relaxed, conversational tone, "You have been in Orison for some time now. I fear that you have seen few of us at our best. Nevertheless you have had time to form impressions, perhaps even to draw conclusions.

"What do you think of us? Is there hope for Orison and Mordant? What is your opinion of King Joyse?"

Baffled and vexed, Terisa was tempted to retort, No, I don't think there's any hope. Not as long as you insist on behaving like this. But she could feel danger around her. Whatever she said would have consequences. Carefully, she replied, "I think he knows what he's doing."

Elega's smile seemed to grow a degree brighter. "And the Congery? What do you think of the Imagers? They have put us in grave peril. Are they honest? Or perhaps I should ask, Are they honorable?"

Terisa shrugged. She wasn't about to begin discussing either Master Eremis' or Geraden's ideas with the King's strange daughter. "Some of them seem to be. Others don't." Then she added, "I don't think very many of them expected the champion to go wild like that."

This answer gave Elega less satisfaction, but she didn't dwell on it. "And the lords of the Cares? What are your opinions of them?"

In reaction, alarm flushed through Terisa. How did—? Trying to cover her fright, she jerked to her feet, went to the wine decanter, and refilled her goblet. How did Elega know she had met the lords of the Cares? Suddenly, the whole room felt threatening, as though the walls were transparent and the floor might yawn open. Elega knew because someone had told her. That was simple enough. Or because she had had a hand in the attack on Terisa. That wasn't so simple. But still somebody must have told her about the meeting. Who would have any reason in the world to do that?

Unexpectedly, Terisa found that she had reached her limit. She was already in distress—and Elega was making no sense at all. Apparently, she was trying to probe Terisa, test her somehow. But for what?

She drained her goblet, faced the King's daughter squarely, and said, "Prince Kragen and I were talking about you. You've made a conquest. He's really quite impressed. What did he say about you?" she asked rhetorically. "He said if you were an Alend you would 'stand high among the powers of the Kingdom.'" Then she stopped to let Elega draw as many inferences as possible.

The lady rose to her feet immediately to meet Terisa's stare. Her smile was like the lights in the dining room of Terisa's mirror-walled apartment: it was on a rheostat which made it brighter at every turn. "Terisa," she said softly, "you take my breath away. Is this what being ordinary means in your world? That place must be brave beyond conception. You have begun working to shape events with a vengeance.

"I understand you," she affirmed. "Do you understand me?"

Terisa didn't answer. She was afraid to open her mouth.

"Terisa," Elega urged in a whisper, "I have said that this charade is not necessary with me. You can no longer pretend passivity—and you need not pretend ignorance."

Still Terisa didn't answer.

Slowly, Elega's brightness dimmed. She didn't give up, however. "Since you have mentioned Prince Kragen, perhaps you will tell me your impression of him."

With an effort, Terisa recovered her voice. "Did you know the Alend monarchy isn't hereditary? It has to be earned. That's what he's doing here. He's trying to earn the right to become the next Alend Monarch." She studied Elega closely, but the lady's expression betrayed nothing except its underlying intensity. "I think that's more important to him than peace."

This riposte was rewarded with a slight widening of Elega's eyes, a slow congealing of her smile. The way her pleasure curdled reminded Terisa that she had no real idea what was going on. Elega clearly understood what Terisa was saying better than Terisa did herself.

In a voice scarcely louder than a whisper, the lady asked, "Do you not believe that you can trust me? We are women, you and I—despised in a world of men. There is no one here whom you *can* trust but me. No one else intends as much good to both Mordant and yourself. What may I do to convince you?"

That, at least, was a question Terisa could meet. Without hesitation, she said, "Tell me what's going on. Before you ask me to trust you, start trusting me."

Slowly, Elega nodded in acknowledgment. She was no longer looking at Terisa, and her smile was gone. "You are better at this than I suspected. I cannot trust you until you have first trusted me. I have more to lose."

Sadly, she turned to go.

In her confusion and frustration, Terisa wanted to demand, What is *that*, exactly? What have you got to lose that's more than every-body else in this mess? But she let it go. Instead, she said before Elega reached the door, "Just tell me one thing. What makes you think I'm lying about Myste?"

The lady paused with her hand on the latch. A different smile touched her mouth, a smile like the affectionate and faintly conde-scending one she had occasionally given her sister. "You do well, as I have said, Terisa. But you do not know Mordant well enough to exert power without risk. Plainly, you do not know that what you have said of Myste is impossible. Romish is too far. In this winter, it would be easier for a lone woman to rebuild our breached wall than to cross the Demesne and Armigite on foot." A suggestion of tri-umph. "I doubt that you intend me to believe my sister has decided to kill herself."

Still smiling, she left the room.

Terisa hardly noticed her departure. She was remembering the way King Joyse had stood in front of her with his eyes squeezed shut and tears spilling down his cheeks, in anguish at the idea that Myste had gone back to her mother. *If you lie to me*, he had said like an appeal. *If you dare lie to me*—But he must have guessed even then that she wasn't telling the truth.

Her stomach heaved. Unfortunately, all the lies and plots and pain she had swallowed refused to be ejected. After a moment, she went to the door and opened it long enough to tell the guards that she didn't want any more visitors today. Then she bolted the door, sat down again in front of the fire, and had more to drink than she had ever had in her life.

EIGHTEEN:
A LITTLE
CONVERSATION

T he next morning, she had the kind of headache that made strong men swear off drink. Internal pressure seemed to be prying the bones of her skull apart, and her brain felt bruised. In addition, her throat had apparently been treated with sandpaper, and her stomach gave the impression that it was sloshing wetly from side to side in her abdomen.

Nevertheless she was no longer so badly baffled by her talk with Elega.

The lady and Prince Kragen must have formed some kind of alliance. Elega knew about Terisa's meeting with the lords of the Cares because the Prince had told her. What they hoped to accomplish, Terisa wasn't sure; but she was sure that whatever it was wouldn't make King Joyse either comfortable or happy.

And they hoped to include her for some reason.

Sometime during her fourth or fifth goblet of wine, she had found —rather to her surprise—that she didn't like what Elega was doing. King Joyse persistently refused to remind her of her own father. He had perhaps sacrificed most ordinary claims on the loyalty of his people, but he didn't deserve to be betrayed by his daughter.

So the question she was left with—the question on which neither too much wine nor a night thick with bad dreams had shed any particular light—was the one that had made her sick in the first place. What was she going to do about Geraden? Or about Master Eremis?

Since she was hung over, the Master's caresses no longer seemed entirely inevitable or convincing. Yet his arguments were still important. In fact, his reasons for distrusting Geraden made more sense than Geraden's for believing the worst of him. On the other hand, the idea that Geraden was a traitor felt absurd.

Groaning more to persuade herself she was alive than because it relieved the pain, she climbed weakly out of the knotted chaos that her dreams had made of the bed. The rooms were cold: by bolting the door, she had locked Saddith out; and she couldn't remember having put wood on the fires herself more than once or twice. But the cold forced her to take better command of the situation. Struggling into her robe, she went deliberately into the bathroom to drink as much water as her stomach could bear. Then she returned to the hearth in her sitting room and began trying to coax a little flame out of the warm coals.

In her condition, blowing on the coals was as painful as batting her head against the wall. Nevertheless she persevered because she was determined not to let anyone into the suite to help her. She didn't want an audience while she suffered the consequences of her folly. So she got the fire going despite the sharp pressure in her brain. She took a bath, even washed her hair out of sheer stubbornness. And she dressed herself alone, working her way into one of Myste's relatively demure gowns, a warm sheath of yellow velvet. Only then did she permit herself to unbolt the door to see if Saddith had left a tray for her.

In fact, the maid had done so. And, as a mercy, there was no one waiting to talk to her. In peace, she was able to eat a little porridge and drink a great deal of a hot beverage which she thought of as tea —although it tasted more like cinnamon and rose petals—before a knock at the door announced that she had a visitor.

She didn't trust her voice, so she moved carefully to the door and opened it.

Geraden stood outside.

Oh, terrific. That was just what she needed.

"I hope I'm not disturbing you," he began at once. "We didn't get a chance to talk yesterday. I wanted to tell you—" Then his smile faded. "Are you all right? You look a little sick."

Thanks to Master Eremis, the sight of the Apt made anxiety throb in her veins—which in turn threatened to split her head. "It's the gown." Her voice came out like a croak. "Yellow isn't my color."

Doggedly, she gave him a smile that felt like a crack across a porce-
lain vase, and invited him in.

Studying her, he said as soon as the door was closed, "I tried to see
you yesterday, but the guards told me to leave you alone. I couldn't
help worrying." Behind his concern, he looked self-conscious.
"How did your talk with Master Eremis go?"

She concentrated on keeping herself from groaning or shutting
her eyes. "Artagel told you."

He nodded. "He might have anyway. But you looked so bad
when you came out of the cell, he felt he didn't have any choice."

"Then he must have told you what happened." Her sudden bitterness surprised her. When had she begun to believe that she had the
right to resent the way she was treated? "I thought I was going to be
able to accomplish something—I thought I was going to make a
difference. I was going to persuade you to start cooperating with
each other." Instead, I'm supposed to spy on you, even though
you're the only friend I've got left, now that Myste is gone. Even
though you're the only one who cares about me enough to *do* anything. "Instead, all I did was make a fool of myself."

No, she wouldn't do it. She couldn't. The promise of a few intimate kisses didn't suffice. Geraden was too important to her. She
would watch him, yes. But she wouldn't tell anyone what she
learned. Not unless he did something that forced her to believe
Master Eremis was right about him. And she would make the decision for herself. No matter what the Master offered her.

Unexpectedly, she felt better. In spite of her resolution, she found
herself saying, "I had too much to drink yesterday," so that his feelings wouldn't be hurt. "I suppose I was trying to drown my sorrows.
My head feels like a football."

This time there was a quirk of relief in his smile. "I've done that a
few times," he admitted, pretending rue. "I still don't know what
made me think it was a good idea. I guess I'd just had more of my
own fumble-footedness than I could stand.

"Anyway, I'm sorry that happened to you," he added in a way that
suggested it wasn't his biggest regret. "For your sake, I wish he had
listened to you.

"Terisa, I—"

He stopped abruptly, and his eyes began to fill with tears. Suddenly, she thought he had come to tell her something terrible. In-

stinctively defensive, she went back to the door and bolted it. Then she faced his troubled brown gaze.

"What's the matter, Geraden?"

"Nothing," he said quickly. "Nothing." Too quickly. "I mean, you survived, didn't you? It turned out all right."

He couldn't sustain his pretense, however. "I'm sorry." His voice rasped, but he didn't turn away to hide what he was feeling. "I'm really sorry. After we were rescued—after they got us out from underneath all that rock—Artagel took me back to my room. I drank quite a bit of wine myself. But when I went to sleep I kept having the same dream over and over again, exactly the same." His expression twisted. "For a long time, I thought it was a nightmare. It was the *worst*—"

He took a breath to steady himself. "But I finally realized it wasn't a nightmare. I wasn't dreaming at all. I was just remembering." He had to grit his teeth to make himself say, "I was remembering that you almost got killed."

Oh, is that all? She tried not to show her relief. What he was saying wasn't terrible after all.

"That only happened because of me."

Now she stared at him.

"I brought you here," he explained miserably. "I don't know how to take you back where you belong. People want you dead. They want to manipulate you. And the champion—

"You went through that whole ordeal—you were buried alive and came within inches of being crushed to death—because of me.

"When I saw Castellan Lebbick harassing you, I wanted to club him with a chair. I'm sorry. That's what I should have done. Just to make him *stop*. It's my fault you got hit.

"If anything happens to you, it'll break my heart."

If she had felt healthier, she might have laughed. Instead, she put her hand on his arm, touched the muscles knotted along his bones. "Geraden," she protested, "he would have snapped you in half. He wants somebody to defy him, so he can crush them."

In response, he looked at her in pain; and she recognized that he needed a better answer than that. No one else had ever declared so much concern for her. It was strange, really—and endearing. He had nightmares because of her?

She did the best she could. "You kept me *sane*. You were in as much trouble as I was. Worse. Master Gilbur nearly knocked your head off. But you were still able to hold me together. If you hadn't helped me, I would have lost my mind hours before we were rescued."

She should have gone on—should have said, You and Myste are the only friends I've ever had. No one has ever been as good to me as you have. I'm glad I'm here. But that was too much for her self-consciousness, her fragile sense of herself. Awkwardly, she dropped her hand.

And yet she had to do something for him that would mean as much as a touch. Rather than attempting to match his declaration, she tried to joke with him. "This has got to stop. I'm going to start rationing you. If you apologize to me more than once a day, I'll kick you."

He peered at her dubiously, uncertain how to take her. "Do you mean that? I know I apologize a lot. If you caused as much trouble as I do, you would too. So far, you're the only thing I haven't been wrong about. You shouldn't have to bear the brunt of my disasters."

There was no question about it: he deserved better from her. Trying to provide it, she looked straight into his eyes and said, "You don't get me in trouble. You save me. Orison is full of disasters, but as far as I'm concerned you haven't caused any of them. You're one of the few people who wants to do something about them.

"You don't have anything to apologize for."

He continued to study her warily. When she didn't drop her gaze, however, he began to relax. His shoulders lifted; the chagrin let go of his face; his eyes brightened as if they had been wiped clean. After a moment, he said softly, "Thank you."

Now her heart was eased. She was willing to fight the pain in her head if that enabled her to make him happier. Smiling more successfully, she sat down in one of the chairs near the fire, then gestured toward her tray. "Have you had breakfast? I've got more than I can eat."

He shook his head. He seemed to be suppressing a burst of exuberance, a desire to shout or sing or hug her. Moving with comic care, so that he wouldn't trip or lose his balance, he turned a chair to face hers and seated himself. Then he gleamed in humorous triumph, as if to say, And you thought I couldn't do it.

What he actually said, however, was, "What did King Joyse want to talk to you about?"

She hoped without much optimism that her sudden surge of anxiety didn't show. In the press of more recent events, she had forgotten the question of what to tell him about her discussion with the King. He might be appalled by what she had discovered, deeply grieved to learn that his father's old friend and his own childhood hero was deliberately embarked on the destruction of Mordant. And Master Quillon had made a point of explaining that Geraden was still in danger from his nameless enemies, still liable to pay a high price for knowing too much. Or had Master Quillon come to Master Eremis' conclusion that Geraden himself was dangerous, not to be trusted? Were Eremis' reasons for his distrust that good?

When she didn't reply at once, Geraden went on, "Being thrown out of his rooms like that wasn't exactly the highlight of my life." He sounded incongruously cheerful, as if he wanted to encourage her. "I didn't think the Tor would take his side." He shrugged. "On the other hand, I don't have any reason to believe I ever know what the Tor is going to do. I just want to understand. I want King Joyse to say something that makes sense."

Terisa wasn't listening. The question in front of her was too complex to be answered casually. She needed more time to think. More time to watch. Unconscious of her own abruptness, she said, "He wanted to talk about checkers some more." Her headache was getting ahead of her. On impulse, she added, "Elega was here."

Geraden waited expectantly. When she didn't continue, he asked, "The lady Elega? My former betrothed? When was that?"

She tried to clear her thoughts. Actually, she had a number of things she wanted to talk to Geraden about. Elega might be a safe place to start. If she could get her hangover under control.

"She was waiting here for me. When I got back from seeing Master Eremis."

"What did she want?"

Terisa hesitated momentarily. Was she sure she wanted to say this to Geraden?

Yes. She was already carrying too many questions alone.

With unexpected ire, she articulated distinctly, "The lady Elega wanted to enlist me in a plot against her father."

Geraden froze. "What kind of plot?"

"I don't have any idea." As fully as she could, she told him what had been said—and what she surmised. His eyes narrowed at Prince Kragen's name, but he listened without interrupting. Sourly, she concluded, "That was why I didn't want any more visitors yesterday.

I didn't want to take the chance I might hear anything else like that for a while."

He frowned without speaking for a moment—long enough to make her wonder whether he believed her. She wanted him to believe her. The more secrets she kept, the more lies she told, the greater her need to be believed became, especially when she was being honest. Fortunately, he began to nod.

"That's always worried me about her," he murmured, brooding. "I've always had the feeling she was more interested in what kings are than in what they do. More interested in the power than in what the power is for. She might be capable of some pretty unscrupulous decisions."

"So you don't think I'm jumping to conclusions?"

"No." His face was tense with thought. "Not after your conversation with Prince Kragen. By that time, they had probably already agreed to approach you."

"I wish I knew what they think I can do," she complained, simply because she felt like complaining. "It's the same problem I have with everybody. Even you. You all think I can *do* something." But her parents had never permitted her to whine, and she found she didn't care for the sound of it herself. "I haven't shown much sign of it yet," she finished.

Geraden went on musing morosely. "What should *we* do?" he wondered. "Should we tell King Joyse?"

Careful not to reveal too much, she countered, "If we could get him to listen, do you think he would pay any attention?"

He let out a dejected sigh. "Probably not." Then he asked, "What about Castellan Lebbick?"

She shrugged. "I don't like telling him anything. I don't like the way he treats me.

"He'll certainly *do* something. He may or may not be able to stop her—but whatever he does will give away the fact that we told him. She'll know she can't trust me. That'll be the end of our chances to find out what she's doing."

The Apt shot her a glance and a quick grin. "For someone who can't do anything, you seem determined to try. What's your suggestion?"

She was about to say, I don't have any idea, when she had what felt like an inspiration. "You could ask Argus and Ribuld to keep an eye on her."

He blinked at the unexpected notion. "They didn't exactly enjoy what happened the last time they did me a favor," he muttered, thinking aloud. "But this time Artagel is here to back me up. They might be willing—especially if they can think of a way to do it without making Castellan Lebbick suspicious." He met Terisa's gaze as he added, "It might be worth it. If we can just learn how she intends to communicate with Prince Kragen, that'll be an improvement.

"I'll ask them." The decision brought back his sense of humor. With a mischievous glint, he commented, "If you do it, they may try to talk you into making it worth their while. You can guess what that means. The worst they can do to me is say no."

Smiling at him was becoming easier. Her headache had begun to recede. And her anxiety had turned to relief again. The sensation that here, at least, was one subject on which she wasn't alone—and on which Geraden agreed with her—was a positive pleasure. When he smiled back, she felt good enough to broach another of her many areas of incomprehension.

"That conversation I had with Prince Kragen reminds me. What's an arch-Imager?"

Her question made Geraden sit up straighter. "It reminds you—? What connection—?" Almost at once, however, he pushed down his confusion, unwilling to give his questions precedence over hers. "An arch-Imager is someone who has mastered what we consider the apex of translation—the ability to pass safely through flat glass. As far as we know, only one man has ever done it—the arch-Imager Vagel.

"In theory, the difficulty is that translation changes whatever it touches. When the translation involves a passage between separate worlds—or, if Master Eremis is right"—he grimaced—"between our world and Images which are known not to exist in our world—the changes are appropriate. For instance, they solve the problems of language and breathing. But when you pass through a flat glass, you don't actually go anywhere. I mean, you move from place to place, but you stay in the same world. So you don't need to be changed. But you are anyway." He looked down at his hands. "It made Adept Havelock mad.

"Theoretically, if you looked into a flat mirror that showed you to yourself—in other words, a mirror that was focused on the exact spot where you were standing, so that you were also in the Image looking out at yourself—you would go into a kind of translation cycle, passing simultaneously back and forth between yourself and your Image, changing literally without going anywhere. Probably nobody who looked at you would be able to see the difference. But your mind would be gone. Not just mad. Taken away.

"I still don't know how I survived seeing myself in that room where I found you. I have to believe mirrors *are* different in your world. Or you're the most powerful Imager we've ever heard of.

"Anyway, the other important point is that the capacity to be an arch-Imager seems to be just that—a capacity. It isn't a skill you can learn, it's a talent you're born with. If it were a skill, Havelock would have mastered it somehow. 'The Adept' isn't an honorary title. He earned it by being better at translations than anybody else. In particular, he was better at working translations with mirrors he didn't make. *I* can't even work them with mirrors I *did* make.

"Does that answer your question?"

Terisa nodded. She was trying to make what he told her fit her experience.

"Then answer mine. What does all this have to do with your conversation with Prince Kragen?"

"Oh, that. I'm sorry. I wasn't trying to be cryptic. It just seems like this is crucial somehow. I was talking to him right before we were attacked. That's why it reminded me."

Then she got to the point of her question. "When Artagel examined the dead men—the ones who vanished later—he said he found an insignia—a 'sigil'—that meant they were Cadwals. They were Apts of the High King's Monomach. But when they attacked, they seemed to come out of nowhere. And when the rest of them were dead, their leader didn't have to run away. He just disappeared.

"He and his men must have come and gone through a flat mirror. But isn't that impossible? The Perdon and Prince Kragen decided Vagel must be involved, but that doesn't explain it. If passing through a flat glass safely is a matter of talent rather than training, then all of those men must have been arch-Imagers."

And, now that she thought about it, how had Master Gilbur contrived to elude the Castellan? If it was conceivable that the man in black and Master Gilbur were allies, surely it was also conceivable that the Master had disappeared in the same way?

For a long moment, Geraden regarded her thoughtfully. "You know," he said with a wry chuckle, "a lifetime ago, when I was still a new Apt, and I believed I was going to accomplish glorious things, I used to lie awake at night stewing about questions like that. And I came up with an idea that might work.

"First you shape a flat glass which just happens to be focused exactly where you want it." He shrugged humorously. "A trivial problem for the Imager I intended to be. Then you make another mirror —a normal one this time—that just happens to show a world which is essentially inert. No people or animals—and preferably no weather —to interfere with what you're doing. Then you translate the first mirror into the second and position it so that it fills as much of the Image as possible. And then, if the first mirror hasn't changed—and if it's actually possible to work two translations almost simultaneously —you might be able to pass through and keep your mind in one piece."

He grinned. "Ingenious, don't you think?"

"Yes." Actually, she thought it was more than ingenious: she thought it was brilliant. But some of the implications—"It would take two people, wouldn't it? One to translate the other?"

"Not to go. But it would to come back. That's true of any translation."

Therefore if Master Gilbur had escaped by the same device that had saved the man in black, then Geraden was proven innocent. Everyone in Orison was innocent (especially Geraden, but also Master Eremis, who was locked up in the dungeon and had no access to mirrors) because they were *here* rather than wherever the mirrors were located. They could not have pulled Master Gilbur away.

Almost shivering, she said, "I wish there was some way we could find out what really happened. If your idea is right, Master Gilbur probably left Orison the same way the men who attacked me came in."

"But who did the translation?"

"Could it have been Vagel? That makes sense now—or it does as long as there actually is some way to move people around Mordant by Imagery without making them lose their minds."

The Apt threw up his hands. "*I* don't know. For years, everybody thought the arch-Imager was dead. Now they all think he's alive.

"But you know," he went on, looking at her appraisingly, a hint of eagerness rising in his voice, "there might be a way to verify that Imagery was involved when you were attacked. There might even" —he sat forward—"be a way to check out my idea."

She watched him closely as he explained. Excitement animated his face, making it more and more attractive to her.

"Obviously, there's a lot we don't know about Imagery. Some things seem like they might be theoretically possible, but we've never had any way to test them. For instance, it's theoretically possible that an Imager with a certain kind of talent might be sensitive to mirrors from the other side. I mean, if he were to walk into a place that you could see in some mirror somewhere else, he would be able to feel it. He would know he was in an Image.

"Of course, you have to assume the Image actually exists. Otherwise what you see in a flat glass is just a copy of something real, and there would be nothing to feel.

"But if he *could* feel it"—Geraden jumped to his feet, no longer able to sit still—"then it's *also* theoretically possible that he might be able to work the translation from the other side. Do you see what that means? He could just step out of the Image into wherever the mirror happened to be."

As he spoke, her heart began to beat faster. His excitement took her with him. "If you're right," she said slowly, "then it wouldn't have to take two people. Master Gilbur could do it alone. He could come and go from Orison whenever he pleased."

"Yes!" returned Geraden impatiently. "But that's not the point. The point is that it might be *possible*." In his enthusiasm, he gripped the arms of her chair so that he could look into her face closely. "It might be possible for *you*."

Unfortunately, he misjudged the distance. Their foreheads cracked together with a sound like breaking bone.

"Oh, Terisa, I'm sorry!" he sputtered. "I'm sorry, I'm sorry." One hand clapped to his head, he reached out to her with the other. "Are you all right? I'm so sorry."

Just for an instant, the whole room looked like it was on fire. Then the hot red and orange flames resolved themselves into flares of pain across her vision, and her skull began to clang as if he had used it for a gong.

But she hadn't been hit as hard as all that: her hangover accentuated the blow. When she was sure that her forehead was neither crushed nor bleeding, she pushed Geraden's apologetic hand away. Rising purposefully to her feet even though she now had an entire carillon ringing between her ears, she did her best to kick one of his shins.

First he gaped at her as though she had lost her mind. Then he let out a shout of laughter.

"I warned you," she muttered through the pain. It was starting to decline. She was almost able to hear herself. "One apology a day. That's all you get." Helpless to spare herself, she was laughing as well. "I'm not some lord or Master you can trifle with."

Gales of glee rose from him.

"Please don't make me laugh." Weakly, she lowered herself back into her chair. "My head is going to split open."

He took a deep breath to control his mirth. When he was able to stop laughing, he came over to her. Cupping his palm to her cheek, he kissed her bruised forehead tenderly.

For a moment, she thought he would lower his mouth to hers. If she could have stifled the throbbing in her skull, she would have tilted her head back to meet him halfway. But the pain wasn't fading quickly enough. She didn't know whether to be relieved or vexed when he withdrew to his chair.

"Terisa," he repeated quietly, "it might be possible for you."

She sighed and closed her eyes. With both hands, she massaged the back of her neck. "You must have broken something in your head. That's the craziest idea you've had yet."

"Not really," he replied good-naturedly. "It's only an idea, of course. But you want to know why you're here—what you can do. Well, we can't teach you enough about making mirrors to find out if you can be an ordinary Imager. The Masters made it clear that they won't stand for it, and they control the laborium. But maybe you have a different kind of talent. Maybe that's why I was drawn to you when all the rules of Imagery should have taken me to the champion.

"We could try to find out, anyway. What have we got to lose?"

Opening her eyes, she stared at him hard. "You're serious, aren't you?" He didn't look like a man who had just become dangerously insane. "You think there might be some way to test what you're saying? To verify—?"

He nodded brightly.

Maybe you have a different kind of talent. Unexpectedly, her headache became less important. "I'm almost afraid to ask how."

Excitement gathered in him again, and his gaze shone. Making an effort to be reasonable, he said, "I hope you understand that I don't really know any more about this than you do. It's only theory. And most of the Masters wouldn't even be interested. Shaping mirrors takes too much practical research and effort." Then his enthusiasm broke out, pulling him once more to his feet. "But all we have to do is go back to where you were attacked. Once we're in the right vicinity, all you have to do is move around slowly and concentrate on what you feel."

The responses he aroused in her were so unfamiliar that she didn't know what to call them. Was this fear or eagerness? Her question was more complex than it sounded as she asked, "What am I expected to feel?"

"Who knows?" he replied, unaware of the extent of her confusion. "But it'll probably be subtle. A slight tugging sensation? An impression that something in front of you looks blurred? That sick feeling some people get when they look down from a cliff?

"If you don't feel anything, it won't prove anything. You might or might not have talent. Imagery might or might not be involved." He chuckled. "We might or might not be in the right place. But if you *do* feel something—" He made a visible effort to appear calm. "*That* would be interesting.

"Do you want to try it? Shall we go?"

For a moment, she couldn't answer. Peering into the fire, she almost heard a voice saying, That's the stupidest thing you've said today. Stop wasting my time. It sounded like her father's voice. And she knew what her mother would have said. Little girls don't do thing like that.

Things like that.

What if Geraden were right?

If he were wrong, there would be no problem. Nothing in her life would change. But if he were right—She would never be the same again.

"It isn't that simple," she murmured. "I don't think I can find the place again. I was only there once. And—and my mind was on other things."

His brief hesitation before he spoke suggested that he was paying strict attention to her now, that he had realized the importance of the issue he raised. "We can solve that problem," he said carefully. "We can ask Artagel to help us. He'll remember the exact spot." Then softly he repeated his earlier question. "Terisa, what have you got to lose?"

She wanted to say, My self. Who I am. But that seemed impossibly melodramatic. Why was she taking all this so seriously? As a treatment for headache, it worked admirably: her head still hurt, but now she was able to forget about it. On the other hand, the danger she apparently feared was so improbable that she should have considered it silly. Really, she ought to have more common sense.

Intending a flippant retort, she faced Geraden.

His intent demeanor stopped her: he was looking at her as he might have looked at someone who was about to risk her life. He had made a leap of empathy that carried him into the center of her fear. In a husky voice, as if he were full of pity, he said, "I would take you back to your world if I knew how. You know that."

For an instant, something like grief rose in her throat. His eyes held a sharp awareness of what she had lost. He had already cost her her former life. Now he asked her to risk her sense of herself, the little she understood about who she was.

Mustering a smile, she said, "Yes, I know. Don't you dare apologize." Then she stood up. Whatever happened, she had no intention of wasting his friendship. "Maybe the exercise will do me good."

The pleasure in his face was so brilliant that she nearly started laughing again.

They found Artagel in one of the halls near her tower. By then, she had discovered that exercise made her head hurt worse at first; but by degrees circulating blood seemed to cleanse her brain, and she began to feel better. Thinking about Geraden's brother, she wondered if he had any system for keeping an eye on her. The hall where they found him didn't look like an especially logical station for a bodyguard. On the other hand, they had no trouble locating him.

He greeted her with a humorous bow and a comradely comment on her questionable appearance. Geraden defended her with mock indignation and received for his pains a cuff on the shoulder which did him no appreciable damage. Then he explained what he had in mind—leaving out, she thought, most of the salient details—and asked for Artagel's help.

Artagel took this more grimly than Terisa had expected. "Thank your good fortune," he snapped, "the lady Terisa *doesn't* remember how to find that place. Did you leave your brains under that pile of rubble? Or maybe you just *forgot* she was attacked down there by Apts of the High King's Monomach. It's even possible Gart himself was among them." He digressed momentarily. "I would hate to think anyone less could give me that much trouble." Then he resumed, "What were you planning to do if she was attacked again? Ask them nicely to go away?"

"Not exactly." His brother's anger clearly didn't trouble Geraden. "I thought I would just ask them to wait until you caught up with us.

"Actually," he explained, "they probably can't attack us. They won't be ready for us. They don't have any way of knowing what we're doing—and I'm sure they don't spend *all* their time crouched in front of the mirror waiting for a likely victim to appear by coincidence. We should be safe."

In spite of himself, Artagel was mollified. "You're too clever for your own good. But it does happen that I don't have anything better to do this morning." Without apparent difficulty, he forgot his anger and grinned at Terisa. "My lady," he said formally, offering her his arm, "shall we go?"

When she accepted, he gave Geraden a smile of good-humored malice and swept her away, leaving his brother to tag along behind.

As he followed, Geraden's face wore an expression of lopsided fondness. After all, she reflected, he had six older brothers—and all of them probably delighted in teasing him. The way he looked now gave another lift to her spirits. He and Artagel made it easy for her to think she was doing the right thing.

As she returned to the damp, disused passages among the foundations of Orison, however, she began to reconsider. She didn't have fond memories of this place. The endless dripping of water promised peril. Although there were enough lanterns to enable Artagel to find his way, their scattered and distant reflections in the puddles and smears of water on the floor gave the stone an evil aspect, as though dark secrets were hidden behind the gleams. The echo of bootheels chased the silence down side passages and around corners until she felt irrationally sure that she was being stalked. The warmth of day never reached down this far, and the air felt colder than she remembered it: certainly, more of the moisture had become ice. Whenever she or her companions broke the surface of a frozen puddle, the ice crackled like fire.

And if Geraden were right—if by some strange chance she had the kind of talent he described—

She clung to Artagel's arm harder than she realized. Apparently thinking she was cold, he draped the edge of his gray cloak over her shoulders.

"Whoever made that mirror," Geraden commented like whistling in the dark, "was either very lucky or very good. It's hard to imagine anyone *accidentally* shaping a mirror that shows this part of Orison. On the other hand, it isn't exactly easy to figure out how he could have made it deliberately. Even the best Masters have to do decades of research to get what they want."

"I hope you know what you're doing," muttered Terisa nervously. "I don't like this at all."

Artagel gave her a little hug. "He probably does. The only time you really have to worry about him is when he looks like he has everything under control."

She wanted Geraden to reply, but he didn't. After a moment, she asked, "Who keeps these lanterns lit?"

Her escort shrugged. "Servants."

"But why?" she pursued. "Hasn't this whole area been abandoned?"

"Well, not quite *abandoned*. I've heard that many of the damp, cold rooms down here are used to store wine. If we just knew which ones, we could die happy. And I know for a fact that the Castellan uses sections of this place to train his guards, especially in winter.

"Besides," he added wryly, "I think he hates the dark. He might put lanterns here even if no one but the people who took care of them came here from one year to the next."

The thought of Castellan Lebbick wasn't much comfort. "How much farther?" she asked.

"We're almost there." Artagel sounded nonchalant, but when she glanced at him she saw wariness in the flick of his eyes, the movement of his head. "Lebbick must have had the floor cleaned. Otherwise you could see the blood by now."

He was right. After another dozen paces, the look of the corridor began to match her memory of it, despite the absence of blood.

"Here," she said softly. Even though she understood that sound didn't pass through mirrors, she was viscerally afraid of being overheard by unfriendly ears. This was the place. She could almost detect the residual tremor of her own fear, vibrations left over from the man in black's assault. "It was here."

"Yes." Artagel stopped, turned. Then he moved her until her back touched one wall. "You were there." With a gesture, he indicated the passage. "We fought there." The obscure illumination made his face as grim as his voice. "The Perdon and Prince Kragen came from the other side. They rescued us." Abruptly, he confronted his brother. "I'm not sure you realize," he grated through his teeth, "that the bastard beat me—whoever he was. The last time that happened, I was a lot younger than you are now."

Light gleamed dimly across Geraden's forehead as though he were sweating in spite of the cold. "Somehow," he muttered, "I'm sure you'll get a chance to try him again. I just hope it doesn't come today. *I* won't be very good at rescuing you.

"But this isn't what we're looking for." He moved past his brother and peered at Terisa through the gloom. "We need to find the exact point of translation. If there is one.

"Where did they come from?"

She closed her eyes. She had been walking with Prince Kragen. He had been talking about Elega. One bodyguard was ahead of them; the other, behind. She heard a quiet leather sound—a sword leaving a sheath? Then the men charged forward. The black leather of their armor made them difficult to see. Their naked swords were more distinct, glinting lanternlight—

"There," she breathed and opened her eyes. She was pointing at what appeared to be a dark side passage diagonally across the corridor from her. "They came out of there."

"Good." Geraden was whispering as though he, too, feared being overheard. "Let's take a look."

His breath left a wreath of steam in the air as he moved away.

Artagel had his sword out. It seemed to flex with the movement of his wrist. He touched her arm with his free hand, and she went with him after Geraden.

The way ahead remained black. If it was a side passage, it was too short to merit a lantern of its own. Illumination reflecting from the main corridor faded rapidly. After a moment, Artagel asked, "Do you want to wait while I get us a light?"

"No," hissed Geraden. "If there is a mirror focused here, light will just make it easier for us to be seen."

Artagel nodded. He was keeping Terisa positioned between him and the wall, to reduce the number of directions from which she could be threatened.

"Concentrate," Geraden said to her over his shoulder. "The point of translation could be anywhere. Try to feel it. Forget everything else and just try to feel it."

"Concentrate yourself," she retorted. Her whisper came out

hoarsely. "I'm not the only one who doesn't know what his talents are."

Geraden paused for a second. "Good point."

Artagel flashed her a grin she could barely see in the thickening dark.

This is silly, she enunciated to herself. All three of them were supposed to be adults—yet here they were, groping their way down a blind hall looking for some place where the air or the stone or who knew what would give one of them twinges. We must be out of our minds. If somebody had jumped at her and said, Boo! she would have screamed.

That idea made her want to giggle.

It distracted her. She didn't realize what was happening until a touch of cold as thin as a feather and as sharp as steel slid straight through the center of her abdomen.

Before she could react—before she could try to shout a warning—a man stepped out of the wall. His body felt like a block of stone as he collided with her heavily, knocking her against Artagel.

Artagel clinched her arm. "Back!" he snapped. "Back to the light!" and flung her away from him.

At once, the cold sensation vanished.

She didn't notice the difference.

She stumbled, caught her balance. Where was Geraden? Every muscle in her body wanted to run, but she turned in time to see Artagel thrust Geraden after her while threatening a shadowy figure with his blade.

Urgently, she raced for the main passage and the lanterns.

Geraden was faster. He was beside her when he reached the corridor. He steered her to the right, toward the nearer lantern. Their momentum took them to the opposite wall, to the place where she had fallen and waited for the man in black to kill her. There they both whirled to see what was happening to Artagel.

He came into the light with his sword still poised between him and the obscure figure. No, it wasn't one figure: she saw two. Three. Four. They moved slowly, massively; the menace of Artagel's blade didn't hinder them.

Four. That was bad. But at least there weren't any more. As they reached the light, she saw that they did in fact look like men. They had the heads and faces and limbs of men. Their nakedness showed that they had the bodies of men. Their arms were extended for embraces.

But their eyes were dead. And under their skin lumps the size of hands moved visibly—lumps that couldn't be muscle.

They carried no weapons, however. And their movements were so leaden that Artagel would surely be able to handle them.

He retreated in the other direction, trying to lead them away. His fighting grin was absent. Behind his perplexity, his eyes hinted at horror.

The four men ignored him. As they emerged from the side passage, they headed for Terisa and Geraden.

Artagel shouted to distract them. They ignored that as well. They might have been deaf. Lumbering woodenly, they went after their chosen object.

In an effort to turn them, he struck. His sword whirled and flashed and came down on the wrist of the leading figure with such force that Terisa winced, expecting to see the hand flop to the stone.

But the hand didn't fall. There wasn't any blood. Instead, the skin of the wrist peeled back from the point of the blow, revealing an insect like a monstrous cockroach where the bones of the hand should have been.

The skin withered away; the insect dropped from the wrist-stump to the floor.

It tasted the air with its feelers for a second, worked its mandibles, then scurried toward Terisa and Geraden.

At the same time, a second insect started to squirm out of the lumbering figure's wrist. The skin of the wrist withered, as if the cockroach inside it were all that had preserved it as living tissue.

Terisa would have screamed if she could have found her voice. But the insect was faster than the heavy body or host that had carried it; and Geraden had shouted at her, grabbed her arm, trying to tug her away; and some residue of the incisive cold that had presaged this assault seemed to knot up her chest, so that she was hardly able to breathe.

While the second insect dropped to the floor from the tattered flesh of the figure's wrist, a third fought into view out of his forearm.

She couldn't tear her eyes away from what was happening. Geraden had to drag her backward. She saw the wild revulsion in Artagel's eyes as he sprang to the attack.

One high hard blow of his sword bit into the nearest figure's shoulder at the base of the neck, cutting deeply through the man's chest. Another swing—so quick that it seemed to be part of the first —came around from the other side, licking murderously far between his ribs.

But there was no blood. He didn't fall.

Like a rotten husk, his torso split open. His head continued staring straight ahead; his legs continued walking stiffly, heavily, down the corridor after his fellows—and dozens and dozens of cockroaches came tumbling out of his ruptured chest and abdomen.

For an instant, they seethed around each other, searching for a scent. Then they ran like a rush of blood after Terisa and Geraden.

Abruptly, the man's head burst, scattering a knot of insects among the rest. After that, his legs seemed to lose their way. They tottered to the side, hit the wall, and fell over, while more and more huge cockroaches swarmed out of the crumbling remains of his waist and hips and thighs.

Soon there was nothing left of him except hurrying insects.

Terisa heard Artagel swearing in vicious desperation, as if he were about to vomit.

"Terisa!" Geraden hauled on her arm. "Run!"

Transfixed by Artagel's attack and its result, she hadn't realized how much she was hindering Geraden—how swiftly the insects were moving. The nearest one had nearly reached the skirt of her gown.

Gasping, she whirled away.

For a few strides, she ran, ran with all her heart. But then she had to stop and turn, to see—

Artagel had put away his sword. With his face clenched and bleak, his lower lip bitten between his teeth, he came up behind one of the remaining figures, stooped rapidly, hooked his hands around the squirming ankles, and pulled as hard as he could.

The man toppled forward with the slow, unreactive violence of felled timber.

When he hit the floor, the impact broke his whole body open. All the insects that had packed themselves into his flesh were released at once.

They flooded the passage from wall to wall. Lanternlight gleamed and glinted on their dark backs; they formed a flowing current as they sped forward, champing their mandibles for the flesh of their victims.

Terisa fled again.

Geraden ran with her. "We can keep ahead of them," he panted. His chest heaved, urgent for air. "Don't stop. We can outrun them."

"How far?" Her heart was on fire, as if she had already run for miles. She seemed to be suffocating on fear and cold. "How far can you run?"

"Far enough," he promised grimly. Yet he sounded like each breath he took hurt his lungs.

She stopped near a lantern and looked back. She and Geraden were twenty or thirty feet ahead of the leading cockroaches. From this angle, the whole floor of the passage seemed to boil with menace as the insects rushed forward. Behind them, the figure Artagel had struck first was just finishing his collapse, releasing the last of his occupants among the swarm. The remaining man increased his pace to keep up with the hunting torrent.

Artagel followed in a frenzy. "Geraden!" His call echoed down the corridor like a wail. "What can I do? Tell me what to do!"

"No," Terisa rasped. She fought for air, but was too frightened to get it. "I can't run far enough. We don't know where we're going. If we get out of here, we'll just lead those things into Orison."

In response, Geraden gave her a look of pure anguish.

"We've got to fight somehow," she said as if a total stranger were talking, someone who had no acquaintance with the panic which hammered in her heart, the dread and revulsion that twisted her stomach. "We've got to fight."

For one more moment while the cockroaches rushed closer, he stared at her as though he were about to start sobbing. Then he gave an inarticulate shout like a cry of battle and leaped for the lantern.

Wrenching it from its hooks regardless of the way the heated iron scorched his hands, he flung it at the insects.

It hit in a splash of burning oil, and a dozen or more of the creatures caught fire.

They burned almost instantly, spouting flames as bright as torches: they were incendiary in some way. After two or three heartbeats, nothing remained of them except bits of charred carapace—

—nothing except a black vapor which rose into the air and spread quickly.

It smelled like a strong combination of formaldehyde and partially digested meat, and it clawed at Terisa's throat and lungs like acid. Gagging, she doubled over: the spasm that gripped her chest was too fierce to let her cough.

The passage had gone dim without the lantern, but she was close enough to the floor to see the nearest cockroaches scuttling rapidly forward, unconcerned by a few deaths. She had to run, *had* to—

She couldn't. It was impossible. She could not break the hold of that black vapor on the inside of her chest.

Retching hard enough to crack his ribs, Geraden got his arms around her and somehow found the strength to lift her off her feet. With her convulsed weight awkward in his embrace, he stumbled away, struggling to outrun the insects again.

In a few strides, he set her down to see if she could carry herself now. She snatched a whooping breath, and the spasm began to unclench. Still clinging to him for support, she fled farther before turning to look back.

She was in time to see Artagel run up with a lantern that he must have retrieved from the opposite direction and throw it like a madman at the head of the last erect attacker.

He didn't know his danger: he was too far away to have seen accurately what had happened to Geraden and her. But she couldn't shout a warning. Her raw throat could barely whisper his name as the lantern hit and broke—and the lumbering figure went up in flames, burning with such sudden fury that he seemed incandescent —and the spouting black exhalations of that many insects engulfed Artagel, causing him to collapse as effectively as a sword-thrust in the belly.

"Artagel," croaked Geraden. "*Artagel.*"

Terisa watched Artagel and the insects while her fear turned to a cold, dark anger. This time, she was the one who grabbed at Geraden's arm and pulled. "Come on." Her voice was only a scrape of pain in her throat, but now the chill seemed to be doing her some good, slowly numbing the hurt of the black vapor. "Come *on.*"

Ahead, she saw that the corridor came to a T, branching left and right. More light seemed to emanate from the right than from the left.

When she reached the T, she scanned both passages to ascertain that there was in fact a lantern nearby off to the right. Then she released Geraden. The cockroaches were after her. They had come through the same mirror that the man in black had used to attack her. She was the only person she knew who had active enemies.

"Get the lantern," she choked out. "I'll lead them away."

He gaped at her as though his brother's fall had cost him his wits.

Urgently, she pushed him into motion. "*Go!* I'll lead them away. You follow. Every lantern we pass, you can kill a few more. Just don't breathe that vapor."

At last, he appeared to understand. He moved into the right-hand corridor a few steps ahead of the cockroaches.

Retreating backward so that she could see what he did, she went to the left.

Unfortunately, her assumption was mistaken. The entire swarm swept after Geraden, ignoring her completely.

Geraden!

Her anger crumbled into horror and incomprehension. The strength ran out of her: she nearly sank to her knees. Slowly, she raised her hands to her mouth, and fear filled her eyes.

He didn't realize his danger until he reached the lantern, unhooked it, and turned back. Then he saw the oncoming rush. For a second, he was paralyzed. Dismay wiped the combative stubbornness off his face. His hands lowered the lantern: it looked like it was about to fall.

One of her knees failed. She lost her balance and stumbled to the floor, breaking the ice that scummed a wide puddle. Water soaked into her gown. She wasn't even on her feet when she heard him howl, "Terisa! Get help!"

But she was watching him, watching with all she had left, yearning for him in voiceless desperation, as Adept Havelock arrived at his side and leveled a beam of light against the onslaught.

Apparently, the mad old Imager had been waiting in the hall for just this purpose. The reflections from his eyes danced insanely, but his movements betrayed none of the erratic frenzy, the hysteria of intent, which she had seen in the past: they were deft and sure, almost calm.

One hand took hold of Geraden's collar and pulled him back; the other directed his beam at the seething cockroaches.

Terisa was past surprise, so she noticed as if it were a matter of course that the Adept's weapon was the same small piece of glass he had used before to light her way and save her life. Now, however, that mirror shone much more hotly: its light was as fierce as fire. More powerfully than burning oil, it ignited the insects. They took flame and were incinerated almost instantly, popping like firecrackers as they died.

Then billowing black vapor filled the corridor so thickly that the illumination of Geraden's lantern was obscured. Only Adept Havelock's fire was bright enough to show through the sudden midnight as the beam swept the floor and cockroaches by the hundreds burned.

At the last moment, Terisa remembered to hold her breath.

For what felt like a long time—a dozen heartbeats, two dozen—the Adept's light moved swiftly and methodically over the stone, boiling the damp to steam in order to achieve the death of each insect. Of course, the creatures simplified this process by marching with mindless determination in Geraden's direction. Adept Havelock didn't need to be concerned that any of them would sneak past him along the walls, or would turn and flee. Nevertheless he was careful, and so the cleansing of the passage took time. She felt her mind going giddy as she wondered whether the Adept had enough sense—or Geraden enough self-awareness—to stop breathing.

Then the vapor became thick enough to block even Adept Havelock's beam. The air began to sting her eyes. She lowered her forehead to the floor. The ache of her bruise against the cold stone gave her a focal point for her concentration, and she clung to it so that she wouldn't breathe.

Unexpectedly, something nudged her shoulder.

Believing in panic that she had been found by one of the cockroaches, she flipped to the side and gasped for air so that she could scream.

Adept Havelock stood over her, dressed as usual in his worn surcoat and tattered chasuble. His light played on the ceiling, filling the corridor.

He looked like a dangerous lunatic. His disfocused eyes bulged; the few remaining tufts of his hair protruded wildly. His fleshy grin was gleeful and lecherous. Behind the dirty stubble on his cheeks, his skin seemed to be turning purple.

As she began to cough, however, he let his own breath out with a burst and started breathing again. The air made him cough as well, and a few tears trickled from his eyes; but his eyes stopped bulging almost at once, and his skin lost its purple intensity.

"I see," he rasped hoarsely, "that the air is now tolerable. It was kind of you to sample it for me."

Geraden stumbled into her range of vision. His eyes were raw, and the difficulty of breathing showed in his face. Nevertheless he was on his feet. As soon as he saw that she, too, would survive, he

THE MIRROR OF HER DREAMS

groaned, "Artagel," and pushed himself into a coughing run toward his brother.

"Artagel?" Although one of Havelock's eyes leered, the other was sane and serious. His nose, as fierce and ascetic as a hawk's beak, made every word he uttered count. "Was he caught in this trap as well?"

"Back there." A spasm of retching wracked Terisa. After that, however, the pain in her lungs eased, and she was able to breathe more normally. With an effort, she climbed to her hands and knees, then to her feet. "He tried to save us. That vapor got him."

"Balls of a goat!" the Adept snapped. At once, he strode away.

Struggling not to be left behind, she reeled after him.

Slowly her balance improved as the effects of the vapor faded. She was nearly steady as she and Adept Havelock reached Geraden.

He didn't notice them. He sat on the floor, cradling Artagel's head in his arms.

Artagel's face was mottled with exertion and pain, and his eyes gaped at the ceiling as though he had gone blind. But he was breathing.

Her relief was so acute that her eyes spilled tears.

Stooping to Geraden, Adept Havelock tapped him crisply on the shoulder. "Come along, Geraden. Carry him if you have to. I don't like staying this close to that translation point. Who knows how many more surprises Vagel has for us? I'll take you somewhere safe."

Geraden hugged his brother harder and didn't move. Terisa couldn't tell whether he had heard the Adept.

As if he were making a concession, the old Imager said, "I have some wine. I think it'll help him." Then he lost patience. "Horror and ballocks, boy! If you're attacked again, I might not be able to save you!"

Still Geraden didn't move. But Artagel jerked his head in a nod as if he understood. When Terisa took hold of his arm and tried to pull him upright, he made a feeble effort to assist her.

Roughly, Geraden rubbed his eyes with the back of his hand. Then he helped Terisa lift his brother off the stone.

"Come along," repeated Havelock. With a brisk stride, he moved away.

Supporting Artagel between them, Terisa and Geraden followed. Artagel was unable to keep his feet under him, but she heard an improvement in his breathing. He was beginning to sound like he would live.

She found that she was completely disoriented: she had no idea where Adept Havelock was taking them. After a short distance, he entered a side passage which led at once to a sturdy wooden door that looked like the entrance to a storeroom. In fact, it was the entrance to a storeroom. The storeroom, however, appeared to be full of nothing but empty crates in various stages of disrepair. Adept Havelock ignored them as he picked his way to another door hidden in a niche at the back of the room.

This door looked ordinary enough from the outside, but inside it held enough bars and bolts to seal a dungeon. Havelock shut it behind Terisa, Geraden, and Artagel, then led them down a passage that opened almost immediately into a room crowded with a disarray of mirrors.

"King Joyse confiscated most of these during his wars," the Adept explained offhandedly as he crossed the room to another corridor. "After he created the Congery, he restored quite a few mirrors to the Masters. But he kept more than he gave up.

"I wish they did me some good."

The sight astonished Geraden out of his distress, at least for a moment. Adept Havelock had the only light, however, and he left the room promptly. Terisa and Geraden followed with Artagel.

After two or three turns, as many short hallways, and another door, they suddenly found themselves in the large, square room where Terisa had listened to Master Quillon explain the history of Mordant's need.

The place appeared unchanged: it was still furnished and cluttered like the study of a man whose mind had gone. Lamps set into the walls and the central pillar shed plenty of light toward the doors that lined the walls, giving admittance to Orison's secret passages.

Perhaps because she was suffering from reaction, Terisa was struck by the odd thought that Adept Havelock resembled a spider. This room was the center of his web; the secret passages were the strands. Now she and Geraden and Artagel had been caught.

She wondered what the Adept was plotting.

He bustled away behind the pillar. While he was out of sight, Terisa and Geraden helped Artagel to one of the chairs at the checker table. Artagel's breathing still had a thick tubercular wheeze that was painful to hear, but he was strong enough to take notice of his surroundings. With an effort, he choked out, "Does he *live* here?"

"Looks like it," replied Terisa vaguely. She still wasn't ready to tell anyone that she had been here before.

"I wish I knew what he was doing with all those mirrors," Geraden muttered. Fear and strain and bafflement gave him a feverish look.

Carrying a large flagon, Adept Havelock returned.

At last she had an opportunity to observe him more closely. He conveyed an impression of suppressed haste, as though he were trying to resist the acceleration of some internal process. His movements were deliberate, tightly controlled; but his eyes flicked from side to side with a discernible rhythm, like a heartbeat being gradually goaded faster by adrenaline.

He handed the flagon directly to Artagel. "Drink it all. It's going to taste terrible. I put some balm in it to heal your throat." Brusquely, he addressed Geraden. "Make sure he drinks it all. If he recovers, make him play hop-board with you." He indicated his empty checkerboard table. "You need the practice. I want to talk to the lady."

Without waiting for a reaction, he took Terisa's arm and drew her away, around the pillar until she could no longer see Geraden and Artagel.

When he stopped, however, he didn't speak. His eyes took turns flicking toward her and off again, flicking—Their rhythm and the aftertaste of black vapor made her stomach queasy. A grimace clenched his sybaritic mouth, as if he had taken a vow not to let himself grin at her. Slowly, he raised his scrawny old arms and folded them across his chest.

From beyond the pillar came harsh gagging noises. The wine must have been worse than terrible. Fortunately, the noises soon ceased.

Facing the Adept alone, Terisa felt a strong desire to become hysterical. That would solve a number of problems. It would give her an escape from his loony gaze. It would provide a much-needed rest. It would free her from the responsibility of trying to figure out what was going on. But he had saved her life. He had saved Geraden. And he clearly had some kind of purpose for bringing her here. In return, she had to make some kind of effort to rise to the occasion.

Swallowing hard to clear her throat, she said, "You're not really as crazy as people think."

In response, he let out a bark of laughter. "Oh, yes I am. This is just one of my lucid moments. Quillon told you I have lucid moments. This is one of them."

Abruptly, he unfolded one age-spotted hand from his chest to stab his index finger in her direction. "The important thing," he whispered intensely, "is, don't ask me any questions. *Don't*. I'm having a hard enough time as it is."

At once, he resumed his stance and went on flicking his eyes at her, back and forth in turn, their rhythm eloquent of mounting pressure, perhaps even of violence.

She felt her mouth hanging open, so she closed it. Apparently, he needed her to help him in some way. But without asking any questions. Did he want her to guess at something? Or did it matter what she said?

Maybe it didn't matter. Cautiously, she ventured, "I haven't thanked you for saving us. I don't know how the arch-Imager or whoever it was managed to spring that trap on us. I can't think of any way for him to know what we were going to do. But if you hadn't come along, we—" She shuddered, unable to complete the thought.

Without warning, he snapped, "Vagel!" He sounded grimly angry, yet his expression conveyed gratitude. "If I could get just one hand on him, I would tear his heart out. But it isn't good for me to lose my temper." Whatever emotions appeared on his face or in his voice had no effect on his posture or the movement of his eyes. "That was just coincidence. The first piece of good luck we've had in a long time. I've seen those creatures before—just once, when I was in a cabal of Imagers High King Festten built around Vagel in Carmag. I saw what they do. But I've never actually seen the glass.

"We were told they're like hunting dogs. If you translate something with the scent of the man you want hunted on it into their world, those insects go wild. But apparently they can't be translated directly. They forget the scent and just attack the first thing they find. So you have to give them living bodies to serve as hosts."

As he spoke, the edges of her vision went dim as if she were about to faint.

"They eat their way into those bodies and breed, and then they can be translated without losing the scent."

"That's what they would have done to Geraden," she murmured weakly. Then she raised a hand to her mouth, fighting to keep her nausea at bay.

"And anybody else who got in their way," added the Adept. He seemed to be growing calmer. "That's why I say we were lucky. If he hadn't happened to be near the translation point when those creatures came through, they would have had to go looking for him. We would have had to fight them in the public halls of Orison. Who knows how many people would have been killed."

Struggling to get her mind off the idea of Geraden as a host for the monstrous insects, Terisa started to ask a question. Fortunately, she caught it in time to rephrase it.

"It's a good thing you were there to rescue us."

She felt an unexpected, poignant desire to say, I saw the riders of my dream in the augury. Geraden thinks I'm an Imager.

"I said I'm crazy," the Adept replied with some asperity. "I didn't say I'm stupid." Then, to her surprise, he smiled, baring his crooked yellow teeth. "It's obvious that Vagel has plans for that translation point. After going to all the trouble to create it, he isn't likely to leave it unused. I've been watching it, more or less ever since you told Quillon about it—the day after Gart came through and almost killed you."

She couldn't help herself: she blurted out, "Gart? The High King's Mono—?"

At once, a spasm of fury twisted his face. He squeezed his eyes shut. As if they weren't under his control, his hands rose into fists and began punching at his temples. She saw that he was holding his breath.

"I'm sorry," she whispered fervently, frightened without knowing why. "I'm sorry. I didn't mean it. I just didn't know it was Gart—" She faltered and fell silent.

Fiercely, he sucked a deep breath in through his nose and opened his eyes. "Of course it was Gart." One muscle at a time, as if by a supreme act of will, he resumed his stance. His mouth grimaced again. He appeared to be in command of himself. "The alliance between Vagel and Festten still holds. Cadwal wants you dead even more than Alend and that treacherous Prince do." The rhythm of his eyes was faster, however, flicking to her and away like the stalking beat of his madness.

He tried to smile again—this time unsuccessfully. Without transition, he said, "You're probably wondering why I brought you here. Well, I can't tell you that. If I knew the answer myself, it probably wouldn't make sense. But I want to tell you a little bit about King Joyse."

Terisa swallowed the change of subject as well as she could and waited for him to go on.

"You know, the relationship between Imagery, augury, and fate is an interesting philosophical question." His tone was peaceful now, but his eyes contradicted it. His manner brought back the idea of a lurking spider. "Before Joyse was born, I was what some people called the 'pet Imager' of the Cadwal prince who ruled Orison and the Demesne. He was a petty tyrant, but imaginative in his cruelties, and I was growing desperate for hope. So I tried to arrange an augury for the coming birth.

"Unfortunately, I was unable to shape a flat glass to show the room where he would be born. The best I could create was an Image of a hill just outside Orison—a hill," he added by the way, "which is now *in* the castle. In fact, it forms the foundation for the tower where he has his rooms.

"But at the time," he resumed, "the focus of my mirror refused to be adjusted any farther than the stables where our prince allowed us to keep our mangy horses.

"Of course, I could have waited until the child was born and grew up enough to go to the stables on his own. But as I say I was growing desperate. So one black night soon after he was born, I stole little Joyse from his cradle and took him down to the stables and risked leaving him there alone in a pile of straw while I raced back to my small laborium to work the augury.

"He took cold and nearly died—but I got what I wanted."

From where he stood, he couldn't see Geraden and Artagel as they crept past the edge of the pillar. Terisa glanced at them to reassure herself about Artagel's condition—and to try to warn them not to interfere. Then she returned her attention to the Adept.

"It was a remarkable augury, unusually distinct in some ways, maddeningly vague in others. On the one hand, it clearly showed Joyse making himself a king. On the other, it proved to have almost nothing to do with the process by which he actually did become King. It didn't show the battles he actually fought, the victories he actually won, the decisions he actually made. So it was no help at all to us along the way. The best it gave us was an occasional bit of confirmation, when the results of something he did—like the cre-

ation of the Congery—unexpectedly matched the Images in the augury.

"Let me give you an example," he said blandly while the pace of
his gaze increased. "According to my augury, he became King as an
old man. Sometime *after* a large, unexplained hole was torn in the
side of Orison."

While Terisa stared—and Geraden and Artagel fought to muffle
their surprise—Havelock permitted himself a stiff shrug. She felt
sure he was trying to tell her something urgent, something she
couldn't possibly understand. "At the time, the idea that I would
have to wait until he was old was so depressing—I almost didn't
bother to go rescue him from the stables. But since then I've had a
lot of time to ask myself what went wrong. Did I falsify my augury
by not allowing the conditions for it to happen naturally? Does the
very act of casting an augury change events? Or are there other
possibilities? Has King Joyse changed his own fate by being stronger
—or weaker—than he would have been if he hadn't taken cold that
night and nearly died?

"We would be better off if we could answer questions like these."

As if he were pausing to briefly become a completely different
person, he relaxed his rigid posture and scratched himself unceremoniously. Whatever dignity and command he possessed vanished at
once. His surcoat looked old and grimy enough to carry lice: perhaps
the itching was unbearable. Then he drew back into his clenched
stance.

"I'll tell you something else that was in my augury. If you promise
never to tell anybody. Never never never." He spoke to the rhythm
of his eyes. "Never never never." The strain of holding on to his
lucidity brought sweat to his forehead, despite the cool of the room,
"His daughters were in it.

"Of course, I didn't know they were his daughters then. But now
it's obvious."

A crafty look broke over his features. "You'll never guess what I
saw Myste doing."

Terisa had to gouge her nails into her palms to keep herself quiet.
At the edge of her attention, she was aware of Geraden's agitation,
but she had no time to spare for him.

With a visible effort, Adept Havelock wrestled his expression back
to sternness. "Of course you'll never guess," he snapped as if she had

just said something insulting. "How could you? That's why I'm going to tell you.

"I saw her," he said sarcastically, "with a figure who bore an astonishing resemblance to Gilbur's champion. She looked like she was begging him not to kill her."

Terisa must have been stronger, more resilient, than she realized. How else was it possible for her to feel such panic, after everything she had already been through? Havelock knew where Myste had gone. Perhaps King Joyse also knew. Perhaps he had known all along. *Begging him not to kill her*. Myste!

Numb with fright, she asked, "Did he kill her? Did she go through all that just to get herself killed?"

But it was likely that Adept Havelock didn't hear her. While she breathed her question, Geraden surged forward, demanding, "Myste is with that champion? Is that why no one's seen her recently? Does King Joyse know about this?"

Rage on his face, Havelock whirled as if he intended to strike Geraden down. Instantly, however, his turn changed into a pirouette, and he spun circles, flapping his arms like an old crow. When he stopped, he looked like he wanted to storm at Geraden, yet he was giggling, and his voice was thick with mirth.

"Do you know what the difference is between an Apt and an Adept?"

Frozen with chagrin, Geraden gaped at the mad Imager.

Lugubriously solemn, Adept Havelock raised his fingers to his fat lips and flapped them, making a *de-de-de-de* sound. Then he cackled appreciation for his own humor and turned to Terisa. "Do you get it? De-de-de-de. *D-e*. A-*d-e*-p-t." But he quit laughing as soon as he saw the dismay on her face. "Women!" he snorted. "Whoever invented women gave them teats instead of brains. By the hoary goat of the arch-Imager! No wonder Mordant is in such a mess."

Suddenly, her throat filled with pain. He was so valuable—and so lost. "I'm sorry," she whispered. "You poor man. I'm so sorry."

But no amount of regret could bring his mind back. He leered at her, smacked his lips, and pronounced in a tone of finality:

"Sheepdung."

When Artagel had recovered sufficiently, he and his companions found their way back up to the public halls of Orison. "You'd better tell Castellan Lebbick about all this," said Geraden glumly as they walked. "He needs to know where that translation point is. And if there's a chance Myste is still alive, he needs to know she's with the champion. Or she will be as soon as she finds him. It's probably too late, but the men hunting him should be warned to look out for her."

Artagel nodded and left. He still carried himself stiffly, as if his lungs were tender, but all he needed now was rest.

The prospect of being alone made Terisa's skin crawl, so she asked Geraden to keep her company in her rooms. Inborn consideration seemed to warn him off sensitive topics: deliberately casual, he whiled away part of the afternoon for her by chatting about his family, giving her brief sketches of his brothers and their life in the Care of Domne. Soothed by his gentle talk and affectionate memories, she began to feel restored enough to consider the implications of the day's events.

Unfortunately, he was called away at that point: one of the younger Apts found him and summoned him to his neglected chores.

The remainder of the afternoon was bad. And the evening threatened to be worse, until she discovered—to her surprise and relief—that she was too exhausted to keep her eyes open. Grateful for small blessings, she went to bed.

The next morning, after a night full of dreams from which Terisa awakened as though she had been screaming, Saddith bustled into her rooms and announced gleefully that Master Eremis had been released.

"Really? Are you sure?" Terisa tried to conceal her emotions, but her heart was pounding. The Master had said, *When I am free, I will come to you*. As if by magic, the events of the previous day became less important. *There will be no part of your womanhood which I have not claimed*. "Why would Castellan Lebbick let him out?"

Saddith looked positively exultant. "I do not know the entire story, my lady. Apparently, the Castellan is teaching his men to keep their mouths closed. But it is rumored"—she lowered her voice dramatically—"that Orison was attacked by Imagery yesterday. Master Eremis had been imprisoned because he was believed to be responsible for such things." The recollection made her indignant. "But of course he could not have attacked Orison by Imagery while locked in the Castellan's dungeon. No proof can be found that he is guilty."

She chortled. "Even our dour Castellan cannot justify imprisoning an innocent man."

Terisa made a conscious effort not to speculate about the meaning of Saddith's pleasure. Her own expectations were already too confused: she didn't want to have them complicated further by memories of the way Saddith had moaned and clung while Master Eremis thrust into her. Instead, she remembered the touch of his lips and tongue on her breasts—the way he had instructed her to betray Geraden—and waited impatiently for the maid to leave.

She wanted the Master—and was afraid to face him with her refusal to take his part against Geraden. Opposing desires made her forehead ache. As soon as Saddith closed the door, she rushed to give herself a quick, intense bath, trying to get ready. But then she forced herself to put on the dingiest gown she had, as if she wished to be unattractive. Master Eremis. Geraden. She yearned for both in different ways and had no idea what to do about the contradiction.

But Master Eremis didn't come.

She had thought she was going to find out who she was. But neither of the men who tried to claim her had given her an answer. She had risked accompanying Geraden to Vagel's translation point for nothing more than the sensation of thin, sharp cold—a sensation that made no difference. And she had known all along that Master Eremis could have any woman he wanted.

Apparently, he didn't want her.

Perhaps for that reason—perhaps simply because she couldn't have him—she found that she wanted him badly.

NINETEEN: THE ADVANTAGES OF AN EARLY THAW

Four days later, the weather broke.

By that time, Terisa had forced down the pain of Master Eremis' implicit rejection. She continued to function, which meant that she spent as much time as possible with Geraden—talking, trying to understand. Nevertheless the knowledge that she didn't have anything better to do, anything more constructive to offer, wore on her constantly. She couldn't shake free of a gray depression that took the edge off everything she thought and felt; her behavior resembled her former existence more than anything she had done since she had come to Orison. As a result, her conversations with Geraden were like many of the sessions she had had with Reverend Thatcher. But now the underlying futility was on her side rather than on anyone else's.

She had lost her fragile sense of purpose, of direction. The conclusions she was occasionally tempted to draw from the appearance in the Congery's augury of the riders of her dream had never seemed so foolish. She had no reason for being where she was. And she didn't seem able to invent one. The real point of her long conversations with Geraden was not to shed any light into the dark corners of her situation, but rather to keep him with her, so that he wouldn't fade from her life like Master Eremis.

So while snow as sharp and brittle as ice rattled against her windows and lorn wind keened past the edges of the tower and all Orison seemed to fall into a kind of static calm, frozen not by peace but by waiting, she did essentially nothing except eat, sleep, and sit in her rooms, talking with the Apt whenever he got free of his duties.

He brought her news from around Orison. The Masters were involved in a fierce and apparently endless debate, trying to decide what to do about their champion—and about their own vulnerability. Castellan Lebbick's guards and every stonemason available were busy using the rubble of the champion's departure to build a wall across the breach in Orison's side. And Argus and Ribuld were doing what they could to keep an eye on the lady Elega.

The rest of the time, Terisa and Geraden talked about their circumstances.

On his side, this meant fighting a steady but subdued, almost covert struggle to raise her spirits. As if he knew that any despondency in him could hurt her, he practiced good cheer. As if he knew that the sore places in her weren't ready to be touched, he preserved a tactful emotional distance. As if he knew that she wasn't strong enough to be pushed, he urged nothing. With a delicate gentleness that made his physical mishaps look like they belonged to a completely separate person, he cared for her.

Even though he needed care himself and wasn't getting it. His enemies were as savage as hers, wanted him dead as badly—and for as little reason. But if he was afraid, he kept his fear to himself.

At one point, he asked rather wistfully, "Did you feel anything at the translation point? Could you tell it was there?"

A touch of cold as thin as a feather and as sharp as steel. That was something she didn't want to talk about; it frightened her too badly. "It was so cold down there, and I was so scared. Just before those"— she shivered involuntarily—"those men appeared, I seemed to get even colder and more scared." She already knew that she was never going to mention it to Master Eremis. "That's probably all it was."

He looked at her hard before glancing away.

"What about you?" she countered. "That would explain a lot. If you have that kind of talent, and Master Gilbur got a hint of it while he was teaching you, we would at least have an explanation for why you were attacked."

He rolled his eyes at the ceiling. "Wouldn't that be fun? I would love an explanation. But all I can remember is thinking that it was a silly idea. I was dragging you and Artagel around in the cold and damp for an empty theory. I didn't even see the translation start."

She sighed morosely.

Several times, they both returned to the matter of their strange session with Adept Havelock. "What was all that about, do you suppose?" he wondered. "Why did he want to tell you all that? Why those specific details?"

She had no idea. "He's crazy. Maybe what he calls 'lucidity' just means he's able to put a few sentences together in order."

But that explanation didn't satisfy either of them. Eventually, an old resolve crumbled, and she found herself telling him about her first night in Orison. She described how Adept Havelock had fetched her to his chamber, what Master Quillon had told her of Mordant's history, and how the Adept had saved her from the man in black.

He listened in mingled astonishment and incomprehension. When she was done, he breathed, "They already knew. The first night you were here, they already knew you were in danger. Master Quillon has been busy." He scowled wryly. "If you told the rest of the Congery about this, they wouldn't believe it. Master *Quillon*? Trying to change what happens to anyone?" Then he said more seriously, "At least now we know who my enemies are. Master Gilbur and arch-Imager Vagel."

She nodded. She could feel herself sinking deeper into gloom.

He didn't let the idea of his enemies dismay him, however. Smiling, he said, "There's one advantage to all this, anyway. Now I know how you feel. You don't understand what everybody thinks you can do. I don't understand why men like that think highly enough of me to consider me worth killing."

She was too despondent to be amused. "I want to know whose side Master Quillon and Adept Havelock are on. Not the King's. Not the Congery's. Not Master Gilbur's." She could have also said, Not Master Eremis'.

How many sides *were* there?

But that brought them back to their encounter with the Adept—and to the presumed hints hidden in what he had said. Finally, she decided to give up another of her few remaining secrets. She was committed to him—not because she knew what she was doing, but because he was her friend. And Master Eremis didn't want her. There would be no harm in telling Geraden about Myste.

He listened in close silence. As she explained Myste's reasons for going after the champion, he held his head up like a salute, and tears stood in his eyes. When she was finished, he remained silent for a long moment before murmuring gruffly, "I always liked her.

"Of course," he added, "I know Elega better. And Torrent is so sweet she makes you want to lie down on the floor for her to stand on so her feet won't get cold. King Joyse doesn't have any unattractive daughters. But Myste—" His voice trailed away.

Begging him not to kill her. Terisa felt like crying herself.

Early in the morning of the fifth day, however, she was awakened from a thin, unrestful sleep by the sound of rain.

Groggy with sleep and surprise, she climbed out of bed and went to the nearest window.

For a moment, she was baffled because she couldn't see any rain. In fact, the sky was completely free of clouds. The early sun cast a genial light over the walls and battlements, and the heavens were a vital blue, shaded closer to purple than azure. The distant hills seemed softer under their thick robes of snow, and the crooked bulk of Orison looked considerably more picturesque than it had the previous day, more like a grand castle in a fairy tale.

Then she realized that the sound came from the melting of the snow.

Water ran thickly from the roofs and towers, streamed off the eaves like a downpour. Already, the courtyard resembled a quagmire: its churned mud lay hidden beneath brown puddles as vast as ponds. Guards and people bustling in and out of the courtyard, to and from the huddled maze of shops and shanties and tents, had to wear cloaks against the runoff and high boots against the standing water; but under the open sky they pushed back their cloaks or doffed them altogether to revel in the new warmth.

The winter had turned to thaw.

A little thrill ran through her as she thought she might get a chance to go outside for a while. It might be possible to stop feeling depressed for a while.

Hurrying, she went to wash her face and put on her clothes.

She wasn't surprised when Geraden arrived before Saddith had brought her breakfast. His cheeks were flushed with exertion, and he was breathing hard. He must have run up the stairs. At first glance, she thought he was simply eager, caught up in a stronger version of her own reaction. But the way his eyes shone was more complex than that.

"Have you seen it?" he panted as soon as she shut the door.

"Yes."

They went to the windows together, drawn by the prospect of sun and warmth and springtime after the long, tense winter.

"Glass and splinters," he muttered while he regained his breath, "this is awful."

She blinked at him like a startled owl. "Awful?"

At once, he started laughing. "Isn't that silly? I feel this eager every spring. Like the whole world is coming back to life. The first thaw always makes me want to go out and play like a boy.

"But it's still awful. Even though I love it." He tried to sound somber. "Terisa, this is *very* bad news."

His laughter drew a smile from her. "It's a good thing I've known you so long. If you were a stranger, I would have to assume you've lost your mind. *Why* is this bad news?"

"You mean, since you know me, you don't have to *assume* I've lost my mind? You can take it for granted?" He dismissed her protest with a chortle. "Because it's early. Too early. Right now, winter is about the only thing protecting us. If too much of the snow melts, there won't be anything to prevent Cadwal and even Alend from marching against us *today*.

"You heard what the Perdon said. High King Festten has already mustered an army. He can do that because Cadwal gets so much less snow than we do. And you can be sure the Alend Monarch didn't send his son on a mission as dangerous as a visit to Orison without having an army prepared to support or rescue him. Or avenge him.

"We're the only ones who aren't ready," he continued. "Oh, I'm sure Castellan Lebbick has done everything he can. But we didn't get ready for war last autumn because King Joyse refused to command it"—now Geraden managed to sound grim—"and we aren't ready now because he hasn't been paying attention all winter. Our only hope has been that the snow would last until he came back to his senses."

Terisa frowned in an effort to concentrate. "If they start marching today, who's going to get here first?"

Unable to preserve an appropriately dire expression, he flashed a grin. "That's complicated. Cadwal is closer, especially if they march up through Perdon from the southeast. Alend's best route comes almost due south through the Care of Armigite. That's nearly twice as far.

"But South Perdon is mostly hills, some of them rugged. Armigite is almost all lowland. To reach us, the High King's army has to cross two rivers, the Vertigon and the Broadwine. The Alends only have to ford the Pestil. And the Perdon will fight Cadwal every step of the way. The Armigite, on the other hand—" Geraden sighed. "We would be lucky, I guess, if he fired a few catapults at Margonal's army while it went by."

Although the air outside was obviously much warmer than it had been, it wasn't balmy: when he leaned close to the window, his words left small, brief ovals of condensation on the glass. "But it's even more complicated than that. How long has Prince Kragen been gone? Six days? I presume he's riding hard, but he won't be able to go very fast. Not even today. This much snow will take days to melt off. So he's still a long way from home. Will the Alend Monarch do anything without him? I don't know.

"Giving you my utmost wisdom"—he grimaced—"I would say at this point anything can happen. With our luck, it probably will."

"Well, that's all right," she murmured. " 'Anything' is what's been happening ever since I got here."

He responded with a chuckle and a bow. "My lady, you have an enviable gift for understatement." Then he added, "We're probably lucky. If it stopped happening, we might get confused."

"Speak for yourself," she replied. "Confusion is my natural state." She feigned puzzlement. "Or I *think* so, anyway."

He laughed. "A kindred spirit. No wonder I like you."

Gazing out at the thaw, he sighed happily, "This really is terrible."

Sometime later, there was a knock on the door.

"I am sorry to be late, my lady," Saddith said as she entered the room carrying a large breakfast tray. "The guards told me that Apt Geraden was with you—already." She winked. "So I went back for more food."

Feeling light-headed and impervious to discomfort because of the thaw, Terisa asked foolishly, "How is Master Eremis this morning?"

Saddith glanced down at her tight bosom. "He has been very busy. Or so it is rumored. But he is well." When she looked up, her face wore a deliberate veil of blandness, but the corner of her mouth quirked. "Or so it is rumored."

Terisa realized that she didn't feel quite as cheerful as she thought.

Geraden watched her with a quizzical expression; however, he

made no comment. He had apparently decided that he didn't want to
know what her present relationship with the Master was.

When the maid had left, Terisa tried to recover her good humor
by eating a big breakfast. Nevertheless her mood had turned restless.
She wanted to *do* something, wanted to go as far away from this room
—and from herself—as she could. Abruptly, she demanded, "Let's
get out of here. Today. This morning."

He stared at her with his mouth full. "Get out? You already know
I can't—"

"I didn't mean that. I meant, out of this room. Out of Orison.
Outside." Trying to make sense, she urged, "Maybe we could rent
some horses. I don't know how to ride, but you could teach me.
Anything. I just want to *get out* for a while."

He struggled to understand. "I'll do anything you want. What is
'rent'?"

For no very admirable reason, she thought it might be fun to
scream at him. Or maybe not *fun*, exactly. Maybe *satisfying*?

Fortuitously, someone chose that moment to knock at her door.

Swallowing her baser impulses, she called, "Come in."

On command, a guard opened the door formally and announced,
"The lady Elega." Then he stepped aside and bowed the King's
eldest daughter into the room.

She was dressed as if for an excursion in a warm, high-collared fur
robe and ornately tooled leather boots.

Geraden jumped to his feet. Instinctively, Terisa did the same.

Elega studied both of them. "I am sorry," she said with an ironic
smile. "I did not mean to frighten you."

"Guilty secrets," Geraden replied promptly. "You know me, my
lady." His smile was no more innocent than hers. "I'm always plotting something."

The lady measured him with a glance. Then she turned to Terisa.
"Whatever he plots, Terisa," she said, "I hope you will not let him
entangle you in it. I do not know what he has in mind, of course. But
surely he plots in the same way he does everything else." She
grinned around the word: "Notoriously."

In response, Geraden bowed. "You're too kind, my lady."

Instead of shouting, Cut it out! Terisa asked Elega, "Would you
like some breakfast?"

"Thank you, no." The King's daughter accepted the change of
subject smoothly. She comported herself as though she were ready

for anything. "I have breakfasted. What I would like—if it would please you—is to take you shopping."

Shopping? Terisa gaped helplessly, struck as much by the familiarity of the word as by the strangeness of hearing it from Elega.

"I fear it will not be a very elegant experience. Because of the mud," explained the lady. "But this thaw is wonderful. If it lasts as much as a day or two, it will open the roads around Orison enough to permit the merchants to replenish their stores. This late in the winter, the shops have become too depleted to be worth visiting. Now they may be resupplied.

"Terisa, I would like to take you to buy cloth and engage a seamster, so that you can have clothes made"—she hesitated almost imperceptibly—"to your own fit and fashion."

"Clothes?"

"Whatever clothes you like. Of course," said Elega firmly, "I will offer you advice as to weather and custom. But what I wish is to help you please yourself."

"But"—it was the first thought that came to her—"I don't have any money."

The lady raised a delicate eyebrow in surprise. "You are a friend of the King's daughter. Why do you need money?"

Terisa couldn't find the words to protest. Fortunately, Geraden was sensitive to the particular character of her ignorance. "The lady Elega is right," he said, supplying more reassurance than the situation superficially required. "As long as you're with her, any merchant or artisan in Mordant will give you anything you want. That's one of the privileges of the ruling family.

"It isn't actually fair." His tone reminded her that most of his friendships were among the workers of Orison, rather than among the lords and ladies. "But the way King Joyse runs the country puts more wealth back than it takes out, so his privileges don't do any harm." He seemed to be urging her to accept Elega's offer.

She made an effort to collect her scattered wits. Really, she ought to be accustomed to surprises by now. They were becoming the story of her life. And when she thought about it, she found that she was excited.

"Thanks," she said to the lady. "That sounds like fun. I was just telling Geraden I wanted to get out of this room. I'm about to start screaming."

Elega smiled. "I know just what you mean. I have felt that way for years at a time. When would you like to go?"

Terisa glanced at Geraden, but his features were composed into a neutral mask. "How about right now?"

"That suits me admirably." Elega looked pleased.

"If you will take my advice from the start, however," she continued, "you will change your garments before we go. The seamsters who serve the ladies of Orison are accustomed to gowns. I suspect that they have scant acquaintance with"—she searched for a graceful description—"the styles of your world. If you wear a gown and carry your own clothing with you, you will be able to leave it for the seamster to use as a pattern. Then they should be able to match it."

Although Terisa wasn't at all sure that she wanted shirts and pants instead of gowns, Elega's advice seemed too reasonable to ignore. "Just give me a minute." From the wardrobe in the bedroom, she quickly fetched her demure gray gown. Then she retreated to the bathroom to change.

"Dress warmly," Elega called. "And be prepared for mud."

As soon as she had worked her way into the gown, Terisa located the thick sheepskin coat and boots that Geraden had supplied for her tour of Orison's battlements. In a few moments, she was ready to go. She carried her old clothes under her coat. Her heart was beating like a schoolgirl's.

"Will you accompany us, Geraden?" inquired Elega. "I doubt that choosing fabrics and studying styles will be of much interest to you. But it is unwise for ladies to go unescorted to the shops." To Terisa, she explained, "Despite Castellan Lebbick's best efforts, the bazaar attracts any number of rude fellows—pickthieves, gypsies, clowns, and ruffians. The guards maintain good order, but they cannot prevent all small crimes." Then she addressed Geraden again. "If you would like an escape from your routine duties, I will be happy to pretend that I have commanded your attendance."

"Again you are too kind, my lady." Behind his deference, he was laughing. "But the King's daughter's pretense is probably as good as a command. I'll go with you, of course."

Elega smiled at him as though he were an amiable child. "Then perhaps you should get a coat."

He was taken aback: he seemed almost suspicious, as if he thought the lady might have some ulterior motive. He swallowed his concern, however. "That's a good idea. Which door are you going to use? I'll catch up with you."

She told him.

Bowing to Terisa, he left.

Brightly, Elega asked, "Shall we go?"

Terisa wasn't sure what she was doing as she followed the King's daughter out of the room.

Chatting easily about trivial subjects, Elega led her around through Orison to the northwest end of the castle. Along the way, she spotted Ribuld and Argus. The two guards were loitering in the hall as if they were off watch and had no better use for their time.

Her eagerness began to change color. What had started as a simple case of spring fever was becoming yet another gambit in the plots and schemes that surrounded Mordant's need.

She accepted this. At the moment, all she really wanted was to *get out* of her recent depression.

Then she and Elega reached a door that gave access to the courtyard. With its massive timbers and thick iron bolts, it was made to be sealed; but it was open, and its guards stood outside, watching the crowd that spilled out of Orison to swirl and mill around the shops and tents.

Geraden was already there: he had been running again. Now, however, he had a coat to keep him warm.

Just for a second, his face showed a relief he couldn't conceal. Apparently, one of his fears had been proved groundless. Then he greeted the two women with a smile.

Terisa inhaled the springlike air deeply and plunged with her companions through the downpour from the eaves out into the mud.

Once again, she was struck by the size of the courtyard. Hidden in its own shadow, the eastern edifice of the castle was dark against the fathomless blue sky; but to the west Orison's whole inward face held the sun and reflected the browns and grays of its stones, making the atmosphere around her warmer than the weather. In this light, the erratic pile of the castle seemed protective, rising high on all sides to keep what it enclosed safe. Windows caught the sunlight and flashed; from oriels and poles and projections among the balconies and walkways, clotheslines had been strung, and drying laundry decorated the walls in particolor; up on the towers, pennons made tiny by distance fluttered and gleamed.

The mud wasn't as bad as she had expected. In this end of the courtyard, away from the area where the guards exercised their horses, gravel had been strewn over the dirt. That didn't solve the problem, but it did make the inevitable muck less deep and cloying. The hem of her gown became soaked and stained immediately, but she was able to walk with unanticipated ease.

Doubtless inspired by their own species of spring fever, the people of the courtyard had flung wide the wooden fronts of their shops, decked their tents with ribbons, brought out carts loaded with refreshments which no one would have braved the cold to enjoy yesterday. They had put on their gay clothes and declared the day a spontaneous festival. Terisa heard the music of pipes and lutes punctuated by tambourines. Somewhere, there was probably dancing. Cooking smells and spices followed the tang of woodsmoke which drifted along the slight breeze from tin chimneys in the roofs of wooden structures, from smoke holes at the tops of tents, and from open fires crackling frequently in the gaps between the buildings.

For no reason except that she suddenly felt wonderful, she began laughing.

Geraden shared her mood. And Elega smiled, although the assessing quality of her gaze suggested that her pleasure was more complex. Terisa grinned at both of them and made an effort not to hurry.

"Here!" Passing among the shops and the crowds, Geraden presumed on his apparent stature as *a friend of the King's daughter* to dash over to a cart and capture some of its wares, which were charred chunks of meat on long cane sticks. "This is my favorite food in the whole world." The vendor bowed again and again like a bobbing cork as Geraden carried his booty triumphantly back to Terisa and Elega. "It's called 'treasure of Domne.' The meat is just lamb, but it's basted with a sauce that will melt your heart." With a flourish, he offered a stick to each of his companions. "Eat! And grieve that you weren't born in the Care of Domne."

"I think," Elega murmured without malice, "we would be more likely to grieve if we *were* born in the Care of Domne."

Juice ran down Terisa's chin as she bit into the tender meat. It was spiced like nothing she had ever tasted before. Stale coriander? Cumin that hadn't been stored properly? For Geraden's sake, she finished the piece she had in her mouth, then tried to think of an excuse not to eat the rest. Luckily, he savored the treat so much himself that he was temporarily deaf and blind to his companions. Elega deftly handed her stick to the nearest passerby. After a momentary hesitation, Terisa did the same. A bit self-consciously, she wiped her chin.

She and Elega walked on. The crowd made too much noise for quiet conversation. People were laughing gaily, shouting rowdy encouragements and insults at each other, greeting friends and hawking merchandise. But she didn't want to talk—she wanted to see everything and absorb it all. The loud bustle seemed entirely unlike the frenetic activity of the city streets with which she was familiar. These people weren't thinking about making fortunes or losing their jobs or fighting off muggers or being evicted from their homes. And they also weren't thinking about war with Cadwal and Alend, the ethics of Imagery, or their King's inexplicable decline. Their minds were on more important things.

Geraden rejoined her, grinning a little foolishly. With Elega, they took the path of least resistance through the throng.

Everything here had been set down or built up unsystematically, without a thought to such questions as ease of access or advantageous display—and with very little concern for sanitation. Apparently Castellan Lebbick's authority didn't entirely rule this little village which had sprung up to serve the demands of Orison. Rickety wooden buildings that looked too tall for their underpinnings, and too hastily hammered together to be more than semi-permanent, leaned against each other, often making it difficult for prospective buyers to find the entrances to the shops. Some of the tents assertively overfilled the available space, with the result that they couldn't be passed except by squatting under or straddling over the ropes. Cooking fires sent up sparks dangerously close to weathered planks and dry canvas. Terisa was jostled so frequently that she began to be glad she wasn't carrying any money.

Around one corner, she and her companions came upon a mountebank selling nostrums from a brightly painted wagon. His shirt was several sizes too small for him; his trousers, far too large. And both had been worn to tatters. But he had made a virtue of necessity by tying himself up from neck to ankles in ribbons of all colors, so that his tatters looked like a deliberate part of his costume. His mustache was as tangled as his hair, which had the added attraction of being streaked with ash. More ash stained his swarthy skin; his eyes rolled feverishly.

His nostrums were contained in crooked little glass bottles, large and uneven clay pots, and baskets woven of reeds. He advertised them with a high-pitched cry like the whine of a half-wit. If he had worn a red sign around his neck that said CHARLATAN, he would have appeared no less reliable than he did now. Large numbers of people showed interest in his wares, but he didn't seem to have many buyers.

"Where does somebody like that *come* from?" Terisa asked Elega. "I can't believe he sells enough to keep himself alive."

"You have never been beyond the walls of Orison." The lady's tone and expression were cool: she obviously didn't share Terisa's curiosity. "Do not let your experiences among us paint a false picture. Away from the Demesne—and, to a lesser extent, from the principal cities of the Cares—Mordant's people include a predictable number of simpletons and gulls. Fellows such as this often live better than you might guess."

Nevertheless Terisa thought the man was fascinating. In fact, she found him more fascinating than she could explain. Something about the way he rolled his eyes and leered made her suspect that he knew what he was doing—that there was cunning in his performance. Was it all an act? Did he disarm suspicion by making himself so plainly untrustworthy?

Her companions wanted to go on, however. After a moment, she let them draw her away.

Shortly, Elega raised her voice and pointed. "All the fabric and tailor shops are there. They have been set almost one on top of the other. It is not usually a quiet place. I think they are often more interested in stealing custom from each other than in attracting buyers. But they will restrain themselves as long as I am with you."

Terisa was tempted to reply, you seem to have that effect on everybody. She bit her tongue, however, and said nothing.

They passed a cart selling what looked like fried bread. Another offered the sort of trinkets that a guard might buy for a serving girl. In an open area where no one had yet built a shop or pitched a tent, a juggler in a voluminous black robe handled sharp, silver pieces of metal shaped like stars as if they were plates or ninepins. His robe whipped and spun around him like a whirl of midnight. Then Terisa and her escorts were near enough to the tailors and cloth merchants to see swaths of material draped invitingly out windows and over doors, and to hear men with measuring tapes around their necks and pins stuck in their clothing haggling over the passersby.

Suddenly, Geraden let out a yelp of surprise and pleasure and took off at a run, splashing mud.

Terisa and Elega stared after him. "I swear to you, Terisa," the lady said, "that man becomes more like a boy every year." Despite her tone, she looked perplexed—perhaps even a little worried. "Surely he knows that it is neither courteous nor wise to abandon us?"

Terisa watched him dodging recklessly through the crowd and held her breath, afraid that he would fall. But he didn't. Instead, he came to a stop as suddenly as he had started.

"Let's go see what he's doing." Without waiting for agreement, she headed in that direction.

Elega sighed audibly and joined her.

Geraden hadn't gone far. They found him with another man, who appeared to be considerably less than delighted by the fact that Geraden had spotted him.

"Terisa," the Apt announced as she and Elega reached him, "this is my brother Nyle."

Then he began babbling.

"Artagel told me you were here, but I almost didn't believe him. I haven't been able to find you. Where have you been hiding? It's great to see you. Why are you here? The last I heard, you were in Houseldon for the winter. You were trying to talk yourself out of—well, never mind that. Is everyone all right? How is father? And Tholden? How about—"

"Let him answer, Geraden," chided Elega firmly. "I am sure he did not come out of 'hiding,' as you call it, specifically so that you could drive him to distraction."

With an effort, Geraden cut off his rush of words.

Unabashedly curious, Terisa studied Nyle. She would have known him as Geraden's brother anywhere. He had Geraden's hair and coloring, Geraden's build, only an inch less than Geraden's height. And he would have had Geraden's face, if his features hadn't been set for brooding instead of openheartedness. He looked like a discontented version of his younger brother, a man whose basically serious nature had curdled.

It was clear that he took no joy in meeting Geraden.

Stiffly, he bowed to the two women. "My lady Elega." He and Elega didn't look at each other. "My lady Terisa. I'm glad to meet you"—Terisa heard no pleasure in his voice—"even though my brother hasn't bothered to introduce us."

Geraden started to apologize, but Nyle cut him off. "You haven't been able to find me because I've been busy with my private affairs." He glared at Geraden, and his tone was acid. "They don't have anything to do with you, so there's no reason why you should be involved in them."

"What do you mean, 'private affairs'?" snorted Geraden. "I'm your *brother*. You don't *have* private affairs. Even Stead"—he laughed shortly—"doesn't have private affairs, and he needs them more than you do. Half the husbands in Domne flinch every time he walks into the room. What can you possibly be doing that doesn't involve your own family?"

A muscle in Nyle's cheek twitched; however, he kept the rest of his face still. Turning from Geraden, he bowed again to Terisa and Elega. "My ladies, I hope you enjoy your outing. We're lucky to have this weather."

With his shoulders squared and his back rigid, he strode away between the shops.

Terisa shot a look at Geraden. His face was knotted: for an instant, he seemed on the verge of chasing after his brother, shouting something. Then he swung toward Elega. "My lady"—he bit down to keep his voice steady—"is this your doing?"

She wasn't taken aback by the accusation. Watching Nyle's departing figure vividly, she murmured, "It may have something to do with me. I should speak to him. Excuse me."

Pulling up her skirts, she hurried after him.

Geraden moved to follow. Instinctively, Terisa put a hand on his arm. Hadn't she heard Elega mention Nyle once? When was that? Oh, yes. When Elega first took her to meet Myste. *Nyle is more to my taste.* Geraden looked at her to see why she had restrained him; she asked, "How could it be her doing?"

Elega caught up with Nyle and stopped him. Their faces couldn't be seen clearly: too many people intervened, moving in both directions. And of course what they said was inaudible.

Distantly, Geraden replied, "He's been nursing a passion for her for years, but he thinks it's hopeless. He thinks—" He frowned in vexation. "I don't understand it. He thinks he isn't grand or special enough for her. He hasn't done anything dramatic in the world. He knows she's ambitious, and he's sure she won't have him. I think it galls him that *I* was the one who was betrothed to her—and I let her get away.

"He told us he was going to stay in Houseldon all winter to talk himself out of asking for her hand."

"So you think he came to Orison to see if she'll have him?"

Geraden nodded. His face was tight with empathy. "But I guess he hasn't asked her yet. If he did, and she turned him down, he wouldn't stick around. So she must have done something to hurt him before he got his courage nailed down tightly enough to actually propose. He can't leave because he hasn't done what he came for. But he's in too much pain to do it.

"Blast her." He glanced at Terisa. "I'm guessing, of course. But look at them. Whatever it is, she knows what's eating at him."

The glimpses Terisa caught through the crowd seemed to confirm Geraden's opinion. Elega was talking to Nyle—pleading with him? —as though she knew what to say. And his answers—brusque as they were—suggested understanding, even approval.

Because she didn't know how to comfort Geraden, Terisa changed the subject. "What did you think of that mountebank? The man in the ribbons and tatters."

At first, Nyle and Elega held Geraden's attention. With an effort, however, he dragged his gaze back to Terisa. "What did you say? I didn't hear you."

"The mountebank we passed a little while ago. What did you think of him?"

"Think of him? Nothing special. Why?"

She could see the difference when he actually *looked* at her. "Just curious," she said casually. "Something about him—"

Another characteristic of Geraden's that she liked was his willingness to accept her whims. He wracked his memory, then said, "I haven't seen him before. I wonder why. He doesn't look young enough to be new at this."

"Well, he isn't exactly old," she began. "He—"

A moment later, the truth struck her.

"He looks familiar." That was why she found him so interesting. "I *have* seen him before."

Geraden stared at her. "You what?"

"I've *seen* him somewhere," she insisted. "I'm sure of it. But not like this. He's in disguise."

"Where was that?" Geraden was instantly ready to believe her. "Was it the man who attacked you?"

Gart? "No." She closed her eyes and tried to calm her excitement. "It's not him." But the hints and pieces didn't come together. "I don't know. Somewhere." The more she pictured the mountebank, the less familiar he looked. "I can't remember."

"Don't try to force it. The quicker you forget about it, the quicker it'll come to you." Then he added, "And thanks."

She shook her head. "Thanks for what?"

He nodded toward Elega and Nyle. "I needed the distraction."

As Terisa looked in that direction, Nyle moved off into the throng and Elega returned to her companions.

Her determined smile and veiled gaze made it clear at once that she had no intention of revealing what had passed between her and Nyle. "I am sorry I kept you waiting," she said before either Terisa or Geraden could speak. "The best of the cloth shops is just over there. Shall we go?"

Taking their acquiescence for granted, she started toward the shop.

Geraden met Terisa's eyes behind Elega's back and shrugged. The twist of his mouth suggested regret rather than anger. After all, this wasn't his first experience with the King's eldest daughter. He seemed to know the trick of not being offended by what she did.

He and Terisa followed her together.

As they approached the fabric and tailor shops, the noise rose to a din. The merchants there fought over possible customers so aggressively that Terisa would never have considered approaching them if she had been alone. The lady Elega wasn't in the least disconcerted, however. Smiling good-naturedly, she walked into the midst of the shopkeepers and said without raising her voice, "Good sirs, you do not need this raucous display. You know that I am not persuaded by it." Her tone was mild but sure. "Perhaps you will indulge me with a bit more moderation."

Almost immediately, quiet spread out around her as people saw who she was and nudged their neighbors.

In response, Elega inclined her head graciously—a gesture that made Geraden roll his eyes. Nevertheless Terisa saw that the deference of the shopkeepers was perfectly serious. The King's daughter's patronage must have been well worth what it cost.

Selecting a shop, Elega sailed toward it as if she were leading a fleet. Like many of the wooden structures, this one was built up a bit so that its flooring didn't rest in the mud. A few apparently reliable steps led to a narrow porch that inspired less confidence; then an open door gave admittance to the small room where the merchant showed his wares.

Most of the room's light came from unglassed windows with their shutters pushed aside, but a brazier in the center of the floor provided some warmth. Scurrying ahead of Elega, the shopkeeper stationed himself behind a counter and began to murmur obsequious enthusiasm for her presence.

Aside from the brazier and the counter, the room was empty. Bare planking without shelves formed the walls. In fact, there was no cloth to be seen in the shop, apart from the swaths hanging out the windows and over the porch.

Elega greeted this fact with equanimity. "I see that I have come to the right place."

The shopkeeper was bold enough to say, "You have, my lady. All my winter stock is sold. I have nothing left except my samples."

"I take that as testimony to the quality of your goods."

He bowed in humble pride. "But I will have everything you wish as soon as the roads are open," he added quickly.

"Very good. Let us see your samples." Elega indicated her companions. "The lady Terisa of Morgan needs to improve her wardrobe."

"At once, my lady."

From beneath the counter, the man started producing long, thin strips of cloth which he spread out for inspection.

Geraden cleared his throat. "With your permission, my lady," he said to Elega, "I'll leave you for a while. My opinions aren't likely to be much help. And if anybody troubles you while you're choosing cloth or talking to tailors, every merchant in the area will leap to your defense."

"Leave Nyle alone," Elega replied by way of assent. "I think he is in no mood to be pestered by his family today." Then she chose two or three of the strips and showed them to Terisa. "What do you think of these?"

Only Terisa noticed the Apt's bow as he left the shop.

Trying to sound casual, she took this opportunity to ask Elega, "Did you know Nyle was in Orison? Geraden was surprised to hear it."

"No. Why?" Elega's disinterest was nearly flawless. "I should
have been more surprised than he was. I did not know Nyle was here
until we saw him. But I fear I am losing the ability to be surprised by
anything the sons of the Domne do."

Terisa shrugged. "I just thought you might have seen him around.
You mentioned him to me once. I got the impression you liked
him."

"I do." Elega was better at nonchalance than Terisa was. "I consider him a friend. And I respect him. He has a—a seriousness of
mind?—no, a seriousness of *desire* which his brothers apparently lack.
It is inconceivable, for instance, that he would spend Geraden's years
trying and failing to become an Imager. And it is also inconceivable
that he would learn Artagel's skills and then refuse to use them—as
Artagel has refused—to rise in command of the King's guards.

"There was a time," she admitted, "when if he had expressed an
interest in my hand I would have taken him as seriously as he took
me." She spoke without any noticeable concern for the shopkeeper's
presence. "Still, I did not know that he had come to Orison. His
'private affairs'—whatever they may be—have nothing to do with
me."

"I was just curious." Lamely, Terisa turned her attention to the
question of fabrics.

Elega proved to have a good eye. The materials she selected for
consideration were excellent—some warm twills and light poplins
for everyday wear, some fine silks and velvets for formal occasions—
and the colors she advised were right for Terisa's hair and eyes and
skin. Soon Terisa had the ten samples she liked best arranged in front
of her. She was trying to pick one or two (or three?) when Elega said
to the shopkeeper, "These will be enough at present. As soon as the
material arrives, deliver it to Mindlin the seamster. He will tell you
how much he needs."

"Certainly, my lady. With pleasure." The prospect of supplying
enough free cloth to make ten outfits didn't appear to distress him.

Terisa herself was too astonished to protest. *Ten* new outfits? What
was she going to do with *ten* new outfits?

Elega seemed to enjoy the look on Terisa's face. "Come," she said
with a smile. "Mindlin has always made my clothes. I am sure he will
be glad to do the same for you."

"Without question, my lady," the shopkeeper put in, "without
question. An outstanding choice, if I may say so. Mindlin's work is

superb. Superb. I'll provide him these fabrics the instant they arrive."

Bestowing a nod, the lady drew Terisa out of the shop.

Mindlin's establishment was nearby. If anything, it was even less elaborate or pretentious than the fabric shop. Mindlin himself was a tall man with sunken gray cheeks and an austere manner, and he spoke in a haughty tone which seemed to come out of a different mouth than the subservient words he actually uttered. In fact, the content of his speech was so fawning that even Elega was embarrassed. "Unfortunately," she explained to Terisa, "he has become wealthy on the strength of his reputation as my seamster."

Terisa was unable to suppress a grin.

Embarrassment, however, didn't cost Elega her command of the situation. Briskly, she told Mindlin what materials would be supplied to him, and by whom. Then she asked Terisa, "What would you like?"

For a moment, Terisa's imagination was paralyzed. "I've never had clothes made for me before."

"Then the experience will be good for you," Elega replied with satisfaction. She thought briefly, then informed Mindlin that the lady Terisa needed two formal gowns, two warm winter gowns, two lighter ones for spring, and—she gave him the bundle of Terisa's old clothes—four outfits made on that unfamiliar pattern, again two for winter and two for spring. She also specified which fabric should be used in each case—a test of memory that would have defeated Terisa.

"But you must choose the details," she told Terisa, "unless you wish to abandon yourself to Mindlin's taste. There is no hurry, however, if you are unsure. He will bring you his work well before it is complete, so that it can be fitted properly. You will have that opportunity to discuss the way your skirts hang, or the amount of lace and finery you wish to display, or even"—she indicated ironic tolerance for the foibles of woman—"the degree of décolletage that interests you."

"That would be nice," Terisa said, feeling shy as well as excited.

"Then I will leave you in his hands," Elega announced smoothly. There seemed to be a hint of anticipation in the way she started toward the door.

At the idea of having to face this situation by herself, Terisa went into a schoolgirl's panic. "Where are you going? Aren't you going to stay with me?"

The lady beamed reassurance. "I must do a few trifling errands of my own. And I have already tried to make too many of your decisions. I will return—almost at once. If I do not, wait for me here. I will be with you soon."

Before Terisa could protest further, Elega was gone.

Terisa wanted to run after the lady. She felt suddenly alone in a hostile world. She had so many questions. How was Mindlin going to measure her? Was she expected to disrobe right here in his shop? How could she?

To make matters worse, the seamster's demeanor changed immediately. His manner became less austere: he even went so far as to attempt a ghastly smile. At the same time, the subservience dropped out of his speech. Holding up her clothes disdainfully, he asked, "Does my lady seriously intend to wear such garments?"

Reduced by alarm—and by echoes of her father's sarcasm—to feeling like a child, she was on the verge of blurting out, No, of course not, not if you don't think it's a good idea, what do you recommend? Fortunately, she caught herself in time. Really, she ought to be ashamed of herself. Hadn't she already stood up to Castellan Lebbick more than once? And now she was going to let herself be driven to drivel by a *seamster*?

With a conscious effort, she raised her eyes to meet his, and as she did so her spirits also rose. Smiling, she asked, "What's wrong with them?"

His expression looked suspiciously like a sneer. "They are not flattering, my lady. Not womanly."

"Do you think so? Where I come from, they're considered"—she rolled the word around in her mouth and realized that she could have fun doing this—"delectable."

Mindlin seemed shocked. She suspected he was afraid of having misjudged her meekness. The haughtiness in his face came up as the self-assertion in his voice went down. "As my lady wishes. I will certainly work to the best of my humble abilities to please her."

There was no question about it: she could have fun doing this. She didn't want to overdo it, however. "But you're probably right," she said as though he had persuaded her. "I don't need four outfits like that. Two should be enough." In a flash of inspiration, she added, "Why don't you use the rest of the material to make me two riding habits?"

"Riding habits?" Suppressed apoplexy constricted his tone. "Does my lady intend to go riding? On horseback?"

"Of course," she answered sweetly. "Where I come from, all the ladies do it. Don't you know how to make clothes like that?"

He dropped his gaze. "I am not accustomed to make such garments for women of rank. But I will do as my lady wishes."

"Good." She was starting to feel inordinately proud of herself.

Still studying the floor instead of her face, he said, "If it pleases my lady, I will take a measure from these"—his fingers twitched her shirt and pants—"and return them to her no later than this evening. Then, sadly, I must await the arrival of the fabrics in order to serve her. As the lady Elega, my illustrious patroness, has said, the details can be discussed when the work is ready for fitting."

"That's fine," Terisa pronounced. Then, because she knew she would never be able to stand where she was and keep her composure, she turned to leave. Trying to emulate Elega's regal bearing, she walked out of the shop into the crowds and the sunlight.

If Geraden had been there, she would have burst out laughing: all she needed was someone to share her humor with. But he was nowhere in sight. And Elega, too, didn't appear. The clamor of the merchants had risen to its former pitch. If anyone had called her name, she might not have heard it. The flow of the throng made it easier to move than to stand still, so she let herself be nudged and jostled slowly away from Mindlin's shop.

Before she had gone far enough to consider turning back, she caught a glimpse of Nyle.

He shifted purposefully through the crowd—not hurrying, but also not wasting any time. His path took him out of view again almost immediately; but a moment later he became briefly visible between shops, still heading in the same direction.

On impulse, Terisa started after him.

She would have been hard pressed to account for what she was doing. He was a familiar face, of course, and she didn't like being alone among all these people. Her curiosity about him as Geraden's brother was probably a more fundamental explanation, however. And more fundamental still was her instinctive interest in his purpose. Whatever it was, it was enough to make him snub Geraden. But not Elega.

Was he unaware that Elega plotted to betray his father's best friend?

Quickly, she walked to the shops between which she had just seen him. Taking that narrow lane, she reached the place where he had passed. Almost at once, she spotted him.

He seemed very far away.

She didn't want to call attention to herself by running. At the same time, she didn't want to lose him. After an instant of hesitation, she decided to run.

It was a fortunate decision, despite the fact that it caused her to bump into people and made total strangers mutter curses at her: it enabled her to gain enough ground so that he didn't vanish when he turned along a row of food stalls and turned again. She reached the row of stalls barely in time to see him clamber over the ropes and disappear behind a tent which had been pitched much too close to the neighboring buildings.

She went as far as the tent; then she had to stop. Could she follow him? Her gown and coat would make her awkward over the tent ropes. And there appeared to be no exit from where Nyle had gone except around one side of the tent or the other. If he knew of another, she had already lost him. And if he came back while she tried to go after him, he would catch her.

Finally she moved to the opening of the tent and made an effort to wait there inconspicuously, watching both sides.

The tent seemed to be about the size of a comfortable cottage. In a ring around the tent pole, rough tables had been set up in the mud (there was no ground cover), and from these tables a number of men and women sold beads and sequins, shawls and trinkets. None of the people behind the tables were particularly busy; one man called out to Terisa, inviting her in. She ignored him and remained at her post.

Several minutes after she began to feel foolish, but still a minute or two before her stubbornness would have given out, a slight quiver ran through the tent as Nyle returned, pushing himself over the ropes.

With her heart pounding, she ducked partway into the tent to avoid being seen, then turned to watch him, holding herself steady with one hand on the canvas.

His face was focused, intent. Whatever he was doing didn't appear to give him any pleasure: his frown was so deep that it seemed to describe the underlying set of his bones. Nevertheless he was obviously not a man who hesitated simply because he wasn't enjoying himself. Perhaps he didn't expect enjoyment from life.

Without noticing her, he strode off the way he had come.

She was about to go after him when another quiver warned her that someone else was climbing over the tent ropes.

She froze in time to get a clear, close look at the man who emerged from the place where Nyle had just been.

It was the mountebank, his ribbons and tatters fluttering extravagantly.

The *mountebank*? That was surprising enough. By itself, it would have astounded her. But the fact that stunned her into openmouthed immobility was that she knew him. He passed so near to her that she was able to recognize him.

Behind the distracting way he dressed, under the ash that marked his face and hair, he was Prince Kragen. The Alend Contender.

Around her, the whole day shifted. Meanings changed everywhere. It *can't* be, she protested. I saw him *leave*. I saw him ride out of Orison with all his men.

But if he wanted to come back secretly, how else could he do it? Pressure filled her throat, rising there until she thought she would choke. How else could he and Elega communicate? How else could they make plans together?

And Nyle was involved with them. Elega had lied. Of course she had lied. His "private affairs" had everything to do with her. No wonder he didn't want to encounter his brother.

He was plotting with Elega and Prince Kragen against the King of Mordant.

And Elega's invitation to Terisa to come here with her wasn't innocent at all. It had nothing to do with any desire for a mere friendly outing. Shopping was just an excuse. Elega was still trying to snare her somehow.

Terisa was so staggered that she didn't notice the black-clad juggler with the sharp silver stars until he began performing directly in front of her, hardly more than twenty feet away.

The midnight whirl of his cloak caught her attention. His stars began to dance in his hands. They cast a glitter of sunshine, lovely and bewitching, as they arced through the air, passing between his fingers like flakes of light. Soon he was surrounded with spangles.

He didn't watch what he was doing. He had no need to watch: his hands knew their skill. Instead, he regarded Terisa narrowly.

The stars cast a trance. For a moment like the touch of a dream, she saw everything.

Here in the middle of the bazaar, a good distance from the torrents of water pouring off the eaves and roofs of Orison, the mud was beginning to dry under the warmth of the sun and the passage of so many feet. The boots of the men were stained, of course, and the skirts of the women were filthy; but they were no longer clogged in mire.

Nyle had disappeared into the throng in one direction; Prince Kragen would soon be out of sight in the other. As if to balance the scene, however, Geraden and Elega were approaching from opposite ends of the row of food stalls.

The sunlight seemed to make the smells from the stalls stronger. Sweets, oils, nuts, pungent meats—they were all part of the arcing dance of the stars.

Elega was apparently looking for someone—maybe for Terisa herself. The way Elega squinted reminded Terisa that sunshine wasn't the lady's natural element, not the kind of illumination that brought out her beauty.

Geraden, on the other hand, had already spotted Terisa. He waved his arm and moved toward her, smiling.

The sky overhead looked as blue as a dream, blue and perfect, the ideal background for the whirl of silver.

But the juggler *had a nose like the blade of a hatchet; his teeth were bared in a feral grin. She had the indistinct impression that there were scars on his cheeks.* His burning yellow eyes were fixed on her—

Then the moment ended, and she didn't see how things happened.

Without forewarning, the stars changed their dance. From the juggler's hands, they began to float straight at her head like bright, metal leaves on a long breeze.

Hardly aware of what she did, she twitched her face away from the first star. The second licked along her cheek.

The rest of them should have hit her. But they were pulled off target when Geraden crashed into the juggler, grappling for his arm.

The juggler delivered a blow with his elbow that crumpled Geraden into the mud. Then his robe swirled aside, and a longsword appeared like a slash of steel fire in his hands.

He sprang at Terisa.

She was already falling backward, stumbling into the tent.

Everything seemed to go dark. People screamed, cursed. She collided with one of the display tables and overturned it. Someone shrieked, bitten by the juggler's blade. In a flurry of trinkets, she fell past the table and hit the tent pole.

Then she was able to see again.

As black and irresistible as midnight, the juggler came after her, wielding his sword like a flail to clear terrified merchants and shoppers out of his way.

Somehow, she got her legs under her, put the tent pole between her and her attacker. Then she lost her footing and went down again.

"Gart!" a man barked.

The shout turned the juggler away from her.

"Don't tell me," drawled Artagel as he sauntered forward, grinning sharply, "that the High King's Monomach can't find a worthier opponent than an unarmed woman. I've already warned you about that."

"Do you think you're worthy?" the man in black hissed like silk. "I already know you aren't."

Artagel kicked a table aside. Almost in the same motion, he jumped to the attack.

Gart wheeled and leveled a blow like the cut of an axe at Terisa.

His swing was hard enough to split her in half. Fortunately, Artagel anticipated Gart's move. He came around the other side of the tent pole in time to parry the blow and save her.

Then he was between her and the High King's Monomach.

The tent was deserted now except for Terisa and the two combatants. Their boots ground beads and lace into the mud as they probed and riposted. Their blades struck sparks from each other, a darkened and baleful version of the sunlit dance of stars. She could hear Artagel's harsh breathing: he sounded as though he hadn't fully recovered from the damage to his lungs. Gart's respiration was so firm and even that it made no noise.

Attack. Parry. The clangor of iron.

Artagel had trouble with the tables. They hampered his strokes, interfered with his parries: they caught his feet so that he nearly fell. His movements were tight with strain. Gart, on the other hand, seemed to float among the obstacles as if he had placed them where they were to suit his training and experience.

Bracing herself on the tent pole, Terisa climbed upright. Her hands were slippery with blood. Where had it come from? Probably from her cheek. Artagel was going to get killed because of her. Because of her. She wanted to run away. That was the only thing she could do. If she distracted Gart by running away, Artagel might have a chance. But the High King's Monomach stayed so close to the opening of the tent that she couldn't escape.

She would have cried out; but the ringing clash of iron and the hoarse rasp of Artagel's breath made every other sound impossible.

As it happened, she didn't need to cry out. Roaring like maddened bulls, Argus and Ribuld charged out of sunlight into the gloom of the tent.

Even if she had known what to watch for, she might not have seen how Gart saved himself. It was too fast. Perhaps he took advantage of the moment their eyes needed to adjust. All she knew was that she heard him snarl as he whirled and met Argus and Ribuld with a blow which somehow forced them to recoil separately, away from each other.

Artagel sprang after him.

Too wild, too desperate. Off balance.

Gart met that onslaught also, caught and held Artagel's blade on his, then slipped it aside and swept his own steel in a slicing cut that laid open Artagel's side and brought blood spurting between his ribs.

Gasping, he staggered to one knee.

That was all the time Ribuld and Argus needed to recover and attack again. Still Gart was too quick for them. Before they could hit him, he leaped for the tent pole—vaulting over the blow Artagel aimed at his legs—and dealt a high cut to the rope that pulled the canvas up the pole.

Then he dove and rolled for the opening, passing as slick as oil between Argus and Ribuld while the tent came down on their heads.

The wet, heavy canvas pushed Terisa into the mud again. She groveled there, smothering slowly. In her mind Gart's blade bit into Artagel's side and the dark blood flowed. She hardly heard the clamor of the onlookers as the High King's Monomach made his escape.

Roused by the tumult, a number of guards arrived almost immediately. They cut Terisa and Artagel, Argus and Ribuld free. They improvised a litter and raced Artagel toward the nearest physician. They picked up Geraden, chaffed and slapped him back to consciousness. They started a search. Soon Castellan Lebbick came on the scene with reinforcements, organization, and tongue-lashings. The whole bazaar was searched.

But no one found Gart.

TWENTY:
FAMILY MATTERS

erisa wanted to go after Artagel with Geraden. She was the one who had seen Artagel hit, seen him fall. Fighting to save her. But even if she hadn't been a witness, as well as the cause—in fact, even if she hadn't known Artagel at all—she would have felt the same. Befuddled by Gart's blow, Geraden let his anguish show nakedly on his face. His concentration on his brother was so urgent that he was blind to everything else. Awkwardly, he struggled to free himself from guards and questions and astonished onlookers so that he could go after Artagel. Seeing him like that made her believe that he needed her. In spite of her own shock and fear, she wanted to go with him.

Elega didn't release her.

The lady came to Terisa's side as soon as the guards had fanned out to search for the High King's Monomach. As she held Terisa's arm and dabbed at the blood on Terisa's cheek, she made soft comforting noises which sounded a little artificial, coming from her. Terisa would have had to repulse her vehemently in order to get away from her.

Terisa didn't have it in her to do that. Not now: not while every muscle in her arms and legs trembled, and her stomach twisted around itself, trying to decide what to do about the sight of Artagel's blood. So she was caught where she was as Geraden stumbled away through the crowd, pursuing the litter that carried his brother.

Touched by something that might have been pity, the Castellan let him go.

On the other hand, Lebbick didn't appear to feel anything as soft as pity when he turned to question Terisa.

Elega shielded her, however. "Castellan," she interposed firmly, "you are not surprised to learn that the lady Terisa has an enemy who wishes her dead. You are only surprised that her enemy is a man as important and dangerous as the High King's Monomach. And you are surprised that he has such freedom of movement in Orison, despite the fact that you are responsible for such matters."

A muscle in the Castellan's jaw twitched.

"You will agree, I am sure," she continued, "that the lady Terisa is the last person likely to relieve your surprise. What does she know of Cadwal's secrets—or of Orison's defenses? If you must question her, do so in her own rooms, when she is stronger."

In response, Lebbick gave Terisa a look that made her heart turn over. Then he bowed stiffly, ordered an escort for the two women, and turned away.

Elega took Terisa back toward the peacock rooms.

At first, she felt no pain in her cheek. With the odd detachment of shock, she wondered if she were cold enough to be numb. Then she wondered whether Gart put poison on the edges of his weapons.

After a while, however, the relative warmth in Orison and the exertion of walking brought back the sensation of bright metal as it licked the side of her face. The cut was too thin to hurt. What she felt now wasn't pain. It was a trail of moisture, a long wet touch like the stroke of a tongue.

Once, trying to explain the way coming here had disrupted her life, she had said to Myste, *It was like dying without any pain. It doesn't hurt.* That idea recurred now in a kind of panic. If her cheek had hurt, she would have known what to do about it. Suddenly, she ached for a mirror, for any looking glass which would have told her whether she had been disfigured.

She didn't realize that Elega was talking until the lady stopped her, took her by the shoulders, and insisted, "Terisa, I know that you are afraid. Nevertheless you must listen to me. It may appear that your reasons for fear become less if you do not think about them, but I assure you they do not. The reverse is true. You can only make your danger less by understanding it and acting against it."

At the moment, Elega didn't appear to be a woman who had much sympathy for fear.

They were standing on the stairs that led up to Terisa's rooms. Elega seemed unconscious of the escorting guards; perhaps she thought that the urgency of her questions outweighed caution. But Terisa didn't want to talk at all: she certainly didn't want to talk in front of two men she didn't know. Somewhere in Orison, a physician was trying to save Artagel's life. And Geraden was there—She was surprised to hear the anger in her voice as she demanded, "What do you think I can do?"

"Put your fear aside and try to grasp the truth," Elega replied at once. "There must be a reason why the High King's Monomach risks his own life in order to threaten yours."

Terisa stared at the lady and thought, She still believes I'm some kind of Imager. That's why she wants me on her side. With Prince Kragen. And Nyle. A moment later, however, she realized that Elega's thoughts were more complex than that. The lady was also considering the idea that Terisa had already involved herself in someone else's machinations—a plot so far-ranging and insidious that High King Festten took it as a personal threat. A plot about which Elega knew nothing; a plot which might undo everything she herself wanted to achieve.

With unfeigned fatigue, Terisa asked, "Do you really want to discuss it here?"

Elega lifted an eyebrow and glanced around her. A flush stained her cheeks. Was she embarrassed by her own carelessness? Abruptly, she moved on up the stairs.

Stifling the temptation to turn and flee in the opposite direction, Terisa followed her.

When they had reached the safety of the peacock rooms and closed the door behind them, Elega poured out a goblet of wine for each of them. By then, she had regained her composure. Watching Terisa over the rim of her goblet, she drank a few swallows. Then, with an air of decision, she put the goblet aside.

"You must forgive me for speaking of such things at such a time. I understand that you have been badly frightened. And I am sure that you are concerned for Artagel. But you must understand that it is madness to ignore my question. Terisa"—her eyes were vivid in her pale face—"you surely have some idea why Gart is here to kill you.

It is inconceivable that you could pose such a threat to the High King without being aware of it."

Terisa sighed. She didn't want to deal with Elega. She wanted to lie down and sleep for a few years. At the same time, she wanted to go find Artagel. The sharp wet sensation of her cut was starting to resemble pain. When she drank, the wine seemed to make the cut worse. Carefully, she raised her hand to her cheek. Her fingers came down marked with dried blood. Her face must be a mess. Afraid of the damage, she asked unsteadily, "How bad is it?"

Elega frowned in vexation, but she quickly smoothed her expression. With a gesture that asked Terisa to wait, she went into the bathroom and returned with a damp towel. Then she motioned Terisa to sit on the couch. When Terisa was settled, Elega began stroking her cut gently with the towel, washing away blood and dirt from the wound.

After studying the cut for a moment, the lady pronounced, "It is clean. It still bleeds a little"—she dabbed the towel at Terisa's cheek —"but that only serves to keep it clean. We can summon a physician if you wish, but I doubt that you need so much care. It is only as long as my finger"—at the moment, her fingers looked exceptionally long —"and rather delicate. When it heals, you will have a fine, straight scar that no one will see except in certain lights." She drew back to consider the matter from farther away. "And no one will see it at all if they do not stand near you."

In a neutral tone, she concluded, "When it heals, I expect that most men will feel that your beauty has been enhanced rather than diminished."

"I wish I could see it," Terisa admitted lamely. "Where I come from, that's all we use mirrors for. To see ourselves."

Still neutrally, Elega replied, "For that reason we have maids, so that women who care for the decoration of their appearance will not make fools of themselves." She couldn't hold down her real interests, however. More quickly, she asked, "Then all the mirrors in your world are flat?"

Terisa tried to swallow another sigh. "Yes."

"And you are not translated by them?"

"No."

The lady rose to her feet. Facing the hearth, she cupped her hands under her elbows, holding her forearms across her midriff as if to restrain herself from an outbreak of emotion. "You insist that you are an ordinary woman. Perhaps that is true in your world. But is it possible that you are translated and do not know it—or take it for granted? Here, we are told that any man who faces a flat glass in which he sees himself facing himself will be lost in a translation which never ends. But what if you—if all the people of your world—possess a power which we lack? A power to master the most dangerous manifestation of Imagery? You might be unaware of it—and yet it would be fundamental enough to alter all our preconceptions."

"No." Terisa denied that idea as she had denied everything like it from the beginning. "Where I come from, mirrors are just *things*. They aren't magic." In an effort to shorten the discussion, she faced what she took to be Elega's point. "I really *do not* know why the High King's Monomach wants to kill me."

Her eyes flaming, Elega turned from the fire. "That is not possible."

Terisa raised the towel to her cheek to hide her anger. "It's still true."

For an instant, Elega was on the verge of a shout. "Then—" But at once she caught herself; calculations ran behind her eyes so clearly that they were almost legible. "Then you must be protected."

"Protected?"

"The King will not do it. He will not understand the need. And because the King will not understand the need, the Castellan *cannot* do it. He is too hampered. He has shown that he cannot even limit Gart's access to Orison.

"The lords of the Cares are useless to you. The Tor has become an old drunkard. The Armigite's foppishness shames the memory of his father. The Fayle does not know where his loyalties should lie. And neither the Perdon nor the Termigan are *here*.

"As for the Congery"—she made a dismissive gesture—"the Masters are too divided among themselves to protect anyone. They all resemble Master Quillon, who is too timid to take risks—or Master Barsonage, who is too concerned for the reputation of the Congery to take action—or Master Eremis, who is too self-absorbed to take interest.

"Terisa—" Elega seemed to hesitate, as if doubting whether she should finish what she had started to say. But hesitation wasn't a prominent part of her nature. Distinctly, like an avowal of faith, she said, "You must let me protect you."

Terisa was so startled that she stared.

"For the present, I admit," Elega hurried on, "I can do little more than hide you. But that I can do very well. My knowledge of Orison's secrets is extensive. Soon, however, I will be able to protect anyone I choose.

"I can provide you safety, if you will entrust yourself to me."

Though she wanted to think clearly—it was important to think clearly—Terisa's head whirled. She believed that she understood Elega. On the other hand, she would gain more information if she pretended ignorance. At the same time, however, her cheek hurt, and she was worried about Artagel and Geraden, and she feared that Elega was too cunning for her. And she was still angry.

With difficulty, she managed to ask, "How?" instead of losing her temper. "I've heard you complain about how left out you are. How little you have to do with what's going on. How are you going to protect me?"

Elega met Terisa's gaze steadily. "I can provide you safety," she repeated, "if you will *entrust* yourself to me." Then she added, "Terisa, I have shown you nothing but friendship. I desire only your well-being, and the preservation of Mordant—and an end to evil in the realm. But if you will not trust me I can do nothing."

You surely have some idea why Gart is here to kill you.

It was too much. "You're going to have power," retorted Terisa harshly. "Where are you going to get it? I can only think of one place. From your father. But he won't just give it to you. That isn't the way he does things. You're going to betray him. You're going to cut his throne out from under him somehow. You and Prince Kragen." She barely stopped herself from saying, And Nyle. You've even turned Geraden's brother against him. But the shock on Elega's face warned her that she had already gone too far. "I don't want to have anything to do with that."

"And why not?" Ire mounted through the lady's surprise. "Do you have any alternative? Are you so pure that you can conceive some answer to Mordant's need that does not require betrayal?"

"He's your father. That ought to make a difference."

Elega drew back her shoulders, straightened her spine. The violet flash of her eyes made her look regal and certain, like a woman who was within her rights. "I assure you, my lady," she said austerely, "that it does make a difference. You understand me so well that I am sorry to find you understand me so little."

Giving Terisa a bow as correct and defiant as an offer of combat, the lady Elega left the room.

Terisa watched the door long after it closed. She had made a serious mistake: she had just ruined her only chance to learn *how* Elega and Prince Kragen intended to take Mordant away from King Joyse. In disgust, she tried to swear at herself. Her heart wasn't in it, however. After all, what Elega had offered her made no sense.

To keep her hidden. For how long? Until the end of winter? Until the Alend army arrived? Until Orison fell to siege? Twenty or thirty or forty days?

It made no sense.

She didn't want to think about such things. They were either irrelevant or impossible. She wanted to know what was happening to Artagel and Geraden.

And she wanted to know what made her so valuable that people were willing to risk their lives over her. What was there about her that made her worth Gart's hate and Artagel's blood?

Outside, the sun shone warmly, as if it were immensely pleased with itself.

If she had been required to wait long alone, she might have done something foolish. That is to say, she might have done *something*; and she felt sure that anything she decided to do would be foolish. Fortunately, while she was still unable to make up her mind, Geraden arrived at her door.

He had a high spot of color in each cheek and a slightly glazed look in his eyes; he was frowning deeply, as if he were in pain; his fingers made small twitching movements, though his hands were held pressed to his sides. Nevertheless he had come to her.

Because she had grown up in a household where she was seldom offered comfort—and was never asked for it—she didn't put her arms around him, either for his sake or for her own. She invited him in quickly, however, and closed the door and swallowed the congestion in her throat to ask, "How is he?"

He made an effort to look at her, to pull himself out of his distress and *look* at her. Gently, he reached out a hand and touched her cut cheek with his fingertips. Somehow, he managed to twist his mouth into a smile. "Does it hurt? It doesn't look too bad. I'm glad you're all right."

"*Geraden.* How *is* he?"

A spasm cracked his control. His smile broke, and his eyes brimmed with tears. "The physician is doing everything he can. He doesn't know what's going to happen. Artagel's lost a lot of blood. He might die."

Slowly, he hunched forward, and his arms rose to his chest as if he were crumpling inwardly, collapsing in on himself.

For just an instant, Terisa remained still. Then, as if she were turning her back on everything she had ever been taught about people and pain, she went to him and caught him in a hug as hard as she could.

They stood that way together for a long time.

When she finally let him go, he didn't look at her at first. Rubbing his face, he murmured, "I don't think I ever told you. My mother died when I was just a kid. A fever of some kind—we never knew what it was, but it dragged on for a long time. *I* thought it was a long time, anyway. I was only five—and I was her baby, so she wanted me with her—and watching her die I thought I was being torn apart. I *swore*—" Slowly, he raised his head, letting Terisa see his grief. "I was only five, but I swore I was never going to let anybody I loved die ever again."

Then he sighed, and by degrees his expression cleared. "I hope Artagel doesn't hold me to it, because there's nothing I can do to save him."

"I'm sorry." She didn't know what else to say. "This is all my fault somehow. I'm the one Gart wants to kill. I just don't understand why."

He sniffed to clear his nose. "Don't be silly. It's Gart's fault, not yours." His frown came back as he tried to reassure her. "Or you could say it's my fault, since I failed to stop him. Or, if you want to look at it that way, it's High King Festten's fault. After all, Gart is the High King's Monomach. He's just following orders." His features clenched. "You could even say it's King Joyse's fault. If he weren't being so detached, the High King wouldn't dare send Gart here.

"In fact"—he tried unsuccessfully to smile for her—"if you look at it right, you're the only one whose fault it *isn't*."

He misunderstood her. What she felt about Artagel's wound wasn't blame, but rather a regret as piercing as iron. The distinction was unimportant at the moment, however. Instead of trying to explain it, she said as if she were still on the same subject, "I'm not so sure. I think I've done something pretty stupid."

His incomprehension seemed to warn him to listen to her closely. "Wait a minute. You mean you think Gart attacked you because you've done something stupid?"

She shook her head. "Elega brought me back here. She offered to protect me."

He scowled at her; his jaws knotted. Unexpectedly, she became aware that it might be possible to be afraid of him: the intensity he focused on her was daunting. As if he were holding back an eruption, he said, "Maybe you'd better tell me the whole story."

As simply as she could, she described her conversation with Elega and watched his anger mount. Then she concluded, "As soon as I mentioned Prince Kragen, I ruined the chance that she would ever tell me what she's doing. She's never going to trust me."

Geraden turned away to hide his face. "Glass and splinters!" he muttered fiercely. "Now she's been warned. She'll be more careful. Before long, she's bound to notice Argus and Ribuld. As soon as that happens, they won't be able to follow her anymore. We've lost before we even got started."

This time, Terisa could have said, I'm sorry, without being misinterpreted. But the apology she owed him now was nothing compared to the one he would deserve soon. For a moment, she quailed. Why not keep *this* a secret as well? At least until his unfamiliar rage declined. Who would be hurt?

Nevertheless she knew the answer. She had learned it in this place of secrets. Whenever he discovered the truth, he would be hurt. And the fact that she had kept the truth from him would cripple their friendship.

Taking a deep breath for courage, she said, "Maybe we haven't lost yet."

He swung around to confront her.

He looked so extreme and vulnerable that she could hardly speak. "She left me alone with her seamster. I was finished before she got back, so I left his shop." Remembering what had happened, a momentary faintness passed over her. "I saw Nyle."

Without transition, Geraden's anger disappeared.

"I followed him—I don't know why. I guess I wanted to know why he snubbed you." A feeling of despair rose in her. Geraden would hate her for this. "He met someone behind that tent. He didn't see me, but I saw him. I saw who it was."

She faltered. Geraden looked nauseous with anticipation.

"It was that mountebank. The one we talked about. This time I recognized him. I know who he is. I'm sure of it." Rapidly, so that she wouldn't break down, she said, "He's Prince Kragen. He met Nyle behind that tent."

For a second, Geraden looked as surprised and wounded as she had feared. His love for his family was one of his sovereign passions —and she had just accused his brother of plotting treason. The stark and intimate dismay on his face was more than she could bear.

After that first second, however, his entire posture shifted. The bones in his spine and shoulders straightened themselves, making him taller. His expression became at once bleaker and stronger, as if all the weaker or more awkward lines of his cheeks and jaw were being honed away. His eyes gave hints of authority.

"That explains it," he said flatly. "No wonder he wants to stay away from Artagel and me."

Then he added, "Elega got him into this."

She knew on some level that his crisis wasn't over—that perhaps it was just beginning—but his immediate reaction relieved her so much that she almost kissed him. "So we haven't necessarily lost," she breathed. "You can tell Argus and Ribuld to forget Elega. They can follow Nyle."

Geraden didn't appear to be listening: he looked like he was concentrating hotly on his own thoughts. But he replied in a murmur, "*If* they can find him. That's going to be the hard part. If they can find him, maybe we can stop him before he does something even King Joyse will have to punish."

Abruptly, he swung into motion. "Come on. We've got to tell somebody about this."

He was already at the door. Starting after him, Terisa blurted, "Tell who? Why?"

"Not King Joyse," he answered as if she were thinking fast enough to keep up with him. "He probably wouldn't listen anyway. And Castellan Lebbick would probably overreact. He might have Nyle cut down on sight. The Tor would be better." The way he held the door for her was like a command for haste. "It's the only thing we can do right now to protect Nyle. If we aren't able to stop him— and he gets caught—he'll be less likely to be executed if what he's doing doesn't come as a surprise."

He said this with such conviction that she believed him. In spite of her mud-streaked clothes and blood-marked skin, she kept pace with him.

He hurried all the way to the King's apartment without tripping once.

They were admitted to the suite readily because King Joyse wasn't there. "Off somewhere with his Imager, I suppose," the Tor muttered in explanation. "His courtesy never fails, but he tells me as little as he can to keep me from howling."

His voice was a subterranean gurgle, as though it emerged from somewhere deep in his great fat, and the passages that let it out were filling up with wine. Days of use were marked on his green robe by wine and food stains. His unshaven jowls and oily hair showed that he had been neglecting his toilet.

"I am a patient man, young Geraden," he confided past his flagon. "I have spent no small number of years in the world, and I have learned that fat is more enduring than stone. But the truth is that my presence here has not accomplished quite what I intended." He flapped one hand in a gesture that made Terisa notice the absence of the King's hop-board table. "He has simply moved his games elsewhere."

He sighed lugubriously, and his eyes misted. "It is a sad thing to be neglected at my age."

Listening to the Tor, Terisa began to lose confidence. Nevertheless Geraden was wound too tightly to be deflected.

"You appointed yourself chancellor, my lord," he reminded the Tor. "You said you would take action in the King's name. That ought to be easy, if he isn't here to contradict you."

The Tor gave Geraden a sour look. "You are too young to understand. If I wish mutton rather than duckling for my next meal, I have only to speak. If I decide to appoint a holiday and make every lady in Orison do without her maid, I can do so without raising my voice. Who here has any desire to oppose the will of the King's old friend?" One fist beat out the words as his anger rose. "If I take it upon myself to declare war tomorrow, I have no doubt that I will be obeyed.

"But the *King*, young Geraden!" He raised his bulk to emphasize his point. "Where is the *King*? Where is the man who ought to be shamed by every command I issue in his name? Off playing *hop-board* with Adept Havelock while his realm *crumbles*."

Slowly, the Tor subsided. "As for Castellan Lebbick," he sighed, "he now holds what little effective power is left in Orison. But even he finds it difficult to ignore me; and he does not want to submit his decisions for my opinion, so he avoids me. I suspect he secretly passes judgment on all my orders before they are carried out.

"It appears I have chosen a foolish way to grieve for my son."

Terisa tried to catch Geraden's eye; she wanted to send him a mental message, urging him not to tell the Tor about Nyle and Elega. The old lord was starting to remind her of Reverend Thatcher.

Geraden refused to receive her signal, however. He was fixed on the Tor, and his expression had softened, although his manner remained grim. "I'm sorry, my lord," he said roughly. "I don't have time for your grief."

Under his fat, the muscles of the Tor's face tightened dangerously, but Geraden went ahead without pausing. "I need to talk to King Joyse. Since he isn't here, I'll have to talk to you. I can't take this to the Castellan. I'm not going to tell it to anybody who isn't a friend of my father's."

He had caught the Tor's attention. "I consider the Domne a friend," the lord rumbled slowly. "And your past courtesy outweighs your present rudeness." He had blinked the blur of wine from his eyes: his gaze was hard. "I am interested in what you need to tell the King."

Terisa was suddenly ashamed of herself. Rather than distrusting the Tor's despondency, Geraden was trying to help.

The perception made her squirm. She had never done anything to help Reverend Thatcher. She had listened to him for hours, but she had never tried to help.

"You've probably heard the rumor that King Joyse thinks the lady Elega has turned against him." Geraden didn't need to feign harshness; the bleak strength that had brought him here rasped in his voice. "Well, he's right."

As gently as the bite of a crosscut saw, Geraden told the Tor what he knew about Elega and Prince Kragen and Nyle. When he had recited the basic facts, he added, "Two of my friends—two guards—are following her around. But she knows we're suspicious of her now. She'll be more careful. I'm going to tell my friends to forget her and concentrate on Nyle." He said his brother's name in a tone of forced impersonality. "Maybe he'll lead us to the answers."

The Tor's gaze held: his eyes looked like bits of glass embedded in pastry dough. "I hear quite a number of rumors," he commented when Geraden was done. "Duty outside this door is dull, and many of the guards liven it with conversation. I have heard a rumor that your brother Artagel, who is reputed to be the best swordsman in Mordant, faced the High King's Monomach and fell." His tone didn't become clear until he asked, "Is he seriously injured?"

Geraden swallowed convulsively. "Yes."

Unblinking, the Tor studied Geraden for a moment. Then he said, "I have lost a son. I will not have it said to the Domne that I sat drunk on my hams while one of his sons was killed by the High King's Monomach and another sold himself to the Alend Monarch. What do you wish me to do?"

At once, Geraden replied, "Don't let Castellan Lebbick interfere. Make him leave Nyle alone." He was plainly relieved to get away from the subject of Artagel. "And tell him to assign Argus and Ribuld to me. Tell him I'm doing you some kind of favor and I need their help." He sounded clear, almost authoritative, as if he had been involved in situations like this all his life. "The last time they tried to help me, he roasted them for it. They'll do a better job if they don't have to dodge him the whole time."

He sounded so sure of what he was doing that Terisa wanted to give him a round of applause.

Nevertheless he was sweating by the time he was done.

The Tor regarded him gravely for a little while longer. Then he turned his head and let out a cheerful yell that made Terisa jump and brought the guards promptly into the room.

"Yes, my lord Tor?" one of them inquired. He was on good terms with the self-appointed chancellor. "You bellowed?"

"Mongrel!" snorted the Tor. "That was not a bellow. That was a polite request for attention." His chuckle sounded like belching. "If you ever have the misfortune to hear me bellow, you will not speak of it so calmly.

"But now that you are here—" He rolled his eyes at the ceiling as though he were contemplating an entire litany of desires. "I want cranberry sauce with that duckling which the cook is already so late in providing. I want more wine. I want peace or war with our enemies, whichever will cause them the most consternation." He rubbed a fat hand over his jowls. "I believe I want a barber. But most of all"—suddenly, his voice seemed to have a knife hidden in it somewhere—"I want the Castellan."

Briskly now, he said, "Be so kind as to inform him that I require a few moments of his time—almost immediately."

"As you wish, my lord Tor." Grinning, the guards withdrew.

The Tor looked at Geraden and shrugged. "He may not come at once, but I will nag until he does."

"Thank you, my lord Tor," the Apt breathed sincerely. "That should make things easier."

With a flutter of his free hand, the Tor waved gratitude aside. After a moment's consideration, he said severely, "Young Geraden, your reputation for mishap is entirely misleading. You have shown me that my King has a need for his chancellor which I did not suspect. I believe I will begin to assert myself."

Pointing a pudgy finger at the Apt, he added in an ominous rumble, "In the meantime, I advise you to stop Nyle before he goes too far. The union of the Cares already grows fragile. An open rupture now between King Joyse and the Care of Domne may bring us all to grief."

Quickly, he emptied his flagon. Then he drawled happily, "While you are otherwise occupied, I will take it upon myself to teach my lady Elega the fear of discovery."

For an odd moment, Terisa felt like laughing. The idea of a confrontation between the huge old lord and the regal princess tweaked her fancy. But her amusement was primarily a reaction to strain: as soon as she glanced at Geraden, it evaporated. His grin was a rather feverish imitation of the smile Artagel wore into combat.

Fortunately, the Tor also noticed his expression. "You may go now, young Geraden," he said firmly, "unless you have more treachery to reveal? I do not mean to share my duckling with anyone. Send me word as soon as you have news of Artagel."

"Thank you, my lord." At once, Geraden headed for the door.

Terisa wanted to thank the Tor more thoroughly, let him know how much he did for Geraden. But she couldn't do that and still follow the Apt.

The old lord seemed to understand, however. "Take care of him, my lady," he muttered, dismissing her. "He has need of you."

Flashing him her best smile, she left the apartment and pursued Geraden down the stairs.

He slowed his pace after a flight or two so that she could catch up with him. "I've been away from Artagel too long," he said. "Will you excuse me? I would take you with me, but the physician won't

let you in. I practically had to threaten his life to see Artagel myself.
You can find your way back to your rooms, can't you? Will you be all
right?"

"Geraden—" She put her hand on his arm to make him hear her.
"You did the right thing with the Tor. You gave him what he
needed." Unaccustomed to saying such things, she sounded terribly
stilted to herself—and she hated it. But she didn't back down. "I'm
proud of you."

That reached him. The muscles around his eyes unclenched, and
something that looked like a smile caught at the corners of his
mouth. "I like him," he explained simply.

"I'll be all right," she promised. "Go see Artagel. Send me a
message right away."

He nodded and immediately took off at a run.

She went back to her rooms alone and spent the rest of the day
trying not to think.

The next morning, Artagel's physician ventured the opinion that his
patient might live.

At once haggard with exhaustion and giddy with relief, Geraden
brought the news to Terisa before going to his own rooms for some
rest. "Now it's just a question of infection," he reported. "If he can
get through that, he's going to make it."

As an afterthought, he added, "The Tor did it. Argus and Ribuld
are working for me now. Castellan Lebbick doesn't like it, but I
guess the Tor told him I had some ideas about how to protect you
from Gart. So far, they haven't been able to locate Nyle."

Terisa wanted him to stay with her. She was losing whatever ability
she once had to support being alone. When she was by herself, the
High King's Monomach and Castellan Lebbick and Master Eremis
seemed to crouch in hiding all around her, waiting for her most
vulnerable moment. And she wasn't much comforted when she succeeded in concentrating on Elega, Nyle, and the Alend Contender,
or worrying about Myste and the champion, or trying to analyze the
relationships between Master Quillon, Adept Havelock, and King
Joyse, or wondering what obscure talent for Imagery either she or
Geraden might have. Every question was dangerous.

But Geraden looked so tired—emotionally drained as well as physically weary—that she took pity on him. As firmly as she could, she

sent him on his way, ordering him not to return until he had caught up on his sleep.

Alone, she turned to meet the day in the same spirit in which she had too often faced her evenings in her old apartment: as if the only thing she could hope to do with her time was cling to a tenuous and necessary sense of her own existence.

The view from her windows interested her for a while. The early thaw was settling in as if for a long stay. Sunlight poured over the piled bulk of Orison, melting more snow, raising more mud. Crowds milled through the bazaar, as eager as they had been the previous day. Carts and wains lumbered down the road to the gate of the castle, their iron-rimmed wooden wheels cutting the snow and mud together. Again, she wanted to go outside. But she couldn't—not alone.

She felt lost in her own company.

Before long, Mindlin the seamster arrived to return her old clothes and announce that he expected to receive the material he needed for her tomorrow, or the day after tomorrow at the very latest, unless something dramatic happened to the weather. As a friend of the lady Elega, she would command his first and best attention, so he believed he could promise with confidence that her new garments would be ready for their first fitting no later than six days from now.

Unfortunately, the question of what her new clothes should look like had no power to divert her. She had other things on her mind.

Where was Master Eremis?

What was she doing here?

How could she know anything about herself without a mirror?

Why was it that the only times she was able to reach out to Geraden were when he was hurt? Why was she still keeping secrets from him as if she didn't trust him?

If she kept this up, she might drive herself crazy. These impossible questions only reminded her of what she lacked. They ignored what she had: Geraden's friendship, and Artagel's; the Tor's respect; perhaps even Myste's gratitude, if Myste were still alive. So she was glad for the distraction when a knock at the door announced that she had a visitor. It could be Master Eremis. And even Castellan Lebbick might be an improvement over her own company.

It was Master Barsonage.

The mediator of the Congery was such an unexpected arrival that at first she didn't notice the change in his appearance. But the vague way he failed to meet her gaze as he greeted her made her look past her surprise and see his distress.

"Master Barsonage. Come in."

"Thank you, my lady." With an aimless air, as if he didn't quite know where he was going, he shuffled into the sitting room.

He appeared *deflated*—that was the only description she could think of to fit him. When she had first met him, his girth had appeared almost equal to his height. His eyebrows had sprouted thickly, like bracken. His skin had had the color and texture of cut pine. Now, however, that yellow hue had turned sickly, and his flesh seemed slack across his bald skull. His eyebrows sagged; lines ran down his cheeks. His movements and his bulk resembled each other: they were flaccid, like bladders without enough substance in them.

"This is an honor." She spoke without sarcasm because he looked so woebegone—and so unconscious of it. "What can I do for you?"

His eyes persisted in missing hers. "I hardly know, my lady."

Well, she couldn't leave him standing in the middle of the peacock rug. "Why don't you sit down?" She gestured toward one of the chairs. "Would you like some wine?"

He accepted the chair. A weak push of his hands rejected the wine. When he spoke, his tone was as aimless as his appearance. "You were attacked, my lady."

At that, she groaned to herself. She had already had this conversation more than she wanted. But then she reflected that it wasn't her fault he was unhappy. With more asperity than she intended, she replied, "Again. That was actually the third time."

He blinked in her general direction. "The third?"

"Didn't Master Eremis tell you about the second? It was right after his meeting with the lords. Prince Kragen and the Perdon almost got killed."

"No," he breathed. His voice also was deflated. "Master Eremis made no mention—He has left Orison. To return to Esmerel, he said. Yesterday—when the thaw began. I had to restore his chasuble, of course. There is no evidence against him. He could not bear our debates, he said." Unconscious of her reactions, he asked simply, as if they were both children, "Why were you attacked, my lady?"

He made her heart flutter against her ribs. So there was a reason why Master Eremis hadn't come to see her since Gart's attack. He

had probably left Orison before it happened. On the other hand, he
hadn't said goodbye—

Painfully confused, she tried to concentrate on the mediator. "Everybody wants to know why I was attacked." Her mother would
have sent her to her room for speaking in that tone. "You, Castellan
Lebbick, Geraden and Artagel, Prince Kragen"—with an effort, she
prevented herself from mentioning Elega—"even King Joyse. Even *I*
want to know why I was attacked. What difference does it make to
you, Master Barsonage?"

Still his gaze wouldn't shift to hers. All the anger seemed to have
gone out of him. In that same simple voice, he answered, "I have
given my life to it. The Congery is ruined, my lady."

"Ruined?" What he said was more unexpected than his appearance. "How? What do you mean?"

"We are disbanded."

She stared at him. "Wait a minute. Say that again. You've *disbanded*
the Congery?"

"The name still exists, of course. King Joyse does not will that we
should come to an end. Therefore we continue. But it has no meaning now. We are done with it—done with our King's impossible
ideals and his abandonment of us. Each of us will go his own way."

"Unless you will tell me why you were attacked."

Her blood felt like cold tallow around her heart, congealed and
sickly.

"My lady, we have debated and debated until we have lost our
voices—and our hearts. I will not trouble you with the arguments.
Without purpose, we are nothing. Either Master Gilbur is a traitor or
he is not. In either case, there is nothing we can do. He is beyond
our reach. Either the translation of the champion was a mistake or it
was not. In either case, there is nothing we can do. We have no glass
to return him to his own life. And we cannot reach him for any other
translation.

"Either the translation that brought you among us was a mistake
or it was not. In either case, there is nothing we can do. Unless we
know."

"Know?"

His limp hands gestured nowhere. "We could serve you, my lady.
If you had a reason for being here. The High King's Monomach
risks his life to end yours. Are you not a threat? Are you not an

Imager? Then turn to us, my lady. Give us your purpose. Let us
serve you."

No. That was too much. No. She backed away from it. "Aren't
you afraid I might be an enemy?"

He shrugged his empty shoulders. "The High King's Monomach
risks his life to end yours," he repeated. "You are not a friend of
Cadwal. That is more certain than anything else we have. We will
trust it—if you will give us purpose."

He couldn't *do* that. She couldn't let him make her responsible for
the Congery—for all those Masters who despised her, despised Geraden. This was the same man who had forbidden her information
when she had first arrived. Bitterly, she retorted, "You haven't got
any easy answers, so you're just going to give up. Have you told
Geraden about this yet?"

Quietly, Master Barsonage admitted, "I have not had the courage." Then he added, "None of the Apts have been informed. They
continue to tend the fires and the laborium, so that we will be able to
do our work—if we are able to find any purpose for it."

For just a moment, she considered telling him what she had never
told Geraden, or anyone else: that she had seen the three riders of
her dream in the Congery's augury. But the thought of what he
might do with the knowledge stopped her.

He might put the responsibility for the Congery on her shoulders
in earnest, making demands that she wouldn't know how to either
meet or refuse.

"Master Barsonage," she said while the pressure increased in her
veins, "don't you think you're asking a little too much? You've
barely been *civil* to me since I got here. You certainly haven't been
decent. You've ignored my ignorance—and what it cost me. And
you're still ignoring it. You're ignoring me. I don't know why Gart
wants to kill me. Where I come from, mirrors just reflect. They don't
do anything. *I am not an Imager.*"

In spite of her vehemence, he still didn't meet her eyes. Instead,
he took several deep breaths, as though he were pumping himself
up, and his hands closed into fists.

"My lady, this is wrong. The Congery is precious, whatever King
Joyse now thinks of it. It stands between us and bloody chaos—
between Mordant and horror. War is only war. Men are killed.
Women are mistreated. Then the struggle shifts elsewhere, and there

is peace for a while. But without the Congery to control it Imagery will wreak such evil upon the innocent—

"It will, my lady. It must. Even if every Imager living is a man of good heart, intending what is beneficial, his Imagery must come to abomination in the end. Because he will fall to High King Festten, or to the Alend Monarch, or to whoever takes power in Orison—and these rulers will require his Imagery for destruction. They must, because they are at war. Yet it is not they who suffer. Their soldiers pay a price—and the rest is borne by the innocent of the world.

"Because King Joyse has turned his back on us, there is no other hope. Only the Congery can prevent this. If it is safe and strong—if it has a purpose to unite it.

"You are the answer, my lady. You must not leave us to ruin."

He moved her. In spite of her anger, her instinctive rejection, he moved her. Perhaps his belief that she could help him was an illusion. Nevertheless the fear that drove him to it was real.

"Master Barsonage," she said softly, "the honest fact is that I don't know what's going on. I don't understand any of this. But I'm like you. I don't think Imagery should be used for destruction.

"I'll tell you the truth about me—as soon as I find out what it is. If it turns out to be an answer, it'll help both of us."

She couldn't tell whether he grasped what she was saying. In fact, she couldn't tell whether he so much as heard her. His eyes stayed away from hers, and his face sagged on his skull as if she had refused his appeal completely.

After a while, he rose from his chair and slumped away.

She was left with one more terrible thing that she would have to tell Geraden.

The advantage was that she no longer had to worry about her grasp on substantiality. She was too worried about him to be in any danger of fading.

Around noon the following day, he came to her rooms to take her to see Artagel.

She had spent the night groping for courage. But there was no kind way to say what needed to be said, so she simply described her conversation with the mediator. Then she bit her lip and held her breath, waiting to see how he would take the news.

To her dismay, he took it laughing.

He laughed so hard that he had to lean against the wall—a strange, silent laughter which shook his whole body but didn't make a noise. He huddled into himself as if he were weeping; tears smeared his face like grief. Yet he was obviously laughing, so astonished with amusement that he was almost hysterical. His hands pounded against each other like applause.

"Well, you have to admit," he cried through his mirth, "it's logical."

She had no idea what to do. Was he really hysterical? He had a right to be: he was under enough strain. Did that mean she was supposed to slap him?

She was supposed to tell him about the riders of her dream. She knew that. Yet she couldn't do it. She was afraid.

"It all comes back to you." Trying to stop himself, he set his teeth into one knuckle hard enough to draw blood. The pain helped him regain a measure of steadiness. "Even if you didn't have anything to do with it. Even if you're just here because I have some amazing new talent no one has ever heard of before. There still has to be a reason. A reason why I translated you instead of somebody else. Otherwise it was only an accident. Doesn't mean anything. One way or another, it's the fundamental question of Imagery.

"You *are* the answer."

Like Master Barsonage, he couldn't meet her gaze.

"Disbanded. My whole life—ever since I came to Orison—"

"Oh, Terisa."

But he didn't let her touch him. "It's probably just as well," he said, making a gallant and miserable attempt to sound gay. "I spent most of my time trying to get out of doing my work anyway. Now I can concentrate on more important things."

Roughly, he insisted on escorting her to visit Artagel.

Along the way, he walked like a man who had something broken in his chest and didn't know what it was. Nevertheless he kept moving. His self-control gave the impression that he had no conception of how much he had been hurt.

Artagel's quarters were in a part of Orison she had only visited once, during Geraden's tour—a vast warren of rooms built every which way around and on top of each other. She wouldn't have taken it for the castle's equivalent of a barracks if she and Geraden hadn't encountered so many guards, and if she hadn't seen interspersed among the rooms the obviously military halls where the guards mustered. From the look of the place, she guessed that each man had at best one room to himself; the larger rooms were probably shared. Artagel, however, had a modest suite—a bedroom, sitting room, pantry, and lavatory which together took up less space than her bedroom.

Most of the suite was unadorned, almost unfurnished: its occupant apparently didn't spend enough time in Orison to care about his rooms. Or perhaps his sense of *home* was focused exclusively on Houseldon. Whatever the reason, his quarters contained only one piece of decoration—a long rack, stretching across two walls of the sitting room, from which hung a clutter of variously snapped and shattered swords.

"They're all blades that failed him," Geraden whispered in explanation as he led her toward the bedroom.

There Artagel lay on an austere bed, a simple wooden frame with strips of cloth woven across it to support a pallet. He had no fireplace, and the air was cool. In addition, he was naked to the waist, except for the bindings wrapped around his middle. Nevertheless sweat streaked his skin, and his eyes smoldered darkly, like secret fires.

Geraden had warned her that he was feverish; but she was still taken aback to see him grinning as though he were about to go down under Gart's next attack.

She had rehearsed a speech for him, wanting to thank him, but it failed her. There was no fat on him: all his muscles were outlined clearly under his skin. And the sweat emphasized his scars, making them catch the light differently so that she couldn't ignore them. He had been cut and cut—Part of his chest looked like someone had once stuck a pole through it, and he hadn't been able to grow enough tissue to refill the wound. And under his bandages was another wound.

Her eyes spilled tears, making him a blur of reflected lamplight. "I'm sorry. I don't know why he wants to kill me. I swear I don't know why he wants to kill me."

"My lady." His eyes glittered through the blur, and his voice sounded like his eyes. "Your cheek is almost healed. That's good. When he hit you, I couldn't see how bad it was. I thought I was too late. Then this idiot"—he was referring to Geraden—"jumped him and nearly got his neck broken. I thought you were both lost. I'm glad you've got quick reflexes."

While Terisa blinked her vision clear, he added, "I've been practicing that counter he used on me. I think I know what to do about it
now."

"If you ever get the chance to find out," Geraden put in gruffly,
"I'm going to tie you down until it's all over. That way, we won't
have to find out whether he can beat you three times in a row. I can't
stand the suspense."

Artagel's smile looked like the fire in his gaze. "That's the trouble
with you. You don't have any confidence in me."

Geraden wasn't having a good day. For a moment, Terisa feared
he might lose his grip on himself. But somehow he managed to smile
back at his brother. "Oh, shut up," he muttered in a thick growl.
"You're breaking my heart."

"You heard him, my lady." Unexpectedly, Artagel began falling
asleep. "If you wake up one morning and find yourself dead, with
me tied up on the floor beside you, you'll know what happened. No
confidence." He closed his eyes, and a subtle tension faded out of
him.

She and Geraden left him to rest.

For two more days, nothing happened. The thaw weakened, but
didn't break. Mindlin sent word that her material had arrived. Argus
and Ribuld found no trace of Nyle. To pass the time, Terisa took
long, aimless walks through Orison; she even revisited the bazaar
because she wanted some fresh air. Now whenever she left her
rooms alone at least one guard accompanied her: Castellan Lebbick
had made his orders for her protection stricter. But she saw no sign
of Prince Kragen or the High King's Monomach anywhere.

Not long after breakfast on the third day, however, Geraden came
to her rooms. "I've just had a talk with the Tor," he announced,
trying to sound cheerful. He was feeling too much stress to carry it
off, however.

She asked the natural question. "What did he want?"

"He wanted to tell me about his conversation with Elega."

"And how did it go?"

"Not very well. I think he underestimated her." Geraden shook
his head. He didn't like what he was thinking. "You remember he
said he wanted to teach her 'the fear of discovery.' Unfortunately,
she doesn't seem to fear discovery. 'She declines to be taught,' he

said. In fact, she defied him to produce one scrap of proof that she was in communication with Prince Kragen.

"That was bad enough," he commented. "Whatever her plan is, it's already at work. And she's sure we can't stop her. But——" He grimaced and met Terisa's gaze glumly. "She was so convincing the Tor isn't sure he believes us anymore."

Terisa winced.

"He made quite a speech about it. He told me that before I aimed any more accusations at my own brother and the King's eldest daughter I should make an effort to produce a witness or two, instead of relying on empty-headed suspicions."

"But I *saw* Prince Kragen and Nyle meet each other," she protested.

He shook his head again. "They both emerged from behind the same tent. Maybe they just happened to go back there at the same time to relieve themselves."

"Do you think I'm wrong?"

"No," he answered at once. "He's behaving too strangely. There has to be an explanation." A moment later, however, he added in a pained tone, "But I wouldn't want Castellan Lebbick to throw him in the dungeon for reasons as thin as what we have."

That expression of certainty did little to make her feel better.

Geraden returned to spend the evening with her. They were together when a guard brought a message from Argus and Ribuld.

It was cryptic:

"Got Nyle. See Artagel."

So Terisa and Geraden went to see Artagel.

He was half sitting up in bed, with several pillows propped behind his back, and he looked clearer and cooler of eye, less feverish. His smile was distant and a little sad, rather than fierce. "He came to visit me," he explained. "They picked him up when he left."

"I don't understand," muttered Geraden. "He's been hiding out for days. Why did he suddenly decide to visit you?"

Artagel tried to shrug; the movement hurt his torso. "If *you* don't understand, don't expect *me* to figure it out." He wasn't being sarcastic. "I don't understand him any better than I understand you."

Geraden ignored that remark. "What did he want to talk about? What did he say?"

The memory emphasized Artagel's unaccustomed sadness. In a

thin voice, he said, "He didn't look glad to see me. I suppose that's because I'm hurt. But he's seen me hurt before. At least I'm not dead. If he was worried about me, wouldn't he be glad to see I'm getting better?

"Anyway, he asked me if there was any news from Houseldon. But he's been there more recently than I have. He asked me"— Artagel's eyes avoided Geraden's—"when you were going to stop embarrassing the family here and go back home where you belong. I didn't try to answer that."

Geraden held himself still.

"Then he asked me what would happen to Orison in a siege, now that we've got that breach. The last time I saw it, the wall Lebbick is building wasn't very impressive. He asked me if we had any defense left. He asked me how long I thought it would be before King Joyse got us into a war with *some*body. But he wasn't listening to the answers.

"Then—" Artagel stared at the ceiling while the lines in his face got deeper, cut by what he remembered. "Then he told me how much he admired me. I was his hero—I was *always* his hero. The first thing he could remember about his own life was wanting to be like me. But he just didn't have the balance, or the reflexes. And his muscles refused to develop the right kind of strength for a long-sword.

"And everybody in the family seemed to be content with him the way he was, when the way he was wasn't what *he* wanted. Having his parents and his brothers content with him did nothing except make his heart ache. Nobody expected him to be *good* at anything. They were proud of me. And they were ambitious for you. They wanted you to marry Elega and become a great Imager. But nobody wanted anything from him. Or for him."

Swallowing hard, Artagel stopped.

"Is that it?" asked Geraden quietly. "He didn't say anything else?"

"I told you," Artagel snarled. "Don't expect me to explain it." But his anger wasn't aimed at Geraden. "The best I could think of was to ask him how he managed to admire me, when I didn't even have a home of my own or a woman who could put up with me, not to mention children, and I was lying here with a stupid *hole* in my ribs after the High King's Monomach had already beaten me twice."

Geraden put a hand on his brother's shoulder. "Don't worry

about it. There was nothing you could have said that would have made a difference. He's already committed." His tone was more reassuring than his expression. "He was just trying to apologize."

"Apologize? For what?"

"For choosing the other side," Geraden sounded like he understood perfectly. "If everything he and Elega and Prince Kragen are planning works out—and you and I don't turn our backs on King Joyse—he might end up being responsible for our deaths." A note of grimness came into his voice. "That's why we have to stop him. He'll hardly be able to stand the rest of his life if he has both of us on his conscience. On top of everything else."

Terisa watched the two brothers study each other. Finally, Artagel managed a crooked smile. "Well, I'm not going to be much help. That physician swore he'll have me clubbed if I try to get out of bed too soon. But there probably isn't a guard in Orison who doesn't know Ribuld and Argus are trying to do you a favor for me. You should be able to get all the support you need."

Somehow, Geraden chuckled. "I would rather have you. But I suppose I ought to be satisfied with one or two thousand of Castellan Lebbick's best men." Then he sighed. "I hope he doesn't keep us waiting much longer. I want to know what's going on."

Terisa felt the same way.

As it happened, Nyle didn't keep them waiting much longer. In fact, if Argus and Ribuld hadn't found him when they did, they probably would have missed him altogether. Before dawn the next morning, while Terisa was still in bed, tangled in sweaty sheets and dreaming that she could see Gart's blade as it came for her like the edge of a star, she was awakened by a wooden pounding and Geraden's voice.

"Terisa. *Terisa*."

Naturally, she decided the noise must be coming from the door to the secret passage. She peeled the sheet off her naked back and climbed, instantly shivering, out of bed to let Master Quillon or Adept Havelock in. But that didn't make any sense. Why were they knocking so loudly, when she had forgotten to put a chair in the wardrobe to block the door?

With a wrench, her perceptions corrected their orientation. Was it really this *cold*, or was she just chilled by the effect of her dreams? Her robe was on the chair that should have been in the wardrobe. She snatched it up, got her arms into the sleeves, knotted the sash around the deep velvet. Geraden? Shivering so hard she nearly lost her balance, she went into the sitting room and unbolted the door.

Light from the lamps outside washed inward, sweeping Geraden with it.

"Come on," he whispered at once. "We've got to hurry. He's leaving."

"Leaving?" Her voice shook wildly. "What are you talking about? What time is it?"

"Almost dawn." He was breathing hard: he had been running. "It's Nyle. This is our chance to find out what he's doing. Maybe it's our chance to stop him."

"Leaving?" she repeated. Her robe seemed to hold no warmth at all. "How can he be leaving? Where can he go?"

"That's what we'll find out," Geraden hissed. "Just *get ready*. He was in the stables when Argus and Ribuld finally figured out what he was doing. He's probably in the courtyard by now. He'll be out the gate by the time you get your clothes on. We've got to *hurry*."

Some of his tension reached her. She turned to look for some clothes. Which clothes? Her old shirt and pants. And the sheepskin coat. The warm boots. There was still a small fire in the hearth. Why was she so *cold*? "How can we follow him?" she asked, trying to get herself under control. "He's practically gone already."

Geraden permitted himself a growl of exasperation. "Argus is waiting for us. Ribuld will follow Nyle. He'll leave us a trail. *Come on.*"

She got herself moving and tried to hurry.

Violent tremors made her hands fumble. As familiar as these clothes were, she had trouble putting them on. From the privacy of the bathroom, she asked, "What's happened to the weather? I'm freezing."

"Bitter, isn't it," he muttered. "The thaw is over—at least for a while. But there's no new snow. We would be better off if there was. It would slow down anybody who might be marching in this direction. And it might make it easier for us to follow Nyle."

A part of her was glad that she was too cold and rushed to think about what she was doing. If she thought about it, it might turn out to be crazy. Her rooms were still full of nightmares. It would be good to escape them.

A moment later, she pulled on her coat and left the bathroom.

"I'm ready," she said, although that was probably nonsense. "Let's go."

He took her hand, and they left.

They went down the stairs almost at a run. Holding his hand gave her the illusion that she could keep him from falling, but he didn't stumble. All she remembered about the stables was that they were somewhere near the warren of rooms where the guards were quartered. And she had never ridden a horse. The route he chose appeared convoluted because it bypassed a number of long, straight halls and passages that ran in the wrong direction. The exercise was just starting to generate a little human warmth inside her coat when he brought her to the place where Orison wintered its horses.

The guard at the side entrance nodded sleepily and said, "Argus is waiting. Keep it quiet. Nobody's supposed to be here this early. Upsets the horses." Then he let them in.

The low ceiling was supported by a great number of stone pillars, as well as by bulky wooden posts which also anchored the sides and rails and gates of the individual stalls. In addition, many of the stalls had been constructed haphazardly, with the result that the aisles between them were crooked. Consequently, the true dimensions of the place were hard to see. Its size was only apparent from one of the main aisles, which met like roads in the center of the stables.

During his tour, Geraden had taken Terisa to the center and showed her that the stalls stretched cavernously for a hundred yards in each direction.

The ceiling multiplied noise; but the place was much quieter now than she remembered it. Still, a constant rustling murmur punctuated with staccato thuds and coughs filled the air as hundreds of horses snuffled in their sleep, broke wind, shifted positions, and knocked their hooves against the slats of the stalls. So many animals put out enough heat to make the cavern warm, one of the most noticeable effects of which was to perfect the sweet, thick stench of horse droppings and urine fermenting in sodden straw. Together, the noise and the warmth and the smell were comforting in an odd way, like a return to a primitive womb. And the womblike atmosphere was increased by the fact that at night the stables were lit only by a few small lanterns placed at considerable intervals along the aisles. Nevertheless the air made Terisa feel that she had fungus growing in her lungs.

Geraden put his finger to his lips unnecessarily and led her forward.

She spared as much attention as she could to keep her feet out of the brown piles that dotted the aisles, but she had a number of other things to think about. Now that she was more awake, she was both excited and fearful. She was going to go *out*. For the first time since this whole experience began, she was going to see the outside of Orison. On the other hand, she believed instinctively that something was about to go wrong.

Geraden spotted Argus. The guard stood near a lantern with three horses, already saddled. They nickered and snorted softly, complaining about being put to work so early in the morning. Geraden waved and hurried toward the grizzled veteran.

Bracing herself to endure Argus' crude sense of humor, Terisa followed.

Over leather clothes, Argus wore a mail shirt and leggings; over his mail, a cloak that looked like a bearskin. His iron cap was on his head. A dagger hung at his belt opposite his longsword, but he had left his pike behind. As Geraden and Terisa reached him, he grinned, showing the gaps where several of his teeth had been knocked out. "Good," he leered. "I have horses. I even have brandy." He indicated a small pouch tied to the back of one saddle. "You have a woman. This is going to be more fun than guard duty."

Geraden brushed that remark aside. "How far ahead do you think he is?"

"She's in my debt, don't you think?" Argus persisted. "I don't care how fine a lady she is. The finer the better. I've risked my life for her twice now. She owes me a little gratitude." He reached a grubby hand toward Terisa's cheek.

"Argus." Suddenly, Geraden clamped a hold on the guard's wrist. Though Argus was much larger, Geraden wrenched his hand down. "Do not trifle with me." Strength echoed in his voice—strength that Terisa hadn't heard for a long time. "Nyle is my brother. How far ahead is he?"

Involuntarily, Argus winced. "He has his own horse," he replied as if he were surprised to find himself backing down. "He didn't have to get permission to take it and go. And he didn't have to stand around here waiting for you. But Ribuld has him. We should be able to catch up."

"Then let's go," said Geraden impatiently. The echo was gone. "Who gets which horse?"

"This one's mine." With a slap to its rump, Argus shifted a rawboned roan stallion out of his way. "You get the mare." He indicated a smaller horse the color of fresh axle grease. "She likes to kick, but you can handle her. At least she's tough.

"The lady can have the gelding."

Terisa found herself staring at a horse with rancid eyes, a mottled coat, and an expression of sublime stupidity.

With an effort, she cleared her throat. Her voice sounded small and lost. "I don't actually know how to ride."

Argus flashed her a look that might have been anger or glee. "Geraden mentioned that. He didn't explain why you have to come with us. I mean, if you can't ride, and you think you're too good to spread your legs for a man who saved your life, why bother?" He gave a massive shrug. "But at least he warned me.

"The only way this gelding can hurt you is if he steps on you. He hasn't got the brains to do anything except follow the nearest thing he recognizes—and the only thing he ever recognizes is another horse. Just hold on to the saddle horn and let him do the rest."

Still she hesitated. Geraden and Argus stared at her. Abruptly, Geraden came and took her to the side of the mount. Holding the stirrup, he said, "Put your left foot here, grab the saddle horn, and swing your right leg over. Leave the reins where they are. We'll adjust the stirrups when you're in the saddle."

She looked at him hard and saw that his eyes were dark with suppressed urgency. Swallowing a lump of alarm, she nodded her head. Then, before she had time to panic, she put her foot into the stirrup and lunged for the saddle.

Argus caught her on the other side and squared her in her seat. The ceiling seemed perilously close. Argus and Geraden made her stirrups longer or shorter without consulting her. The gelding shifted its weight. She gripped the saddle horn until her knuckles ached. To no one in particular, she said, "Why am I doing this?"

"Because"—Argus flashed his remaining teeth—"you've heard it said that a few hours on a horse make a woman desperate for a man."

Geraden was already on the mare. "If you don't stop harassing her," he muttered, "I'm going to wait until we're several miles from here, and then I'm going to break all your legs and leave you to walk back."

Argus let out a guffaw which made several of the nearby horses whinny in protest and brought an angry insult from a watching stablehand whom Terisa hadn't noticed before. Argus wasn't daunted, however. Chuckling to himself, he took hold of the gelding's reins and tugged the beast into motion behind him.

Terisa clung to the saddle while Argus led her and Geraden out to one of the main aisles and along it toward the closed passage that went in the direction of the courtyard.

The guards at the main entrance lifted the gate without a word: apparently, Argus had already spoken to them. But when he and his companion reached the gate to the courtyard—with Terisa shivering again at the sudden drop in temperature—he had to stop and speak to the sentries for several minutes. She saw him point at Geraden, heard him mention Artagel. Finally, the gate opened, and the horses crunched out into the frozen mud of the courtyard.

"One more gate," Geraden told her softly. "Then we can start hurrying."

The sky was clear above the high, dark walls of Orison, but most of the stars were gone, washed out by the oncoming gray flood of dawn. The air was so sharp it cut her throat: she could feel it in the bottom of her lungs, pricking like needles. From horseback, the ground looked faraway and dangerous. The cold seemed to make the leather of her saddle slick; because she couldn't stick to it, she had trouble keeping her balance over the stiff-legged lurch of the gelding's stride. Geraden looked like a shadow beside her. Argus was nearly invisible against the darkness of the wall ahead.

Other people moved in the courtyard, waking up, getting ready for another day. Small lights flickered on the inner balconies. A few more showed in the bazaar. One or two cooking fires had been started. Terisa barely noticed them.

The predawn gloom and the shadow of the walls hid the gate, but she remembered it—a massive shutter raised or lowered by winches. Because Mordant was said to be at peace, the gate stood open during the day. At night it was down.

When the horses reached it, Argus dismounted and went to talk to its guards. For some reason—perhaps because his back was turned—his voice was an indeterminate murmur, but the sentry could be heard clearly.

"You're out of your mind, Argus."

Argus made some response.

"We *had* to let him out. He's a son of the Domne. We don't have any orders to keep him in."

Again.

"Try explaining *that* to the Castellan."

Geraden shifted in his saddle, fretting. Terisa could feel her face freezing stiff.

Then: "All right. He's a son of the Domne too. And you're assigned to him. And we thought it was just some strumpet with you. If you don't back us up, I'll personally see to it you never have children."

A faint call rose. Geraden let a breath of relief through his teeth as Argus came back to his horse. His boots on the mud sounded like he was striding through broken glass. After a moment, Terisa heard a long creaking noise as rope began to stretch between the winches and the gate.

She saw the gate go up, a deep darkness lifting off the lighter background of the road.

"Come on," Argus muttered. Taking Terisa's reins again, he put his heels to the stallion and started forward so sharply that she let out a yelp and nearly lost her seat.

When they were outside, Geraden caught up with Argus. "Well done," he rasped sarcastically. "Do you *want* her to fall?"

"Don't be so prickly," replied the guard. "*I* didn't know she's a squealer." Terisa had the impression he was grinning.

She unknotted her muscles, flexed her grip on the saddle horn, and began making a conscious effort to find the point of balance on the gelding's back.

Overhead, the paling sky seemed impossibly open. The gradual hills immediately around the castle were naked of trees, kept that way so that Castellan Lebbick could watch his enemies approach him; in the dawn twilight the bareness of the slopes made them feel as expansive as the heavens, wide and unmeasured to the extreme horizons after the relative constriction of Orison. In spite of her precarious perch, she felt her excitement rise.

If anything, the air was even colder here. Most of the road had been chewed to mud and iron ruts by days of wagon wheels, but whenever the hooves of the horses hit a patch of snow, the distinct clatter of horseshoes against hard dirt changed to an oddly resonant crumpling sound, a break-and-echo, as the hooves stamped to the ground through the iced surface, the snow melted by the thaw and then refrozen. The graying of the sky grew stronger, enabling her to see the black trees that lined the road after it branched. One branch, she remembered, went south; another, northwest; the third continued northeast toward the Care of Perdon: roads running toward secrets and surprises in every direction. The world was something she had hardly begun to discover.

Although spring was drawing closer, the sun was still so far to the south that she couldn't glimpse the source of the dawn past Orison's bulk until she had ridden almost to the road's branching. By then, the trees were tipped with light as if they were catching fire. Sunshine glowed coldly on the towers and battlements behind her, making Orison look less dire—but larger somehow, as though a sense of its true size were impossible from inside. Its gray stone appeared stronger and more enduring than she had expected.

From the branching, she watched the sun come up and wished she were a little less cold so that she could feel its touch on her face.

"Now what?" Geraden demanded of Argus. His mind was clenched to what he was doing. "How do we know which way to go?"

"That's Ribuld's job." Argus scanned the area. "He's supposed to leave signs. Probably in the snow beside the road." Tossing her reins to Terisa, he moved toward the left edge of the road. "Start looking."

Geraden took the other side. The two men began to work around the branching. Experimentally, Terisa picked up her reins, gripped them as her companions did, and gave the gelding a tentative kick, trying to make it follow Geraden. But it went after Argus instead.

When Argus burst out laughing, she looked where he pointed and saw a mark shaped like an arrow in the snow. It had been drawn rather unsteadily with a warm, yellow liquid.

Northwest.

Geraden came to look at the sign and grinned in spite of himself. "That's got to be him."

"Right. Now we can start moving faster." The guard glanced at Terisa as if he anticipated entertainment. "But we've got to be careful. They might turn off."

Geraden nodded and cantered his mare to the northern side of the road. Although he didn't appear especially smooth or self-contained in the saddle—his elbows flapped, and his weight bounced with the horse's gait—his experience was evident. He knew how to ride well enough to do so without thinking about it.

Argus hadn't resumed his hold on Terisa's reins. "Come on. You've got to learn sometime." Watching her over his shoulder, he started away, matching Geraden's pace along the western margin of the road.

She was still trying to decide how hard to kick her mount when it lumbered ahead, following the stallion.

For one moment that seemed to last a long time because it was frozen by panic and cold, she dropped the reins and clutched for the saddle horn, but the gelding's gait hit her so hard that she missed her grip and started to fall.

When she failed to fall, she didn't immediately understand why. By degrees, however, the strain in her legs made her aware that she was clenching the beast with her knees.

This development amazed her so thoroughly that she only put one hand back on the saddle horn. With the other, she retrieved the reins. Then, borne along by a burst of exhilaration, she kicked the gelding to make it catch up with Argus.

The guard gave her a nod of disappointed approval and turned his attention to the road.

Her mount's spine pounded her up and down. Its tack jangled so loudly—and her legs and rear slapped the leather so hard—that she wanted to shout, Do we have to go this fast? But a residue of common sense told her that for her sake Argus and Geraden were already going more slowly than they wished. She closed her mouth so that she wouldn't bite her tongue and held on.

Orison looked surprisingly far away. She had to glance back over her left shoulder to see the castle. A purple flag flew from the King's tower now, raised to meet the day. Then the road crested a hill, dipped into a hollow, and Orison was gone.

A short distance later, a spur of the road ran north to a village nestled picturesquely in a little glen. Most of the twenty or thirty houses had wooden frames, but a few had obviously been constructed of stone. The snow had melted off their slate roofs; smoke curled from their chimneys as fires were built up for cooking and warmth. The angle of the sunlight enabled her to make out cattle pens in the shelter of the hills. These people raised meat for the castle.

In a war, a siege, they would have to evacuate their homes and live in Orison.

Geraden found no indication that Ribuld had taken the spur. The three riders went on.

Terisa's hands were red and freezing, despite the exertion of holding herself on her mount's back. Her face was so stiff it felt like it might break. Whenever a scrap of breeze caught her eyes, tears ran to ice on her cheeks. Gradually, she understood that it would actually be easier to keep her seat if the horse moved a bit faster. But Argus and Geraden now seemed to be going as fast as they dared. They had to watch for Ribuld's signs.

Over the rise of another hill, they came suddenly upon a wain loaded—Terisa would have said overloaded—with barrels of all sizes. Although it faced toward Orison, it was stopped by the side of the road for no apparent reason. At a glance, Terisa couldn't tell which looked more miserable, the shaggy, club-headed workhorse in the traces, or the driver huddling on the wagonbench, clutching his reins with hands that barely protruded from the mound of wool blankets wrapped around him. A moment later, however, the driver explained himself by croaking, "Argus? One of you Argus?"

The stallion skittered to a halt beside the wain. "I'm Argus," the guard said, studying the driver.

"Guard like you gave me a silver double to wait here." The driver sounded like he was being strangled by the weight of his blankets. "Too cold for that. About to give you up."

"Now why would Ribuld do that?" drawled Argus.

The man's eyes glittered shrewdly. "Too cold. One silver double—" His horse snorted vapor. "Not enough."

At that, Argus guffawed. "Pigshit! Taking this load into Orison won't earn you more than half a dozen coppers. You've already tripled your take. Don't push your luck."

The mound of blankets moved in a shrug. The driver made a clucking noise, and his horse pricked up its ears. When he twitched the reins, the horse leaned into its harness, and the wagon started to move.

Geraden swore under his breath. Argus was unperturbed, however. Over the groaning of the wain's axletrees, he commented amiably, "I'm thirsty. Before you leave, I think I'll knock a few holes in some of these casks." He drew his longsword. "Most of it's probably swill, but you may have something drinkable back there."

The driver tugged his horse to a halt. He considered for a moment, then said, "Glad to help the King's guards. Guard like you left the road here. Asked me to mark the place."

"Which direction?" demanded Geraden.

"North."

The Apt fisted his mare to the north side of the road. Almost at once, he called, "I've got his tracks. It looks like at least two riders went this way."

Argus sheathed his sword and gave the driver an elaborate bow. In a tone of gratitude, he said, "I'm sure it's *all* swill," and went to join Geraden.

Terisa's gelding followed with an air of lugubrious endurance.

As soon as she and her companions left the road, she was surprised by the noise they made. Crunching through the frozen white crust and thudding to the ground beneath, the horses' hooves were loud enough to be heard half a mile away—a sound like a cross between shattering glass and a distant cannonade. Nevertheless Argus set a somewhat faster pace and pulled ahead. After a moment, she realized that he was trying to match the stallion's gait to Ribuld's trail, riding as much as possible on already broken snow. When Geraden swung in behind him, and the gelding transferred its affections from the stallion to the mare, their progress became noticeably less noisy.

Ribuld's trail ran along a shallow valley between small hills, then crossed a ridge and began to descend a series of slopes marked with brittle thickets and black copses. Woods filled a fold in the terrain ahead, and the fold deepened as the ground around it rose into sharper hills. Argus followed the trail straight into the woods.

There he had to slow down. The ground between the trunks wasn't particularly cluttered; the wood itself wasn't thick. But many of the branches grew low enough to swipe at riders.

Barely cantering now, listening to the way the metallic sound of tack seemed to echo delicately back from every tree because of the steeper hills on either side, and wondering why she felt so much like holding her breath, Terisa followed Geraden into a gully which became a rocky streambed with its bottom less than half full of ice and crusted water. The trees on the slopes grew more thickly together, pointing their dark twigs like fingers at each other; but the bed remained clear. Now when the horses broke fresh crust their hooves clicked and clattered on stone.

Her legs ached. Her hands hurt like raw ice. She had the impression that the cold had begun to peel her face back from the bone. How else could she explain the sensation of numb pain in her cheek and chin and nose? She should have been as miserable as the driver and his workhorse.

But she wasn't.

For some reason, she expected to hear horns.

Then the streambed debouched into a valley where its waters joined a larger stream which had cut a ravine for itself among the hills. The ravine went roughly from east to west, and its northward wall especially was steep but climbable. As soon as Argus hissed a warning and pointed, she saw the horse tethered in the low flat made by the joining of the streams.

Ribuld crouched at the crest of the northward wall, peering over the rim: his cloak made him look like a shaggy rock. He turned his head, gazed downward, and waved.

"This is it," muttered Geraden. "That ridge probably blocks the sound. But we still need to be quiet."

"Right." Argus dismounted, and Terisa did the same. While he tethered his stallion as Ribuld had done to an old piece of deadwood sticking up out of the snow, she nearly collapsed because her legs were suddenly knotted with cramps. She had forgotten how cold her feet were. And her feet had forgotten the ground: she expected it to wobble like the gelding.

Her companions were already laboring up the side of the ravine.

Determined not to be left behind, she struggled after them.

The climb was easier than she expected. There was enough rock under the snow and dirt and the autumn's layer of fallen leaves to give her secure footing; and her legs were glad to do almost anything that didn't involve clutching at a horse. She reached Ribuld only a moment or two behind Geraden and Argus.

"Good timing," Ribuld whispered, grimacing around the old scar that ran from his hairline between his eyes almost to his mouth. "He's been here awhile. The others just arrived."

Kneeling in the snow at Geraden's side, she looked past the edge of the ridge into another ravine like the one behind her. Directly below her, a horse champed at the cold. Near it, a man with his back to her stood beside a small fire that burned almost without smoke.

She took him to be Nyle. His fire seemed so wonderful to her that she could practically taste its warmth.

On the other side of the bottom, four men were busy securing more horses. Three of them looked like bodyguards.

The fourth was Prince Kragen.

TWENTY-ONE:
AT LEAST ONE
PLOT DISCOVERED

N yle," the Prince said.

Geraden's brother returned the greeting. "My lord Prince."

Terisa could hear them perfectly. It was astonishing how well the cold and the ravine wall brought the sound up to her.

"I hope you were not kept waiting long."

"Just long enough to build a fire."

Like his men, Prince Kragen was wrapped in a white robe, with boots of white fur on his feet and a white fur cap on his head, using the winter itself for concealment. At first glance, Nyle's black-brown garb, his half-cloak and leggings, looked like a bad choice by comparison. But his clothes were indistinguishable from the colors of the driftwood in the ravine, the dark trunks of the trees. If he stood still, no one would see him.

"What news do you have of Orison?"

"What's the news of Alend, my lord Prince?"

A fringe of black hair showed around the rim of Prince Kragen's cap, hair as black as his eyes. He studied Nyle for a moment, then turned to his men and gave them a gesture that set them in motion. Two of them went in opposite directions to keep watch up and down the ravine. The third began to unpack bundles tied to the back of his saddle.

A bit sadly, Prince Kragen commented, "You still do not really trust me, do you, Nyle?"

"Yes and no, my lord Prince." Nyle's voice emerged from a clenched throat. "I'm committed to you. But we're traditional enemies. That's hard to forget."

At Terisa's side, Geraden picked up a handful of snow and rubbed it across his face to cool a reckless inner fire.

"I understand," replied the Prince evenly. "But I am more at risk here. You can ride back to Orison and resume your life. As soon as we separate, you are innocent. If *I* am caught, Castellan Lebbick might have me executed before anybody can explain to him that killing foreign princes is rarely wise.

"What news do you have of Orison?"

Argus turned away. Ribuld hissed at him for silence; he ignored the warning and began to pick his way back down the slope. Fortunately, the wall cut off the noise he made.

Grudgingly, Nyle answered, "Elega is in trouble."

Prince Kragen flashed a glance. "What trouble?"

"For some reason—I don't know how—that woman Terisa of Morgan decided you and Elega are plotting against the King. She convinced my brother Geraden. And he convinced the Tor.

"I told you the Tor has set himself up as some kind of chancellor. He issues orders as if he has the King's authority behind him, and no one questions him. It might be true. After all, he *is* the Tor—the lord who gave King Joyse his start."

"He is also," the Prince put in, "a drunken fool."

"He is. That's probably why he believed Geraden. There aren't many people left who can muster that much optimism."

Geraden heard this with a grimace that reminded Terisa of Artagel's fighting grin.

"And what trouble has this drunken fool caused for the lady Elega?" pursued Prince Kragen.

"He told her he knows what she's doing. Then he went off on a long lecture about the loyalty children owe their parents." Nyle shrugged. "She says it wasn't much. She gave him a piece of her mind and left him looking—she says he looked cowed. And she *says* he won't be able to interfere with her part of your plan. I'm not so sure. All he has to do is drop a few hints to Lebbick, and she won't be able to take a step without half the guards in Orison watching her."

"I see." Prince Kragen thought for a moment. "I regret that she is at hazard. But she has assured me many times that her role is secure

—and she is a woman who conveys conviction." In a decisive tone, he concluded, "We must trust that she will do what she has said."

Nyle's voice sounded like he had both fists knotted around it. "I'm still waiting to hear exactly what that is."

The Prince stiffened. With misleading casualness, he said, "My lord Prince."

"My lord Prince."

Prince Kragen's nod advised, Remember it. His mouth commented, "The lady Elega's safety and success depend upon secrecy."

"Then maybe you'll tell me the news of Alend. My lord Prince." Nyle's anger was controlled, but unmistakable. "Maybe you'll tell me why we had to meet today. Not sooner. Not later. All I've had so far are assurances and rhetoric. Maybe you'll tell me what's going on."

Geraden bobbed his head in approval. "Good," he breathed. "Make him tell you what's going on."

Ribuld glowered at the Apt for speaking.

"In a moment." Prince Kragen's composure was equal to the occasion. "I will answer a number of your questions in a moment. First, however, I prefer to tell you what I want you to do."

Nyle still had his back to the eavesdroppers: Terisa couldn't see his face. But his shoulders hunched as though he were strangling things inside himself.

"I asked you to meet me here on this particular day," the Prince said steadily, "and I asked you to be prepared to leave Orison, because I want you to ride to Perdon. I want you to find the Perdon and offer him the kingship of Mordant."

Breathing too loudly, Argus came back up the hill carrying his pouch of brandy. His companions paid no attention to him. At Prince Kragen's announcement, Geraden's whole body twitched. Terisa stared. At least temporarily, even Ribuld was too interested in what he heard to be interrupted by liquor.

Nyle's surprise showed in the way he stood. "Why?"

"Why the Perdon?" Prince Kragen hid a trace of amusement under his black mustache. "Why the kingship? Or why you?"

Nyle seemed unable to do anything except nod.

"The Perdon is my only reasonable choice. You see, I profited from my meeting with the lords, although it did not have the outcome I desired. The Fayle is too old—and too loyal. The Tor has become a drunken fool. The Domne would refuse. The Armigite—"

Prince Kragen snorted. "As for the Termigan, he is too far away. Also he is concerned only for the fate of his own Care.

"The Perdon must be offered the kingship to prove our good faith."

Furiously, Geraden whispered, "Not to mention the fact that the Perdon is the only lord with an army close enough to threaten you, my lord Prince."

"Despite what King Joyse and Castellan Lebbick believe," Prince Kragen continued reasonably, "it has never been the Alend Monarch's intention to conquer Mordant for himself. His first priority—his only overriding commitment—is to fill the vacuum of power in Mordant so that the Congery of Imagers will not fall into the hands of Cadwal. To accomplish that, we will conquer Mordant because we have no alternative. What else can we do? The King insulted my mission. The lords refused the union Master Eremis and I offered them.

"But we will not take Mordant for ourselves if the Perdon can be persuaded to be King. That will be your job. He might not listen to such a proposal from me. We are traditional enemies, as you have said. But a son of the Domne—a lifelong friend of the lady Elega—may perhaps persuade him. For the good of all who oppose Festten and Cadwal.

"Will you do it, Nyle?"

Nyle was silent for a long time. When he spoke, he sounded both astonished and relieved.

"Yes." In spite of its softness, the word came out with too much steam, as if it were exploding from inside him. "Yes, my lord Prince. I'll do it."

Geraden covered his head with his hands, inadvertently smearing snow into his hair.

"Good." Prince Kragen stepped closer to the fire to warm his hands. "Then you will need to know what's going on, in order to convey that information to the Perdon."

Argus put his brandy pouch down in front of Terisa. Noticing it, she realized that she was miserably cold. With a shiver, she loosened the neck of the pouch and raised it to her mouth. Like her cheeks, her lips were too numb to know what they were doing, but her tongue verified that the brandy was going into her mouth rather than down her chin. It tasted like badly perfumed tarnish remover, but it did what it was supposed to do: it raised the temperature of her blood several degrees.

She passed the pouch to Geraden.

Down in the ravine, Prince Kragen crooked a finger at the bodyguard who had unpacked the bundles. The man came to him and handed him a stylus and a small writing tablet. Standing by the fire, Prince Kragen began to write. His fingers held the stylus as though they knew nothing about swords and had never helped save Terisa's life.

"Is that a message to the Perdon, my lord Prince?" Nyle's tone suggested impatience.

The Prince shook his head. "To my father. The Alend Monarch needs to know that you have agreed to approach the Perdon for us."

"What will he do?"

"What he is already doing." Prince Kragen's mind was on his message. "In the bazaar of Orison during the first morning of the thaw, you brought me the lady Elega's word that she had learned a way to fulfill her part of our plans. You noticed, I think, that I was pleased by this news.

"I was pleased because much hinges on her role. While you and I spoke together—while we chose the day and place for this meeting— my father and his armies were already crossing the Pestil into Armigite."

Argus, Ribuld, and Geraden became still: all movement was sucked out of them. They didn't blink or glance around; they didn't appear to breathe. Every part of them—their arms and legs, the angles of their backs, the set of their shoulders—concentrated on what they were hearing.

So it was all a lie, thought Terisa. His *peaceful* mission. His meeting with the lords. A lie. The Alend Monarch had begun marching before he even had time to learn the outcome of his son's mission. He had never intended to do anything except invade Mordant.

Like an echo of her shocked thoughts, Nyle articulated softly, "You never wanted peace. You never meant King Joyse to take your mission seriously. You just came here looking for people to help you betray him." Both arms leaped outward in a gesture full of violence, fiercely truncated. "This is what you call good faith."

Distinct and sibilant in the cold, a sword came out of its sheath. Prince Kragen's bodyguard moved forward, aiming the tip of his blade at Nyle's throat.

Ribuld clutched at his own sword.

But a quick wave of the Prince's hand stopped the bodyguard. The man shrugged stiffly and resheathed his longsword.

"I understand your anger, Nyle." Prince Kragen spoke calmly, almost casually, but his tone warned Nyle not to push him too far. "You misunderstand me, however. The problem is one of communication, is it not? Knowing that I spent nearly thirty days in the worst of this winter making my way from the Alend Monarch's seat in Scarab to Orison, you believe that we have had no time to exchange messages since my arrival here. Therefore you conclude that I have come merely to serve plans which he made before I left him."

Nyle didn't move.

With a faint smile, the Prince continued, "Those unruly barons, the Alend Lieges, are always striving to gain the advantage over each other. At last their petty wrestling has produced something useful." Another gesture to his bodyguard brought the man forward carrying a bundle that appeared to be a swath of cloth wrapped around a rigid frame.

Prince Kragen rolled his message tightly and tied it into a tiny packet with a piece of thread. When he was done, his bodyguard unveiled the bundle, revealing a bird in a square cage.

"A carrier pigeon," Terisa breathed in astonishment. "They're using *carrier pigeons*."

Argus, Ribuld, and Geraden all stared at her for an instant, then snapped their attention back down into the ravine.

The bird was unmistakably a pigeon. It cooed comfortably as the bodyguard removed it from the cage and held it so that Prince Kragen could bind his message to its leg. "One of the Lieges," the Prince explained, "discovered that these birds have the ability to find their way over any distance back to the place they have been trained to recognize as home. This one has learned to identify a combination of tents, standards, and wagonlines that invariably occurs in my father's encampments. It will fly to him when it is released.

"Now do you understand?" Prince Kragen's tone was hard, a threat behind his amicable manner. "I brought a number of these birds from Alend. They bear messages to my father in a day—perhaps less. In this way, I make decisions for him.

"I came to Orison charged with the responsibility of resolving the dilemma of the Congery, Cadwal, and war—the dilemma of your King's strange weakness. I am the Alend Contender. I wish strongly to earn the throne. For that reason, my mission of peace was sincere, I assure you. But when King Joyse rejected it, I began to think of war. I sent messages accordingly. Then, however, both Master Eremis and the lady Elega offered me hopes that were much preferable to war. Again I sent messages. When the lords of the Cares refused the pact Master Eremis suggested to them—and most especially when I experienced how vulnerable Orison, and therefore the Congery, was to attack from Cadwal—I determined to act on the possibilities the lady Elega and I had discussed.

"The Alend Monarch is doing what I ask of him. And I ask it because I believe it to be the least bloody and most effective answer to an intolerable danger. *High King Festten must not gain control of the Congery.* The breach of Orison's wall is an opportunity I *can not* ignore."

Firmly, the Prince concluded, "What is your answer now?"

Nyle looked like he was swallowing hard, trying to adjust his preconceptions to fit new information. At the moment, Geraden appeared to have no opinion about what his brother should do. He seemed to be scrambling to catch up with the implications of what he had just heard. Both Argus and Ribuld watched the encounter below with trouble in their eyes.

"My lord Prince," Nyle began thickly, "I should probably apologize. I didn't know this was possible." His hands moved helplessly at his sides. "Of course I'll go to Perdon. I'll persuade the Perdon somehow."

Prince Kragen studied Nyle for a moment. Then he nodded.

His bodyguard released the pigeon.

It took to the air in a flash of gray, a hint of blue and green. Terisa watched it go, an easy labor of wings against the chill sky—watched it as if it were on its way to bring bloodshed down on Orison. After circling briefly, it turned north.

Ribuld glared at her. "You knew about that bird," he murmured.

"We have them where I come from." Defensively, she added, "We have horses, too, but I've never ridden one before."

Geraden nudged the guard silent.

Nyle was still struggling to improve his grasp on the situation. "But is there time?" he asked after some thought. "When do you think the Alend Monarch will get to Orison? I don't know where the Perdon is. He might not be in Scarping. He might be anywhere along the Vertigon, fighting Cadwals."

"I have chosen the time with some care," replied Prince Kragen as if this would reassure Nyle. "It is important that you not reach the Perdon too soon. If you do, and he is not persuaded, and so he brings his forces against us, he might be able to block us from Orison. For that reason, we did not meet until today. I calculate that if you find him immediately—and he rejects you and comes against us in furious haste—he will not reach Orison until after we have mastered it."

Geraden shook his head. "It's not that easy," he whispered.

"You think it's going to be that easy?" The idea seemed to incense Nyle. "A siege might take all spring. Even with that breach in the wall. You can't just—"

"Nyle," the Prince cut in. "I am not a child. Do not harangue me about sieges. I have studied them deeply. And I assure you that we will be able to master Orison."

Nyle received this assertion like a man struggling not to let what he heard stun him. "Still, my lord Prince," he said slowly, "it seems to me you're trying to control events too delicately. What if the weather turns against you? We're almost sure to get another storm."

Prince Kragen shrugged. His patience was wearing thin. "Then you and the Perdon will be hindered as much as we are."

"And what about the Armigite?" Nyle seemed unable to keep his anger down. "Is he going to let you march your army—and *supply* it —straight through his Care without making at least an effort to slow you down?"

At that, Prince Kragen laughed shortly. "I doubt that I need to concern myself with the Armigite." His laugh held a note of scorn that made Terisa feel suddenly colder. "Nevertheless I have done so. He and I have negotiated a pact.

"Sweating fear all the while, he offered me an unhindered passage through his Care for as many armies as I chose to name. And what did he ask in exchange? That we do no violence to his people in their towns and villages? That we leave untouched the cattle pens and storehouses that feed his Care? No. He asked only that he be allowed to remain safe and ignorant—*ignorant*, Nyle—while the fate of Mordant was decided."

Argus swore under his breath. But Terisa had met the Armigite: she wasn't surprised.

"Personally," the Prince went on with more nonchalance, "I would enjoy damaging his ignorance a little. His Care deserves bet-

ter of him. But we will respect the pact. And we will do no harm to
his people or his cattle or his stores. Our aim is to find an answer to
your King's weakness—and to oppose Cadwal—not to worsen the
old enmity between Mordant and Alend.

"Have I satisfied you, Nyle?"

From the back, Nyle didn't look satisfied: there was too much
tension in his stance. Terisa would have expected him to be grateful
to Prince Kragen for giving him so few causes for mistrust, so many
reasons to believe he was doing the right thing. Why was he still
angry? Why did he sound almost livid with fury as he replied, "Yes,
my lord Prince."

For a moment, Prince Kragen regarded his ally as though he, too,
didn't understand Nyle's mood. But apparently what he saw in
Nyle's face assured him. "Good," he said, suddenly brisk. "The
Perdon will listen to you. Let us begin."

At once, he signaled to his bodyguards.

The men watching either end of the ravine returned to their
horses. Moving stiffly, Nyle readied his own mount. At last, Terisa
saw his face. His features were set and implacable, as if nothing—not
even his own passion—could dissuade him from the course he had
chosen.

Argus rose into a crouch and loosened his sword. "We'll jump
them before they get out of the ravine. Maybe we'll be able to stop
them." The grimace that exposed his missing teeth didn't show much
fear. Fighting was his job; he and Ribuld seemed to take it for
granted.

But Geraden stopped them. "Don't be stupid. There are four of
them. And if the Prince has any sense, he has more men nearby.

"You." Speaking quickly so that the guards had no chance to argue with him, he stabbed an index finger at Argus. "Follow the
Prince. Find where he's camped. Keep an eye on him. And leave a
trail.

"Ribuld, you get back to Orison." The lines of Geraden's face
were as sharp as the cold. Frost in his eyebrows and snow in his hair
made him look strangely feral. "Tell Castellan Lebbick what you
heard. Lead him here. Tell him if he captures the Prince we can use
him as hostage. We still have a chance to get out of this mess.

"Go." He gave the guard an urgent push.

Ribuld looked once at Argus and back at Geraden, puckering his scar in concentration. Then he launched himself down the steep slope almost at a run.

Prince Kragen and his bodyguards swung up into their saddles. Nyle began dousing his fire with handfuls of crusted snow.

"Thank's a lot," Argus whispered sarcastically to Geraden. "You gave *me* the hard job. If they go west, these two ravines join. I can pick up their trail there. But if they go east—" He jerked a thumb behind him. "That one ends. The other opens out of these hills. I won't be able to get my horse over the ridge. I'll have to follow them on foot."

"Then you're in luck." Geraden pointed downward.

Below him, Nyle mounted his horse. The son of the Domne and the son of the Alend Monarch faced each other, and Prince Kragen raised a salute. Together, the Alends turned to the left and started along the frozen stream.

Argus punched Geraden lightly on the arm and left, bounding down the side of the ridge toward his mount.

Terisa continued watching Nyle. Over her shoulder, she heard Ribuld ride away.

Nyle remained where he was for a moment, perhaps considering the best route to Perdon, perhaps wondering what he could say to persuade Perdon's lord—perhaps simply hesitating. Then he urged his mount forward with his heels and went east.

Geraden caught hold of Terisa's hand. "Come on. We've got to stop him." He almost pulled her off balance as he followed Argus toward the horses.

At once, he fell. Fortunately, some instinct inspired him to let go of her hand as he went down. And he caught himself before he had a chance to break any bones on the rocks. He reached the bottom of the ravine several strides ahead of her.

Awkward with haste, he leaped into the saddle of his mare. From the low valley where the streams met, Ribuld had disappeared along the streambed in the direction of Orison. At a more cautious pace, Argus was going west, toward the joining of the ravines. Flapping his boots against the mare's sides, Geraden goaded her into a gallop eastward.

Terisa reached out a hand to him, called as loudly as she dared, "Wait!"

He didn't see or hear her.

By the time she had descended to her gelding, she had decided to forget everything else and just follow Ribuld home. She was chilled to the heart; she didn't know how much more of this cold she could endure. She was afraid of everything she had heard.

Ignoring her own decision, she continued to hurry as fast as she could. Somehow, she untethered the gelding; somehow, she got her left foot into the stirrup, her right leg over its back. With the reins, she hauled its head toward the east.

Gritting her teeth, she kicked it.

She nearly panicked when the gelding went from a trot into a canter and then a run, trying for reasons of its own to catch up with Geraden's mare.

This speed felt tremendous. And the bottom of the ravine was treacherous. She ought to control her mount somehow—slow it; steer it to safer footing. Of course. And while she was at it, she ought to defeat the Alend Monarch's army, take care of Master Gilbur and the arch-Imager Vagel, and produce peace on earth. While composing great music with her free hand. Instead of doing all that, however, she concentrated with a pure white intensity that resembled terror on simply staying in the saddle.

The northern wall of the ravine became sheer gray stone, then relaxed its slope a little. Along the top, it was thick with brush. The south side was much more gradual, held down by heavy black trees with their roots gripped in the soil. But soon the trees drew back, and the side became steeper.

While the gelding hurtled along, she promised and promised herself that if she ever got off it alive she would never ride again, never as long as she lived, never.

All at once, as if the terrain itself had taken pity on her, the walls of the ravine jumped up and came together, ending the watercourse. At one time, it must have continued on to the east, but apparently its sides had fallen inward, forcing the water to find another channel. The horses had nowhere to go.

Roughly, Geraden wrenched his mare to a halt and sprang from her back. He hit the ground too fast: he fell again, slamming his whole body into the snow. He looked like a wild man as he regained his feet and charged the north slope.

She had no breath to shout at him, call him back, so she had to figure out how to make the gelding stop by herself.

Unintentionally kind, it took care of that detail for her. Having rejoined the mare, it seemed suddenly content with its lot in life. At the mare's side, it nuzzled her once, then lowered its head and lapsed into a state of impenetrable stupidity.

Terisa was still in one piece. Amazing.

It would have been nice to sit there and enjoy her survival for a moment. But Geraden was scrambling frantically up the slope. At first, the climb looked too steep for him. Then she saw that he was going to make it. Soon he would be out of sight.

She struggled off her horse, took a few tentative steps to test the solidity of the world, then pushed herself into a tight run.

The ridge side was certainly steep. It was well supplied with embedded rocks and protruding roots, however. And Geraden's upward scramble had cleared away a remarkable amount of snow. She found that if she didn't hurry—and didn't look down—she could make the ascent quite easily.

On the way, she tried not to think about how far ahead he was. Or what he intended to do.

Gasping at the icy air, she reached the crest.

The spine separating the two ravines was much the same here as it had been back where she and Geraden had eavesdropped on Nyle and Prince Kragen: a bit gentler down its northward face; marked with brush, jutting piles of rock, a few trees; but still steep. The stream that had cut the ravine clung to the base of the spine, wandering slowly out of sight to the east. The ravine itself was gone, however. Its own north side had slumped down and opened up into a wood which filled the lower ground between this spine and another ridge of hills. The ridge was plainly visible through the bare treetops, although it appeared to be some distance away.

Geraden, on the other hand, was nowhere to be seen.

She would have panicked, but she had no time. Almost at once, she spotted Nyle.

He rode at a trot along the streambed. He was still off to her left, coming eastward; but in a moment he would be directly below her. If she were the kind of person who did such things, she could have hit him with a rock.

More because Nyle's movement drew her gaze in that direction than because she had recovered her common sense, she looked at the slope in front of her and saw the marks of Geraden's descent. They went straight into a thick clump of brush poised above the streambed.

She figured out what was happening just in time to control her
surprise as Geraden sprang out of the brush at his brother.

His elevation and proximity gave him an advantage: he could
hardly have missed. And he jumped hard. His momentum carried
Nyle out of the saddle and plunged both of them into the snow on
the far side of the horse with a sound that made Terisa think of
snapped arms and broken backs.

She started down the slope, a shout locked in her throat.

Geraden's experience with falls stood him in good stead. He was
on his feet again almost instantly. Scattering flurries of snow, he
dashed after the startled horse and struck the beast on its rump,
sending it away at a gallop, out of reach. Then he turned back to his
brother.

Nyle lifted his head. For a moment, he didn't appear to realize that
he was blind because his face was caked with snow. When he scraped
his features clear, however, he was able to see.

"Are you all right?" asked Geraden. "I didn't mean to hurt you. I
just wanted to stop you."

Blinking fiercely, Nyle shook his head. In a series of jerks, he
moved each of his arms, then his legs. He slapped snow off his half-
cloak. All at once, he yanked himself to his feet like a knife blade
opening.

"If you think this is a joke," he said between his teeth, "it isn't
funny."

Terisa's exhausted legs nearly failed her; she stumbled and had to
catch herself on a tree. But she was almost there.

"It isn't a joke." Geraden was so caked and white that he looked
like he had been rolled together by children. Nevertheless there was
nothing childlike in his manner. "I'm not going to let you do it."

Terisa reached the streambed and skittered across the frozen surface toward the two brothers.

"Do *what*?" snapped Nyle. "You've lost your mind. I was just
riding. On a *horse*. Remember horses? You act like that's a crime
against humanity."

"Nyle." Geraden held himself still. Even his voice became still. "I
heard you. I was there." He included Terisa. "We were there. We
heard everything you said. And Prince Kragen."

For just a second, Nyle gaped at his brother. He gaped at Terisa.
Mutely, she nodded in confirmation.

He straightened his shoulders, and anger closed his face like a shutter.

"So you've decided to stop me. Full of moral superiority, you've decided to stop me because you cling to the astonishing belief that King Joyse and chaos and terrible Imagery and a fresh start to the wars that crippled Mordant for generations are somehow *preferable* to putting the Perdon on the throne and saving the entire kingdom. You—"

"No." Geraden shook his head, suppressing violence. "It won't work. The Perdon will never accept Prince Kragen's offer—he knows that. He's sending you to do this to confuse the issue, so the Perdon won't have a chance to fight for Orison when Alend attacks."

"You're wrong, Geraden." Terisa was surprised to hear herself speak. Her voice was like a small animal huddling against the cold and barely alive. "I'm sorry. I've met the Perdon. I've seen him and Prince Kragen together. He's desperate. He won't turn the Prince down."

Geraden gave her a quick look of dismay; but Nyle didn't glance away from his brother. "Even if that's not true," he resumed, "you're acting like a child. Prince Kragen is right. The Alend Monarch is right. The *worst* thing that can happen to us is for High King Festten to get his hands on the Congery.

"We're already being torn apart by an Imager no one can find or stop. Cadwal will be able to decimate everything west of the Vertigon if the Congery falls. On our mother's grave, Geraden, we ought to *beg* Margonal to invade us.

"Instead of interfering, why don't you figure out what you're going to say to all the families who are going to be butchered—all the children who are going to be bereaved—all the men and women who are going to be maimed and massacred when King Joyse finally collapses and no power strong enough to hold the realm together takes his place?

"In the meantime, get out of my way."

Thrusting between Geraden and Terisa, he stamped off after his horse.

The dismay on Geraden's face got worse. For a moment, he seemed unable to move. Confused and alarmed, Terisa reached out a hand to him. "Geraden?"

Abruptly, his features knotted, and he swung into motion.

Chasing Nyle, he yelled, "That's great! Wonderful! You're right, of course. You're being perfectly reasonable. Our father is going to be very proud of you."

Nyle flinched, but kept on walking.

"There's just one thing. What about loyalty? King Joyse is our father's *friend*. What about self-respect? You're betraying your *King*, the man who made Mordant and peace out of nothing but bloodshed. How are you planning to live the rest of your life without loyalty or self-respect?"

"Loyalty to *whom*?" Though Nyle's stride didn't falter, his shout was like a cry. "King Joyse? When was he ever loyal to *me*?

"He met all of us. He must have seen me dying for his notice, his approval. But *you're* the one he invited to Orison. When he decided to betroth Elega, he chose *you*. And a brilliant choice it was, too. You've certainly vindicated his good judgment, haven't you? Forgive me, but I find it a little difficult to feel warm and sentimental about that man.

"And he's going to get us all *killed*!" Small pieces of his distress echoed back from the tree trunks. "Don't you understand that? How much *self-respect* are you going to get out of giving your life for a man who sacrificed you simply because he *couldn't be bothered* to hold his realm together? If you want to talk about self-respect, ask yourself why you place so little value on your own blood. I won't even mention the blood of all the people you claim to care about."

"Then why—"

Geraden caught up with Nyle and grabbed his arm. Nyle flung off Geraden's grip. The two brothers faced each other, their breath steaming furiously.

"Then why," Geraden repeated, "are you so angry about it?" He was no longer shouting. His voice sank to a whisper. "You're doing what you know is right. Doesn't that make you feel good? And you're doing what Elega wants. She'll love you for it. She won't be able to help herself. Doesn't that make you feel good?"

"No." Like Geraden, Nyle lowered his voice as if he didn't want the trees or the snow to hear him. "No, it doesn't." Each word hurt. "That's how I got into this, but it doesn't help. She doesn't love me. She'll never love me. She loves Prince Kragen."

All around him, the wood was silent. The only noise came from Terisa's boots as she neared the brothers. The sunlight out of the leaden sky seemed to have no weight, no effect against the cold.

Geraden spread his hands in a gesture of appeal. "Then give it up.

Please. This is all craziness anyway. There's no way the Alend Monarch can take Orison without a terrible siege—without killing any number of people. I don't care what Prince Kragen says. The Tor and Castellan Lebbick won't give up. The only lives you're going to save are Alend's, not ours. Don't throw yourself away for a woman who wants to betray her own father."

Terisa saw at once that Geraden had made a mistake. He should have left Nyle's grief to gnaw at him unaided—shouldn't have mentioned Elega again. But it was too late now: the damage was done. As if the bones of his skull were shifting, Nyle's face took on the implacable set that had persuaded Prince Kragen to trust him. His eyes were as dull as weathered stone.

"If you want my advice"—he had a white-knuckled grip on himself—"go home while you can. And take Artagel with you. He isn't going to enjoy losing his famous independence."

"*Nyle*," Geraden protested.

Nyle glanced over his shoulder. "I see my horse. He'll let me catch him—if you haven't spooked him too badly." He returned his gaze to Geraden's. "You're going to stay here while I go get him. Then I'm going to ride away. If your mind is as weak as your talent for Imagery, you'll go back to Orison and tell Lebbick the whole story. It won't do him any good, but at least he'll have something to fret about for a few days. But if you have any sense, you'll keep your mouth shut."

Softly, Geraden replied, "No." Clogged with snow, he looked white and foolish beside his dark-clad brother. Pain came from him in gouts of vapor, but his voice and his eyes and his hands were steady. "No, Nyle. I won't let you go."

Briefly, Nyle's features twisted as though he were trying to smile. Then his shoulders and arms relaxed. "I guess I knew you were going to say that." He made an unsuccessful effort to sound casual. "You always were pretty stubborn."

Terisa struggled to give warning, but her voice failed her. As if she were helpless, she watched Nyle start into a full-circle spin which seemed to lift him off the ground, out of the snow, bringing one of his boots to Geraden's head.

His kick slammed his brother down.

For a moment, Geraden arched his back and clawed at the crust. Then he lay still as if his neck were broken.

Quickly, Nyle bent to examine his brother.

When he was satisfied, he swung to face Terisa. Now he couldn't contain his fury. His hands clenched and unclenched spasmodically at his sides. The muscles of his jaw worked.

"Take care of him. If you let him die out here, I'll come back and throttle you with my bare hands."

He headed for his horse at a run, as though there were hounds at his heels.

She never saw him go. Her hands were too cold; she couldn't find any sensation in her fingers. She was weeping with fear and frustration when she finally located the pulse in Geraden's throat and understood that he wasn't dead already.

A long time seemed to pass before she noticed that her surroundings looked familiar.

Through the black-trunked trees, she saw a ridge of hills. She had seen it earlier without paying any attention to it, but now its crisp line against the wintery sky tugged at her memory. Where—? It had been slightly different. What was different? The snow. The snow was different. She remembered dry, light flakes frothing like steam, churned to boiling by the haste of horses. She remembered the creaking of leather, the jangle of tack. And she remembered—

She remembered horns.

Her dream. This place was in her dream, the dream that had come to her the night before her life changed—come as if to prepare her for Geraden's arrival. The trees and the cold were the same. The ridge was the same. And Geraden was here, the young man in her dream who had appeared, coatless and unarmed, to save her life. All she lacked were three riders who hated her and drove their mounts through the snow for a chance to strike her dead. And the sound of horns, reaching her through the chill and the wood like the call for which her heart waited.

She didn't hear any horns. Though she yearned and strained for it, she couldn't conjure that hunting music out of her mind and into the air.

Nevertheless she heard the labor of horses in the distance, crashing through the snow crust. The cold brought every sound off the ridge into the wood, as edged as a shard of glass.

The sensation that she had wandered into her dream made everything distinct and slow: she had time to see clearly, time to hear every sound except the horns she desired. There they were, where she knew they would be: three men on horseback charging along the skirt of the ridge. She saw them through the wide gaps between the trees. She saw steam trailing furiously from the nostrils of the mounts. Each plunge of their hooves, each crunch-and-thud through ice and snow reached her ears.

Unheralded by the high, winging call that would have made the dream complete, the three riders swung abruptly away from the hills and aimed their mounts in her direction.

She was watching them so hard that she didn't realize Geraden was conscious until he gained his feet beside her, rubbing his head.

Caught up in the double experience of what was happening and what she had dreamed, she was unable to speak, unable to shift her concentration from the riders. Like hers, however, his attention was on them. "You recognize them?" His voice was dull with the aftereffects of his brother's blow.

The riders were still too far away to be recognized, although she already knew the look of their hate. She shook her head.

"They're probably after you." He didn't need to speak quickly; there was no hurry, he had plenty of time. "It wouldn't be impossible for somebody to find us. If they asked the right questions at the stables and the gates. And they met that wagon driver." He turned away, then back again. "There's no point in trying to run. Our horses are too far away."

Swords appeared in the hands of the riders—blades as long as sabers, but viciously curved, like scimitars. They were going to hack her into the snow where she stood. She ought to move. She and Geraden ought to do something. At the moment, however, she was more interested in the odd recollection that the swords raised against her in her dream had been straight, not curved.

Geraden seemed equally out of touch with reality. He was too calm. For some reason he chose this moment to kick at lumps in the snow. Then his behavior began to make sense. From the snow, he uncovered fallen branches. They were crooked and dead; but two of them were stout, as thick as her arm, long enough to be useful.

This wasn't right. This wasn't the way it happened in her dream. But there was still plenty of time. He gave one branch to her, kept one for himself.

"When they reach that tree"—he pointed—"we'll separate. If they split up, we might have a better chance against them. If they don't, I'll be able to hit them from the side when they attack you."

She had the impression that if she really *looked* at him, she would see that he was terrified. Yet her ears insisted on hearing him as if he were calm.

"Don't worry about the riders. Go for the horses. Try to hit one of them in the face. If we get lucky, the rider will fall and hurt himself."

She didn't respond. Her attention was on the riders while she waited to hear horns.

Then their faces came into focus for her, and she saw that she was wrong about them. They weren't the riders in her dream.

They weren't men at all.

They had eyes in the wrong places. Long whiskers sprouted around the orbs. Snouts hid their mouths, but not their tusks. She was able to see their heads because the hoods of their riding capes had been swept back. Their heads were covered with mottled red fur.

They seemed to have more limbs than they needed. Each of them seemed to be waving two swords.

No. It wasn't like this.

Nevertheless the sensation that she was acting out a dream grew stronger.

She remained motionless, waiting. The air was whetted with cold, as hard as a slap and as penetrating as splinters. She could hear the separate sound made by each pounding hoof.

When the riders reached the tree Geraden had indicated, he hissed, "Now!" and dashed away as if he had decided at the last moment to flee. He ran kicking his feet high to break them free of the icy surface. But she didn't move.

Without hesitation, all three of the riders turned their mounts and plunged after him. None of their strange eyes so much as glanced at her.

Out of nowhere, a pang of fear nailed her.

Geraden? *Geraden?*

So suddenly that he nearly fell, he turned and saw his danger. He flung a look like a cry in her direction, then raised his club. The riders were almost on top of him.

Gripping his branch in both hands, he broke it across the forehead of the first horse.

The mount squealed in pain, tried too late to leap aside. Wrenched off balance, the rider spilled into the snow in front of the second attacker.

Frantically trying to avoid a collision, the second horse and rider went down.

Geraden hit the downed rider with the remains of his club, then dodged around the struggling horse to evade his third attacker—and tripped. He landed on his face in an untrampled patch of snow.

As he fell, the first rider hacked at him from the ground. But the crusted snow hampered movement: the blow missed. Geraden and his attacker struggled to their feet at the same time, while the third rider turned to come in for another charge.

Awkwardly, Geraden stumbled out of reach long enough to snatch up a sword from the rider he had stunned. He obviously didn't know how to use it, however. Clenching it like a bludgeon, he turned to face his attacker.

The creature let out a snort of scorn and started swinging.

Geraden blocked the first cut.

He was helpless to parry the second.

In her dream, Terisa had watched a man hazard his life to save her. Despite his evident lack of experience with weapons, he had downed one assailant for her sake. Then another. And she had watched. Nothing more. She had seen the third rider come up behind him. Sword held high, the rider had positioned himself to cut her rescuer down. And she had made no effort to help him. She had startled herself out of the dream altogether by shouting a warning.

But it was Geraden who was being attacked, Geraden who needed rescuing. And she still had the branch he had given her. She felt that she had been running for a long time, that the distance was too great, she would never reach him in time; but she ran harder than she had ever run in her life, and before his attacker could kill him she swung her club against the side of that furred head.

Several things seemed to be happening simultaneously. Nevertheless she saw them all.

She saw a flat patch appear in the mottled red fur. While the attacker stumbled to his knees, the patch began to bleed, first slowly, then in a sickening gush. He hit the snow, and his life splashed a red-black stain across the crust. He was never going to move again.

Geraden gaped at her, momentarily astonished.

At the same time, she saw the third rider come up behind him. Swords held high, the rider positioned himself to cut Geraden down.

Geraden was looking at her. He had forgotten the third rider entirely.

There was no time for warning, no time for her to move, no time for him to duck or dodge.

Yet there was time for her to see another horseman reach the creature and drive a long poniard like a spike into the center of his back. She saw him cough blood onto Geraden's shoulders and pitch from his horse, almost knocking Geraden down as he dropped.

Nyle hauled his mount to a stop and sprang out of the saddle. "Are you all right?" Without waiting for an answer, he began to check the fallen riders. "Where did you get enemies like *this?*" When he found that the first attacker was still alive, he produced a length of rope from one of his saddlebags and lashed the creature's wrists and ankles together. "I saw them heading this way. Since they were in such a hurry to get to the place where I just left you, I decided I ought to follow them."

Geraden and Terisa stared at him as if he had arrived from the moon.

"Are you all right?" he repeated. There was concern in his eyes; but there was also a glint of humor, a suggestion of pride; for a moment he looked so much like Artagel and Geraden that the resemblance closed Terisa's throat. "I get the impression you aren't used to fighting enemies like this."

"Thank you," said Geraden as if he felt the same way she did. A nauseated expression distorted his features. With a shudder of disgust, he dropped the sword he was holding. "Thanks for coming back."

In the same motion, he picked up another sturdy branch and knocked his brother unconscious in front of him.

Then he stood hunched over Nyle with his chin thrust out and his face like the winter, breathing in great gasps that seemed to hurt his chest.

Terisa strained her ears for the distant calling of horns. But it was all in her mind.

TWENTY-TWO:
QUESTIONS ABOUT
BEING BESIEGED

Eventually, Terisa and Geraden were found by a squad of Castellan Lebbick's guards.

By that time, both Nyle and the attacker were conscious. Nyle wasn't particularly amused to discover that he was trussed with his own rope; but after a few minutes of bitter cursing—which did nothing to warm the bleak cold of Geraden's expression—he lapsed into silence.

The attacker snarled periodically and twisted his strange features. He didn't waste his strength on futile efforts to break his bonds, however.

The guards brought Geraden's mare and Terisa's gelding along with enough of their rough brandy to push the worst of the chill back from her vitals—and enough questions to make her ache for sleep. Fortunately, Geraden took charge before anyone—perhaps including the Apt himself—realized what he was doing; he quickly established that the guards' questions were less important than the need to join the men on Argus' trail, pursuing Prince Kragen.

All Terisa wanted was to get out of this weather and lie down somewhere warm, where it might be possible to forget the way that flat patch in the mottled red fur had begun to gush blood—or the way Geraden had struck Nyle down. Chasing after Argus and the Prince would only prolong her misery.

But at least no one had time to insist on questions.

Although she had promised she would never ride again, she soon

found herself mounted on the gelding. Ignoring the reins, she clung
to the saddle horn and went wherever her horse took her.

Once Nyle and Geraden's attacker had been secured on their own
beasts, and the guards were mounted again, her horse took her with
everyone else back the way they had come.

Eager for more speed, Geraden surged ahead.

"Relax," one of the guards advised him. "There are already at
least a dozen men on that trail. They'll catch him. It won't happen
any sooner just because you're in a hurry."

Terisa caught the look Geraden flashed at the guard. It was wild
and sick; and she understood almost automatically why he wanted to
go faster. He didn't want to help capture Prince Kragen. He wanted
to get away from what he had done to his brother.

Instinctively, she straightened her back and tried to improve her
balance, as if that would enable the gelding and all the horses to go
faster.

The guards swung east and didn't cross the stream until a fold in
the south wall provided them access to those hills. Their route back
to the southern ravine was circuitous, but quicker than walking—and
much quicker than getting lost, as Terisa would have done if she had
tried to find her own way. Still, it took long enough to make her
numb. She was blind to herself, and the passing of the dark tree
trunks on either side, and the tight mood of the riders around her as
they reached the joining of the streambeds where Ribuld had ridden
south to rouse Orison and Argus had gone west after Prince Kragen
—blind enough to be surprised by the fact that the valley was full of
guards.

Although they were mounted, they didn't appear to be doing anything except waiting.

All their eyes were on Geraden and her. None of them spoke.

Ribuld sat erect on his horse with his head high, brandishing his
scar as though he were about to let out a yell.

Involuntarily, Geraden jerked his mare to a halt. The men with
him stopped. Terisa's gelding blundered against the mare's rump and
stopped also.

"What is it? Why aren't—?" Geraden's voice caught.

Near Ribuld stood a horse without a rider. But not without a
burden: the man on its back hung from his stomach; his wrists and
ankles had been tied to the girth so that he wouldn't fall. His back

was wet. Blinking stupidly, Terisa recognized Argus' stallion before she recognized Argus himself.

"I'm sorry," a guard with a captain's purple band knotted around his bicep rasped. "I know he was a friend of yours."

"What—?" Geraden tried again, but couldn't make the words come out. "What—?"

The captain was a stocky, middle-aged man with a face that suggested more decency than imagination. "We found him about a mile down the ravine. I guess he wasn't careful enough. There wasn't even a struggle. He was just there on the ground with a hole in his back. Probably made by an arrow."

The captain spat a curse into the snow, then continued, "After that, the trail gets confused. When that Alend butcher found out he was being followed, he knew what to do. He and his men did a good job of it, I'll give them that. I've got my best trackers working on it, but I think it's hopeless. By the time we locate his trail, he'll hit a road or a stream and disappear."

Geraden wasn't listening. He stared at the body hanging from the stallion. Terisa could see the contours of his face aging. "Argus," he said thickly. "I got you killed."

"Very good," Nyle snarled at him. "This is wonderful. Now you've got the worst of both sides. Without Prince Kragen, you can't stop Margonal's army. But you insisted on stopping me. This way, the Alend Monarch won't have any choice. After he breaks Orison, he'll have to keep it for himself."

Geraden flinched; but he didn't answer his brother. Kicking his horse into motion, he went to face Ribuld.

"I'm sorry," he said. "It's my fault. I should have sent you with him."

Ribuld lowered his head. For a moment, Terisa feared he was going to strike Geraden; he looked savage enough for that. Without thinking, she urged her mount after Geraden so she would be near him.

"Nyle is right," Geraden went on. "I should have let him go. We should have concentrated on catching the Prince."

Ribuld clenched his fists. "Do I look like the kind of man who takes orders from an inexperienced puppy?" he growled. "I thought he was smart enough to watch his back."

Geraden bowed his head and couldn't speak.

The only sounds in the valley were the stamping of the horses, the jangle of tack. Then one of the guards pointed at the bound creature and asked in dismay, "What kind of thing is *that*?"

The Apt turned. Terisa could hardly recognize him: he appeared more dangerous than Artagel had ever been.

"I intend to find out."

"Come on, men," the captain ordered. "The Castellan is going to shit brass when he hears about this. The longer we make him wait, the worse it's going to get. Form up."

He spent a moment arranging more support for the trackers, assigning men to carry messages. Around the streambed, the guards pulled into formation. Terisa found herself beside Geraden between two files of riders who, among other things, clearly wanted to know what she was doing there.

She glanced back at Nyle; his face was closed and locked. Any resemblance between him and his brother had been struck away by Geraden's blow.

Her attacker had eyes in the wrong places, surrounded by long whiskers; he had a snout and tusks. But she didn't notice those things. Instead, she saw blood seeping to a rush out of mottled red fur, blood and death spilling to the white snow.

She was hardly aware of the way her seat and legs hurt as the gelding lumbered into a trot to keep up with the rest of the horses.

The ride back to Orison was cold and gloomy; it might as well have been interminable. Terisa lost track of herself and didn't regain her bearings until she realized that the host of red-furred riders waving scimitars that swept toward her every time she turned her head was just a hallucination, the product of too much gray sunlight glaring deceptively off too much snow. Orison wasn't as far away as her physical condition seemed to indicate, however. Eventually, the riders entered the courtyard of the castle and stopped.

Sliding off her mount's back, she planted her feet in the churned mud and stood on her own, trembling.

The guards dismounted. For a moment, she was surrounded by confusion—men moving here and there, muttering to each other. For reasons of their own, more men came out of Orison, hurrying in groups. The whole courtyard appeared full of guards who ran in one direction or another. Peasants or merchants pushed wagons about. She didn't know what to do with her horse. There was warmth nearby now: it was somewhere in the high walls looming around her. She couldn't imagine how to get to it.

Then the captain barked an order. His squad sorted out its disarray, came to attention.

Castellan Lebbick strode toward them.

Disdaining winter gear, he wore only his characteristic mail and leather, with his purple sash draped diagonally down his chest and his purple band knotted above his eyebrows. Cold steamed off his skin, but he didn't appear to notice it: he had enough fire inside to keep him warm. Though he was shorter than Terisa, he dominated her and the men and even the horses as if he were much taller. Ire glinted in his eyes.

Brusquely, he returned the captain's salute, but didn't speak. Instead, he surveyed the men before him. When he spotted Ribuld with Argus' body, he went abruptly in that direction.

Geraden put a hand on Terisa's arm as if to steady or comfort her. But his expression was too harsh to be convincing.

Rigid with silence, the guards waited as Castellan Lebbick thrust among them to Argus' side. Roughly, he clenched a fist in Argus' hair and lifted the dead man's head as if to check his face, verify his identity. The look the Castellan gave Ribuld was enough to make the veteran turn away.

Lebbick aimed a glare at Nyle's sealed belligerence. Then he considered the inhuman attacker. For a moment, the two measured each other across the gulf of their antagonism and strangeness. Without turning his head, he demanded unexpectedly, "Is this his horse?"

"Yes," answered Geraden between his teeth. "There were three of them. One was killed. Terisa and I would have died, but Nyle killed the other."

The Castellan, however, wasn't interested in how many red-furred creatures had been killed. "*This* horse?" he insisted. "*This* tack?"

"Yes."

Castellan Lebbick moved toward Geraden. In a soft voice, hardly louder than a whisper, which nevertheless sounded like it could be heard on the highest ramparts, he said, "I don't like losing men. Do you understand me, boy? I don't like it."

Geraden didn't try to respond. In any case, the Castellan turned away without waiting for a reply. To the captain he snapped, "Put Nyle and that monster of Imagery in the dungeon. I'll see you, Geraden, and"—he sneered her name—"the lady Terisa of Morgan in the south guardroom."

Trailing wisps of vapor from his shoulders, he stalked away.

"The dungeon," Geraden groaned to himself. He put his hands over his face. "Oh, Nyle. What am I doing to you?"

Nyle raised his voice sharply. "Don't worry about it, little brother. This isn't any different than what you've done with the rest of your life. And Lebbick probably hasn't had anybody to torture for a long time. For him, this will be more fun than a carouse."

Geraden's shoulders tightened. Terisa stared at Nyle numbly. But it was Ribuld who spoke.

"I advise you to keep your mouth shut." He tried to sound casual in spite of the way his voice shook. "Nobody cares what happens to you. If you weren't a son of the Domne—and if your brothers weren't so much better men than you are—we would have let you ride off and make a shitass of yourself in front of the Perdon. You talk about *fun*."

"Ribuld," warned the captain, "that's enough."

But Ribuld couldn't stop. "I'm sure the Perdon would have thought it was fun to be offered the kingship of Mordant"—he was ventilating a vicious grief—"if we captured that fornicating Prince, and the whole Alend army was helpless against us. Geraden did you a *favor*."

Nyle avoided the guard's gaze.

"*Argus* did you a favor, you rotten—"

"*Ribuld!*" The captain's voice cut like a whip. "I said, that's enough."

Ribuld rolled the whites of his eyes, glaring like a wounded predator. His scar flamed with blood. Nevertheless the captain's command caught and held him. He turned his back on Nyle, began untying Argus' wrists.

"He doesn't have any family. Somebody has to bury him."

Lifting the body in his arms, he carried his friend away, out of the courtyard.

Terisa feared that if she didn't get inside soon she would begin to cry.

Dourly, the captain issued instructions to his men. Nyle and Geraden's attacker were escorted rather ungently in the direction of the dungeon. The remaining guards took charge of the horses while the captain himself guided Geraden and Terisa toward the south guard-room.

She seemed to have no sensation left in her. What was going on made no sense, and she was afraid of the Castellan. How had she survived being so cold? It was probably a lie that there was warmth in Orison. She was afraid of Castellan Lebbick because of his relent-less anger. Or was it because she had lied to him?

When had she lied to him? How many times? She had killed one of Geraden's attackers, and all these falsehoods were going to de-stroy her.

In spite of lies and cold, however, a door opened and closed, and suddenly something blissful touched her face. She was inside the castle; she was still cold, frozen almost to the marrow, carrying her misery with her like a cocoon of ice; but the air was warm, warm. She could breathe it. She could stretch out her fingers to it. She tried to clear her throat, and a snuffling noise like a sob emerged.

"Here." Geraden stopped her and undid the front of her coat to let more warmth reach her. "You aren't used to this." He took her hands and slapped them, firmly but not too hard, then rubbed her wrists. "I'm sorry. I didn't realize you were feeling it so much."

She began to shiver again.

He put his arm around her and helped her toward the guardroom.

It proved to be a low hall with a bare stone floor and all its walls unadorned except one, which supported a large slate chalkboard. Most of the space was taken up by rows of wooden benches facing the chalkboard: apparently, this was where Castellan Lebbick ex-plained their orders to his captains and men. The warmth was stronger here; it made her shivering worse.

The Castellan arrived a moment after she entered the guardroom. Slamming the door behind him, he confronted her and Geraden. For some reason, she noticed his hands were curled. At first, she thought that was because he was angry. Then she realized he had spent so much of his life with a heavy sword in his grasp that he could no longer completely straighten his fingers.

He was looking at her closely, and something strange happened in his face. His expression softened; his constant, simmering rage let go of his features.

As abruptly as he had entered the guardroom, he left again.

Mystified, she and Geraden turned to the captain. He shrugged and tried to keep his own surprise from showing.

They waited. Geraden glowered at the ceiling. Terisa shivered.

When Castellan Lebbick returned, he was followed by a maid carrying a tray. There were three brass goblets on the tray. Whatever was in them gave off a sweet, heavy steam.

"Mulled wine," he announced without quite meeting anyone's stare. His manner suggested that he was ashamed of himself. "You look like you could use it."

The maid delivered the goblets to Terisa, Geraden, and the captain, then withdrew.

Straining to conceal his surprise, the captain emptied his goblet with unceremonious haste. Then he gaped into it as though he were fervid for more wine to occupy his attention until someone else spoke.

Geraden looked at his drink suspiciously, as if he were wondering if it was drugged.

Terisa couldn't wait for him to make up his mind. Wrapping her hands around the heat of the metal, she sipped at the dark liquid as though she were sampling nectar.

Mulled wine. She sipped some more. She had never had mulled wine. In fact, she had never had hot wine before. It was lovely. She drank a large swallow. It ran down into her, as delicate as the guards' brandy was rough; and it tightened her shivering into a knot and then released it, so that all the strain seemed to flow suddenly out of her muscles. She was warm again, warm in places that had given up hope. Mulled wine. Her goblet didn't hold enough, but she drank what there was down to the last drop.

In sudden resolution, Geraden tossed down several swallows too quickly, with the result that he inhaled some of the spiced liquid and went into a spasm of gagging and coughing. Trying to help, the captain pounded him discreetly between the shoulderblades.

"Thank you," Terisa said to Castellan Lebbick as she lowered the goblet. "Thanks."

"Don't thank me." The Castellan sounded bitter, but his expression was still soft and ashamed. "You should be more like Geraden. He thinks I put something in it to make you talk."

She sighed—and was relieved to hear no quaver or catch in her breathing. "That's all right. You didn't bring it for him. You brought it for me. I'm grateful."

Scowling, Castellan Lebbick turned to the captain.

"Your report?"

Back on familiar ground, the captain regained his poise. Without wasting time, he conveyed what he knew, described what he had done, and pointed out—rather unnecessarily—that he himself still had no idea what had happened to Geraden and the lady Terisa after Ribuld had left them.

The Castellan absorbed the details, nodded once. "All right. Muster a squad. Send them back where your men found Geraden and her. I want them to backtrack those three creatures. As far as possible. I want to know where they came from. I want to know how creatures of Imagery happened to be mounted on horses and saddles like that.

"While you're at it, set up supplies and relays for your trackers. Prince Kragen isn't going to make any mistakes—but if he does, I want him to pay for them.

"And," he concluded, "find me a falconer. I want to know more about these"—he snarled the words, glancing at Terisa—"carrier pigeons."

The captain saluted. With an unmistakable air of relief, he left the guardroom.

For a long time, Castellan Lebbick didn't say anything. Initially, he didn't look at Terisa and Geraden: he acted like a man lost in thought. Then he began to study them carefully, scrutinizing each of them in turn while his choler mounted. He seemed to be waiting for one of them to speak first, to blurt out something he could use. Or he might have been giving himself a chance to recover from his unaccustomed charity.

The expression with which Geraden met the Castellan's scrutiny wasn't belligerent, but it was tight and wary, and he didn't open his mouth.

For her part, Terisa had nothing to say. The hate in the strange faces of her attackers held her.

Finally, the Castellan pulled up a chair for himself and sat down, folding his arms on his chest. His manner didn't invite Terisa and Geraden to do the same. "So," he said. His gaze was aimed somewhere between them, ready to strike in either direction. "Again something strange happens, and again the lady Terisa of Morgan is involved." He articulated each word with hard-edge consonants and blunt vowels, so that it had an almost tangible impact. "This time, at least one mystery is solved. I don't know who she's plotting with. I don't know why. But finally I know how."

"Plotting?" Geraden was immediately incensed. "Terisa? What are you talking about?"

Castellan Lebbick looked at the Apt. A baleful light was growing in his eyes. "I'm talking about carrier pigeons."

"But that's crazy! She doesn't have any pigeons. Where would she keep them?"

"Perhaps they bring messages to her first and carry her answers back. Then all she has to do is open her window to hatch treachery with anyone in the world."

"No," Geraden insisted. "No, that's still crazy. They would still have to be trained. When has she had a chance to do that?"

"We don't know how much training they need." Lebbick's face had been forged out of iron and extremity. He seemed deaf to the impossibility of what he was saying. "But that's really unimportant. Didn't she come here out of a mirror? A mirror that couldn't possibly have anything to do with her? She's an Imager of some kind." His tone slapped down contradiction. "How do you know how much chance she's had? For all you know, she's already spent years here secretly, getting ready to betray King Joyse."

Terisa shook her head. "You don't understand." She couldn't take Lebbick's charge personally. It was too loony. And she was too tired. "Carrier pigeons only work one way. You take them away from home, and they fly back. That's all. Prince Kragen can send messages to his father. He can't receive them." Then she stopped because the effort of explaining to him that he ought to concentrate on Elega was beyond her.

"You see?" demanded Geraden. "It's crazy. The Alend Monarch is marching an army through Armigite *right now*, and you're wasting your time on impossible accusations. We're going to be *besieged*. Don't you understand *that*?"

For just a moment, the muscles in Castellan Lebbick's neck corded, and his arms clamped hard across his chest. He was at the edge of his self-control. Nevertheless he shifted his glare deliberately to Terisa, as if Geraden hadn't spoken.

"A falconer may be able to tell me whether you're telling the truth. If you are, I'll have to assume that your pigeons are being kept for you by an ally here in Orison."

Geraden threw up his hands, but the Castellan ignored him. "How do you communicate with an ally, when you're reasonably well watched by my men? Through the secret passage in your wardrobe. A child could do it.

"But let that pass for now. In the meantime, my lady, why don't you tell me how you happened to know Nyle was going to meet with Prince Kragen this morning?"

Terisa blinked at him, her heart suddenly quailing.

"For someone as innocent as you are, I call it remarkable that you managed to be in just the right place to spy on that meeting. May I take it as proven that the people you're plotting with aren't Alend? Or are you exposing your own allies to conceal your real plans?"

Worn down by exposure and lulled by wine, she couldn't meet his eyes. Maybe she was as guilty as he thought. That seemed possible. She understood the secret of recrimination: it was deserved because it was received; accusations instilled the sense of guilt that justified them. Because the Castellan looked at her so harshly, spoke to her so bitterly, she deserved it. She had no defense.

But Geraden was already speaking for her.

"Listen to me." His voice lacked Lebbick's clenched and whetted capacity for violence. "I'm going to explain a few things to you." Yet he made the Castellan heed him.

"The first day of the thaw, Terisa and I went out to the bazaar with the lady Elega. You know that." And the more he spoke the more he seemed to push back the pall that Castellan Lebbick had cast over her. "While we were there, we saw a mountebank. Terisa recognized him. He was Prince Kragen."

Terisa felt rather than saw the Castellan's gaze shift to Geraden.

"Purely by chance," the Apt went on, "she happened to see the mountebank and Nyle"—he said the name as if it didn't hurt him— "come out from behind a tent as if they'd just had a private conversation. That was before Gart attacked her.

"I decided the best way to find out what was going on was to have Nyle followed. So I asked the Tor to get Argus and Ribuld released from their duties, and I put them to work on Nyle's trail."

Lebbick's jaw jutted ominously.

"It's that simple." Geraden stood his ground as though he were the Castellan's equal in courage and determination. "She isn't plotting with anyone. If she were using carrier pigeons herself, it would be incredibly stupid of her to let us know she knew anything about them."

Terisa hung her head and kept quiet.

"Very interesting, boy." Lebbick's tone was like the thrust of a dagger. "She told you what she saw, and you decided what to do about it. But I'm the Castellan of Orison. Defending the King from all enemies is my job. If there's any danger in the Demesne or Orison, I need to know it." He was a coiled spring, tightened to the point of outbreak. "Why didn't you tell *me*?"

"Because, good Castellan," a familiar voice rumbled, "you are prone to excess."

Terisa looked up in surprise as the Tor entered the guardroom.

He seemed to be in an affable mood—a bit unsteady on his feet, perhaps, but full of good will. He came into the room wearing a fleshy smile that appeared to have nothing behind it except more fat. The way he walked suggested that he had filled every cavern and crevice of his bulk with wine before venturing out of the King's suite.

"My lord Tor," said Castellan Lebbick between his teeth. He didn't get up. "I'm surprised you trouble to join us. Today would be a good day for men with nothing better to do to stay in bed."

"Ah, true," replied the lord amiably. "Very true. It is my extreme misfortune that there is a voice which brings me the news of this stone pile—brings me the news implacably. Its custom is to whisper, but the closer I drowse toward sleep, the louder it shouts. This morning I thought it imaginable that King Joyse himself would awaken.

"Alas," he went on, "the King seems unlikely to take an interest in the great events of the day. Therefore the burden falls to his chancellor."

Lumbering forward to the nearest bench, he seated himself with a sigh. The stout plank groaned under him.

"That's very diligent of you, my lord Tor," grated Lebbick. "It also happens to be unnecessary. I'm perfectly capable of handling 'the great events of the day' myself."

"Certainly you are." The Tor was like a lump of pastry dough, impervious to sarcasm—and immune to argument. "Doubtless you understand sieges as well as most men understand their wives. I am sure you will do everything that must be done to prepare for the coming of the Alend Monarch. Nevertheless, good Castellan, I must point out"—he sounded kindly, almost avuncular—"that if the matter had been left to you, you would still be unaware of Margonal's approach. As I say, you are prone to excess."

Castellan Lebbick's eyes bulged slightly in their sockets. "In what way, my lord?"

The Tor spread his plump hands. "Suppose young Geraden had come to you with his suspicions of his brother? What would you have done? Why, you would have arrested Nyle, of course. Instead of following him to his assignation and overhearing his plans, you would have tried to take those plans from him by persuasion or force. And if he had resisted both persuasion and force—" The lord rolled his thick shoulders.

"Or suppose again that young Geraden had given you his *reasons* for suspecting his brother? Suppose he had mentioned that hints dropped by the King's daughter Elega led the lady Terisa to suspect that she was involved with Prince Kragen?" Now the lord was no longer pastry dough talking. His voice became like the grinding of heavy stones against each other. "Suppose he had revealed that the guards Argus and Ribuld were following Elega—that in fact they had no other reason for being near enough to save Artagel's life when the High King's Monomach assailed the lady Terisa?" His hands lay limp on his fat thighs, but his eyes grew harder. "Suppose he had informed you that the lady Terisa had rejected Elega's effort to win her support for the Prince—and that, forewarned by this rejection, Elega had made herself fruitless for Argus and Ribuld to trail? What would you have done then, good Castellan?

"Would you have raised a cry against her?" At last he was not an obese old drunk: he was the lord of the Care of Tor, King Joyse's first ally in the campaign that had created Mordant. "Would you have sent men to arrest her so that she could be hailed before her father and publicly accused of treason?"

The Castellan's face was dark with blood, but he didn't unclose his teeth. "It's already done."

For a moment, the Tor looked like he might rise to his feet and shout something. Instead, however, he smiled sadly and slumped back into softness. "Just so. And what is the result?"

"We can't find her."

"Certainly you cannot. She has gone into hiding. And she has bragged, good Castellan, that she knows the secrets of Orison well enough to remain hidden for a long time. And so the opportunity has been lost to learn her intent—the intent on which Prince Kragen's plans hinge, the intent which will deliver Orison to the Alend Monarch without a protracted siege.

"Good Castellan, you have a greater need of me than you realize."

Geraden looked like he wanted to applaud.

The muscles at the corners of Castellan Lebbick's jaws bunched. His eyes scanned the guardroom as though he were looking for the perfect stretch of bare wall against which to spill the Tor's blood. But he didn't rise from his chair.

Slowly, he said, "Geraden, my lady Terisa—you haven't told us where you got those creatures of Imagery. In fact, you haven't told us how you managed to catch Nyle. He's your brother. He knows you. Surely he didn't let you just trip and fall on him. You've been telling the Tor so many stories. Why don't you tell him that one?"

" 'Creatures of Imagery'?" The lord smiled pleasantly at Geraden. "Yes, young Geraden. Do tell us."

Geraden glanced back and forth between the two men, gauging where he stood with each of them, before he shrugged and said, "All right."

Just a few minutes ago, Terisa would have sworn it was impossible, but now she found that she was too warm. She loosened her coat a bit, shifted it back from her neck.

"I wasn't thinking straight," admitted Geraden stiffly. "Nyle wasn't the real danger. I should have let him go so we could concentrate on trying to catch Prince Kragen. But that never crossed my mind. Stopping him was too important—" In an awkward way, he seemed to be asking for understanding. "He's my brother. I couldn't let him make a traitor of himself."

The Tor nodded in an absentminded fashion; his attention appeared to be elsewhere. Sourly, Castellan Lebbick muttered, "It was a little late for that, don't you think?"

Geraden flushed. He didn't permit himself to react, however.

"But I made a mess out of that, too. He got away, and we were stuck out there without our horses.

"That was when those 'creatures of Imagery' attacked. They came from the east, but that could have just been because of the terrain. I thought they were after the lady Terisa, so I wasn't ready for it when they came for me."

"*You?*" demanded the Castellan. "They came for *you*, boy?"

Until then, Terisa hadn't remembered that Castellan Lebbick probably knew nothing about the earlier attempt on Geraden's life, when he had been saved by Adept Havelock.

"That's what it looked like." With a visible effort, Geraden held himself steady. "We separated. They ignored her. All three of them chased me."

Although he still didn't seem to be paying attention, the Tor's expression was beatific, as if he had just received a piece of good news. "Young Geraden, you are a wonderment. I have mentioned—have I not?—that you underestimate yourself. Even the lady Terisa of Morgan does not have such enemies."

"Oh, yes," snarled Lebbick. "That seems especially plausible because you're still alive. You were alone against the three of them. What did you do? *Accident* them to death?"

Somehow, Geraden retained his self-command. Carefully, he said, "I used a club on their horses. Two of them went down. One was killed. The other is your prisoner."

"No," Terisa breathed.

Castellan Lebbick ignored her. "And the third?"

"Nyle got him. He saw them heading toward us, so he came back. Terisa and I might both be dead if it weren't for him. While he was still thinking about that, I knocked him out. I hit him with a tree branch. That was how I caught him."

"No," Terisa repeated. She couldn't help herself: it all came back to her. It was as vivid as dreaming in front of her.

"He was fighting for his life," she whispered. "I had to help him. Didn't I? I can't spend my whole life just sitting on my hands and wondering when I'm going to fade. I can't. That's worse than doing something wrong. Isn't it?

"He got two of them off their horses. He stunned one of them. The other went after him with those swords." She shivered as though she had become cold again, but the truth was that she could hardly bear the weight of her coat. "I had to help him. I killed—With a club. I hit him from behind and broke his skull." A small patch of red fur on the back of the skull had turned wet and begun to gush blood. "Then Nyle came.

"Geraden didn't kill anybody."

She ran out of words and fell silent.

The men stared at her. Geraden's throat worked as if he were choking on her name. After a moment, the Tor rumbled gently, "My dear lady, of course you had to help him. You would not forgive yourself if you had not helped him. And perhaps you would both be dead."

Castellan Lebbick turned away. "Women." Every line of his posture was knotted and bitter. "Always women. It's indecent. If I'm ever saved by a woman, I'll do away with myself."

Then he rasped, "But the horses. That's the point. The saddles and *tack*, my lord Tor. Tell him about the horses and saddles and *tack*, Geraden."

In his uncertainty, Geraden faced the Castellan while he spoke to the Tor. "Our attackers were obviously creatures of Imagery. But their horses looked normal to me. I didn't notice anything else."

Abruptly, Lebbick jerked to his feet. "*Normal* horses, my lord Tor. *Normal* saddles and tack. What do you make of that?"

The lord pursed his lips. "These creatures were mounted after their translation. Either they stole mounts and gear for themselves, or they were equipped by their translators. Equipped and instructed."

"Exactly." Castellan Lebbick faced the lord like a fuse burning dangerously close to powder. "The horses were normal. The saddles definitely didn't come from Cadwal—in Cadwal they use barbed stirrups—but they could have come from anywhere in Mordant or Alend."

"And the tack?" asked the Tor obligingly.

"The tack—" Lebbick stifled a furious gesture by clenching his fists on his hips. "The tack includes a hackamore you won't find anywhere in Cadwal or Alend or Mordant—anywhere except the Care of Tor." His glare was hard enough to strike sparks from flint. "Only your people use it, my lord Tor."

The Tor gazed back at the Castellan as though Lebbick were a curious specimen pinned to a mounting board.

"Perhaps," the Castellan gritted, "you think this is just another of my *excesses*."

He took Terisa so completely aback that a moment passed before she grasped how serious he was. The *Tor*? In league with Vagel against Geraden and King Joyse and Mordant? Her legs were weaker than she realized: she had to sit down. Riding a horse wasn't easy. Without quite noticing what she was doing, she went to the nearest bench and seated herself beside the lord.

Geraden was aghast. "You can't mean that," he protested. "Do you know what you're saying?"

Without warning, Castellan Lebbick grinned. His teeth flashed fiercely.

"Oh, I am sure that our good Castellan knows entirely what he is saying." The Tor had resumed his pastry dough aspect, impervious to affront. "One of Mordant's greatest problems has always been that the vile attacks of Imagery which harass us come from no known source. My son was killed by an enemy who might be hidden anywhere in Alend or Cadwal—or Mordant."

"If indeed your son was killed," the Castellan interrupted. "I only have your word for that—and the word of your men. The corpse you showed us could have been anybody."

Geraden went white at this insult to the lord. The Tor, however, shrugged it aside. "But now," he persisted, "we have taken a great step forward. Now we know where to look."

"In the Care of Tor." Lebbick was remorseless. "In your domain, my lord."

The Tor permitted himself a subtle flare of anger. "Astonishing, is it not?"

"Unquestionably," the Castellan grated with pleasure.

"Unfortunately"—the Tor's ire was instantly gone—"a search is impossible at present. We are otherwise occupied. Please tell me what you are doing to prepare Orison for siege. It is reported that Prince Kragen places great faith in the Alend Monarch's ability to master us almost without difficulty. That seems absurd on its face—and yet I doubt that Prince Kragen is given to trusting the absurd. It is a pity that we cannot question—or observe—the lady Elega. That is beyond help, however. We must be very ready, good Castellan."

"I'll be ready," retorted Castellan Lebbick. "By my estimation, we still have a few days left, but I've sent out scouts to make sure. The fact that the Armigite is a traitor probably has one advantage for us." As he spoke, he seemed to fall unconsciously into the manner of an old soldier delivering a report. "We can assume Margonal will use the main roads through Armigite. They're the easiest, quickest route. So his army shouldn't be hard to find.

"Also, I've sent messengers to the Cares that ought to help us. Fayle. Perdon." Glowering at Geraden, he commented, "What the Perdon hears isn't going to be what your dear brother had in mind." Then he resumed his report. "I've sent men to the Termigan, but he's too far away to do us much good.

"I haven't had time to talk to the Congery yet, but I'll do that soon. Maybe I'll finally be able to scare some sense into those Imagers."

Apparently, none of the Masters had seen fit to announce their intention to disband the Congery.

"In the meantime, I'm calling my garrisoned troops into Orison. Most of the men hunting for the Congery's *champion*"—he was snarling—"have come back, and I won't send them out again. The only men I'm going to risk outside are the ones who still have a chance to locate Prince Kragen before he joins his father, and the ones who're trying to backtrack those creatures. I'll have all my strength here and organized by dawn tomorrow."

The Tor nodded, but didn't interrupt.

"Because we're near the end of winter, our stores are low. That's a problem. But there are quite a few merchants and villages we can call on for supplies. That won't cause them any unfair hardship—with a war about to start, most of them are going to want sanctuary in Orison anyway, so they might as well pay for their safety with food. If Margonal gives us three days, we should be as well stocked as possible.

"But our biggest problem is that breach in the wall."

Again, the Tor nodded. This time, however, his eyes were closed. He looked like he was going to sleep.

"Without that," Castellan Lebbick rasped, "I could hold Orison against anybody. Long before our stores were gone, at least one of the lords of the Cares would take it into his head to come to our rescue. But that breach changes things. I've had all the stonemasons I could find working to build a rough curtain wall across the gap. It's serviceable, but it won't take the kind of pounding Margonal is going to give it.

"Am I boring you, my lord Tor?"

The lord opened one eye. "Not at all, good Castellan. I am merely resting my mind from the chore of trying to imagine the source of Prince Kragen's confidence."

The Castellan's mention of the champion reminded Terisa that she wanted to ask a question. She felt that she was coming back to herself now, recovering some presence of mind and attention. But this wasn't her chance to speak.

"Young Geraden," the Tor went on, "can you remember exactly what Nyle and the Prince said to each other?"

"Pretty much," Geraden answered. "Prince Kragen was worried about Elega. Nyle told him about your talk with her. That shows she knew you were suspicious of her. And it proves she and Nyle were in communication before he left this morning. Then he said that she said that you won't be able to interfere with her part of the plan."

Castellan Lebbick grunted. The Tor raised an eyebrow.

"Nyle had trouble believing that. But—let me try to get it right." Geraden looked at the ceiling while he searched his memory. "Prince Kragen said, 'I regret that she is at hazard. But she has assured me many times that her role is secure. We must trust that she will do what she has said.' "

"Is that all?" demanded the Castellan.

Geraden shrugged. "Nyle still wasn't convinced. But Prince Kragen said, 'The lady Elega's safety and success depend upon secrecy.' He was pretty careful. I'm not sure Nyle realized how many of his questions weren't being answered."

"Poor Nyle," the Castellan sneered.

"Unfortunate," contributed the Tor thoughtfully. "What can one woman hidden in Orison do to ensure the success—the *instant* success—of the Alend Monarch's siege? I confess that I am baffled. I need wine."

With an effort, he heaved himself to his feet. The bench under Terisa flexed in relief.

"Good Castellan," he murmured, "I suggest that you question your prisoners. But try not to harm them. You really must curb your instinct for excess. I suspect that Nyle will be more amenable to persuasion than force. Perhaps he will speak frankly if he can be made to believe that Elega has been caught—that the only way to spare her distress is by revealing what he knows. And the creature of Imagery may let slip something helpful."

"Thanks for the advice, my lord Tor," Castellan Lebbick replied. "Question the prisoners. I would never have thought of that.

"While you're waiting for me to tell you what I've found out, what will you be doing?" His question was an obvious reference to the lord's drinking.

The Tor sighed. For a moment, his thick flesh dropped into lines of sorrow. "Good Castellan, I trust you more than you know. I am sure that you have done everything in your power. Nevertheless I am not content with matters as they stand. I will make one more attempt to interest King Joyse in the fate of his kingdom."

With that, he waddled out of the guardroom.

At once, Lebbick turned a glare like the cut of a hatchet at Terisa and Geraden. "I *like* that. I've been wrestling with this problem for years, and one fat old man thinks he can solve it by howling outside the King's door."

Here it comes, Terisa thought glumly. Now he's really going to tear into us.

She was wrong: the Castellan had more imagination than that. There was malice and anticipation in his tone as he said, "You two still haven't told me what I want to know. But I don't want to be accused of *excess*. And you won't be leaving Orison anytime soon. You'll have plenty of time to talk yourselves into telling me the truth.

"In the meantime, I want you to help me question the prisoners. You should enjoy that."

She and Geraden looked at each other. The room wasn't so warm after all; she no longer wanted to take off her coat. His face held an expression of alarm that worried her. She was so full of her own problems that she tended to forget how much he was suffering. *Help me question*—Did the Castellan really intend to use him against his brother? After what he had already done?

Because she believed Geraden needed her, she rose to her feet and met Castellan Lebbick's scowl.

"You're searching for Elega." She was still afraid of him. Nevertheless she had stood up to him in the past; she could do it again. "Do you think there's any chance you'll find her?"

His jaws chewed iron. Yet in spite of his ire he answered her. He looked oddly helpless, as if he didn't have any choice. "That depends on how many secret passages she knows. I can't spare enough men to search them all at the same time."

"I understand." She had expected that. It was unimportant, however. Her next question was the one that mattered. As if she weren't going off in a completely different direction, she asked, "Is it true that your men never found the champion?"

Is it true that your men never found Myste?

"Those pigshit Imagers," he rasped. "No, my men never found the *champion*. And that doesn't make sense. He must have left a trail. He needs to eat, doesn't he? He must have raided villages for food. That's not the kind of thing a farmer or cattleherd forgets. Even if he went straight for Cadwal, we should have been able to follow him at least that far. But my men couldn't even find *rumors* about him.

"Either he's dead under a snowdrift somewhere, or Gilbur and Vagel translated him to safety. Or he sprouted wings and flew away. *You* tell *me*.

"As for the firecat"—Lebbick gave a bleak shrug—"it just disappeared. They must have sent it back where it came from."

But what about Myste? What happened to Myste?

If the man she risked her life to find had disappeared, what did she do?

"Castellan," Geraden interposed. Terisa had given him enough time to recover his self-possession. "If you're planning to tell Nyle lies about Elega, you don't want me with you. He knows me too well. He'll see the truth in my face. I won't be able to hide it."

Lebbick looked at the Apt. For the second time, his face went through a strange transformation. Terisa expected him to be livid, but he wasn't. Taken by surprise, he was open, accessible to pain: Geraden had hurt his feelings. "I have no intention of lying to anyone." He spoke sternly, but his sternness wasn't anger. "I don't tell lies."

"I'm sorry," Geraden said at once, abashed by the change in the Castellan. "I knew that. I'm just not thinking straight."

"It wouldn't make any difference if you were." Castellan Lebbick's tone was rude, yet his intent may have been kind. "No matter how important the Tor thinks you are, you didn't cause this mess. Prince Kragen told your brother a lot of hogslop. I know Margonal. He hasn't suddenly been converted to benevolence and peace. He's been planning to invade Mordant ever since he heard about King Joyse.

"Come on."

Dismissing Geraden's apology along with his own odd vulnerability, the Castellan strode toward the door.

The guardroom that gave access to Orison's dungeon was unaltered from the time when Terisa had passed through it with Artagel, going to talk to Master Eremis. Despite its resemblance to a crude tavern— its trestle tables and rough benches, its beds and hearth, its refreshment bar—its defensive function was unmistakable. The racks fixed along all the walls held enough pikes and swords to equip forty or fifty fighting men. And the room itself was the only way into or out of the passages that led to the cells.

Remembering Master Eremis made her heart feel weak. He had left Orison without coming to her, without fulfilling his promise. An ache of desire passed over her.

If the room hadn't changed, however, the men in it had. They weren't ill-disciplined and resting: they were on their feet, at attention to meet the Castellan's arrival.

He saluted their captain and stalked on through the guardroom without speaking.

Geraden shrugged and grimaced companionably at the guards as he and Terisa followed the Castellan. One or two of them nodded to him slightly, little signs that they understood his circumstances.

The air beyond the guardroom remained dank, foul with rotting straw and recollections of torture, fretted with hints of old blood. The infrequent lanterns seemed to create more gloom than illumination; the passage wandered as if it led down into the dark places of Orison's soul. Castellan Lebbick took one turn, then another, and reached the region of the cells.

Past his shoulders, Terisa saw two guards coming along the corridor. They walked in single file, apparently lugging something heavy between them.

An instant later, she realized that they were carrying a litter.

Panic leaped in Geraden's face.

She thought dumbly, Nyle?

When Castellan Lebbick shifted to one side of the passage, however, and the guards took the other, she saw that the man lying in the litter wasn't Nyle.

"Artagel!" Geraden cried in relief and consternation. "You're supposed to be in bed."

The guards stopped, and Artagel hitched himself up on one elbow.

"What're you doing here?" snapped the Castellan. "This is none of your business. I've already lost one man today, along with my best chance to catch Margonal's pigslime son. I don't need you bleeding to death on top of my other problems."

"Are you all right?" Geraden put in. Suddenly, he had so much to say that it all tried to tumble out at once. "There was no other way I could stop him. I couldn't talk him out of it. He saved us. He could have let us be killed, but he didn't. It makes me sick. I hit—" His voice caught; he couldn't go on. His whole face burned for Artagel's forgiveness.

But Artagel didn't glance at Geraden. "He's my brother," he replied to the Castellan in a voice like a dry husk. He looked like he had suffered a relapse of fever; his mouth had lost its humor, and his eyes glittered like polished stones. "I had to see him."

One of the guards shrugged against the weight of the litter. "We couldn't talk him out of it, Castellan. He was going to walk if we didn't carry him."

Castellan Lebbick ignored the guards. Facing Artagel, he demanded, "What did he say?"

With surprising strength, Artagel reached out, caught at Lebbick's sash, pulled the Castellan closer to him. "He told me the truth. He got into this because he loves that crazy woman. And because he thinks it's right. Somebody has got to save Mordant. He thinks Margonal is our only chance." Staring at him, Terisa understood that he wasn't angry. He grinned when he was angry. No, what he felt now was closer to despair. "She talked to him about everything in the world except her part in Kragen's plans. He doesn't know where she is, or what she's going to do."

On the other hand, Castellan Lebbick was angry enough for both of them. "Do you expect me to believe that?"

"Artagel?" Geraden insisted. "Artagel?"

Artagel met the Castellan's glare. Slowly, he let go of the sash and eased himself onto his back in the litter. "I don't care whether you believe me or not. I don't even care if you torture him. He's a son of the Domne. No matter what you do, this is going to kill my father."

Geraden raised a hand and clamped it around his mouth to keep himself still.

The Castellan drew himself up. His face showed no softening. Nevertheless he said, "All right. I'll try believing him for a while and see what happens."

For the first time, Artagel turned his eyes to Geraden. The angle of the light from the one lantern filled his face with shadows.

Geraden flinched. Terisa had never seen him look more like a puppy cringing because he had offended someone he loved and didn't know what to do about it. He needed understanding if not forgiveness, needed some kind of consolation from his brother.

He didn't get it.

"You're the smart one of the family." Artagel's voice was still as dry as fever. "You find that woman and stop her. If you don't—and she betrays us—I swear to you I'm not going to let Margonal's men in here, no matter who tells me to surrender. I'll fight them all if I have to."

In response, Geraden's face twisted as if he were about to throw up.

"Oh, get him out of here," Castellan Lebbick rasped to the guards.

"Put him back in bed. Tie him down if you have to. Then call his physician. This air is making him crazy. Right now, he couldn't fight a pregnant cripple."

"Yes, Castellan." The guards settled their shoulders into the load and took Artagel in the direction of the guardroom.

"Geraden?" Terisa put her hand on his arm and felt the pressure that knotted his muscles. "He didn't mean it. He still has a fever. He shouldn't have gotten out of bed." He was so hurt that she wanted to embrace him, but Castellan Lebbick's presence prevented that. "Listen to me. He didn't mean to blame you."

The Apt turned to her. Gloom hid his eyes. He had his back to the lantern; the lines of his face were dark. He didn't respond to what she said. But he continued to face her as he addressed the Castellan.

"That just leaves the creature who attacked us." His tone was as empty as one of the cells. "What do you think you can learn from him?"

"That depends," replied Lebbick. "You're the student of Imagery. You tell me. Is there any chance he speaks a language we can understand?"

Geraden had once discussed that subject with Terisa; he didn't go into it now. "Let's find out."

He and Lebbick started down the passage—and a shadowy figure brushed past them, hurrying toward the creature's cell. "Nobody tells me anything," the man muttered into the air as he passed.

Terisa caught a glimpse of his face and recognized Adept Havelock.

Adept Havelock?

Automatically, the Castellan grabbed at his sword; then he slapped it back into its scabbard. With Geraden, he pursued the mad old man.

Jumping to sudden conclusions, Terisa ran after them.

They were moving too quickly: she couldn't catch up with them in time. In the grip of a sudden alarm, she called, "Don't ask him any questions."

Castellan Lebbick whirled toward her so unexpectedly that Geraden ran into him. Their collision sent the Apt staggering against the bars of a cell. Swearing viciously, Lebbick took hold of Terisa's coat and snatched her to him.

"Don't ask him any questions?"

"That's right. Questions just make him worse." The Castellan's breath was dry and sour. She wanted to explain herself clearly, but everything was happening too fast. "He might tell us something. But not if we ask him any questions."

"My lady," Castellan Lebbick whispered through his teeth, "how do you know that?"

"He told me."

"He *told* you?"

Fortunately, she had no chance to think about what she would say. A chance to think would also have been a chance to make a mistake, to reveal something accidentally. Almost without hesitation, she repeated, "He told me. I guess he wanted to talk to me. But I didn't understand. When I didn't obey, he nearly had a fit."

The Castellan tightened his grip on her. His grin made him look mad, nearly out of control. A second later, however, he dropped his hands and went after Adept Havelock again.

Geraden had caught up with the Adept. They stood together in front of a cell. Lamplight glowed from inside the grid wall.

A snarl throbbed down the corridor. Four furred arms with claws on their fingers sprang between the bars, reaching for Geraden. He jerked backward just in time.

Vehemently, Adept Havelock shoved the last digits of both hands up his nostrils and waggled the rest of his fingers at the creature like a child trying to make his face as horrible as possible.

Castellan Lebbick grabbed Havelock by the scruff of his surcoat and pulled him a safe distance away from the bars. When Terisa joined the three men, the creature was clinging to the grid with all four hands. His chest heaved, and the whiskers around his eyes bristled like weapons. Maybe they're poisoned, she thought, staring at him. Though his features were completely alien, they plainly promised violence.

Swept away from rationality by the creature's strangeness, the Adept's unexpected appearance, the pressure of too many unanswered questions, she observed in a tone of lunatic calm, "The weather sure got cold today."

Trying to lure Havelock into talking with her.

He didn't look in her direction. First he pinched his lips with his fingers and pulled them apart, making a wild grimace. Then he commented, "I've heard of these, but I've never seen one before."

The Castellan started to explode. Geraden slapped a hand against his chest to stop him.

All at once, Terisa's throat went dry. She had to swallow several times before she was able to say, "We went riding today. I nearly froze to death."

Havelock experimented with another monstrous face, but it had no discernible impact on the creature. "A couple of Vagel's Imagers talked about them," he muttered. "Not Vagel himself. But he was eager. In the mirror, all they did was hunt for things to kill. And they seemed to be able to find what they were after without seeing it. They went past the mirror in swarms. But obviously intelligent. They had domesticated animals they used for mounts. He wanted a whole army of them."

In an effort to keep the Adept going, she said the first words that popped into her head. "We were following Geraden's brother Nyle. He went to meet Prince Kragen."

Geraden winced.

"That's right," replied Havelock as though he were in complete agreement. "Festten kept interfering." He bared his teeth in a hu-morless grin, then put his thumbs in his ears and stretched his eyes to slits with his fingers. "If Vagel had his own army, he wouldn't need the High King. Festten found ways to interrupt the research before those two Imagers could finish it. One of them finally disappeared. I think he was killed."

Terisa did her best to pull her thoughts together. Her concentration was in tatters. She had killed—

What were the Imagers researching? What kept them from trans-lating the army the arch-Imager wanted?

Was it language?

Aiming a mute apology at the Apt, she said, "We tried to stop Nyle. That was when they attacked us. They were after Geraden. Not me."

The Adept gave her a smile as high-pitched and unexpected as a giggle. "I know exactly what you mean." The lamplight made his eyes look milky, as if he were going blind.

From one of his sleeves, he produced the palm-sized bit of mirror that Terisa had twice seen him use as a weapon.

For a piece of time that seemed to have no measurable duration, she gaped at him while he murmured to the glass and passed his hand over it. Then a sting of intuition warned her, and she wrenched herself forward, grabbed at his wrist.

She missed. He had already turned away.

Blissfully unaware of her, he focused his glass and shot out a beam so hot that the creature went up in flames like a bundle of kindling.

With a howl of inarticulate frustration and rage, the Castellan flung Havelock aside. Instantly, the beam stopped as Adept Havelock stumbled against the wall and fell to the floor.

But the creature burned like a torch. No sound came from him; he didn't recoil or wave his arms or loose his grip on the bars. Slowly, slowly, he slumped down the grid.

As if in slow motion, Terisa felt a blast of heat. The stench of scorched fur and sizzling flesh filled the air.

Unable to control her reactions, she staggered to her knees. Down near the floor, the air was still cool. The rotten stink of the straw was too much for her, however. Adept Havelock had risen to his hands and knees to watch the creature. When he saw that she was looking at him, he gave her a huge, conspiratorial wink.

Then darkness welled up in her, and she fainted as though she were fading inward.

TWENTY-THREE: ANTICIPATING DISASTER

S he had the distinct impression that she was gone for a long time.

A man bending over her: she remembered that. But who was he? Master Eremis? The idea gave her a liquid feeling in the pit of her stomach. She didn't want to be unconscious. If he were to touch her in any way, she didn't want to miss it.

Now, however, the figure with her was more like a woman. Gradually, she became aware that she wasn't lying on the floor in the dungeon. For one thing, she was warm, really warm—warm all the way down to her toes. There must be a bed under her; no stone was this soft. And blankets—

With an effort, she got her eyes open.

Over her hung the familiar peacock-feather canopy of her bed.

Saddith met her bleary gaze and called softly, "Geraden, I think she is waking up."

At once, Geraden came to her side. His face was stretched with fatigue and worry, and his expression was harried; but when he looked into her eyes he smiled as though she made everything in the world all right. "Thank the stars," he murmured in a husky voice. "I'm glad to see you conscious again."

She coughed at a throat full of gluey cotton. "How long have I been out?"

"Long enough."

Saddith gave a light laugh. "My lady, the Apt is sotted with you.

Every moment that your eyes are not open for him is 'long enough' to fill him with alarm. You have had a much-needed rest. When you have had food and"—she wrinkled her nose—"a bath, you will feel well enough to be amused by his concern."

Terisa smelled the faint rotten scent. It seemed to be in her hair. And in—Her coat was draped over the back of another chair, but she was still wearing her clothes under the blankets. The smell was in her shirt and pants as well. When she lifted the covers, it wafted delicately into her face.

She pushed the blankets away and let Saddith and Geraden steady her in a sitting position on the edge of the bed. A bright fire crackled in her hearth, and the creature had burned—

"What happened?" she asked.

Geraden's smile twisted. "Not much. You passed out. Adept Havelock left. The Castellan swore at everybody. One of the physicians and I brought you here. He said you were going to be all right, but I didn't believe him." He looked away. "Saddith has been telling me her life story to keep me from screaming while you slept."

"Why did—?" Terisa ran her fingers into her hair, then grimaced at the odor which clung to them. She had to breathe deeply to make her head stop spinning. "Why did Adept Havelock kill that poor—?"

At that, Geraden's expression turned harsh. "He's crazy. Even if we knew why he does anything, it wouldn't make sense."

"I can explain it," said Saddith in a teasing tone. "If the rumors are true, the Adept has not had a woman since he returned from Cadwal." With her elbow, she nudged Geraden's ribs. "All men become madmen if they do not bed women often enough."

For no very clear reason, Geraden appeared to be blushing.

Terisa had to get the creature's immolation out of her mind. She had to get the stink out of her clothes and hair. Ignoring Saddith, she said to Geraden, "I don't understand. Why didn't those Imagers who worked with Vagel translate the army he wanted? What research did they have to do?"

Promptly, as if he were relieved by her question, he answered, "I don't have any way of knowing, of course—but I'm pretty sure I can guess. We've talked about language." He watched Terisa's face intently. "When the arch-Imager's cabal came up with an Image of what looked to them like the ideal warrior, they had no way of knowing whether they would be able to talk to him. They didn't believe the question of language would be resolved by the translation itself. That's what they needed to research."

He snorted a sour laugh. "It's funny, in a way. Either High King Festten or the arch-Imager could have had an entire army of those creatures, if they just believed the same thing King Joyse believes. They might have been able to beat him.

"Now we'll never know the answer," he concluded bitterly.

Terisa nodded, letting Geraden push back the memories she wanted to escape from. For her part, however, Saddith didn't appear particularly pleased by this turn of the conversation. As soon as Geraden stopped, she said, "My lady, I have no food or bathwater ready for you. I did not know when you would awaken. But both can be provided almost immediately. With your permission, I will go to bring what you need."

"Thanks." As usual, Terisa's eyes were drawn to Saddith's open blouse and bursting breasts. She made an effort to raise her head so that she felt less like she was talking to Saddith's chest. "I would like that."

In response, Saddith swung a saucy gaze at Geraden. "Be warned," she said slyly. "I will be back too soon for what you desire. Even the hottest youth must have a certain amount of time."

Laughing, she left the rooms.

Terisa eased herself experimentally to her feet.

In a hurry to steady her, Geraden jerked forward. Unfortunately, he missed his balance and nearly fell onto the bed. Terisa found herself holding him up rather than being supported.

Swearing at himself, he pulled away. Apparently, he had lost his balance in more ways than one. Now he looked like he was on the verge of tears.

Geraden? What's the matter? She wasn't sure of what she was seeing. Or she wasn't sure of herself. She wasn't in particularly good shape. In fact, she felt lousy. Where was the Geraden who always took care of her as if she were the most important person in his life?

Inanely, she said the first words she could think of that had nothing to do with what she felt. "I thought I saw you blush. What were you and she really doing while I was asleep?"

He stiffened. Retreating to his chair allowed him to turn his face away from her for a moment. When he sat down, his features were set into hard lines, as if he were angry. Nevertheless she knew he wasn't angry. His eyes were hot with grief.

"I don't understand that woman," he muttered without meeting her gaze. "I mean, I understand. I'm not as ignorant as she thinks. It just doesn't make sense to me." He scowled at the vista of his confusion. "While you were asleep, she wasn't telling me her life story. She was trying to persuade me to bed her right here on the floor."

For some reason, Terisa didn't find this amusing. All at once, the muscles around her heart felt tight.

"She said she hadn't had a man for a while. She talked about it like it was just scratching a complicated kind of itch. Of course, there are probably two hundred men within a stone's throw of us right now who would be glad to oblige her. But she didn't want to do anything that might get back to the man she's really interested in. I got the impression he's been away. Whoever he is." He sighed, but still couldn't bring himself to look at Terisa. "She said I was safe because my heart was set on you, not her. And she would be doing me a favor by teaching me what to do with your body when I finally got my hands on it.

"I couldn't get it through her head that if she kept talking like that she was going to make me throw up."

"Why?" Terisa tried to sound casual, but didn't succeed. "Don't you think she's attractive?"

His gaze turned cold as he faced her. "Sure, she's attractive. A stone wall would be attractive if it looked like that. It's her attitude I don't like. There's more to love than just getting your itches scratched.

"Tell me something." Now he was angry. "Some time ago—I think it was the first morning of the thaw—I was here with you, and Saddith came in. You asked her how Master Eremis was."

The knot around Terisa's heart pulled tighter.

"At the time, I thought that was a strange question. I just didn't want to pry. But the more I think about it, the stranger it gets. Why ask *her*? What would she know about Master Eremis?"

Saddith had tried to seduce Geraden. Terisa sat back down on the bed to conceal the fact that she was trembling—and to control it. In a small voice—putting her emotions at a distance because she was afraid of them—she said, "She's having an affair with him. She tells me about it." She would never be able to admit that she had seen Master Eremis and Saddith together. "I think she believes if she sleeps with enough men she'll end up queen of Mordant."

After a moment, he murmured, "That explains it." He no longer sounded angry. He sounded frayed and alone.

Abruptly, he rose to his feet. "I got a message earlier. Artagel has had a relapse. His physician says it's temporary. He'll be all right. But I ought to go see him. Saddith will be back soon. That may not cheer you up, but at least you'll get some food and a hot bath."

Unable to keep his distress from showing, he turned to leave.

"Geraden, wait." The sight of his departing back seemed to pull everything inside her in a different direction. She jumped upright, reached a hand he couldn't see toward him. "Don't go."

He paused in the doorway. His voice was cramped in his throat. His shoulders hunched as if he were huddling over a pain in his chest. "I have to."

"Please," she said. "I've been very selfish. You're always so good to me that I let myself forget you have problems of your own. Please tell me what's the matter."

He didn't move. Slowly, he put out one hand to brace himself on the doorframe. "Terisa," he said, aching, "this mess really is my fault."

"No, it isn't." She was ready to defend him at once. "You aren't Prince Kragen. You aren't Elega."

He raised his free hand to his face. "Nyle was right. I've been a fool about everything. He was doing what he thought was right. But he was also doing something that wouldn't do any serious damage if he turned out to be wrong. That's important. We didn't need to worry about him. He didn't pose any threat. You and I should have gone back to Orison so that Ribuld could stay with Argus. We should have told Castellan Lebbick about Elega right away."

Slowly, his voice became edged with iron, like the hit of a chisel. He cut off words like chips of stone. "You wouldn't be here if I hadn't gone wrong with that translation. The champion would be here instead. Or else he would have refused, in which case he wouldn't have been translated against his will. Orison's walls would be intact. And Myste would still be here. If anybody could stop Elega, she could."

"Geraden." Terisa went to him; tentatively, she rested her hands on his back. It felt like it had been bound with cords to keep him from exploding. The boyish side of him was dying. He was being taken apart piece by piece, deprived of the things he loved, the things that sustained him. "Please, Geraden."

She would have to tell him.

He had gone too far to stop. "The Alend Monarch is going to take Orison. It's impossible—it *ought* to be impossible—but he's going to do it. And it's my fault. I was *betrothed* to that woman. Maybe we don't have much in common, but I thought I knew her better than this. First Nyle. Now her. Everything I love—"

His throat closed. She felt him struggle to open it. Then he said, "Artagel is right. This is going to kill my father."

She should have told him long ago. "Geraden, don't do this to yourself."

Without warning, he turned to face her. His cheeks were wet with tears, but he didn't look like he was weeping: he looked flagrantly unhappy, almost demented with contempt for himself and his mistakes.

"Artagel thinks it's my fault." He spoke quietly—so quietly that he sounded unreachable. "I expected that from Nyle. But Artagel thinks it's my fault too."

"*Geraden.*" She had passed the limit of what she could stand. To steady herself—because she was afraid—she took hold of the front of his shirt with both hands. "You aren't wrong. I don't know why—or how. But you aren't wrong.

"Do you remember the augury? Do you remember seeing riders?" *Three riders. Driving their mounts forward, straight out of the glass, driving hard, so that the strain in the shoulders of their horses was as plain as the hate in the keen edges of their upraised swords.* "I saw them— I dreamed them before I ever saw the augury. Before I ever met you. I had a dream that was exactly the same as one Image in the augury."

Searching his face, she saw surprise and bafflement dawn into joy. "So there *is* a reason," he breathed in wonder. "I didn't go wrong. You *are* the champion."

"I don't know why," she repeated, insisted. It was the only gift she had to give him, the only consolation. "I don't know how. But there is a reason. You didn't go wrong."

In response, he became brighter and brighter, as if he were burning. His arms closed around her; his mouth came down to hers.

Ardently, she put her arms around his neck and kissed him.

They hugged and held each other until Saddith returned with a tray of food and a porter carrying bathwater.

After a meal, they did what they could to get ready for the coming siege.

By noon the next day, Castellan Lebbick had deployed virtually all the King's guards in Orison, sorting them according to their responsibilities for the defense and maintenance of the castle, and billeting them wherever he could find room. When the barracks became overcrowded, some of the abandoned passages and quarters under the main habitation were brought back into use. Cooks complained about the extra work. Servingmen and -women whose jobs included sanitation complained vehemently. Nevertheless Orison swallowed the additional troops.

Work on the curtain wall across the breach continued.

At the same time, scouts crossed from the Demesne into the Care of Armigite. Although they would have been appalled to encounter the Alend Monarch's army so soon, they began to travel with more caution.

During the night, the men tracking Prince Kragen had returned. The Alend Contender had lost his pursuers in the simplest way possible—by riding onto a road, where his trail couldn't be distinguished from anyone else's. This report inspired the Castellan to curse extensively, but there was nothing he could do to change it.

Nothing was heard from the guards who were trying to find out where Geraden's alien attackers had come from.

Most of the farmers and merchants in the nearer environs of the castle had started to empty their sheds and warehouses and pens and barns toward Orison. Plenty of people still alive in the villages remembered what life had been like before King Joyse had taken power over Mordant and created peace by the strength of his good right hand. They goaded the folk around them into motion.

Grandmothers and flocks of goats didn't move quickly—but they were on their way.

As a result, the courtyard was crowded with activity, and an atmosphere of bustle pervaded the halls. The situation could easily have degenerated into chaos and choler. Castellan Lebbick knew his job, however—and his men knew their orders. Most of the incoming populace found places and got settled without noticing how closely they were supervised. And those who did notice probably didn't guess that the highest priority of the guards wasn't to preserve order, but rather to make sure that Alends or spies didn't sneak into Orison.

Satisfied with the progress of his preparations, Castellan Lebbick paid a visit to Master Barsonage.

The outcome of that visit was less satisfactory. Since the Masters had seen fit to interfere in Mordant's affairs by translating their champion, the Castellan argued that they couldn't now claim to be detached from what was happening. It was their responsibility, therefore, to assist in the defense of Orison and their King. That seemed clear enough.

But Master Barsonage replied with the almost treasonous information that the Congery had disbanded itself. Paralyzed by the very ideals that had brought them together, the Masters couldn't agree on anything. They had no credible purpose. Castellan Lebbick was free to approach individual Imagers as he saw fit—unlike Master Eremis, most of them had remained in Orison—but he couldn't look for concerted decision or action. King Joyse's abandonment of the Congery had finally arrived at its logical conclusion.

Fuming, Castellan Lebbick left.

For his part, the Tor spoke to King Joyse. Or, more precisely, he spoke *at* King Joyse. He wheedled and demanded; he whispered and shouted. He made himself lugubrious, and he tried sincerely to make himself noble. Unfortunately, he received nothing for his pains except a rather strained smile and the absentminded assertion that the King was sure his old friend the Tor would do whatever he, the Tor, thought best. King Joyse himself was really too busy trying to solve the latest hop-board puzzle Adept Havelock had set for him to be distracted by a mere siege. Nevertheless he became irrationally angry when the Tor risked mentioning the lady Elega. The Tor eventually gave up and retreated to the solace of his chancellor's flagon.

As for Elega, two squadrons of guards had searched what they called twenty-five miles of hidden passages in Orison without finding her. The Castellan sent them back to the beginning to start over again.

Pacing the peacock rug in Terisa's sitting room, Geraden demanded, "But what can she *do*?" Terisa had forgotten how many times he had asked the same question, but at least he had the decency not to expect an answer. "I mean, stop and think about it. She has essentially promised that she'll deliver Orison to Prince Kragen single-handed. And she made him believe it. But he knows what a siege is. And he's seen Orison. What could she possibly have said to him that he would believe?"

Terisa sighed and gazed glumly out the window.

As he had promised, Mindlin brought her new clothes for a preliminary fitting. She made a few arbitrary decisions, accepted a few adjustments; he went away.

She returned to the window. Although she loved the springlike sunshine which made the hillsides sparkle and the roads treacherous, she was hoping for snow.

In fact, most of Orison's burgeoning population was hoping for snow. But the next morning brought, not clouds and cold, but a warming trend. Apparently, the weather was on Alend's side.

Castellan Lebbick wasted no time cursing the weather, however. He had other things to swear about.

The influx of people and livestock and supplies was actually going quite well. Of course, life in the courtyard was little better than thinly structured chaos; and people who found themselves quartered in the once unused depths of the castle had to contend with a damp that only grew worse as the walls were warmed by fires and bodies. But there was room for everybody somewhere. And the added livestock and supplies compensated for the increased number of people who had to be fed.

The causes of Castellan Lebbick's compressed fury lay elsewhere.

He had heard nothing from his scouts—but that was good news, not bad. On the other hand, he had also heard nothing from the men who were backtracking Geraden's attackers. As news, that was uncontestably bad. It left open the ominous possibility that an entire horde of creatures was gathering somewhere to sweep down on Orison at the worst possible moment.

Unfortunately, the Castellan also had other provocations. One was that the Tor refused to leave him alone. Having failed to dent King Joyse's detachment, the fat old lord now insisted on knowing everything about Orison's defenses. He wasn't content with generalities: he wanted specifics—the names of officers who had been given certain orders; the quantity and disposition of certain stores; the important routes for moving men and weapons (and water—was the Castellan ready in case of fire?) through the castle. The lord's interference was enough to make a kind man savage.

As another provocation, King Joyse refused to take seriously Lebbick's report from Master Barsonage. "Disbanded?" he snorted. "Nonsense. Barsonage has just lost his nerve. Find Master Quillon." The King hopped a piece on his board and studied the resulting position. "Tell him he's the new mediator. I need those Imagers."

Although Castellan Lebbick gnawed at an outrage that was starting to taste like despair, King Joyse refused to say anything further.

And the lady Elega appeared to have vanished without a trace. The guards not only failed to find her, they also failed to find any sign of her—any little stores of food and water; any clothes; any lamps or candles; any (the guards were thorough) carrier pigeons. All they found was Adept Havelock, who appeared at awkward intervals and treated them to displays of wisdom and decorum that would have embarrassed the ruffians at a carnival. The Adept seemed to be having the time of his life. Nevertheless Castellan Lebbick wasn't diverted.

Behind his anger, and his concentration on his duty, and his determined belief that no one woman could deliver him and Orison to the King's enemies, he was beginning to sweat.

"Do you think," Geraden asked Terisa, "it's something stupid and obvious, like suborning the guards? That might work if nobody suspected her. It's at least imaginable that she could arrange to have the gates opened in the middle of the night."

He was calmer today, which relieved her sense of responsibility for him and freed her to feel worse herself. Perhaps his obsession was starting to soak into her, making her tense and irritable for no good reason. Or perhaps there was something—She ground her teeth at the idea. Something she knew and couldn't remember? Something she ought to understand?

Damn it.

Scowling at the Apt as if he were to blame, she tried to make sense out of the little she knew.

"Tell me something. Why haven't Alend or Cadwal—or both—attacked Mordant long before this?"

"They were afraid of King Joyse. They were afraid of what he would do with the Congery."

She nodded. "And why is Margonal attacking now? Why isn't he still afraid?"

"Because he's heard"—this was painful for Geraden to say—"from Prince Kragen and probably a few dozen other sources that King Joyse doesn't care anymore."

"No." She felt that she was pouncing. "That's not good enough. So what if the King doesn't care? Why isn't Margonal still afraid of the Congery? Why isn't he afraid the Masters will defend themselves no matter what King Joyse does?"

"Because they've disbanded."

"He doesn't know that. *She* probably doesn't know it."

At that, Geraden faced her with an awakening light in his eyes, as if she had suddenly become more beautiful or brilliant. "In that case, she's promised to do something that will keep the Masters from fighting back."

"Yes." That made sense to her. For a moment, she felt vindicated, sharply triumphant.

But she was misleading herself, of course. After scrutinizing what she had suggested, he asked, "What, exactly? What *can* she do? What power does she have over the Congery?"

Terisa had no idea.

This time, it was Geraden who stared morosely out the window. "I told you an early thaw was dangerous," he muttered for no particular reason.

The next day was overcast and gloomy, full of cold wind: it seemed to promise a return of winter. Castellan Lebbick kept an eye cocked at the sky while he fretted at the Tor's persistent attention and stewed over the fact that his scouts hadn't come back. Without realizing it, he fell into the pattern of announcing, when he had nothing more direct or withering to say, that he intended to have the Armigite charbroiled at his earliest convenience.

From a superficial point of view, Orison demanded a great deal of him. The castle was overcrowded—and overcrowding bred quarrels as well as vermin. People were angry because they had been forced to leave their homes. Some merchants were angry because everything they owned had been commandeered; others were angry because almost no one could afford to pay the exorbitant prices dictated by scarcity. Guards were angry because they were being cooped up, or drilled too hard, or assigned to duties they didn't like. Lords and ladies were angry because anger was in the air. Everybody was angry because everybody was afraid. And fear made anger seem more urgent, righteous, and justified.

The truth was, however, that Castellan Lebbick now had the castle organized to function almost entirely without him. His men knew what to do; their officers knew what to do. Everybody was angry, but virtually no one got hurt. The Castellan really had nothing to do but fret and stew—and keep an eye on the weather.

That night, what was left of the squadron backtracking Geraden's attackers rode into Orison: two battered veterans with wounds that still bled, kept open by hard riding. The squadron had been ambushed by a number of the same creatures. And the ambush had taken place not far south of the Broadwine—not far into the Care of Tor.

To commemorate the occasion, the Tor broached a new hogshead of wine. But Castellan Lebbick concentrated on snow. If the weather turned to snow, the men he had sent to the Perdon, the Fayle, even the Termigan might have time to get through.

In the morning, the weather turned to spring.

Sunlight poured through the windows, leaving a gold largesse on the stone floors and the thick rugs. A breeze like a harbinger of flowers wafted through the courtyard. A few patches of bare ground appeared on the hillsides, and some of the distant trees looked distinctly like they intended to bud. Unexpected flocks of birds swirled over the roofs of the castle, lit in loud clusters on the tiles and gutters, and sang.

Shortly after noon, the Castellan's scouts returned to report that the Alend army was already in the Demesne. Barring a cataclysmic disaster or a miraculous reprieve, Orison would be under siege no later than noon the next day.

The scouts gauged that Margonal had ten thousand men—two thousand mounted, eight thousand on foot—and enough engines of war to take the castle apart stone from stone. As it happened, many of the engines were of Armigite design. Apparently, Prince Kragen's dealings with the Armigite hadn't been as simple as the story he had told Nyle.

Unfortunately, that wasn't the only bad news.

Shortly before sunset, a trumpet announced the arrival of riders. Nearly a hundred soldiers came down the road from the Care of Perdon. They looked old and weary, as if they had been traveling for an indecent length of time. They carried the Perdon's banner and wore the Perdon's insignia, and they moved slowly. All of them were injured: limbs were missing; heads and chests, bandaged; faces, haggard. Many of their horses supported litters bearing dead men.

When he realized who the riders were, the trumpeter changed his note to the wail of a dirge.

"Oh, no," Terisa groaned, watching from her window as the procession approached. "He said he was going to do this."

"Cadwal is marching," muttered Geraden grimly. "The Perdon isn't going to come to our rescue. He's already at war."

Then he bit his lip. "We have got to stop her. If she betrays us now, we don't have any hope."

Castellan Lebbick and the Tor met the riders at the gate. The Tor made a short speech. The Castellan didn't know how to express grief or compassion, so he remained silent.

To Orison's welcome and the Tor's speech, the captain of the riders replied only, "We are dying. The Perdon commanded us to come."

The sunset that evening was especially glorious.

Terisa pushed her supper away untasted. Geraden picked at a piece of bread, rolling bits of dough into pellets and tossing them at the hearth. The mood in the room was as dark as the night outside the window. Neither of them had spoken for a long time.

At last, he murmured, "It isn't enough."

"Hmm?" she asked vaguely

For no special reason, they had both neglected to light the lamps. The only illumination came from the hearth. Flickering firelight cast streaks of orange and shadow across the Apt's face; bits of flame echoed in and out of his eyes.

"It isn't enough," he repeated. "Suppose Elega knows some way to neutralize the Masters. For example, suppose—just for the sake of supposing—that she has some kind of acid that eats glass. And she knows a way to sneak into the laborium where the mirrors are kept. *And* she knows where all the Masters keep all their private mirrors. Suppose she has time to ruin every mirror in Orison. That's a lot—but it isn't enough."

As he spoke, she was gradually struck by the impression that his face had changed. The firelight seemed to emphasize an alteration in the line of his jaw, the planes of his cheeks, the shape of his frown. The pressure of the past few days had ground the puppy out of him. He no longer looked like a man who tripped over his own feet and smiled lopsidedly at the results.

"It wouldn't defeat Orison," he mused into the fire, talking mostly to himself. "Castellan Lebbick wouldn't surrender for a reason like that. There has to be some other answer."

Yes, she said inside herself. There has to be some other answer. But she wasn't agreeing with him. She was consciously and explicitly angry. She was angry at Artagel and Castellan Lebbick and Nyle. She was angry at King Joyse, who knew what he was doing to people who had spent their lives trusting him. She was angry at the Masters for their derision, their unwillingness to understand. She had *liked* Geraden's puppyish look. She had *liked* his ability to tumble all over himself without feeling that he was to blame for the destruction of everything he loved.

Why are *we* responsible for Elega? Why is it *our* fault she's probably going to betray everybody?

A moment later, however, her memory brought another image back to her, as vivid as Geraden's face—an image of the lady Myste. Sitting in this same room, Myste had explained to Terisa why she wanted to go after the champion. *I have always believed,* she had said, *that problems should be solved by those who see them. This is more true rather than less for a king's daughter.*

Myste! Terisa murmured with a silent ache. What happened to you? Where are you?

What is Elega doing?

Without thinking, she said aloud, "Water."

Geraden's face shifted through patches of light and darkness until he was looking at her. "Water?"

"Where do we get water?"

His brows knotted in perplexity. "I told you about that during our tour. Orison was built over a spring. But of course it's grown a lot. And we use a lot of water. I think I mentioned Castellan Lebbick has strong ideas about sanitation. The spring has been inadequate for a long time. So we store rainwater and melted snow. Gutters and pipes from all the roofs take water to the reservoir—I showed you the reservoir."

"And now," she said slowly while a keen pulse began to beat in her temple and a hand of tension closed around her heart, "we have all these extra people. And we haven't had any more snow."

"That's one of the dangers of an early thaw." He was watching her closely. "Until the rains start, we won't have anything except the spring to keep us going."

She took a deep breath and held it to prevent her head from spinning. When she was ready to speak steadily, she asked, "What if something happens to the reservoir?"

He still didn't understand. "Happens? What could happen?"

"Is it guarded?"

"No. Why should it be guarded?"

Unable to suppress the excitement or fear charging through her, she jumped to her feet. With both hands, she took him by one arm and pulled him upright.

"What if she *poisons* it?"

The idea hit him as if she had thrown open a window and shown him a completely alien world. His lips shaped the words *poisons it* while he scrambled to catch up with her. In a strangled tone, he argued, "There's always the spring."

"What difference does that make? Fresh water won't help. We'll all be *poisoned*. As long as nobody knows we're in danger, we'll all be *poisoned*. There won't be anybody left to fight. Even if we aren't killed—even if we're just sick for a few hours—Margonal will be able to take Orison almost without a struggle."

"That's right." His face twisted as his thoughts raced. "We've got to warn Castellan Lebbick."

"*Geraden.*" For just a second, she wanted to yell at him. He was being so obtuse.

Almost at once, however, her mood changed, and she wanted to laugh. She wasn't used to being ahead of him. Carefully, she said, "Don't you think it would be better if we *stopped* her?"

He stared at her momentarily with his mouth wide open. Then he let out a whoop that sounded like glee. The firelight was as bright as laughter in his eyes. "Excuse me, my lady." He hugged himself and chortled. "I've got wax in my ears. I'm not sure I heard you right." But joy and relief weren't the only emotions reflecting from his gaze. The flames were warm and glad—and they were also fierce, burning sharply. "Did you say, Don't you think it would be better if we saved Orison all by ourselves? Just you and me?"

She nodded.

"Why should we tell Lebbick? We're just guessing. He might not believe us. If he believes us, we might be wrong. But if we're right this is our chance to prove that you're innocent—that you aren't secretly plotting Orison's destruction."

She nodded again, more because she liked the life in his face than because she thought the Castellan would believe any demonstration of her innocence.

"Blast all glass to splinters!" He hissed the words between his teeth, grinning like Artagel. "Get your coat. It's going to be cold up there."

Terisa got her coat.

It was cold up there.

The reservoir had been built in the highest part of Orison's main body—a labor of construction that was justified by the amount of work saved by being able to distribute water around the castle with gravity instead of pumps. The towers, of course, required pumps; and the waters of the spring had to be pumped up to the reservoir. But those were relatively simple jobs compared to the chore of supplying water for all of Orison.

Terisa had to fill in many of the details from memory. The place was dark: the only light came from the screened openings that let rain and snow and the night air into the reservoir while keeping birds out; and the bright moon outside did little more than glint vague silver across the surface of the water. But she remembered that the reservoir had been built like a pool, deep and rectangular, with a smooth stone walk on all four sides.

Around the walk rose heavy timbers, crisscrossing toward the roof to hold up the network of pipes that carried rainfall and melted snow and even dew from the roofs of Orison—and to support also the scaffolding that made possible the cleaning and repair of the screens. Because of these timbers, the reservoir resembled a cathedral. Against the faint, wet, lapping susurrus, the overarching silence felt like awe. In the darkness, the water looked vast.

It seemed to absorb whatever warmth endured after the onset of night. The reservoir was cold enough to make her chill despite her coat.

"We need a light," she whispered unsteadily.

"She'll see us," answered Geraden, putting his mouth close to her ear so that he wouldn't be overheard.

Terisa nodded. She had hoped she would never have to be cold again in her life.

"Where can we hide?"

For a moment, he didn't move. "How long do you think we'll have to wait?"

"How should I know? I'm just guessing about all of this."

"Well, guess some more."

She made an effort to control her shivers. "All right. Whatever she

562   THE MIRROR OF HER DREAMS

puts in the water will need time to dissolve—or spread out—or whatever it does. But if she does it too soon, people will start getting
sick"—or dying—"too soon. The Castellan or somebody might have
time to figure out what's going on. Before Margonal is ready.

"If I were her, I might wait until the siege starts." No later than
noon the next day. "We might be stuck here all night."

"No." Geraden was thinking too hard to be polite. "If she does
that, practically all our forces will already be on duty. She'll get the
farmers and servingwomen and cooks, but that will just warn Lebbick. She needs to strike tonight, so the water will be bad when the
guards get out of bed tomorrow morning. Tomorrow morning
early."

That made sense. "Where can we hide?" she repeated.

He took her by the arm and pulled her softly into motion. "There
may be any number of ways in here. The floor is riddled with pipes.
Maybe it's riddled with passages, too. But we can't do anything
about that. And there really isn't anyplace to hide. We'll just put
ourselves where we can watch the entrances—the way we came in,
and the other one"—he pointed across the reservoir—"and hope we
get lucky."

"That should be fun," she retorted simply because she needed to
say something. "We're famous for our good luck."

He let out a breath of stifled laughter. "Very true."

Muffled though it was, his laugh made her feel better.

She wanted to test her way with her feet to be sure she didn't fall
into the pool, but he urged her forward as if he were afraid of
nothing. He didn't lead her into the water, however. Instead, he
guided her to a place where a pair of timbers met the floor close
together. They were located roughly midway between the entrances
to the reservoir, and the gap between them was just wide enough for
two people. In this dark, she and Geraden would be effectively invisible as long as they stood near the timbers.

Side by side in the gap, they were pressed against each other a bit
at the shoulder and hip. Initially, she tried to squeeze away from him,
so that he wouldn't feel her shivering. But she would be warmer if
they were closer together. She would be warmer still if he put his
arm around her. After a moment, she found that she didn't mind
letting him know how cold she was.

Turning his head, he breathed her name into her hair and gave her a companionable hug. Almost at once, the pressure that made her shiver seemed to grow less.

She quickly got tired of straining her eyes into the deep dark of the pool, of trying to tell the difference between the light lap-and-slap of water and the possible sound of footsteps. Shifting more toward Geraden so that she fit better against his side, she whispered, "What're we going to do when she comes?"

"Stop her."

She poked at his ribs through his coat. "I know that, idiot. *How* are we going to stop her?"

"Not so loud," he cautioned. "Water carries sound."

She wished she could see his face. He sounded tense and far away, caught up in his responsibility for what happened to Orison. Stopping Elega was like stopping Nyle for him: she was his King's daughter, a childhood friend, and his former betrothed. Precisely because the situation was so painful for him, he couldn't afford to fail.

Almost in spite of herself, Terisa understood his allegiance to King Joyse and Mordant.

"She'll have a light," he went on softly. "She doesn't expect to be caught. And she needs to see what she's doing." Like his attention, his voice seemed to be aimed out into the dark. "When we see her light we'll try to sneak up on her."

Terisa nodded, but her mind was elsewhere. Her head nestled against his shoulder; his coat warmed her cheek. Was it really better for him to remain loyal to the people and ideas he loved? Was that preferable to facing the truth when those people and ideas failed him? preferable to doing what Nyle and Elega were doing—what Master Eremis had been trying to do all along? *How are you planning to live the rest of your life without loyalty or self-respect?* Of course it was always better to face the truth. Wasn't it? Nyle and Elega and Master Eremis had all faced the truth. But she couldn't shake the odd feeling that what Geraden was trying to do was harder.

For that reason, it was a good thing he hadn't been able to return her to her old life. Maybe the sense of unreality that had dogged her for so long was the result of living in the wrong world: maybe she truly had never been a solid being until she came here. Or maybe her evanescence was the result of striving for the wrong things—despite what Reverend Thatcher might have taught her—of not understanding what Geraden understood so well. It was even possible—

Across the water, she saw a wink of light.

Geraden stiffened.

It was no larger or brighter than a candle flame—it flickered like a candle flame. But it flickered because it was moving, passing behind the timbers on the opposite side of the pool. When it stopped, she saw that it was a small lantern.

The hand that carried it set it down on the flat stone near the lip of the pool. The light shone on a woman's features. She seemed to be cloaked in midnight: nothing of her was visible except her hands and face.

Elega.

She scanned the reservoir for a moment, and Terisa cowered; but the lady's lamp was too weak to reach so far. Almost at once, Elega withdrew into the darkness.

Geraden drew a hissing breath. "Now." He shrugged himself out from the timbers. With his mouth at Terisa's ear, he whispered, "You go that way." He gave her a slight nudge in the direction he meant. "When you get close enough, distract her. I'll come up behind her. "Go."

She felt rather than saw him fade into the dark.

Go. Yes. Good idea. But how? One misstep would take her into the pool. Dragged down by her coat, she would drown. She would never learn whether she was right about Elega.

Cautiously, she turned and put one hand on the nearest timber.

The timbers were all the same distance from the edge of the pool. If she felt her way along them, she would be safe. And she had another sign to navigate with: the reflection of the lamp in the water. That gleam was tiny, but it helped her keep her bearings.

Hoping that the pool's wet noises would cover the sound of her steps, she concentrated all her attention on the timbers and the reflection and started moving.

Elega was still nowhere to be seen.

Geraden had disappeared completely.

More quickly than she would have believed possible, Terisa reached the corner of the pool. This side; another corner; a straight walk to the lamp. She was cold, but she had no time for that. She wasn't conscious of shivering.

Elega returned to the light.

Instinctively, Terisa froze.

The lady brought with her a sack about the size of a large purse.

She supported it with both hands as though it were heavy. In contrast, however, her walk and posture didn't betray much strain. Apparently, she feared that the material of the sack might tear, spilling its contents. Her care was obvious as she put the sack down beside the lamp.

I'm going to be too late. With an effort of will, Terisa forced herself into motion again.

But she wasn't too late. Instead of opening the sack, Elega retreated once again into the dark.

This side; another corner. How long would Elega be gone? How far did the light reach?

Where was Geraden?

The lamp made everything behind it blank, impenetrable.

She felt that she was breathing louder than the sound of the water; the effort of muffling her respiration made her want to gasp. Now she didn't need to guide herself by the timbers: the lamp showed her the rim of the pool. But she had to be quiet, *quiet*. No sound from her boots on the stone; none from her heart; none from the tense fear that constricted her chest.

How long would Elega be gone?

Not long enough. While Terisa was still too far away, the lady reentered the reach of her light.

She was carrying a second sack. It was just like the first one. She cradled it with both hands.

Terisa wanted to freeze again.

Instead, she began to run.

At the noise of Terisa's boots, Elega whirled. The cowl of a cape flipped back from her head, and her eyes seemed to gather up all the light, flaring like violet gems. Her face was whetted and intense.

"Terisa, *stop*!"

Terisa jerked to a halt.

"Come no closer!" the lady warned. "You cannot prevent me from flinging my sack into the water. That is not the best way to distribute the powder—but it will suffice." In this light, with such extremity in her eyes, her beauty was astonishing. She looked as certain as a queen. "And one sack will suffice, though I have brought two for safety. Do not interfere with me."

"Elega—" Terisa had to gasp hard to clear her throat, unlock her chest. "Don't do this. It's crazy. You're—"

"Who is with you?" demanded Elega.

"You're going to kill thousands of people. Some of them are your friends. A lot of them know and respect you."

"*Terisa!* Who is with you? Answer me!"

"*You're going to kill your father.*"

Deliberately, Elega adjusted her grip on her sack and started to swing it toward the water. The sack appeared to be made of some unusually supple leather.

Geraden hadn't come. There was nothing beyond the lamp except the dimly silvered night of the reservoir. "I'm alone!" Terisa cried urgently.

The lady checked her swing.

"There's nobody with me. I'm alone."

Elega's eyes burned. "How can I believe that?"

Helpless to do anything else, Terisa replied bitterly, "No one trusts me. Who would believe me if I told them you were going to do this?"

"Geraden trusts you. Together, you persuaded the Tor to be suspicious of me."

"I know," Terisa shot back in desperation. "But you made him back down." Where was Geraden? "And Geraden *can't* believe anything like this about you. You're the King's daughter."

For a moment, Elega studied Terisa. Slowly, she straightened her back; she faced Terisa regally. She didn't put down her sack, however.

"If no one else would believe this, why do you? How do you come to be here?"

Terisa met the lady's scrutiny as well as she could and struggled to hold down her panic. "I guessed. We talked about the water supply. I think I suggested it." Her self-control was fraying. In another minute, she would begin to babble. "Elega, *why*? This is your home. You're the King's daughter. You're going to kill—"

"I am going to kill," cut in Elega impatiently, "a few of Orison's oldest and most infirm inhabitants. That is regrettable. Perhaps my father will be one of them." She grimaced. "Even that is regrettable. But no one else who drinks this tainted water will die. They will simply be too sick to fight.

"Orison will fall with little loss of life." Her voice rose. "At small cost to the realm, my father will be deposed, and a new power will take his place. Then Mordant will be *defended*"—she had to shout in order to hold back an uprush of passion—"defended against Cadwal and Imagery, and the dreams with which King Joyse reared his daughters will be restored!" Her cry was strong—yet it echoed like mourning in the high silence of the reservoir. "To accomplish that, I am willing to cause a few deaths."

She might have continued: the force of what she felt might have impelled her to say more. But she didn't get the chance. All the illumination behind her condensed at once, transforming Geraden instantly out of the dark; and he charged wildly.

In fact, he charged so wildly that he caught his foot on the butt of one of the timbers.

The sound alerted Elega. As quick as a bird, she leaped aside while he crashed to the stone on the spot where she had been standing.

"Geraden!"

The impact seemed to stun him: he looked hurt. Although he bounded up almost instantly to his hands and knees, into a poised crouch, his balance shifted as if the flat stone under him were moving, and his head wobbled on his neck.

Nevertheless he was between Elega and the water.

Terisa hurried to his side. She wanted to help him up, find out how badly he was hurt. But she couldn't take her eyes off the lady.

The two women studied each other across a space of no more than ten feet. Elega's face was dark around the violet smolder of her eyes; she clutched her sack with both hands. Despite the fear pounding in her head, Terisa braced herself to block Elega's approach to the pool.

The corners of the lady's mouth hinted at a smile. In a formal tone, as if she wanted the reservoir to hear her, she said, "My lady Terisa, I am sorry that I did not persuade you to join me. I believed you when you said you were alone. Clearly, you are a better player of this game than I realized."

Nothing about her gave the impression that she was caught or beaten.

Geraden, get up!

Abruptly, he wrenched himself to his feet, stumbled sideways, then recovered. His gaze appeared oddly out of focus, as if his eyes were aimed in slightly different directions. Breathing heavily, he bent over and braced his hands on his knees to support the weight of his sore head.

"Blast you, Elega," he panted, "don't you know we caught Nyle? Castellan Lebbick has him. I don't expect you to care what happens to anybody as minor as a son of the Domne, but you ought to care about the fact that he didn't get through to the Perdon.

"You made a nice speech about defending the realm and restoring dreams. But you can't pretend that anymore. You aren't doing this for Mordant. You're doing it for Alend."

The lady's eyes flared.

"Or you're doing it for Prince Kragen, which comes to the same thing. When you're done, we'll all be ruled by the Alend Monarch. Then it won't be you who decides what happens to your dreams. It won't even be your personal Prince. It'll be Margonal. Once Orison falls, you won't be anybody except the oldest daughter of the Alend Monarch's worst enemy.

"Give it up before you get hurt."

As if she were in pain, Elega lowered her gaze. "Perhaps you are right," she murmured. "You have caught me. I was a fool to believe the word of an Alend." Her grip on the sack shifted.

Terisa shouted a warning—too late, as usual—as the lady flung her sack over Geraden's head.

At the edge of the light, it arched toward the still, dark water.

Geraden leaped for it.

So did Terisa.

Before they collided with each other, his reaching fingers hooked the soft leather and deflected it.

They fell tangled together. His arms and legs were all around her: she couldn't sort her way out of them.

After an interminable instant, she found herself on the floor while he scrambled to regain his feet. She was gazing straight along the smooth stone at the sack. It had landed right at the rim of the pool—so close that she could have put her hand on it.

But it had split open when it hit. A strange green powder was already pouring into the water. As she watched, the sack slumped empty.

Then the light went out.

A heavy splash cast sibilant applause around the reservoir as the other sack sank into the pool.

Across the dark, Elega said, "Prince Kragen is a truer man than you are, Geraden fumble-foot. He will not be false to me."

Small waves continued to slap and echo against the sides of the pool long after the King's daughter was gone.

TWENTY-FOUR:
THE BEGINNING
OF THE END

ater that night, a small band of men on horseback launched an attack that no one understood at the time against the heavy gates of Orison. With a great whooping and hallooing, the men charged forward, shot burning arrows into the wood or up at the parapets, then brandished their swords and challenged the defenders to come out and fight instead of cowering inside the walls like girls.

Their arrows had no effect on the gates: some of Castellan Lebbick's guards had spent the past four days soaking the wood with water. And the attackers themselves seemed more drunk than dangerous. Nevertheless they made enough noise to be heard by every man on duty around the walls.

While the captain in command of the watch readied a sortie, the riders escaped. They could be heard laughing derisively for a few moments after the night had swallowed their retreat.

When this was reported to the Castellan, he had less to say about it than might have been expected. By that time, he had passed from his usual fulminating outrage into a tightly coiled fury that resembled equanimity. He looked almost cheerful as he went about his work, preparing Orison to meet an Alend siege with a totally inadequate supply of clean water.

Sometime earlier, Terisa and Geraden had had the disconcerting experience of appearing to improve his mood by telling him about their encounter with the lady Elega.

When they first approached him, he acted like a man who was savage with lack of sleep. His eyes had a harried cast, and some of his gestures seemed aimless, as if he weren't aware of making them. His personality changed stress and fatigue into ire, however. His problem was that he had nothing to do: Orison was as ready as possible for a struggle he had no expectation of winning. Because he couldn't rest, he was in danger of driving his own forces ragged before the real test of their strength began.

He had never been very good at resting. The strict urgency inside him kept him on his feet. Now, however, he couldn't rest because rest meant sleep—and sleep meant dreams.

His dreams were haunted.

As a younger man, he had occasionally had nightmares about his revenge on the Alend garrison commander who had raped and tortured his wife of four days with such relish and variety. But over the years the stable mildness of her companionship—and the clear worth of the work he did for his King—had taken the sting out of those dreams.

But now she was dead. He was alone—effectively abandoned even by King Joyse. And when he dreamed, he didn't dream of revenge.

He dreamed that he was an Alend garrison commander with a young Termigan sod's nubile bride tied helpless in front of him. He dreamed of all the things that could be done to her to make her scream and her husband mad.

He dreamed of relish.

And he awoke trembling—*he*, Castellan Lebbick, *trembling*, a man who hadn't quailed in the face of any dread or danger since the day when King Joyse had cut him free and let him take his revenge.

At the sight of Geraden's stiff-faced determination and the woman Terisa's stubbornly controlled alarm—alarm which he instinctively wanted to justify—something leaped through him like fire in a mound of dry brush.

By the time Geraden finished describing what Elega had done, Castellan Lebbick was smiling.

"Congratulations," he said almost genially, "Here's another triumph for you. The lady Terisa"—he spoke as if she weren't present—"gave you the perfect chance to do something right for a change—and what did you do? You decided to be a hero by saving Orison alone. You must be particularly proud of yourself."

"That's not fair," the woman put in unexpectedly. Despite her alarm and her downcast gaze, she had courage. "You make it impossible for anybody to tell you anything. If I turned out to be wrong—if Elega did something else while you were guarding the reservoir—you would accuse us of conspiring to distract you."

Yes, the Castellan mused, she was an interesting woman. And her turn was coming. Someday soon he would have her in his power. Then she would learn what it really meant to be accused. He would teach her thoroughly.

He still found it difficult to distrust the Apt: as the Domne's son and Artagel's brother, Geraden had an automatic claim on Castellan Lebbick's good opinion. And he had stopped Nyle. That may have been stupid, but it was certainly honorable.

The woman, on the other hand—

Curious, wasn't it, how she just happened to be the one who became suspicious of Elega—how she just happened to be the one who figured out what Elega was doing. All Lebbick knew of her was that she was an Imager. And that she acted like an enemy of Alend. And that High King Festten wanted her dead. And that she lied to him when the truth would have helped him serve his King. The rest was inference, speculation, dream.

The smile with which he regarded her would have curdled milk. Still addressing Geraden, he asked, "Do you know what I'm going to have to do now?"

"Yes, Castellan." The Apt sighed as though he anticipated more abuse. "You're going to have to face this whole siege with only the spring for water."

"That's right. We've doubled our population. That spring doesn't give a tenth of what we need. We're going to have to ration water severely. I'm going to have to put pregnant women and tired old men and children on rations that will make them ache with thirst. Because you thought it would be fun to be a hero for a change. And that's not all."

"No, it's not."

Regardless of what Geraden felt, he faced Lebbick without flinching. The Castellan liked that. Not so long ago, the Apt would have flinched.

"You're also going to have to flush out the reservoir and all the pipes. If you don't do it—and do it soon—people who get thirstier than they can stand are going to start sneaking drinks. If they're weak enough, they'll die.

"Flushing everything will use water, too. You won't have much left to ration."

The Castellan nodded. No matter how stupidly he behaved, the Apt wasn't stupid. In fact, considering his obvious intelligence, it was amazing how consistently he managed to go wrong.

"Are you sure she poisoned the water?"

Geraden frowned. "Do you mean, am I sure she knew what she was doing? No. And I haven't tested it. But whatever was in those sacks was a powder, and it was green. I only know one kind of green powder. It's a tinct the Masters use. They call it 'ortical'—it was first mixed by an Imager named Ortic. There must be a hundredweight of it stored in the laborium." He didn't look away. "That stuff will make you sick if you just get too much of it on your hands."

"Is there a counteragent?"

"Who knows? Imagers don't *eat* tinct. And they don't spend their time trying to cure people who do."

"If I ask your Master Barsonage, will he be able to tell me if any ortical is missing?"

"No. Nobody supervises the Masters when they're working. Quite a few of them still like to keep the ingredients they use secret. But one of the younger Apts might have noticed a sudden drop in the amount of ortical on the shelves."

Again, the Castellan nodded. Without warning, he addressed Terisa for the first time. "How did you know what the lady Elega was going to do?"

In a small voice, she replied, "I guessed."

"You *guessed*?"

"I put together some things she said." She became stronger as she spoke. "They weren't even enough to be called hints. I put them together and just guessed."

"My lady," Castellan Lebbick announced in a contented tone, "I don't believe that." Then he dismissed her and Geraden.

He didn't need to plan what had to be done. It was already clear to him, step by step. He was the Castellan of Orison; he knew how to serve his King. In the end, it made no difference what the odds were against him. How badly Orison was damaged. How much he was outmanned. How far King Joyse failed. Castellan Lebbick had made himself more like a sword than a man—and a sword knew nothing about surrender.

In the meantime, he had something to look forward to. That woman's turn was coming.

Geraden took her back to the peacock suite, then went to his own rooms to try to get some sleep. But neither of them slept much.

No one in Orison slept much.

Of course, many of the castle's inhabitants were awake because they were too tense to sleep. A large number of people didn't have that problem, however. They were guards who were either too experienced or too tired to stay awake; parents whose overexcited children had worn them out; merchants who knew that their own survival—and even their profits—would probably be more rather than less valuable after the siege, regardless of who won. They were servants who were so badly overworked that they couldn't afford sleeplessness; Masters who lacked imagination; lords who didn't understand and ladies who were philosophical.

These people didn't get much sleep because Castellan Lebbick and his men woke them up.

Despite his quickness, the Castellan was too late to save two old men who were accustomed to make several trips to the lavatory during the night, a handful of guards who came off watch and refreshed themselves before they were warned, and several children who roused their parents crying for water. But these unfortunate incidents at least served to confirm that Elega *had* poisoned the reservoir —that the harsh measures which Lebbick imposed on the castle were necessary. The children were desperately sick, but no one died except one of the old men.

And in the morning nearly everybody tried to crowd out onto the battlements or around a window to watch for the Alend army.

In that respect, Terisa and Geraden were fortunate. They had no trouble gaining access to the top of the tower that held her rooms.

During the night, the weather had turned cold again. A featureless gray cloud wrack had closed down over Mordant, turning the castle and the landscape the color of gloom; a chill wind blew like a scythe, reaping away every sign of an early spring. The nearby hills lost depth; the ones farther away looked higher, more dangerous. The black trees tossed their limbs as if they were writhing. Corrupt snow still clung to most of the slopes, making the bare ground appear unwell. At first, she could hardly see: the cold felt like a slap, and the wind in her face made her eyes tear. Gradually, however, her vision improved until she was able to scrutinize the horizons in the direction of Armigite and Alend just as the crowds on the lower battlements and the people on the other towers did.

There was nothing to see.

For a long time, there was nothing to see. By degrees, the crowds thinned. Twice, Terisa and Geraden broke their vigil and returned to her rooms to get warm.

"When are they coming?" she asked.

"How should I know?" he replied with uncharacteristic asperity. He was taking his failure to stop Elega hard.

She knew how he felt and didn't blame him.

"Which direction are they going to come from?"

He repented his testiness. "Along the road. That's longer, but it should be quicker. And it's the only way they can bring their supplies. Or the 'engines of war' we keep hearing about."

When they went back outside, she learned that he was right. Warned by an indefinable stiffening of attention around her, she peered harder into the harsh wind and saw the vanguard of the Alend army coming.

It was on the northwest road from the Care of Armigite.

The Alend Monarch's flags flew in the hands of his standard-bearers. The gray light and the distance made them look black.

Slowly, the army marched toward Orison—a body of men that seemed huge beyond counting. Soldiers on horses. Soldiers on foot. Dozens of drivers goading the mules that dragged the supply wains. Swarms of transformed servants and impressed peasants who steered and tended the lumbering siege engines. And a second army of porters and camp followers.

All come to take Orison away from Mordant's King.

Held by a kind of awe, she stared out from the tower and tried to imagine the amount of bloodshed King Joyse's actions threatened to bring down on his people.

Perhaps he was imagining the same thing. Geraden nudged her and pointed toward the north tower. Squinting in that direction, she saw King Joyse standing before the parapets with Castellan Lebbick.

He looked small across the length of Orison, despite his heavy fur cloak. Both he and his Castellan studied the Alend advance without moving. Perhaps there was nothing they could do. The flags of Mordant had been raised over the battlements, but the King's personal banner snapped painfully from the end of a pole on the tower where he stood. It was a plain purple swath that might have appeared jaunty and brave under bright sunlight. Now it looked as if it was about to be torn away by the wind.

After a while, he and Castellan Lebbick left the tower.

For no reason that Terisa could see, Orison's trumpeter winded his horn. He may have been blowing a call to arms; it sounded more like a wail.

With ponderous precision, like a display of inevitability, Alend's army invested the castle.

Ten thousand soldiers surrounded the walls and presented their weapons. The siege engines were rolled into position. Then the Alends bugled a signal of their own, and a party of riders formed around the Alend Monarch's standard-bearer. The standard-bearer added a flag of truce to Margonal's assertive green-and-red pennon. Together, the flags and the riders approached the gates of Orison.

Orison's trumpeter responded. The gates rose.

With six men behind him, Castellan Lebbick rode out to meet the Alend party.

He wasn't surprised to see that the Alends were led by Prince Kragen. Nor, after his conversation with King Joyse, was he surprised by the fact that one of the riders was the lady Elega.

The two groups stopped and eyed each other across a short distance. The Prince was steady, but Elega didn't meet Castellan Lebbick's glare.

After a long silence, Prince Kragen said, "Greetings, Castellan. Your King's folly has brought us to this."

The Castellan was holding his horse with too tight a rein: the beast couldn't stand still. As it shied from side to side, he rasped, "Say what you came to say and be done with it, my lord Prince. I have better things to do with my time."

Prince Kragen's gaze darkened. "Very well," he snapped. "Listen carefully, Castellan."

In a formal tone, he announced, "Margonal, the Alend Monarch and Lord of the Alend Lieges, sends greetings to Joyse, Lord of the Demesne and King of Mordant. The Alend Monarch asks King Joyse to meet with him under a flag of truce, so that together they may find some way to avert this conflict. King Joyse has refused to hear requests for peace from the Alend Monarch's ambassador. Nevertheless it is peace the Alend Monarch desires, and he will pursue that desire openly and fairly with King Joyse, if the King will consent to meet him."

"A pretty speech," Castellan Lebbick retorted without hesitation. "Why should we believe you?"

"Because," the Prince shot back, "I do not need to make pretty speeches. Your wall is broken—and not well repaired, I observe. You have no stores of clean water. Your men are too few. You cannot endure a siege, Castellan. The Alend Monarch has no reason to offer you peace—no reason except the sincerity of his desire."

" 'The sincerity of his desire.' " Lebbick jerked at his mount. "I like that—from an Alend.

"All right. Here's your answer.

"King Joyse asks me to point out to you—and to your illustrious father—that neither of you understands hop-board. You wouldn't have gotten as far as a stalemate without help. Instead of waving your swords at us, you ought to remember what happened the last time you went to war with Mordant."

The wind cut between the horses. "By the stars, Lebbick," cried out the lady Elega, "is he *still* playing hop-board? Tell him to *surrender*!"

The Castellan didn't shift his gaze from Prince Kragen's face. "The King's daughter," he remarked. "That attack last night was a diversion, so she could get out of Orison." As soon as King Joyse had said this, Lebbick had cursed himself for not realizing the truth immediately. "What do you plan to do with her now? Is she a hostage?"

Prince Kragen spat an oath. With an effort, he resumed his formal tone. "The Alend Monarch welcomes the lady Elega as a friend. He has no intention of offering any harm, either to her, or to her father in her person. This courtesy, also, he provides as a demonstration of his desire for peace."

"I have an answer for that, too." For the first time, Castellan Lebbick used the exact words he had been given. "King Joyse replies, 'I am sure that my daughter Elega has acted for the best reasons. She carries my pride with her wherever she goes. For her sake, as well as for my own, I hope that the best reasons will also produce the best results.' "

The lady Elega stared at Castellan Lebbick as if he had said something horrible.

"*That* is an *answer*?" demanded the Prince.

"Take it and be satisfied," the Castellan replied. "You ought to like it better than the denunciation she deserves. Ask her"—King Joyse had specifically forbidden him to say this—"if she wants to know how many people died this morning."

Prince Kragen ignored that jibe. "You misunderstand me deliberately, Castellan. Have you given me your King's answer to the Alend Monarch's desire for truce? Is he that far out of his senses?"

Riding the strength of the fact that King Joyse had actually talked to him—however strangely—Castellan Lebbick had no trouble finding a retort. "I don't advise you to put it to the test."

"Then hear me. Hear me well, Castellan." Prince Kragen's anger was fierce. "This is my last word.

"Your King leaves us no choice. We *cannot* 'be satisfied.' Cadwal is marching. You know that Cadwal is marching. Where we stand, we are more vulnerable than you to the High King's great force. We cannot defend you, or your people, or the Congery—"

"Or yourselves."

"—or *ourselves* if we do not take Orison. King Joyse compels us all to a war he cannot win, regardless of the cost to us. He *must* offer peace. By peace or by blood, we *must* have Orison."

The Castellan fought his horse still. "*That* is your *last word*?" He was grinning.

"Yes!"

"Then here's mine." Lebbick knew what to say, although he didn't understand it. "King Joyse assures the Alend Monarch that he has more choices than he realizes. King Joyse suggests you withdraw to the west of the Demesne and await developments. If you do that, he'll be glad to meet the Alend Monarch under a flag of truce and offer more suggestions.

"If you don't"—the Castellan could barely conceal his own surprise at the threat he had been instructed to deliver—"King Joyse intends to unleash the full force of the Congery against you and rout you from the earth!"

At the moment, he didn't care whether or not the King's gambit would succeed. He was simply glad that he had been allowed to say those words.

Silence seemed to shock the gathering. For a time, no one could respond. In spite of himself, Prince Kragen gaped in anger and dismay.

Then the lady Elega whispered intensely, "Castellan Lebbick, you lie." Her face was pale in the harsh wind. "My father would never do such a thing."

As if she had commanded it, the Prince snatched the flag of truce from the standard-bearer, broke its shaft across his knee, and threw the pieces into the road. Wheeling his mount, he led his party back to the Alend lines.

Castellan Lebbick and his men returned to Orison. The gates thudded shut behind them.

The Alend bugler sounded another call. All around the castle, camp followers and servants began to unpack wagons and pitch tents. The siege of Orison had commenced.

"I've got to go see Artagel," Geraden said as if he were proposing to have his legs broken. "He'll want to hear what's happened." The cold made his nose run; he sounded congested and miserable. "If he can't forgive me for letting Prince Kragen get away, at least there isn't anything worse he can do to me for letting Elega poison the water."

Terisa offered to go with him, but he declined her company. He wanted to face his distress alone.

When he left, she went back to her rooms.

She had a great deal to think about. She needed to decide where she stood in relation to what was happening around her. She needed to define her own loyalties. She needed to decide how far she was willing—or able—to pursue the commitment she had apparently given Geraden by telling him about the connection between her dream and the augury.

Instead, she found herself thinking about Reverend Thatcher.

She had worked for him for almost a year—long enough to forget why she had originally accepted the job as his mission secretary. Since then, what she tended to remember about him was his dogged ineffectuality. But she hadn't seen him that way at first. No, at first she had gone looking for a mission job to make up for the emptiness and wealth of her background, the uselessness which eroded her sense of herself. And she had taken the job Reverend Thatcher offered because of his dedication against impossible poverty and callous disregard.

At the time, of course, she hadn't realized that he was ineffectual. Now, however, she began to wonder whether that perception was accurate. In his place, wouldn't Geraden have done just what he did?

Wouldn't Geraden have held true in the face of any failure? Wasn't the real failure of her mission work in her? A failure of heart?

Wasn't it possible to live as if she could hear horns?

What she was thinking didn't solve anything. But it was necessary, and she stayed with it. At least it taught her to understand that she owed Reverend Thatcher an apology.

Later, she became aware that she was tired enough to sleep.

The idea of a nap was unexpectedly appealing. She hadn't slept well the night before. And no amount of fatigue or wakefulness was going to do Orison any good. Humming to herself, she added wood to both fires to keep her rooms warm. Then she took off all her clothes, tossed them onto a chair, and slipped herself into bed.

For a while, she listened to the hungry wind scraping its claws on her window, on the corners of the tower. But as soon as the cool sheets gained heat from her skin, she fell asleep.

Deep in dreams, she received the delicious impression that she was being kissed.

A strong mouth covered hers. A tongue stroked her lips, probing delicately between them. She tasted cloves.

Under the blankets, a hand caressed her belly, then moved up to her breasts. Its touch was just cool enough to make her nipples harden.

When she realized that she wasn't dreaming, she opened her eyes.

Master Eremis was bending over her; his pale gaze met hers. Her father had eyes like that. But the crinkles around them suggested that he was grinning.

He startled her so much that she clutched at the blankets and jerked her head away from him.

Pulling back a little, he withdrew his hand from her body. The ends of his chasuble swung carelessly against the front of his accustomed jet cloak. He was definitely grinning. In fact, he seemed to be in excellent spirits.

"My lady," he said, "I fear I have frightened you. Do forgive me."

Staring up at him through the gray light from the windows, she thought that he was uglier than she remembered: his face was too much like a wedge; his hair sprouted too far back on his skull. Yet that only made the lively intelligence of his expression more magnetic.

She pulled the covers tightly over her shoulders and blinked at him in confusion. "How—?"

"The wardrobe." His smile stretched wider. "I was exploring hidden passages and had the good fortune to find your room."

"Where—?" She sat up a bit. Her mind refused to function. She had been more deeply asleep than she realized. How had she gotten out of the habit of putting a chair in that wardrobe? "Where were you? I thought I would see you."

He seated himself on the edge of the bed, then reached out a hand and ran his fingertips down the line of her neck from her ear to her shoulder. "I was required at home. I think I have mentioned Esmerel?" His touch felt like a signature on her skin. "My grandfather called it our 'ancestral seat,' though Esmerel is not really as grand as that. My father is still less grand, however, and does not use such language."

Master Eremis plucked lightly at the sheet she held in front of her. "In his blunt way, he demanded my presence. It seems that one of my brothers killed the other—although with that pair the truth has often been difficult to determine. My father wanted me in front of him while he decided whether to disinherit the survivor in my favor.

"Esmerel is in the Care of Tor—fortunately a ride of only two days beyond the Broadwine. I have just returned."

She could hardly swallow. If he went on looking at her like that, she was going to forget everything that had happened while he was away. His fingers were curled gently over the edge of the sheet covering her. Soon he would begin to pull it down, and she wouldn't be able to resist. She didn't know that she wanted to resist. Her head seemed to be full of forgotten dreams. It was impossible to think.

With an effort, she asked, "What did he decide?"

The Imager shrugged to show his disinterest. "My father hates me. As do—or did—both my brothers. So it is remarkable that they have always done what I wished. I have no use for Esmerel at present. Therefore my brother will inherit it. If my father has the good sense to die soon."

He leaned toward her, and his mouth took hers again. The scent of cloves seemed to fill her senses. His hand urged the sheet downward, and his tongue had to be answered. No, she couldn't resist. His palm rubbed her nipple until she shivered at his touch; then he cupped her breast possessively. She was his—

Somehow, she pushed him back. A flush on her cheeks, and

breathing raggedly, she faced him as well as she could. "Why does your family hate you?"

His smile was gone: his eyes burned with an intensity that made her melt. "My lady, I did not come here to discuss my family. I came to claim you at last."

Without thinking, she rolled away from him and got out of bed. Momentarily defying her nakedness, she went to the chair where she had left her robe. Her hands shook as she pulled the velvet onto her shoulders and knotted the sash; her voice shook as she spoke.

"You were gone for a long time. I waited for you. I wanted to help you. I was ready—" Ready to do almost anything. "But you didn't come. I didn't hear from you."

Despite her resistance, she was close to panic at the thought that he might take offense and leave, that by retreating from him she had sacrificed her chance to be touched and kissed. He didn't look offended, however. His smile was too acute to be affectionate; yet he gazed at her with a new eagerness, as if she had become a challenge.

"My lady," he said thoughtfully, "I regret that you did not hear from me. That was not my intention. I sent word to you several times. But perhaps my messages were intercepted."

She started to ask, Who would intercept—? before she understood what he was saying. He hadn't meant to leave her without saying goodbye. That changed everything. Didn't it? Almost babbling, she said, "You sent messages with Saddith. But she's your lover. She wants you for herself, so she didn't give me any of your messages."

For an instant, the Master's eyes widened as if she had surprised him. A grin quickly altered his expression, however. Now his excitement was unmistakable. His tone was both careful and jocose as he said, "My lady, you cannot possibly be jealous of a maid like Saddith. Nearly all the men she has ever known have been between her legs. I can believe that she did not deliver my messages. But I cannot believe it matters that I have taken advantage of her crass charms."

Terisa's emotions were in an alarming muddle. Her relief that he had tried to send word to her lasted only a moment. It was replaced almost at once by the sense that the information came too late. It didn't change anything after all. She had made her commitment without him—had put herself on Geraden's side. And not just by default: not just because the Apt was present and Master Eremis was absent. She had chosen Geraden because to distrust him—to spy on him, to betray him, as the Master had demanded—was intolerable. If only Eremis had come to her sooner. She bit her lip to try to keep her distress from showing on her face.

Still smiling, he studied her narrowly. After a moment, he said, "Saddith is of no importance, however. I will dispense with her to please you. You asked about my family."

She nodded dumbly, hanging on every word he said while her heart hurt.

"It is a small family. Esmerel is a small estate, though beautiful. My grandfather was a man of high intelligence—and even higher refinement. He had an exceptional understanding of both knowledge and pleasure. And he dabbled in Imagery. In truth, one of our family legends is that he was acquainted with the arch-Imager Vagel. Of course, that was before the wars for Mordant, during which the arch-Imager went into High King Festten's service.

"Unhappily, my grandfather had but one son, and that one son was a lout. Beauty and refinement were as blank as stone walls to him. He understood nothing except violence—and the pleasures of violence. When he came into possession of Esmerel, he spent years debauching its beauties as well as himself. Then he became a petty brigand to preserve some semblance of wealth in his 'ancestral seat.'

"The accidental result of his debauchery was that he had three sons. The first was an exact duplicate of himself—therefore much loved. The second was a bit smaller, a bit less muscular, and a bit more cunning—therefore tolerable.

"I was the third."

The Master's voice was part of his spell. Terisa expected him to move toward her. The way he studied her made her feel that he was moving toward her. Her pain seemed to hypnotize her. But he remained motionless beside the bed.

"Fortunately," he observed, "I was a good deal stronger than I looked. To all appearances, I was the runt of the litter, and my father despised me accordingly. For that reason, my brothers sought to earn his approval by tormenting me." He spoke calmly, but the glint in his eyes was as calm as a hatchet. "On one occasion, I recall, they locked me in a wooden shed and set it afire to see what I would do."

Breathing through parted lips as if she were rapt—or appalled— she asked, "What did you do?"

He chuckled. "I tricked them. I was no heir to Esmerel, but I was my grandfather's heir in intelligence. Before I was old enough to be afraid, I was clever enough to protect myself. And soon I learned that the surest protection was to turn them all against each other. So I set out to teach each of them that he needed my help against the others. With a little judicious prodding, I was able to make them do whatever I wished."

Drawn by what he described—things that must have been acutely painful, things that reminded her of closets and fading—she took a step toward him. "What did you make them do?"

He betrayed a glint of anticipation. "I made them all good citizens of the Care of Tor. I tamed my brothers. I deprived my father of his debaucheries. And I made them restore the resources of knowledge which Esmerel had once boasted, so that I could claim my grandfather's true inheritance. It was his interest and researches that led me into Imagery.

"Since leaving Esmerel, I have done what I can to keep my family from bestiality. But a distance of two days' ride seems like the world to men like them. I regret that there was nothing I could do to prevent the altercation that left my father's firstborn dead." His manner suggested that his regret wasn't especially profound.

She took another step. His pale gaze seemed to be devouring her. "You came to claim me. What do you want me to do?"

He opened his hands as if to show her their strength. "Take off your robe."

She touched her sash as a giddy acquiescence swept through her. But she shook it away. "I mean after that. What do you want me to do for Mordant?"

"Why must there be an 'after that'?" he countered. "I will content your womanhood in ways you have not dreamed."

In a small voice, she insisted, "I want to help you. I want to help Mordant."

"Very well." As though he were confident that she already knew and had accepted the answer, he replied, "Together, we will persuade Castellan Lebbick and the Congery that Geraden has betrayed us."

When he said that, her heart gave a lurch—and then her courage was gone, as if he had kicked out the bottom of her spirit. Geraden? Was he back to Geraden? Still arguing that Geraden was in league with Gilbur and Vagel? Or did he have some new accusation to level against her only friend? She barely had the fortitude to ask, "What has he done?"

"Done? What has he not done? Has he not convinced you that *I* am a traitor?"

She shook her head.

"Then he is wiser than I thought. You would have become suspicious of him if he had tried to turn you against me."

The Master considered her for a moment, then said, "Because he has been wise, you will probably not believe that he arranged to leave you alone in the bazaar so that Gart could attack you. You will probably not believe that his failure to stop Elega was no accident."

She stared at him in frank horror.

"Those are subtle points," he went on. "I grant it is difficult to credit him with such subtlety. But I will tell you something you must believe. Cadwal is marching. Have you never asked yourself *why* Cadwal is marching? Have you never wondered why High King Festten feels he must attack *now*?"

Terisa didn't reply. Her mind was blank with dismay. A new accusation. New reasons to believe that the only man who cared about her and encouraged her and stayed with her was a traitor.

"In the ordinary course of events," Eremis explained, "the High King's spies must have told him that Alend was coming to Orison. What would he do?" His voice was like the wind, growing harsher as it filled the room. Light from the hearth made his face unnaturally ruddy. "On one side is the risk that Orison might fall, giving the Congery into the Alend Monarch's hands. But with Castellan Lebbick—if not our good King—defending the castle, that is unlikely. On the other side is the certainty that the forces of Perdon would be drawn to Orison's support. Alend and Mordant might easily cripple each other in that battle—and then everything the High King wants could be taken almost without cost. *Why* did he not wait for his enemies to destroy each other?

"I will tell you why, my lady." The Master made a short, brutal gesture with both hands. "He did not wait because he knew of Elega's intentions. He knew our danger was greatly increased by the fact that Orison would be betrayed from within by Prince Kragen's allies.

"Think, woman. How could High King Festten have known that Orison would be betrayed to Alend? By Imagery, his Monomach can enter or leave the castle—although how this is done remains a mystery. But access to our halls does not give him access to our secrets. Who but a traitor would tell Gart that Elega meant to poison the reservoir, depriving us of water and exposing us to summary defeat?"

"No," Terisa murmured. She wanted to collapse into a chair. "No."

Master Eremis ignored her protest. "And who but Geraden knew the danger?"

"But he was attacked," she objected. "By Imagery. Twice. They tried to kill him—Gilbur, Vagel—"

"Whelp of a bitch!" Eremis sounded furious. "Those were *ploys*, woman. Tricks. They show only that Gilbur and Vagel are desperate that you do not turn against their ally. By attacking Geraden, they make him appear innocent. The truth is that they feint his death for the same reason that they actively desire yours—so that you will not expose him.

"If he had not been rescued as he was, I assure you that they would have recalled their insects before he was slain."

She was no longer looking at the Imager. She wasn't looking at anything. Tears streamed down her cheeks. "How could I expose him?"

"You have been with him for many days. You have watched him, spoken to him, studied him. And you met in private in your own world, before he translated you here. You alone possess the knowledge—the experience—that will persuade the Congery of his treachery."

"No," she repeated softly. She wasn't speaking to him, however. She was speaking to herself. She hardly heard what he said: she heard only his voice, his anger, the threat of losing him. Geraden was no traitor. Of course not. She knew that precisely because she had spent so much time with him. But she was being forced to a choice. No, more than that. She was being forced to do something about what she believed. She couldn't defend Geraden without turning her back on Master Eremis and everything he represented.

"You said you wished to help Mordant." He spoke in a hectoring tone that reminded her of her father. "While you protect the man who betrays us, we are doomed."

What could she do? She couldn't argue with him. She had never been able to argue with her father. She could only take his side or refuse. That was clear enough.

Quietly, she asked, "What are you going to do to me?"

"Take off your robe," he snapped. "Your body, at least, will not disappoint me."

Now at last she understood the anger and secret triumph she had so often heard in her father's voice, the desire to inflict pain. For that reason, what she had to do was clear to her in the end—clear and simple—and so difficult that it was nearly impossible.

Her hands were on the sash of her robe. Deliberately, she pulled it tighter.

"No," she said to the Master.

She thought that he would shout at her or strike her. He started toward her, and his expression sharpened into a grin of violence. Instead of shouting, however, he whispered intensely, "My lady, I have claimed you. I have placed my hands and my kisses where you will never forget them." He was close enough to grasp her shoulders. Echoing firelight, his hot gaze held her. "Every curve of your flesh and pulsebeat of your womanhood desires me, and I will not be refused."

He pulled her to him and kissed her forcefully. Somehow, her robe was gone from between them. He felt as hard as iron against her inexperienced belly.

She didn't struggle: she was too weak to struggle. But her body had gone cold; her nerves and her sore heart no longer responded to him. His kiss was only pressure against her face, nothing more. His hardness had lost its fascination.

No, she protested. I said *no*.

Someone knocked at her door so hard that it thudded against the latch.

Swearing viciously, Master Eremis pushed her away. For an instant, he measured the distance to the wardrobe. "Do not answer!" he hissed.

She was about to faint. "I forgot to lock it."

Without waiting for admission, Geraden burst into the room and slammed the door behind him.

But when he saw Terisa standing near the entryway to the bedroom with her robe open and Master Eremis near her, he stopped as if he were turned to stone.

Convulsively, she jerked the robe closed and sashed it. Surprise and mortification made her feel like a lunatic. She sounded like a lunatic as she asked, "How is Artagel?"

The Master's eyes were savage.

Geraden stared at Terisa as though she were appalling. "I didn't go see him."

"Then what *did* you do, boy?" inquired the Imager. "It must have been quite interesting, if it drives you to enter a lady's bedchamber so discourteously."

"Terisa." With the light of the hearth behind him, Geraden's features were dark. His gaze glittered at her out of the shadows. "Tell him to leave."

Master Eremis made a snickering noise in the back of his throat. She was facing Geraden: she didn't know that the Master had moved until she felt him beside her. He put one arm around her waist. With the other, he slid his hand into her robe and began to fondle her breast. "The lady Terisa," he said, "does not wish me to leave."

Shame flushed down the length of her body. "Please," she breathed to Eremis, to Geraden, on the verge of weeping. Don't do this to me. It doesn't mean what you think. "Please."

"In fact, it *was* interesting," Geraden replied in a voice thick with blood. "I had a talk with Saddith."

Terisa felt Master Eremis stiffen. Slowly, he took back his hand, although he didn't release her. "What an odd thing to do. Almost as odd as the urgency you attach to it. Are you quite sure you are well, boy?"

With an effort, she swallowed the distress that clogged her throat. She felt that she was fighting for her life. "What did Saddith say?"

Without a glance at the Imager, Geraden retorted, "Your guards told me you were alone. How did he get in here?"

She knew immediately that Master Eremis didn't want her to answer. She could feel his will in the harsh strength of his grasp.

"The wardrobe," she said thinly. "The secret passage."

Geraden nodded once, abruptly. "And how did he know it was there?"

In an even tone, as though he were in danger of becoming bored, Eremis drawled, "He had no idea it was there. He was exploring a passage new to him and found the lady Terisa's rooms by chance."

The Apt turned a gaze like stone on the Master. Shadows shifted along his jaw. "Actually, that's not true." Then he addressed Terisa again. "How did Saddith become your maid?"

She was having difficulty breathing: the pressure growing in her chest seemed to cramp her lungs. "King Joyse told her to take care of me."

"Did he choose her himself?"

It was astonishing how vividly the memory came back to her. The King had said, *Saddith will attend upon you as your maid.* He had even greeted her by saying, *Just the one I wanted.* But he hadn't looked pleased.

"I don't think so. He didn't ask for her by name. He just told the guard I needed a maid."

"I begin to see why you found this so interesting," commented Master Eremis. He seemed to be laughing to himself. "Trivial matters always interest men who fail at everything else."

"Terisa"—now Geraden's tone cast hints of authority, as if he stood taller under the weight of the Master's derision—"do you remember what we talked about after the first time Gart tried to kill you?"

Dumbly, she shook her head. She couldn't think. That memory was gone, as blank as the previous one was distinct. The dim gray light from the windows appeared to be failing.

"We talked about how he found you."

How he found me.

"It was obvious that he had an ally in Orison. Somebody must have told him where you were."

"That is very good, Geraden," Master Eremis sneered, "A prodigious display of reasoning. Somebody must indeed have told him. Perhaps it was you. You knew where she was. I have heard that her room was guarded at your request."

Terisa didn't look away from Geraden.

He met her gaze to the exclusion of everything else. "Saddith didn't tell me as much as I wanted. But she told me enough so I can guess the rest. She volunteered to be your maid."

Volunteered?

"I wondered about that. Why would she volunteer, when the only people who knew you were here—and knew you were important— were King Joyse and the Masters? With a little prodding, she told me. She did it to please one of her lovers. Or rather someone she wanted for a lover. One of the Masters. He asked her to take care of you for his sake, and she did it to make him grateful."

A log fell in the hearth; flames spurted higher. Gently, Master Eremis wrapped his long fingers around the back of Terisa's neck.

"That's also how he found out about the secret passage to your room," Geraden went on. "From her. She could hardly help noticing you kept a chair in your wardrobe."

"This is outrageous, boy." The Master's grip on the back of Terisa's neck tightened. "Have you lost your mind? Do you seriously mean to accuse me—*me!*—of being in league with the High King's Monomach?" Beneath his scorn ran an undercurrent of mirth.

Still Geraden kept his hard gaze on Terisa, away from Master Eremis. "He's one of the few people who knew where you were that first night. He's one of the few who know about that secret passage. And he's the only one who could have set up that ambush for you after the lords met Prince Kragen. He's the only one who knew you would be there. He *took* you.

"He put you right in front of the champion so you might get shot. You were together—but *he* escaped. He could have taken you with him. He could have stopped me. Why didn't he?"

The fires seemed to be dying. The suite was filling up with gloom.

Geraden, help me. He's going to break my neck.

"Geraden," said the Master casually, "this is inexcusable. You have gone beyond insult." The pressure of his fingers began to make Terisa light-headed. "You cannot place the blame for your own crimes on my shoulders. I will not carry it."

Geraden shifted his glare to Eremis.

"All of this is silly supposition except the question of Gart's attempt on her life after the meeting of the Lords. And *that* you could have arranged as well as I. Your brother Artagel was following her. You knew at all times where she was. It is only good fortune that Gart did not come upon all the lords together. Some of them would surely have died."

"Let her go," the Apt said in a voice like a piece of granite. "If you have to have a hostage, take me. I'm a lot more dangerous than she is."

At that, Master Eremis laughed like a splash of acid. "Oh, you flatter yourself, boy. You flatter yourself."

Before she could try to twist free, she heard the sound of someone thrashing his way through clothes. In a sudden flurry, her wardrobe disgorged most of its contents, and a man burst out from the hidden passage.

His cloak and leather armor were so black that he seemed like an incarnation of the darkness behind him; he moved like a shadow. But the long steel of his sword caught reflections of fire and scattered them in front of him. His nose jutted between his yellow eyes like the blade of a hatchet.

He sprang into the room, coiled for bloodshed.

Nevertheless he was unmistakably surprised to find Master Eremis, Terisa, and Geraden all in front of him. Despite himself, he checked his attack. The aim of his sword wavered.

"Gart!" Master Eremis shouted. "Whelp of a dog! Your timing is miraculous!"

So quickly that his movement staggered her, he released Terisa and bounded to the bed. While Gart swung into motion, Master Eremis snatched down the peacock-feather canopy and flung it over Gart's head.

At the same moment, Geraden grabbed Terisa and jerked her away, thrust her into the sitting room behind him. She stumbled toward the fire, barely caught her balance.

With a wet sound like water on hot iron, Gart's sword swept the canopy to shreds. Feathers settled to the floor on all sides: their eyes watched everything.

Master Eremis jumped up onto the bed.

As he faced the Monomach, firelight glared across his features. The red flash gave him a look of almost ghoulish glee as he pitched a pillow at Gart.

Snarling, Gart separated the pillowcase from its stuffing with the tip of his sword so fiercely that the pillow appeared to explode. Feathers billowed toward the ceiling and came snowing down on him.

Instantly, a second pillow followed the first.

This one, however, he caught on the flat of his blade. Swinging his longsword like a bat, he sent the pillow back at Master Eremis.

It hit him in the chest hard enough to knock him against the wall.

Gart turned on Geraden and Terisa.

"Guards!" roared Master Eremis before the High King's Monomach could strike. "*Guards!*"

For the second time, Gart was startled enough to hesitate. He stopped the driving swing which had carried him into the sitting room—the swing which would have carried Geraden's head from his body. Swiftly, the Monomach gauged the distance past Geraden to Terisa; he looked at the door as the latch lifted; he glanced over his shoulder at Eremis.

With his left hand, he reached to his belt and produced a keen iron dirk.

As the door pounded open and the first guard started into the room, Gart cocked his arm.

A third pillow thumped against his shoulder and spoiled his aim. He missed Terisa.

Master Eremis let out a cackle of laughter.

Now the Monomach had no time for hesitation. Cursing vehemently, he met the first guard's blow with his sword, then kicked the man's legs out from under him. While the second struggled to avoid trampling his comrade, Gart retreated into the bedroom.

Without a glance at Master Eremis, he dove into the wardrobe.

"After him!" Eremis yelled at the guards. "That passage leads to Havelock's chambers! *Go!* I will summon reinforcements!"

Terisa saw the guards falter distinctly before they plunged into the wardrobe. Perhaps they didn't want to face the High King's Monomach in a narrow place. Or perhaps they were reluctant to intrude on Adept Havelock's private domain—especially if, as Master Eremis seemed to suggest, the Adept were in league with Gart.

With a bouncing stride, Master Eremis left the bed and came into the sitting room. The glow of the fire and his own mirth lit his face, but Terisa thought he had never looked more dangerous. Briskly, he approached Geraden and stabbed a finger at the Apt's chest.

"I intend to call a meeting of the Congery." Despite his humorous expression, his tone was savage. "You will answer me for this in front of the Masters, boy."

"No, I won't," Geraden replied unsteadily. "They've disbanded themselves."

Master Eremis snorted. "Again you are mistaken. Quillon holds them together with the King's authority."

Flourishing his chasuble like a threat under Geraden's nose, he left the room.

Geraden's features twisted as if he had just been kicked in the stomach.

Terisa sat straight down on the floor. The noise of the guards' boots echoed dimly out of the wardrobe, but she heard nothing that sounded like the clash of swords.

TWENTY-FIVE:
MASTER EREMIS
IN EARNEST

re you all right?" Geraden asked. His tone wasn't sympathetic.

Sitting cross-legged on the rug, Terisa clamped her hands to the sides of her head to keep her mind from flying apart. She didn't understand: none of it made any sense. Master Eremis. Gart. What were they doing to her?

"Terisa?"

And why was Geraden so angry at her? He was her friend. Why was he suddenly blind to her pain?

"Did he hurt you?"

He was her friend. He must have a good reason for snarling at her as if she had broken his heart. She struggled to concentrate. The room was full of disaster. She had to *think*.

Heavy boots hammered the stone. Three guards burst into the room with their swords out. Master Eremis had certainly gotten their attention. Once in the room, however, they hesitated, waving their blades warily, until Geraden snapped, "There's a wardrobe in the bedroom with a passage behind it." Then they charged away. The boards of the wardrobe resounded as they went through it.

How many different kinds of pain were there? There was the dull ache where Master Eremis had gripped the back of her neck. There was the grief that seemed to throb in the secret places of her heart. There was the sharp strain around her chest which grew tighter every time Geraden spoke to her in that clenched and bitter tone.

There was the belabored sensation inside her skull, as if her mind had been beaten with clubs.

And somewhere else—somewhere indefinable—there was a new certainty as pure as a knife. It needed a name. Perhaps that was why it hurt so much: because she had no name for it.

Dully, she said, "At least now we know he and Gart aren't working together."

"*Terisa.*" That word would have sounded like a cry if Geraden hadn't whispered it so softly.

Before she could reply, another voice intervened. "Don't torture yourself, Geraden," Castellan Lebbick said from the doorway. Four more guards clattered past him on their way to the wardrobe. "She isn't worth it."

She scrambled to her feet so that she wouldn't appear so defeated in front of the Castellan.

Geraden stood with his back to the wall, his arms folded like fetters across his chest. His face looked like a stone mask from which all the joy had been chipped away. Firelight reflected out of his eyes, as dry as fever.

"Save your insults, Castellan," he rasped quietly. "We don't need them."

Castellan Lebbick cocked an eyebrow. "All right. I'll be civil. You be cooperative. For a change. What happened?"

Geraden seemed to shrink slightly, as if he were being compacted by the pressure of his grip on himself—as if he were squeezing himself down to his essence. "We were attacked. The High King's Monomach tried to kill her again."

A grin pulled the Castellan's lips back from his teeth. "And you're still alive? How did you manage that?"

"Master Eremis saved us. He fought Gart off until the guards could get in."

"Master Eremis? What was *he* doing here?"

Bitterly, Geraden didn't look at Terisa.

With an effort, she met Lebbick's gaze. "He came to see me."

"And do you always receive him dressed like that?"

In shame, she bit her lip. Shame was yet another kind of pain. Somehow, she murmured, "He came when I was asleep."

The Castellan turned back to Geraden. "Apparently, Master Eremis was welcome. In that case, what were *you* doing here? I doubt that either one of them invited you."

"When I arrived," Geraden said like a piece of the wall where he stood, "her guards said she was alone. Don't you want to know how he got in? Don't you want to know how Gart got in?"

"Go on. Tell me."

"Both of them used the secret passage behind her wardrobe."

At that, Castellan Lebbick drew a hissing breath through his teeth. "Ballocks! How did they know about it?"

"Saddith and Master Eremis are lovers. In fact, she volunteered to be Terisa's maid to please him. She noticed the chair in the wardrobe and told him about it. I presume he told Gart."

"Wait a moment. You said Master Eremis saved you. Now you say he is in league with Gart?"

"Where else could Gart find out about the passage?" retorted the Apt. "Who else knew enough to tell him? There's just me and Terisa. Saddith and Master Eremis. And you, Castellan. Even Artagel doesn't know about it."

Involuntarily, Terisa remembered that Myste knew.

Clenching his fists on his hips, the Castellan rasped, "All right. If Gart knew, why didn't he use it to kill her long ago?"

"At first," Geraden said, "he didn't know. Saddith told Master Eremis where Terisa was, but she didn't know any more than that. I don't know when she found the passage. And I don't know when he got her to tell him about it. I certainly don't know how busy Gart is. But I think Master Eremis decided he wanted to let her live because he wanted her for himself. He didn't tell Gart about the passage until the Alend army arrived and they both ran out of time."

Abruptly, Castellan Lebbick turned on Terisa. "Is this true? Have you been making it worthwhile for Master Eremis to keep you alive when he really wants you dead?"

His tone made her wince. She was starting to understand Geraden's hurt, and his reasons dismayed her. Nevertheless she met the Castellan squarely.

"He did save us." And her certainty was precise, if only she could put a name to it. "He said he's going to make Geraden answer for this in front of the Congery."

She wasn't prepared for the virulence with which Lebbick snarled under his breath, "Bitch!" Fortunately, he swung back to Geraden too soon to see her flinch.

"I have a few questions myself. I want to know how you suddenly became an expert on what Saddith does or doesn't tell her lovers. And I want to know some of the things you haven't told me yet.

"But as it happens, you're not my only problem right now. I have the rest of Orison to worry about. I'll wait until the Congery meets.

"When my men come back from not finding Gart, tell them to report to me."

Brusquely, Castellan Lebbick strode to the door and left.

Without thinking about what she was doing, Terisa turned toward the fire so that she wouldn't have to look at Geraden. She was afraid to look at him. He was so hurt— And almost everything he believed about her was true. He had saved her from her own weakness. Master Eremis had claimed her—and she had resisted him so little. Even choosing against him, she had been unable to struggle. Shame seemed to demoralize her; she couldn't face the accusation of his pain.

Yet her cowardice disgusted her. He had never let fear prevent him from doing anything for her. At last, she forced herself to turn again and meet his distress.

"Geraden, I—"

He hadn't shifted his stance an inch. Dim gray from the windows and dull red from the hearth lay along the stone lines of his cheeks and jaw, his straight nose, his strong forehead. Not a muscle moved. His hair curled into darkness.

But his eyes were closed.

This was her fault: he was in so much pain because of her. Because he had found her nearly naked with Master Eremis. Because he had seen the Master touch her so intimately. Helplessly, she asked, "What're we going to do?"

He didn't open his eyes. Perhaps the sight of her was intolerable. When he spoke, he couldn't restrain his voice. It shook as if he were freezing.

"I need to know whose side you're on. You don't have to tell me anything else. You have to make your own choices. I can't tell you who to love. But I'm going to have to stand up in front of the Masters and tell them everything I can think of. They aren't going to want to believe me. I've spent too many years making too many mistakes.

"You're my only witness. You're the only one who can tell them I'm telling the truth. If you're planning to call me a liar—" He couldn't go on.

She wanted to reply at once, but his distress closed her throat. What could she say? Nothing was adequate. He had touched her near the point of her certainty, but she still didn't know what to call it.

Yet she was unable to bear his rigid silence. Somehow, she mustered an answer.

"I didn't invite Master Eremis here. He came while I was asleep. That's why I'm dressed like this.

"He wanted me to choose between you."

A muscle twitched in Geraden's cheek, a knot of pain.

"I think he's probably the only man in Orison who has a chance to save Mordant. He has the ability to make things happen." That was the limit of her honesty. "But I chose you."

His eyes popped open. A subtle alteration of the planes and lines of his expression made him appear both astonished and suspicious. His voice continued to shake.

"Your robe was open."

"He did that. I didn't."

For a long moment, he remained motionless—and yet, in spite of the fact that he wasn't moving, she seemed to see the entire structure of his face being transfigured, the whole landscape behind his eyes and emotions reforming. He didn't smile: he wasn't ready for that. But the potential for a smile was restored.

Slowly, he unbent his arms from his chest. Slowly, he reached out his hand and stroked her cheek as if to wipe away tears she hadn't shed.

Unable to hold back, she flung her arms around him and hugged him desperately, as if he could cure her shame.

The embrace with which he answered her was as tight and needy as hers, as hungry for solace. And somehow, because he wanted so much from her, he gave her what she needed.

A short time later, nine guards came trooping up out of the passage behind her wardrobe. They had nothing of any use to report.

The gray afternoon wore down toward evening. All around Orison, campfires glimmered against the wind. Tents everywhere formed a ripple of hillocks over the bare ground. Even the siege engines looked small in this light, at this distance. Wind thudded without remorse at the windowpanes of Terisa's rooms, until the atmosphere felt crowded and bitter, full of threats.

Late afternoon brought her an incongruous visitor: the seamster, Mindlin, come to deliver her new clothes. He wanted to give them a second fitting, to be sure that she was satisfied—perhaps he thought her approval would have some value when the siege was over—but she accepted them and sent him away.

For the fourth or fifth time, she said, "We've got to *do* something."

Geraden sighed. "I know the feeling. But I'm not exactly brimming with ideas."

She needed to put her certainty into words, so that it would be good for something. It would come to her, she told herself, if she stopped pushing it. Or if she pushed it in the right way. Abruptly, she shook off her irresolution.

"You wanted to talk to Artagel, but you didn't get the chance. Why don't you do that now?"

The suggestion surprised him. "What's that going to accomplish?"

"It might make you feel better."

"And you think I might not get another chance? You think I might have a little trouble getting my brother to forgive me after I've been tossed in the dungeon for treachery?"

She couldn't suppress a grin. "I didn't say that."

"You didn't have to." In spite of himself, he caught her mood. "I said it for you."

"So you did. If you think it's such a terrible idea"—now she was grinning broadly—"I'm afraid I'll have to apologize for bringing it up."

At once, he waved his hands defensively. "No, no. Anything but that. I'll do it." His playfulness faded almost immediately, however. "Do you want to come with me?"

She shook her head.

"What *are* you going to do?"

Firmly, as if she were sure of herself, she said, "I'm going to make sense out of this. Somehow."

He spent a moment studying her. Then, in a purposely sententious tone, he said, "My lady, I've got the strongest feeling you'll succeed."

"Oh, get out of here," she returned.

Nevertheless she hoped he was right. As soon as he was gone, she got dressed, putting on her warm new riding clothes and her winter boots because she didn't want to be hampered by her more ladylike gowns. Then she went to see the King.

She had no clear plan in mind. She simply wanted him to intervene on Geraden's behalf.

As she climbed the stairs toward the royal suite, however, she remembered more and more vividly that she had lied to the King the last time she had talked to him. And she still had no idea how he had guessed that she had helped his daughter Myste sneak out of Orison. Before she reached his door, she was tempted to turn back.

The ordeal Geraden had ahead of him determined her to keep going. He needed answers. She needed answers in order to help him. If King Joyse would do nothing else for her, or for the Domne's son, or for Mordant, he might at least supply a few answers. The chance was worth what it might cost her.

And if the King refused to see her, she could always talk to the Tor.

The guards outside the suite saluted her. Practicing steadiness, she asked them if she could be admitted. One of them stayed at the door while the other entered the suite. A moment later, she was given permission to go in.

Her pulse was laboring enough to make her regret her temerity. Blind to the room's luxurious appointments, she had eyes only for the three old men sitting like bosom companions before the ornate fireplace.

King Joyse lay as much as sat in an armchair with his legs stretched over a hassock toward the fire. His purple velvet robe showed the benefits of a recent cleaning, and his cheeks were freshly shaved: his appearance, if not his posture, suggested readiness.

In contrast, the Tor slumped as if his skeleton no longer had enough willpower to support his fat. Like his flesh, his robe spilled over the arms of his chair; the green fabric was stained with splotches of wine. Too plump to look haggard, his face sagged like wet laundry. He gave the impression that he had become so involved in Orison's preparations for defense that he had stopped taking care of himself.

Between the two old friends sat the King's Dastard, Adept Havelock, looking grimier and loonier than ever in his ancient surcoat, with his unruly tufts of hair and his disfocused gaze.

All three men held large, elegant goblets.

All three turned their heads toward Terisa as she was announced.

The Tor peered at her through a haze of exhaustion and wine. Adept Havelock licked his lips salaciously. King Joyse nodded but didn't smile.

She had been hoping that he would smile. It would have done her good to see his luminous smile again.

He greeted her casually; his tone implied that he was a bit the worse for drink. "My lady, come join us." His cheeks were red, scraped raw with shaving, but behind their color his skin looked pale. "Pour yourself some wine." He nodded toward a decanter and extra goblets on a table against the paneled wall. "It's quite good—a fine wine from—" A look of perplexity crossed his face. "Where did you say this wine is from?" he asked the Tor.

The Tor shook himself as if he were in danger of falling asleep. "Rostrum. A small village near the border of Termigan and Domne, where the babes drink wine instead of milk from their mothers' breasts, and even the children can do exquisite things with grapes. Rostrum wine."

King Joyse nodded again. "Rostrum wine," he said to Terisa. "Have some. We're celebrating."

She stood in the center of the thick blue-and-red rug and tried to watch all three men simultaneously. "What're you celebrating?"

Adept Havelock giggled.

"Are we celebrating?" The Tor's voice sounded damp. "I thought we were grieving."

"Grieving? My old friend." King Joyse glanced at the Tor kindly. "What for? This is a celebration, I tell you."

"Oh, of course, my lord King." The Tor waggled a hand. "A celebration. I misspoke." His fatigue was plain. "Orison has been invested by the Alend Monarch. Your daughter has poisoned our water. While we sit here, the men of Perdon die, spending themselves without hope against Cadwal. And the royal Imager, Adept Havelock"—he inclined his head courteously in Havelock's direction—"has burned to death our only clue as to where—and who—our chief enemy is. We do well to celebrate, since we can accomplish nothing with sorrow."

"Nonsense," replied the King at once. Although his expression was grave, he appeared to be in good spirits. "Things aren't as bad as you think. Lebbick knows a trick or two about sieges. We still have plenty of Rostrum wine, so we don't need much water. As soon as he realizes we can't reinforce him, the Perdon is going to back off and let Festten through. That will stop the killing."

He seemed unaware that what he was saying didn't convey much reassurance.

"And the death of the prisoner?" inquired the Tor glumly.

King Joyse dismissed that question. "Also, we have another reason to celebrate. The lady Terisa is here. Aren't you, my lady?" he asked Terisa, then went on speaking to the Tor. "Unless I've gotten it all wrong, she's here to tell us that she has found a new cure for stalemate."

Again Adept Havelock giggled.

For a second, Terisa nearly lost her head. A *cure*? A cure for *stalemate*? She wanted to laugh feverishly. Did King Joyse really think this was all just one big game of hop-board? Then they were all doomed.

Fortunately, she caught hold of her reason for being here before all her thoughts veered off into panic. Geraden. That was the important thing. Geraden.

"I don't know anything about stalemates. Or cures." Her tone was too curt. She made an effort to moderate it. "My lord King. I came because I'm worried about Geraden. Master Eremis is going to try to ruin him in front of the Congery."

The King gave her his attention politely. "Ruin him, my lady?"

"He and Master Eremis are going to accuse each other of betraying Mordant."

"I see. And don't you call that a stalemate?"

"No." She wasn't getting through. She had to do better. "No, my lord King. The Congery will believe Master Eremis." And yet she was certain— "But he's lying."

The Tor twisted in his seat to study her more closely. With a show of effort, Adept Havelock picked up his chair, turned it, and plumped it down again so that he could sit facing her.

King Joyse, however, gazed toward the fire. "Master Eremis?" he asked as if he were losing interest. "Lying? That would be risky. He might get caught. Only innocent men can afford to tell lies."

"My lady," said the Tor quietly, "such accusations are serious. Master Eremis is a man of proven stature. The Congery might have some justification to take the word of one of their own number over the charges of a mere failed Apt. How do you know that Master Eremis is lying?"

She opened her mouth, then closed it again. What could she say? The piece of information lodged in her brain refused to come clear. Something Master Eremis had said, or revealed—Or was it Geraden? After a moment, she admitted, "I haven't figured that out yet."

"I see, my lady." The old lord returned his attention to the fire. "You simply trust Geraden. That is understandable. I trust him myself. There is no help that I can give you, however. I am no longer my lord King's chancellor."

What?

Adept Havelock grinned at her.

King Joyse sighed and leaned his head against the back of his chair. "My old friend was wearing himself toward his grave with the business of Orison. He doesn't want to admit he's no longer young. Sadly, it's true."

"My lord King," the Tor explained, "has given instructions that I am not to be obeyed, except in matters of my personal comfort. With the arrival of Alend's army, my power ended." He snorted to himself. "You may imagine Castellan Lebbick's delight. Remember, he thinks it possible that I am a traitor myself. He did not like my interest in our defenses. Though my lord King does not say so, I believe he has taken away my position to protect himself in case the good Castellan's suspicions prove correct."

At that, King Joyse jerked up his head. His watery eyes were suddenly acute, and his mouth twisted. He didn't reply to the Tor, however. Glaring at Terisa, he demanded, "Just what is it you want, my lady?"

She was startled: for a moment, she had lost herself in empathy for the old lord. Almost stammering, she said, "Geraden doesn't stand a chance in front of the Masters. Master Eremis will chew him to pieces. You've got to stop them. Don't let them do this to him."

"But if Master Eremis is telling the truth," returned the King in a voice like a rasp, "Geraden deserves to be caught and punished."

"No." She couldn't think. It was maddening. "You don't believe that."

King Joyse aimed his gaze at her like a nail and spoke as if he were tapping his words into wood. "That is not the point, my lady. At the moment, it isn't him I doubt. It's you."

She blinked. Her heart began to labor again, pounding alarm in all directions. "Why?"

"Are you surprised? You underestimate me. I warned you this game is dangerous.

"After we talked, I had Myste's rooms searched. She took nothing personal with her—none of her little mementos of childhood, none of her favorite gifts. Does that seem likely to you? If she had gone back to her mother, she would have taken everything she could carry.

"You lied to me, my lady. You lied to me about my daughter."

Inside her chest, a cold hand knotted into a fist. Both the Tor and Adept Havelock squinted at her as if she were being transformed to ugliness in front of them.

"Where did she really go?"

This was what Terisa had feared: King Joyse had found her out. She had learned the danger of lies when she was still a child. Falsehood had been exquisitely tempting to her; her dread of being punished had made her ache to deflect every manifestation of parental irritation, discontent, or disapproval. She had learned, however, that the punishment was worse when she got caught.

In simple defensiveness, she tried to counter as if she had cause to complain. "How did you know she came to see me? Were you having your own daughter spied on?"

Adept Havelock swung his chair back to face the fire, sat down again, and began to twiddle his fingers.

The King continued to glare at her for a moment. She met his gaze because she was afraid to do anything else. Then, abruptly, he too turned away. "You were warned," he muttered. "Remember that. You were warned.

"My lord Tor, be so good as to summon the guards. I want this woman locked in the dungeon until she condescends to tell me the truth about my daughter."

"No!" The cry burst from her before she could stop it. "I'll tell you. I'll tell you anything. Geraden needs me. If I'm not there, he'll have to face the Congery alone."

None of the men were looking at her. The Tor emptied his goblet, but didn't trouble to refill it.

Terisa took a deep breath, squeezed her eyes shut for a second. "She went after the champion. She thought he needed help." She swallowed hard. "I'm sorry."

To Terisa's astonishment, King Joyse's profile quirked toward a smile. But almost at once his expression turned sorrowful, and he leaned his head morosely to rest against his chair again. "More wine would be nice, don't you think?" he commented in the direction of the ceiling.

The Tor seemed to slump farther down in his seat.

With a strangled chortle, Adept Havelock tossed his wine into the fire. While the wine hissed and burned, he threw his goblet behind him, narrowly missing Terisa.

"Fornication," he pronounced, "is hard to do well alone."

"My lady," the King breathed as if he were going to sleep, "I didn't *know* Myste went to see you. I *reasoned* it. If you were more honest, I would have less trouble trusting you. You ought to try using a little reason yourself."

Terisa had expected him to be appalled and angry. Obviously he wasn't. Preconceptions were being jerked out from under her. This new surprise seemed to knock the last bit of sense out of the situation. Myste was doing something that had been foreseen in Havelock's augury of King Joyse. Was that why a lie made the King furious and the truth had nearly made him smile?

"I don't understand," she murmured weakly. "Don't you care?"

King Joyse reached out a swollen, unsteady hand and nudged Adept Havelock, who in turn nudged the Tor. "My lord, I said, 'More wine would be nice.' "

Sighing, the Tor pried his bulk out of his chair and moved to fetch the decanter.

"You want me to use a little *reason*." Terisa had difficulty holding her voice down. "How about giving me some information to reason *with*? Myste is probably dead. If the cold didn't kill her—and the champion didn't kill her—then that firecat probably did. You act like the only thing you care about is that she didn't go see her mother!"

"No." The King sounded sad, but he answered without rancor. "What I care about is that she did something I can be proud of."

Like an echo, Terisa seemed to hear Castellan Lebbick quoting King Joyse to Prince Kragen: *She carries my pride with her wherever she goes. For her sake, as well as for my own, I hope that the best reasons will also produce the best results.*

She wanted to yell, But that doesn't make any *sense*! Elega betrayed you! Myste is probably dead! The words died in her throat, however: they were hopeless. The thought that she would have to go support Geraden with nothing except more confusion made her feel sick.

The Tor refilled the King's goblet and his own, then eased himself into his chair. "The lady Terisa is distressed," he remarked distantly. "It would be a kindness, my lord King, if you gave her what she desires."

King Joyse lifted his head once more, scowling sourly as if he meant to say something acid to the Tor.

But he didn't. Instead, he growled, "Oh, very well."

Over his shoulder, he addressed Terisa. "The reason I told Geraden not to talk to you when you were first brought here is the same reason I didn't intervene when the Masters decided to translate their champion. It's the same reason I'm not going to intervene now. I'm trying to protect you. Both of you."

"Protect us!" She was too upset to restrain herself. "How does it protect me to keep me ignorant? How does it protect us to let that champion be translated? We were buried alive." I almost lost my mind. "How does it protect him to let Master Eremis destroy him? All you're doing is making us look foolish."

The King turned his head away and sketched a frail gesture with both hands. "You see?" he observed to the Tor. "She doesn't reason." Then his tone grew bitter.

"You're still alive, aren't you? Do you have any conception how unlikely that was when you first arrived? Better minds than yours were sure neither of you would last for three days. A little foolishness is a small price to pay for your lives."

Terisa stared at the back of his head with her mouth open as if he had taken all the air out of the room.

" 'Better minds'!" crowed Adept Havelock like a man addressing a crowd of admirers. "He means me. *He means me.*"

"If I had welcomed you with open arms," King Joyse went on, "my enemies would have formed a higher estimate of how dangerous you are. They would have put more effort into killing you." He sounded querulous and old, peevishly incapable of the things he ascribed to himself. "As long as they thought I had no interest in you—that I was too stupid or senile to have an interest in you—they could afford patience. Wait and see. Gart attacked you that first night because my enemies hadn't had time to find out I hadn't welcomed you. But as soon as people heard that I wasn't treating you like an ally, Gart held back for a while.

"Are you satisfied?"

His demand took her by surprise. She scrambled to ask, "Do you mean the reason you can't help Geraden now is that if you do your enemies will know you're his friend and they'll start trying even harder to have him killed?"

"I mean much more than that," he snapped. "I mean that if I had given him permission to tell you whatever you wanted to know I would have doomed you both. My enemies would have taken anything like that as a sign that you were on my side.

"*Now* are you satisfied?"

"But what—?" It was too much: his explanation increased her confusion. It had all been an elaborate charade. "Who *are* your enemies? Why can't you protect anybody you want in your own castle?" Images of Geraden and Myste and Elega and Queen Madin and Master Barsonage and even Castellan Lebbick rose in her, all of them lost and aggrieved. "*Why do you have to make everybody who's loyal to you think you don't care what happens?*"

"My lady." His tone was no longer petulant. Now it was as keen and cutting as ice. "If I had any desire to answer such questions, I would have done so earlier. As a courtesy to your distress, I have already told you more than I consider wise." Like Geraden's, his speech became more formal as it gathered authority. Despite his years, his voice still had the potential to lash at her. "I advise reason and *silence*, my lady. You will not prolong your life by speaking of what you have heard."

He dismissed her without a glance. "You may go."

But—? But—? She knew she should have been stronger. She should have demanded a better explanation. But what she wanted to ask couldn't get past her mental stutter into words. She had no sure ideas left to stand on. King Joyse knew what he was doing—he knew with a vengeance. He was being passive and obtuse on purpose—hurting the people who loved him on purpose. But what purpose was that? It was inconceivable. He—

"My lady," he said again, "you may go."

In a tone of faraway sadness, the Tor murmured, "My lady, it is generally unwise to disregard the will of a king." He spoke as if from personal experience.

With a fierce effort, Terisa quelled her insistent incomprehension. The exertion left her angry and panting, but in control of herself.

"Thank you, my lord Tor," she said stiffly. "My lord King, I'm sorry. I lied to you about Myste because she trusted me. She was afraid somebody would try to stop her. She asked me to protect her. I lied to you because I didn't know you would have let her go."

None of the three men looked at her. They stared vacantly into the fire, as if they had used up their allotment of words for the day and had nothing left to think with. King Joyse let her get as far as the door before he breathed softly, "Thank you, my lady."

She left as if she were escaping.

Geraden joined her in her rooms for supper.

His expression was a strange mixture of relief and dread. His conversation with Artagel made his spirits soar; the upcoming meeting of the Congery hung on him like lead. The good news, he reported, was that Artagel was healing well after his earlier setbacks. And Artagel was still his friend. The bad news was that the swordsman was still in no condition to stand up in front of the Masters and defend his brother.

"When will the meeting be?" she asked.

"I don't know what kind of mediator Master Quillon is. I used to think he wasn't assertive enough to pull a meeting together. But now—" He shrugged.

Fervently, he listened while she described her session with King Joyse, the Tor, and Adept Havelock. Unfortunately, it changed nothing. "You know," he commented after a while, "all this would do us a lot more good if we had any idea why we're so important."

"I don't think so." She felt sour and imperfectly resigned. "It doesn't cheer me up to believe King Joyse is really our friend only he can't risk doing anything about it. What good are friends who treat you just like your enemies do?"

He nodded slowly without agreeing with her. "The important thing is, it's hope. He certainly sounds like he has reasons for what he's doing." Geraden's mood seemed to improve as hers deteriorated. "And if he has reasons, we can at least *hope* they're good ones."

"On the other hand," she countered, "look at the way he's treating the Tor."

That made Geraden scowl. "You heard King Joyse say he 'defies prediction.' There's probably a danger he'll do something to mess up one of the King's plans. So King Joyse is trying to keep him under control."

A moment later, he added in a black tone, "I don't like plans that hurt the Tor."

"Neither do I," said Terisa.

After a while, he remarked with more humor, "It's too bad nobody much cares what we think of their plans."

Damn you, Geraden, she thought, you're starting to cheer up again. I don't understand it.

In spite of his improved humor, however, he didn't smile when one of the younger Apts knocked on the door and announced that the Congery wanted him. When the Apt used the words "at once," Geraden's eyes widened slightly.

"That was fast," he muttered to Terisa. "Master Eremis knows how to get action."

The young Apt avoided looking at Geraden. "The lady Terisa isn't invited."

"The lady Terisa," she snapped, "is coming anyway."

The Apt didn't look at her, either.

Geraden tried to give her one of Artagel's combative grins; but its failure only made him appear sick. "Let's go get it over with."

Together, they followed the young Apt through Orison down to the laborium.

Until her knuckles began to ache, she didn't realize that she was clenching her fists.

Although she was warmly dressed, she felt the chill as soon as she crossed the disused ballroom and descended into the domain of the Masters. Castellan Lebbick's new curtain wall defended the breach the champion had made, but didn't seal it. Because of the strong wind outside, there was a noticeable breeze in the passages. As a result, the atmosphere was cold enough to make her wish she had brought a coat.

If Geraden noticed the cold, he didn't show it. His manner was distracted. As he entered the laborium, he grew tense. He had spent all his adult life—and a good part of his adolescence—trying to earn a place for himself in these halls and passages, and now his failure threatened to become so dramatic that it would be considered treason.

For his sake as well as her own, Terisa was getting angrier.

The young Apt led her and Geraden to a part of the laborium where she had never been before—to the room the Masters had used for their gatherings ever since the champion had destroyed their meeting chamber.

This room was small by comparison, but still more than large

enough. It was a long rectangle; and something in the color or cut of
its cold, gray stone, in the worn but uneven floor, in the number of
black iron brackets set into the walls created the impression that it
had originally served as a storeroom for the instruments of torture. It
was the kind of place where ways of inflicting pain might wait while
they weren't needed: racks and iron maidens being taken to and
from the interrogation chamber might have rubbed those hollows in
the floor; thumb-screws and flails might have hung in the brackets. A
few of the brackets had been adapted to hold lamps, but the rest
were empty. The empty ones seemed especially grim.

The Masters were already gathered.

They sat in heavy iron-pegged chairs which lined the two long
walls, roughly half of them on either side facing each other as if they
had deliberately set out to form a gauntlet. Because of the length of
the room, however, a sizable space at each end was unused. The
doors were there, several strides from the nearest seats.

Two guards on strict duty held the door through which Terisa and
Geraden entered the chamber. Neither man acknowledged the Apt's
glum nod.

As the door closed behind her, she scanned the room. At first, the
only face she recognized was that of Master Barsonage. Since she had
last seen him, the former mediator seemed to have developed a nervous tick: one of his thick, stiff eyebrows twitched involuntarily. Under the pressure of the Congery's mistakes and indecision, his face
had taken on a jaundiced hue. She saw no hope there.

Looking for Master Quillon, her eye was caught by Castellan Lebbick.

When she saw him, her throat suddenly went dry.

He had Nyle with him.

Geraden's brother sat beside the Castellan at the far end of one
row of chairs. He wore a brown worsted cloak over his clothes.
Inside it, his arms bunched across his chest, holding the cloak shut.
His head hung at a dejected angle. He didn't look up at Terisa and
Geraden.

Geraden was frozen with shock. All expression had been wiped
from his face. The spark that animated his features most of the time
was gone—hidden or extinguished—and he seemed smaller, as if he
were shrinking in on himself. He stared blankly at Nyle while two
bright spots of color slowly spread in his cheeks. She had never seen

him look so lost. The glazing of his eyes made her irrationally afraid that he was having a heart attack.

"The lady Terisa was *not* invited," said one of the Masters loudly.

"But she *is* welcome," rasped Castellan Lebbick. "Isn't she, Master Quillon."

The rabbity mediator rose to his feet, gazing brightly at everything and nobody. Wrinkling his nose, he answered, "As welcome as you are, Castellan."

Castellan Lebbick grinned like a snarl.

Master Eremis was sitting on the other side of the Castellan. "Oh, I insist," he said at once. "If Castellan Lebbick and Nyle are permitted, it is only fair to permit the lady Terisa also." His expression was difficult to read. For no clear reason, he looked pleased.

"Why is he here?" Geraden asked. He sounded like a sleepwalker.

Everyone understood to whom Geraden was referring. Master Quillon started to reply, but Castellan Lebbick spoke first. Still grinning, he said, "Master Eremis claims he's going to support the accusations against you."

"Nyle!" Terisa cried softly.

All the Masters were staring at her, but none of them seemed to have faces. She didn't know who they were.

Geraden moved to the nearest chair and sat down as if he were crumbling.

Nyle tightened his grip on his cloak. He didn't raise his head.

"Castellan Lebbick," Master Quillon said as if he were thinking about something else, "this is the meeting of the Congery, not a congregation of your guards. You have no authority here. You are permitted only because you refuse to let Nyle among us without you. Please be quiet."

The Castellan accepted this admonition without retort, but also without acquiescence.

"My lady," the mediator continued in the same tone, "will you sit down so that we may begin?"

Terisa wrestled with an impulse to start shouting. Abruptly, she turned and took a seat beside Geraden.

He looked so stunned that she whispered, "What is Nyle going to say about you?"

He didn't answer.

Master Eremis watched Geraden curiously, as though he were genuinely interested in what the Apt was thinking.

"Very well," said Master Quillon. He took one or two quick steps out into the middle of the floor between the rows of chairs. "Let us begin."

The chairs were old; perhaps they were left over from the days when the lords and ladies of Orison liked to watch the way prisoners were questioned. The wood was dry and porous enough to hold bloodstains.

"We hold this meeting to consider a question which I will not attempt to soften." His manner suggested that he might be looking for a place to hide, yet his voice was firm. "As you all know, Master Eremis claims that Apt Geraden is a traitor—a traitor to the Congery and to Orison, to King Joyse and to Mordant. He also says that Apt Geraden will make the same claim of him. We will hear both speak. They will give their reasons. They will provide what corroboration they can. And we will try to determine the truth."

"And when the truth has been determined," Castellan Lebbick put in casually, "I'll act on it."

Master Quillon ignored the interruption. "This matter must be dealt with speedily. There is a blot on the honor of the Congery, and it must be removed at once. Orison is under siege because of us— because we are desirable to the King's enemies. And we are not much trusted at the best of times. Therefore it is urgent that we determine the truth—and that any traitor is delivered to the Castellan.

"Apt Geraden"—the mediator's eyes sparkled—"will you speak first?"

Everybody turned to look at Geraden—everybody except Nyle, who slumped in his chair as if he were contemplating suicide.

Terisa wanted to say, demand, No. Make Master Eremis go first. But the words didn't come. She watched like one of the Imagers as Geraden got slowly to his feet.

The spots of color in his cheeks had darkened until they resembled a flush of exertion. His movements were tight, constrained. His chest rose and fell as if he were trying to take a deep breath and couldn't. He didn't look at Nyle: in fact, he didn't look at anybody. He had been given a shock he didn't know how to face.

Terisa found herself thinking, Nyle is doing this because Geraden stopped him.

"Masters—" The Apt had to swallow hard to clear his throat. His voice seemed to be choking him. His life's ambition had been to belong to the Congery. He had spent years obeying and honoring these men. "We've all been betrayed. I can't prove any of it."

Oh, Geraden.

Master Eremis appeared to be suppressing a desire to laugh.

"You must make the effort, Geraden." The mediator's words were sterner than his tone. "Master Eremis will prove everything he can. Are you speaking of Master Gilbur, or of someone else?"

Geraden nodded aimlessly. His gaze stumbled to the floor. Yet he said nothing.

At the sight of his pain, something turned over in Terisa. He had suffered too much, borne too much. And now his brother hurt him like this—personally, deliberately. He was finally breaking under the strain.

"It's simple, really," she said in a voice she hardly recognized. "There *has* to be a traitor. Someone else—not just Master Gilbur."

Master Quillon swung toward her. His nose seemed to twitch with eagerness, but the rest of his face was still.

"It's simple, really," Geraden echoed like a ghost. "There *has* to be a traitor. Someone else."

Then he raised his head.

"It has to be somebody here."

Terisa held her breath, praying that he would go on.

"She's been attacked by Gart four times." His tone was a little slurred, but the glaze in his eyes seemed to be fading. "The third time was out in the bazaar. That doesn't prove anything. But the fourth time Gart came through a secret passage in her room. Somebody must have told him about that passage."

He stopped.

"That is true," Master Eremis observed as if he were agreeing with Geraden. "Someone must have told him. I was there to feel his attack. It is possible, I suppose, that I was his intended victim."

"Master Eremis," said the mediator with unexpected force, "you will be given all the time you need to speak. Defend yourself then. The Apt must be left to say what he will."

A Master with a heavy paunch and no eyebrows interposed, "You were there, Master Eremis? How did you survive? How did any of you survive?"

Smiling, Eremis made a deferential gesture for silence.

Without hesitation, Master Quillon prompted Geraden, "Continue, Apt. Who knew of the secret passage?"

At once, Geraden said, "The Castellan, of course. King Joyse. His daughters. Terisa. Her maid. And Master Eremis."

Terisa released an inward sigh of relief because he hadn't mentioned Master Quillon or Adept Havelock. He still had enough sense to keep that secret.

The mediator, however, gave no sign that he had noticed Geraden's restraint. "And what does this prove?"

"Everybody knew about the passage all along. Except Master Eremis. He only found out about it recently. Soon after he found out about it, Gart used it."

"That means nothing!" protested Master Eremis at once. "What opportunity have I had to confer with the High King's Monomach? I have been away, as you all know. I have been visiting Esmerel."

Geraden straightened his back. "But that's not the crucial one." At last he began to sound stronger. He was breathing more easily, and his gaze had come into focus. "It's the second attack that's crucial. It was right after Master Eremis and Master Gilbur met with Prince Kragen and the lords of the Cares."

A look of outrage jerked across Castellan Lebbick's face as old suspicions were confirmed. "They *met*—?"

Geraden overrode the Castellan. "That lets out everybody else. Everybody who didn't know about the meeting. But Master Eremis took her to it. When it broke up, he left her with Prince Kragen. Gart came out of a mirror with four of his men to attack them. The Perdon and Artagel saved them. Only Master Eremis could have arranged that. He's the only one who knew she would be there. He's the only one who had any control over where she would be after the meeting."

An expression of mock horror widened Master Eremis' eyes and stretched his mouth.

"And," Geraden insisted, "he may be the only Master who knew where she was that first night, when Gart broke into her rooms to kill her. He's Saddith's lover. She volunteered to be her maid because he asked her to.

"Master Eremis is the only man in Orison who could have told Gart where and when to attack Terisa."

As if he were having trouble keeping his balance, Geraden sat down and braced his hands on his knees.

Castellan Lebbick was on his feet, dangerously calm. "I suspected something like this. Tell me about that meeting."

"Is that *all*, Apt?" demanded an Imager with a red complexion and bad teeth. "Do you expect us to *believe* that?"

"Be seated, Castellan," advised Master Quillon. "This does not concern you."

"What does Artagel say?" someone else asked.

"I still do not understand why the High King's Monomach wants to kill the lady Terisa. What threat is she to Cadwal?"

"Why weren't we told about the second attack?"

"He hasn't done anything right since I've known him. I think we can take it for granted that if he says something it must be wrong."

"Ballocks and pigsoil!" Castellan Lebbick roared over the babble. *"Tell me about that meeting!"*

Silence echoed after his shout.

"You have reached a hasty conclusion, Castellan," Master Eremis volunteered without rising from his seat. "The Perdon suggested a meeting between the lords of the Cares and the Congery so that we could discuss our mutual problem—the inaction of our good King. He arranged the coming of the lords to Orison. Master Gilbur and I were chosen to represent the Congery—I because I favored the meeting, he because he opposed it. I took it upon myself to invite Prince Kragen, believing his mission of peace to be sincere."

He shrugged eloquently. "Nothing came of it. The Fayle and the Termigan were too stiff-necked, the Tor too drunk, the Armigite too cowardly. Only the Perdon and Prince Kragen displayed any understanding of each other.

"Incidentally, if I am trusted by Alend, I am unlikely to be a servant of Cadwal. Don't you agree?

"I believe," he concluded, "that the blood you found belonged to Gart's men. Their bodies left as they came—by Imagery. We can only assume that Master Gilbur escaped in the same way, as the arch-Imager Vagel's ally."

His explanation was so close to the truth that it made Terisa squirm. The air in the room seemed to be getting colder. She wondered if she would ever be warm again.

"It was treason," Castellan Lebbick breathed through his teeth. "You were plotting treason."

"It was nothing of the kind," sighed Master Barsonage, speaking for the first time. His weariness cut deep. "The truth is that we were hoping the lords would give us cogent reasons not to risk the translation of our champion. We only took the risk of that translation because the lords convinced us they had no answer to Mordant's plight."

"In any case," Master Eremis said more sharply, "it came to nothing. There is no cause for your outrage, Castellan, because no harm was done. In retrospect, it is clear that the gravest danger arose simply from the presence of so many lords—and Prince Kragen—here at the same time. If the champion had chosen to blast his way in some other direction"—Master Eremis rolled his eyes humorously, but his tone didn't lose its edge—"he might have brought Orison down on the head of every important man in the kingdom."

Castellan Lebbick muttered a few dark oaths.

"Can we get on with it?" Terisa asked, still speaking in the voice she hardly knew. "I want to hear why Nyle thinks Geraden is a traitor."

The Master with the paunch snapped, "My lady, what you want is not of great consequence to us at present."

With a gesture, Master Quillon demanded silence. Facing Lebbick, he inquired acerbically, "Castellan, may we continue? Or do you wish to go on abusing us because we see our circumstances and Mordant's need differently than you do?"

Castellan Lebbick spat another curse, then clamped his mouth shut. Like a coiled spring, he returned to his seat.

The mediator rubbed his nose, trying to stop its twitch. "Apt Geraden, have you finished what you wish to say?"

Geraden gave an abrupt nod.

"Do you have any corroboration? Is there anything you can show us or tell us to support your assertions?"

Geraden shook his head.

An odd thought crossed Terisa's mind. Geraden, she realized, had done what King Joyse wanted her to do: he had used his reason. His accusation against Master Eremis was based on reason rather than on proof.

Unfortunately, it was proof the Masters wanted. "Master Eremis was the only one who knew I would be at the meeting," she said. "I was there. Everyone else was surprised to see me."

"No, my lady," Master Eremis put in immediately. "That is incorrect. You cannot be sure that I did not mention my intent to Master

Gilbur—or even to Prince Kragen. You cannot be sure that the surprise you saw did not have another cause.

"But even if your assertion is true, what does it mean? Master
Gilbur and I left the meeting together, going—as you know—to
report what had happened to our fellow Masters. But he parted from
me almost at once, saying that he had an urgent need to visit his
rooms. Knowing now that *he*, at least, is a traitor, how can you believe that he did not take that opportunity—unforeseen though it
may have been—to translate Gart against you?"

"Because," someone Terisa didn't know remarked incisively,
"such an attack could not have been done without preparation. The
necessary mirror could not have been made on a whim. Indeed, the
location of the meeting must have been chosen to match the proximity of the mirror. Was it not you who chose the location of the meeting, Master Eremis?"

Almost instantly, everyone in the room fell still. Attention concentrated the atmosphere. Geraden took a deep breath, and some of the
unnatural color left his face.

Master Eremis, however, wasn't daunted. "Of course it was," he
snapped. "I had that responsibility because neither the Perdon nor
Prince Kragen knew Orison well enough to make the choice themselves. But you assume that the mirror was created for the sake of
Gart's attack on the lady. There were only six days between the
planning of the meeting and the meeting itself. Do you think such a
mirror could be conceived and researched and shaped in six days? Is
it not more probable that the mirror was created for an entirely
different purpose—perhaps to give Gart access to Orison whenever
he wanted it—and that the opportunity to attack the lady was merely
fortuitous, an accident of circumstance which Master Gilbur hurried
to turn to his advantage?"

Several of the Imagers shuffled their feet; few of them met Eremis'
gaze. The ease with which he had turned the accusation made Terisa's thoughts spin.

"Very well, Master Eremis," the mediator murmured after a long
pause. "I presume that Geraden has no more to say. Since you have
already begun to defend yourself, please continue."

"Thank you, Master Quillon," Eremis said as if he were deliberately suppressing contempt. He didn't trouble to rise. "I will give
you my reasons. Only if they do not persuade you will I call on Nyle

to prove what I say. He is understandably reluctant to condemn his
brother."

That statement may have been true. Nyle did look reluctant: he
looked reluctant to go on living.

"I have been curious about Apt Geraden since the moment when
he brought the lady Terisa to us from a mirror which could not have
performed that translation." The Master sat nonchalantly, half
sprawled in his chair with his legs outstretched. While he spoke, his
long fingers played with the ends of his chasuble. His manner was so
negligent that Terisa had to study him closely to notice that he was
watching the entire room. "The link between him and Master Gilbur
turned my curiosity to suspicion. When Master Gilbur finally proved
himself false, my worst doubts were confirmed."

No one interrupted him as he recited the arguments he had already presented to Terisa. She had to admit that they sounded plausible, almost inevitable. It was Master Gilbur who shaped the glass
which first showed the champion, Master Gilbur who guided every
step of Geraden's attempt to match that mirror. Therefore if Geraden's abilities had made a mirror which could do things no mirror
had ever done before, Master Gilbur must have been a witness to
them. Or else Master Gilbur must have been responsible for the
mysteries of that mirror himself, guiding Geraden to accomplish-
ments which the Apt couldn't have achieved for himself. In either
case, the two men were confederates. Geraden's difficulties had always been ones of talent rather than of knowledge: Master Gilbur
couldn't have employed him to do something unprecedented without the Apt's awareness of it.

"No," Geraden murmured. "I had no idea." But no one paid any
attention to him.

Master Eremis also explained his theory about why Cadwal was
marching. On that basis, he claimed, the rest was obvious. Who was
the only man who always knew exactly where the lady Terisa was?
Apt Geraden, of course, who first arranged to have her rooms
guarded, then persuaded his brother Artagel to follow her. Who was
the man most likely to have aided Master Gilbur in translating Gart
after the meeting of the lords? Apt Geraden, of course, Master
Gilbur's confederate. Why was it that all Geraden's apparent loyalty
to King Joyse came to nothing? Because it was only a clever disguise
to help him hurt those who most trusted him. He was in league with
Gart and High King Festten.

Listening to this made Terisa feel sick.

The pain in Geraden's eyes was acute, but he said nothing.

When Master Eremis was done, the rest of the Imagers were slow to speak. A few of them looked shocked. More were relieved, however, as if they had been rescued from believing that a member of the Congery had betrayed them. And some were plainly delighted by the prospect of finally being rid of Geraden.

After a moment, however, a slightly cross-eyed young Master countered, "But this is inconsistent, Master Eremis. If I understand rightly, it is Geraden who has kept the lady alive by providing her with defenders."

"Nonsense," retorted Master Eremis shortly. "The guards he first arranged for her could not be a match for the High King's Monomach. And since then his duplicity has been more profound than you realize. He has put Artagel at the lady's side so that Mordant's best swordsman might also be killed, thus freeing Cadwal of two important enemies with one betrayal."

"You can't believe that!" Geraden's protest was like a groan. At once, however, he closed his mouth again.

"No, Geraden." Master Barsonage heaved his bulk upright. His gaze lingered momentarily, sadly, on Terisa. "I do not believe that." His face had the color and texture of prolonged strain. "The truth is that I do not believe anything I have heard here. You and Master Eremis denounce each other as though what you say cannot be doubted, but you do not answer the most important question, the question on which all else stands or falls. You do not explain *why*.

"*Why* does the High King's Monomach go to such lengths to attack the lady Terisa? *Why* does Master Eremis wish her killed?" Over his shoulder, he demanded, "Master Eremis, *why* does Geraden wish her killed?" Then he addressed the Congery. "Nothing that these men have said has any meaning unless they can tell us *why*."

Before either accuser could answer, Terisa stood up. "I'll tell you why." A shiver ran through her voice—a shiver of anger rather than of cold. She wasn't cold: she was sure. The frustrating certainty that she hadn't been able to name was suddenly clear. "I'll tell you exactly why." *If he had not been rescued*—She wasn't talking about Master Barsonage's question; she had no answer to that. But it gave her a way to say what she meant.

"Geraden doesn't have any reason to want me dead. He's spent enough time with me since I got here to know I'm no threat to anybody. If he were in league with Gart, I would never be attacked. He wouldn't risk the High King's Monomach on someone like me.

"But Master Eremis has a reason."

The Master sat up straighter. He appeared to be taken aback. "My lady," he said wonderingly, "I have saved your life. I have done everything a man can do to gain your love. How can you think that I wish you harm?"

She wanted to throw up. "Because I know you're lying."

At that, his expression darkened. She heard a hiss of indrawn breath from the Imagers behind her as he rose ominously to his feet. "Be sure of what you say, my lady," he murmured in warning.

"I'm sure," she flung back at him. Pressure mounted in her voice. She didn't want to yell, but she needed passion to control her fear, to keep her going despite the fact that she had never defied anyone like this before and didn't believe she could do it, certainly not Master Eremis, he was too much for her, he was like her father, he had been too much for her from the start. "You know all about the attack after the meeting. I told you that. I've made a lot of mistakes. But you left without coming to see me again." *If he had not been rescued*—"I never had a chance to tell you about the attacks on Geraden. Who told you about them?

"You could know about those riders in the woods. That's common knowledge now. Anybody could have told you."—*rescued as he was, I assure you*—"But you knew about the first time, too."

Master Eremis stared at her as if she had caught him completely by surprise.

"Nobody knew about that except Artagel, Geraden, and me. And Adept Havelock. *He* didn't tell you." Master Eremis had made a mistake. Under the pressure of Geraden's accusations, he had made a mistake. "None of us told you. You weren't *here*. But you still said that attack was just a ploy. You knew all about it. You said, 'If he had not been rescued as he was, I assure you that they would have recalled their insects before he was slain.'

"You said 'their insects.' How did you know he was attacked by insects?"

A light of amazement and vindication broke across Geraden's face.

Struggling for self-control, she concluded, "You're trying to accuse Geraden for the same reason you want me dead. Because we're dangerous to you. We know you're the traitor."

For just a moment, Master Eremis continued to gape. Then he began chuckling.

His mirth didn't sound particularly cheerful.

"My lady," he said, "you are outrageous. You told me about the attack youself."

"That's another lie," she shot back in fury.

"No, my lady. The lie is yours. I had the story from your lips between kisses."

"I don't think so, Master Eremis." Geraden stood at Terisa's side. Her audacity had galvanized him: he was poised for battle, and his eyes burned. "She doesn't have any reason to lie. She doesn't have anything to gain here."

"Does she not?" Master Eremis' mouth twisted scornfully. "You are naive, boy—or a fool. You are her reason. She has you to gain."

That argument stopped Terisa: it set her back on her heels, like a dash of cold water in her face. It was true—

It was true enough to make her look foolish.

Nevertheless it was a miscalculation. Before Eremis could go on, several of the Masters burst out laughing.

"With *your* reputation for women?" said the Imager with the bad teeth. "Do you ask us to credit that she prefers Geraden fumble-foot?"

"I would not have believed any other proof," another Master put in, "but I believe this. If Master Eremis is reduced to claiming that he could not win a woman away from the Apt, then there is no truth in him."

"On the contrary," someone else returned uproariously. "If Master Eremis is reduced to admitting that he could not win a woman away from the Apt, then he must be speaking the truth."

"Enough!" barked Master Eremis. He slashed the air with his hands, demanding silence. "I have endured *enough!"*

His shout made the walls ring fiercely. The fury in his voice and the relish in his eyes stilled the room, commanding everyone's attention.

"It is intolerable that all my service to Mordant and the Congery is met with distrust. It is *intolerable* that any of you will believe this weak boy when I am accused. Now I will prove what I say. I will ask Nyle to speak."

The Masters stared. Geraden opened his mouth, closed it again;

the color seeped out of his skin. Down inside her, Terisa's shivering suddenly got worse.

Master Quillon cocked his head reflectively. After a moment, he commented in a tone that almost sounded threatening, "For the sake of everyone here, Master Eremis, I hope that you are sure of what he will say."

"I am sure." Eremis' certainty was absolute, as unshakable as his grin.

Everyone looked at Nyle.

Geraden's brother seemed unaware of what was going on. His dejected posture didn't shift: his head didn't rise. The grimace that distorted his features was as deep as despair.

Abruptly, he turned and whispered in Castellan Lebbick's ear.

The Castellan listened, frowned—and said, "Masters, Nyle wants a private word with Geraden."

Nyle returned his gaze to the floor.

No one moved. Terisa's heart pounded against the base of her throat. Geraden knotted his fists and kept his head high; his jaw jutted. Master Eremis turned a measuring gaze on Nyle, but didn't say what he was thinking. The Imagers glanced uncertainly at each other, at the Castellan, at Master Quillon.

At last, the mediator asked curiously, "Why?"

Castellan Lebbick shrugged. "Maybe he thinks he can persuade Geraden to confess."

"Do you object?"

Lebbick shook his head. "The room is guarded." Then he added sarcastically, "Anything Geraden has to confess is bound to be fascinating."

Once again, Master Quillon looked as though he wanted to run and hide. Nevertheless he said, "Then let us be seated. Nyle and Geraden may go to the end of the room."

Master Eremis shrugged and complied. The other Masters resumed their seats.

Terisa turned to Geraden. What is Nyle going to say about you? Oh, Geraden, what's wrong?

But Geraden didn't meet her gaze. Everything in him was focused on his brother—the brother he had tried to save from committing treachery; the brother he had humiliated to the bone.

"Be careful," Terisa breathed. She could feel disaster gathering around him. There was no way to forestall it. "Please."

Aching with suspense, she sat down.

Stiffly, Geraden moved to stand in front of Nyle.

When he saw Geraden's boots near his own, Nyle wrenched himself to his feet. Without releasing his grip on his cloak, he strode away to the far end of the room—as far as he could get from the Masters; the farthest point from Terisa.

There he waited for Geraden to join him.

The Masters watched without moving. Castellan Lebbick's jaws chewed indigestible thoughts; his gaze didn't shift an inch from the brothers.

They stood with Geraden's back to the room. Terisa could see Nyle's face: it was set and savage, more implacable—and more desperate—than it had been when he had ridden away to betray Orison. He looked at once homicidal and appalled, as if he were involved in a crime which made every inch of him cringe.

Whispering, he said something to Geraden.

It must have been something hurtful: Geraden reacted as though he had been struck. He flinched; he surged forward. From the back, he appeared to have taken hold of Nyle's cloak.

Between the brothers, an iron dagger dropped to the floor, clattering metallically on the stone.

It was covered with blood.

Nyle slumped against the wall. His eyes rolled shut. Then his knees bent. Geraden tried to catch him, but he collapsed on his back. His cloak fell open, exposing the red mess the knife had made of his abdomen.

Like the dagger, Geraden's hands were covered with blood.

TWENTY-SIX:
FRATRICIDE

In the stunned silence of her mind, Terisa started screaming. Fortunately, she didn't scream aloud.

For a moment, no one said anything aloud. No one did anything at all. Everyone simply gaped at Geraden and Nyle.

Then Geraden made a constricted noise like a sob, and the Congery erupted.

Masters jumped out of their chairs and headed in all directions. Castellan Lebbick burst into motion, hurtling like a destructive projectile toward Geraden. Geraden cowered against the wall as if he were cornered.

Over the chaos, Terisa cried out, "Geraden! *Run!*"

As if she had set him on fire, he flung himself at the door.

He was too late, too slow: he was in a state of shock and couldn't match the Castellan's instinct for action. But a few of the Masters were also rushing at him, perhaps wanting to capture him, perhaps hoping to help Nyle. One of them was Master Quillon.

As fast as a rabbit, he dove after Geraden—and stumbled.

He fell directly in front of Castellan Lebbick, accidentally cutting the Castellan's legs out from under him. Lebbick plunged to the stone.

Geraden reached the door and jerked it open.

"*Stop him!*" Castellan Lebbick roared at the guards outside. "*Stop Geraden!*"

The door slammed shut in time to cut off his shout.

Master Barsonage stood alone in the middle of the confusion. While Imagers shouted at each other and tried to decide which way to run, he clasped his hands together and gaped at nothing. Even his involuntary tic was paralyzed.

Still roaring, the Castellan sprang upright, heaved Masters away from him on both sides, charged the door.

Master Eremis wasn't the first to reach Nyle. Nevertheless he shoved everyone else aside, swept the bloody form up in his arms, and began dodging toward the far exit. "A physician!" he barked although no one was listening to him. "He must have a physician!"

Automatically, Terisa followed Master Eremis and Nyle.

Without warning, someone caught her by the arm. Forced to turn, she found herself facing Master Quillon.

His bright eyes shone; his nose twitched extravagantly. "Come!" he demanded in a voice that seemed to pierce straight through the confusion into her heart. "We must help him!"

At once, he started forward, hauling her into motion toward the door Master Eremis had just taken.

The two guards assigned to that door were in the room, shouting for order and answers. Master Quillon ducked past them. They made an effort to stop Terisa, then let her go: the turmoil of the Congery demanded their attention.

With his gray robe flapping against his knees, Master Quillon broke into a run.

She had no idea where he was going: she followed him simply because he had used the word *help*. But suddenly she began to recognize this part of the laborium. Down a corridor, then along an intersecting passage, Master Quillon brought her to a door small and heavy enough to be the door of a cell.

This door also was guarded.

"Quickly!" Master Quillon shouted at the men. "Someone has been killed!" He pointed back the way he and Terisa had come. "The Castellan needs you!"

His urgency was so convincing that both guards left their post at full speed, drawing their swords as they ran.

Immediately, Master Quillon swung the door open, ushered Terisa through it, and closed it again.

They had entered the antechamber of the network of cells that had been rebuilt for the storage and display of the Congery's mirrors.

"Will he come here?" she asked. She was panting hard.

With unintended brutality, Master Quillon replied, "He has nowhere else to go." Taking her arm again, he impelled her through the nearest entryway into the warren of showrooms.

But he didn't accompany her.

When he stopped, she turned back to question him.

"Go!" he snapped. "Help him! I will gain as much time as I can. I will be believed when I say he did not come here—at least for a minute or two."

She stared. *Help* him?

"*Go*, I say!" He gave her a push.

She stumbled, caught her balance, and fled the antechamber.

Help him? Geraden?

Nyle was dead. His belly had been cut open with a knife.

Why?

So he wouldn't speak to the Congery. So he wouldn't support Master Eremis' accusations.

Geraden!

As soon as she found the room where the mirror that had brought her to Orison was on display, she spotted him. He was trying to dodge past an entryway, trying to hide, but he wasn't quick enough to avoid her.

Master Gilbur's original glass had been destroyed by the champion, of course: this mirror was Geraden's copy. Because it was covered, she couldn't see what scene it showed.

"Geraden!" she whispered. She was afraid to shout. "It's me. Terisa."

After a moment, he came out of hiding to confront her.

He had become a different person. His face was iron; his eyes were steel. He spoke as if he could call up authority against her at any time.

"Have you come to persuade me to surrender?"

"No." She could hardly force out words. Something inside her was breaking. "He told me to help you."

"He?"

"Master Quillon."

"He should have come himself."

The sound of a door echoed faintly through the rooms. Terisa heard a distant murmur of voices.

"If you are an Imager, my lady," Geraden went on, "you may be able to help me. Otherwise, I have no escape."

"You know I'm not an Imager." Oh, my love! "What was Nyle going to say about you?"

He looked unreachable—too hard and inhuman to be touched. Yet something in her voice or her face or the way she stood must have penetrated him. His defenses cracked.

"Nothing," he said as if he had arrived without transition on the verge of tears. "Nothing at all. It's a trick. Something Master Eremis cooked up against me.

"Terisa, I did not kill my brother."

She heard Castellan Lebbick clearly. "Spread out! He's got to be in here. I want him alive."

"I'm not an Imager!" she cried. "I can't help you!"

In misery, she flung her arms around Geraden's neck.

He clung to her until they both heard the sound of hard boots approaching them from one of the other rooms. At once, they sprang apart.

He had become iron again.

Without hesitation, he turned to the mirror and swept off its cover.

The glass showed the bitter alien landscape where the champion and his men had failed.

"No, Geraden!" she gasped. "You'll be lost! You'll never get back."

He didn't heed her. "As soon as I am translated, my lady," he said as if she were a stranger, "please shift the focus of the mirror. If I am visible in the Image, I will be pursued."

He said something she didn't understand. His fingers stroked the wooden frame in parting; his hands made a gesture of farewell.

Then he stepped into the mirror and left her alone.

But he didn't appear in the Image.

She searched the scene feverishly: there was no sign of him. Once again, his glass had performed an impossible translation. It had taken him to a place it didn't show.

This time, however, no one was holding on to his foot. He had no way to come back. He was gone completely.

Castellan Lebbick came upon her so suddenly that she would have wailed if she hadn't been in such dismay.

He looked around the room, peered into the glass. Then he put

his hands on her arms and ground his fingers into her weak flesh. A
ferocious triumph burned in his face.

"Now you've done it, woman," he said almost cheerfully.
"You've done something so vile that nobody is going to protect you.
You've helped a murderer escape."

She should have said something to defend herself. A denial would
have cost Geraden nothing. He was beyond harm. But she only held
her head up and met the Castellan's flagrant gaze as well as she could
with her own distress and didn't speak.

"Now," he said through his teeth, "you are *mine*."

This is the end of
THE MIRROR OF HER DREAMS.
Mordant's Need
will be concluded in the next volume,
A MAN RIDES THROUGH.